The Western Women's Reader

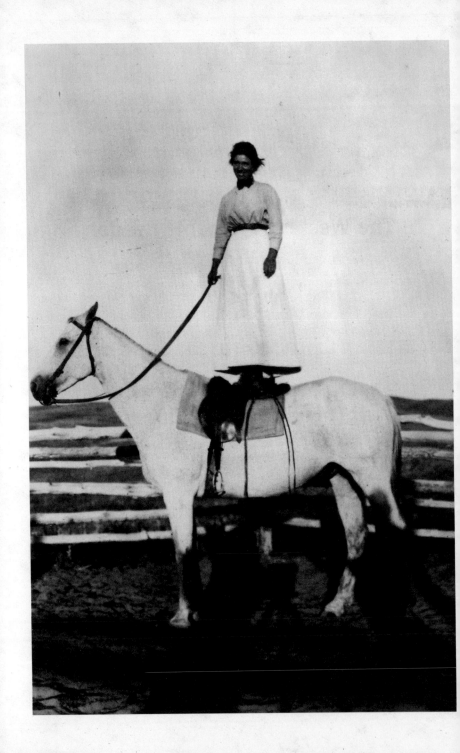

The Western Women's Reader

Lillian Schlissel and Catherine Lavender

HarperPerennial
An Imprint of Harper Collins*Publishers*

Cover Images (from top): Barbara Van Cleve, *Sandy Cook Rosenlund,
Blue Jay Ranch*, 1986; Evelyn Cameron, *Self-Portrait Standing on Jim*, 1912.
This art also appers as frontispiece. Amelda Ann Mansfield, 80, at the
wheel of the car in which she retraced her overland journey by covered
wagon; Unidentified Woman on a Burro in the Southwest.

HarperCollins books may be purchased for educational, business, or
sales promotional use. For information please write: Special Markets
Department, HarperCollins Publishers Inc., 10 East 53rd Street, New York,
NY 10022.

First HarperPerennial edition published 2000.

Designed by Antoinette Anderson

Library of Congress Cataloging-in-Publication Data has been applied for.
ISBN 0-06-09533-3-73

00 01 02 03 04 ❖/RRD 10 9 8 7 6 5 4 3 2 1

Contents

Acknowledgments

I have been absent from the field of Western women's writings for a decade; *Far From Home*, with Elizabeth Hampsten and Byrd Gibbens, was published in 1989, and *Women's Diaries of the Westward Journey* in 1982. I can see now that I have always been drawn to writings outside the narratives called literature—or rather, that I accept literature as including texts that are drawn by "amateur" voices. They are less elegant but often impassioned; in this collection, readers will find some unusual sources and I have relied on colleagues from a range of disciplines. To Ellen Tremper my gratitude for the bright intelligence that met all questions and for the patient good will to stay until an answer was sighted. Howard Lamar always has my admiration and thanks for being a friend willing to stop and think about a question in a new light.

Sue Armitage and Elliott West were generous readers when the shape of this collection was not yet clear; their critical insights helped us understand our own directions. Vera Norwood and John Faragher extended their help at different stages along the way, and their input was gratefully received. To Susan Rabiner, long-time friend and agent, thanks for being a constant support and in seeing this book through to its conclusion. To our editor at HarperCollins, Trena Keating, and her assistant Bronson Elliott, thanks for their willingness to make editorial decisions with flexibility, to understand at all times the vision of the book that we were trying to develop.

To the Tattered Cover—that Taj Mahal of book lovers—and to their dedicated staff, my deepest gratitude. William Harwood, director of the Idaho State University Library, and the staff of the Montana Historical Society—Brian Shover and Kathryn Otto—their help was generously offered. They were distant editors, and friends.

Catherine Lavender, my coeditor, my gratitude for her keen eye and for the conviction with which she spoke for the views she brought to the task. A writer is always indebted to family, who take on the daily tasks that make possible the hours spent at the computer. To my daughter Rebecca and my son Daniel, always, my thanks and my love.

—*Lillian Schlissel*

■ ■ ■

My thanks to our editor at HarperCollins, Trena Keating, and to her assistant, Bronson Elliott, who were unfailingly encouraging and patient. To Susan Rabiner, many thanks for her stamina and kindness. My most heartfelt thanks to my co-editor, Lillian Schlissel, for her generosity and openness, which has been a great inspiration, and for her laugh, which has kept me going.

Several colleagues provided comments on the manuscript at various stages in its development, and their input has been tremendously important to the final version which is published here. Sue Armitage and Elliott West provided crucial perspectives on the project, and the final cohesion of the collection owes much to their input. Thanks also to Paul Lauter, John Mack Faragher, and Vera Norwood for their generosity and guidance.

As a Westerner who has moved to New York City to teach Western women's history, I often feel as if I am living in the hinterland, far from the center of action. They say you can get anything you want in New York, but that "anything" must not include easy access to information about the West. I would like to thank the staff of my hometown bookstore, Denver's Tattered Cover, for the books which keep me connected, and my Mom and Dad for mailing me library books and newspapers. Many thanks, also, to the Denver Public Library's Western History Collection for being my research home.

I would like to thank all of my History Department, American Studies, and Women's Studies colleagues at The College of Staten Island of The City University of New York for their generous support and encouragement. In particular, Frederick M. Binder, Luther Carpenter, Kate Crehan, Manuela Dobos, Ellen Goldner, Michael Greenberg, Calvin Holder, Eric Ivison, Richard Lufrano, François Ngolet, Richard Gid Powers, and Jonathan Sassi have helped me immeasurably. The History Department's senior staffperson,

MaryAnn Pandullo, has made everything run more smoothly. Deborah and Frank Popper have made me feel welcome here, and I thank them both for their stimulating companionship, their senses of humor, and for sharing my passions about the West (and about bison). Thanks especially to my colleagues and friends Alyson Barsdley and Jeff Ewing for everything; their excellent California sensibilities infuse my work, and their friendship has been my foundation.

Many thanks to my students at both the College of Staten Island and the CUNY Graduate Center, who hike in the rain with me, who understand that *The Grapes of Wrath* is a western, and whose questions force me to figure out what I really think. As always, they have taught me a lot.

I would also like to thank the many far-flung friends who continue to be my excellent Western history colleagues, especially Rebecca Bales, Sam Matthews-Lamb, Kenneth Orona, and Clark Whitehorn. Thanks also to my teachers at the University of Colorado at Boulder and to those who were always willing to offer assistance to one who was just starting out: Lee Chambers-Schiller, Sarah Deutsch, Yvette Huginnie, Albert Hurtado, Betsy Jameson, Patricia Nelson Limerick, Marjorie McIntosh, Ralph Mann, Phil Mitterling, Maria Montoya, Peggy Pascoe, George Phillips, Robert Pois, Lee Scamehorn, Virginia Scharff, and Martha Tocco. I'd like also to celebrate the memory of two teachers, James Folsom and Page Smith, who continue to be inspirations.

My deepest appreciation goes to my family. To my parents, James and Evelyn Lavender, thanks for their support and advice, and most of all, for their stories. To my parents-in-law, Terry and Diana Bell, of Hamilton, New Zealand, who traveled halfway around the world to let me share the West with them from the Grand Canyon to Yellowstone and from Disneyland to the Mitchell Corn Palace, my thanks. Finally, to my marvelous husband, Warrick Bell, who always carries far more than his fair share, my thanks, respect, and love.

—*Catherine Lavender*

Introduction
THE ANGLE OF VISION
Lillian Schlissel and Catherine Lavender

The task of editing a Reader is really a process of self-education—all that is known is offset by all that is out there to discover. It is sometimes a dangerous undertaking; what one has safely tucked away as "certain" is jarred loose, and the discoveries that make the task exciting also upset one's mental apple cart.

At the beginning of our work, there were questions about whether there was enough writing to support a *Western Women's Reader*. Women's writings have so often figured at the fringes of a genre that is heavily masculinized. Both the historical and the literary West have been drawn in studies like Richard Slotkin's *Regeneration Through Violence* and *Gunfighter Nation*, and people all over the world recognize the signature of the American West in images of cowboys and outlaws. The traditional canon has imprinted ideas of conquest as emblematic of the region, and the writings of women have seemed somehow smaller, less significant, narrower, an alternative voice that played at the margins of larger, more compelling stories.

By the 1980s, however, women's writing experienced a new growth and a new surge of energy. Not only was there an outpouring of writing, but in university departments of Asian American Studies, Chicano/a Studies, Native American Studies, and Women's Studies, there was place and time to read the new writing. What was once marginal assumed new visibility and drew new interest. It seemed the right time to collect the "old" and the "new" and to consider new directions.

Our original intention was to offer a single volume devoted to women's writing in historical perspective. We intended that the *Reader* would hold selections that had taken their place in the literary canon, but we also knew that it would include writing beyond the literary canon. There were discussions about what merited inclusion, and what did not. As the editors of the *Norton Anthology of African American Literature* debated whether to include rap as an extension of oral tradition, we debated the inclusion of folksong and folkstory, of taped interviews and mem-

oirs, of political writings and of autobiography, of photograph and
of sculpture, of fiction and testimony. In the end, we agreed that
these writings and images are "texts" from which the history of
western women can be drawn. This collection is offered, therefore, to western historians, to historians of western women's history, to literary critics, and to all readers. The angle of vision, the
eye of the artist, belongs only to women, and the images in focus
are sometimes different from what we are accustomed to seeing
and reading.

We know we will not have satisfied all readers. Thus,
"Calamity Jane's Letters to Her Daughter" are included in spite of
the "taint" of fraudulence because Calamity Jane is part of western women's folklore, and though the "Letters" are most likely fiction, the story deserves telling. Other pieces included seem
hardly to qualify as "literature." Barbara Kingsolver's taped interviews with the Latina women who walked the Arizona picket
lines against Phelps-Dodge, or the songs of Los Angeles cannery
workers, or Mother Jones's description of the workers at Cripple
Creek, Colorado, or Tillie Olsen's passionate account of the San
Francisco longshoremen's strike—none of these are, in the formal sense, literary, but they bring literature closer to the urgent
voices of western women who lived on the land and were determined to feed their children and to earn a living. Those experiences are part of the history of women in the West, and part of
this undertaking.

The operative factor in making choices for the *Reader* has
been the authenticity of the image and of the voice—whether that
image be drawn out of fiction or out of historical event. In some
cases, the choices were made on the basis of literary excellence,
and in others the choices were made on the basis of the participation of women in an extraordinary historical event. The *Reader*,
then, has been assembled so that selections become historical
texts. William Deverell has called Western history the record of the
"hurts and heartbreaks" of the past.[1] In memoir, autobiography,
newspaper article, union song, oral history, political tract, short
story, novel, photograph, and illustration, there are some voices of
women that would not be set aside.

The photographs of Laura Gilpin, Dorothea Lange, Evelyn
Cameron, Joan Myers, Carole Gallagher, Toba Tucker, Barbara

Van Cleve, and Teresa Jordan, and the "clay people" of Roxanne Swentzell—these are also "texts" of the western experience. Women artists "speak" through the silence of the photograph or the clay figure. The photographs we have chosen are not "chapter candy" for readers who may be comfortable with illustrations. As the West has been home to the Navajo weaver, to sharecroppers, and to ranch women, the images we have chosen are part of the story. Images bring past and present together. In the woodcuts of Mary Hallock Foote, women's loneliness finds expression. The image makers are part of the story we have tried to tell.

Our intention has been to follow the curve of literary tradition and visual image when women were center stage. Yet even that "simple" direction has led us to complex questions. We asked who is a western woman writer. Is it location in the West that makes a writer western? Is it the result of having been born there, or dying there, or making a choice to pitch one's battles for and in it? Elizabeth Hampsten wondered about the "affinity to place and people that so mystifies me . . . [the] alchemy to belong, in some secret way, to the mountains and canyons and small towns of northern Arizona."[2] We have been guided by the sense that western women writers are western by virtue of something intangible, by their identity with the west, by some personal "alchemy," as much as by birth or location.

We have organized the *Reader* into a kind of historical chronology, focusing on the thematic development of women's history in the region. From the first settlements to the arrival of outsiders, we trace the origins of women's experience in the West. We examine western paradoxes—the gift of good land and the promises of success, as well as the harshness of life in the region's unforgiving extremes. From these origins and from this landscape have emerged several traditions of western women's writing. We start with storytelling, the most conventionally "literary" of the ways women have written about the West, and move to oral histories and memoirs. Women have challenged the standard histories of Western expansion by writing biographies of their own "heroes." Women have raised their voices against class and racial injustice. Finally, there is a gathering of the rich harvest of Western women's writing today.

Homesites

Here are the stories of the West before it was called "the West," when it was "home" to the Native Americans and "el norte" to the Spanish colonists who lived there. Native American tribes called themselves "the people," and the land was the place where creation stories were enacted by the mountains and the animals, by the sky and the clouds and the forest. In those stories, mothers and daughters played principal roles, and the world was often in their keeping. Some stories grow out of Spanish settlements, when parts of modern-day New Mexico, Arizona, Nevada, Utah, Texas, California, and Colorado were Spanish-speaking provinces. In those stories, the earth was the stage where divinities worked out the destinies of men and women, where women were charged with keeping the histories of their people alive.

Landfall

Still, "getting there" is part of the historical construction of the West. The quest for the West is built into the American national myth, our homespun version of *The Odyssey*. Western journeys have been made by every possible conveyance, from foot to wagon train, from handcart to automobile, from horseback to airplane. Contrary to images of the passive westering woman who accompanied her husband going West, we found women who chose their own destinations, from the boisterous ladies of mishaps and jests Clementine and Sweet Betsy from Pike, to women like newspaper reporter Emma Kelly, climbing the awful Chilkoot Trail, determined to "get the scoop" on the Klondike Gold Rush, and Chinese American journalist Sui Sin Far, not entirely choosing her way, but determined just the same to make this country—this particular landfall—her home. And for the glint of her eye, we affectionately pay tribute to Amelda Mansfield, who, after westering in a wagon train as a child, bought herself a Model T Ford in her eighties and made the same journey again—at the wheel!

The Gift of Good Land

Western women have understood their connection with the land more in terms of love than of possession. Hector St. John de Crevecoeur believed that the immigrant became a "new man" when he owned the land, yet the gift of good land has always been more ambiguous when it refers to the inheritance of daughters. Willa Cather's descriptions of fields of Nebraska wheat and Mary Austin's clear-eyed precision in her descriptions of the desert do not entail conquest so much as stewardship or, indeed, seduction. Elinore Pruitt Stewart's joyful acceptance of the homesteader's life includes the claim that she had become a "bloated landowner," but as a woman, she was setting work on the land against work in a factory, and she preferred one to the other; as she wrote, "I was glad because I really like to mow."[3] And camp cook Anne Ellis found the West a place where a woman could do any job she turned her hand to and reap the rewards. For Yankton Sioux writer Zitkala Sa, as for other Native Americans, the gift of good land was complicated by the fact that the good land had been taken away.

Hardscrabble

The gladsome face that nature wears is sometimes exchanged for landscapes filled with terror, with seasons of dust bowl and locusts, of howling winds and snows, of years when bringing in a crop sapped the spirit and stupefied the mind. Women write about farming and of watching their men worry about survival as their children bend beneath the labors thrust upon them. Drawing from literary roots outside the region, such as Edith Summers Kelley's Kentucky novel *Weeds*, hardscrabble literature stretches west in Mari Sandoz's history of the women of Niobrara County, Nebraska, in *Old Jules*. "Starve-to-death" farming fills the pages of Hope Williams Sykes's *Second Hoeing*, where Hannah Schreissmiller tried to break free from the stoop labor of the Colorado sugar beet growers. Echoing West Virginia stories of "starve-to-death" mining captured in Rebecca Harding Davis's *Life in the Iron Mills*, the Western mining story resonates in Agnes Smedley's *Daughter of Earth*. In the hardscrabble novels of western women writers, one hears the stories of frontier violence turned into domestic violence, of houses on lonely prairies which hold secrets told only in whispers.

Storytellers

The West has always fostered legends, and women write the stories that have helped to shape the popular perceptions of the

West. Here one of the most famous characters of Western lore, Calamity Jane, appears both as a folkloric wild woman and in a new incarnation as a long-suffering mother. Here, too, are the works of some of the most literary of Western storytellers: Katherine Anne Porter, whose stories of Texas and Mexico gained her fame far beyond the West; Helen Hunt Jackson, whose best-selling novel *Ramona* inspired films and popular songs; Mary Hallock Foote, whose stories of her "exile" in Idaho were illustrated with her own drawings; and Mourning Dove, author of *Cogewea*, the first Native American woman's novel, whose collection of oral tradition informed her fiction. Modern-day storytellers draw on these oral traditions as inspirations for their work, as in the moving retelling of Athabaskan legend by Gwich'in writer Velma Wallis of Alaska, and in the thoroughly modern refiguring of tradition by Chickasaw poet and novelist Linda Hogan.

First Person

Our angle of vision is unavoidably shaped by the contours of memory, by what is remembered and what is recorded. Oral histories and memoirs expand and extend what we know of Western women's pasts. Here are stories from the broad sweep of Western memory, from former slaves now free, from daughters and granddaughters who come to understand elder women relatives only after time and youth have passed, and from Chinatown daughters who find the strength within themselves to become woman warriors. First person accounts sometimes come to us through the mediating voice of the anthropologist, historian, or writer; and yet, the first voice remains clear and audible. Through the oral histories of ranching women and of Native American women and through western women's memoirs told directly run stories of resistance, survival, and acceptance.

Rewriting History

At the beginning of this introduction, we spoke of "upsetting one's mental apple cart." The women writing history—here the biographies of Crazy Horse, Geronimo, Sitting Bull, and Red Cloud—revised the national disposition to describe Indians as "savages." Mari Sandoz, Angie Debo, Dorothy Johnson, and Delphine Red Shirt understood the injustices done to peoples driven from their homelands. Like George Catlin's elegant portraits of people he saw as the "aristocrats" of the Plains, these biographies were executed with accuracy and flair—and respect. Mari Sandoz's *Crazy Horse* is a literary triumph, and set against her *Old Jules*, provides a subtle indictment of the old pioneer. Crazy Horse, on his wedding day, is followed by Black Shawl, "in her buckskin dress, deep-yoked in beads," her "vermillioned face woman-strong and proud."[4] It was Black Shawl, not the women of Niobrara County, that Sandoz saw as inheriting the promise of western lands. Dorothy Johnson and Angie Debo, their voices restrained by the historian's task of accuracy and objectivity, also called for a revision of the tendency to depict enemies where heroes stood. Delphine Red Shirt's evocation of her memories of Red Cloud brings women's revisions into the present, as Native American peoples stake their claims to tell their own histories.

Walking the Line

The chronicle of working-class women in the West is held in a slim shelf of books, but the labor movement west of the Mississippi had its share of fiery women. Mary "Mother" Jones was part of major strikes in Cripple Creek (1903) and Ludlow (1913), her union sympathies born of her work with the women and children of mine workers' families, and of her outrage—carried West with her—at the working conditions of children in Eastern textile mills. Industrialism spread across the country, and the West, no less than the East, witnessed the widening separations between the working and the middle classes. Workers, often foreign-born, were being displaced as surely as had the Sioux and the Cheyenne. In San Francisco in 1934, Tillie Olsen wrote about the longshoremen's strike, and in Arizona in 1983, Barbara Kingsolver taped her interviews with the Latina women who "held the line" against the Phelps-Dodge mining corporation as their men went out of state to earn a living. The women were determined to make a better life for their children and to live in the West as westerners, not as "lousy foreigners."[5]

Talking Back

Native American writer Paula Gunn Allen speaks of herself as a "maverick," and Western women writers often find their identities in resistance. For Mary Crow Dog and Angela Davis, resistance is born in a political movement; it means defense of the tribe and of the race. For seventeenth-century Mexican nun Sor Juana Inés de la Cruz, resistance means not submitting the mind to social and religious protocol. For Jeanne Wakatsuki Houston, resistance lies in the refusal to let memory die, or to maintain silence about the past. For Nancy Mairs, resistance is the refusal to allow physical pain to limit the act of social protest. For Terry Tempest Williams, protest means bearing witness to the impact of human cruelty on the land and its inhabitants. Each of these writers describes resistance as the path to self-realization; each finds that identity as a western woman has something to do with being heard. Teresa Jordan has said that she thought the "westerness" of the women in her family lay in their refusal to be silent: "They wanted to be in control of their own lives."[6]

Looking Within Myself I Am Many Parts: Western Women's Writing Today

The title "Looking Within Myself I Am Many Parts" derives from a painting by the late Santa Clara Pueblo painter Helen Hardin, and we heard that sentiment in the writings of women who affirm identities shaped by "border-crossings." Western borders are different and deeper than those defined by lines of latitude and longitude. In the West, borders are more than lines in the sand or fences stretched across the desert; they are also redefinitions, lines in the heart, connections between and through identities, blendings and marblings of inheritances drawn from the past. These writings reaffirm traditions that stretch back to the first practices of intertribal marriages, making new families of old enemies. In recent memory, this tradition emerges in the more troublesome heritage of the "halfbreed" or "mixed blood," whose stories hold both the promise and the danger of inheriting multiple legacies. Today's western women's writings celebrate these personal border crossings, choosing the person of many worlds as the new ideal.

Contemporary western women's stories have been described as modern or even postmodern, but they spring from Mabel Dodge Luhan's life in Taos and her marriage to Tony Luhan, from Helen Hunt Jackson's romance *Ramona* and from Mourning Dove's *Cogewea*, from Mari Sandoz's praise-song to Crazy Horse and from

Fabiola Cabeza de Baca's evocation of the Llano. Western women writers people their art with characters representing the diversity of western communities. From these many points of origin and many traditions of writing have emerged stories drawn from the intersection of people and land, from roots which converge finally in the West as a place in the real world. Paula Gunn Allen calls herself the "global Indian" with friends and family members from every corner of the planet; "as the years roll by, we take more and more of the human strains into the family lines."[7] Gloria Anzaldúa writes of the "mestiza way," and of the woman with a

> tolerance for contradictions ... [and] for ambiguity. This assembly is not one where severed or separated pieces merely come together. Nor is it a balancing of opposing powers. ... [The] self has added a third element which is greater than the sum of its severed parts. That third element is a new consciousness—a mestiza consciousness.[8]

This new mestiza consciousness permeates beyond Latina sensibilities. Western literary critic Melody Graulich imagines herself a script writer for a new television show where "my great-grandmother, a Danish immigrant, grows ... artichokes with her common-law Californio husband and raises eight children, just enough to marry newly arrived immigrants from Guatemala, the Basque Country, Korea, Mexico, Oklahoma, the Badlands of South Dakota, Cambodia, Harlem and—what the hell—Kosovo."[9] Kay Walkingstick (Cherokee Winnebago) asks in her painting, "You're an Indian? I thought you were a Jewish girl from the Queens who changed her name."[10]

Like western borders, the landscapes embraced in contemporary western women's writings are full of instabilities; and they are often as unlovely as they are beautiful or fertile. Hardscrabble land like the bitter stretches of South Dakota take a lot of loving, and even the "solace of open spaces" can be trampled in the rush to control what nature has given freely. But women rarely come to the West driven by dreams of mastery. Women find in themselves a quiet humor for "things as they are," from Mary Austin's desert scavengers to Molly Ivins's Texans who go around "impersonating the Lord," from Roxanne Swentzell's "clay people" to Sylvia Watanabe's "Talking to the Dead."

The figure that emerges from the pages of western women writers and from the images of photographers is one poised in motion, seldom still. Her angle of vision is broad and takes in multiple vistas. Where Ulysses travelled, the new Western woman will travel too. Her American odyssey has just begun.

Notes

1.William Deverell,"Fighting Words: The Significance of the American West in the History of the United States," in Clyde A. Milner II. ed., *A New Significance: Re-Envisioning the History of the American West* (Oxford University Press, 1996): 29–55, p. 38.

2. Elizabeth Hampsten, *Mother's Letters: Essays* (University of Arizona Press, 1993), p. 24.

3. Elinore Pruitt Stewart, *Letters of a Woman Homesteader* (University of Nebraska Press, 1961), p. 7.

4. Mari Sandoz, *Crazy Horse: The Strange Man of the Oglalas* (University of Nebraska Press, 1992), p. 254.

5. Agnes Smedley, *Daughter of Earth* (The Feminist Press, 1973), p. 95.

6. Teresa Jordan, *Riding the White Horse Home: A Western Family Album* (Pantheon Books, 1993), p. 194.

7. Paula Gunn Allen, *Off the Reservation: Reflections on Boundary-Busting, Border-Crossing, Loose Canons* (Beacon Press, 1998), p. 5.

8. Gloria Anzaldúa, *Borderlands/La Frontera: The New Mestiza* (Aunt Lute Books, 1987), pp. 79–80.

9. Melody Graulich, "Valley Girl," *Western American Literature* Vol. 34, No. 2 (Summer 1999): 223–227, p. 227.

10. Kay Walkingstick, "Talking Leaves, 1993," quoted in *Indian Humor,* ed. Sara Bates (American Indian Contemporary Arts, 1995), p. 95.

1

Homesites

Before the West was called "The West," it was called either "home" or "el norte" by Indian and Spanish colonial women. Beginning in the 1840s, "free land" and the prospect of gold brought massive Anglo-American settlement into the region. But before that happened, Native American and Spanish-American women had already begun to tell their own stories of the West as home. Writings by these women before the 1840s often take the form of origin stories, a tradition of Western American writing which continues today.

Western origin stories take several forms. Some are stories of having been created in the West, or tell of emerging from another world. Many Native American peoples who live today in the West carry with them oral traditions of creation. The Navaho, for example, tell of being led to this world from another world below it by Grandmother Spiderwoman. The Caddo tell of being saved from a great flood by a giant turtle who carried them to this world on its back. The Ute tell of the first man, formed from a clot of blood by the playful kicks of a rabbit. The Modoc tell of being brought in a basket out of the underworld by an old spirit and his daughter who missed seeing the sun. The Maidu tell of Earth-Maker, who descended from the sky on a rope to create the people. The Arapaho tell of Whirlwind Woman who created the earth from a ball of mud. Like all oral traditions, they have changed subtly over the years of their telling, like the banks of a long-running river. The twentieth-century anthropological collection of these stories, and their retelling by contemporary Native American writers, provide glimpses of the stories that came before. The origin stories carried forward by Native American women writers writing today preserve oral traditions even while they are new creations, as much products of the times in which they are written as the literary traditions they recreate.

The commonly-known story of the overland journey from the eastern United States is familiar to most readers. Less familiar are stories of Spanish settlement in the West. Long before the Mayflower's first landfall, Spanish settlers from New Spain expanded their colony north into what is today Utah, Nevada, Texas, California, and Colorado. By the 1600s, New Spain was the center of a booming and culturally rich settlement which stretched from the Philippines to the Caribbean, and from Panama north into the Rocky Mountains. From its capital in Mexico City, settlers from New Spain fanned out into the region to establish churches, schools, and cities. While the Puritans struggled through their first winters at Plymouth, Spanish settlers maintained large permanent settlements in the American Southwest—including Santa Fé, in today's New Mexico, and the booming Pacific coast settlements of Los Angeles, San Diego, and San Francisco in California. For many of the Spanish (and later Mexican) women who wrote about their lives in this early period, the West was home. Their writing reflects their sense of belonging to this new land, and of their fears at its being taken away from them.

Willa Cather (1873–1947)

The Song of the Lark was Willa Cather's third novel, following *O Pioneers!* and *Alexander's Bridge.* The story framed more clearly Cather's concern with the dilemmas faced by a woman who wanted to be an artist. Where Alexandra Bergson in *O Pioneers!* was able to live at home and devote herself to her farm, the heroine of *Song of the Lark*, who is a singer, must choose a life that separates her from the women of her generation. Cather modeled Thea Kronborg on the life and career of Olive Fremstad, the reigning Wagnerian soprano at the Metropolitan Opera, a Swedish-born immigrant who had grown up in Minnesota. Each woman came from obscure beginnings, possessed a special genius, and moved toward international acclaim. The woman who was an opera singer and the woman who was a writer knew what it meant to live in the characters they created, and to leave behind family and friends.

The scene in the novel when Thea Kronborg recognizes that beauty is everywhere comes, ironically, when she imagines the life of a woman who belonged to the Ancient People of Arizona, called the Anasazi. There is irony, perhaps, in the fact that her awakening to art should come from an experience of the past, with the Cliff Dwellers, who left only a few shards of pottery as clues to their history. Nevertheless, epiphanies come when they will, and *Song of the Lark* remains Cather's *kunstlerroman*, her novel of awakening.

THE ANCIENT PEOPLE

The faculty of observation was never highly developed in Thea Kronborg. A great deal escaped her eye as she passed through the world. But the things which were for her, she saw; she experienced them physically and remembered them as if they had once been a part of herself. The roses she used to see in the florists' shops in Chicago were merely roses. But when she thought of the moon-

---

Willa Cather, "The Ancient People," from *The Song of the Lark* (1915).

flowers that grew over Mrs. Tellamantez's door, it was as if she had been that vine and had opened up in white flowers every night. There were memories of light on the sand hills, of masses of prickly-pear blossoms she had found in the desert in early childhood, of the late afternoon sun pouring through the grape leaves and the mint bed in Mrs. Kohler's garden, which she would never lose. These recollections were a part of her mind and personality. In Chicago she had got almost nothing that went into her subconscious self and took root there. But here, in Panther Canyon, there were again things which seemed destined for her.

Panther Canyon was the home of innumerable swallows. They built nests in the wall far above the hollow groove in which Thea's own rock chamber lay. They seldom ventured above the rim of the canyon, to the flat, wind-swept tableland. Their world was the blue air-river between the canyon walls. In that blue gulf the arrow-shaped birds swam all day long, with only an occasional movement of the wings. The only sad thing about them was their timidity; the way in which they lived their lives between the echoing cliffs and never dared to rise out of the shadow of the canyon walls. As they swam past her door, Thea often felt how easy it would be to dream one's life out in some cleft in the world.

From the ancient dwelling there came always a dignified, unobtrusive sadness; now stronger, now fainter,—like the aromatic smell which the dwarf cedars gave out in the sun,—but always present, a part of the air one breathed. At night, when Thea dreamed about the canyon,—or in the early morning when she hurried toward it, anticipating it,—her conception of it was of yellow rocks baking in sunlight, the swallows, the cedar smell, and that peculiar sadness—a voice out of the past, not very loud, that went on saying a few simple things to the solitude eternally.

Standing up in her lodge, Thea could with her thumb nail dislodge flakes of carbon from the rock roof—the cooking-smoke of the Ancient People. They were that near! A timid, nest-building folk, like the swallows. How often Thea remembered Ray Kennedy's moralizing about the cliff cities. He used to say that he never felt the hardness of the human struggle or the sadness of history as he felt it among those ruins. He used to say, too, that it made one feel an obligation to do one's best. On the first day that Thea climbed the water trail she began to have intuitions about the women who had worn the path, and who had spent so great a part of their lives going up and down it. She found herself trying to walk as they must have walked, with a feeling in her feet and knees and loins which she had never known before,—which must have come up to her out of the accustomed dust of that rocky trail. She could feel the weight of an Indian baby clinging to her back as she climbed.

The empty houses, among which she wandered in the afternoon, the blanketed one in which she lay all morning, were haunted by certain fears and desires, feeling about warmth and cold and water and physical strength. It seemed to Thea that a certain understanding of those old people came up to her out of the rock shelf on which she lay; that certain feelings were transmitted to her suggestions that were simple, insistent, and monotonous like the beating of Indian drums. They were not expressible in words, but seemed rather to translate themselves into attitudes of body, into degrees of muscular tension or relaxation; the naked strength of youth, sharp as the sun-shafts; the crouching timorousness of age, the sullenness of women who waited for their captors. At the first turning of the canyon there was a half-ruined tower of yellow masonry, a watch-tower upon which the young men used to entice eagles and snare them with nets. Sometimes for a whole morning Thea could see the coppery breast and shoulders of an Indian youth there against the sky; see him throw the net, and watch the struggle with the eagle.

Old Henry Biltmer, at the ranch, had been a great deal among the Pueblo Indians who are the descendants of the Cliff-Dwellers. After supper he used to sit and smoke his pipe by the kitchen stove and talk to Thea about them. He had never found any one before who was interested in his ruins. Every Sunday the old man prowled about in the canyon, and he had come to know a good deal more about it than he could account for. He had gathered up a whole chestful of Cliff-Dweller relics which he meant to take back to Germany with him some day. He taught Thea how to find things among the ruins: grinding-stones, and drills and needles made of turkey-bones. There were fragments of pottery everywhere. Old Henry explained to her that the Ancient People had developed masonry and pottery far beyond any other crafts. After they had made houses for themselves, the next thing was to house the precious water. He explained to her how all their customs and cere-

monies and their religion went back to water. The men provided
the food, but water was the care of the women. The stupid women
carried water for most of their lives; the cleverer ones made the
vessels to hold it. Their pottery was their most direct appeal to
water, the envelope and sheath of the precious element itself. The
strongest Indian need was expressed in those graceful jars, fashioned slowly by hand, without the aid of a wheel.

When Thea took her bath at the bottom of the canyon, in the
sunny pool behind the screen of cottonwoods, she sometimes felt
as if the water must have sovereign qualities, from having been the
object of so much service and desire. That stream was the only living thing left of the drama that had been played out in the canyon
centuries ago. In the rapid, restless heart of it, flowing swifter than
the rest, there was a continuity of life that reached back into the
old time. The glittering thread of current had a kind of lightly worn,
loosely knit personality, graceful and laughing. Thea's bath came to
have a ceremonial gravity. The atmosphere of the canyon was ritu-
alistic.

One morning, as she was standing upright in the pool, splashing water between her shoulder-blades with a big sponge, something flashed through her mind that made her draw herself up and
stand still until the water had quite dried upon her flushed skin.
The stream and the broken pottery: what was any art but an effort
to make a sheath, a mould in which to imprison for a moment the
shining, elusive element which is life itself,—life hurrying past us
and running away, too strong to stop, too sweet to lose? The Indian
women had held it in their jars. In the sculpture she had seen in
the Art Institute, it had been caught in a flash of arrested motion. In
singing, one made a vessel of one's throat and nostrils and held it
on one's breath, caught the stream in a scale of natural intervals.

Yes, Ray Kennedy was right. All these things made one feel that
one ought to do one's best, and help to fulfill some desire of the
dust that slept there. A dream had been dreamed there long ago, in
the night of ages, and the wind had whispered some promise to the
sadness of the savage. In their own way, those people had felt the
beginnings of what was to come. These potsherds were like fetters
that bound one to a long chain of human endeavor.

FURTHER READINGS

Sherrill Harbison, "Introduction" to Willa Cather, *The Song of the Lark* (Penguin Books, 1999); Joseph R. Urgo, *Willa Cather and the Myth of American Migration* (University of Illinois Press, 1995); Philip L. Gerber, *Willa Cather* (Twayne, 1995); Harold Bloom, ed., *Willa Cather: Modern Critical Views* (Chelsea House, 1990); Sharon O'Brien, *Willa Cather: The Emerging Voice* (Oxford University Press, 1987); Judith Fryer, *Felicitous Space: The Imaginative Structures of Edith Wharton and Willa Cather* (University of North Carolina Press, 1986).

Beverly Hungry Wolf (1950–)

In this collection of short myths gathered from elder women of her tribe, the Blood Blackfoot writer Beverly Hungry Wolf tells about the origins of women and of their ways of interacting with the world around them. Beverly (Little Bear) Hungry Wolf grew up on the largest Indian reservation in Canada, the Blood Indian Reserve. She learned English when she was sent to Catholic boarding school, where she later worked as a teacher after graduating from college. While she continued to live in contact with elderly tribe members who maintained tribal traditions, she wrote that she and her friends "felt ashamed to be with our old-fashioned grandparents in public." In the late 1960s, she married a European-born Indian man, Adolf Hungry Wolf, who encouraged her to learn traditional practices from her grandmothers. She recorded those practices and stories in her book, *The Ways of My Grandmothers,* originally published in 1980.

Hungry Wolf wrote the book in part to make traditional practices available to Blood women born too late to meet the grandmothers. But she also wanted to correct the published record of Blood and Blackfoot lifeways, which told only, she wrote, about "horse stealing, buffalo hunting, and war raiding." A reader who relied on the published record to understand Blood women's lives "would have to assume that Indian women lived boring lives of drudgery, and that their minds were empty of stories and anecdotes." In this selection from that book, "The Myths and Legends of My Grandmothers," Hungry Wolf presents Blood women with full and storied lives. She documents the emergence of the first women, traces the struggles that emerged between the first women and first men, and explains how men and women came to appreciate each other.

With her husband, Adolf Hungry Wolf, Beverly Hungry Wolf has written numerous studies and guides to Northern Plains Indian cultures including *Shadows of the Buffalo* (1983) and *Indian Tribes of the Northern Rockies* (1991). Her *Daughters of the Buffalo Women* (1997) is a sequel to *The Ways of My Grandmothers.*

In these short tellings of myths, Hungry Wolf shares the moral landscapes of Blood women, tracing out the ways that they came to live on the land and to make peace with it. She presents a complex picture of carefully negotiated relations between men and women, and between women and the animals upon which they depend for survival.

THE MYTHS AND LEGENDS OF MY GRANDMOTHERS

How the Old People Say We Women Were Made

The way I have heard our ancestral stories told, the first woman was made as a companion for the first man. The Creator took a piece of buffalo bone and some sinew, then he covered them with mud and shaped them. When the Creator blew on the body it came to life. He did the same with the woman, and he taught them both how to make more of their own kind. While this was going on a wolf came along and offered to help out. He blew on the woman and at the same time he made a wolf howl, and the old people say that is why women have higher voices than men.

This first man and woman are said to have lived together happily for quite some time. They had two children, both boys. Every day the man went out hunting and the woman gathered firewood and hauled the water. But one day the man came home earlier than usual and he found that his wife was still not at home. He became suspicious, and he told the boys to be prepared for trouble.

The next morning the husband told his wife that he was going hunting again, but instead he went up on a high ridge where he could look down and keep watch on his camp. Soon he saw his wife going for wood, and then for water. Just before she got to the river the husband saw a large snake crawl behind a rock and change into a handsome man. Then he knew what was going on, so he rushed back to camp to tell his children. He gave them four magic articles that had great power. He said to the boys that their mother was under the snake's spell and that she would turn into a

Beverly Hungry Wolf, from *The Ways of My Grandmothers* (1980).

mean monster when she learned that they knew about it. He told them to run for their lives.

As the two boys were running away they heard a commotion back at their camp, and soon they saw a terrible monster following them. They threw one of the magic articles behind them and a great mountain range formed. The monster had to climb these mountains, but soon it caught up to the boys again. They threw behind another of the magic articles and a great forest formed. The monster had to make its way through the thick trees and brush, but soon it was behind them again. They threw back the third magic article and behind them formed a big swamp through which the monster had a hard time to wade. Finally the boys threw back their last magic article and a huge body of water formed over which the monster was not able to pass. They say this was the ocean. The two boys were now on the other side of the ocean.

Some years passed and finally one of the boys said to the other: "My brother, I am lonesome over here. You stay here and help out the people, while I go back to the other side and see what I can do there." This one that came back over here was named Napi, which means Old Man in Blackfoot. Napi came over and did many mysterious things, some of them very helpful and some of them very cruel and mean. His exploits have been handed down through the ages in a series of tribal legends that are still told today. Many of these legends are so vulgar that only the adults tell them to each other. Napi was the first man to use and abuse women for his own fun and pleasure. He is also credited with making many changes in nature. His favorite camping place was along the foot of the Rocky Mountains, at a place where modern maps show the start of the Old Man River, in southern Alberta, Canada.

How Men and Women Were Brought Back Together

By the time Napi came over to this side of the ocean the Creator had already made more people. They had a hard time to live, because all the country was still covered with mountains, forests, and swamp. So Napi covered the swamp with land, and he divided up the people into different tribes. But the women couldn't get along with the men, so Napi sent them away in different groups. Not long after, he got together with the chief of the women so that they could decide about some important things.

The chief of the women told Napi that he could make the first decision, as long as she could have the final word. He said that was all right, and the old people say that ever since then it has been this way between men and women.

Napi said that his first decision was to have people's bodies covered by hair so that they could stay warm. But the woman said: "They can have hair, but only on their heads to keep the rain and snow off. If they want their bodies warm they will have to wear furs and hides."

To this, Napi said: "Then the people have to learn to use tools so they can tan the furs and hides. The men will be able to tan quickly but the women will take a long time." The woman replied: "Yes, they will learn to tan. When the men tan quickly their furs will be stiff and poor, but when the women take a long time their furs and hides will be nice and soft."

Then Napi decided that the people would have to learn how to cook their food. He said: "The men will be able to cook quickly over an open fire, while the women will cook slowly and they will need utensils." The woman agreed, but added: "When the men cook quickly over their open fires their meals will taste plain and get burned, while the slow food that women cook will be of all different kinds and it will taste much better."

Finally they decided about life and death. Napi picked up a buffalo chip and threw it into the river, then he said: "The people will have to die, or there will be too many of them. But, just as this chip floats on top of the water, so will the people float for four days and then they will be reborn." The woman picked up a stone and threw it into the river, saying: "Yes, they will have to die, but just as this stone sinks and stays gone, so will the people stay gone once they have died."

Time went by, and one day Napi met the chief of the women again. She was crying because her only daughter had died. She said to Napi: "Let us change one thing that we agreed on: let the people float four days, like you said, and then let them come back to life again." But Napi told her: "No, we agreed that you would have the last word, and you have already decided." So the woman lost her daughter.

The next time Napi met the chief of the women she told him: "You are the one that decided for men and women to live separate, and now I want to have the last word about that. From now on the men and women will live together so they can help each other. I want you to bring all the men to the camp of my women so that they can choose partners." Napi agreed that it would be done.

Now, at that time the men were living real pitiful lives. The clothes they were wearing were made from stiff furs and hides, hardly tanned at all. They couldn't make moccasins or lodges, and they couldn't even keep themselves clean. They were nearly starved because the food that they ate was always plain and usually burned. When Napi told them what had been decided, they were very anxious to join the women.

The women got dressed up and perfumed for the grand occasion. Only their chief did not. Instead she put on stiff old furs and took off her moccasins, thinking she would be most appealing like that for the one that she wanted. She told the other women they could pick any man that they wanted, except for Napi. She wanted him for herself.

Then the men came to the camp of the women, and the women chose them, one by one, for their partners. The chief of the women went over to Napi and took his arm to lead him to her lodge. Napi yanked his arm away and cursed at her: "Get away from me, you awful-looking woman, I wouldn't have anything to do with someone like you." Then he turned the other way and admired all the good-looking women, and wondered which one was going to choose him.

The chief of the women was insulted by his reaction, so she went back to her lodge and put on her finest clothes. She cleaned herself up, braided her hair and put on perfume, and then she went out to look for another man. When Napi saw her he thought: "My, she sure looks good, and I think she is coming for me." Instead, she took the man next to him, and soon all the men and women were paired off except for Napi. He wandered off into the hills, crying, and they say that he became ornery from then on because of his loneliness.

FURTHER READINGS

Beverly Hungry Wolf, *Daughters of the Buffalo Women* (Book Publishing Co., 1997); Beverly Hungry Wolf and Adolf Hungry Wolf, *Indian Tribes of the Northern Rockies* (Book Publishing Co., 1991); Beverly Hungry Wolf and Adolf Hungry Wolf, *Shadows of the Buffalo* (Book Publishing Co., 1983); Beverly Hungry Wolf, *The Ways of My Grandmothers* (William Morrow & Co., 1980).

Leslie Marmon Silko (1948–   )

Leslie Marmon Silko, who identifies herself as of mixed ancestry—"Laguna Pueblo, Mexican, and White"—was born in Albuquerque, New Mexico, in 1948. She grew up at the Laguna Pueblo, where she learned of Laguna culture from her grandmother and great aunt who, she later wrote in *Storyteller* (1981), gave her "an entire culture by word of mouth." After receiving her English degree from the University of New Mexico, Silko has gone on to teach at universities throughout the West, including Navajo Community College, the University of New Mexico, and the University of Arizona. Although she wrote from childhood, she began publishing her poetry and short stories in the late 1960s, and is best-known for her novels, including *Ceremony* (1977), *Storyteller* (1981), and *Almanac of the Dead* (1991), and several collections of her poetry, including *Laguna Woman* (1974).

Silko has been a central figure in the Native American literary renaissance which started in the 1970s with her work and that of James Welch, Paula Gunn Allen, and N. Scott Momaday, telling the stories of contemporary Native American lives. Silko's concern with rebirth and continuity emerges in part from her own life experience, and in part from Laguna tradition. Growing up so near to Los Alamos, the site of the explosion of the first atomic bomb, had a deep effect on Silko; as she has said, "The Pueblo people have always concentrated upon making things grow, and appreciating things that are alive and natural, because life is so precious in the desert. The irony is that so close to us . . . scientists began the scientific and technological activity which created the potential end to our whole planet, the whole human race." This irony is imbedded in most of Silko's work, especially *Ceremony* and *The Almanac of the Dead.*

In the poetry included here, Silko illuminates the traditions which have resonated in her Laguna past. As she has said, "What I know is Laguna. This place I am from is everything I am as a writer and human being."

TS'ITS'TSI'NAKO, THOUGHT-WOMAN

Ts'its'tsi'nako, Thought-Woman,
is sitting in her room
and whatever she thinks about
appears.

She thought of her sisters,
Nau'ts'ity'i and I'tcts'ity'i,
and together they created the Universe
this world
and the four worlds below.

Thought-Woman, the spider,
named things and
as she named them
they appeared.

She is sitting in her room
thinking of a story now

I'm telling you the story
she is thinking.

SLIM MAN CANYON

early summer Navajo Nation, 1972 for John

700 years ago
people were living here
water was running gently
and the sun was warm
on pumpkin flowers.
It was 700 years ago
deep in this canyon
with sandstone rising high above
The rock   the silence   tall sky and flowing water

Leslie Marmon Silko, "Ts'its'tsi'nako, Thought-Woman" (1977) from *Ceremony* (1977); "Slim Man Canyon" and "Prayer to the Pacific" (1972) from *Voices of the Rainbow,* ed. Kenneth Rosen (1975).

> sunshine through cottonwood leaves
> the willow smell in the wind
> > 700 years.

The rhythm
> the horses feet   moving strong through
> > > white deep sand.

Where I come from is like this
> the warmth, the fragrance, the silence.
Blue sky and rainclouds in the distance
> > we ride together
> > > past cliffs with stories and songs
> > > painted on rock.
> > > > 700 years ago.

PRAYER TO THE PACIFIC

1

I traveled to the ocean
> distant
> > from my southwest land of sandrock
> > to the moving blue water
> Big as the myth of origin.

2

Pale
pale water in the yellow-white light of
> > sun   floating west
> > > to China
> > where ocean herself was born.
Clouds that blow across the sand are wet.

3

Squat in the wet sand and speak to Ocean:
> I return to you   turquoise   the red coral you sent us,
> > sister spirit of Earth.
Four round stones in my pocket   I carry back the ocean
> > to suck and to taste.

4
Thirty thousand years ago
             Indians came riding across the ocean
             carried by giant sea turtles.
Waves were high that day
             great sea turtles waded   slowly   out
                              from the gray sundown sea.
Grandfather Turtle rolled in the sand   four times
                   and disappeared
                        swimming into the sun.

5
And so   from that time
             immemorial,
                   as the old people say,
rainclouds drift from the west
                   gift from the ocean.

6
Green leaves in the wind
Wet earth on my feet
             swallowing raindrops
                   clear from China.

FURTHER READINGS
Gregory Salyer, *Leslie Marmon Silko* (Twayne, 1997); Louise K. Barnett and James L. Thorson, eds., *Leslie Marmon Silko : A Collection of Critical Essays* (University of New Mexico, 1999); Donna Perry, *Backtalk: Women Writers Speak Out: Interviews* (Rutgers University Press, 1993); Laura Coltelli, ed., *Winged Words: American Indian Writers Speak* (University of Nebraska Press, 1990); Per Seyersted, *Leslie Marmon Silko* (Boise State University Press, 1980); Edith Blicksilver, "Transitionalism vs. Modernity: Leslie Silko on American Indian Women," *Southwest Review* 64 (Spring 1979): 149–160; Lawrence J. Evers and Dennis W. Carr, eds., "A Conversation with Leslie Marmon Silko," *Sun Tracks* 3 (Fall 1976): 28–33.

Elsie Clews Parsons (1875–1941)

Born in New York City, Elsie Clews Parsons was the eldest of three children and the only daughter of Henry Clews, the son of a Staffordshire potter who had emigrated to the U.S. and founded a New York bank, and Lucy Madison Worthington, a descendent of President James Madison. Her life followed the usual contours of her social position, but Parsons demonstrated a great degree of independence. Although her family pressed her to become a debutante, she chose instead to attend Barnard where she received an A.B. in 1896, and then went on to Columbia University, where she received a Ph.D. in sociology in 1899.

Though married and the mother of four children, Parsons turned her seemingly limitless reserves of both energy and cash to pacifism, socialism, feminism, and anthropology. After a brief appointment as an instructor in the Sociology Department at Barnard College from 1902 to 1905, she taught graduate courses on the family and gender at Columbia University. She spent a good deal of her time with young radicals and intellectuals, and wrote occasionally for Max Eastman's *Masses*. She also became involved with Heterodoxy, a feminist network in Greenwich Village. Later, she helped found The New School for Social Research in New York City.

Parsons's scholarship falls mostly into two categories: sociological studies, with a special interest in the politics of sex and gender; and folkloric and ethnographic writings, focusing on the Native Americans of the American Southwest especially. Parsons's ethnographic studies, the result of tireless research in the American Southwest from the early 1910s until her death in 1941, include *Pueblo Indian Religion* (1939) and *Tewa Tales* (1926). With rare generosity, she funded the work of numerous other women anthropologists working in the region, and was the first woman elected to the presidency of the American Anthropological Association.

Parsons's impressive folkloric work in the American Southwest is not without detractors who criticize her for encouraging informants to share information about secret sacred ceremonies.

However, Parsons's tireless collection of Southwestern Indian traditions has provided a written record of the distinctive traditions of
the Pueblo peoples. This Hopi origin story, collected in the 1920s, is
an account of how some of these peoples came to call the West
their home.

A HOPI CREATION STORY

When the [people] were way underneath, they were ants. Then
they came to another place and turned into other creatures. At still
another place they became like people but with long tails. They
knew they had tails and were ashamed.

They were very crazy; the women would not mind their husbands. They said, "We are not dependent on marriage to live." There
was a river, and they divided; the men went across the river, and the
women stayed where they were, at their village. In springtime
the women planted their corn and melons by themselves, and the
men planted, too. The men raised lots of crops, and the women, too.
But next year the women raised only half of what they raised
before. In the third year, the women got very little corn and few
melons, but the men got more than before. In the fourth year the
women had no crops, but the men had large crops. "Throw us some
corn, some watermelons!" the women called across. "We can't
throw anything to you," the men answered.

About that time a flood was coming closer and closer, and the
women began to build a tower. They built and built, but they never
reached the sky. The women thought they were braver than the
men, smarter than the men; but the men thought women could not
do much. The tower fell down.

Then the men began to think about it, for the flood kept on
coming. They were thinking about what would reach the sky. First
they planted pine, it grew and reached the sky, but could not go
through. [Grandmother Spiderwoman told them to plant reeds.]
Next they planted reeds, and sang a song to make the reeds grow.
They sang and sang, and the reeds grew and grew and reached the
sky and went through.

Elsie Clews Parsons, from *Pueblo Indian Religion* (1939).

It was Badger they sent up first, and he stepped on the reeds and went up and up and up. Pretty soon Badger went through and was looking around. But there was not enough light to see. Then Badger went back. "What did you see?" said the men. "Did you find the earth?" Badger said, "I could not see much up there. It was dark." [Next they sent Shrike up.]

It was dark where Shrike came out and very cold. He saw a little stick and perched on it. He looked around in search of someone. Soon he saw a fire to the northeast, a very small fire. "I guess someone lives over there," he said to himself. He flew toward the fire and soon reached it. There was a little house and a little field with very high corn in it. The cornfield was a very small place. Someone was watching the fire. He was sitting with his back to the fire, eating green corn. Shrike went by, flying slowly. He was soon close to the man; the man did not hear him. Shrike came up to him, stood there, and asked him: "Who are you living here?" The man turned round suddenly, saw Shrike, and started up to get something. Close by him was a mask which he had taken off and left near him. He stretched out for it but could not reach it to put it on. "Oh, oh! oh, oh!" he said. "I did not know anybody was coming." It was Masauwü.

"Where did you come from?"—"From over there."—"All right; you outsmarted me. I cannot put on my mask. I did not know you were coming. It is all right; it makes no difference. Sit down! Sit down!" His mask was a large one with only a little hair on it and with big eyes. Whenever he hears people, he puts on his mask and frightens them away, so they do not catch him. Soon Masauwü gave Shrike something to eat. He had watermelon, muskmelon, pumpkin, and squash. He gave Shrike a lot to eat. Shrike took his pipe, put in the tobacco, took four puffs and handed it to Masauwü, saying, "My friend!" Masauwü took four puffs and gave the pipe back to him, saying, "My friend!" Masauwü asked, "Whence come you? Perhaps you are looking for something. I have never heard of you. I live here alone."—"Yes, I came out of the earth."—"Is that true?"—"Yes, I came out of the earth."—"Oh! I have heard that people live down in the earth."—"That is where I came from."—"What has happened there?"—"A great deal of trouble. A great many people, especially the young people, pay no heed to anyone, they respect no one. They are continually fighting and killing and causing sickness.

They are always doing medicine man tricks, always planning how to make someone sick. They get power, [they change into coyotes.] None is concerned for the consequences of what he does. If a man meets a girl, he will take her off to have intercourse. There is much sickness, too much trouble. The chief does not like this state of things. That is why he told us to hunt for the way out. I found it."— "All right; you outsmarted me. You saw my mask; I could not reach it. Had I heard you coming, I should have put on my mask, and your people would not be able to get out. But now when you go down, tell the people to come out, you have got the better of me. I will give you my land. When you come out, send me word!"

"Four days from today we go up," said the chief. Then, just when the flood was close to their village, they went up—they all went up.

"I think we are ready to start," said Town chief as he came out and stood in front of them. The War chief was much farther back, watching the bad people in order to keep them from coming out of the earth. The other people now sang a long song.

Spider Woman, the War Twins, and Mockingbird are the first to climb up and out. Mockingbird was sitting close to the hole where the people were coming out. He gave them a language. That is how they got their language, Hopi, American, Navaho, Paiute, Shoshone, and all the other Indians.

There was no light. They talked about it at the hole where they came out. "How can we get a light?" Somebody said, "We will make stars." So they made stars. Coyote was sitting with them (different kinds of animals came out with them), he could understand them, but he could not talk. They said to two boys, "Go to a certain place and place these stars properly!" Coyote said to himself, "I will go with the two boys." They put the Seven together, the Pleiades, in a good position, and those six, Orion, they put them together, and the biggest one they put toward the east, and another they put on the south side, and another on the west side, and another on the north side. Then they put up the Dipper. Just when they had put all these up, Coyote said to himself, "It is a big job!" He said to the boys, "We shall never finish this work, we shall all die first, why can't we do this?" And he took the stars and threw them in every direction, improperly. So they came back, the boys and Coyote. Next night they were watching and they saw the Big Star come out, before daylight. That will be Dawn Star. Soon another star came out from the south. Then they said, "We will call that star Ponu'chona." Then two came up, but did not give much light. When they were going down in the west, another big star was going ahead of them. "We will give [that star] a name," they said. "We will call him Tasupi," they said. About that time a north star came out. About that time the Pleiades came out from the east, then the six came out; it began to get cold. They did not give much light. Then they saw stars scattered all over the sky. The people said, "Bad Coyote, you did that?" — "Yes," he said. "If you had not gone with them, all the stars would be well placed. But you are bad Coyote; you scattered them all over the sky." They were very angry. But Coyote said, "That's all right. It's a lot of work to put them all into good positions, better to scatter them around."

Well, those stars did not give much light, so they thought about what they could do for more light. So somebody said, "We will make Moon." They asked him what they could make it of. "We will make it of a wedding blanket." So they sent for those same boys who put up the stars. They put up the wedding blanket in some way. Then they saw a light coming out, and it was Moon, and they gave it a name. It gave them some light, but not enough, they said. Then they thought about it again. "We will make something else for a better light," somebody said. He gathered a blanket, a buckskin, a white foxskin, and a parrot tail and he sent for the same two boys, brave boys, and they took the things to the east and they put them up in some way, somehow. Well, when the moon came out and went down, about the time daylight would first come, out came the foxskin for daylight, next came the parrot tail, making it yellow. Then the sun came out, but it could not move. "Something is wrong. Why can it not move?" Then they asked one another, "What can make it go?" At last Coyote said, "Nothing is wrong with it. All is fixed as it should be. Nothing is wrong, but if somebody should die right now, then it would move." Just then a girl died, and the sun began to move. When it got to the middle of the sky, it stopped again. "Well, what is the matter?" Coyote said, "Nothing is the matter, nothing is wrong. If somebody die[s] right now, it will move." Then the son of one of the head men died, and that made the sun go again. "It is only by somebody dying every day—morning, noon, and evening—that the sun will move every day," said Coyote. Coyote thinks more than anybody. Smart fellow!

First a girl died, then a boy, then a woman. After four days she came back again. "Well, if somebody dies, in four days they will come back again." Then Coyote said, "I don't think that will be right for us. If we die and come back in four days, we won't be afraid to die. I will die and never come back." Then he overate and died, and after four days he did not come back. He never came back. About that time another woman died, and they counted four days, but she did not come back because Coyote died and did not come back.

This made the people feel very bad. The husband of the woman was very unhappy, and he went back to the place where they came out; they had put a round cactus over the hole. He pulled away the cactus and looked down into the hole. His wife was way down underneath, she was combing her hair. And Coyote was there too. Hearing something, he raised his head and said, "You know I am dead and your wife died too, but we came back here. And after this, when anybody dies, he will come back here and live forever. So do not feel so bad about your wife!"

The world was still soft, muddy from the flood; so the [War] Twins shot their lightnings and made canyons for the waters to drain into. The Twins made the mountains and everything that is of stone. They hardened the mud into rocks, spraying with medicine from Spider Grandmother. The chief suggested to all the horned animals to tear the earth into valleys.

FURTHER READINGS
Desley Deacon, *Elsie Clews Parsons: Inventing Modern Life* (University of Chicago Press, 1997); Rosemary Levy Zumwalt, *Wealth and Rebellion: Elsie Clews Parsons, Anthropologist and Folklorist* (University of Illinois Press, 1992); Peter H. Hare, *A Woman's Quest for Science: Portrait of Anthropologist Elsie Clews Parsons* (Prometheus Books, 1985); Harold Courlander, *Hopi Voices: Recollections, Traditions, and Narratives of the Hopi Indians* (University of New Mexico Press, 1982); Gerald Hausman, *How Chipmunk Got Tiny Feet: Native American Animal Origin Stories* (HarperCollins, 1995).

Fabiola Cabeza de Baca
(1894–1991)

Fabiola Cabeza de Baca was born near Las Vegas, New Mexico, in 1894, part of a family which held a land grant from Spain. In this section from her memoir, *We Fed Them Cactus*, Fabiola Cabeza de Baca tells of growing up on the Llano, plains that stretch across northeastern New Mexico and northwestern Texas. Surrounded by her family and with a sense of connection to the land from which they drew their living, Cabeza de Baca writes of the fundamental transformations of her life created by the coming of the railroad, urbanization, and the resultant new prominence of *Americanos* in the region. Many New Mexican families who held Mexican land grants faced struggles to maintain possession of land they knew as home. Cabeza de Baca's family shared this uncertainty. Nonetheless, her stories of the Llano show the everyday patterns of living on a large ranch, where a rodeo was a cattle roundup, and sheepherding required bravery as well as patience.

A woman's life on the Llano was more than waiting for the men to come home. Certainly, one of Fabiola Cabeza de Baca's duties as a daughter was to pray for the safety of men away hunting buffalo, or to pray for the rain upon which the inhabitants of the Llano depended. Beyond that, though, a girl was expected to take part in all the necessary activities of a ranch, from lambing to herding. Elder women, like her grandmother, might serve as overseers for hired men's work.

Cabeza de Baca earned a bachelor's degree from New Mexico Normal in 1921, and a BS degree in home economics from New Mexico State University in Las Cruces. For more than thirty years, she worked for the Agricultural Extension Service in New Mexico as a home economist, and in 1950 she worked with UNESCO to set up extension service training centers for Tarascan Indians in Mexico. In her work as an extension agent, she went against the norm in emphasizing the importance of maintaining local foodways, arguing that native diets were often nutritious and well-balanced. She is best remembered, however, as a writer; some critics have called *We Fed Them Cactus* the first Chicana novel. She published the first New Mexican cookbook, called *Historic Cookery* (1931), which popularized the use of chile and the New Mexican cuisine which is now familiar throughout the United States. She also published *The Good Life: New Mexico Traditions and Food* (1949), a collection of folklore and recipes. She died in Albuquerque in 1991 at the age of ninety-seven.

LONELINESS WITHOUT DESPAIR

The Llano is a great plateau. Its sixty thousand square miles tip almost imperceptibly from fifty-five hundred feet above sea level in northwest New Mexico, to two thousand feet in northwest Texas.

From the Canadian River, the Llano runs southward some four hundred miles. The Pecos River and the historic New Mexican town of Las Vegas mark its ragged western edge, while two hundred miles to the east lie Palo Duro Canyon—once the goal of Spanish buffalo hunters—and the city of Amarillo, steeped in the traditions of Texas cattle-raising.

Between these boundaries are the settlements, whistlestops, trading posts, chapels, ranch headquarters and homesteader's houses—some new, some old, many abandoned—which tell the story of more than a hundred years of living on the Llano.

Curving along the Llano's high northern and western rim is the Cap Rock, the rough-hewn Ceja, or eyebrow, above the plain.

No other land, perhaps, is more varied in its topography than the Ceja and the Llano country. As one descends Cañon del Agua Hill from Las Vegas, a full view of this great stretch of country greets the sight. There are myriads of hills, peaks, wooded mesas, canyons and valleys. The Montoso, wooded land, extends for miles and miles. In the distance one can see Conchas Mesa, Corazón and Cuervo peaks, the Variadero Tableland, and many other hillocks. Traveling on, descending hills, crossing arroyos, one reaches Cabra

---

Fabiola Cabeza de Baca, "Loneliness Without Despair" and "The Night It Rained," from *We Fed Them Cactus* (1950).

Spring. This is an oasis, a spring of sweet water which saved many a traveler from dying of thirst on his way to the buffalo and Comanche country. Later it was a watering place for an overnight stop on the way to the sheep and cattle territory.

It is unbelievable that in a country where rain is scant, there can be so many springs gushing from the earth in the most secluded places. There are lakes all along the land, some made by rains, some fed by springs from the hills. If rains are plentiful, these lakes may be filled the year round; if rains are few, the lakes may dry up from evaporation.

There are deep canyons in the hills, seemingly inaccessible, yet the old-timers knew every canyon, spring and lake from Las Vegas to the Panhandle of Texas.

After passing Cabra Spring, one comes in view of the Luciano and Palomas mesas, Tucumcari Peak, Cuervo Hill and, in the distance, Pintada Mesa. Bull Canyon of the Luciano Mesa presents one of the picturesque panoramas of the area. Its red coloring, from red earth and rocks surrounding it, is typical of the land and a sight comparable, perhaps, to the Grand Canyon of Arizona.

From Cañon del Agua Hill to Luciano Mesa, the vegetation includes juniper, piñon, yucca, mesquite, sagebrush, gramma and buffalo grasses, as well as lemita, prickly pear, and pitahaya. There are wild flowers in abundance, and when the spring comes rainy, the earth abounds in all colors imaginable. The fields of oregano and cactus, when in full bloom, can compete with the loveliest of gardens.

It is a lonely land because of its immensity, but it lacks nothing for those who enjoy Nature in her full grandeur. The colors of the skies, of the hills, the rocks, the birds and the flowers, are soothing to the most troubled heart. It is loneliness without despair. The whole world seems to be there, full of promise and gladness.

Leaving the Luciano and Palomas, the Ceja country, and traveling east and south, one comes upon the great Llano, so extensive that one must see it to realize its vastness. For miles and miles, as far as the eye can see, is the expanse of level land. Here are mesquite, prickly pear, yucca, and grass, grass, grass.

There is little similarity between the Llano of today and that of the last century. The Llano, then, was an endless territory of grass and desert plants, with nothing to break the monotony except the horizon and the sky. In the days of the buffalo and the Comanche, the Llano was uninhabited and dangerous. The buffalo hunters knew the waterholes and springs, yet they had to be careful to follow the right trails; otherwise they would perish.

The early Spanish colonists had settled along the rivers in north central New Mexico, using the surrounding land for pasturing their sheep and cattle. They did not extend their grazing because of the aridity of the country south and west of the Rio Grande, and because northern pastures along the smaller rivers lie in the cold belt where rigorous winters make it more difficult for stock to survive. The frequent raids of the Navajos were another deterrent to increasing the herds.

While the colonists had received all protection available against warring Indian tribes during Spanish rule, when Mexico gained its independence from Spain in 1821, the New Mexicans were left to survive by their own resourcefulness. They found it prohibitive to augment their livestock. Indians came down on the settlements, killing herders and driving off sheep, cattle and horses. Between 1821 and 1840, flocks and herds had to be reduced to numbers small enough to be tended close to the settlements. At night all livestock had to be corralled in the *placitas,* the squares within the walls of houses.

The New Mexican home of the *rico,* or landowner, as I heard my grandmother describe it, was a fortress in itself. It was built around a square, with living quarters on one side. Another side comprised storerooms, granaries and workshops. On the third side was constructed the *cochera* for the family coach, *carretas,* and wagons. The fourth end, which completed the square, was a high wall with one entrance—a massive gate of hand-hewn timbers. Through this gate, the horses, mules, cattle, sheep, goats, and pigs were driven at night. The outer walls of the flat-roofed adobe houses were built high and pierced with troneras, loopholes for fighting Indians.

Livestock had to be kept close to the settlements and under close surveillance of the herders. Consequently, the range near the towns and villages became denuded of the natural browse, which for years had pastured the stock. Traditionally, meat had been the main fare on New Mexican tables, but with the decrease in livestock, the supply became more and more scarce.

The Llano and Ceja country were well known to the New Mexicans who ventured forth as Indian fighters and to hunt the buffalo. They brought back tales of the good pastures and the extensive territory beyond the mountains.

The sheep and cattle owners traveled eastward, and on the Ceja and the Llano found the Promised Land. There, where the mountains end and the plains begin, they found grama and buffalo grass growing as tall as the cattle.

The best pastures were on the Ceja, the Cap Rock area at the top of the Staked Plains. As one descends south and east from Las Vegas, all the country is known as the Llano, and it is the history of this section, of its people and their lives, which this book tells. To one living on the American plains of the Middle West, so level and flat, the land on the bluffs of the Staked Plains, with its rocky hills, juniper, mesquite, and piñon, may not seem a llano, but to New Mexicans, because of the drop of two or three thousand feet from the peaks, it is not the Sierras, and they have called it the Llano— the wide open spaces.

In 1840, the sheep owners started sending herders with their flocks into the Ceja and the Llano, and the Hispanos continued to prosper in the sheep industry for more than half a century.

In those days a man had to be courageous to face the many dangers confronting lonely living far from the populated areas, yet there seems to have been no lack of men who were willing to follow the herds for the employers, the *patrones*. In feudal times, there were many poor people who became indebted to the *ricos*, and the rich were never at a loss to find men to be sent with flocks of sheep. Then, of course, herding was one of the few kinds of employment available in New Mexico. If a man became indebted to a *rico,* he was in bond slavery to repay. Those in debt had a deep feeling of honesty, and they did not bother to question whether the system was right or wrong. Entire families often served a *patrón* for generations to meet their obligations.

If the flock of the *patrón* ran into thousands, he employed a *mayordomo,* or manager, and several overseers, called *caporales.* The *caporal* was in charge of the herders, and had to see that the sheep were provided proper quarters in the different seasons. He furnished the sheep camps with provisions, and it was his duty to make sure that water was available for the *partidas* under the care of each herder. A *partida* usually consisted of a thousand head of sheep. The *caporales* worked under the *mayordomo,* or directly under the *patrón* if no manager were employed.

I can remember my paternal grandfather's sheep camps and the men who worked for him. They were loyal people, and as close to us as our own family. They were, every one of them, grandfather's *compadres,* for he and grandmother had stood as sponsors in baptism or marriage to many of their children.

Lambing season was a trying one, since the range was extensive. This happened in the early spring, and the weather on the Llano can be as changeable as the colors of the rainbow. If the season was rainy, it went hard with the sheep and many lambs were lost. If there had been a dry spell the year before, the ewes came out poorly and it was difficult for the mothers bringing in young lambs. Sheep raising was always a gamble until the day when feed became plentiful with the change in transportation facilities.

In order to save ewes and lambs during a cold spell, the herders built fires around the herds. The fires were kept burning day and night until better weather came to the rescue. Quite often the *patrones* and their sons, who might have just come back from Eastern colleges, helped during lambing.

Shearing the sheep was done in the summer and there were professional shearers who went from camp to camp each year. This was a bright spot in the life of the herders, for then they had a touch of the outside world. Among the shearers and herders there were always musicians and poets, and I heard Papá tell of pleasant evenings spent singing and storytelling, and of *corridos* composed to relate events which had taken place. These poets and singers were like the troubadours of old. The *corridos* dealt with the life of the people in the communities and ranches; they told of unrequited love, of death, of tragedies and events such as one reads about in the newspapers today.

The sheepherder watched his flock by day, traveling many miles while the sheep grazed on the range. As his flock pastured, he sat on a rock or on his coat; he whittled some object or composed songs or poetry until it was time to move the flock to water or better pasture. Many of the *corridos* are an inheritance from the unlettered sheepherder. At night he moved his flock to camp, a solitary tent where he prepared his food and where he slept. If there were several camps close to each other, the herders gathered at one tent for companionship.

In winter the sheepherder's life was dreary. Coming into his old tent at night, he had to prepare for possible storms. The wood for his fire might be wet, and with scarcely any matches, perhaps only a flint stone to light it, his hands would be numb before he had any warmth. He might not even have wood, for in many parts of the Llano there is no wood, and cowchips had to serve as fuel.

He went to sleep early to the sound of the coyote's plaintive cry, wondering how many lambs the wolves or coyotes might carry away during the night. The early call of the turtle dove and the bleating of lambs were his daily alarm clock, and he arose to face another day of snow, rain, or wind. Yet he always took care of his sheep, and I have never known any mishap due to the carelessness of the herder. The *caporales* traveled on horseback from camp to camp in all kinds of weather to make sure that all was well with the herders and the flocks.

I knew an old man who worked for my maternal grandmother for many years. Often I accompanied my grandmother to the sheep camp on the Salado, and I always came back with a feeling of loneliness. Yet, at camp, the old man always seemed happy. If he was not at camp when we arrived, we found him by listening for his whistling or singing in the distance. When I think about the herders on the endless Llano, I know that they are the unsung heroes of an industry which was our livelihood for generations.

THE NIGHT IT RAINED

We had just finished branding at the Spear Bar Ranch. For a whole week we had been rounding up cattle and branding each bunch as they were brought in from the different pastures.

As we sat out on the patio of our ranch home, I watched Papá leaning back in his chair against the wall of the house. He always did that when he was happy. The coolness of the evening brought relief from the heat and dust in the noisy corrals during the day.

The hard dirt floor of the patio always had a certain coolness about it. Just a few nights before, the boys had been in the mood to renovate it. They brought a load of dirt, which we sprinkled with water and spread over with burlap sacks. We had such fun tramping it down. We made it a game by jumping on it until the soil was packed hard. This was repeated until we had a solid, even patio floor. Around it the boys built a supporting wall of rock filled in with mud.

Our home was a rambling structure without plan. It was built of the red rock from the hills around us, put together with mud. The walls were two feet thick. Viewed from front, the house had an L shape, but from the back, it appeared as a continuous sequence of rooms.

We had pine floors in the front room and dining room and the other rooms had hard-packed dirt floors. The *despensa* occupied a space of twelve hundred square feet. This room served as a store-room, summer kitchen, and sleeping quarters when stray cowboys dropped in on a snowy or rainy night. The windows had wooden bars and so had the door.

The *cochera* adjacent to the *despensa* was a relic of the days of carriages and horses. When automobiles came into use, it became a garage, but we always called it the *cochera*. The front had two large doors which opened wide for the carriage to be brought out, and the hole for the carriage tongue always remained on the doors to remind us of horse and buggy days.

The roof on our house was also of hard-packed mud. Many years later, it boasted a tin roof. The dirt roof had been supported by thick rectangular *vigas,* or beams, which remained even after we had the tin roof.

All the rooms were spacious and our home had a feeling of hospitality. We had only the most necessary pieces of furniture. We had Papá's big desk in the front room and dozens of chairs with wide arms. Over the mantel of the corner fireplace, in the dining room, hung a large antique mirror. Grandmother's wedding trunk, brought over the Chihuahua Trail, stood against a wall. It was made of leather, trimmed with solid brass studs. We had no clothes closets, but there were plenty of trunks in every room. Mamá's wedding trunk, made of brass, tin and wood, was the shape of a coffer. Papá's trunk was very similar. We all had trunks.

The most necessary pieces of furniture were the beds. Of these, we had plenty, but many a night three of us slept in one bed, and if we were inconvenienced we were recompensed. Our sudden guests came from different *ranchos,* and they always had wonderful tales and news to relate.

Tonight we had no guests. We were a happy family enjoying the evening breeze with hopes for rain. The cowboys did not need chairs; they were stretched out on the ground with their hands clasped behind their heads as a protection from the hard dirt floor of the patio—a typical relaxation from the day's labors.

I can never remember when Papá was not humming a tune, unless his pipe was in his mouth. Tonight he was just looking up at the sky. As the clouds began to gather towards the east, he said, "We may have some rain before morning. Those are promising clouds. If rain does not come before the end of the month, we will not have grass for winter grazing. Our pastures are about burnt up."

From the time I was three years old—when I went out to the Llano for the first time—I began to understand that without rain our subsistence would be endangered. I never went to bed without praying for rain. I have never been inclined to ask for favors from heaven, but for rain, I always pleaded with every saint and the Blessed Mother. My friends in the city would be upset when rain spoiled a day's outing, but I always was glad to see it come. In the years of drought, Papá's blue eyes were sad, but when the rains poured down, his eyes danced like the stars in the heavens on a cloudless night. All of us were happy then. We could ask for the moon and he would bring it down.

Good years meant fat cattle and no losses, and that, we knew would bring more money. We had never been poor, because those who live from the land are never really poor, but at times Papá's cash on hand must have been pretty low.

If that ever happened, we did not know it. Money in our lives was not important; rain was important. We never counted our money; we counted the weeks and months between rains. I could always tell anyone exactly to the day and hour since the last rain, and I knew how many snowfalls we had in winter and how many rains in spring. We would remember an unusually wet year for a lifetime; we enjoyed recalling it during dry spells.

Rain for us made history. It brought to our minds days of plenty, of happiness and security, and in recalling past events, if they fell on rainy years, we never failed to stress that fact. The droughts were as impressed on our souls as the rains. When we spoke of the Armistice of World War I, we always said, "The drought of 1918 when the Armistice was signed."

We knew that the east wind brought rain, but if the winds persisted from other directions we knew we were doomed. The northwest wind brought summer showers.

From childhood, we were brought up to watch for signs of rain. In the New Year, we started studying the *Cabañuelas*. Each day of January, beginning with the first day, corresponded to each month of the year. Thus, the first of January indicated what kind of weather we would have during the first month. The second day told us the weather for February and the third for March. When we reached the thirteenth of January, we started again. This day would tell us the weather for December. After twenty-four days, we knew for sure whether the *Cabañuelas* would work for us or not. If the days representing the months backward and forward coincided, we could safely tell anyone whether to expect rain in April or in May. The *Cabañuelas* are an inheritance from our Spanish ancestors and are still observed in Spain and Latin America.

From the Indians we learned to observe the number of snowfalls of the season. If the first snow fell on the tenth of any month, there would be ten falls that year. If it fell on the twentieth, we would be more fortunate: there would be twenty snowfalls during the cold months.

We faithfully watched the moon for rain. During the rainy season, the moon had control of the time the rains would fall. April is the rainy month on the Llano, and if no rain fell by the end of April, those versed in astrology would tell us that we could still expect rain in May if the April moon was delayed. There were years when the moons came behind schedule.

Whether these signs worked or not, we believed in them thoroughly. To us, looking for rain, they meant hope, faith, and a trust in the Great Power that takes care of humanity.

Science has made great strides. Inventions are myriad. But no one has yet invented or discovered a method to bring rain when wanted or needed. As a child, prayer was the only solution to the magic of rain. As I grew older and I began to read of the discoveries of science, I knew that someday the Llano would have rain at its bidding. On reaching middle age, I am still praying for rain.

My mind still holds memories of torrential rains. Papá would walk from room to room in the house watching the rain from every window and open door. I would follow like a shadow. My heart would flutter with joy to see Papá so radiant with happiness.

Often before the rain was over, we would be out on the patio. I would exclaim, "We are getting wet, Papá!" "No, no," he would say. He wanted to feel the rain, to know that it was really there. How important it was in our lives!

After the rain subsided, off came my shoes and I was out enjoying the wetness, the rivulets. The arroyo flood would be coming down like a mad roaring bull. Papá and I would stand entranced watching the angry red waters come down. The arroyo, usually dry and harmless, would come into its own defying all living things, enjoying a few hours of triumph. A normally dry arroyo is treacherous when it rains.

If the rain came at night, we were cheated of the pleasure of enjoying the sight. Yet there was a feeling of restfulness as we listened to the rain on the roof. The raindrops on the windows showed like pearls, and to us they were more valuable than the precious stones themselves.

A few rains and then sun, and the grass would be as tall as the bellies of the cows grazing upon it. And Papá was happy.

A storm on the Llano is beautiful. The lightning comes down like arrows of fire and buries itself on the ground. At the pealing of thunder, the bellowing of cattle fills the heart of the listeners with music. A feeling of gladness comes over one as the heavens open in downpour to bathe Mother Earth. Only those ever watching and waiting for rain can feel the rapture it brings.

Papá never saw the lightning. He was too busy watching for the raindrops.

FURTHER READINGS

Tey Diana Rebolledo, "Introduction," *We Fed Them Cactus* (University of New Mexico Press, 1994); Genaro M. Padilla, "Imprisoned Narrative? Or Lies, Secrets, and Silence in New Mexico Women's Autobiography," in Héctor Calderón and José David Saldívar, eds., *Criticism in the Borderlands* (Duke University Press, 1991); Erlinda Gonzales-Berry, ed., *Paso por aquí: Critical Essays on the New Mexican Literary Tradition, 1542–1988* (University of New Mexico Press, 1989); Genaro M. Padilla, "The Recovery of Chicano Nineteenth-Century Autobiography," *American Quarterly* 42 (1988).

Sarah Winnemucca Hopkins (1844–1891)

Sarah Winnemucca was born a member of the Northern Piute tribe near Truckee, in what is now Nevada. In the late 1840s, when Winnemucca was a small girl known as Thocmetony, her tribe first came into contact with white settlers in the region. During the 1840s, she learned English and Spanish in addition to three Indian languages, and assumed the name Sarah Winnemucca when she lived among whites in Genoa, Nevada. While in her teenage years, she became an interpreter between the Piutes and U.S. military officers and Indian agents, who oversaw the tribe on its reservation. After the Bannock War, Winnemucca traveled to San Francisco in 1879, where she began a speaking tour throughout the West campaigning for peace and security for the Piutes and for all Indians. In San Francisco, she was known in the newspapers as "Princess Sarah," and through the newspaper accounts, she attracted the attention of Eastern reformers concerned about the fate of the Indians. With their encouragement, she traveled to Washington, DC, in 1880, where she met with President Rutherford B. Hayes.

In 1883, Winnemucca and her husband, Lewis Hopkins, traveled East, where she delivered a series of well-attended public lectures about the Piutes. Frustrated by the limitations of the lecture format, she decided to tell a fuller version of Piute lifeways. Published with the editorial assistance of Mary Peabody Mann, her book was *Life Among the Piutes: Their Wrongs and Claims* (1883). The first known work published in English by a Native American woman in North America, *Life Among the Piutes* combined tribal history, personal narrative, folklore, and political tract, ending in a petition to the U.S. Congress on behalf of the Piute people.

Returning to Nevada in 1884, Winnemucca established a school in Lovelock where Indian children could learn their own Indian languages and preserve their own cultures. After four years, however, the school closed. Exhausted and in ill health, Winnemucca went to live with her sister in Henry's Lake, Idaho, where she died not long after in 1891. So influential had she been in her lifetime that newspapers throughout the country, including the *New York Times,* carried her obituary.

FIRST MEETING OF PIUTES AND WHITES

I was born somewhere near 1844, but am not sure of the precise time. I was a very small child when the first white people came into our country. They came like a lion, yes, like a roaring lion, and have continued so ever since, and I have never forgotten their first coming. My people were scattered at that time over nearly all the territory now known as Nevada. My grandfather was chief of the entire Piute nation, and was camped near Humboldt Lake, with a small portion of his tribe, when a party travelling eastward from California was seen coming. When the news was brought to my grandfather, he asked what they looked like? When told that they had hair on their faces, and were white, he jumped up and clasped his hands together, and cried aloud,—

"My white brothers,—my long-looked for white brothers have come at last!"

He immediately gathered some of his leading men, and went to the place where the party had gone into camp. Arriving near them, he was commanded to halt in a manner that was readily understood without an interpreter. Grandpa at once made signs of friendship by throwing down his robe and throwing up his arms to show them he had no weapons; but in vain,—they kept him at a distance. He knew not what to do. He had expected so much pleasure in welcoming his white brothers to the best in the land, that after looking at them sorrowfully for a little while, he came away quite unhappy. But he would not give them up so easily. He took some of his most trustworthy men and followed them day after day, camping near them at night, and travelling in sight of them by day, hoping in this way to gain their confidence. But he was disappointed, poor dear old soul!

I can imagine his feelings, for I have drank deeply from the same cup. When I think of my past life, and the bitter trials I have

---

Sarah Winnemucca Hopkins, "First Meeting of Piutes and Whites," from *Life Among the Piutes* (1883).

endured, I can scarcely believe I live, and yet I do; and, with the help of Him who notes the sparrow's fall, I mean to fight for my down-trodden race while life lasts.

Seeing they would not trust him, my grandfather left them, saying, "Perhaps they will come again next year." Then he summoned his whole people, and told them this tradition:—

"In the beginning of the world there were only four, two girls and two boys. Our forefather and mother were only two, and we are their children. You all know that a great while ago there was a happy family in this world. One girl and one boy were dark and the others were white. For a time they got along together without quarrelling, but soon they disagreed, and there was trouble. They were cross to one another and fought, and our parents were very much grieved. They prayed that their children might learn better, but it did not do any good; and afterwards the whole household was made so unhappy that the father and mother saw that they must separate their children; and then our father took the dark boy and girl, and the white boy and girl, and asked them, 'Why are you so cruel to each other?' They hung down their heads, and would not speak. They were ashamed. He said to them, 'Have I not been kind to you all, and given you everything your hearts wished for? You do not have to hunt and kill your own game to live upon. You see, my dear children, I have power to call whatsoever kind of game we want to eat; and I also have the power to separate my dear children, if they are not good to each other.' So he separated his children by a word. He said, 'Depart from each other, you cruel children;—go across the mighty ocean and do not seek each other's lives.'

"So the light girl and boy disappeared by that one word, and their parents saw them no more, and they were grieved, although they knew their children were happy. And by-and-by the dark children grew into a large nation; and we believe it is the one we belong to, and that the nation that sprung from the white children will some time send some one to meet us and heal all the old trouble. Now, the white people we saw a few days ago must certainly be our white brothers, and I want to welcome them. I want to love them as I love all of you. But they would not let me; they were afraid. But they will come again, and I want you one and all to promise that, should I not live to welcome them myself, you will not hurt a hair on their heads, but welcome them as I tried to do."

How good of him to try and heal the wound, and how vain were his efforts! My people had never seen a white man, and yet they existed, and were a strong race. The people promised as he wished, and they all went back to their work.

The next year came a great emigration, and camped near Humboldt Lake. The name of the man in charge of the trains was Captain Johnson, and they stayed three days to rest their horses, as they had a long journey before them without water. During their stay my grandfather and some of his people called upon them, and they all shook hands, and when our white brothers were going away they gave my grandfather a white tin plate. Oh, what a time they had over that beautiful gift,—it was so bright! They say that after they left, my grandfather called for all his people to come together, and he then showed them the beautiful gift which he had received from his white brothers. Everybody was so pleased; nothing like it was ever seen in our country before. My grandfather thought so much of it that he bored holes in it and fastened it on his head, and wore it as his hat. He held it in as much admiration as my white sisters hold their diamond rings or a sealskin jacket. So that winter they talked of nothing but their white brothers. The following spring there came great news down the Humboldt River, saying that there were some more of the white brothers coming, and there was something among them that was burning all in a blaze. My grandfather asked them what it was like. They told him it looked like a man; it had legs and hands and a head, but the head had quit burning, and it was left quite black. There was the greatest excitement among my people everywhere about the men in a blazing fire. They were excited because they did not know there were any people in the world but the two,—that is, the Indians and the whites; they thought that was all of us in the beginning of the world, and, of course, we did not know where the others had come from, and we don't know yet. Ha! ha! oh, what a laughable thing that was! It was two negroes wearing red shirts!

The third year more emigrants came, and that summer Captain Fremont, who is now General Fremont.

My grandfather met him, and they were soon friends. They met just where the railroad crosses Truckee River, now called Wadsworth, Nevada. Captain Fremont gave my grandfather the name of Captain Truckee, and he also called the river after him. Truckee is an Indian word, it means *all right*, or *very well*. A party of twelve of my people went to California with Captain Fremont. I do not know just how long they were gone.

When my grandfather went to California he helped Captain Fremont fight the Mexicans. When he came back he told the people what a beautiful country California was. Only eleven returned home, one having died on the way back.

They spoke to their people in the English language, which was very strange to them all.

Captain Truckee, my grandfather, was very proud of it, indeed. They all brought guns with them. My grand-father would sit down with us for hours, and would say over and over again, "Goodee gun, goodee, goodee gun, heap shoot." They also brought some of the soldiers' clothes with all their brass buttons, and my people were very much astonished to see the clothes, and all that time they were peaceable toward their white brothers. They had learned to love them, and they hoped more of them would come. Then my people were less barbarous than they are nowadays.

That same fall, after my grandfather came home, he told my father to take charge of his people and hold the tribe, as he was going back to California with as many of his people as he could get to go with him. So my father took his place as Chief of the Piutes, and had it as long as he lived. Then my grandfather started back to California again with about thirty families. That same fall, very late, the emigrants kept coming. It was this time that our white brothers first came amongst us. They could not get over the mountains, so they had to live with us. It was on Carson River, where the great Carson City stands now. You call my people bloodseeking. My people did not seek to kill them, nor did they steal their horses,— no, no, far from it. During the winter my people helped them. They gave them such as they had to eat. They did not hold out their hands and say:—

"You can't have anything to eat unless you pay me." No,—no such word was used by us savages at that time; and the persons I am speaking of are living yet; they could speak for us if they choose to do so.

The following spring, before my grandfather returned home, there was a great excitement among my people on account of fearful news coming from different tribes, that the people whom they called their white brothers were killing everybody that came in their way, and all the Indian tribes had gone into the mountains to save their lives. So my father told all his people to go into the mountains and hunt and lay up food for the coming winter. Then we all went into the mountains. There was a fearful story they told us children. Our mothers told us that the whites were killing everybody and eating them. So we were all afraid of them. Every dust that we could see blowing in the valleys we would say it was the white people. In the late fall my father told his people to go to the rivers and fish, and we all went to Humboldt River, and the women went to work gathering wild seed, which they grind between the rocks. The stones are round, big enough to hold in the hands. The women did this when they got back, and when they had gathered all they could they put it in one place and covered it with grass, and then over the grass mud. After it is covered it looks like an Indian wigwam.

Oh, what a fright we all got one morning to hear some white people were coming. Every one ran as best they could. My poor mother was left with my little sister and me. Oh, I never can forget it. My poor mother was carrying my little sister on her back, and trying to make me run; but I was so frightened I could not move my feet, and while my poor mother was trying to get me along my aunt overtook us, and she said to my mother: "Let us bury our girls, or we shall all be killed and eaten up." So they went to work and buried us, and told us if we heard any noise not to cry out, for if we did they would surely kill us and eat us. So our mothers buried me and my cousin, planted sage bushes over our faces to keep the sun from burning them, and there we were left all day.

Oh, can any one imagine my feelings *buried alive*, thinking every minute that I was to be unburied and eaten up by the people that my grandfather loved so much? With my heart throbbing, and not daring to breathe, we lay there all day. It seemed that the night would never come. Thanks be to God! the night came at last. Oh, how I cried and said: "Oh, father, have you forgotten me? Are you never coming for me?" I cried so I thought my very heartstrings would break.

At last we heard some whispering. We did not dare to whisper to each other, so we lay still. I could hear their footsteps coming nearer and nearer. I thought my heart was coming right out of my mouth. Then I heard my mother say, "'T is right here!" Oh, can any one in this world ever imagine what were my feelings when I was dug up by my poor mother and father? My cousin and I were once more happy in our mothers' and fathers' care, and we were taken to where all the rest were.

FURTHER READINGS
Gae Whitney Canfield, *Sarah Winnemucca of the Northern Paiutes* (University of Oklahoma Press, 1988); Doris Kloss, *Sarah Winnemucca: The Story of an American Indian* (Dillon Press Inc., 1981); Katherine Gehm, *Sarah Winnemucca: Most Extraordinary Woman of the Paiute Nation* (O'Sullivan Woodside, 1975).

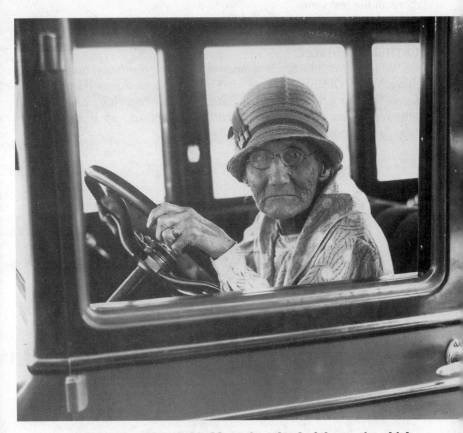

Amelda Ann Mansfield, 80, at the wheel of the car in which she retraced her overland journey by covered wagon. Used by permission of The San Antonio Light Collection, The Institute of Texan Cultures, University of Texas–San Antonio.

2

Landfall

Few events in American history have been as celebrated as the westward journey, the mid-century migration of a quarter of a million American families from "jumping off" places along the Missouri River to the Pacific Ocean. That thousand-mile excursion meant that families were leaving "the States" and that good-byes might last for a lifetime. The Trail was a wrenching break with the life that had gone on before, and many women in their childbearing years had just borne a child, carried with them an infant still nursing, or faced the fearful prospect of being delivered on the road. But land fever and gold fever were powerful aphrodisiacs and Americans were betting everything that the future lay in the West.

Between 1847 and 1865, the Overland Trail was a testing ground of hardihood and courage and innovation. In the early years emigrants had little help from surveys or maps—some guide books promised that the trip was only a summer's vacation, and that the Great Salt Lake emptied into the Pacific Ocean! And between 1851 and 1853 cholera ravaged the travelers and the Plains Indians alike.

The letters and diaries collected here attest to the fact that "the West," wherever one might find it, held very different experiences. Emma Kelly found the "West" in the "North," as she and thousands of gold-seekers struggled up the perilous Chilkoot Trail in Alaska, and the Chinese who settled on the Pacific Coast, found a land of incomprehensible customs. Against all challenges, women were as tenacious as men in mustering the courage to prove themselves equal to the challenges of the road.

Elizabeth Smith Dixon Geer

Elizabeth Smith Dixon Geer, her husband, and seven children, were in the vanguard of emigrants crossing the continent in 1847. Mrs. Dixon writes matter-of-factly of the daily tasks of travelers crossing mountain ranges and rivers, stretching supplies and "hiring" Indians to help them hunt. It was a rainy summer and children were almost always wet, adults were sick with dysentery or "mountain fever," and sometimes emigrants were buried along the road in unmarked graves. Against the ills of the road, most emigrants had only laudanum, tabasco, and whiskey.

The diary tells of one woman who burned the tarpaulin of the family wagon when her courage gave out, Elizabeth noting only that the husband, seeing his wagon in flames, "mustered spunk enough to give her a good flogging." Mrs. Dixon herself was sorely tested; the wagon party was caught in "snow, mud, and water." They managed to come into Oregon with the help of Indians who took them across the swollen Deschutes River in October. In Portland by Thanksgiving, Elizabeth found her family shelter in a "small, leaky concern with two families already in it. I got some of the men to carry my husband up through the rain and lay him in it." She nursed him through January and February, and watched him die. At her journey's end, she was a widow, "poor as a snake."

Undaunted by the hardship of the journey, Elizabeth found herself a new husband, a "stout, healthy man," the father of ten, and "a Yankee from Connecticut." They were married the very next year, and when her diary was printed, he appended a note telling all that she had made him a "first-rate wife."

OVERLAND DIARY, 1847

JAN. 31.—Rain all day. If I could tell you how we suffer you would not believe it. Our house, or rather a shed joined to a house, leaks

Elizabeth Smith Dixon Geer, *Overland Diary, 1847,* from *Transactions of the Oregon Pioneer Association* Vol. 26–35, (1907), pp. 153–179.

all over. The roof descends in such a manner as to make the rain run right down into the fire. I have dipped as much as six pails of water off of our dirt hearth in one night. Here I sit up, night after night, with my poor sick husband, all alone, and expecting him every day to die. I neglected to tell you that Welch's and all the rest moved off and left us. Mr. Smith has not been moved off his bed for six weeks only by lifting him by each corner of the sheet, and I had hard work to get help enough for that, let alone getting watchers. I have not undressed to lie down for six weeks. Besides all our sickness, I had a cross little babe to take care of. Indeed, I cannot tell you half.

FEB. 1.—Rain all day. This day my dear husband, my last remaining friend, died.

FEB. 2.—Today we buried my earthly companion. Now I know what none but widows know; that is, how comfortless is that of a widow's life, especially when left in a strange land, without money or friends, and the care of seven children. Cloudy.

FEB. 3.—Clear and warm.

FEB. 4.—Clear and warm.

FEB. 5.—Clear and warm.

FEB. 6.—Clear and cool.

FEB. 7.—Clear and warm.

FEB. 8.—Cloudy. Some rain.

FEB. 9.—Clear and cool. Perhaps you will want to know how cool. I will tell you. We have lived all winter in a shed constructed by setting up studs 5 feet high on the lowest side. The other side joins a cabin. It is boarded up with clapboards and several of them are torn off in places, and there is no shutter to our door, and if it was not for the rain putting out our fire and leaking down all over the house, we would be comfortable.

FEB. 10.—Clear and warm.

FEB. 11.—Clear and warm.

FEB. 12.—Cool and cloudy.

FEB. 13.—Rainy.

FEB. 14.—Cloudy. Rain in the afternoon.

FEB. 15.—Cool. Rain all day.

FEB. 16.—Rain and snow all day.

FEB. 17.—Rain all day.

FEB. 18.—Rain all day.

FEB. 19.—Rain all day.

FEB. 20.—Rain and hail all day.

FEB. 21.—Clear and cool. You will think it strange that we do not leave this starved place. The reason is this—the road from here to the country is impassable in the winter, the distance being 12 miles, and because our cattle are yet very weak.

FEB. 22.—Clear and cool.

FEB. 23.—Clear and cool.

FEB. 24.—Clear and warm. Today we left Portland at sunrise. Having no one to assist us, we had to leave one wagon and part of our things for the want of teams. We traveled 4 or 5 miles, all the way up hill and through the thickest woods I ever saw—all fir from 2 to 6 feet through, with now and then a scattering cedar, and an intolerably bad road. We all had to walk. Sometimes I had to place my babe on the ground and help to keep the wagon from turning over. When we got to the top of the mountain we descended through mud up to the wagon hubs and over logs two feet through, and log bridges torn to pieces in the mud. Sometimes I would be behind out of sight of the wagons, carrying and tugging my little ones along. Sometimes the boys would stop the teams and come back after us. Made 9 miles. Encamped in thick woods. Found some grass. Unhitched the oxen; let them feed two hours, then chained them to trees. These woods are infested with wild cats, panthers, bears and wolves. A man told me that he had killed 7 tigers; but they are a species of wolves. We made us a fire and made a bed down on the wet ground, and laid down as happy as circumstances would admit. Glad to think we had escaped from Portland—such a game place.

Butteville, Oregon Ty., Yamhill County, Sept. 2, 1850.

Dear and Estimable Friends, Mrs. Paulina Foster
and Mrs. Cynthia Ames:

I promised when I saw you last to write to you when I got to Oregon, and I done it faithfully, but as I never have received an answer, I do not know whether you got my letter and diary or not, consequently I do not know what to write now. I wrote four sheets full and sent it to you, but now I have not time to write. I write now to know whether you got my letter; and I will try to state a few things again. My husband was taken sick before we got to any settlement, and never was able to walk afterwards. He died at Portland, on the Willamette River, after an illness of two months. I will not attempt to describe my troubles since I saw you. Suffice it to say that I was left a widow with the care of seven children in a foreign land, without one solitary friend, as one might say, in the land of the living; but this time I will only endeavor to hold up the bright side of the picture. I lived a widow one year and four months. My three boys started for the gold mines, and it was doubtful to me whether I ever saw them again. Perhaps you will think it strange that I let such young boys go; but I was willing and helped them off in as good style as I could. They packed through by land. Russell Welch went by water. The boys never saw Russell in the mines. Well, after the boys were gone, it is true I had plenty of cows and hogs and plenty of wheat to feed them on and to make my bread. Indeed, I was well off if I had only known it; but I lived in a remote place where my strength was of little use to me. I could get nothing to do, and you know I could not live without work. I employed myself in teaching my children: yet that did not fully occupy my mind. I became as poor as a snake, yet I was in good health, and never was so nimble since I was a child. I could run a half a mile without stopping to breathe. Well, I thought perhaps I had better try my fortune again; so on the 24th of June, 1849, I was married to a Mr. Joseph Geer, a man 14 years older than myself, though young enough for me. He is the father of ten children. They are all married, but two boys and two girls. He is a Yankee from Connecticut and he is a Yankee in every sense of the word, as I told you he would be if it ever proved my lot to marry again. I did not marry rich, but my husband is very industrious, and is as kind to me as I can ask. Indeed, he sometimes provokes me for trying to humor me so much. He is a stout, healthy man for one of his age.

The boys made out poorly at the mines. They started in April and returned in September, I think. They were sick part of the time and happened to be in poor diggings all the while. They only got home with two hundred dollars apiece. They suffered very much while they were gone. When they came home they had less than when they started. Perley did not get there. He started with a man in partnership. The man was to provide for and bring him back, and he was to give the man half he dug; but when they got as far as the Umpqua.

River, they heard it was so very sickly there that the man turned back; but Perley would not come back. There were two white men keeping ferry on the Umpqua, so Perley stayed with them all summer and in the fall he rigged out on his own hook and started again; but on his way he met his brothers coming home, and they advised him for his life not to go, and so he came back with them.

At this time we are all well but Perley. I cannot answer for him; he has gone to the Umpqua for some money due him. The other two are working for four dollars a day. The two oldest boys have got three town lots in quite a stirring place called Lafayette in Yamhill County. Perley has four horses. A good Indian horse is worth one hundred dollars. A good American cow is worth sixty dollars. My boys live about 25 miles from me, so that I cannot act in the capacity of a mother to them; so you will guess it is not all sunshine with me, for you know my boys are not old enough to do without a mother. Russell Welch done very well in the mines. He made about twenty hundred dollars. He lives 30 miles below me in a little town called Portland on the Willamette River. Sarah has got her third son. It has been one year since I saw her. Adam Polk's two youngest boys live about wherever they see fit. The oldest, if he is alive, is in California. There is some ague in this country this season, but neither I nor my children, except those that went to California, have had a day's sickness since we came to Oregon.

I believe I will say no more until I hear from you. Write as soon as possible and tell me everything. My husband will close this epistle.

ELIZABETH GEER.

Butteville, Sept. 9, 1850.

Dear Ladies:

As Mrs. Geer has introduced me to you, as her old Yankee husband, I will say a few words, in the hope of becoming more acquainted hereafter. She so often speaks of you, that you seem like old neighbors. She has neglected to tell you that she was once the wife of Cornelius Smith. She has told you how poor she became while a widow, but has not said one word about how fat she has become since she has been living with her Yankee husband. This is probably reserved for the next epistle, so I will say nothing about it.

Of her I will only say she makes me a first-rate wife, industrious, and kind almost to a fault to me, a fault, however, that I can cheerfully overlook, you know.

We are not rich, but independent, and live agreeably together, which is enough. We are located on the west bank of the Willamette River, about 20 miles above Oregon City, about 40 yards from the water—a very pleasant situation. Intend putting out a large orchard as soon as I can prepare the ground; have about ten thousand apple trees, and about 200 pear trees on hand. Trees for sale of the best kinds of fruit. Apple trees worth one dollar, and pears $1.50 apiece. I have not room to give you a description of this, the best country in the world, so I will not attempt it; but if you will answer this I will give you a more particular account next time. I will give a brief account of myself. I left my native home, Windham, Conn., Sept. 10, 1818, for Ohio; lived in Ohio till Sept. 9, 1840, when I left for Illinois. Left Illinois April 4, 1847, for Oregon; arrived here Oct. 18, 1847. Buried my first wife Dec. 6, 1847.

Now I wish you or some of your folks to write to us and let us know all about the neighbors, as Mrs. Geer is very anxious to hear from you all.

Direct to Joseph C. Geer, Sen., Butteville, Marion County, Oregon Territory.

My best respects to Mr. Ames, and if there is a good Universalist preacher there, tell him he would meet with a cordial welcome here, as there is not one in this Territory.

I must close for want of room.

Yours respectfully,
JOSEPH C. GEER, SEN.
Mrs. P. Foster, and Mrs. C. Ames.

FURTHER READINGS

Lillian Schlissel, *Women's Diaries of the Westward Journey* (Schocken, 1982, 1992); Kenneth L. Holmes, ed, *Covered Wagon Women: Diaries from the Western Trails, 1840–1890*, 11 volumes (Arthur H. Clark Company, 1983–93).

Abigail Malick

The Malick family made the overland journey in 1848, the summer following the journey of Elizabeth Smith Dixon Geer. Abigail and George Malick had six children, all of them old enough to help with the chores, and the Malicks were seasoned pioneers. They had already moved by wagon from Lancaster, Pennsylvania, to Tazewell County, in Illinois. After farming in Illinois for a dozen years, George decided it was time to "move on." When the Malicks started west, they were leaving behind a married daughter, Mary Ann Albright, her husband, and children. They promised each other they would all meet in Oregon Territory the very next year.

The Albrights never went west, and Abigail Malick wrote to her daughter for the next seventeen years, until her death in 1865. In letters they exchanged recipes, seeds, pieces of birthday cakes, coins, fabric, and family news good and bad. But it took Abigail two years before she could tell Mary Ann that seventeen-year-old Hiram had drowned in plain sight on the journey west.

LETTER FROM OREGON TERRITORY, 1850

I never shal see eney of you eny More in this world. We Are Almost three thousand Miles apart. I would like to see My sweet littl Ann And Homer And the other two but I never Shall. . . . And you never Will see Hiram. . . . Hiram drounded in [the] Plat River At the Mouth of Dear Krick. He went Aswiming with some other boys of the Compeny that we Trailed with And he swum Acrost the river and the Water run very fast And he could not reach this side. The young Men tried to save him but he [had the Cramp] And Could swim no more. And they Said o hiram do swim but he said I cannot swim eney More. And one young Man took A pole And started to him And the water ran so fast that he thought he Could not swim eney more so he returned And left him to his fate. And the other

Abigail Malick, *Letter from Oregon Territory, 1850,* in Malick Letters, Manuscript collection, Yale University Library, New Haven, Connecticut.

boys Called to him and said O hiram O swim. And he said o my god I cannot eney More. They said that he went down in the water seven or eight times before he drounded. And then he said o my god O lord gesus receive My Soul for I am no More. Oyes I think that if ever A young Man went to their lord gesus that he Did for he Always Was A very good boy and that [all who] knew him liked him. So you know All about Hiram's death now. So you need not ask enything About him eney More for it will not do us eney Good to trouble ourselves About him eney More. It has Almost kild Me but I have to bear it. And if we Are good perhapes then we can meete him in heven.

FURTHER READINGS

Malick Letters, Manuscript Collection, Yale University Library, New Haven, Connecticut; Lillian Schlissel, et al., *Far From Home: Families on the Westward Journey* (Schocken, 1989); Kenneth L. Holmes, ed, *Covered Wagon Women: Diaries from the Western Trails, 1840–1890*, 11 volumes (Arthur H. Clark Company, 1983–93).

Gold Rush Women

Even in Indiana, Margaret Frink heard "talk of money in California." She had heard "rumors a woman could get $16 a week for cooking for one man." She and her husband joined the rush to the goldfields, and in Sacramento, they built and ran Frink's Hotel. By 1851, they sold the hotel at a profit, left the gulches and the "dirty tents and cloth shanties," and set themselves up in a "cottage" they ordered built in New England, shipped around Cape Horn, and delivered to Sacramento.

Luzena Stanley Wilson heard the clink of coin when she arrived in Nevada City, California, even though it was no more than "a row of canvas tents [that] lined each of the two ravines. . . . The gulches [were] alive with moving men." When her husband left to find some wood to build them a place to live, Luzena lost no time in setting herself up in business.

> As always occurs to the mind of a woman, I thought of taking boarders. There was a hotel nearby and the men [who] ate there paid $1 a meal. . . . With my own hands, I chopped stakes, drove them into the ground, and set up my table. I bought provisions at a neighboring store and when my husband came back at night he found . . . twenty miners eating at my table. Each man as he rose put a dollar in my hand and said I might count on him as a permanent customer. I called my hotel "El Dorado."

Luzena and her husband served between seventy-five and two hundred boarders at twenty-five dollars a week. More than an innkeeper, Luzena wa a banker, handling gold dust for the men.

> Many a night have I shut my oven door on two milk pans filled high with bags of gold dust and I have often slept with my mattress lined. . . . I must have had more than two hundred thousand dollars lying unprotected in my bedroom.

In 1849, Mary Jane Megquier and her husband, a physician, left their children with relatives in Maine, took a ship down the Atlantic Coast to Panama, where they crossed the isthmus by mule-drawn carriage. Then they continued on the Pacific to San Francisco. Megquier wrote home that "women's help is so very scarce that I am in hopes to get a chance by hook or crook to pay my way. . . . A woman that can work will make more money than a man, and I think now that I shall do that. . . . For the quicker the money is made, the sooner we shall meet."

In San Francisco, the doctor and his wife opened a hotel, though the work was stupendous. Mary Jane wrote from San Francisco, on June 30, 1850:

Dear Daughter:

I should like to give you an account of my work if I could do it justice. We have a store the size of the one we had in Winthrop, in the morning the boy gets up and makes a fire by seven o'clock when I get up and make the coffee, then I make the biscuit, then I fry the potatoes then broil three pounds of steak, and as much liver, while the woman is sweeping, and setting the table, at eight the bell rings and they are eating until nine. I do not sit until they are nearly all done. I try to keep the food warm and in shape as we put it on in small quantities after breakfast I bake six loaves of bread (not very big) then four pies, or a pudding then we have lamb, for which we have paid nine dollars a quarter, beef, and pork, baked, turnips, beets, potatoes, radishes, sallad, and that everlasting soup, every day, dine at two, for tea we have hash, cold meat bread and butter sauce and some kind of cake and I have cooked every mouthful that has been eaten excepting one day and a half that we were on a steam-boat excursion. I make six beds every day and do the washing and ironing you must think that I am very busy and when I dance all night I am obliged to trot all day and if I had not the constitution of six horses I should [have] been dead long ago but I am going to give up in the fall whether or no, as I am sick and tired of work. . . . The woman washes the dishes and carpets which have to be washed every day and then the house looks like a pig pen it is so dusty. . . . Write. Write. Write.

SOURCES

Luzena Stanley Wilson, *Forty-Niner: Memories Recalled for Her Daughter, Correnah Wilson Wright* (Eucalyptus Press, 1937); Margaret Frink, *Journal of the Adventures of a Party of Gold-Seekers: Indiana to Sacramento, March 30 to September 1850* (1897); Mary Jane Megquier, *Apron Full of Gold: Letters From San Francisco, 1849–1856*, ed. Robert Glass Clelland (Huntington Library, 1949).

FURTHER READINGS

Lillian Schlissel, *Women's Diaries of the Westward Journey* (Schocken, 1982); Kenneth L. Holmes, ed, *Covered Wagon Women: Diaries from the Western Trails, 1840–1890*, 11 volumes (Arthur H. Clark Company, 1983–93).

Sweethearts of the Road

The popular songs *Clementine* and *Sweet Betsy from Pike* celebrate the overland experience as a grand adventure, with rollicking tales of doughty heroines and stalwart suitors. Trail laughter has a certain grim resonance, as real-life tragedies and tales of woe become comic commentary on the plight of all overlanders.

Clementine

In a cavern, in a canyon, excavating for a mine,
Lived a miner, forty-niner, and his daughter Clementine.

Oh my darlin', oh my darlin', oh my darlin' Clementine,
You are lost and gone forever, dreadful sorry Clementine.

Light she was and like a fairy, And her shoes were number nine;
Herring boxes without topses, Sandals were for Clementine.
(Chorus)

Drove she duckling to the water, Every
*   morning just at nine,*
Hit her foot against a splinter, Fell into
*   the foaming brine.*
(Chorus)

Ruby lips above the water, Blowing
*   bubbles soft and fine,*
Alas for me, I was no swimmer, So I
*   lost my Clementine.*
(Chorus)

In a churchyard near the canyon,
*   Where the myrtle doth entwine,*
There grow roses and other posies,
*   Fertilized by Clementine.*
(Chorus)

In my dreams she oft doth haunt me,
   With her garments soaked in brine;
Though in life I used to hug her, Now
   she's dead I draw the line.
(Chorus)

Then the miner, forty-niner, Soon
   began to peak and pine;
Thought he 'oughter jin'e his daughter,
   Now he's with his Clementine.
(Chorus)

Sweet Betsy from Pike

Oh don't you remember sweet Betsy from Pike,
Who crossed the big mountains with her lover Ike,
With two yoke of oxen, a big yellow dog,
A tall Shanghai rooster, and one spotted hog?

Chorus:
Singing dang fol dee dido,
   Singing dang fol dee day.

One evening quite early they camped on the Platte.
'Twas near by the road on a green shady flat.
Where Betsy, sore-footed, lay down to repose—
With wonder Ike gazed on that Pike County rose.

The Shanghai ran off, and their cattle all died;
That morning the last piece of bacon was fried;
Poor Ike was discouraged and Betsy got mad,
The dog drooped his tail and looked wondrously sad.

They stopped at Salt Lake to inquire of the way,
Where Brigham declared that sweet Betsy should stay;
But Betsy got frightened and ran like a deer
While Brigham stood pawing the ground like a steer.

They soon reached the desert where Betsy gave out.
And down in the sand she lay rolling about;
While Ike, half distracted, looked on with surprise,
Saying, "Betsy, get up, you'll get sand in your eyes."

Sweet Betsy got up in a great deal of pain,
Declared she'd go back to Pike County again;
But Ike gave a sigh, and they fondly embraced,
And they traveled along with his arm round her waist.

The Injuns came down in a wild yelling horde,
And Betsy was scared they would scalp her adored;
Behind the front wagon wheel Betsy did crawl,
And there fought the Injuns with musket and ball.

They suddenly stopped on a very high hill,
With wonder looked down upon old Placerville;
Ike sighed when he said, and he cast his eyes down,
"Sweet Betsy, my darling, we've got to Hangtown."

Long Ike and sweet Betsy attended a dance;
Ike wore a pair of his Pike County pants;
Sweet Betsy was dressed up in ribbons and rings;
Says Ike, "You're an angel, but where are your wings?"

'Twas out on the prairie one bright starry night,
They broke out the whiskey and Betsy got tight,
She sang and she howled and she danced o'er the plain,
And showed her bare legs (arse) to the whole wagon train.

The terrible desert was burning and bare,
And Isaac he shrank from the death lurkin' there,
"Dear old Pike County, I'll come back to you."
Says Betsy, "You'll go by yourself if you do."

They swam wild rivers and climbed the tall peaks,
And camped on the prairies for weeks upon weeks,
Starvation and cholera, hard work and slaughter,
They reached Californy, spite of hell and high water.

A miner said,"Betsy, will you dance with me?"
"I will, you old hoss, if you don't make too free.
But don't dance me hard, do you want to know why?
Doggone ye, I'm chock full of strong alkali.

Long Ike and sweet Betsy got married, of course,
But Ike, getting jealous, obtained a divorce,
While Betsy, well satisfied, said with a shout,
"Goodbye, you big lummox, I'm glad you backed out!"

Mary Ann Hafen

Mary Ann Hafen was born in Berne, Switzerland in 1854. Her family converted to the Mormon Church, and decided to join the Mormons who were moving to Utah, but their journey was dogged by bad luck. An ocean storm cracked the mast of their ship, but they somehow managed to reach New York and then Nebraska, a journey they accomplished by handcart, two-wheeled affairs with two shafts and a tarpaulin to cover the top. "The carts were very much like those the street sweepers use in the cities today, except that ours were made entirely of wood without even an iron rim." Between 1856 and 1860, ten different handcart companies made up of almost 3000 people pushed or pulled over 600 handcarts to Salt Lake City. "Father and Mother [Samuel and Magdelena Stucki] pulled [the handcart]; Rosie (two years old) and Christian (six months old) rode; John (nine) and I (six) walked. Sometimes, when it was down hill, they let me ride too."

The family took up a section of land in Southern Utah, and through the first years of settlement, they lived in a wigwam, a thatched hut, a dugout, and an adobe. Mary Ann married at nineteen, but after her husband died on their honeymoon, she agreed to a polygamous marriage with John Hafen, and together they raised seven children. Of all her work, Mary Ann was perhaps most proud of the fact that, by rising before dawn to pick and dry peaches, she bought herself a sewing machine for forty-two dollars. Hafen's story is filled with harsh detail and with the pride of survival.

A HANDCART PIONEER

Our company was the tenth and last to cross the Plains in handcarts. It contained 126 persons with twenty-two handcarts and three provision wagons drawn by oxen. We set out on July 6,

Mary Ann Hafen, from *Recollections of a Handcart Pioneer of 1860* (1938).

1860, for our thousand-mile trip. There were six to our cart. Father and mother pulled it; Rosie (two years old) and Christian (six months old) rode; John (nine) and I (six) walked. Sometimes, when it was down hill, they let me ride too.

The first night out the mosquitoes gave us a hearty welcome. Father had bought a cow to take along, so we could have milk on the way. At first he tied her to the back of the cart, but she would sometimes hang back, so he thought he would make a harness and have her pull the cart while he led her. By this time mother's feet were so swollen that she could not wear shoes, but had to wrap her feet with cloth. Father thought that by having the cow pull the cart mother might ride. This worked well for some time.

One day a group of Indians came riding up on horses. Their jingling trinkets, dragging poles and strange appearance frightened the cow and sent her chasing off with the cart and children. We were afraid that the children might be killed, but the cow fell into a deep gully and the cart turned upside down. Although the children were under the trunk and bedding, they were unhurt, but after that father did not hitch the cow to the cart again. He let three Danish boys take her to hitch to their cart. Then the Danish boys, each in turn, would help father pull our cart.

Of course we had many other difficulties. One was that it was hard for the carts to keep up with the three provision wagons drawn by ox teams. Often the men pulling the carts would try to take shortcuts through the brush and sand in order to keep up.

After about three weeks my mother's feet became better so she could wear her shoes again. She would get so discouraged and down-hearted; but father never lost courage. He would always cheer her up by telling her that we were going to Zion, that the Lord would take care of us, and that better times were coming.

Even when it rained the company did not stop traveling. A cover on the handcart shielded the two younger children. The rest of us found it more comfortable moving than standing still in the drizzle. In fording streams the men often carried the children and weaker women across on their backs. The company stopped over on Sundays for rest, and meetings were held for spiritual comfort and guidance. At night, when the handcarts were drawn up in a circle and the fires were lighted, the camp looked quite happy. Singing, music and speeches by the leaders cheered everyone. I remember that we stopped one night at an old Indian camp ground. There were many bright-colored beads in the ant hills.

At times we met or were passed by the overland stage coach with its passengers and mail bags and drawn by four fine horses. When the Pony Express dashed past it seemed almost like the wind racing over the prairie.

Our provisions began to get low. One day a herd of buffalo ran past and the men of our company shot two of them. Such a feast as we had when they were dressed. Each family was given a piece of meat to take along. My brother John, who pushed at the back of our cart, used to tell how hungry he was all the time and how tired he got from pushing. He aid he felt that if he could just sit down for a few minutes he would feel so much better. But instead, father would ask if he couldn't push a little harder. Mother was nursing the baby and could not help much, especially when the food ran short and she grew weak. When rations were reduced father gave mother a part of his share of the food, so he was not so strong either.

When we got that chunk of buffalo meat father put it in the handcart. My brother John remembered that it was the fore part of the week and that father said we would save it for Sunday dinner. John said, "I was so very hungry and the meat smelled so good to me while pushing at the handcart that I could not resist. I had a little pocket knife and with it I cut off a piece or two each half day. Although I expected a severe whipping when father found it out, I cut off little pieces each day. I would chew them so long that they got white and perfectly tasteless. When father came to get the meat he asked me if I had been cutting off some of it. I said 'Yes, I was so hungry I could not let it alone.' Instead of giving me a scolding or whipping, father turned away and wiped tears from his eyes."

Even when we were on short rations, if we met a band of Indians the Captain of our Company would give them some of the provisions so the Indians would let us go by in safety. Food finally became so low that word was sent to Salt Lake City and in about two weeks fresh supplies arrived.

At last, when we reached the top of Emigration Canyon, overlooking Salt Lake, on that September day, 1860, the whole company stopped to look down through the valley. Some yelled and tossed their hats in the air. A shout of joy arose at the thought that our long trip was over, that we had at last reached Zion, the place of rest. We all gave thanks to God for helping us safely over the Plains and mountains to our destination.

■ ■ ■

We stayed here all that winter and though we were poor we did not suffer for food and shelter. While we lived here my brother and I used to go fishing. One Sunday the bank on which John was standing caved off and he fell in. The river was deep and he could not swim. I ran and called Mother. She brought a long pole for him to hold to but he could not hear her call. He was washed down stream until he came to a bridge. He happened to catch hold of one of the posts supporting the bridge and was able to climb out. As soon as he was safe he fainted and Mother had a hard time bringing him to.

■ ■ ■

Many of those who had covered wagons used their wagon boxes for their first shelters. We had none, so father built a sort of wigwam out of willows. To mother this seemed a poor substitute for the nice house left behind.

"Oh, these red hills! this roily water!" she would sometimes say as she remembered the green hills and clear mountain streams of Switzerland.

But when the lots were plowed up and set to vineyards, a dam built across the creek, and irrigation ditches dug, things looked more promising.

■ ■ ■

With the help of the neighbors, father built us an adobe house. A hole about four feet deep was dug. Rocks were quarried in the hills nearby. With sand-and-clay mortar they were laid up in a rock foundation. With this same smooth plaster the adobe walls were laid up—two adobes deep, making a substantial wall a foot thick. Instead of the sand roofs of the old houses, wooden rafters covered with sheeting and shingles hauled in from the North made a water-tight shelter. In each room was a window or two with panes of glass.

By this time, along each side of the wide street ran a little irrigating ditch of water. Upon the banks, to shade the sidewalks, cottonwood trees were set out. Every morning while the water was still cool and clean, each family dipped up barrels of water for household and drinking purposes. After a storm the water was roily and had to settle before it was fit to use.

Water for laundry purposes was generally softened by pouring in cottonwood ashes. Soft rainwater we generally used to wash our hair and our nicest clothes. But of course we couldn't get rain water always. A favorite substitute for soap was the root of the "oose," or yucca sometimes called "soap root." This root looked about like a sugarbeet. Cut up and left in water it soon made a fluffy suds. Colored clothes came out fresh and bright because the cleanser did not harm the dyes. White clothes however were turned slightly yellow by it and therefore were not generally washed with oose. I remember how soft, fluffy, and sweet-smelling my hair always felt after a shampoo with oose suds. For mopping the wooden floors the oose root served not only as soap but as scrubbing brush as well. And how white and beautiful those floors would look.

■　■　■

This very same year I learned how to weave. Father made me a loom. My arms were too short to reach both sides of the loom to shove my shuttle through the web, so I had to lean from side to side. I was proud of the first dress I wove. It was made in a checkered pattern one inch across of brown, blue, and white, from cotton yarn. I also made what we called jeans out of cotton warp with wool. This was used for men's suits and was very heavy cloth.

Before this, father made me a spinning wheel. I was so glad that father was a carpenter; he could make us so many nice things that others did not have. After we had gathered the cotton, picked out the seeds and carded it, I spun it into threads on my wheel. We dyed our yarn different colors. We used evergreen brush for dye. Also we used dock roots for brown, adding a little coperas for dark brown. We made blue with indigo; red from the red berries which grew along the creek.

When I was a girl I helped father harvest a lot of grain. We cut it with a sickle and bound it by hand. In addition to our own grain, we cut for others on shares, receiving four bushels to the acre. Father, John, Rosie and I would cut an acre in a day, by working early and late. My, how our backs would ache and how the sweat would roll off us. One year, I remember, I helped father sickle nine acres. That was the last year before I was married.

When I was fourteen, Mother had a baby girl. It was the first baby in our family for so long that we all loved her. But when she was a year and a half old she died with black canker. Two years later a fine baby brother was born but he also died, with chills and fever. We did not know much about medicine because, in the old country, we had always relied upon a doctor. Gradually we learned home remedies after much sad experience.

FURTHER READINGS

Mary Ann Hafen, *Recollections of a Handcart Pioneer of 1860: A Woman's Life on the Mormon Frontier* (University of Nebraska Press, 1938, 1983); Leroy Reuben Hafen and Ann W. Hafen, *Handcarts to Zion: The Story of a Unique Western Migration, 1856–1860* (Arthur H. Clark, 1960); Kenneth L. Holmes, ed, *Covered Wagon Women: Diaries from the Western Trails, 1840–1890*, 11 volumes (Arthur H. Clark Company, 1983–93).

Emma L. Kelly

Emma Kelly was a correspondent for the Kansas City *Star* when she set out in late fall of 1897 for the Klondike, determined to put herself on equal footing with newsmen who were following the "stampeders" in what was thought to be the story of a lifetime. "Rushers" jostled and pushed their way into Alaska, although the Klondike "highway" tested the endurance of even hardened gold-seekers. The Chilkoot Trail was only 3550 feet in elevation, but it rose 1,000 feet in a little more than a half mile on the final ascent. In summer, the trail was filled with boulders, and in winter, it was almost impassable with snow and ice. Pack horses, loaded with provisions, were of little use, and goods had to be carried by rushers in backpacks. Every packer was required by the Canadian government to bring 1,000 to 2,000 pounds of goods so that they were provisioned for a year. A person travelling alone often had to make the round trip fifteen to twenty-five times.

Facing cruel weather and packers who were uneasy at being led by a woman, Kelly described a blizzard and astonishing hardships. At the top of the pass, at the Canadian border, Kelly found the Northwest Mounted Police (without their mounts) collecting customs in a tiny tent flying the British flag.

A WOMAN'S TRIP TO THE KLONDIKE

I left Topeka, Kansas, for the Klondike, and, sailing from Seattle, reached Dyea with a thousand pounds of goods and provisions to be transported seven hundred miles to Dawson.

The winter blizzards had set in on the summit, and experienced packers could not be induced to try the pass. All with whom I came in contact attempted to discourage me in the undertaking at that season, as it was supposed to be too late for the water route and too early for the winter trail over the snow and ice. I knew no

Emma Kelly, "A Woman's Trip to the Klondike," in *Lippincott Monthly,* (November 1901), pp. 625–633.

person in Dyea and was unable to secure packers of experience, and, facing this dilemma, I determined to try for packers among the inexperienced deck-hands of the vessels in the harbor.

By promising to feed them and pay each man fifty cents a pound for all he carried over, I secured a motley crew of ten men of various shades of color and nationalities to take my goods to Lake Linderman, where I learned a party of men had built some boats and would soon start across the lakes and down the river to Dawson, my great anxiety having been to reach the lakes in time to secure passage in one of the boats.

After securing my packers I waited a day in Dyea for the subsidence of the storm, keeping my men herded away from the old packers, who were full of fearful accounts of the dangers of the storm on the pass.

On the following day I secured Healy & Wilson's pack train to take my goods to Sheep Camp at the foot of the pass, twelve miles from Dyea, and with my packers I fell in immediately behind the horses, and after plodding all day through slush and muck, in the face of a terrific storm of sleet which drove into our faces like tacks, we reached Sheep Camp at five o'clock in the evening. As the storm was still raging I had to lay over a day waiting for it to subside, having again to herd my packers from those at the camp.

The trail from Dyea to Sheep Camp, always terrible, was in wretched condition, the entire distance being through snow, slush, and muck, up sharp elevations, down precipitous cañons, and over rocks and bowlders covered with snow and ice. Up to the winding cañon the trail crosses one stream sixty-one times, and when the water was too deep for me to wade, I would have a packer carry me over on his back.

Some of my men wanted to turn back from Sheep Camp, but I told them they could make the trip if I could, and so I held them to their contracts.

The following day the sun came out warm and there was but little wind. I was up at five o'clock and got breakfast, and by seven the men were packed and we all set out across the summit for Lake Linderman, eighteen miles distant. At ten o'clock we reached Stonehouse, at the foot of the steep climb, where the elevation rises for two and a half miles at an angle of forty-five degrees to the summit, which is usually enveloped in mist and clouds. An immense glacier is crossed by the trail and travel is impeded by great bowlders which cross the narrow, winding footway.

At one o'clock the summit was reached, and with a feeling of exultation I sat down with my packers for a rest and to look back over that fearful trail from Sheep Camp. I was safely over the worst part of the trip, and with all my goods.

We made the descent with comparative ease, and after ferrying three small lakes reached Linderman, where my packers put down their loads at half-past nine o'clock, all worn out and ready for a hearty supper of bacon and beans, after an eighteen-mile tramp over one of the most dangerous and terrible mountain passes in the world.

However, I was too anxious to think much of eating or of sleeping, and so after a few mouthfuls I started out among the tents on the lake shore, stopping wherever I observed a light in quest of the parties who had completed their boats. At one tent at which I called a good-natured-looking young man opened the flap door of his tent, and the inside looking so warm and comfortable, I asked the privilege of entering, sitting down, and resting. I found the young man to be one of the party with the boats ready for a start on the following day. On stating to him my business, he assembled the rest of the company, which consisted of twenty-two men, with three boats, ready for the start next day.

As their little crafts, ordinary row-boats, were to carry seven men in each of two of them and eight in the other, each man having seven or eight hundred pounds of food, it was not certain that they would be able to take me with my thousand pounds and my dog "Klondike," a fine Newfoundland shepherd I had brought from the States. They doubted if there would be room, but as they were about out of money and must pay the Canadian custom duties at Taggish Lake, my offer of one hundred and twenty-five dollars for passage for myself, dog, and luggage was accepted.

One of the party, whom I later learned was constitutionally disagreeable, grumbled a good deal, and said it would be too much trouble to have a woman along in the "gang," as I would likely be cranky, require a good deal of attention, and want things just so;

would want my own tent pitched at night and taken down in the morning, and this would require time and delay them. But I told them that I did not expect anything of the kind on such a trip, that I could take my blanket and, rolling up in it, could lie on the snow as well as any man in the company, which I would do before putting them to any trouble.

At about ten o'clock on the following morning one of the party came to my tent and told me they would start at noon. I was lying on the ground, rolled up in my blanket, and was so sore and stiff, and ached so from my long climb and walk in the water, mud, and snow of the previous day, that I was unable to get up without help. One of the men helped me, and I had almost to crawl about that day, but I made no complaint that I felt badly and said nothing of my condition, for fear I would be thought a nuisance from the start.

We loaded our outfits into the boats, and at one o'clock pushed out across Linderman, which is seven miles long, and which connects with Bennett Lake by a river about half a mile in length, the water of which is shallow and filled with large, sharp rocks, necessitating the lining through of our boats. The men packed the goods around to the shores of Lake Bennett, and as I walked along the shore I came across a newly made grave with the following inscription, "J. Mathews, age 26." I learned that after losing his all on the summit he went back to Dyea, put his last dollar into a second outfit, and tried to carry his loaded boat through this channel, when it was dashed to pieces on the rocks and everything lost. He was so discouraged after his second loss that he shot himself through the heart.

I gathered a few green boughs from the spruce-trees near, placed them in the snow over his grave, and if I could have learned where his mother was would have sent her word, as she will be waiting and watching many winters for mail from the Klondike, another lone watcher grieving for the absence of one who will never return.

■ ■ ■

I returned to where the men were lying on the beach, and, waking them, told them we had better get an early start, as the lake was calm that morning.

■ ■ ■

As we reached Miles Cañon on this stream we noticed the current was growing much swifter, and swinging around a bend in the river we almost ran into a nicely built and fine-appearing boat which lay upon its side against the rocks with a hole in the centre-board. I made such inquiry as I could, but was unable to learn anything of those who had doubtless met death with the disaster encountered.

I announced that I would ride through the cañon in a boat, but the men vehemently protested against my doing so, and pleaded with me to walk around. I was informed that no man who ever guided a boat through Miles Cañon had yet consented to take a woman through its seething, foaming waters; but I insisted, and went through. I wanted to see and experience this so-called danger, which men freely court, but which women may only read or hear of.

The stream is very swift for a long distance before the entrance to the cañon is reached, and as the prow of our boat was turned into the stream and caught by the current I felt as if being swung around by some mighty engine and then shot forward at a terrific rate. I felt as if the boat would certainly glide out from under me. Faster and faster we went, until it seemed as if we had been speeding along for at least two or three minutes, while in fact, the distance made required but thirty seconds. When we slowed up a little we felt the waters swell beneath us, churning the boat on all sides. At that point the cañon widens a little; the waters thrown out of the main channel are dashed, foaming and seething, against the projecting sides of the granite walls which hold them in their narrow course. Then if you succeed in keeping in the narrow channel you glide into a very narrow part of the rapids, and in a second more shoot down and out of the mouth of the cañon into the turbulent waters below. After hard pulling a landing is effected; and the passage is accomplished, leaving a mad desire for its repetition.

After making the first trip through I walked back over the trail to again go through in the second boat. When near the summit of the trail, where it runs very close to the edge of the cliff, I slipped on the ice and rolled down the cliff about fifteen feet on to the rocks, the shock rendering me unconscious. As the men were returning for a second load they heard my dog barking, and looking, saw him jumping around. One of them with his rifle came up, thinking the dog had treed a squirrel, and found me lying in an unconscious condition. However, I soon revived, and, though feeling pretty badly shaken up, determined to go on with the men and pass through the cañon again.

The last ten days before we reached Dawson we made but six or eight miles a day, and to save time morning and evening we did not put up our tents at night, but rolled in our blankets and slept in the snow with a piece of canvas spread over us, my dog always lying on my feet to keep them warm.

One evening while at the Pelley we saw moose-tracks in the snow. The moose is very much like the buffalo of the plains, the flesh very rich and juicy. One of the men, who was quite a good shot, tracked the animal and killed it, so we had plenty of fresh meat for the remainder of our trip. We saw many black bears along the river, two of which we killed, keeping the skins for robes and eating the meat, which, though a little coarse, was very good. We saw many red foxes and numberless squirrels in the spruce forests which abound along the river.

On the first day of November the river was nearly blocked, and with much difficulty we worked our boat through the drift, and, floating into Dawson, entered the great Klondike district, the goal for which so many had striven and risked all to gain.

We were tired and worn out with our long ride in the small boats. Never a day passed that I did not sit, singing at the top of my voice coon songs and others, partly to brace myself up and also because I thought it would help the rowers a little and cheer them as well. Always as a child when alone in the dark I would sing or talk to myself. And though the dangers through which I had passed were different from any I had ever experienced, singing seemed to lessen my fear and give me more heart.

Just at dark we made a landing on the banks of the Yukon, directly in front of the little town of Dawson, and, pitching our tents in the snow, we camped for the night under our first shelter, even of a tent, for ten days. All were so pleased and happy that good fortune had enabled us to escape the perils which threatened as well as the danger of an ice-block in the river that the men proposed a celebration of their good fortune. They were going up-town, but I told them it was not right to leave me alone the first night in a strange place, and that if they would remain in camp I would pay enough for them to drink and have their celebration in their tents. To this they agreed, and one of them went to the town and shortly returned, stating that whiskey, Canadian case goods, was ten dollars a quart. I sent him back and purchased a couple of bottles, which the men drank without becoming boisterous. I then went to my war-sack, and taking out my guitar, which I had carried over the summit, we sat on the ground around the little tent stove and all joined in singing the songs of home.

FURTHER READINGS

Charlene Porsild, *Gamblers and Dreamers: Women, Men, and Community in the Klondike* (University of British Columbia, 1999); Elizabeth Robins, *The Alaska-Klondike Diary of Elizabeth Robins, 1900* ed. Joanne E. Gates (University of Alaska Press, 1999); Frances Backhouse, *Women of the Klondike* (Whitecap Books, 1996); Cynthia Brackett Driscoll, ed., *One Woman's Gold Rush: Snapshots from Mollie Brackett's Lost Photo Album 1898–1899* (Oak Woods Media, 1996); Melanie J. Mayer, *Klondike Women: True Tales of the 1897–98 Gold Rush* (Swallow Press/Ohio University Press, 1989).

Eighteen Men and One Woman Nearing the Summit of Chilkoot Pass, Alaska, 1898.

Photo from Alaska State Library, Winter and Pond Collection, Photo Number PCA87–707.

Sui Sin Far/Edith Maude Eaton (1865–1914)

Sui Sin Far was christened Edith Maude Eaton when she was born in Cheshire, England, the daughter of an English father and a Chinese mother. When she was a small child, her family moved first to New York and then to Montréal. When she later emigrated to Vancouver, British Columbia, and then down the West Coast of the United States, she adopted the pen-name Sui Sin Far. Living for several years in San Francisco, and then settling in Seattle, she made her living as a journalist, publishing in a number of newspapers and magazines, including *Good Housekeeping, Ladies Home Journal, Century Magazine, Overland, Land of Sunshine,* and *Sunset.* In addition to her journalism, she wrote in several genres, leaving behind forty short stories, six essays, twenty-five journalistic pieces, and numerous letters. She also claimed to have written a novel, although the manuscript disappeared when many of her papers, stored in a trunk during a cross-continental journey, were lost when the train she was riding in crashed.

Sui/Eaton is best remembered for her portraits of North American Chinatowns at turn of the century, which described bustling, vital communities made up largely of families, correcting the common misperception of Chinese American communities as "bachelor" societies. Her Eurasian perspective made her aware of prejudices which existed in both cultures; while many Chinese immigrants saw themselves as the heirs of the world's oldest civilization and viewed Europeans as culturally backward and barbaric, most Anglo Americans saw the Chinese as "inscrutable" and so alien that they passed laws excluding them from entering the United States. In her journalism about Chinese American communities, Sui/Eaton traced cultural traditions to China, making the behavior of Chinese Americans understandable to her Anglo American readers, while at the same time she championed Chinese American rights. A collection of her writings, published in 1912 as *Mrs. Spring Fragrance,* represents the first publication of a book in English by an Asian American woman. Sui/Eaton's sister, Winnifred, shared her concern about the mistreatment of Asians in North America, but she expressed this through adopting the Japanese-sounding pen name of Onoto Watanna and publishing several successful romantic novels set in Japan.

Sui/Eaton felt herself at odds in both Anglo American and Chinese American society. Although she could "pass" for Caucasian, she chose to embrace and emphasize her Chinese heritage, which excluded her from Anglo American society; at the same time, she was unable to speak Chinese and, raised as she was outside the Chinese or Chinese American communities, she was viewed as an Anglo in those communities. In 1914, she finally succumbed to the rheumatic fever she had contracted as a child.

ITS WAVERING IMAGE

Pan was a half white, half Chinese girl. Her mother was dead, and Pan lived with her father who kept an Oriental Bazaar on Dupont Street. All her life had Pan lived in Chinatown, and if she were different in any sense from those around her, she gave little thought to it. It was only after the coming of Mark Carson that the mystery of her nature began to trouble her.

They met at the time of the boycott of the Sam Yups by the See Yups. After the heat and dust and unsavoriness of the highways and byways of Chinatown, the young reporter who had been sent to find a story, had stepped across the threshold of a cool, deep room, fragrant with the odor of dried lilies and sandalwood, and found Pan.

She did not speak to him, nor he to her. His business was with the spectacled merchant, who, with a pointed brush, was making up accounts in brown paper books and rolling balls in an abacus box. As to Pan, she always turned from whites. With her father's people she was natural and at home; but in the presence of her mother's she felt strange and constrained, shrinking from their curious scrutiny as she would from the sharp edge of a sword.

When Mark Carson returned to the office, he asked some questions concerning the girl who had puzzled him. What was she? Chinese or white? The city editor answered him, adding: "She is an unusually bright girl, and could tell more stories about the Chinese than any other person in this city—if she would."

Sui Sin Far/Edith Maude Eaton, "It's Wavering Image," from *Mrs. Spring Fragrance* (1912).

Mark Carson had a determined chin, clever eyes, and a tone to his voice which easily won for him the confidence of the unwary. In the reporter's room he was spoken of as "a man who would sell his soul for a story."

After Pan's first shyness had worn off, he found her bewilderingly frank and free with him; but he had all the instincts of a gentleman save one, and made no ordinary mistake about her. He was Pan's first white friend. She was born a Bohemian, exempt from the conventional restrictions imposed upon either the white or Chinese woman; and the Oriental who was her father mingled with his affection for his child so great a respect for and trust in the daughter of the dead white woman, that everything she did or said was right to him. And Pan herself! A white woman might pass over an insult; a Chinese woman fail to see one. But Pan! He would be a brave man indeed who offered one to childish little Pan.

All this Mark Carson's clear eyes perceived, and with delicate tact and subtlety he taught the young girl that, all unconscious until his coming, she had lived her life alone. So well did she learn this lesson that it seemed at times as if her white self must entirely dominate and trample under foot her Chinese.

Meanwhile, in full trust and confidence, she led him about Chinatown, initiating him into the simple mystery and history of many things, for which she, being of her father's race, had a tender regard and pride. For her sake he was received as a brother by the yellow-robed priest in the joss house, the Astrologer of Prospect Place, and other conservative Chinese. The Water Lily Club opened its doors to him when she knocked, and the Sublimely Pure Brothers' organization admitted him as one of its honorary members, thereby enabling him not only to see but to take part in a ceremony in which no American had ever before participated. With her by his side, he was welcomed wherever he went. Even the little Chinese women in the midst of their babies, received him with gentle smiles, and the children solemnly munched his candies and repeated nursery rhymes for his edification.

He enjoyed it all, and so did Pan. They were both young and light-hearted. And when the afternoon was spent, there was always that high room open to the stars, with its China bowls full of flowers and its big colored lanterns, shedding a mellow light.

Sometimes there was music. A Chinese band played three

evenings a week in the gilded restaurant beneath them, and the louder the gongs sounded and the fiddlers fiddled, the more delighted was Pan. Just below the restaurant was her father's bazaar. Occasionally Mun You would stroll upstairs and inquire of the young couple if there was anything needed to complete their felicity, and Pan would answer: "Thou only." Pan was very proud of her Chinese father. "I would rather have a Chinese for a father than a white man," she often told Mark Carson. The last time she had said that he had asked whom she would prefer for a husband, a white man or a Chinese. And Pan, for the first time since he had known her, had no answer for him.

It was a cool, quiet evening, after a hot day. A new moon was in the sky.

"How beautiful above! How unbeautiful below!" exclaimed Mark Carson involuntarily.

He and Pan had been gazing down from their open retreat into the lantern-lighted, motley-thronged street beneath them.

"Perhaps it isn't very beautiful," replied Pan, "but it is here I live. It is my home." Her voice quivered a little.

He leaned towards her suddenly and grasped her hands.

"Pan," he cried, "you do not belong here. You are white—white."

"No! no!" protested Pan.

"You are," he asserted. "You have no right to be here."

"I was born here," she answered, "and the Chinese people look upon me as their own."

"But they do not understand you," he went on. "Your real self is alien to them. What interest have they in the books you read—the thoughts you think?"

"They have an interest in me," answered faithful Pan. "Oh, do not speak in that way any more."

"But I must," the young man persisted. "Pan, don't you see that you have got to decide what you will be—Chinese or white? You cannot be both."

"Hush! Hush!" bade Pan. "I do not love you when you talk to me like that."

A little Chinese boy brought tea and saffron cakes. He was a picturesque little fellow with a quaint manner of speech. Mark

Carson jested merrily with him, while Pan holding a tea-bowl between her two small hands laughed and sipped.

When they were alone again, the silver stream and the crescent moon became the objects of their study. It was a very beautiful evening.

After a while Mark Carson, his hand on Pan's shoulder, sang:

> *"And forever, and forever,*
> *As long as the river flows,*
> *As long as the heart has passions,*
> *As long as life has woes,*
> *The moon and its broken reflection,*
> *And its shadows shall appear,*
> *As the symbol of love in heaven,*
> *And its wavering image here."*

Listening to that irresistible voice singing her heart away, the girl broke down and wept. She was so young and so happy.

"Look up at me," bade Mark Carson. "Oh, Pan! Pan! Those tears prove that you are white."

Pan lifted her wet face.

"Kiss me, Pan," said he. It was the first time.

Next morning Mark Carson began work on the special-feature article which he had been promising his paper for some weeks.

"Cursed be his ancestors," bayed Man You.

He cast a paper at his daughter's feet and left the room.

Startled by her father's unwonted passion, Pan picked up the paper, and in the clear passionless light of the afternoon read that which forever after was blotted upon her memory.

"Betrayed! Betrayed! Betrayed to be a betrayer!"

It burnt red hot; agony unrelieved by words, unassuaged by tears.

So till evening fell. Then she stumbled up the dark stairs which led to the high room open to the stars and tried to think it out. Someone had hurt her. Who was it? She raised her eyes. There shone: "Its Wavering Image." It helped her to lucidity. He had done it. Was it unconsciously dealt—that cruel blow? Ah, well did he know that the sword which pierced her through others, would carry with it to her own heart, the pain of all those others. None knew better than he that she, whom he had called "a white girl, a white woman," would rather that her own naked body and soul had been exposed, than that things, sacred and secret to those who loved her, should be cruelly unveiled and ruthlessly spread before the ridiculing and uncomprehending foreigner. And knowing all this so well, so well, he had carelessly sung her heart away, and with her kiss upon his lips, had smilingly turned and stabbed her. She, who was of the race that remembers.

Mark Carson, back in the city after an absence of two months, thought of Pan. He would see her that very evening. Dear little Pan, pretty Pan, clever Pan, amusing Pan; Pan, who was always so frankly glad to have him come to her; so eager to hear all that he was doing; so appreciative, so inspiring, so loving. She would have forgotten that article by now. Why should a white woman care about such things? Her true self was above it all. Had he not taught her that during the weeks in which they had seen so much of one another? True, his last lesson had been a little harsh, and as yet he knew not how she had taken it; but even if its roughness had hurt and irritated, there was a healing balm, a wizard's oil which none knew so well as he how to apply.

But for all these soothing reflections, there was an undercurrent of feeling which caused his steps to falter on his way to Pan. He turned into Portsmouth Square and took a seat on one of the benches facing the fountain erected in memory of Robert Louis Stevenson. Why had Pan failed to answer the note he had written telling her of the assignment which would keep him out of town for a couple of months and giving her his address? Would Robert Louis Stevenson have known why? Yes—and so did Mark Carson. But though Robert Louis Stevenson would have boldly answered himself the question. Mark Carson thrust it aside, arose, and pressed up the hill.

"I knew they would not blame you, Pan!"

"Yes."

"And there was no word of you, dear. I was careful about that, not only for your sake, but for mine."

Silence.

"It is mere superstition anyway. These things have got to be exposed and done away with."

Still silence.

Mark Carson felt strangely chilled. Pan was not herself tonight. She did not even look herself. He had been accustomed to seeing her in American dress. Tonight she wore the Chinese costume. But for her clear-cut features she might have been a Chinese girl. He shivered.

"Pan," he asked, "why do you wear that dress?"

Within her sleeves Pan's small hands struggled together; but her face and voice were calm.

"Because I am a Chinese woman," she answered.

"You are not," cried Mark Carson, fiercely. "You cannot say that now, Pan. You are a white woman—white. Did your kiss not promise me that?"

"A white woman!" echoed Pan her voice rising high and clear to the stars above them. "I would not be a white woman for all the world. *You* are a white man. And *what* is a promise to a white man!"

When she was lying low, the element of Fire having raged so fiercely within her that it had almost shriveled up the childish frame, there came to the house of Man You a little toddler who could scarcely speak. Climbing upon Pan's couch, she pressed her head upon the sick girl's bosom. The feel of that little head brought tears.

"Lo!" said the mother of the toddler. "Thou wilt bear a child thyself some day, and all the bitterness of this will pass away."

And Pan, being a Chinese woman, was comforted.

FURTHER READINGS:

Sui Sin Far, "Leaves from the Mental Portfolio of a Eurasian," *Independent* (21 January 1909); Annette White Parks, *Sui Sin Far/Edith Maud Eaton: A Literary Biography* (University of Illinois Press, 1995); Amy Ling and Annette White-Parks, eds., *Mrs. Spring Fragrance and Other Writings* (University of Illinois Press, 1995); Amy Ling, *Between Worlds: Women Writers of Chinese Ancestry* (Elsevier Science Ltd, 1990); Amy Ling, "Chinese American Women Writers: The Tradition Behind Maxine Hong Kingston," in *Redefining American Literary History*, eds. A. LaVonne Brown Ruoff and Jerry W. Ward (Modern Language Association of America, 1990).

Evelyn Cameron, *Children's Day at Church*, 1913.

The Haynes Foundation Collection, The Montana Historical Society, Helena, Montana.

3
The Gift of Good Land

The poet Wendell Berry spoke of "the gift of good land" when he wanted to describe the American experience of abundance. This continent gave up bountiful crops, and crowned the farmer with title to land he could leave to his sons. Hector St. John de Crevecoeur wrote that the immigrant became "a new man" when he owned the land that he had tilled by the sweat of his brow.

But the gift of good land has been more ambiguous as it came to mean the inheritance of daughters. Mary Austin, Zitkala Ša, Willa Cather, Elinore Pruitt Stewart, and Anne Ellis write about their lives on the land, but only Stewart speaks of the land in terms of ownership. Austin embraced socialism, so profoundly did she believe that ownership did not devolve on those with legal title, but on those who live and work the land, who perceive its beauty and its fine webs of life. Zitkala Ša saw herself as intimately connected to the land where she was born, and yet, she also wrote about it more out of her sense of loss than a sense of ownership. Cather wrote of a landscape that was a secret source of ecstasy and mystical experience, but beyond human control: "We come and go, but the land is always here. And the people who love it and understand it are the people who own it for a little while." Ellis wrote with adoration for the respite she found in the landscapes surrounding Rocky Mountain mining communities, but never felt she owned anything more than a temporary stopping place.

Cather and Austin, often described as quintessentially Western writers, traveled widely and each saw herself as a professional writer and artist at a time when that role yielded a woman only a fragile foothold in the world. The kept close the company of women who gave them emotional and professional support. Sarah Orne Jewett, in Maine, was Cather's mentor and guide. Jewett's New England landscapes, especially in *The Country of the Pointed Firs* (1896), collapsed the continental distances between herself and Cather and deeply influenced Cather's work.

Zitkala Ša, who grew up to become an Indian rights advocate, and Anne Ellis, who turned to writing after poor health prevented her from working as a cook, were professional writers of a different kind. Zitkala Ša used her stories (and her non-fiction work) to advocate for the rights of Native American peoples, and crafted a career out of carefully assessing the best audience before which to present her arguments. For her, the gift of good land was one complicated by the fact that that land had also been largely taken away from her Yankton Sioux people, leaving her to ask to whom the gift of good land had been given. Anne Ellis became a writer out of financial desperation, but her frank and often funny discussion of her adventures reached a popular audience. For Ellis, the land— and the birds and animals it held—afforded her rare moments of quiet in an otherwise noisy and hectic life. In casting herself as its protector, she embraces a special variety of female authority. Elinore Stewart urged other women to choose a life on the open land rather than in the workforce of the cities. The land for her was an uncomplicated gift, there to be taken by men and women with enough ingenuity and courage to build their lives upon it, and show their gratitude by careful husbandry.

Mary Austin (1868–1934)

Mary Hunter was born in Carlinville, Illinois when that state was still "frontier" country. She went to Blackburn College in Carlinville, and after graduation, she moved with her family to California and married Stafford W. Austin. They homesteaded in and around the Owens Valley, but the marriage was unhappy; economic hardship and the care of a retarded child combined to make domestic life an apprenticeship in misery. Austin began to turn her early training as a naturalist into a role she designed for herself, that of chisera, or medicine woman. She learned from the desert-dwelling Shoshones and Paiutes that the barren landscape held creative energy and beauty, and that nature's smallest forms—the wildflowers and the seeds—and ordinary tools—baskets and pots—hold the secrets of the interconnectedness of all life.

She published her first book, *The Land of Little Rain*, in 1903. Immediately successful, the book has remained an American classic. Among her twenty-seven books and over 250 articles, it is the most idiosyncratic, being neither short story nor essay, but a kind of naturalist's poetry. She used Indian and Spanish names for plants and for places and in *The Land of Journey's Ending* (1924), she added to the text a glossary of over 800 Spanish words. Austin traveled widely in Italy, France, and England, and she was committed to the ideals of Socialism because she believed only living on the land could bestow ownership. In 1924 Austin came back to the desert and settled in Santa Fé, New Mexico. She died ten years later in 1934.

Her descriptions of the desert glow with amazing acuity. As a stylist, and a philosopher, she reaches back to Emerson and Thoreau in finding that the smallest detail of the natural world holds the spark of mystical oneness with the universe. She is the precursor of John Muir and Rachel Carson in comprehending that nature is the metaphor for all human life.

THE LAND OF LITTLE RAIN

East away from the Sierras, south from Panamint and Amargosa, east and south many an uncounted mile, is the Country of Lost Borders.

Ute, Paiute, Mojave, and Shoshone inhabit its frontiers, and as far into the heart of it as a man dare go. Not the law, but the land sets the limit. Desert is the name it wears upon the maps, but the Indian's is the better word. Desert is a loose term to indicate land that supports no man; whether the land can be limited and broken to that purpose is not proven. Void of life it never is, however dry the air and villainous the soil.

This is the nature of that country. There are hills, rounded, blunt, burned, squeezed up out of chaos, chrome and vermilion painted, aspiring to the snow-line. Between the hills lie high level-looking plains full of intolerable sun glare, or narrow valleys drowned in a blue haze. The hill surface is streaked with ash drift and black, unweathered lava flows. After rains water accumulates in the hollows of small closed valleys, and, evaporating, leaves hard dry levels of pure desertness that get the local name of dry lakes. Where the mountains are steep and the rains heavy, the pool is never quite dry, but dark and bitter, rimmed about with the efflorescence of alkaline deposits. A thin crust of it lies along the marsh over the vegetating area, which has neither beauty nor freshness. In the broad wastes open to the wind the sand drifts in hummocks about the stubby shrubs, and between them the soil shows saline traces. The sculpture of the hills here is more wind than water work, though the quick storms do sometimes scar them past many a year's redeeming. In all the Western desert edges there are essays in miniature at the famed, terrible Grand Cañon, to which, if you keep on long enough in this country, you will come at last.

Since this is a hill country one expects to find springs, but not to depend upon them; for when found they are often brackish and unwholesome, or maddening, slow dribbles in a thirsty soil. Here you find the hot sink of Death Valley, or high rolling districts where the air has always a tang of frost. Here are the long heavy winds

Mary Austin, "The Land of Little Rain," "The Scavengers," and "The Basket Maker" from *The Land of Little Rain* (1903).

and breathless calms on the tilted mesas where dust devils dance, whirling up into a wide, pale sky. Here you have no rain when all the earth cries for it, or quick downpours called cloud-bursts for violence. A land of lost rivers, with little in it to love; yet a land that once visited must be come back to inevitably. If it were not so there would be little told of it.

This is the country of three seasons. From June on to November it lies hot, still, and unbearable, sick with violent unrelieving storms; then on until April, chill, quiescent, drinking its scant rain and scanter snows; from April to the hot season again, blossoming, radiant, and seductive. These months are only approximate; later or earlier the rain-laden wind may drift up the water gate of the Colorado from the Gulf, and the land sets its seasons by the rain.

The desert floras shame us with their cheerful adaptations to the seasonal limitations. Their whole duty is to flower and fruit, and they do it hardly, or with tropical luxuriance, as the rain admits. It is recorded in the report of the Death Valley expedition that after a year of abundant rains, on the Colorado desert was found a specimen of Amaranthus ten feet high. A year later the same species in the same place matured in the drought at four inches. One hopes the land may breed like qualities in her human offspring, not tritely to "try," but to do. Seldom does the desert herb attain the full stature of the type. Extreme aridity and extreme altitude have the same dwarfing effect, so that we find in the high Sierras and in Death Valley related species in miniature that reach a comely growth in mean temperatures. Very fertile are the desert plants in expedients to prevent evaporation, turning their foliage edgewise toward the sun, growing silky hairs, exuding viscid gum. The wind, which has a long sweep, harries and helps them. It rolls up dunes about the stocky stems, encompassing and protective, and above the dunes, which may be, as with the mesquite, three times as high as a man, the blossoming twigs flourish and bear fruit.

There are many areas in the desert where drinkable water lies within a few feet of the surface, indicated by the mesquite and the bunch grass (*Sporobolus airoides*). It is this nearness of unimagined help that makes the tragedy of desert deaths. It is related that the final breakdown of that hapless party that gave Death Valley its forbidding name occurred in a locality where shallow wells would

have saved them. But how were they to know that? Properly
equipped it is possible to go safely across that ghastly sink, yet
every year it takes its toll of death, and yet men find there sun-dried
mummies, of whom no trace or recollection is preserved. To under-
estimate one's thirst, to pass a given landmark to the right or left, to
find a dry spring where one looked for running water—there is no
help for any of these things.

Along springs and sunken watercourses one is surprised to
find such water-loving plants as grow widely in moist ground, but
the true desert breeds its own kind, each in its particular habitat.
The angle of the slope, the frontage of a hill, the structure of the soil
determines the plant. South-looking hills are nearly bare, and the
lower tree-line higher here by a thousand feet. Cañons running
east and west will have one wall naked and one clothed. Around
dry lakes and marshes the herbage preserves a set and orderly
arrangement. Most species have well-defined areas of growth, the
best index the voiceless land can give the traveler of his where-
abouts.

If you have any doubt about it, know that the desert begins
with the creosote. This immortal shrub spreads down into Death
Valley and up to the lower timberline, odorous and medicinal as
you might guess from the name, wandlike, with shining fretted
foliage. Its vivid green is grateful to the eye in a wilderness of gray
and greenish white shrubs. In the spring it exudes a resinous gum
which the Indians of those parts know how to use with pulverized
rock for cementing arrow points to shafts. Trust Indians not to miss
any virtues of the plant world!

Nothing the desert produces expresses it better than the
unhappy growth of the tree yuccas. Tormented, thin forests of it
stalk drearily in the high mesas, particularly in that triangular slip
that fans out eastward from the meeting of the Sierras and coastwise hills where the first swings across the southern end of the
San Joaquin Valley. The yucca bristles with bayonet-pointed
leaves, dull green, growing shaggy with age, tipped with panicles
of fetid, greenish bloom. After death, which is slow, the ghostly
hollow network of its woody skeleton, with hardly power to rot,
makes the moonlight fearful. Before the yucca has come to
flower, while yet its bloom is a creamy cone-shaped bud of the
size of a small cabbage, full of sugary sap, the Indians twist it

deftly out of its fence of daggers and roast it for their own delec-
tation. So it is that in those parts where man inhabits one sees
young plants of *Yucca arborensis* infrequently. Other yuccas,
cacti, low herbs, a thousand sorts, one finds journeying east from
the coastwise hills. There is neither poverty of soil nor species to
account for the sparseness of desert growth, but simply that each
plant requires more room. So much earth must be preëmpted to
extract so much moisture. The real struggle for existence, the real
brain of the plant, is underground; above there is room for a
rounded perfect growth. In Death Valley, reputed the very core of
desolation, are nearly two hundred identified species.

If one is inclined to wonder at first how so many dwellers
came to be in the loneliest land that ever came out of God's hands,
what they do there and why stay, one does not wonder so much
after having lived there. None other than this long brown land lays
such a hold on the affections. The rainbow hills, the tender bluish
mists, the luminous radiance of the spring, have the lotus charm.
They trick the sense of time, so that once inhabiting there you
always mean to go away without quite realizing that you have not
done it. Men who have lived there, miners and cattle-men, will tell
you this, not so fluently, but emphatically, cursing the land and
going back to it. For one thing there is the divinest, cleanest air to
be breathed anywhere in God's world. Some day the world will
understand that, and the little oases on the windy tops of hills will
harbor for healing its ailing, house-weary broods. There is promise
there of great wealth in ores and earths, which is no wealth by reason of being so far removed from water and workable conditions,
but men are bewitched by it and tempted to try the impossible.

For all the toll the desert takes of a man it gives compensa-
tions, deep breaths, deep sleep, and the communion of the stars. It
comes upon one with new force in the pauses of the night that the
Chaldeans were a desert-bred people. It is hard to escape the sense
of mastery as the stars move in the wide clear heavens to risings
and settings unobscured. They look large and near and palpitant;
as if they moved on some stately service not needful to declare.
Wheeling to their stations in the sky, they make the poor world-fret
of no account. Of no account you who lie out there watching, nor
the lean coyote that stands off in the scrub from you and howls
and howls.

THE SCAVENGERS

Fifty-seven buzzards, one on each of fifty-seven fence posts at the rancho El Tejon, on a mirage-breeding September morning, sat solemnly while the white tilted travelers' vans lumbered down the Canada de los Uvas. After three hours they had only clapped their wings, or exchanged posts. The season's end in the vast dim valley of the San Joaquin is palpitatingly hot, and the air breathes like cotton wool. Through it all the buzzards sit on the fences and low hummocks, with wings spread fanwise for air. There is no end to them, and they smell to heaven. Their heads droop, and all their communication is a rare, horrid croak.

The increase of wild creatures is in proportion to the things they feed upon: the more carrion the more buzzards. The end of the third successive dry year bred them beyond belief. The first year quail mated sparingly; the second year the wild oats matured no seed; the third, cattle died in their tracks with their heads towards the stopped watercourses. And that year the scavengers were as black as the plague all across the mesa and up the treeless, tumbled hills. On clear days they betook themselves to the upper air, where they hung motionless for hours. That year there were vultures among them, distinguished by the white patches under the wings. All their offensiveness not-withstanding, they have a stately flight. They must also have what pass for good qualities among themselves, for they are social, not to say clannish.

It is a very squalid tragedy,—that of the dying brutes and the scavenger birds. Death by starvation is slow. The heavy-headed, rack-boned cattle totter in the fruitless trails; they stand for long, patient intervals; they lie down and do not rise. There is fear in their eyes when they are first stricken, but afterward only intolerable weariness. I suppose the dumb creatures know nearly as much of death as do their betters, who have only the more imagination. Their even-breathing submission after the first agony is their tribute to its inevitableness. It needs a nice discrimination to say which of the basket-ribbed cattle is likest to afford the next meal, but the scavengers make few mistakes. One stoops to the quarry and the flock follows.

There are three kinds of noises buzzards make,—it is impossible to call them notes,—raucous and elemental. There is a short croak of alarm, and the same syllable in a modified tone to serve all the purposes of ordinary conversation. The old birds make a kind of throaty chuckling to their young, but if they have any love song I have not heard it. The young yawp in the nest a little, with more breath than noise. It is seldom one finds a buzzard's nest, seldom that grown-ups find a nest of any sort; it is only children to whom these things happen by right. But by making a business of it one may come upon them in wide, quiet canons, or on the lookouts of lonely, table-topped mountains, three or four together, in the tops of stubby trees or on rotten cliffs well open to the sky.

It is probable that the buzzard is gregarious, but it seems unlikely from the small number of young noted at any time that every female incubates each year. The young birds are easily distinguished by their size when feeding, and high up in air by the worn primaries of the older birds. It is when the young go out of the nest on their first foraging that the parents, full of a crass and simple pride, make their indescribable chucklings of gobbling, gluttonous delight. The little ones would be amusing as they tug and tussle, if one could forget what it is they feed upon.

One never comes any nearer to the vulture's nest or nestlings than hearsay. They keep to the southerly Sierras, and are bold enough, it seems, to do killing on their own account when no carrion is at hand. They dog the shepherd from camp to camp, the hunter home from the hill, and will even carry away offal from under his hand.

The vulture merits respect for his bigness and for his bandit airs, but he is a sombre bird, with none of the buzzard's frank satisfaction in his offensiveness.

The least objectionable of the inland scavengers is the raven, frequenter of the desert ranges, the same called locally "carrion crow." He is handsomer and has such an air. He is nice in his habits and is said to have likable traits. A tame one in a Shoshone camp was the butt of much sport and enjoyed it. He could all but talk and was another with the children, but an arrant thief. The raven will eat most things that come his way,—eggs and young of ground-nesting birds, seeds even, lizards and grass-hoppers, which he catches cleverly; and whatever he is about, let a coyote trot never so softly by, the raven flaps up and after; for whatever the coyote can pull down or nose out is meat also for the carrion crow.

And never a coyote comes out of his lair for killing, in the country of the carrion crows, but looks up first to see where they may be gathering. It is a sufficient occupation for a windy morning, on the lineless, level mesa, to watch the pair of them eying each other furtively, with a tolerable assumption of unconcern, but no doubt with a certain amount of good understanding about it. Once at Red Rock, in a year of green pasture, which is a bad time for the scavengers, we saw two buzzards, five ravens, and a coyote feeding on the same carrion, and only the coyote seemed ashamed of the company.

THE BASKET MAKER

"A man," says Seyavi of the campoodie, "must have a woman, but a woman who has a child will do very well."

That was perhaps why, when she lost her mate in the dying struggle of his race, she never took another, but set her wit to fend for herself and her young son. No doubt she was often put to it in the beginning to find food for them both. The Paiutes had made their last stand at the border of the Bitter Lake; battle-driven they died in its waters, and the land filled with cattlemen and adventurers for gold: this while Seyavi and the boy lay up in the caverns of the Black Rock and ate tule roots and fresh-water clams that they dug out of the slough bottoms with their toes. In the interim, while the tribes swallowed their defeat, and before the rumor of war died out, they must have come very near to the bare core of things. That was the time Seyavi learned the sufficiency of mother wit, and how much more easily one can do without a man than might at first be supposed.

Seyavi made baskets for love and sold them for money, in a generation that preferred iron pots for utility. Every Indian woman is an artist,—sees, feels, creates, but does not philosophize about her processes. Seyavi's bowls are wonders of technical precision, inside and out, the palm finds no fault with them, but the subtlest appeal is in the sense that warns us of humanness in the way the design spreads into the flare of the bowl. There used to be an Indian woman at Olancha who made bottle-neck trinket baskets in the rattlesnake pattern, and could accommodate the design to the swelling bowl and flat shoulder of the basket without sensible disproportion, and so cleverly that you might own one a year without thinking how it was done; but Seyavi's baskets had a touch beyond cleverness. The weaver and the warp lived next to the earth and were saturated with the same elements. Twice a year, in the time of white butterflies and again when young quail ran neck and neck in the chaparral, Seyavi cut willows for basketry by the creek where it wound toward the river against the sun and sucking winds. It never quite reached the river except in far-between times of summer flood, but it always tried, and the willows encouraged it as much as they could. You nearly always found them a little farther down than the trickle of eager water. The Paiute fashion of counting time appeals to me more than any other calendar. They have no stamp of heathen gods nor great ones, nor any succession of moons as have red men of the East and North, but count forward and back by the progress of the season; the time of *taboose,* before the trout begin to leap, the end of the piñon harvest, about the beginning of deep snow. So they get nearer the sense of the season, which runs early or late according as the rains are forward or delayed. But wherever Seyavi cut willows for baskets was always a golden time and the soul of the weather went into the wood. If you had ever owned one of Seyavi's golden russet cooking bowls with the pattern of plumed quail, you would understand all this without saying anything.

Before Seyavi made baskets for the satisfaction of desire,—for that is a house-bred theory of art that makes anything more of it,— she danced and dressed her hair. In those days, when the spring was at flood and the blood pricked to the mating fever, the maids chose their flowers, wreathed themselves, and danced in the twilights, young desire crying out to young desire. They sang what the heart prompted, what the flower expressed, what boded in the mating weather.

"And what flower did you wear, Seyav"

"I, ah,—the white flower of twining (clematis), on my body and my hair, and so I sang:—

> *"I am the white flower of twining*
> *Little white flower by the river,*
> *Oh, flower that twines close by the river;*
> *Oh, trembling flower!*
> *So trembles the maiden heart."*

So sang Seyavi of the *campoodie* before she made baskets, and in her later days laid her arms upon her knees and laughed in them at the recollection. But it was not often she would say so much, never understanding the keen hunger I had for bits of lore and the "fool talk" of her people. She had fed her young son with meadowlarks' tongues, to make him quick of speech; but in late years was loath to admit it, though she had come through the period of unfaith in the lore of the clan with a fine appreciation of its beauty and significance.

FURTHER READINGS

Melody Graulich and Elizabeth Klimasmith, eds., *Exploring Lost Borders: Critical Essays on Mary Austin* (Univ of Nevada Press, 1999); Esther F. Lanigan, *Mary Austin: Song of a Maverick* (University of Arizona Press, 1997); Esther Lanigan, ed., *A Mary Austin Reader* (University of Arizona Press, 1996); Rueben J. Ellis, ed., *Beyond Borders: The Selected Essays of Mary Austin* (Southern Illinois University Press, 1996); Vera Norwood and Janice Monk, eds., *The Desert is No Lady: Southwestern Landscapes in Women's Writing and Art* (Yale University Press, 1987); Augusta Fink, *I-Mary: A Biography of Mary Austin* (University of Arizona Press, 1983); Vera Norwood, "The Photographer and the Naturalist: Laura Gilpin and Mary Austin in the Southwest" in *Journal of American Culture* 5 (Winter 1982): 1–27.

Zitkala Ša (Gertrude Bonnin) (1876–1938)

Zitkala Ša was born Gertrude Simmons, the daughter of a Yankton Sioux mother and a white father, on the Pine Ridge reservation in South Dakota in 1876. Raised by her mother in traditional Yankton Sioux fashion, she didn't speak English until she was sent at eight years of age to a Quaker-run Manual Labor Institute in Indiana. Although she later wrote of her great unhappiness at this school, she went on to attend Earlham College in Richmond, Indiana, where she studied music and rhetoric. She later studied violin at the Boston Conservatory. In 1900, she traveled to Paris with the Carlisle Indian Band, and played the violin at the Paris Exposition.

Returning to the U.S., she embarked on a literary career. Her autobiographical writings appeared in 1900 and 1902 *Atlantic Monthly* and *Harper's Magazine*, and were later collected and republished as *American Indian Legends* (1921). These autobiographical writings include accounts of "Why I am a Pagan," as well as memoirs of the contrast between her mother's teachings and those of the Quakers at school. In 1902, she translated and published her mother's traditional Yankton stories as *Old Indian Legends* (1901).

In 1902, she married Raymond Talesfase Bonnin, also a Sioux, and they moved to the Uintah and Ouray reservation in Utah. There, she wrote an opera with William Hanson in 1913, titled *Sundance*, based on Sioux rituals and melodies. On the reservation, she undertook a political career as well, serving as the secretary of the Society of American Indians in 1916, and traveling extensively to lecture on Native American rights. From 1918 to 1919, she edited the *American Indian Magazine*, and in 1924, she published a study entitled, *Oklahoma's Poor Rich Indians, An Orgy of Graft and Exploitation of the Five Civilized Tribes, Legalized Robbery*. In 1926 she founded the National Council of American Indians, and served as its president until her death in 1938.

In this selection, which originally appeared in *Atlantic Monthly* in 1900, Zitkala Ša remembers her first years of life with her mother, the changes that her mother told her came from the arrival of whites in the West, and of her father's decision that she would leave her mother and go away to school.

IMPRESSIONS OF AN INDIAN CHILDHOOD

The Ground Squirrel

In the busy autumn days, my cousin Warca-Ziwin's mother came to our wigwam to help my mother preserve foods for our winter use. I was very fond of my aunt, because she was not so quiet as my mother. Though she was older, she was more jovial and less reserved. She was slender and remarkably erect. While my mother's hair was heavy and black, my aunt had unusually thin locks.

Ever since I knew her, she wore a string of large blue beads around her neck,—beads that were precious because my uncle had given them to her when she was a younger woman. She had a peculiar swing in her gait, caused by a long stride rarely natural to so slight a figure. It was during my aunt's visit with us that my mother forgot her accustomed quietness, often laughing heartily at some of my aunt's witty remarks.

I loved my aunt threefold: for her hearty laughter, for the cheerfulness she caused my mother, and most of all for the times she dried my tears and held me in her lap, when my mother had reproved me.

Early in the cool mornings, just as the yellow rim of the sun rose above the hills, we were up and eating our breakfast. We awoke so early that we saw the sacred hour when a misty smoke hung over a pit surrounded by an impassable sinking mire. This strange smoke appeared every morning, both winter and summer; but most visibly in midwinter it rose immediately above the marshy spot. By the time the full face of the sun appeared above the eastern horizon, the smoke vanished. Even very old men, who had known this country the longest, said that the smoke from this pit had never failed a single day to rise heavenward.

Zitkala Ša (Gertrude Bonnin), "The Ground Squirrel" and "The Big Red Apples" from "Impressions of an Indian Childhood," *Atlantic Monthly* (1900).

As I frolicked about our dwelling, I used to stop suddenly, and with a fearful awe watch the smoking of the unknown fires. While the vapor was visible, I was afraid to go very far from our wigwam unless I went with my mother.

From a field in the fertile river bottom my mother and aunt gathered an abundant supply of corn. Near our tepee, they spread a large canvas upon the grass, and dried their sweet corn in it. I was left to watch the corn, that nothing should disturb it. I played around it with dolls made of ears of corn. I braided their soft fine silk for hair, and gave them blankets as various as the scraps I found in my mother's workbag.

There was a little stranger with a black-and-yellow-striped coat that used to come to the drying corn. It was a little ground squirrel, who was so fearless of me that he came to one corner of the canvas and carried away as much of the sweet corn as he could hold. I wanted very much to catch him, and rub his pretty fur back, but my mother said he would be so frightened if I caught him that he would bite my fingers. So I was as content as he to keep the corn between us. Every morning he came for more corn. Some evenings I have seen him creeping about our grounds; and when I gave a sudden whoop of recognition, he ran quickly out of sight.

When mother had dried all the corn she wished, then she sliced great pumpkins into thin rings; and these she doubled and linked together into long chains. She hung them on a pole that stretched between two forked posts. The wind and sun soon thoroughly dried the chains of pumpkin. Then she packed them away in a case of thick and stiff buckskin.

In the sun and wind she also dried many wild fruits,—cherries, berries, and plums. But chiefest among my early recollections of autumn is that one of the corn drying and the ground squirrel.

I have few memories of winter days, at this period of my life, though many of the summer. There is one only which I can recall.

Some missionaries gave me a little bag of marbles. They were all sizes and colors. Among them were some of colored glass. Walking with my mother to the river, on a late winter day, we found great chunks of ice piled all along the bank. The ice on the river was floating in huge pieces. As I stood beside one large block, I noticed for the first time the colors of the rainbow in the crystal ice. Immediately I thought of my glass marbles at home. With my bare fingers I tried to pick out some of the colors, for they seemed so near the surface. But my fingers began to sting with the intense cold, and I had to bite them hard to keep from crying.

From that day on, for many a moon, I believed that glass marbles had river ice inside of them.

The Big Red Apples

The first turning away from the easy, natural flow of my life occurred in an early spring. It was in my eighth year; in the month of March, I afterward learned. At this age I knew but one language, and that was my mother's native tongue.

From some of my playmates I heard that two paleface missionaries were in our village. They were from that class of white men who wore big hats and carried large hearts, they said. Running direct to my mother, I began to question her why these two strangers were among us. She told me, after I had teased much, that they had come to take away Indian boys and girls to the East. My mother did not seem to want me to talk about them. But in a day or two, I gleaned many wonderful stories from my playfellows concerning the strangers.

"Mother, my friend Judéwin is going home with the missionaries. She is going to a more beautiful country than ours; the palefaces told her so!" I said wistfully, wishing in my heart that I too might go.

Mother sat in a chair, and I was hanging on her knee. Within the last two seasons my big brother Dawée had returned from a three years' education in the East, and his coming back influenced my mother to take a farther step from her native way of living. First it was a change from the buffalo skin to the white man's canvas that covered our wigwam. Now she had given up her wigwam of slender poles, to live, a foreigner, in a home of clumsy logs.

"Yes, my child, several others besides Judéwin are going away with the palefaces. Your brother said the missionaries had inquired about his little sister," she said, watching my face very closely.

My heart thumped so hard against my breast, I wondered if she could hear it.

"Did he tell them to take me, mother?" I asked, fearing lest Dawée had forbidden the palefaces to see me, and that my hope of going to the Wonderland would be entirely blighted.

With a sad, slow smile, she answered: "There! I knew you were wishing to go, because Judéwin has filled your ears with the white men's lies. Don't believe a word they say! Their words are sweet, but, my child, their deeds are bitter. You will cry for me, but they will not even soothe you. Stay with me, my little one! Your brother Dawée says that going East, away from your mother, is too hard an experience for his baby sister."

Thus my mother discouraged my curiosity about the lands beyond our eastern horizon; for it was not yet an ambition for Letters that was stirring me. But on the following day the missionaries did come to our very house. I spied them coming up the footpath leading to our cottage. A third man was with them, but he was not my brother Dawée. It was another, a young interpreter, a paleface who had a smattering of the Indian language. I was ready to run out to meet them, but I did not dare to displease my mother. With great glee, I jumped up and down on our ground floor. I begged my mother to open the door, that they would be sure to come to us. Alas! They came, they saw, and they conquered!

Judéwin had told me of the great tree where grew red, red apples; and how we could reach out our hands and pick all the red apples we could eat. I had never seen apple trees. I had never tasted more than a dozen red apples in my life; and when I heard of the orchards of the East, I was eager to roam among them. The missionaries smiled into my eyes, and patted my head. I wondered how mother could say such hard words against them.

"Mother, ask them if little girls may have all the red apples they want, when they go East," I whispered aloud, in my excitement.

The interpreter heard me, and answered: "Yes, little girl, the nice red apples are for those who pick them; and you will have a ride on the iron horse if you go with these good people."

I had never seen a train, and he knew it.

"Mother, I'm going East! I like big red apples, and I want to ride on the iron horse! Mother, say yes!" I pleaded.

My mother said nothing. The missionaries waited in silence; and my eyes began to blur with tears, though I struggled to choke them back. The corners of my mouth twitched, and my mother saw me.

"I am not ready to give you any word," she said to them. "Tomorrow I shall send you my answer by my son."

With this they left us. Alone with my mother, I yielded to my tears, and cried aloud, shaking my head so as not to hear what she was saying to me. This was the first time I had ever been so unwilling to give up my own desire that I refused to hearken to my mother's voice.

There was a solemn silence in our home that night. Before I went to bed I begged the Great Spirit to make my mother willing I should go with the missionaries.

The next morning came, and my mother called me to her side. "My daughter, do you still persist in wishing to leave your mother?" she asked.

"Oh, mother, it is not that I wish to leave you, but I want to see the wonderful Eastern land," I answered.

My dear old aunt came to our house that morning, and I heard her say, "Let her try it."

I hoped that, as usual, my aunt was pleading on my side. My brother Dawée came for mother's decision. I dropped my play, and crept close to my aunt.

"Yes, Dawée, my daughter, though she does not understand what it all means, is anxious to go. She will need an education when she is grown, for then there will be fewer real Dakotas, and many more palefaces. This tearing her away, so young, from her mother is necessary, if I would have her an educated woman. The palefaces, who owe us a large debt for stolen lands, have begun to pay a tardy justice in offering some education to our children. But I know my daughter must suffer keenly in this experiment. For her sake, I dread to tell you my reply to the missionaries. Go, tell them that they may take my little daughter, and that the Great Spirit shall not fail to reward them according to their hearts."

Wrapped in my heavy blanket, I walked with my mother to the carriage that was soon to take us to the iron horse. I was happy. I met my playmates, who were also wearing their best thick blankets. We showed one another our new beaded moccasins, and the width of the belts that girdled our new dresses. Soon we were being drawn rapidly away by the white man's horses. When I saw the lonely figure of my mother vanish in the distance, a sense of regret settled heavily upon me. I felt suddenly weak, as if I might fall limp to the ground. I was in the hands of strangers whom my mother did not fully trust. I no longer felt free to be myself, or to voice my own feelings. The tears trickled down my cheeks, and I buried my face in the folds of my blanket. Now the first step, parting me from my mother, was taken, and all my belated tears availed nothing.

Having driven thirty miles to the ferryboat, we crossed the Missouri in the evening. Then riding again a few miles eastward, we stopped before a massive brick building. I looked at it in amazement, and with a vague misgiving, for in our village I had never seen so large a house. Trembling with fear and distrust of the palefaces, my teeth chattering from the chilly ride, I crept noiselessly in my soft moccasins along the narrow hall, keeping very close to the bare wall. I was as frightened and bewildered as the captured young of a wild creature.

FURTHER READINGS
Doreen Rappaport, *The Flight of Red Bird: The Life of Zitkala Ša* (Puffin, 1999); D.K. Meisenheimer, Jr., "Regionalist Bodies/ Embodied Regions: Sarah Orne Jewett and Zitkala Ša," in *Breaking Boundaries: New Perspectives on Women's Regional Writing*, ed. Sherrie A. Inness and Diana Royer (University of Iowa Press, 1997); Hazel W. Hertzberg, *The Search for an American Indian Identity: Modern Pan-Indian Movements* (Syracuse University Press, 1971).

Willa Cather (1873–1947)

Willa Cather, who grew up in the Shenandoah Valley of Virginia, was nine when her family moved west to Webster Country, Nebraska. Her father settled his family in a railroad town called Red Cloud, where he opened an office, made farm loans, wrote legal abstracts, and sold insurance. Eldest of seven children, Cather frequently called herself "Willie," dressed in overalls and dreamed of becoming a doctor. She graduated from the University of Nebraska, and began writing for the literature magazines. In an age when few women attained advanced education or professional responsibilities, Cather worked as a journalist and then as a school-teacher. There was nothing insular about her. In 1902, she and Isabelle McClung sailed from New York for a European tour, living for some time in Avignon and Provence. She was deeply moved by the landscape and by the ways in which lives were shaped by work on the land. Back in New York, Cather was managing editor of *McClure's* magazine, and she met Edith Lewis, the friend who would be her lifelong companion.

The friendship and support of women were of critical importance to Cather and to the other women who were beginning to think of themselves as artists. Elizabeth Sergeant, the writer, and playwright Zoe Atkins formed a circle of trusted friends. Sarah Orne Jewett became her mentor and guide. Jewett, author of *The Country of the Pointed Firs* (1896) taught her how regional detail could be drawn into literature. Cather acknowledged her literary apprenticeship when she later wrote the forward to Jewett's collected stories, and dedicated *O Pioneers!* to Jewett in 1913.

In 1912 Cather went back to the West, this time to Arizona and New Mexico, a landscape that critic Judith Fryer has called the "felicitous space." The visit was an awakening, an outpouring of energy and memory and complex emotion that provided the seedground for the novels *O Pioneers!* and *The Song of the Lark* (1915).

During the decades when Henry James and Edith Wharton established the tone of the American novel, Cather was writing about immigrant women, about the Swedish Alexandra Bergson and the pretty young Bohemian Antonia Shimerda. The characters whose lives filled the novel plough and sweep and feed the animals. They are humble figures that resemble the canvases of realist painters like Jules Breton, and Jean-François Millet. They express Cather's feeling that the land belongs to those whose lives are shaped by it.

Two different strains compete in *O Pioneers!*—a lyric mysticism and ecstatic joy, and a shadowed fatalism, as human passions lead to murder and despair. The erotic passage where Alexandra, Cather's pioneer heroine, imagines the land as her lover, is muted by the narrative where human effort—and love—are doomed to frustration.

Cather won the Pulitzer Prize in 1922 for her novel *One of Ours*. She was a prolific writer, who published seventeen novels over the course of her writing career.

THE WILD LAND

For the first three years after John Bergson's death, the affairs of his family prospered. Then came the hard times that brought every one on the Divide to the brink of despair; three years of drouth and failure, the last struggle of a wild soil against the encroaching plowshare. The first of these fruitless summers the Bergson boys bore courageously. The failure of the corn crop made labor cheap. Lou and Oscar hired two men and put in bigger crops than ever before. They lost everything they spent. The whole country was discouraged. Farmers who were already in debt had to give up their land. A few foreclosures demoralized the county. The settlers sat about on the wooden sidewalks in the little town and told each other that the country was never meant for men to live in; the thing to do was to get back to Iowa, to Illinois, to any place that had been proved habitable. The Bergson boys, certainly, would have been happier with their uncle Otto, in the bakery shop in Chicago. Like most of their neighbors, they were meant to follow in paths already marked out for them, not to break trails in a new country. A steady job, a few holidays, nothing to think about, and

---

Willa Cather, "The Wild Land," from *O Pioneers!* (1913).

they would have been very happy. It was no fault of theirs that they had been dragged into the wilderness when they were little boys. A pioneer should have imagination, should be able to enjoy the idea of things more than the things themselves.

That night, when the boys were called to supper, they sat down moodily. They had worn their coats to town, but they ate in their striped shirts and suspenders. They were grown men now, and, as Alexandra said, for the last few years they had been growing more and more like themselves. Lou was still the slighter of the two, the quicker and more intelligent, but apt to go off at half-cock. He had a lively blue eye, a thin, fair skin (always burned red to the neck-band of his shirt in summer), stiff, yellow hair that would not lie down on his head, and a bristly little yellow mustache, of which he was very proud. Oscar could not grow a mustache; his pale face was as bare as an egg, and his white eyebrows gave it an empty look. He was a man of powerful body and unusual endurance; the sort of man you could attach to a corn-sheller as you would an engine. He would turn it all day, without hurrying, without slowing down. But he was as indolent of mind as he was unsparing of his body. His love of routine amounted to a vice. He worked like an insect, always doing the same thing over in the same way, regardless of whether it was best or no. He felt that there was a sovereign virtue in mere bodily toil, and he rather liked to do things in the hardest way. If a field had once been in corn, he couldn't bear to put it into wheat. He liked to begin his corn-planting at the same time every year, whether the season were backward or forward. He seemed to feel that by his own irreproachable regularity he would clear himself of blame and reprove the weather. When the wheat crop failed, he threshed the straw at a dead loss to demonstrate how little grain there was, and thus prove his case against Providence.

Lou, on the other hand, was fussy and flighty; always planned to get through two days' work in one, and often got only the least important things done. He liked to keep the place up, but he never got round to doing odd jobs until he had to neglect more pressing work to attend to them. In the middle of the wheat harvest, when the grain was overripe and every hand was needed, he would stop to mend fences or to patch the harness; then dash down to the field and overwork and be laid up in bed for a week. The two boys balanced each other, and they pulled well together. They had been good friends since they were children. One seldom went any-where, even to town, without the other.

To-night, after they sat down to supper, Oscar kept looking at Lou as if he expected him to say something, and Lou blinked his eyes and frowned at his plate. It was Alexandra herself who at last opened the discussion.

"The Linstrums," she said calmly, as she put another plate of hot biscuit on the table, "are going back to St. Louis. The old man is going to work in the cigar factory again."

At this Lou plunged in. "You see, Alexandra, everybody who can crawl out is going away. There's no use of us trying to stick it out, just to be stubborn. There's something in knowing when to quit."

"Where do you want to go, Lou?"

"Any place where things will grow," said Oscar grimly.

Lou reached for a potato. "Chris Arnson has traded his half-section for a place down on the river."

"Who did he trade with?"

"Charley Fuller, in town."

"Fuller the real estate man? You see, Lou, that Fuller has a head on him. He's buying and trading for every bit of land he can get up here. It'll make him a rich man, some day."

"He's rich now, that's why he can take a chance."

"Why can't we? We'll live longer than he will. Some day the land itself will be worth more than all we can ever raise on it."

Lou laughed. "It could be worth that, and still not be worth much. Why, Alexandra, you don't know what you're talking about.

River Farms

Alexandra and Emil spent five days down among the river farms, driving up and down the valley. Alexandra talked to the men about their crops and to the women about their poultry. She spent a whole day with one young farmer who had been away at school, and who was experimenting with a new kind of clover hay. She learned a great deal. As they drove along, she and Emil talked and planned. At last, on the sixth day, Alexandra turned Brigham's head northward and left the river behind.

"There's nothing in it for us down there, Emil. There are a few fine farms, but they are owned by the rich men in town, and couldn't be bought. Most of the land is rough and hilly. They can always scrape along down there, but they can never do anything big. Down there they have a little certainty, but up with us there is a big chance. We must have faith in the high land, Emil. I want to hold on harder than ever, and when you're a man you'll thank me." She urged Brigham forward.

When the road began to climb the first long swells of the Divide, Alexandra hummed an old Swedish hymn, and Emil wondered why his sister looked so happy. Her face was so radiant that he felt shy about asking her. For the first time, perhaps, since that land emerged from the waters of geologic ages, a human face was set toward it with love and yearning. It seemed beautiful to her, rich and strong and glorious. Her eyes drank in the breadth of it, until her tears blinded her. Then the Genius of the Divide, the great, free spirit which breathes across it, must have bent lower than it ever bent to a human will before. The history of every country begins in the heart of a man or a woman.

Alexandra reached home in the afternoon. That evening she held a family council and told her brothers all that she had seen and heard.

"I want you boys to go down yourselves and look it over. Nothing will convince you like seeing with your own eyes. The river land was settled before this, and so they are a few years ahead of us, and have learned more about farming. The land sells for three times as much as this, but in five years we will double it. The rich men down there own all the best land, and they are buying all they can get. The thing to do is to sell our cattle and what little old corn we have, and buy the Linstrum place. Then the next thing to do is to take out two loans on our half-sections, and buy Peter Crow's place; raise every dollar we can, and buy every acre we can."

"Mortgage the homestead again?" Lou cried. He sprang up and began to wind the clock furiously. "I won't slave to pay off another mortgage. I'll never do it. You'd just as soon kill us all, Alexandra, to carry out some scheme!"

Oscar rubbed his high, pale forehead. "How do you propose to pay off your mortgages?"

Alexandra looked from one to the other and bit her lip. They had never seen her so nervous. "See here," she brought out at last. "We borrow the money for six years. Well, with the money we buy a half-section from Linstrum and a half from Crow, and a quarter from Struble maybe. That will give us upwards of fourteen hundred acres, won't it? You won't have to pay off your mortgages for six years. By that time, any of this land will be worth thirty dollars an acre—it will be worth fifty, but we'll say thirty; then you can sell a garden patch anywhere, and pay off a debt of sixteen hundred dollars. It's not the principal I'm worried about, it's the interest and taxes. We'll have to strain to meet the payments. But as sure as we are sitting here to-night, we can sit down here ten years from now independent landowners, not struggling farmers any longer. The chance that father was always looking for has come."

Lou was pacing the floor. "But how do you *know* that land is going to go up enough to pay the mortgages and—"

"And make us rich besides?" Alexandra put in firmly. "I can't explain that, Lou. You'll have to take my word for it I *know,* that's all. When you drive about over the country you can feel it coming."

Oscar had been sitting with his head lowered, his hands hanging between his knees. "But we can't work so much land," he said dully, as if he were talking to himself. "We can't even try. It would just lie there and we'd work ourselves to death." He sighed, and laid his calloused fist on the table.

Alexandra's eyes filled with tears. She put her hand on his shoulder. "You poor boy, you won't have to work it. The men in town who are buying up other people's land don't try to farm it. They are the men to watch, in a new country. Let's try to do like the shrewd ones and not like these stupid fellows. I don't want you boys always to have to work like this. I want you to be independent, and Emil to go to school."

Lou held his head as if it were splitting. "Everybody will say we are crazy. It must be crazy, or everybody would be doing it."

"If they were, we wouldn't have much chance. No, Lou, I was talking about that with the smart young man who is raising the new kind of clover. He says the right thing is usually just what everybody don't do. Why are we better fixed than any of our neighbors? Because father had more brains. Our people were better people than these in the old country. We *ought* to do more than they do, and see further ahead. Yes, mother, I'm going to clear the table now."

Alexandra rose. The boys went to the stable to see to the stock, and they were gone a long while. When they came back Lou played on his *dragharmonika* and Oscar sat figuring at his father's secretary all evening. They said nothing more about Alexandra's project, but she felt sure now that they would consent to it. Just before bedtime Oscar went out for a pail of water. When he did not come back, Alexandra threw a shawl over her head and ran down the path to the windmill. She found him sitting there with his head in his hands, and she sat down beside him.

"Don't do anything you don't want to do, Oscar," she whispered. She waited a moment, but he did not stir. "I won't say any more about it, if you'd rather not. What makes you so discouraged?"

"I dread signing my name to them pieces of paper," he said slowly. "All the time I was a boy we had a mortgage hanging over us."

"Then don't sign one. I don't want you to, if you feel that way."

Oscar shook his head. "No, I can see there's a chance that way. I've thought a good while there might be. We're in so deep now, we might as well go deeper. But it's hard work pulling out of debt. Like pulling a threshing-machine out of the mud: breaks your back. Me and Lou's worked hard, and I can't see it's got us ahead much."

"Nobody knows about that as well as I do, Oscar. That's why I want to try an easier way. I don't want you to have to grub for every dollar."

"Yes, I know what you mean. Maybe it'll come out right. But signing papers is signing papers. There ain't no maybe about that." He took his pail and trudged up the path to the house.

Alexandra drew her shawl closer about her and stood leaning against the frame of the mill, looking at the stars which glittered so keenly through the frosty autumn air. She always loved to watch them, to think of their vastness and distance, and of their ordered march. It fortified her to reflect upon the great operations of nature, and when she thought of the law that lay behind them, she felt a sense of personal security. That night she had a new consciousness of the country, felt almost a new relation to it. Even her talk with the boys had not taken away the feeling that had overwhelmed her when she drove back to the Divide that afternoon. She had never known before how much the country meant to her. The chirping of the insects down in the long grass had been like the sweetest music. She had felt as if her heart were hiding down there, somewhere, with the quail and the plover and all the little wild things that crooned or buzzed in the sun. Under the long shaggy ridges, she felt the future stirring.

Winter Memories

There were certain days in her life, outwardly uneventful, which Alexandra remembered as peculiarly happy; days when she was close to the flat, fallow world about her, and felt, as it were, in her own body the joyous germination in the soil. There were days, too, which she and Emil had spent together, upon which she loved to look back. There had been such a day when they were down on the river in the dry year, looking over the land. They had made an early start one morning and had driven a long way before noon. When Emil said he was hungry, they drew back from the road, gave Brigham his oats among the bushes, and climbed up to the top of a grassy bluff to eat their lunch under the shade of some little elm trees. The river was clear there, and shallow, since there had been no rain, and it ran in ripples over the sparkling sand. Under the overhanging willows of the opposite bank there was an inlet where the water was deeper and flowed so slowly that it seemed to sleep in the sun. In this little bay a single wild duck was swimming and diving and preening her feathers, disporting herself very happily in the flickering light and shade. They sat for a long time, watching the solitary bird take its pleasure. No living thing had ever seemed to Alexandra as beautiful as that wild duck. Emil must have felt about it as she did, for afterward, when they were at home, he used sometimes to say, "Sister, you know our duck down there—" Alexandra remembered that day as one of the happiest in her life. Years afterward she thought of the duck as still there, swimming and diving all by herself in the sunlight, a kind of enchanted bird that did not know age or change.

Most of Alexandra's happy memories were as impersonal as this one; yet to her they were very personal. Her mind was a white book, with clear writing about weather and beasts and growing things. Not many people would have cared to read it; only a happy few. She had never been in love, she had never indulged in sentimental reveries. Even as a girl she had looked upon men as workfellows. She had grown up in serious times.

There was one fancy indeed, which persisted through her girl-hood. It most often came to her on Sunday mornings, the one day in the week when she lay late abed listening to the familiar morn-ing sounds; the windmill singing in the brisk breeze, Emil whistling as he blacked his boots down by the kitchen door. Sometimes, as she lay thus luxuriously idle, her eyes closed, she used to have an illusion of being lifted up bodily and carried lightly by some one very strong. It was a man, certainly, who carried her, but he was like no man she knew; he was much larger and stronger and swifter, and he carried her as easily as if she were a sheaf of wheat. She never saw him, but, with eyes closed, she could feel that he was yel-low like the sunlight, and there was the smell of ripe cornfields about him. She could feel him approach, bend over her and lift her, and then she could feel herself being carried swiftly off across the fields. After such a reverie she would rise hastily, angry with herself, and go down to the bath-house that was partitioned off the kitchen shed. There she would stand in a tin tub and prosecute her bath with vigor, finishing it by pouring buckets of cold well-water over her gleaming white body which no man on the Divide could have carried very far.

As she grew older, this fancy more often came to her when she was tired than when she was fresh and strong. Sometimes, after she had been in the open all day, overseeing the branding of the cattle or the loading of the pigs, she would come in chilled, take a con-coction of spices and warm home-made wine, and go to bed with her body actually aching with fatigue. Then, just before she went to sleep, she had the old sensation of being lifted and carried by a strong being who took from her all her bodily weariness.

FURTHER READINGS
Joseph R. Urgo, *Willa Cather and the Myth of American Migration* (University of Illinois Press, 1995); Philip L. Gerber, *Willa Cather* (Twayne, 1995); Harold Bloom, ed., *Willa Cather: Modern Critical Views* (Chelsea House, 1990); Sharon O'Brien, *Willa Cather: The Emerging Voice* (Oxford University Press, 1987); Judith Fryer, *Felicitous Space: The Imaginative Structures of Edith Wharton and Willa Cather* (University of North Carolina Press, 1986).

Elinore Pruitt Stewart
(1878–1933)

Elinore Rupert Pruitt was a widow with a young daughter when her minister suggested she might find a position as a housekeeper for some rancher. She did just that and her new employer, in Burnt Fork, Wyoming, was a Scotsman who played the bagpipes. After only six weeks' time, she and Clyde Stewart decided that "ranch work seemed to require that we be married first and do our sparking afterward." Almost immediately, she filed a claim on an adjoining parcel of land, and considered she had become not only a wife but "a bloated landowner."

Elinore wrote a series of twenty-six letters to her friend in Colorado. The letters were published as a book, and the book became the basis of the film *Heartland* (1980). Pruitt wrote that she was lucky to have "healthy, well-formed children, my clean, honest husband, my kind, gentle milk cows, my garden, flowers, chickens, turkeys and pigs." She ran a mowing machine, learned to shoot and to fish, rode a pack-horse through a snowstorm, and when there was no preacher to be found, she read from the Bible and buried one of her own children. She was proud of the work she had done, but most of all, she was proud of land that she owned. "I am thinking of the troops of tired, worried women, sometimes even cold and hungry, scared to death of losing their places to work, who could have plenty to eat, who could have good fires by gathering the wood, and comfortable homes of their own, if they but had the courage and determination to get them. To me, homesteading is the solution of all poverty's problems. . . ." Elinore Stewart had a husband whose help contributed to her success, but other women in Northern Colorado and Wyoming, most of them widows and spinsters, began to file their own claims for land and their rate of success was approximately the same as men's.

LETTERS OF A WOMAN HOMESTEADER

The Arrival at Burnt Fork, Wyoming

April 18, 1909.

Dear Mrs. Coney,—

Are you thinking I am lost, like the Babes in the Wood? Well, I am not and I'm sure the robins would have the time of their lives getting leaves to cover me out here. I am 'way up close to the Forest Reserve of Utah, within half a mile of the line, sixty miles from the railroad. I was twenty-four hours on the train and two days on the stage, and oh, those two days! The snow was just beginning to melt and the mud was about the worst I ever heard of.

The first stage we tackled was just about as rickety as it could very well be and I had to sit with the driver, who was a Mormon and so handsome that I was not a bit offended when he insisted on making love all the way, especially after he told me that he was a widower Mormon. But, of course, as I had no chaperone I looked very fierce (not that that was very difficult with the wind and mud as allies) and told him my actual opinion of Mormons in general and particular.

Meantime my new employer, Mr. Stewart, sat upon a stack of baggage and was dreadfully concerned about something he calls his "Tookie," but I am unable to tell you what that is. The road, being so muddy, was full of ruts and the stage acted as if it had the hiccoughs and made us all talk as though we were affected in the same way. Once Mr. Stewart asked me if I did not think it a "gey duir trip." I told him he could call it gay if he wanted to, but it didn't seem very hilarious to me. Every time the stage struck a rock or a rut Mr. Stewart would "hoot," until I began to wish we would come to a hollow tree or a hole in the ground so he could go in with the rest of the owls.

At last we "arriv," and everything is just lovely for me. I have a very, very comfortable situation and Mr. Stewart is absolutely no trouble, for as soon as he has his meals he retires to his room and plays on his bagpipe, only he calls it his "bugpeep." It is "The Campbells are

---

Elinore Pruitt Stewart, from *Letters of a Woman Homesteader* (1914).

Coming," without variations, at intervals all day long and from seven till eleven at night. Sometimes I wish they would make haste and get here.

There is a saddle horse especially for me and a little shotgun with which I am to kill sage chickens. We are between two trout streams, so you can think of me as being happy when the snow is through melting and the water gets clear. We have the finest flock of Plymouth Rocks and get so many nice eggs. It sure seems fine to have all the cream I want after my town experiences. Jerrine is making good use of all the good things we are having. She rides the pony to water every day.

I have not filed on my land yet because the snow is fifteen feet deep on it, and I think I would rather see what I am getting, so will wait until summer. They have just three seasons here, winter and July and August. We are to plant our garden the last of May. When it is so I can get around I will see about land and find out all I can and tell you.

I think this letter is about to reach thirty-secondly, so I will send you my sincerest love and quit tiring you. Please write me when you have time.

> Sincerely yours,
> Elinore Rupert.

Filing a Claim

May 24, 1909.

Dear, dear Mrs. Coney,—

Well, I have filed on my land and am now a bloated landowner. I waited a long time to even see land in the reserve, and the snow is yet too deep, so I thought that as they have but three months of summer and spring together and as I wanted the land for a ranch anyway, perhaps I had better stay in the valley. So I have filed adjoining Mr. Stewart and I am well pleased. I have a grove of twelve swamp pines on my place, and I am going to build my house there. I thought it would be very romantic to live on the peaks amid the whispering pines, but I reckon it would be powerfully uncomfortable also, and I guess my twelve can whisper enough for me; and a dandy thing is, I have all the nice snow-water I want; a small stream runs right through the center of my land and I am quite near wood.

A neighbor and his daughter were going to Green River, the county-seat, and said I might go along, so I did, as I could file there as well as at the land office; and oh, that trip! I had more fun to the square inch than Mark Twain or Samantha Allen ever provoked. It took us a whole week to go and come. We camped out, of course, for in the whole sixty miles there was but one house, and going in that direction there is not a tree to be seen, nothing but sage, sand, and sheep. About noon the first day out we came near a sheep-wagon, and stalking along ahead of us was a lanky fellow, a herder, going home for dinner. Suddenly it seemed to me I should starve if I had to wait until we got where we had planned to stop for dinner, so I called out to the man, "Little Bo-Peep, have you anything to eat? If you have, we'd like to find it." And he answered, "As soon as I am able it shall be on the table, if you'll but trouble to get behind it." Shades of Shakespeare! Songs of David, the Shepherd Poet! What do you think of us? Well, we got behind it, and a more delicious "it" I never tasted. Such coffee! And out of such a pot! I promised Bo-Peep that I would send him a crook with pink ribbons on it, but I suspect he thinks I am a crook without the ribbons.

The sagebrush is so short in some places that it is not large enough to make a fire, so we had to drive until quite late before we camped that night. After driving all day over what seemed a level desert of sand, we came about sundown to a beautiful cañon, down which we had to drive for a couple of miles before we could cross. In the cañon the shadows had already fallen, but when we looked up we could see the last shafts of sunlight on the tops of the great bare buttes. Suddenly a great wolf started from somewhere and galloped along the edge of the cañon, outlined black and clear by the setting sun. His curiosity overcame him at last, so he sat down and waited to see what manner of beast we were. I reckon he was disappointed for he howled most dismally. I thought of Jack London's "The Wolf."

After we quitted the cañon I saw the most beautiful sight. It seemed as if we were driving through a golden haze. The violet shadows were creeping up between the hills, while away back of us the snow-capped peaks were catching the sun's last rays. On every side of us stretched the poor, hopeless desert, the sage, grim and determined to live in spite of starvation, and the great, bare, desolate buttes. The beautiful colors turned to amber and rose, and then to the general tone, dull gray. Then we stopped to camp, and such a scurrying around to gather brush for the fire and to get supper! Everything tasted so good! Jerrine ate like a man. Then we raised the wagon tongue and spread the wagon sheet over it and made a bedroom for us women. We made our beds on the warm, soft sand and went to bed.

It was too beautiful a night to sleep, so I put my head out to look and to think. I saw the moon come up and hang for a while over the mountain as if it were discouraged with the prospect, and the big white stars flirted shamelessly with the hills. I saw a coyote come trotting along and I felt sorry for him, having to hunt food in so barren a place, but when presently I heard the whirr of wings I felt sorry for the sage chickens he had disturbed. At length a cloud came up and I went to sleep, and next morning was covered several inches with snow.

Proving Up

October 14, 1911.

Dear Mrs. Coney,—

I think you must be expecting an answer to your letter by now, so I will try to answer as many of your questions as I remember. Your letter has been mislaid. We have been very much rushed all this week. We had the thresher crew two days. I was busy cooking for them two days before they came, and have been busy ever since cleaning up after them. Clyde has taken the thresher on up the valley to thresh for the neighbors, and all the men have gone along, so the children and I are alone. No, I shall not lose my land, although it will be over two years before I can get a deed to it. The five years in which I am required to "prove up" will have passed by then. I could n't have held my homestead if Clyde had also been proving up, but he had accomplished that years ago and has his deed, so I am allowed my homestead. Also I have not yet used my desert right, so I am still entitled to one hundred and sixty acres more. I shall file on

that much some day when I have sufficient money of my own earning. The law requires a cash payment of twenty-five cents per acre at
the filing, and one dollar more per acre when final proof is made. I
should not have married if Clyde had not promised I should meet all
my land difficulties unaided. I wanted the fun and the experience.
For that reason I want to earn every cent that goes into my own land
and improvements myself. Sometimes I almost have a brain-storm
wondering how I am going to do it, but I know I shall succeed; other
women have succeeded. I know of several who are now where they
can laugh at past trials. Do you know?—I am a firm believer in laughter. I am real superstitious about it. I think if Bad Luck came along, he
would take to his heels if some one laughed right loudly.

Marriage And A Funeral

December 2, 1912.

Dear Mrs. Coney,—

Every time I get a new letter from you I get a new inspiration,
and I am always glad to hear from you.

I have often wished I might tell you all about my Clyde, but have
not because of two things. One is I could not even begin without
telling you what a good man he is, and I did n't want you to think I
could do nothing but brag. The other reason is the haste I married in.
I am ashamed of that. I am afraid you will think me a Becky Sharp of
a person. But although I married in haste, I have no cause to repent.
That is very fortunate because I have never had one bit of leisure to
repent in. So I am lucky all around. The engagement was powerfully
short because both agreed that the trend of events and ranch work
seemed to require that we be married first and do our "sparking"
afterward. You see, we had to chink in the wedding between times,
that is, between planting the oats and other work that must be done
early or not at all. In Wyoming ranchers can scarcely take time even
to be married in the springtime. That having been settled, the license
was sent for by mail, and as soon as it came Mr. Stewart saddled
Chub and went down to the house of Mr. Pearson, the justice of the
peace and a friend of long standing. I had never met any of the family and naturally rather dreaded to have them come, but Mr. Stewart
was firm in wanting to be married at home, so he told Mr. Pearson he

wanted him and his family to come up the following Wednesday and serve papers on the "wooman i' the hoose." They were astonished, of course, but being such good friends they promised him all the assistance they could render. They are quite the dearest, most interesting family! I have since learned to love them as my own.

Well, there was no time to make wedding clothes, so I had to "do up" what I did have. Isn't it queer how sometimes, do what you can, work will keep getting in the way until you can't get anything done? That is how it was with me those few days before the wedding; so much so that when Wednesday dawned everything was topsy-turvy and I had a very strong desire to run away. But I always did hate a "piker," so I stood pat. Well, I had most of the dinner cooked, but it kept me hustling to get the house into anything like decent order before the old dog barked, and I knew my moments of liberty were limited. It was blowing a perfect hurricane and snowing like midwinter. I had bought a beautiful pair of shoes to wear on that day, but my vanity had squeezed my feet a little, so while I was so busy at work I had kept on a worn old pair, intending to put on the new ones later; but when the Pearsons drove up all I thought about was getting them into the house where there was fire, so I forgot all about the old shoes and the apron I wore.

I had only been here six weeks then, and was a stranger. That is why I had no one to help me and was so confused and hurried. As soon as the newcomers were warm, Mr. Stewart told me I had better come over by him and stand up. It was a large room I had to cross, and how I did it before all those strange eyes I never knew. All I can remember very distinctly is hearing Mr. Stewart saying, "I will," and myself chiming in that I would, too. Happening to glance down, I saw that I had forgotten to take off my apron or my old shoes, but just then Mr. Pearson pronounced us man and wife, and as I had dinner to serve right away I had no time to worry over my odd toilet. Anyway the shoes were comfortable and the apron white, so I suppose it could have been worse; and I don't think it has ever made any difference with the Pearsons, for I number them all among my most esteemed friends.

It is customary here for newlyweds to give a dance and supper at the hall, but as I was a stranger I preferred not to, and so it was a long time before I became acquainted with all my neighbors. I had not thought I should ever marry again. Jerrine was always such a dear little pal, and I wanted to just knock about foot-loose and free to see life as a gypsy sees it. I had planned to see the Cliff-Dwellers' home; to live right there until I caught the spirit of the surroundings enough to live over their lives in imagination anyway. I had planned to see the old missions and to go to Alaska; to hunt in Canada. I even dreamed of Honolulu. Life stretched out before me one long, happy jaunt. I aimed to see all the world I could, but to travel unknown bypaths to do it. But first I wanted to try homesteading.

Little Jamie was the first little Stewart. God has given me two more precious little sons. The old sorrow is not so keen now. I can bear to tell you about it, but I never could before. When you think of me, you must think of me as one who is truly happy. It is true, I want a great many things I haven't got, but I don't want them enough to be discontented and not enjoy the many blessings that are mine. I have my home among the blue mountains, my healthy, well-formed children, my clean, honest husband, my kind, gentle milk cows, my garden which I make myself. I have loads and loads of flowers which I tend myself. There are lots of chickens, turkeys, and pigs which are my own special care. I have some slow old gentle horses and an old wagon. I can load up the kiddies and go where I please any time. I have the best, kindest neighbors and I have my dear absent friends. Do you wonder I am so happy? When I think of it all, I wonder how I can crowd all my joy into one short life. I don't want you to think for one moment that you are bothering me when I write you. It is a real pleasure to do so. You're always so good to let me tell you everything. I am only afraid of trying your patience too far. Even in this long letter I can't tell you all I want to; so I shall write you again soon. Jerrine will write too. Just now she has very sore fingers. She has been picking gooseberries, and they have been pretty severe on her brown little paws.

> With much love to you, I am
> "Honest and truly" yours,
> ELINORE RUPERT STEWART.

Dear Mrs. Coney

When I read of the hard times among the Denver poor. I feel like urging them every one to get out and file on land. I am very enthusiastic about women homesteading. It really requires less strength and labor to raise plenty to satisfy a large family than it does to go out to wash, with the added satisfaction of knowing that their job will not be lost to them if they care to keep it. Even if improving the place does go slowly, it is that much done to stay done. Whatever is raised is the homesteader's own, and there is no house-rent to pay. This year Jerrine cut and dropped enough potatoes to raise a ton of fine potatoes. She wanted to try, so we let her, and you will remember that she is but six years old. We had a man to break the ground and cover the potatoes for her and the man irrigated them once. That was all that was done until digging time, when they were ploughed out and Jerrine picked them up. Any woman strong enough to go out by the day could have done every bit of the work and put in two or three times that much, and it would have been so much more pleasant than to work so hard in the city and then be on starvation rations in the winter.

To me, homesteading is the solution of all poverty's problems, but I realize that temperament has much to do with success in any undertaking, and persons afraid of coyotes and work and loneliness had better let ranching alone. At the same time, any woman who can stand her own company, can see the beauty of the sunset, loves growing things, and is willing to put in as much time at careful labor as she does over the washtub, will certainly succeed; will have independence, plenty to eat all the time, and a home of her own in the end.

Experimenting need cost the homesteader no more than the work, because by applying to the Department of Agriculture at Washington he can get enough of any seed and as many kinds as he wants to make a thorough trial, and it does n't even cost postage. Also one can always get bulletins from there and from the Experiment Station of one's own State concerning any problem or as many problems as may come up. I would not, for anything, allow Mr. Stewart to do anything toward improving my place, for I want the fun and the experience myself. And I want to be able to speak from experience when I tell others what they can do. Theories are very beautiful, but facts are what must be had, and what I intend to give some time.

Here I am boring you to death with things that cannot interest you! You'd think I wanted you to homestead, would n't you? But I am only thinking of the troops of tired, worried women, sometimes even cold and hungry, scared to death of losing their places to work, who could have plenty to eat, who could have good fires by gathering the wood, and comfortable homes of their own, if they but had the courage and determination to get them.

I must stop right now before you get so tired you will not answer. With much love to you from Jerrine and myself, I am

Yours affectionately,
Elinore Rupert Stewart.

FURTHER READINGS
Elinore Pruitt Stewart, *Letters on an Elk Hunt* (1915); Katherine Harris, *Long Vistas: Women and Families on Colorado Homesteads* (University Press of Colorado, 1993); Susanne K. George, *The Adventures of the Woman Homesteader: The Life and Letters of Elinore Pruitt Stewart* (University of Nebraska Press, 1992); H. Elaine Lindgren, *Land in Her Own Name: Women As Homesteaders in North Dakota* (1991).

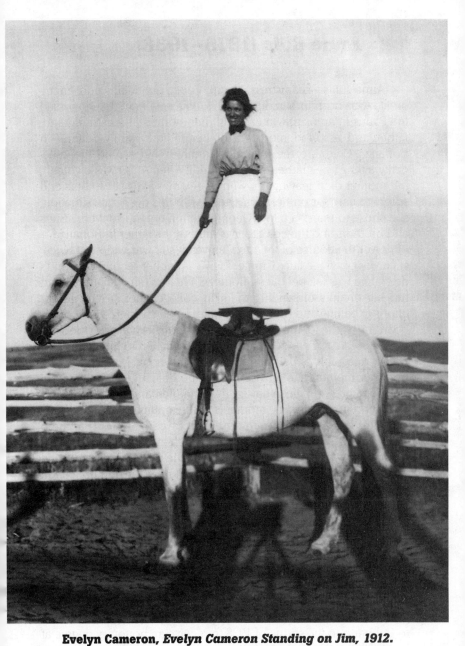

Evelyn Cameron, *Evelyn Cameron Standing on Jim, 1912.*

The Haynes Foundation Collection, The Montana Historical Society, Helena, Montana.

Anne Ellis (1875–1938)

Anne Ellis—seamstress, camp cook, politician, and memoirist—was born in Missouri in 1875. As a small child, she crossed the Plains in an ox-drawn cart with her mother, father, sister, grandfather, and assorted members of her father's family. Settling in Bonanza, Colorado, the extended family found a hard life, especially after Anne's father deserted them. When Anne was eighteen, her mother died, leaving her with three cows and six brothers and sisters to care for on her own. Faced with this desperate situation, she chose to marry a miner, George Flemming, and sent her sisters and brothers and the cows to live with Anne's father in Bonanza.

Over the course of the next ten years, she was widowed twice; such was often the fate of miner's wives. After her second husband's death, she was left penniless, alone with her two small children and her big dreams of sending them to college. After several of her efforts at baking and sewing for money failed, she agreed to open a boarding house for the Vindicator Mine, and later she used the skills she learned running the boarding house kitchen to hire herself on with a telegraph building crew as a camp cook. In this selection from her memoir, she tells of life on the trail, the vast quantity of foods she prepared each day for the workmen, and of the pleasures she found in her rare free moments in the mountains.

After her asthma prevented her from continuing as a camp cook, Ellis ran a sheep shearing camp kitchen, and later, she ran for office on a whim as Treasurer of Saguache County, Colorado, and won, despite the fact that she did not know the multiplication tables or how to write a check. But the job paid well, and it allowed her to put both her son and daughter through college. After two successful terms as county treasurer, she retired to move to a lower altitude, and settled into a sanitorium in Albuquerque, New Mexico. There she made friends who encouraged her to write down her memoirs, and Ellis, desperately needing the money, did. Income from her three volumes of memoirs—*The Life of an Ordinary Woman* (1929), *Plain Anne Ellis* (1931), and *Sunshine Preferred* (1933)—supported her for the rest of her life. Returning to Colorado in the spring of 1938 to receive an honorary degree at the University of Colorado, Ellis settled in Denver, where she died the same year at the age of 63.

COOKING IN A TELEGRAPH CAMP

I usually rode with Primo, a born gentleman, who always waited for me to start the conversation. I tried always to talk of things that would interest him—his team mostly. For hours we would never speak. Then I would say, 'I believe I will walk for a while, Primo,' and he would stop, let me off, drive on out of sight; then, gentleman that he was, halt the horses, and wait for me to come up to him. Once, while waiting, he went into an old abandoned cabin, and found a tattered mildewed magazine. In it was a poem by Ella Wheeler Wilcox, called, I think, 'Crucifixion,' which was to the effect that we make such a fuss over crucifying Christ and yet go on doing it each day in our treatment of laboring children, animals, and other races. Also in it was a picture of Christ on the cross. I hung it on the wall of the tent, and felt that it was a sort of a protection, and I always keep it in my bedroom now.

We made camp beside the Los Pinos, just as full of fish now as when Mr. Townshend was there. One day Earl was fishing and had a line with three hooks on it. I called him and he dropped his pole for the moment. When he returned, he had three fish.

The first things we unloaded were the cook-tent and the dining-tent, the stove, and the supplies. Our tables were boards on trestles. All the tables were white-oilcloth-covered, all the dishes were white enamel. In our camp there was a place for everything, and there it was placed. Now, many years later, if we were unloading, I'm sure both the Boss and I would know where every box, dish, knife and fork, pan, and kettle should go. Our case goods were stacked on one side of the cook-tent, till it seemed almost like the shelves in a store. My opened sacks of sugar, flour, cornmeal, and so on were kept in a large mouse-fly-proof grub-box. Above my work-table, in boxes supplied with shelves, I kept lard, salt, pepper, extracts, soda, baking powder, and so on. As far as I know, I was the only one in camp who had whiskey, which was used in case of emergency and for pudding

---

Anne Ellis, from *Plain Anne Ellis* (1931).

sauce. In the dining-tent were the long table and my bed, which last was always covered with a white sheet. It was a sanitary cot with folding sides. No man in all my years of camping ever sat on my bed except an underbred forest ranger, who rode up one day, and, leaving the saddle and pack on his tired horses, came in to wait for dinner. He threw himself full length, spurs and all, on my bed. And when I told him it wasn't done and suggested he feed and water his horses, he looked at me, hurt, and in an 'ain't-women-fools' manner.

Our fresh meat was brought by the quarter or half, and in the daytime was kept rolled in canvas. At night it was hung high in a tree.

At each new camp, men were set to digging a pit for a toilet; also a second pit in front of the cook-tent, into which all waste, empty cans, and wash-water was thrown. Before leaving a camp, both these pits were filled in and covered over with dirt; also all débris was burned.

In spite of the hard work, getting up before daylight, and not getting to bed before ten, I loved it all—the restfulness of running water and rustling leaves, the dancing shadows of leaves on the tent, either in sunlight or moon-light; grasses swaying in the wind, frost-painted bushes, the twitter and song of birds, the buzz of flies, the daring and triumphant whine of mosquitoes, the rasping call of blue jay and camp robber, the chirrup of chipmunks, the whistle of conies and the rustle and squeak of mice, men's voices in narrative and argument, usually laughing, seldom quarreling, better-behaved than in their own homes—I don't know why, except that they had most of the home comforts and no home irritations. Then, too, being close to nature brings out the best in humanity. But, after all, the main cause of their contentment was that they were well-fed. I felt my position as providing their muscle and morale.

Food was as carefully selected, cooked, and decorated as though we were in an expensive hotel. And (this is a secret) desserts, although lots of work, are much cheaper than beans, meat, and bread. Once, one of the men called me a 'workin' fool,' but you see I enjoyed it. I was expressing myself. Somewhere I have a season's menu—more Government red tape—and you'd be surprised to read it. This would be a sample—Breakfast: Hot, well-cooked cereal, a different kind each day of the week so they would not tire; coffee; stewed dried fruit, each day different; either bacon, ham and eggs, or fresh fish, fried potatoes, hot biscuits always, and either coffee cake, doughnuts, or cookies. Dinner: Soup, tea and coffee, a meat of some kind, with gravy, potatoes, another vegetable—if canned, cooked differently from the usual manner; hot rolls, a salad—yes, a salad, in the mountains where there was no lettuce, but there were canned vegetables, cabbage, potatoes, apples, and fish. For dessert we'd have pie with hard sauce and cheese. Supper would be much the same as dinner, except that we would have no soup, and have cake and pudding for dessert.

For Sundays I planned something special, and always made lemon pie—and I make good ones! I'd also make a huge platter of candy.

Holidays were observed by decorations on salads or cakes. Once, on Primo's birthday, I baked and decorated a cake for him, and when they were all seated at the table, I took it in and put it beside his plate. There was much talk and shouting from every one except Primo—he only smiled up at me—his winning smile.

Instinctively, Mexicans are well-mannered. When they had finished eating, Primo asked me for a clean knife, then stood and cut his cake, walked along the benches and passed it to each man there, then to me. When the men were all gone, he came to me and thanked me for my kindness.

We had few camp rules. Of these I remember only that there was to be no swearing, no wrestling in cook- or dining-tent, and that it was a crime for a man to call my attention by tapping on a cup. If a newcomer swore in cook- or dining-tent—really they both were one—the men looked at him and maybe frowned; anyway, he was made to understand he had committed a *faux pas*. I don't know how to spell or say it, but I know what it means. And no birds or chipmunks were to be killed.

One Sunday, after the dinner work was done, I climbed a nearby mountain. I wanted to be alone. The men were doing their Sunday cleaning-up, washing their clothes, cutting hair, shaving, and so on. After a time I heard the crack of guns, and thought they were shooting at a mark, but when I returned, in the pit I saw, sticking out from loose new dirt, the tips of bushy tails, and the gray and blue of jay and camp-robber wings. I didn't say anything (out loud), but for two Sundays they had no candy.

FURTHER READINGS:
Catherine Lavender, "Not-So-Plain Anne Ellis," in *Plain Anne Ellis* (University of Nebraska Press, 1997); Elliott West, "Foreword," in *Life of an Ordinary Woman* (University of Nebraska Press, 1980); Anne Ellis, "'Plain Anne Ellis': Master of Letters," *Colorado Quarterly* Vol. 6, No. 1 (Summer 1957): 31–45; Anne Matlack, "The Spirit of Anne Ellis," *Colorado Quarterly* 4/1 (Summer 1955): 61–72.

Barbara Van Cleve, *Chinks, Oxbow and Jinglebobs,* **1984.**

Copyright © 1984 Barbara Van Cleve.

4

Hardscrabble

Emerson and Thoreau, Willa Cather and John Muir, provide us with landscapes where abundance is the reward for raising the City on the Hill, and Thanksgiving is the national ritual for remembering the blessings of rich land—the golden wheat and fresh-flowing rivers, the broad horizons and snow-capped peaks, and the promises of tomorrow.

But there are other landscapes that recall the brooding scenes of Thomas Hardy, where nature is an inimical and elemental force. The sea in Stephen Crane's "The Open Boat" tosses men about like toys and in Ole Rölvaag's *Giants in the Earth*, the winter snows cover the living and the dead. In the poetry of Linda Hasselstrom, Wyoming and Montana landscapes carry something of that blind power. —"In the ditch/ a deer's dead eyes/ give back the night's confusion." The poet writes of a land that keeps its nighttime secrets —"The rock snorted/ shook himself, became a buffalo."

And Americans know still other haunting images—like those in Steinbeck's *Grapes of Wrath*, and in Agee and Evans's *Let Us Now Praise Famous Men*, where men and women are captive to despair. In that "other" tradition of nature writing in America, nature is a hard scrabble place that sucks away the spirit. Those are the pictures caught in Rebecca Harding Davis's *Life in the Iron Mills* (1861) where toil deforms the miners of West Virginia, and in Edith Summers Kelley's *Weeds* (1923) where the stupefying labor of tobacco-growing in Kentucky dulls the mind and glazes the eye. Nature in these works holds no benediction.

In *Daughter of Earth*, *Old Jules*, and *Second Hoeing*, the land offers only "starve-to-death" farming and "starve-to-death" mining, and for women and children, the West means isolation and loneliness. Good men, desperate to survive, curse the land and turn their fears against the family. Sykes's Hannah Schreissmiller "tried to dodge away but the whip always met her. At last she sank to the floor, covered her face with her arms and crouched." Smedley writes that "secrecy and shame settled like a clammy rag over everything." And Sandoz tells of her father, who "tore a handful of four-foot wire stays from the bundle in the corner and the children huddled at the back window," and of her mother, "blood dripping from her face where she had been struck with the wire whip."

In Richard Slotkin's trilogy—*The Fatal Environment*, *Regeneration Through Violence*, and *Gunfighter Nation*—western violence is the subtext of national culture, played out in rituals of masculinity and justice. But in the work of Sandoz, Sykes, and Smedley, domestic violence has no regenerative reward. It is violence hidden, and to speak or write of it is a betrayal of western values. Nebraska neighbors of Mari Sandoz's still bristle at the stories in *Old Jules* that were "undaughterly," "vulgar," and better kept secret. *Second Hoeing* was removed from local libraries in Colorado. As they are gathered in this chapter, the novels pose questions which, if they are not exactly new, still raise troubling thoughts, just when we thought we had figured out how the West has shaped the national identity.

Agnes Smedley (1892–1950)

Agnes Smedley grew up in the mining town of Trinidad, Colorado, in poverty that gave the lie to American promises of wealth and success. The degradation of her mother's life and her sister's marriage at sixteen and death in childbirth less than a year later were haunting memories. Smedley had little formal schooling—she attended the Normal School in Tempe, Arizona, for a single year in 1911, and spent a single summer at the University of California in Berkeley. After a brief, unhappy marriage, she moved to New York City in 1917, where she attended classes at New York University. In Greenwich Village, she joined Margaret Sanger's birth control movement, opposed American entry into World War I, and joined the Socialist Party.

Like Emma Goldman, Smedley became a political radical. She supported India's independence from British rule, and in 1918, she was arrested and held in the Tombs in New York as an agent for Indian Nationalists. When charges were dismissed, she fled to Berlin and then to China, where she worked as a correspondent for the Manchester Guardian. She traveled with the Red Army during the Sino-Japanese war, filing war dispatches as she moved. In 1938, she wrote, "I lay ill [of malaria and malnutrition] for nearly three years. For whole days I remained in a coma, unable to move or speak, longing only for oblivion." It was at that low point in her life that she began to write *Daughter of Earth*, trying to purge awful memories, and as a testament to "those of the earth, whose life is a struggle for survival." The Chinese women who "stormed the opium dens" were sisters to the women and children who worked for the Rockefeller's Colorado Fuel and Iron Company of her youth.

In *Daughter of Earth*, Smedley tells of her mother's unrelenting work and the physical abuse she suffered at home. But she tells also of the moment of resistance. When women in the town voted for the first time, her mother refused to tell her husband how she had voted. Her silence against his towering rage marked the beginning of a new determination never to be beaten again.

In the 1930s and '40s, Smedley published five books about China, and she wrote for the American magazines, *The Nation,* the

New Republic, American Mercury, and the *New Masses.* She died in Oxford, England, in 1950, and her ashes were interred in the National Revolutionary Martyrs Memorial Park in Peking.

THE EARLY YEARS

At home I found many changes. We now lived in a little frame house of four rooms. Helen and Annie occupied one of these alone because they worked and paid for their board and room. Annie pretended to be very grown-up; she refused to work in the house or to respect the opinions of my father or mother, and Helen was taking on the ways and speech of a city girl. She stopped saying "ain't" and used "have" or "have not." As sensitive as a photographic plate, she was taking on new manners. She bought sheets, and she slept in thin nightgowns instead of in her underwear like the rest of us. My mother respected her mightily and seemed to identify herself with her in all she did; perhaps through Helen she was living all that was denied her in her own life. On Saturday nights I would often hear the two of them arguing.

■ ■ ■

The church stood on Commercial Street, the main thoroughfare that twisted its way like a snake through the city. It was also a part of the ancient Santa Fé Trail. The church and the saloon were the two landmarks on Commercial Street. The saloon was across the street from the church and a little way up the hill. There I could find my father at all times when he was not at work. It was a small, one-story building with swinging doors and behind these doors men gambled, drank and "swopped yarns." Next to it stood the cigar store in front of which men lounged, smoked and spat all day long, exchanging obscenities and blasphemies.

Across the bridge at the foot of Commercial Street, beyond the railway station that was the boast of the city, stood the boarding house where I now worked. From school I went directly there. Its

---

Agnes Smedley, from *Daughter of Earth* (1929).

owner, Mrs. Hampton, was a young widow whose beauty and cooking made it possible for her to charge such high prices for board and room that only firemen or engineers on the railway could afford to live there. She had a parlor with an organ in it. Her bedroom was big and sunny and was connected with it, for she was a luxurious lady who demanded the best for herself.

One night, from the couch in the parlor where I slept, I heard voices from her room. I listened—surely my name had been mentioned! Yes . . . she . . . she was talking with that engineer. She was saying:

"I think she drinks some of the milk each morning before I get up."

"Why don't you fire her?" The engineer's voice was authoritative and complaining, like that of a husband.

"Yes . . . but she does such a lot of work—as much almost as a regular hired girl."

". . . but if she's not honest!"

I heard no more. For hours I lay awake. The charge against me was true—I took a sip of her milk each morning when I brought it in from the back steps. Often I was hungry, for I got only what the boarders did not eat. Mrs. Hampton was an important woman and she sat at the head of the table herself with her boarders. She was a kind woman and I did not feel lonely in her house; but she did not always notice if there was food enough left over for me. She had no time for the female sex. I ate up what was left as I stacked and washed the dishes in the kitchen.

To wipe out my crime I arose very early the next morning, boiled water and washed out dish cloths, hand towels and pillow cases. By the time she was up, the clothing was flapping on the line and the milk bottle was standing on the table in all its pristine fullness. At the end of the day I secretly took a pail from the kitchen and went down across the tracks. For my mother had been taking in washing for some time and, together with help from Helen, had saved enough to buy a cow. Although she sold the milk, I would tell her the truth and ask her to give me a pailful of milk to pay back my debt to Mrs. Hampton. Then I would tell Mrs. Hampton I was sorry—my crime would be wiped out. I even contemplated returning to the church as a punishment.

With a light conscience I approached our house. But at the

gate I stopped. My father was cursing and dragging my sister Annie
into the house by her hair. Annie was screaming and struggling.

"I'll maul hell out of you if you're twenty-five years old an' as
big as th' side of a house!" he was shouting.

My mother's voice was filled with anguish. "Oh, Annie, tell me if
you was in a roomin' house last night!"

Annie was coarse and vulgar. "Have I got to tell you a hundred
times I went to a dance an' stayed all night with Millie? Go an' ask
her ma if I didn't!"

"You're lyin'!"—but my father's voice was cooling.

"I'm lyin', am I? Then whatdye ask me for?"

"Well, I'll let you go this time, but th' next time I hear of you
goin' to that ornery low-down dance hall an' dancin' with pimps
an' stayin' out all night, I'll maul hell out of you!"

"You look out fer yourself, Pa, and I'll take care of myself! You're
always in the saloon . . . you ain't got nothin' to say to me! . . . I'm
makin' my own money now!"

Annie was fifteen and a woman of the world. And, by the standards of our world, a woman who earned her own money was a
free woman. Only married women had to take orders. By touching
Annie my father had violated the code of honor beyond the tracks.
He was bellowing back at Annie in a voice loud enough for all the
neighbors to hear:

"Yes, you earn yer own money, an' it's a lot o' good it does us!
Helen gives yer mother her money but you spend yours on duds
fer gaddin' about the streets!"

"Why don't you give Ma *yer* money, I'd like to know, instead of
spendin' it in th' saloon?"

"No back talk from you, missy! You do as I say, not as I do, or I'll
maul hell out of you if yer're twenty-five years . . ."

The back door slammed violently. . . . Annie had replied con-
temptuously and left in the middle of his threat.

There I stood at the gate with a pail in my hand. A thousand
emotions had swept over me as I listened to the quarrel in the
house—hateful, bitter emotions. Memories rushed to consciousness, forming an indistinct, vague picture of repulsion. "Annie in a
rooming house all night" . . . that meant sex. My father and mother
on the verge of beating her for it . . . what right had they . . . they
were liars and hypocrites themselves! I had heard them in the mid-

dle of the night . . . and now *they* were shocked! What liars grown-up people are! How dishonest! And that Annie . . . growing up . . . with fat breasts and hips, and proud of them! How disgusting! I did not like to be near her . . . nausea almost overcame me. Growing up and doing what all other grown-up people did—wallowing in sex!

On the one hand stretched my world of fairy tales, the song of "The Maple Leaves Forever," the tales of good little girls being kind to animals, of color, dancing, music, with happiness in the end even if things were not all right now. On the other hand stood—a little house with a rag pasted over a broken window-pane; a lone struggling morning-glory trying to live in the baked soil before the porch; Annie being dragged by her tousled streaming hair; my father, once so straight and handsome, now a round-shouldered man with tobacco juice showing at the corners of his mouth.

Turning, I retraced my steps without even opening the old gate leading into the yard. Along the banks of the Purgatory, over the tracks, across the arroyo flowing into the river, past the round-house back to Mrs. Hampton's. I crept into the kitchen and replaced the pail on the shelf. Then I went to bed and waited.

Mrs. Hampton was saying:

"Marie, I think I can do my own work alone from now on. I don't need you any more."

I looked through the back door into the yard beyond where washing was flapping in the wind. So I was being discharged for having taken a sip of her milk. I thought she had forgotten. I had worked so bard for the past few days and had tried to make up for things. It did not seem possible for her to do it . . . no, it must be that engineer who made her do it; she was going to marry him. He was going to make her a "respectable" married woman now, with standards such as Christians have. And she would have to obey him.

"Can't I stay another month fer nothin'? You won't have to pay me nothin'." My chest felt as tight as a skin stretched over a drum-head.

She thought that over for some time. "No. I can do my own work!" Her voice was sad, but it was final.

It took me hours to reach home. I sat down under a cotton-wood tree near the big round-house for a time, then when it was darker, under a weeping willow hanging sadly over the arroyo. I knew I had either to make up a story or get a whipping from my mother. She would scream that she would "stomp me into the ground" if she ever caught me stealing again. Or that she would whip me "until the blood ran down my back." I had to have time to think and to get rid of the weight in my chest. Perhaps it would be best to jump in the river and drown; then Mrs. Hampton and my mother would be sorry. The river rolled on mercilessly, dark and troubled against the gleam of the gray sand bank beyond. It was talking to itself . . . how strange that voice . . . it was like the night of the flood when it rushed upon us. This was one thing that you could not make love you . . . it was worse than an animal. That voice . . . fear held me back. . . . I could not trust a thing with no feeling in it.

It was late and very dark . . . it must have been hours since I left Mrs. Hampton's . . . it must be nearing midnight now. I dragged my feet homeward, up to the kitchen door, and pushed it open. I didn't care about telling a lie now.

But what was wrong? Helen and Annie were standing together near a corner where it was darkest. My mother was sitting on a chair, her head in her arms, her body shaking with sobs. Like a bull ready to charge, my father stood near the door. They all looked up as I came in. My father saw that my eyes were on my mother, and he perhaps remembered that I could never endure her weeping. Perhaps he felt in a weak position, as if he were author of this misery, for he shouted at me:

"Lookie, Marie, at your . . . your Aunt Helen. . . . I caught her layin' in the corner of the porch with that Dago beau of hers! Payin' fer that there brooch on her dress an' fer her fine duds! That's what she's been doin'!"

"John . . . what in God's name do you mean talkin' to a child like that!" my mother gasped in horror.

"She's got to know what kind of sister her mother's got . . . that's what!"

There was silence. Within my skull it seemed that a brush had made one complete sweep. . . . I could hear it as it made the circle. We all stood where we were. Helen's face was filled with white bitterness.

"You, John Rogers, to talk like that! You treat Elly like a dog! You've got nothin' to say to me when you spend all your money in the saloon."

"God . . . ! You that's a whore to . . ."

Helen rushed at him with a wild scream. Like a flash of lightning her hand struck and left a bloody streak down one side of his face. Then he caught her arms and held them savagely, high in the air. She, frail as she was, struggled viciously, kicking at his stomach, trying to reach him with her teeth. Only by the most violent effort could he hold her from him. My mother arose and in terror ran to them; she put her arms around the writhing Helen, stroking her hair and clinging to her. "Let her go, John! Helen . . . Helen . . . little sister . . . come here to me!"

She separated them and dragged Helen, white and panting, to the other side of the room.

"Takin' the part of a whore agin yer own husband!"

Helen made another lunge, but my mother's arms were around her and the weight of her body stayed the rush. "Elly"—Helen was panting like an animal—"let me go! let me go, Elly!" She and my mother rocked with the struggle, but my mother clung fast. Over her shoulder Helen turned her white face to my father.

"If you call me that agin . . . you low-down dog . . . I'll choke you to death with my own hands, an' Elly can't stop me!" My mother's trembling voice tried to soothe her, stroking her lovely bronze hair and her white cheek. But Helen's voice came, low and passionate.

"An' if I *was* a whore, John Rogers, I want to know who made me one! *You,* John Rogers! You! Elly ain't had enough money to buy grub and duds for herself and the kids. I've give her my wages each pay-day. Yes, an' you know it! If 'twasn't for my money, she'd have starved to death. You in the saloon . . . you comin home on Saturday night when every cent's gone, then lyin' or threatenin' if she complained. How d'ye think she was to live? . . . Washin'? . . . damn you! You're an ornery low-down dog! *You* to call me names! You! Where did you think I could git money for my duds. . . . I *won't* go in rags. . . . I *won't* get married and let some man boss me around and whip me and let me starve! *I've* a right to things. If I'm a whore . . . *you* made me one, you, John Rogers, . . . you . . . you . . . you!"

"You pack up yer duds an' march, an' don't you ever dare darken my door agin!" My father was livid with rage. Helen had spoken the truth. "Git out now . . . to yer Dago pimp! Yer're not fit fer a dog!"

"And you *are* I suppose! And you call this *your* house, do you . . . you don't even pay the rent. You don't bring in *nothin'!*"

"Git out of my house or I'll throw you out!"

My mother had her arms about Helen. "If she goes out in this night, John, I go with her."

"Yer're a nice wife to talk of goin' out in the streets with a woman like that! You let her go an' come here!"

My mother stood, straight and slender, her face ashen-colored like the face of a wounded coal miner I had seen long ago, a few minutes before he died. Her blue-black eyes glistened . . . where had I seen such horrible eyes before. . . .

"Come here!!" my father bellowed at my mother.

But she stood with her arms about Helen.

"You come here or I'll break all the furniture in this God damned house!"

My mother continued standing in icy silence, her eyes glistening. With a grunt my father flung out of the back door and we heard him fumbling in the dark. Helen's voice was tense with passion and misery.

"I'll go alone, Elly. I'll go now. John'll break up everything you've got . . . an' then he might kill you."

"*He* can go . . . not you."

"He won't go . . . he'll kill us all first."

"Then let him break up everythin'. And I'd rather be dead than alive anyway!"

"Don't, Elly. I'll go. I'll send you money an' things fer the kids. No! Stay here, I'm goin' alone. Stay here, I say! Think of the kids! What'll they do without you! Wait until I'm makin' enough for all of us . . . just wait!"

Helen pushed my mother away from her and backed into the room where she and Annie slept. Annie crept in after her, and the key turned in the lock. There were fumbling noises, quick steps, fugitive whispers from behind the door. My mother had sunk to the floor in a heap and lay, face downward, with her head in her arms. Her breath came in hard gasps. The back door opened and my father tramped in with an ax in his hands. His eyes fell on my mother on the floor. He stood listening . . . from behind the bedroom door hasty steps were moving about. He lowered the ax to the floor and waited . . . waited.

There was the sound of an outside door opening and closing . . . two steps on the porch outside, one step downward onto the hard earth, three steps more to the street. The old gate, hanging on one hinge, squeaked and flapped to with a dull rotten sound as if a spirit had passed that way. The rag pasted over the broken window-pane bulged inward from a wind that swept down the canyons in late autumn. My father breathed heavily, turned without a word, and slammed the kitchen door behind him. The click of his steps crossed a ditch leading toward the railway tracks . . . the tracks that wound through the city within a few steps of the saloon. The silence of the kitchen was broken only by the beat of my mother's sobs as if they had always been and would always be.

Weeks passed and then the sword fell. My father carried out his oft-repeated threat and left home. He knew my mother was too frail to support us all. No word had come from Helen.

After my mother had defied him about Helen and showed with each passing day that she no longer cared for life, he had become more and more violent. At night I heard hard, bitter weeping, but the door leading into their bedroom was locked. The horror of uncertainty hung over everything.

That year women were given the vote in our State. My mother's chin raised itself just a bit but she held her peace. She was not a talking woman.

"Howrye goin' to vote?" my father asked her.

She did not reply. Quarrels followed . . . he did the quarreling. At last a weapon had been put into her hands. At least she felt it so. He threatened her, but still she would not answer. On election day he threatened to leave home if she didn't tell him. But, without answering, she walked out of the house as if he did not exist. That night he asked a question that was a command:

"D'ye mean to tell me how you voted or not?"

"I don't mean to!"

The next morning she stood on the kitchen porch and he sat on his wagon outside, holding the reins, ready to drive away. My heart was heavy and I felt sick. He asked one more question, but she just stood quietly with her hands folded, and did not answer. Then he went. My mother's frail body braced itself anew. She decided it was better to go out to wash instead of taking washing in at home, for when she went out she got coffee and dinner; it saved food. Each morning she crossed the Purgatory to the comfortable homes bordering regular streets, with the high school rearing its head amidst them. She knocked at back doors and informed women that she did very excellent washing and ironing. Thus she became a regular washerwoman. Each morning she left home at seven, and she returned at eight at night. Her charges were one dollar and thirty cents a day. Yes, she said, she was frail, but she washed things white—all people had to do was to just give her a trial. The women looked at her eyes and wistful face and shook their heads; but then they saw her hands, big-veined and almost black from heavy work. That convinced them.

She washed all that winter. At night she was, as she herself admitted, "tired as a dog," but never too tired to relate in detail just the kind and quality of food she had had for dinner. It was sent to the wash kitchen on a plate to her. She sometimes had meat. She lingered over the memory, and was so thankful for such good treatment that she offered to wash extra things or stay half an hour later. The only thing that worried her was the neuralgia pains that tortured her in the face and head.

FURTHER READINGS
Janice R. MacKinnon and Stephen R. MacKinnon, *Agnes Smedley: The Life and Times of an American Radical* (University of California Press, 1988); Paul Lauter, Afterword, *Daughter of Earth* (Feminist Press, 1973).

Mari Sandoz (1896–1966)

When she had finished writing *Old Jules,* Mari Sandoz explained to Walter Frieze, editor of Hastings House, that she had written the biography of her Swiss-born father, Jules Ami Sandoz, but she had done much more than that. Her account of his life is also a history of Niobrara County in Western Nebraska between 1884 and 1905. Early settlers in the Sand Hills lived in dugouts, in a land of "starve to death farming." Sandoz grew up with stories of men with "both hands froze, fingers rotting off," driven crazy by blizzards. She wrote of women like George Klein's wife who took gopher poison and killed her three children with an old knife. The shock of reading *Old Jules* does not diminish with time. It is a haunting account of the struggle between settlers and the harsh new land, and of the tormented human relationships on that fierce landscape of "wind and desolation." Mari Sandoz was the little girl at the end of this selection trained by her father to be his hunting dog, to catch the fallen birds and bring them back.

In a country where there was a "tragic scarcity of women," where a man "had to marry anything that got off the train," the history of Jules and his wives is offered without apology. *Old Jules* is the chronicle of Rosalie, Estelle, Henriette, Emelia, and Mary, the women he married and divorced, the women who ran away and swore they never wanted to hear of him again. Mary, Sandoz's mother, was timid and obedient, "neat and quick as a blue-wing teal," but when Jules beat her with barbed wire, she tried to swallow cyanide. The memoir with its unrelenting detail was denounced in the community as an "undaughterly" book, full of detail that should have been kept private.

Sandoz went to school only through the eighth grade, though she attended the University of Nebraska irregularly between 1922 and 1930 and was awarded the Doctor of Letters from the University in 1950. She was married briefly but most of her life she earned her own living as a rural schoolteacher, as a self-taught historian with the Nebraska State Historical Society, and as an associate editor of the *Nebraska History Magazine.* She worked at writing as hard as any homesteader worked the land. "Whenever I had $50 in the bank, I'd quit and start writing for a while."

Sandoz shared her life's work and her friendship with Eleanor Hinman. In the 1920s in Lincoln, Nebraska, they read James Joyce's *Ulysses,* and had few women friends to offer support during discouraging times—*Old Jules* was turned down by publishers thirteen times, and Jules himself told his daughter that he thought "writers and artists the maggots of society." But before he died, Jules asked that his daughter write about him, and of his struggles to plant orchards on the wild Nebraska land. The portrait that emerges of Jules and his times is a mix of admiration and despair, an appraisal of the "pioneer spirit" that was at once brilliant and cruel.

Sandoz was a prolific writer of fiction and non-fiction. Among her books were *Cheyenne Autumn* (1953), *These Hunters* (1954), *The Beaver Men* (1954), *The Cattlemen* (1958), *Hostiles and Friendlies* (1959), *Son of the Gamblin' Man* (1960), *Love Song to the Plains* (1961), and *These Were the Sioux* (1961).

A FATHER'S PORTRAIT

"Well, I be hung for a horse thief! You oughter see the woman Old Jules has wrangled himself," Jed Brown remarked to Big Andrew, to whom he had hurried with the news. "Got a few hundred dollars of her own, Jules was telling me, and he shore needs that. Good enough looker too, and dressed in silks like a fancy woman, but she ain't that kind. She's refined."

"No!—Well, Jules, he write a good letter and is not bad to look on when he is clean like to-day, before he go to the train. If I do not have to come home to look after my mare and foal, I stay. He look fine, like judge, maybe, or senator. And he know how to talk with big words and make you believe," Big Andrew admitted.

Yes, everyone knew how he could talk, and everyone, particularly the women, wondered how this venture could end.

Jules did not take Henriette to his dugout immediately. After considering a photograph of this woman with lace at her wrists, he

---

Mari Sandoz, from *Old Jules: Portrait of a Pioneer* (1935).

decided it should not be so, at first. The dugout was full of muddy traps gathered in from the river, a few green hides, and all the accumulated filth since Paul went to the Platte. Later Henriette would clean it. For the present he made arrangements to use the Rutter shack, near the river, and all above ground.

It was dark when Jules and his bride arrived, and because he had forgotten to buy kerosene he ate crackers and cheese and drank part of a bottle of wine by the light of the cook-stove. He scarcely noticed that Henriette did not eat or that she was as a stick of wood, her hands fastened on the lace handkerchief in her lap. When it was time for bed she roused herself and slowly, with uncertain movements, she spread new linens from her trunk over the blankets she suspected were dirty if she could see them clearly. Once she stopped and looked about as one just awakening. It could not be true—this. This moulting crow could not be the eagle she had seen in the letters from Elvina's brother.

Train-weary, her body aching from the jolting lumber wagon, she crept into bed.

Towards morning it began to rain. The roof leaked, a little at first, then more. Soon everywhere. Henriette sat on the wet straw tick all the next day with a purple umbrella over her head, crying noiselessly while Jules raged that there was no fuel. Plainly the white hands of his wife would be incapable of wielding a successful axe against the toughness of wet wood. So he plunged out, dragged in a fallen ash tree, and chopped it into appropriate lengths on the floor. At last he got the fire going and while one stoveful burned he dried another in the rusty oven, his socks steaming behind the stove. He made half a gallon of coffee and dug out the remainder of the crackers and cheese. As he pushed a cup towards Henriette he warned her that he was not the man to wait on a woman. She shook her head. She was not hungry.

Fed and warmed, Jules filled his pipe and listened to the rain as the dusk gathered. He watched the fire-tinted drops run along the rafters and bound off the umbrella.

Suddenly Henriette laughed aloud. "It is like Chopin—'The Raindrop,'" and she hummed a bit of it.

Jules liked that. Their piano teacher at home had played it sometimes when he stayed to chocolate after lessons. They all practised a little, but only Emile and Nana had the ear. Reminiscently he hummed tunes of the homeland, sang a song Rosalie taught him in the spring:—

> *Ach, bleib' bei mir, und geh' nicht fort.*
> *Dein Herz ist ja mein—*

a lonely sadness creeping into his voice. But a new leak hit his cap, streamed down his neck, and cut the song short.

"*Sacré!*—and they try to tell me this is a dry country!" he exploded in English, laughing as at a huge joke. He hung his wet cap on the stove hook to dry and crawled into bed beside Henriette, rubbing his stubbly cheek against her arm.

■ ■ ■

The woman was intelligent, quick to recognize the potency of silence. With his wife's money Jules wanted to build, like the peasants he saw in France, a grainery, a horse stable, a chicken coop, and a pigpen, in a succession of lean-to's against the living quarters. Henriette waited until he was away on a hunt. Then she hired two men to build a story-and-a-half house, and laid out a yard with outbuildings. Emile abetted her.

■ ■ ■

Gradually the neighbors came back. They talked land and crops and shot target at Indian Hill, high over the Freese house, just as though he did not live there. Sometimes they stayed into the night and then Henriette brought out a loaf of bread, a platter of cold game, and a pot of coffee or a jug of new wine, still sweet. Silent, she was always there, in the dark corner near the stove.

■ ■ ■

November and December were a chain of clear blue days, with a thin powdering of frost on the grass along the river in the mornings. Cattlemen from Dakota said this was more like the old days, when stock rustled all winter and came through strong and in good meat. The roads were open and the towns doing a booming business. Then, after a week of spring weather in January, snow began to fall quietly at daylight. By three in the afternoon the wind was blowing forty miles an hour, sifting fine snow into the tightest soddy, settling a white film over the floors and beds, hissing on the hot stove lids and sucking the fire from the rusty pipes.

By ten o'clock the thermometer was down to thirty-three below zero. Cattle, even horses, their eyes snow-caked, drifted before the wind to pile up and freeze in gullies and in fence corners. No one familiar with the West ventured out without a rope tied about his waist and securely anchored to the door. The settlers hunched over their stoves, their faces dark. There were few words.

Jules, always put in a good humor by vagaries of earth and sky, stuck his head out of the door and jerked it back. "Forty below by morning," he predicted. "I guess I hole up like a bear."

Henriette, a woolen shawl about her shoulders, her feet on a box, off the cold floor, made no answer. The house ivy she had kept with her ever since she left Switzerland was black, frozen behind the stove.

She tried to read, to sew, but always she was back at the hole scratched in the frost of the window. Suddenly she ran out and tore armloads of sticks from the buried wood-pile, dumped them on the kitchen floor, and chopped and sawed until she had a big pile of stove lengths in the corner. Then she shoveled the snow from the chicken-coop door, found all but three of her hens dead. These she brought in to warm and feed behind the stove. She separated the cow from her calf so there would be cream for the coffee in the morning. Finally she went to look at Jules's coyote traps in a side-hill cow trail. Last week there was a big eagle there, fighting the Old Country bear trap. To-day there was an eight-foot drift over the path.

And always she shaded her eyes toward the bluff where the men had disappeared that morning. At last, tired and cold, she forced herself to sit quietly at the open oven door and wait.

Towards evening Jules limped slowly into the yard, his bad foot sore from three miles of crusted snow. Henriette set out his supper and met him at the door. "The woman?" she cried.

"Heah? Oho, she's all right. But my foot hurt. Pull the stuff off." Henriette dug at the crusting of snow and ice and cut the wire holding the gunny-sack wrapping Dickerson put about the tender foot.

"The woman was bad. I have to pack her in snow. Couldn't leave until she stop bleeding."

"What was then wrong?"

"Baby backward," Jules said, scraping out his cob pipe.

"Oh, but that is serious, is it not?—Even for a doctor? What'd you do?"

He tested the draw on his pipe. "Turn him."

"The poor woman!"

"Heah? Oh, hell, that's nature. Woman have to have children to keep healthy."

Henriette hurried out of doors to shake the snow from the gunny-sack wrappings and did not return to the house until her hands were whitening with cold. Jules looked up when she came in. "Where you been?" he demanded. "I want the table cleaned so I can work on my stamps." Silently Henriette went about her task.

Many of the settlers lost their cattle, even milk cows, and some their horses and pigs. Two men and a woman were sent to the insane asylum on the first passenger East. Down at the edge of the hills a mother of three hung herself. North of Hay Springs a man killed his brother with an axe, sneaking up behind him and splitting his skull almost to the neck. There was much lawing. Contest sharks, swooping like buzzards about those with a few dollars left, had to be reminded of Akins and his checkered suit.

■ ■ ■

On Pine Ridge in 1890 the Messiah craze was spreading among the agency-starved Sioux. A holy man had risen far to the west, one who promised the old buffalo days again, with the white man swept from the earth as the chinook clears the snow from the red grass. John Maher, of Chadron, kept the New York papers full of stories of depredations and atrocities. Jules complained. "Eastern people don't know better. They may believe them." But the stories made good reading.

And down in the Niobrara a feud was started, a feud that was to keep Jules's community in turmoil for years, break officials, undermine banks, almost bankrupt the county, drive three people to the asylum, and arouse hatreds that would live long after the leaders were dead.

From Baltimore Dr. Walter Reed wrote that he was studying his beloved bacteriology at last. Jules read the letter while the fire licked the lead kettle. He did not recall the doctor's prediction: "This country will develop, but not until the soil is soaked in misery and in blood."

■ ■ ■

By the fifteenth of November, 1890, the town of Rushville, the nearest railroad station to Pine Ridge, was swarming with war correspondents; even Theodore Roosevelt, writing for *Harper's*, was there. Buffalo soldiers, as the Indians called the curly-haired colored troops, swaggered through the little town. Impatient to shed blood and emboldened by the potent frontier whiskey, they declared a little war among themselves, whacking a few dark heads with revolvers and smashing a few mouths. After a week of this the citizens began to wonder if they didn't prefer the Indians, even ghost-dancing Indians. The Rushville *Standard* noted sadly that some of the high privates seemed less civilized than the Sioux. "If they are able to punish the red-skins as they are red liquor there will not be an Indian left in two weeks." But the midwinter march of sixty miles to the wind-swept Pine Ridge cooled the buffalo soldiers.

December first the citizens of Rushville and vicinity called a meeting to which Jules was particularly invited. What had the Sioux done to justify troops on their reservation? But the business men saw that an Indian war meant freighting, a good market for local produce. A Rushville miller contracted 68,000 pounds of flour for the troops. "Big government are always bulldozing somebody," Jules complained. A petition of protest was signed and sent to Washington. The Indians had withdrawn to the Bad Lands.

By the middle of December the excitement among the settlers had quieted down. Not an Indian had been seen, not a warwhoop heard, and the thermometer hovered about twenty below zero.

Then came the news of the shocking annihilation of Big Foot's band at Wounded Knee: men, women, and children mowed down by Hotchkiss guns while they and their sick chief were surrendering their pitifully inadequate arms and asking for the peace they had not broken.

Jules heard the news the same day at Rushville and rode up in the face of a coming storm. From a hill to the north he looked down over the desolate battlefield, upon the dark piles of men, women, and children sprawled among their goods. Dry snow trailed little ridges of white over them, making them look like strange-limbed animals left for the night and the wolves. Here, in ten minutes, an entire community was as the buffalo that bleached on the plains.

Although Jules shivered in the torn old army coat, he did not move for a long time, did not even know he was cold. When Old Jim snorted impatiently the man suddenly knew that he was very sick, sick as he had been at Valentine, six years before. Slowly he turned his horse with the storm.

That evening at Pine Ridge he heard of a wagonload of whiskey that came up from Rushville the day before the battle, and of the drunken soldiers. The next morning he started home. At the Rushville post office he wrote to Rosalie, the first letter in a long time. In it he poured out all the misery and confusion of what he had just seen. A deep pessimism held him. There was something loose in the world that hated joy and happiness as it hated brightness and color, reducing everything to drab agony and gray.

Back on the river Jules let rumor wash over him as he hunched over his bad foot beside the stove. Pushed for his opinion, "A blot on the American flag," was all he would say.

■ ■ ■

Various reports of the encounter reached the river, and somehow all of them conveyed the impression that the judge had been bested. At least others had not got off so well. When Freese had Jake Morse arrested for attacking his fourteen-year-old girl the community had been aroused. Murder they might overlook, but not this. When half a dozen silent men armed with Winchesters tied their horses in Jules's yard he went out to meet them. They talked a long time, sitting on their heels, drawing figures in the dust with sticks, not lifting their eyes.

For once Jules counseled caution. He was pleased that they came to him, but they had better wait a week. Jake Morse was a steady man and a good farmer with a little money in the bank. There was the Kapic case a couple of years ago. Only quick work by the sheriff saved Kapic from a lynching, but before the case came to trial it turned out to be plain blackmail—an attempt to get money from a settler who had a few dollars. The men nodded to each other. It was so.

"When I see need for a mob I'll lead you," Jules told them.

The settlers scattered to their homes. Before long Freese offered to settle out of court. Everyone knew by now that Morse was innocent. On the advice of the men who would have hung him not long before, he gave Freese enough for shoes for the family, and the case was dropped.

■ ■ ■

Much usually of moment to Jules went unnoticed that summer and fall. The new ranches deep in the hills were infested with road agents and hide-outs. Shooting, knifing, and disappearances became common as sand lizards and wind. The Northwestern was held up, the mail sacks found slit and rifled in a blowout. The divorces of the community were offset by shotgun weddings. A neighbor on the south table hanged himself in his well curbing and dangled unnoticed for two days in plain sight of the road, so nearly did his head resemble a windlass swinging.

Up on Box Butte a woman was fined five dollars and cost for horsewhipping her neighbor over a prairie fire he set. "There is the woman to teach The Black's wife something!" William said, sucking his moustache in anticipation. But unfortunately Tissot's frightened little wife was no such Amazon.

[As time passed, Henriette became postmistress and divorced Jules, who married Mary, Mari Sandoz's mother.]

■ ■ ■

Mary's practical eye appraised the homes on the Flats, soddies, dugouts, unpainted frame houses, often with dead sunflowers choking the yards. To her Jules's weathering house with its two blank windows and a door towards the road was not so much of a shock. But Jacob was not there; no one was there.

"Have you then brought me out here alone?" she demanded.

"I'm no wild man. I won't hurt you," he laughed. "Besides, it will be only a few minutes until somebody comes."

One look inside the house firmed Mary's long chin. "Have you no water and no soap in this country?"

Without waiting for an answer she rolled up the velvet-trimmed cuffs of her brown traveling dress and scoured pots, pans, knives, and forks with wood ashes spilling from the hearth of the cookstove. She piled the catalogues and newspapers into an old box and prepared to sweep the litter from the door.

"Don't throw me anything valuable away!" Jules warned from his chair. "You had better then keep what you want from the floor," she answered as she sprinkled water to lay the dust. Jules escaped into the yard and brought his young antelope to the door. The animal nozzled Mary's palm and tried to follow her into the house.

"No, not inside," she shooed, but she stopped to watch the beautiful animal trot away.

After supper Jules interrupted the cleaning again. The entire west was a sheet of rose, with the Minten house and barn two dark blocks against the sky. A path of red gold rippled on the river. It recalled a childhood rhyme to Mary. Something about "Fire, O! The Rhine is burning!" with a final quenching by a hundred thousand croaking frogs.

"That is a fine sight," Jules pointed out, hoping to please.

But the pain for Switzerland and all it once meant to her closed the woman's throat.

Three horsebackers clattered over the plank bridge, but Jules met them in the yard with their mail. When he came back into the neat, orderly kitchen the two talked of Mary's predicament. There was no telling what delayed her brother. "A woman maybe?" Jules asked. Mary did not know. She had given him the money to come to America six or seven years before and he had not yet repaid her. He was frankly without the initiative she thought any self-respecting person should show.

But she, a town woman, couldn't make a living here on a claim alone, and with scarcely enough money to pay for a shack and a team. And work for pay there was probably none. Of course she could have her position in St. Louis again. "Both Dr. and Frau Geiger told me I was a fool," she moaned, into a sensible handkerchief.

"Marry me and you always have a good home," Jules suggested a bit timidly.

Mary looked at him, her blue eyes perplexed, uncertain whether this was a Frenchman's idea of romance or a joke.

"But I know nothing of you. You may then be a divorced man or a drunkard."

"Do I look like a whiskey soak?"

No, there was nothing of the drunkard about those sharp eyes, the smooth, fine-textured skin.

Sifting the chaff from Jules's accounts of himself and his country as well as she could, Mary decided that if she married him she would have a house to live in, a garden, trees, brush with wild fruit, a team for the heavy work, a big roan milk cow with a deep udder coming fresh, and the river.

Soon it was known that Jules's new wife was neat and quick as a blue-wing teal and gay when she could be. The neighbor women invited her to their homes, asked her to join their *Kaffeeklatsche*. But Jules rose in anger when she would go, and so she faced him with tear-swollen eyes across the table for a meal or two.

Mary had three anæmic, undernourished children very close together, without a doctor. She lost her teeth; her clear skin became leathery from field work; her eyes paled and sun-squinted; her hands knotted, the veins of her arms like slack clothesline. There was little of the city woman about her now, little for the Peters women to envy. She still combed her hair the first thing in the morning, wetting it back, and it still blew out in unruly curls. She still used clean linen tablecloths for Sunday and company, and had a fringed spread on her bed every day.

In order that their names might not die from the Running Water, Jules named the first two children for their parents. The third and ever the favored he called James, Jim. To Mary's curious inquiry he gave some reply, forgotten immediately. Then, with his gun across his knees, he sat long on Indian Hill, Freese Hill, as he called it now, and watched a flock of powdery-blue mountain jays circle about the patch of sweet corn below. He wondered about the man who had found him afoot in the Big Horn country. And if he would be pleased that this fine new son would also be Jim.

Mary had little milk even for her beloved first-born son, and so the little Jule was taken from his father's bed and became his grandmother's charge and favorite. But there was no such escape for the mother from her first girl child. When the little Marie was three months old and ill with summer complaint, her cries awakened Jules. Towering dark and bearded in the lamplight, he whipped the child until she lay blue and trembling as a terrorized small animal. When Mary dared she snatched the baby from him and carried her into the night and did not return until the bright day.

But the night's work was never to be undone. Always the little Marie hid away within herself. She never cried out in the terror of her dreams or walked the house in her sleep as did the little Jule, but from the time she could walk she hid away, retreating into fancy. With Jule it was little better. Even behind the protecting skirts of Mary and the grandmother he could not escape the father's hand entirely.

The little James was more fortunate from birth. He was spared the sex animosity that is the inevitable heritage of the first-born son and daughter. There was more rain, more mother's milk, and his pretty girl face won him praise that the other two saw and envied darkly.

■ ■ ■

Mary avoided crossing him or bothering him for help in anything she could possibly do alone. But there were times when she must have his help, as when the roof leaked or the calves were to be castrated. It took weeks of diplomatic approach to get him to look after the two bull calves before they were too big for her to handle at all. And when she couldn't hold the larger one from kicking, Jules, gray-white above his beard, threw his knife into the manure and loped to the back door. "I learn the goddamn balky woman to obey me when I say 'hold him.'" He tore a handful of four-foot wire stays from the bundle in the corner of the shop and was gone towards the corral, the frightened grandmother and the children huddled at the back window.

They heard the banging of the gate, Jules's bellow of curses. Then Mary ran through the door, past the children and straight to the poison drawer. It stuck, came free, the bottles flying over the floor. Her face furrowed in despair, blood dripping from her face and her hand where she had been struck with the wire whip, the woman snatched up a bottle, struggled with the cork, pulling at it with her teeth. The grandmother was upon her, begging, pleading, clutching at the red bottle with the crossbones.

Jules burst in. "*Wo*'s the goddamned woman? I learn her to obey me if I got to kill her!"

"You!" the grandmother cried, shaking her fist against him. "For you there is a place in hell!"

With the same movement of her arm she swung out, knocking the open bottle from the woman's mouth. It rolled over the floor, strewing the white crystals of strychnine in a wide fan. Then she led Mary out of the house and to the brush along the river.

Jules limped away, saddled up Old Daisy himself, and with his rifle in the scabbard headed for Pine Creek.

And hidden far under the bed the three children cowered like frightened little rabbits, afraid to cry.

■ ■ ■

Jules's orchard was becoming quite an important feature in the settlement of the country, denying the cattleman contention that nothing would grow. By crossing selected wild plums with choice tame varieties, but not quite hardy, he developed a new plum that stood the winter, was free of insect pests, of delicate flavor, and tender-skinned. In addition he experimented with cherries and apples, and grew all kinds of small fruit between the trees to hold the sand and the snow. Every spring he gave away wagonloads of shrubbery, sucker plums, asparagus, horseradish, and pie-plant roots to anyone who would promise to care for them. And in these activities he caught once more something of the early vision he had upon the top of the hill as he looked across Mirage Flats in 1884.

In recognition of his services, Jules's place was designated an experiment station and he was made director of the eighth district, from Cherry County to the Wyoming line. A bushel of Russian macaroni wheat was on the way for trial. Fruits, flowers, and grains for tryouts were available in reasonable quantities, from Washington.

"Well, Mary, you married an important man," he boasted.

"Yes, but I still have to wear men's shoes and carry home the wood."

■ ■ ■

Jules taught [the children] useful things: to pick the thick green worms from his trees and to trap the wily gopher. When a particularly clever one wouldn't be caught, Jules ordered the boys to bring the spade and help dig along the gopher's tunnel, leaving only a very thin crust over it, and a point of light at the end.

"Now fetch me my twelve-bore," he ordered. With the gun aimed upon the tunnel, Jules waited, and the boys behind him. Ten minutes, twelve, of absolute silence. Then suddenly the top of the tunnel boiled with fresh earth. The twelve-gauge roared and the boys ran through the black powder smoke to the hole splattered across the gopher's runway. Jule dug with his fingers, brought up a shattered mass that was gopher.

"Ach, your papa is so nervous he can't wait a minute on anybody, but he can sit still for hours hunting," Mary complained.

Often Jules took the two eldest, seven and eight, small, twin-like, to trail noiselessly behind him when he went on a hunt. Carefully they stepped through the rose-brush thickets, stooping to pull sand burrs and cactus from their feet. At his motion of command they ran ahead to scare up quail, dropping at the first whir of wings and watching where the birds fell. When the gun was silent they ran to retrieve the game, catching all the cripples, crushing the backs of the brittle skulls between their teeth as they had seen Jules do.

"Why, I never saw anything like it! Those children are better than any dog!" an Eastern hunter exclaimed.

"I learn my kids to obey instantly or I lick hell out of them," Jules chuckled.

FURTHER READINGS

Jami Parkison, *Scribe of the Great Plains: Mari Sandoz* (Acorn Books, 1999); Helen Winter Stauffer, ed., *Letters of Mari Sandoz* (University of Nebraska Press, 1992); Melody Graulich, "Violence Against Women: Power Dynamics in Literature of the Western Family," in *The Women's West*, eds. Susan Armitage and Elizabeth Jameson (University of Oklahoma Press, 1987); Helen W. Stauffer, *Mari Sandoz* (Boise State University Press, 1984); Helen Winter Stauffer, *Mari Sandoz: Story Catcher of the Plains* (University of Nebraska Press, 1982).

Hope Williams Sykes
(1901–1973)

Born in 1901 in a sod house near Kanorado, Kansas, Iris Hope Williams grew up close to what she called "the farmer's battle with the elements." The family moved west to Colorado when she was a teenager. She attended Colorado Agricultural College (now Colorado State University) and taught school close to the fields German-Russian families called "the jungles," where men, women and children labored in the fields relentlessly planting, thinning, hoeing, and harvesting sugar beets.

Marriage in 1925 brought her to Fort Collins where the sugar factory processed beets from the outlying fields, and she began to keep notebooks of the families around her. "For seven years I just absorbed the feeling and undercurrent of the beet industry and these people." Notebooks suggest the writer's dispassionate objectivity, but her fiction shows her outrage at the culture that saw women and children as living only to work.

In *Second Hoeing,* Hannah Schreissmiller is the fourth oldest daughter in a household of twelve children doomed to stoop-labor from the age of six until they marry and begin toiling in their own families. *Second Hoeing,* along with Agnes Smedley's *Daughter of Earth,* Rebecca Harding Davis's *Life in the Iron Mills* (1861), about workers in West Virginia, and Edith Summers Kelley's powerful novel *Weeds* (1923), about workers in the tobacco fields of Kentucky, form a body of feminist proletarian fiction now almost forgotten.

When *Second Hoeing* was published in 1935, families who felt themselves embarrassed by accounts of their lives in the book kept it out of circulation in local libraries. But in Washington, DC, where people were setting up the National Child Labor Board, the book was applauded. Rose Feld, in the *New York Times,* called *Second Hoeing* a "powerful proletarian drama of the American soil." And Sykes herself received a letter of congratulations from First Lady Eleanor Roosevelt.

Hope Williams Sykes received a fellowship to the Bread Loaf Writer's Conference in Vermont, and in 1937 G. P. Putnam's Sons published her second novel, *The Joppa Door*. It is the first novel, however, with its defiant heroine Hannah Schreissmiller, that has captured the imagination of the reading public. Sykes died in 1973.

PLANTING AND THINNING

Planting

The farmers had signed contracts to grow so many acres of beets at a certain price to be paid in the fall of the year. Nothing but work, work, work.

She'd never forgive her father. Never. He coulda just as well let her gone to school to finish her eighth grade.

Every jiggle of the harrow over the freshly plowed beet ground added to her hate and resentment. In her mind she went back over the sixteen years of her life, as far as she could remember, as she fought the wind and dirt.

She'd been just four years old when she was left at the end of a beet field to look after two-year-old Tabia, and two-months-old Alec. There, in the shade of a gunny sack stretched over four upright sticks, she had tried to hush the squalling Tabia, and the wailing Alec, while her mother went up and down the rows of beets chopping with the long-handled hoe. Hannah had cried for her mother who could not stop work. The beets had to be thinned.

"Yeah, an' now he cries about how hard he's worked, and how big a succeed he's made. We all worked an' Mamma worked harder than all of us put together, and he'll work her in the beets this year too!" Hannah savagely yanked the horses around at the end of the field. She slapped the lines, smartly across their backs, shouting, "Gid-ap."

She thought of the time when she was six, big enough to crawl behind her father and mother and Lizzie and Mary, who swung their hoes up and down, blocking the tiny sugar beet plants.

On the ground among the dirt and clods, she had crawled on hands and knees, grasping the plants with dirty fingers, pulling the extra ones out so the biggest and strongest would be left to grow.

Hope Williams Sykes, from *Second Hoeing* (1935).

Her fingers had become stiff and dirt-caked. Sweat had run down her body. There was no rest. Adam eternally yelled that the beets had to be thinned. He got them up before daylight and kept them in the field until it was too dark to see.

It was when she was ten that she'd cut her knee with the bright-bladed beet knife while haggling the top off of a big beet in harvest. She'd been too little to lift the heavy beet; so she'd held it on her knee. Swish, the knife had cut through the beet into her knee. That same fall Fritz had broken his arm when he was thrown by a runaway team. Adam had cursed day and night because Fritz couldn't top beets. It took two good arms and hands to top a sugar beet.

Adam had driven all the rest of them, screeching that the beets would be frozen in the ground.

"Yeah, and he still drives us. He thinks we're cattle that he owns!" Hannah spit the words into the wind. "And he'd buy us gum and break the stick in two pieces so we'd work harder. No wonder he saved money so he could rent!"

Hannah looked bitterly into the south. "Nothin' but a dump," she thought, as she compared their place with the Boswell house across the road. "The Boswells' got it easy." Then she saw Jim's coupé turn on two wheels into the circular driveway.

Hannah went sprawling across the harrow. She got up quickly, yanking at the horses to turn them around. They'd stopped suddenly at the end of the field.

"All I'm good for is to grub in the field," she half cried as she rubbed her barked shins. "I bet the hide's took off," she said aloud. "I'm not gonna stay here. I'll leave. Papa can't keep me till I'm twenty-one!" But even as Hannah spoke she thought how he'd kept Lizzie and Mary, and how he was still keeping Fritz.

It was getting dark. She hurried her horses from the field before Adam could speak to her.

As she came into the barnyard she met Alec and Solly bringing in the two cows. At the same time Ana, white kerchief tied over her head, came out of the house carrying two milk pails.

Hannah called to her. "You go back, Mamma, I'll milk."

"Ach, Hannah, all mine life I am milk the cow."

"All her life," Hannah muttered as she threw hay to the horses. "Papa'll work her till she drops in the field."

At the table, that night, Hannah helped Reinie with his food.

"Drink your milk, Reinie," she coaxed.

"Me want some milk," shouted four-year-old Chris.

"Me, too," chimed in six-year-old Coonie.

"Ach, eat the supper. The pigs, he don't got milk enough so he grow good," commanded Adam.

"He even puts the pigs before us!" Hannah thought. She watched her father as he shoveled his food into his mouth. As he chewed, the ends of his straggly mustache moved up and down across his leathery cheek. His sharp beak of a nose wiggled. Industriously, he piled potatoes onto his knife blade using his fork as a pusher. Raising it to his mouth, he stopped the loaded knife in mid-air, and roared:

"Solly! Drop that cat! We don't eat mit cats on the tables!"

"Hannah, tomorrow you drill mit beet seeds, und Olinda, you ride the harrow. Hannah, she got you skinned one mile for work. Gott, I wish it rain, oncet."

Hannah couldn't sleep after she went to bed. She felt gritty and dirty all over from the dust of the field. Her mouth was parched and dry. Dirt-caked. She slid out of bed and crept down the narrow stairs.

Feeling her way to the water bucket, she stopped. Adam was praying in the bedroom off the kitchen.

"Gott, make it rain so mine last beets come themselves up. Gott, you make it rain und next fall I pay twice over mine church dues. Yah, I make him up mit you. Too many acre I think I am farm, und I worry so I don't can think, und I need the rain so I raise good beets. Make him rain und I praise you all mine days, Gott. Sure, I done it."

Grimly Hannah dipped her cup into the water bucket. "Hypocrite," she muttered. "His word don't mean nothin'. He won't keep his word even with God. All he wants is something for himself, and he's scared to death he's gonna make a failure, so he can't crow to everybody how swell he is."

The next morning she started drilling. The factory field man had come in March with the contracts and Adam had signed to grow forty acres of beets. Twenty acres had been planted first week of April, then ten days later, the south field had been planted. Rain had come and the first beets were up in long slender rows of green.

It was dry now and there was not enough moisture to bring up beet seed. Adam held up the lid of the drill box for Hannah to empty the gunny sack of beet seeds, and said: "We got make space between time of plantings so we got time to done the thinnings before the plants get too big in the other fields, but Gott, he don't rain, und the beets come themselves up all to oncet."

The big bulky sack sagged against her knees. Adam roughly put a hand under it, watching the brown, curly seed tumble into the narrow red drill box. Hannah grabbed for a firmer hold and lost her grip. The sack slipped sideways and the light, sponge-like tiny seeds scattered on the dry ground.

"Spill seed, will you?" Adam sent her tumbling to the dirt.

Hannah got up, hating him. She stooped and tried to gather up the seeds with her trembling hands.

Adam's foot struck her on the hip. She fell flat in the dirt.

She gathered herself up and faced him.

"You hit me again, and I go to the house. I don't work. You ain't in Russia." Hannah shrank away from him, defiant, but also fearful.

"Ach, mein Gott im Himmel! Make shut the mouth." He advanced upon her shaking his fists. "Get the drill on, und get busy! Expenses I got on mine back mitout spilling seeds. Fifteen cents a pound I pay for him!"

Sullenly, Hannah climbed on the drill and clucked to the horses. "I'm goin' to leave. I'm goin' to get out," she declared to herself. "He's made me dig manure out of the sheep pens and ride on the old manure spreader. I've plowed and harrowed. I've rolled his old fields with the roller. And now I'm drilling. He makes us all work, Fritz, and Olinda and me, and he keeps the other boys home whenever he thinks he can get by without the truant officer getting him. He keeps us all till we're twenty-one, but he won't keep me."

Adam's voice roared up the field. *"Hannah! Make them horse go faster! You hear?"*

Hannah paid no attention. "Let him yell," she muttered.

Thinning

Hannah slipped stealthily behind a car parked in front of the German church. With this protection between herself and the church she dodged in and out along the cars parked at the curb.

She glanced backward to see if any one might be watching, but she saw no one. She had waited in the dim entryway until the church services had commenced.

Now, as she walked rapidly toward the street corner south of the church, she wished that she didn't have on such a conspicuous white dress, but she had nothing nicer than her confirmation dress. And tonight she had wanted to look her very best. Her first date with Jim Boswell.

Half-fearfully, she wondered if he would be waiting. It had taken her so much longer to get away from the church.

She breathed a sigh of thankfulness as she saw Jim's black coupé waiting at the corner. She slipped gratefully into the seat beside him. Her heart was pounding.

"I see you got away."

"Yes, I come with Katie Heist and Fritz. Papa stayed home from church." Still breathing deeply from her haste, Hannah was glad that Jim said no more. The quiet silence gave her a chance to get hold of herself.

"We mustn't go very far. I've got to be back by the time church lets out," she said quickly when she noticed he was driving steadily toward the mountains.

Jim nodded and immediately turned into a tree-bordered side lane. He stopped the car. Without saying any word whatever he put his arm around Hannah.

She stiffened. Jim tried to draw her closer.

"Don't be afraid. Just tuck that bright head of yours over here on my shoulder." There was soft laughter in his voice. Hannah felt ashamed of her rigid primness. Half fearfully, she let him draw near.

"Glad you came?"

She nodded her head against his shoulder, content. This was heaven, she thought. The intimate silence, the quiet dusk of evening, Jim with his arm around her. She couldn't really believe it was Jim.

Gently, he moved his arm, and turning her sideways started to pull her over against him. Hannah stiffened, resisting him.

"I'm not going to hurt you," Jim reassured her. "I'm just making you more comfortable. You know, Hannah, I don't believe you've had much real loving in this world."

Hannah laughed shakily, and partly relaxed, letting Jim have his way. She was crazy to be afraid of Jim, she knew, but she felt bewildered as he lifted her and held her against him so that she lay in his arms. Unconsciously, she was braced ready for flight but Jim held her quietly, unmoving, silent.

Hannah could feel her heart pounding. The odor of tobacco came to her from the soft wool of Jim's dark suit, filling her with his nearness. Gradually, she became calm.

"Comfortable?" Jim bent his face to hers. She could feel his breath upon her cheek, warm, faintly tobacco.

"Like me a little?" he questioned. His voice was low, husky. Timidly, Hannah touched his cheek with her fingers. It was smooth, clean shaven. Jim laid his face against hers as he whispered, "So you do like me a little."

"No, I don't like you a little," Hannah's whisper held a tremulous, half-laughing note.

"You little devil!" Jim set his lips full against hers with a slow pressure that increased. He held her even more tightly. She hadn't known he was so strong. She felt that she couldn't stand another minute of that embrace, yet she couldn't pull herself away. At last Jim released her and she slumped against his shoulder, tired.

"Like me a little, now?" Jim's hand touched her cheek, lifted her chin.

"Not a little, a whole lot," Hannah whispered.

"You know you're such a little thing." Jim cradled her close in his arms. "When I see you in the field in overalls and blue shirt you look like a husky boy, but now you're all cuddly, soft, and warm. I think you must be two persons, Hannah." He smoothed her cheek with his hand. Hannah caught his fingers and held them tightly.

She felt that she never wanted to move. If she could always rest in Jim's arms, she'd ask no greater happiness. She loved him. She adored him. He was hers; hers alone. There was no world, no time, nothing but Jim, and his soft lips. Hannah pressed his fingers tighter. She suddenly wanted him closer, his lips, his arms. An inward trembling shook her as his lips touched hers.

She could feel the fast beating of his heart. Hear the quickness of his short breaths. Her hand dropped limply from his strong fingers. She must tell him to stop kissing her but she couldn't. His lips were against hers. She'd push his face away but her hand wouldn't move. Her hand didn't want to move. What was the use? He was her Jim. She loved him. His arms held her tightly and she was tired, blessedly tired.

"Hannah." She heard his voice, tender, low. She felt his cheek hot against hers, his lips press hers again, briefly, gently, his muscles tighten. Her body lay as if lifeless, while thoughts flowed swiftly through her suspended mind.

"Whither thou goest, I will go. Thy people shall be my people. No—that can't be. His people are American, mine are German-Russian. No matter."

Her mother's words illogically came to her. "Go often to the Communion and take of the Lord's Supper so you don't backslide. Remember, Hannah, the church comes first." Yes, the church. The church.

Hannah flung herself from Jim's arms. "Jim, Jim, what time is it? I've got to be back at the church by the time it's out."

In the flare from his cigarette lighter, Jim looked at his thin gold watch. "Time we were going," he agreed, reaching forward to turn the switch of the car.

Back on the main highway, he put his arm around Hannah. "You're trembling?" His voice was concerned.

"I feel funny and I can't stop shaking," Hannah stammered.

"Put your head on my shoulder. You'll be all right in a minute." Jim's voice was reassuring. His arm tightened around her shoulders.

When they reached the church, they found the cars still parked along the curbs. From inside the building came the final deep tones of the closing hymn. Jim stopped near Adam's car which Fritz had driven.

Hannah started to move from Jim's encircling arms but he held her a moment and kissed her tenderly.

"All right, honey?"

"Yes, I'm all right." Hannah touched his cheek gently before slipping from the car.

She curled up in the back seat of Adam's car and waited for Fritz and Katie to come from the church.

"Gee, we lost you, I guess," Katie laughed.

"I had a headache and I come out early," Hannah told her.

"Oh, gee, that's too bad." Katie turned to Fritz. "I bet part of her headache is because Jake's not here." She laughed loudly. Hannah didn't answer. She wanted to be alone with her thoughts. As the car bounced over the five miles to the Schreissmiller home, she enfolded the image of Jim close in her arms. But beneath all the breathless wonder of Jim's love, there was fear. Fear of her father finding out. And still another fear she could not have defined, even if she had had the courage to do so.

"Hey, Hannah, get out. We're home. I'm going to take Katie over to her home so she can get some of her things to bring back to Boswells'." Fritz's voice was loud and rather excited.

Hannah thought of Fritz and Katie as she let herself silently into the kitchen. Her own experience with Jim caused her to smile with warmth and good will. It seemed right to her that Fritz would not come home right away.

She made her way on tiptoes to the mirror above the wash-stand. She scrutinized her face. Did she look different than ever before? She felt different. It seemed to her that every one could see the new Hannah shining forth from her sparkling eyes, her happy lips. Would her father notice a difference? She glanced quickly toward the closed door that led from the kitchen to his bedroom. He was sound asleep. She had nothing to worry about.

But maybe some one had seen her running down the street from the church. Maybe some one had seen her getting into Jim's car. Maybe some one had seen her getting out of Jim's car and slip-ping into Adam's to wait for Fritz and Katie. Hannah shivered and looked down at her fragile white dress. Its whiteness would show so plainly in the early evening light. Though she was now safely at home, an acute uneasiness filled her.

The sound of a car coming up the lane startled her. Who would it be at this time of night? It must be Fritz coming back for some-thing. Anxious to do something that would be an excuse for still being in the kitchen, she took a cinnamon roll from the bread box. She took one bite and stood waiting.

"Well, what'd you forget?" she asked as the door opened. But it wasn't Fritz. It was her father who stood framed there.

In the first brief second Hannah took in her father's threaten-ing face, gimlet eyes, thin drawn lips. Little chills ran down her back. Her breath came in short gasps. She shivered, trying to move her gaze from her father's accusing face. But she couldn't. She could only stand and stare into his hard cruel eyes. The cinnamon bun dropped from her trembling fingers as Adam came slowly toward her. As he advanced she began to back away.

"So-o. You sneak mit that Jim Boswell."

The words struck Hannah as if they were blows. This wasn't her father's high pitched shrieking voice. This was a deeper, colder, cruel voice full of hard, condemning hate.

"You go mit that girl-chaser, Jim. Und you lay mit him like that hussy, Olinda, lay mit Henry." Adam's still, accusing face came closer to the girl backed against the wall. Hannah felt as if her throat were paralyzed. She couldn't speak. She couldn't move. She could only look into her father's hating, furious eyes.

"You think that Jim marry you like Henry marry Olinda? You think he marry you? No. He lay mit you but he don't marry mit you. Yah, he lay mit you. You, in your white confirmation dress."

She wanted to run, but she couldn't move. She wanted to scream for help, but her lips wouldn't move. It was as if she were dumb, paralyzed with fear.

"Now, you tell it to me. You tell me how you lay mit Jim Boswell."

She opened her lips but only the sound of her breathing came forth. She couldn't answer, for in her father's eyes she saw death lurking.

"Und I say you tell it." With slow deliberate movement Adam reached for the blacksnake whip which stood in the corner nearest Hannah. Thick at the butt, tapering to a fine flexible thinness at its tip, the whip lay balanced in Adam's horny, work-cracked hands. This was the whip that was used to drive the cows, to lash fractious horses, and sometimes to discipline the older boys.

"You tell it, true." Adam raised the whip. A sharp whistling sound hissed through the room as it snapped on the floor near Hannah's white clad ankles.

"Answer it oncet, or I beat you so you don't can talk. Say how you lay mit him. Say how you sin. Before God you sin. Yah, don't I go by church mit old Heist und I see you running away? Und don't I see you come back mit that landowner's son what don't marry mit you. Yah, he lay mit you but he don't marry mit you. Tell it true."

The whip curled through the air once more. With sure, deadly aim, it circled Hannah's shoulders and flicked across her face.

Hannah screamed.

The baby in its basket in the front room started crying. The door to Adam's room off the kitchen, opened, and showed Reinie's and Chris's heads peeking out. As if by magic Tabia, Alec, Solly and Coonie appeared in the doorway leading to the front room.

"Tell it true!" Adam roared at Hannah. But that first lash had released Hannah's fear-bound muscles. She dodged past her father and into the front room. As she brushed past Tabia she spoke, "Call the minister." She tried to reach the front door and the safety of outdoors, but Coonie got in her way. She tripped, and Adam barred her way to escape. The whip struck across her shoulders.

She turned, thinking to wrest the whip from her father's hand but its lash sent her reeling. She was forced to turn her back to protect her face. He was crazy. She knew it by the inhuman gleam in his eyes, by the deep, rasping tones of his voice. She tried to dodge away from him but the whip always met her. At last she broke and sank to the floor beside the old green couch. She covered her face with her arms and crouched.

"You tell it now?" Adam's voice was rising. "Disgrace mit mine head. Better you been in the grave over laying mit one American what don't marry you mit your shame. You tell it now? You tell where that Jim take you. You tell how you lay mit him. Gott, mit shame it bring on mine head! Mit shame it bring on mine head!" Once more the lash fell across Hannah's shoulders.

Hannah could make herself no smaller. He could kill her. He probably would. Nothing she could say would stop him. Pain was beginning to numb her mind.

"Tell it true! Tell. . . ."

"Mr. Schreissmiller! What are you doing!" The minister's deep stern voice broke in upon Adam's fury.

Hannah lifted her head. She saw her father lower his arm.

"Mr. Schreissmiller, no man will mistreat his grown daughter."

"Gott, she lay mit Jim Boswell, und no minister even let mine daughter disgrace me. *Me! Adam Schreissmiller!* In Russia she would been whipped to death. 'Till she die, she would been whip!"

"This is not Russia, Mr. Schreissmiller. In America, people are put in jail and kept there for whipping a person as you are whipping your daughter. No matter what your daughter has done, you must not whip her as you are doing!"

"Hell! Hell! I don't let no minister . . ."

The minister raised his hand. "Stop, Mr. Schreissmiller. If you continue as you are doing, I'll see that you are put where you can never do this again. You hear me?"

Adam's whip dropped from his hands. With a quick motion he turned and went toward the door. "Hell. Hell," he muttered. "I go mit Boswell und I tell him—" The door slammed behind him.

Hannah put her hands to her welted face. Tears began to run down her cheeks. She heard the minister speak gently to the smaller children. Then she felt his firm hand upon her shoulder and heard his deep, kind voice speaking to her.

"Hannah, child, are you all right? Can you stand?"

"I hate him! I hate him!" Hannah brushed the tears from her eyes. "I'll hate him as long as I live."

"Hannah, you must not. In his way he thinks of your happiness."

"Happiness? Him? He don't! He don't think of nothing but himself. I don't have any happiness. I don't have nothing."

"Yes, Hannah, you have God, and if you take your troubles to Him, he will give you peace."

"I don't want peace. I'm young. I want happiness. I want to live, and when I'm happy, he beats me. *He beats me!*"

"Hannah, you must not. No matter what you have done, you still have a friend who believes in you. Will you believe me, Hannah, when I tell you that?"

"You mean you believe I'm all right no matter what I've done?"

"Yes, Hannah. I've known you since you were a little girl. I knew your mother. I know how she taught you. I have faith in you."

Hannah's eyes softened. "You don't know what knowing that means to me. I didn't do anything wrong. We just went riding."

"Why didn't you tell your father?"

"He wouldn't've believed me."

"If he ever lifts his hand against you again, call me, Hannah."

"He won't touch me again."

Hannah got slowly to her feet and followed the minister to the door. She returned to the front room and stood there looking at the overturned chairs, at the baby in her basket. She heard the kitchen door open. She saw her father standing there.

"Go mit bed," he muttered. He did not look at her, and turned away to his own bedroom.

Hannah looked down at her white confirmation dress. The delicate silk was cut and torn. She could never wear it again.

She started slowly for the stairs—quietly, deliberately, she felt her way up the steep darkness to her own bedroom. She lighted the kerosene lamp and, with Tabia lying in bed looking on, she gathered her few gingham dresses from the hooks. She folded her two Sunday dresses—faded and old—and laid them with her few possessions.

She paid no attention to Tabia when she spoke to her. She did not consciously hear the words, "I don't blame you for leavin' the old fool. But where you goin', Hannah? And what's to become of us? You gotta stay, Hannah."

Hannah gathered her belongings and went downstairs, leaving Tabia crying in her bed.

In the front room she took off her torn confirmation dress. For a moment she held its soft folds to her face. The strong fragrance of tobacco came to her from it. Jim. She'd lain in Jim's arms. There'd been beauty and love, and sweetness, and now her father had made it foul. Never again would he have the chance to do it. She put on another dress, slipped her feet into her broad everyday shoes. The five miles to Valley City would be a long walk.

With her bundle in her arms Hannah turned the knob of the front door. At the same moment Martha, in her basket placed on two chairs, let out a thin wail. The sound of that cry halted Hannah. She hesitated. Once more she turned the doorknob. But she could not go and leave the baby crying. It was time for her feeding.

Hannah laid her bundle upon a chair. Through the room, dimly lighted by the low-turned lamp, she went to the kitchen. When she had put the bottle of milk in its pan of water to warm, she went back and picked up the baby.

She'd feed Martha, *then* she would go. Poor little motherless thing. No one to care for her. The thought startled Hannah from her own deep abstraction.

There was no one to care for Martha. She looked at the helpless baby cuddled in her arms.

Sitting on a battered chair in the kitchen, she knew that she could not abandon this baby. This baby which had been her mother's, which she, Hannah, had cared for since its birth.

Leaving her bundle of clothes lying on the chair, she took the baby to the front room. Lying down on the old couch she cuddled the baby in her arms and tucked an old quilt about them both.

FURTHER READINGS

Hope Williams Sykes, *Second Hoeing* (G. P. Putnam's Sons, 1935); Hope Williams Sykes, *The Joppa Door* (G. P. Putnam's Sons, 1937); Timothy J. Kloberdanz, "Introduction" to Hope Williams Sykes, *Second Hoeing* (University of Nebraska Press, 1982); Ronald B. Taylor, *Sweatshops in the Sun: Child Labor on the Farm* (Beacon Press, 1973); Carey McWilliams, *Ill Fares the Land: Migrants and Migratory Labor in the United States* (Little, Brown and Company, 1942).

Linda Hasselstrom

Linda Hasselstrom has written numerous books of both poetry and non-fiction prose. She is also an editor, a teacher, and a publisher. She is a rancher, whose enthusiasm for the West is undiminished by chasing a disgruntled bull or by the need to feed cattle in thirty-degree- below-zero weather. But most of all, she is a poet, and poets are tricky birds to catch by description. Her poetry reflects her life in South Dakota and in Wyoming, and the knowledge that life on the High Plains is neither romantic nor easy. Often it is harsh and unforgiving of frailty, human or animal. Beauty is only a transient moment. If the poet is lucky, beauty can be caught in the resin of the right word, in the quixotic turn of the right phrase.

Linda Hasselstrom moved to South Dakota when she was nine. She graduated from the University of South Dakota at Vermillion, and went to graduate school at the University of Missouri. She married and moved back to ranch in South Dakota, where she and her first husband founded a literary magazine, *Sunday Clothes*, and the Lame Johnny Press (after a local and celebrated thief). After a divorce, she remarried, though that marriage ended when her husband died of the effects of Hodgkin's Disease.

In 1991 she published *Land Circle*, a collection of poetry and essays, and in 1992, her collected poems, *Dakota Bones*. The landscape she writes about is an expression of western life; it confronts the reader at every turn with some stark image or sudden surprise.

STAYING IN ONE PLACE

Riding fence last summer
I saw a meadowlark caught by one wing.
(My father saw one caught so, once;
in freeing it, taught me compassion.)
        He'd flown

Linda Hasselstrom, from *Dakota Bones* (1997).

futile circles around the wire, snapping bones.
Head folded on yellow breast,
he hung by one sinew, dead.

Gathering cattle in the fall
I rode that way again;
his yellow breast was bright as autumn air
or his own song.

I'm snowed in now, only a path
from the house to the cows in the corral.
Miles away he still hangs,
frost in his eyesockets
swinging in the wind.

I lie heavy in my bed alone, turning, turning,
seeing the house layered in drifts of snow
and dust and years and scraps of empty paper.
He should be light, light
bone and snowflake light.

BONE

—for Georgia O'Keeffe

I am a saguaro, ribs thrust gray
against blue hot sky.
            I am
a polished jawbone, teeth white
against the grass.
I have become all that I see:
an elegant bone gnawed clean,
leaving only bone the end,
bone the beginning,
bone the skyline mountain.

SPRING

Spring is here:
the first skunk lies dead
at the highway's rim,
white fur still bright,
nose stained with one drop of blood.

A calf born dead yesterday
was found by coyotes in the night:
only the head and one front foot remain.
The cat preens in a pile of meadowlark feathers.
A blue jay is eating baby robins.
The hens caught a mouse in their corn
this morning; pecked it to shrieking shreds.

It's spring;
time to kill the kittens.
Their mewing blends with the meadowlark song.
I tried drowning them once;
it was slow, painful.
Now I bash each with a wrench,
once, hard.

Each death makes a dull sound,
going deep in the ground
without
reverberations.

SEASONS IN SOUTH DAKOTA

—for Rodney, who asked

I
Dirty snow left in the gullies, pale
green spread overnight on the hills
mark spring.
            Taking corn to the hens

I hear a waterfall of redwing blackbird song.
When I open the windows to their raucous mating
I let in something else as well:
soon I'll pace the hills under the moon.

II

Watching struggling heifers birth,
greasing the tractor, I may miss
summer.
        Like spring, it bursts open:
blooming hay demands the mower,
All day I ride the tractor,
isolated by roar.
it's time to turn the bulls out
to the cows, check leaning fences.
Even in summer nights' sweat
I hate to sleep alone.
When I'm too tired to care,
I still hear the larks, feel
the cold flow in each window at dawn.

III

Autumn whistles in some day when I'm
riding the gray gelding
bringing in fat calves for sale:
the air quick-chills, grass turns brown.
Last fall I found two gray hairs;
just as quick, winter came:

I was hurrying to pile fresh wood
from the one-woman crosscut saw
when the first flakes crowded the sky.

IV

Despite the feeding, pitching hay to
black cows with frost-rimmed eyes,
cutting ice on the dam under the eyes
of sky and one antelope,
there's still time to sit before the fire,
curse the dead cold outside,
the other empty chair.

GRANDMOTHER

I always see her hands first, turning
the handle of the Foley food mill.
The veins are knotted over old bones;
spicy tomato steam rises around
her white hair. A worn gold ring turns on
her finger but never will slide off
over the knuckle. Solid as a
young woman, she grew thin, forgot our
names. Hands that fed four daughters lay still.
She left us little: brown unlabeled pictures,
a dozen crocheted afghans, piles of patched jeans.
In the cellar, crowded shelves bear jars of beans,
peas, corn, meat.
Labels like white silent mouths
open and close in the dark.

MEMORIAL DAY

I'm on the hill above the town, with
buffalo grass and graves. Nothing else
grows here. These thrive, deep-rooted, pulling
some thin life from the thick clay soil.

Propriety demands the sod turn
once a year above these ancestors.
They're just bones to me. I'd rather let
buffalo grass grow. There's alfalfa
on Charley Hasselstrom's mound; he'd like
that, says my father, his son.
He worked all his life to grow the stuff,
mow it, stack it, feed it to his cows;
worried about it getting hailed out,
burned out, eaten up by grasshoppers.
Now I have to turn under six plants
that volunteered for him.

Dust blooms below the hill: another makes
the yearly journey. I'll leave the spade
against Martha's rock, try the hoe, hack
at the stubborn roots worked deep in clay.
The shock moves up my arm, down the hoe,
drumming to bones I'll never see, deep
in the earth, deep inside my flesh.

BLACKBIRDS

—for Tom

I
In spring, redwing blackbirds are the first back,
raucous clouds in the trees,
gold-rimmed red wings sparkling,
inundating the prairie
in waterfalls of sound.

II
When the tractor chugs into the field in June,
mowing the alfalfa their nests hang on,
blackbirds hover directly overhead,
calling.

III

The sickle blade cuts down the nest;
four blackbird chicks ride it, cheeping,
into the grass. The hovering pair flies away.
A buzzard circles.

IV

I walk through willows where more nests hang:
a male hunches his shoulders and hisses,
flaring his red plumage.

V

I walk across a field after mowing blackbird nests;
that grinding sound just behind my head
is a male blackbird flying within an inch,
then darting away.

VI

I sit in the truck drinking coffee,
wondering if science has studied blackbirds.
A hawk bursts from the cottonwood tops; two
blackbirds dart in above him, strike, screech.
He ducks, tries to slash them with his claws.
In relays, from territory to territory,
the blackbirds drive him toward the next field.
Two more rise to meet him.

VII

A Department of Agriculture pamphlet
suggests poisoning blackbirds with Avitrol.
Birds ingesting it react with "distress symptoms and calls."
It may not be used on crops intended for human food.
Blackbirds may be killed when "committing
or about to commit serious damage to agricultural crops."

VIII

I see a newspaper story on a man who
eats blackbirds; they taste, he says,
somewhat like doves. They have no
distinct taste. "Usually" he advises,
"you have to serve blackbirds with martinis."

MIDNIGHT IN MISSOURI

The radio says, "Fifty degrees tomorrow."
But I know that windsound, that nighthowl
clear from the Dakotas, across the Badlands,
prairie creeks, hunting grounds, down across Kansas stubble,
swoosh across the rivers, flatlands, through Missouri's little woods
around my house, still screeching.

How many coyote cries, wolf voices, joined to make that sound?
Spruces whip, wind scours granite rock faces,
pine needles whistle along rock trails,
deer pause, hides twitching, hair blown up straight.
How many mountain lions breathe in that clear keen,
pace along a rock ledge, crouch, flick tail, spring?
Ghosts rise out of prairies where they fell alone,
lay in the sun and rain before the wolves came
and the buzzards circled.

The screams go on within their dusty brains,
ride the wind to mine.

HOMESTEADING IN DAKOTA

It was a typical prairie homestead:
a hundred sixty dusty acres
with not one tree.
Mr. Fisher put up a soddy for his wife, five kids,
and dug a well by hand the first month.
The kids and the woman worked the winch
after the well got below ten feet.
               He cut logs

in the hills ten miles away for a solid barn,
log-roofed. Once they were settled he went
to the mines in Deadwood, seventy miles away,
for winter cash.
           She stayed in the soddy,
milked the cow, dug out a little garden,
struggling with the sod laced together by buffalo grass
roots. Now and then she'd stop for breath, shade
her eyes, look at the horizon line
drawn smooth against the sun.

Mr. Fisher—she called him that—
came home when he could,
once or twice a month all summer. Neighbors
helped her catch the cow, fight fire, sit up
when the youngest child died.
                    Once
he got a late start, rode in at midnight.
Fumbling at the low door, he heard struggle inside.
The kids were all awake, pale blank faces
hanging in the dark.
                When he pushed aside
the curtain to the double bunk
he saw the window open,
a white-legged form running in the moonlight,
his wife's screaming face.
He shot once out the window, missed;
shot her and didn't.

The neighbors said Black Douglas, on the next claim,
walked for a month like he had cactus in his feet.
The kids grew up wild as coyotes.
                He never went to trial.
He'd done the best he could;
not his fault the dark spoiled his aim the first time.

JOHN NEIHARDT

Without the eyes you might mistake him for
a tree root, flung from earth by flood some years
ago. The storms have raged, the torrents' roar
receded, borne the soft wood with his tears
and left the hard. The skin, like water wind-
blown, wrinkles over bone, and soft white hair
springs up like drying grassblades, clean and thin,
sun-bright. The nostrils, like a spearhead, flare;
cracked lips like rivulets in bark close tight.
Weeds tangled grow above the hollows for
his eyes—histories are in his eyes, alight
with noon sky prairie blue, where eagles soar.
And from these eyes all he has seen will come—
gnarled shaman writing to a midnight drum.

THE BUFFALO AT MIDNIGHT

I prefer midnight walks. There's less to see.
All matter casts its forward shadow.
Walking in the dark, under the trees, I tired.
The ground was damp; a large dark rock lay by the path.
"I'll sit on that." I sat.
        The rock snorted,
shook himself, became a buffalo.
Somewhat out of breath two hundred yards away
I paused to reconsider.

A buffalo may weigh a ton,
stand six foot at the shoulder, be nine feet long,
covered with coarse brown hair, smell
like a ton of angry meat. Mane heavy with night
he lies beside the path, moonlight on the blades
of his horns.

Wherever I walk now,
I become a nerve end, seeking the shape
of whatever lies ahead. Sometimes,
like birds twittering toward sleep, signals
are faint. But I know the buffalo waits.

ELEGY ON A DEAD COW

She hunched her back against the north wind,
searched out a little grass every winter.
She tried to get up one last time, meet it on her feet.
Legs tucked under her she lies dead in thigh-deep mud.
Her brown bucolic eye is glazed, her hip bones draped
with shrinking hide, her sides mud-smeared where we worked
to lift her free. She was too weak, finally, to pull herself
out of the muck. Her lower teeth were gone; she didn't get enough
of the feed we've pitched for sixty days of unremitting snow
and wind.

Fifteen springs she's birthed a calf,
licked him to life, lifting him clear of the grass
with her rough tongue. Fifteen hot June days she's marched
to summer pasture, the calf's head against her side;
grazed, fed her calf, protected him and brought him home
to sell in fall, growing another in her womb.

Now she's
a problem she never was in life: stuck in mud too deep
for any truck, and frozen solid. We find thirty feet
of log chain, drag her to the boneyard to join her sisters.
Coyotes will feast tonight, howling her praises.
We shake our heads and give her funeral oration,
summing up seventeen cold winters, seventeen springs:
    "She was a good old cow."

CALVING TIME

A living calf,
instructed by mother and instinct,
hides like a rabbit
behind two blades of grass.
Eyes roil as I walk past
but he knows he's safe
from me, and from the coyotes.
He's invisible. From a distance,
he is a rock, a bush,
a yucca plant. He's
part of the wildness,
part of the earth.

A dead calf
needs no disguises.
He's alone, exposed,
no options—stark black
or red in melting snow
and greening grass.
His eyes are dusty.
His mother waits awhile,
moves off to graze.
He's part of the wildness,
becoming rock, bush,
yucca plant;
becoming earth.

SAYING GOODBYE

takes a long time. I've made
fruitcakes for everyone I know, shirts
for men I don't care much
about (but none for you), crocheted potholders, baked bread,
doughnuts,
fed the birds, dipped candles, mended jeans,
darned socks, cleaned house—twice.

            I say
you weren't gentle enough, never touched
my hand just in passing,
smoothed my hair. Perhaps the next man (there's
always another man) will. I baked
my love for you in loaves of bread, put
it like garlic in jars
of pickles, sharp as wild grape jam, rich
brown soup tureened in white.
I thought there would be more: mounds of clean
blue shirts, morning coffee,
supper waiting on the oak table by
the west windows.
            But these
are all: that bread, those jars, like silent
mouths opening, closing in
the still dark cellar.

SETTLERS

—for Charles, Feb. 29, 1864 and for John, July 8, 1909

They came from England, Ireland, Germany, Sweden—
from lands that held twelve generations' bones.
Where boundaries cramped and eldest sons inherited,
younger sons walked bravely off to Stockholm, London,
bought steerage tickets, carried one small bag (all they
possessed, including socks and muffler, knit
by sisters never to be seen again), endured
the harbor stench, the heaving sea, the weary months.
They stared at Liberty, and pondered stern advice:
"Go West, young man, and vote Republican."
Learning, they worked repaying uncles' loans
for tickets to their freedom. Set loose from
bondage to the land at last—old Europe, the soft
fat lands of Iowa—they headed West.
("Go West, young man, and vote . . . ") No voting yet,
only struggling six-horse teams that dragged reluctant

wagons past the Badlands to the Hills, claims selected
with memories of boundaries cramped, of land
that held the bones of generations.
They settled uneasily at first, stared at miles
of undulating grass, seeking neighbors, seeking
even the smoke of enemy fires, sought
trees and roofs and villages; sought in vain.

One by one, the earth touched them;
they touched the earth, stretched
to crumble clods, to smell the soil.
They met the land, made it neighbor, friend,
respected enemy; partner, brother, father, wife—
a home, a land to hold the generations' bones.

CORING APPLES

Today I'm preparing apples for the freezer—
ones my mother picked off the ground around a neighbor's tree.
"Too good to waste," she said, handing me a bucket full.
I've got a hand-cranked machine that peels, cores and slices
in one swift turn. Peels spiral down on the table top,
juice drips, sweet red slices fall into the bowl.

Mother tried it once, says it wastes too much.
She prefers bending over the sink for hours,
carefully paring. I've done fifty pounds
in an hour or so; she'll be days finishing hers.
I'll go on to other jobs.
Daughters always go on to other things;
probably she knows that.

I pull off another core, and drop it in the bucket.
At the sink, she finishes slicing, then nibbles
the last scraps of flesh from the core with her own teeth,
she reminds me, until not a drop of sweetness is left. Perhaps
she smiles.

Yesterday she called as I was finishing breakfast.
"I'm not going to church today," she said. "I'm going
to make a lemon pie instead." Given the quality
of her pies, that's a religious act.
I never go to church, except on Easter, my annual gift
to her; instead I'm writing a poem.

DRYING ONIONS

They hung in the cellar's dark all winter
untouched by wind and snow white as they are,
until long green shoots reached for light.
You helped me slice them; crackling
brown skins thin as dragonfly wings covered the floor.

Sweet bitter fruits of the earth—
spread on racks to dry, they became
more part of us than we knew or wanted.
Our eyes began to burn. Our clothes took on the taint.
When we made love, your tongue and mine, this mound
of flesh and that, all flavors
disappeared in onion.
All flesh is onion,
all sweat and juice part of us, fruit of our love.

Outside, the snow has melted, crusted,
sagged toward the earth. We hack through it, peel back
layer after layer, searching for the white heart,
for earth warm enough to take our seed.

HAPPY BIRTHDAY

When I was five
I learned about running away.
I heard train wheels clacking in the dark.
My mother cried while I slept.

At nine, I had visions of horses.
Blaze was fat and slow.
I dreamed her swift.

At twelve, I learned country schoolyards
aren't ruled by brains. Tired of running,
I socked a nose and found friendship
through violence.

When I was sixteen
I realized my breasts would be smaller,
my hands larger, than I had hoped;
my hair would never be waist-length
or black. But I still learned to say "No,"

At seventeen, I learned boys don't date
girls who live thirty miles from town.
At eighteen, I learned college girls
with cars have friends even when they say "No."

At twenty-one, I discovered rape.
At twenty-three, I married; heard
about open marriages at twenty-six,
at thirty discovered divorce may not be fatal.
I was much better at "No"
but not always
at the right time.

At thirty-five, I found three black hairs
on my chin and clipped them off.
"No! No! No!"

At thirty-six I understood
I'd never have children.
At forty, I resolved
never to spend another birthday
on an island
with people who like to fish.

On my forty-first birthday
I dug two latrines and visited
my Mormon relatives. They had no beer.
They loved the knife in my belt.
"No," I said gently.

Today I'm 42.

DOWN THE HIGHWAY: YOUR TAX DOLLARS AT WORK

I travel a lot, can't afford to fly. So I load my poems,
three notebooks, a sleeping bag, coats, coffee, sunflower seeds,
a pistol, a few clothes and 347 books in my orange pickup
and head down the highway. I see a lot of live animals,
drive over dead ones, and write poems.
I see many things I do not understand.

In Pennsylvania, I saw the sun rise over a huge
lavender barn with red hex signs painted on one side,
and a dead Holstein cow lying in front.

In Rapid City, South Dakota, I saw a militant Indian leader,
often photographed with a rifle, jogging along the highway
in a black and silver jumpsuit. His braids and bearclaw necklace
flopped from shoulder to silver shoulder.

Near Custer, South Dakota I saw a red Corvette backed
into a turnoff at dawn. On the other side of the fence,
in a warm half-circle, lay six Hereford cows,
chewing their cud, batting their long eyelashes,
hoping it would wake up.

In a rest area in Montana, I saw,
scrawled on the bathroom wall,
"Sept. 15, 1982, Charley with a kilo of Panama Gold."
"Sept. 16: Charley: Which way are you going?"

One sunset, I rounded a bend on a gravel road
in western South Dakota and saw a dinosaur, knee deep in alfalfa,
head raised. Usually, signs announce concrete dinosaurs
in this state, but none appeared. I speeded up,
just in case.

In Columbia, Missouri, I saw a lumber wagon
pulled by an ancient mule, driven by a gnarled black Methuselah.
I swerved, slowed. No other driver even glanced his way,
causing me to wonder. Maybe no one sees
any of these sights but me.

That's all I needed. From now on I'll keep these sights to
myself, and suggest you do the same. I don't want to know about
your favorite restaurant in Tulsa, called the Terminal Cafe.
I don't care to speculate on why teenagers in northern South
Dakota all drive pickups with rifle racks mounted on the rear
window, or think about the hairy, upright creatures leaving
man-like tracks around Eagle-Butte.
          They're all mysteries to me,
and they can stay that way.

FIRST NIGHT ALONE ON THE RANCH

The only bootprints in the snow are mine.
The dog you never liked trots at my heels.
The horse looks wary as I pitch his hay;
from here the windows are goldlit,
reflecting on the snow,
but it's only sunset.
The cats are silent mounds.
They are always alone in the night,
their children and mates transient.

I wash the single bowl and cup,
sit by the fire with a book—
remembering how I resented dishes for five,
loud laughter when I wanted to read.
Television tells me that families have husbands,
children, smiling mothers doing the wash.

My family is darkness
before the flickering fire,
the cow calving in the barn.

WALKING THE DOG

  —for Frodo, March 1989

Walking a dog in the city humbles me;
we're used to acres of prairie privacy.
I pretend to walk for my health, striding up the walk
past clipped lawns, fenced trees, flower beds,
tugging the dog toward the curb.
"He was my husband's dog," I explained as I left the meeting,
as if being true to George's memory
meant nothing more than taking his dog
to mark territory four hundred miles from home.

You've seen us, or a similar pair:
the human studies the sky, historical plaques, treetops,
apparently unaware of and not responsible for
what the dog at the other end of the leash is doing.
The dog plays his part: stares at bicycles,
challenges windowed cats,
barks at children on a merry-go-round.
He lifts his leg as a cardinal
might lift a hand over a crowd of pilgrims,
with immense dignity, a modicum of grace,
and an expression of concentrated rectitude.
He's a short dog, but his eyes
focus on higher things: the heavens, and
flying squirrels which he—and I—
believe to be ghosts of those caught by larger dogs
whose mark he senses when he stands beside a tree.

Without George I'm like a dog,
dangling at the end of a leash
held by someone I hardly know,
looking and sniffing for a familiar tree,
some landmark among fumes from asphalt, exhaust,
and unknown legs. Neither of us could scent
our real home from here.

It's lost behind us
with the man who put our collars on
and whose identity we shared
as we sat beside his campfires.
Back in the car
the dog curls up on his back seat blanket
dreaming of a place where he catches rabbits—
instead of only smelling the ozone of their passage,

where George tosses chunks of fresh venison
over the campfire's coals at night,
and in the morning leads him beside still waters
waiting for a dry fly to land, a trout to rise.
I keep awake, read maps, watch the gas gauge,
try to determine where we go from here.

FURTHER READINGS

Linda Hasselstrom, *Feels Like Far: A Rancher's Life on the Great Plains* (Lyons Press, 1999); Linda Hasselstrom, *Bison: Monarch of the Plains* (Graphic Arts Center Pub Co, 1998); Linda Hasselstrom, Gaydell Collier, and Nancy Curtis, eds., *Leaning Into the Wind: Women Write From the Heart of the West* (Houghton Mifflin, 1997); Linda Hasselstrom, *Roadside History of South Dakota* (Mountain Press, 1994); Linda Hasselstrom, *Dakota Bones* (Spoon River Poetry Press, 1992); Linda Hasselstrom, *Land Circle: Writings Collected from the Land* (Fulcrum, 1991); Linda Hasselstrom, *Caught by One Wing* (Spoon River Poetry Press, 1990); Linda Hasselstrom, *Roadkill* (Spoon River Poetry Press, 1987); Linda Hasselstrom, *Windbreak: A Woman Rancher on the Northern Plains* (Barn Owl Books, 1987); Linda Hasselstrom, ed., *Horizons: A Collection of Poetry, Fiction & Essays by 55 South Dakota Writers* (Lame Johnny Press, 1987); Linda Hasselstrom, *Going Over East: Reflections of a Woman Rancher* (Fulcrum, 1987); Linda Hasselstrom, ed., *A Bird Begins to Sing* (Lame Johnny Press, 1979).

Calamity Jane with Rifle.

Montana Historical Society, Helena, Montana.

5

Storytellers

Storytelling is a long-standing tradition in the American West. Stories and storytelling have always been important ways for new arrivals and old timers to find common ground. Through stories, women have taught each other ways to survive and ways to overcome difficulties. Stories provide affirmation and laughter, and sometimes, they are told merely to relieve the tedium of women's work and lives. In this chapter, we have selected many examples of Western women's storytelling. Some of these stories have made their tellers famous, while others leave behind many questions even as to who told the story in the first place.

Sometimes stories are ways to continue traditions, as in Velma Wallis's *Two Old Women*. Sometimes stories show us how to remember traditions in new ways, as in Linda Hogan's "Making Do." The stories of Mary Hallock Foote give us a glimpse of a time now gone. Katherine Anne Porter's story, "The Journey," lets us remember the past in a new way. Included here as well are two stories of being of mixed heritage in the West. Helen Hunt Jackson's *Ramona* was a brave examination of this topic, at a time when women of mixed heritage were routinely portrayed as "tragic mulattas," for its sympathetic presentation of the main character. Mourning Dove (Christal Quintasket) tells a similar story with a different voice in *Cogewea*, the first published novel by a Native American woman. Finally, the story-telling tradition allows for folklore, and here, we present a glimpse at the power of legend, in this case a revision of the legend of Calamity Jane.

In these renderings of women's storytelling are glimpses of another kind of women's literary tradition, one which is inherited woman to woman, and which only sometimes gets translated to paper so that the story outlives its teller.

Velma Wallis (1969–)

This is the story of two old women long before the arrival of an outside culture. According to Velma Wallis, it has been handed down "from generation to generation, from person to person, to my mother, and then to me. . . . The point of the story remains the way Mom meant for me to hear it." Velma Wallis grew up one of thirteen children in a Gwich'in (one of the 11 distinct ethnic peoples of Alaska) family, near Fort Yukon, Alaska. She retells an old Athabaskan story from the remote Yukon River region of northeast Alaska. Two Old Women tells of Ch'idzigyaak and Sa', abandoned by their tribe because food is scarce and the old seem a burden on the young. At first the old women believe they will die; they feel betrayed and are fearful of the death that must soon come. Yet, day by day, they survive by ingenuity and cleverness and a stubborn refusal to let death overtake them. When the tribe returns in the spring from its winter journey, the two old women are reunited with the children who abandoned them and with the people who consented to let them die. The story of the two old women teaches that the old have inner strength and independence, and that the young, when they would lose the burdens of caring for the aged, lose something of themselves.

Velma Wallis spent part of her life alone in a trapping cabin twelve miles from the nearest village, living off the land as her ancestors had done. *Two Old Women* won the Western States Book Award in 1993, and the Pacific Northwest Booksellers' Award in 1994. Wallis has also written *Bird Girl and the Man Who Followed the Sun: An Athabaskan Indian Legend from Alaska* (1996).

AN ALASKA LEGEND

The air stretched tight, quiet and cold over the vast land. Tall spruce branches hung heavily laden with snow, awaiting distant spring winds. The frosted willows seemed to tremble in the freezing temperatures.

Velma Wallis, from *Two Old Women: An Alaska Legend of Betrayal, Courage, and Survival* (1993).

Far off in this seemingly dismal land were bands of people dressed in furs and animal skins, huddled close to small campfires. Their weather—burnt faces were stricken with looks of hopelessness as they faced starvation, and the future held little promise of better days.

These nomads were The People of the arctic region of Alaska, always on the move in search of food. Where the caribou and other migrating animals roamed, The People followed. But the deep cold of winter presented special problems. The moose, their favorite source of food, took refuge from the penetrating cold by staying in one place, and were difficult to find. Smaller, more accessible animals such as rabbits and tree squirrels could not sustain a large band such as this one. And during the cold spells, even the smaller animals either disappeared in hiding or were thinned by predators, man and animal alike. So during this unusually bitter chill in the late fall, the land seemed void of life as the cold hovered menacingly.

During the cold, hunting required more energy than at other times. Thus, the hunters were fed first, as it was their skills on which The People depended. Yet, with so many to feed, what food they had was depleted quickly. Despite their best efforts, many of the women and children suffered from malnutrition, and some would die of starvation.

In this particular band were two old women cared for by The People for many years. The older woman's name was Ch'idzigyaak, for she reminded her parents of a chickadee bird when she was born. The other woman's name was Sa', meaning "star," because at the time of her birth her mother had been looking at the fall night sky, concentrating on the distant stars to take her mind away from the painful labor contractions.

The chief would instruct the younger men to set up shelters for these two old women each time the band arrived at a new campsite, and to provide them with wood and water. The younger women pulled the two elder women's possessions from one camp to the next and, in turn, the old women tanned animal skins for those who helped them. The arrangement worked well.

However, the two old women shared a character flaw unusual for people of those times. Constantly they complained of aches and pains, and they carried walking sticks to attest to their handicaps. Surprisingly, the others seemed not to mind, despite having been taught from the days of their childhood that weakness was not tolerated among the inhabitants of this harsh motherland. Yet, no one reprimanded the two women, and they continued to travel with the stronger ones—until one fateful day.

On that day, something more than the cold hung in the air as The People gathered around their few flickering fires and listened to the chief. He was a man who stood almost a head taller than the other men. From within the folds of his parka ruff he spoke about the cold, hard days they were to expect and of what each would have to contribute if they were to survive the winter.

Then, in a loud, clear voice he made a sudden announcement: "The council and I have arrived at a decision." The chief paused as if to find the strength to voice his next words. "We are going to have to leave the old ones behind."

■　■　■

The large band of famished people slowly moved away, leaving the two women sitting in the same stunned position on their piled spruce boughs. Their small fire cast a soft orange glow onto their weathered faces. A long time passed before the cold brought Ch'idzigyaak out of her stupor. She was aware of her daughter's helpless gesture but believed that her only child should have defended her even in the face of danger. The old woman's heart softened as she thought of her grandson. How could she bear hard feelings toward one so young and gentle? The others made her angry, especially her daughter! Had she not trained her to be strong? Hot, unbidden tears ran from her eyes.

At that moment, Sa' lifted her head in time to see her friend's tears. A rush of anger surged within her. How dare they! Her cheeks burned with the humiliation. She and the other old woman were not close to dying! Had they not sewed and tanned for what the people gave them? They did not have to be carried from camp to camp. They were neither helpless nor hopeless. Yet they had been condemned to die.

■　■　■

The moonlight shone silently upon the frozen earth as life whispered throughout the land, broken now and then by a lone wolf's melancholy howl. The women's eyes twitched in tired, troubled dreams, and soft helpless moans escaped from their lips. Then a cry rang out somewhere in the night as the moon dipped low on the western horizon. Both women awoke at once, hoping that the awful screech was a part of her nightmare. Again the wail was heard. This time, the women recognized it as the sound of something caught in one of their snares. They were relieved. Fearing that other predators would beat them to their catch, the women hurriedly dressed and rushed to their snare sets. There they saw a small, trembling rabbit that lay partially strangled as it eyed them warily. Without hesitation, Sa' went to the rabbit, put one hand around its neck, felt for the beating heart, and squeezed until the small struggling animal went limp. After Sa' reset the snare, they went back to the camp, each feeling a thread of new hope.

Morning came, but brought no light to this far northern land. Ch'idzigyaak awoke first. She slowly kindled the fire into a flame as she carefully added more wood. When the fire had died out during the cold night, frost from their warm breathing had accumulated on the walls of caribou skins.

Sighing in dull exasperation, Ch'idzigyaak went outside where the northern lights still danced above, and the stars winked in great numbers. Ch'idzigyaak stood for a moment staring up at these wonders. In all her years, the night sky never failed to fill her with awe.

■ ■ ■

"We have learned much during our long lives. Yet there we were in our old age, thinking that we had done our share in life. So we stopped, just like that. No more working like we used to, even though our bodies are still healthy enough to do a little more than we expect of ourselves."

Ch'idzigyaak sat listening, alert to her friend's sudden revelation as to why the younger ones thought it best to leave them behind. "Two old women. They complain, never satisfied. We talk of no food, and of how good it was in our days when it really was no better. We think that we are so old. Now, because we have spent so many years convincing the younger people that we are helpless, they believe that we are no longer of use to this world."

Seeing tears fill her friend's eyes at the finality of her words, Sa' continued in a voice heavy with feeling. "We are going to prove them wrong! The People. And death!" She shook her head, motioning into the air. "Yes, it awaits us, this death. Ready to grab us the moment we show our weak spots. I fear this kind of death more than any suffering you and I will go through. If we are going to die anyway, let us die trying!"

Ch'idzigyaak stared for a long time at her friend and knew that what she said was true, that death surely would come if they did not try to survive. She was not convinced that the two of them were strong enough to make it through the harsh season, but the passion in her friend's voice made her feel a little better. So, instead of feeling sadness because there was nothing further they could say or do, she smiled. "I think we said this before and will probably say it many more times, but yes, let us die trying." And with a sense of strength filling her like she had not thought possible, Sa' returned the smile as she got up to prepare for the long day ahead of them.

■ ■ ■

Many days went by before the women caught more rabbits. It had been some time since they had eaten a full meal. They managed to preserve their energy by boiling spruce boughs to serve as a minty tea, but it made the stomach sour. Knowing it was dangerous to eat anything solid after such a diet, the two women first boiled the rabbit meat to make a nourishing broth, which they drank slowly. After a day of drinking the broth, the women cautiously ate one ham off a rabbit. As the days passed, they allowed themselves more portions, and soon their energy was restored.

With wood piled high around the shelter like a barricade, the women found that they had more time to forage for food. The hunting skills they learned in their youth reemerged, and each day the women would walk farther from the shelter to set their rabbit snares and to keep an eye out for any other animals small enough to kill. One of the rules they had been taught was that if you set snares for animals you must check them regularly. Neglecting your snareline brought bad luck. So, despite the cold and their own physical discomforts, the two women checked their snares each day and usually found a rabbit to reward them.

Joan Myers, *Crossed Arms*, 1992.

From the exhibition, Women of a Certain Age. *Copyright ©1999 Joan Myers, used by permission of artist.*

■ ■ ■

Looking into the air, Ch'idzigyaak took note of a warmth in the air. "The weather gets better," Sa' said softly and the older woman's eyes widened in surprise. "I should have noticed. Had it been cold, I would have frozen in my position of a sneaky fox." The women found great laughter in this as they went back into the shelter to prepare the meat of a different season to come. After that morning, the weather fluctuated between bitter cold and then warm and snowy days. That the women did not catch another bird failed to dampen their spirits, for the days gradually grew longer, warmer, and brighter.

■ ■ ■

The darkness grew longer, and the land became silent and still. It took much concentration for the two women to fill their long days with work. They made many articles of rabbit-fur clothing such as mittens, hats, and face coverings. Yet, despite this, they felt a great loneliness slowly enclose them.

■ ■ ■

Suddenly, out of the stillness, the women heard their names called. From across the campfire, their eyes met, and they knew what they heard was not their imagination. The man's voice became loud, and he identified himself. The women knew the old guide. Perhaps they could trust him. But what of the others? It was Ch'idzigyaak who spoke first. "Even if we do not answer, they will find us."

Sa' agreed. "Yes, they will find us," she said as her mind raced with many thoughts.

"What will we do?" Ch'idzigyaak whined in panic.

Sa' took a while to think. Then she said, "We must let them know we are here." Seeing the look of hysteria enter her friend's eyes, Sa' hastened to say in smooth, confident tones, "We must be brave and face them. But my friend, be prepared for anything." She waited a moment before she added, "Even death." This did not comfort Ch'idzigyaak, who looked as frightened as her friend ever had seen her.

The two women sat a long time trying to gather what courage

they had left. They knew they could run no longer. Finally, Sa' got up slowly and went outside into the cold night air, hollering rather hoarsely, "We are here!"

For a while no one broke the silence. Finally, Daagoo said, "The chief believed that you survived, so he sent us to find you."

"We are starving, and the cold gets worse. Again we have little food, and we are in the same shape as when we left you. But when the chief hears you are well, he will ask you to come back to our group. The chief and most of The People feel as I do. We are sorry for what was done to you."

As he spoke, Daagoo realized that in these two women, whom he once thought of as helpless and weak, he had rediscovered the inner strength that had deserted him the winter before. Now, somehow, he knew that he never would believe himself to be old and weak again. Never!

■ ■ ■

At first, people wanted to help the old ones in any way they could, but the women would not allow too much assistance, for they enjoyed their newly found independence. So The People showed their respect for the two women by listening to what they had to say.

More hard times were to follow, for in the cold land of the North it could be no other way, but The People kept their promise. They never again abandoned any elder. They had learned a lesson taught by two whom they came to love and care for until each died a truly happy old woman.

FURTHER READINGS
Velma Wallis, *Bird Girl and the Man Who Followed the Sun: An Athabaskan Indian Legend from Alaska* (Epicenter Press, 1996).

Anonymous/Martha Cannary Burke, aka Calamity Jane (1852–1903)

There are almost as many stories about Calamity Jane (Martha Cannary Burke) as there are about Billy the Kid, or Daniel Boone, or Davy Crockett, or Kit Carson. She was born in Iowa or in Missouri in 1852, grew up in Montana, and she worked there and in Dakota, Utah, Wyoming and Kansas for most of her vagabond life. She was a pioneer roustabout in men's clothing, doing men's work; she was a dishwasher, a construction worker, a "bullwhacker" or teamster, an army scout, and, according to her account, a rider for the Pony Express and a member of Buffalo Bill's Wild West Show. There are stories of her scouting for Custer in 1872, and of her being the first white woman in the Black Hills. She was a big-boned, strong woman who boasted she could out-ride and out-shoot any man she knew. In mining towns, she was often remembered less kindly as a woman of low reputation.

In 1875 or 1876, Martha Cannary met "Wild Bill" Hickok and fell in love. She claims they were secretly married and that a daughter, Janey, was born in the following year. She said she divorced Hickok a year later and that in 1885 she married a Texan named Clinton (Charley) Burke and they had a daughter in 1887. The question of Calamity Jane's daughters is further complicated by her "confession" that she also raised Jesse Elizabeth Oakes, whom she called "the meanest child I ever knew," daughter of Calamity Jane's sister, Belle Starr.

What makes Calamity Jane interesting is that she stands between two traditions of Western folklore. One applauds the rogue woman of the dime novels, the heroine called "The White Devil of the Yellowstone," who could shoot and ride and drink like a man. In that guise, Calamity resembled Mary Fields, the black woman who hauled supplies for a mission of Catholic nuns outside of Cascade, Montana. "Stagecoach Mary" drove a team of horses, and kept her rifle and her jug of whiskey beside her on the wagon seat. The idea that the West would tarnish a "lady," that she would learn to drink and to swear, was alive among the new settlers coming west. Annie

Oakley—"Little Sure Shot"—was only five feet tall and ninety-eight pounds, and she retained her popularity by proving she could shoot straight while looking demure. Calamity Jane was more disreputable than Christian charity could abide.

In 1941, the appearance of Jean Hickok McCormick, claiming to be Calamity's long-lost daughter, offering an album of unmailed "letters" from her mother, suggested another side of the story. By Jean Hickok McCormick's reckoning, Calamity was really America's first Stella Dallas, the self-sacrificing, working-class mother who gave her child to be raised as a "lady" by elegant folk in Richmond, Virginia, and in Liverpool, England. Even if the letters were written by the daughter to retrieve her mother's reputation after Calamity's death in 1903, they suggest that the Wild West reprobate might also have been a woman who shared with her daughter her recipe for a "20 year cake" that used 25 eggs, 2 1/2 pounds of sugar and flour and butter, 7 1/2 pounds of raisins, 6 1/2 pounds of currants and citron, and cloves, cinnamon, mace, nutmeg, yeast, baking soda and cream of tartar. "The cake is unexcelled and will keep good to the last crumb for 20 years.—Pour (over) a pint of brandy."

Calamity Jane continues to capture the western imagination. Larry McMurtry wrote about Calamity in *Buffalo Girls* (1990), and Anjelica Huston played the role in the CBS television film in 1995. In Hollywood, Calamity was played at different times by Jean Arthur, Jane Russell, and Yvonne de Carlo. No version, however, is as interesting as the story of humble sacrifice—however fraudulent—of a mother for her daughter described in *Calamity Jane's Letters to her Daughter*, published by Shameless Hussy Press in 1976.

CALAMITY JANE'S LETTERS TO HER DAUGHTER

Jim O'Neil—Please give this album to my daughter, Janey Hickok, after my death.

Jane Hickok

Anonymous, from *Calamity Jane's Letters to her Daughter* (1976).

Sep. 25, 77 Deadwood, Tery Dk.

My Dear—this isnt intended for a diary and it may even happen this will never be sent to you but i like to think of you reading it some-day page by page in the years to come after I am gone. I would like to hear you laugh when you look at these pictures of meself. I am alone in my shack to night and tired. I rode 60 miles yesterday, to the post office and returned home to night this is your birthday and you are 4 years old to day. You see your Daddy Jim promised me he would always get a letter to me on your birth day each year. Was I glad too hear from him? He sent the tiny picture of you—You are the dead spit of Meself at your age and as I gaze on your little photo to night I stop as I kiss you and then remembering tears start and I ask God to let me make amend some how some day to your father and you. I vis-ited your fathers grave this morning at Ingleside. They are talking of moving his coffin to Mount Moriah Cemetary in Deadwood. A year and a few weeks have passed since he was killed and it seems a cen-tury—without either of you the years ahead look like a lonely trial.

Tomorrow I am going down the Yellowstone Valley just for Adventure and excitement. The O'Neils changed your name to Jean Irene but I call you Janey for Jane.

September 28, 1877

Another day had gone, dear, in fact three days have passed since I wrote last—I am sitting beside my campfire tonight. My horse Satan, is picketed nearby. You should see him the light from the campfire playing about his sleek neck and satiny shoulders of mus-cle, white feet and diamond of white between his eyes. He looks an object of all beauty. I am so proud of him. Your father gave him to me and I have his running mate, King. I use him for a pack horse on long trips but I havent got him with me this trip. I can hear coyotes and wolves and the staccato wail of Indian dogs near their camps— There are thousands of Sioux in this vally I am not afraid of them— They think I am a crazy woman and never molest me.

I followed a new trail today it must be the new mail route being built by Bozeman's trail blazers. I expect to catch up with them tomorrow, they are on a dangerous mission and it wont hurt any-thing to be nearby just in case they need someone to help scare away the Sioux. I guess I am the only human being they are afraid of.

On this page you will find a photo of your grandmother Cannery my mother. She & your grandfather came across the plains in a covered wagon when I was just a small child. We lived for years in Missouri. Your Daddy Jim sent me a pen & a bottle of ink so I could write to him some times. He is one man who has some respect for your mother even if others dont. This pen was made in Ireland. I carry it with this album tied to the saddle & the ink in my pocket so I can write to you beside my campfire.

Dear Janey—I sometimes find it impossible to carry the old album to write in so you will find now & then extra pages. My ink has been frozen so many times it is almost spoiled. It is precious to me because your Daddy Jim sent it to me. You are getting to be such a big girl now, almost 6 years old. It only seems such a little while since I met your Daddy Jim & mother Helen O'Neil & gave you to them. Some day I am going to see you. I felt so bad when I heard of Helen's death. You are destined never to have a mother to live with. May God keep old Mammy Ross with you darling. I am looking after a little boy. His name is Jackie, he is five years older than you, his father & mother were killed by the indians. I found him the day your Father was killed. He thought your Father the greatest hero on earth & saw him shot, He is a nice boy & will be a great man someday. The Sioux indians are still troublesome. I went to the battlefield after Custer's battle & I never want to see such a sight again. In a house which had been dismantled was the carcass of a man apparantlly hidden there to escape the Indians seeking revenge. The squaws had cut legs and arms from the dead soldiers, then heads were chopped, then eyes probed out. You see, Custer had molested an Indian village, running the squaws & children from their camps, so one cant blame them for getting even in their own way. Your Uncle Cy was in that battle Janey. I found him hacked to pieces, his head in one place, legs & arms scattered about. I dug a grave & put his poor poor old body in my saddle blanket & buried him. I can never think of him without crying. Good night dear till next time.

July 1880, Coulson

Dear Janey—I am here in Coulson. It has been one year since I have heard from your Daddy Jim. You should see Coulson. I met a man here today from Deadwood who knew my best friend there,

Mister Will Lull. I was sick with a fever of some sort while rooming at his Hotel. The Hotel Baby Face Lull took over from a New Orleans man, Porter, & Lull was so good to me. He knows his business. I like him very much, He always greets me with, "Howdy Jane, little girl. Keep a stiff upper lip, remember youre a good girl." He & your Daddy Jim are the only 2 men who have faith in me. Queer the men I could like are Easternrs. I went up stage to Cheyenne awhile back & had quite an exciting time. The stage is run by Luke Voorhees. He is a relative of Clark—Lewis & Clark—we had quite a conversation. He was so interested in the time your Father & I went by horseback to Deadwood Gulch from Abilene. We stayed all night in the old station in Virginia Dale. I dressed in mens pants & posed as Wild Bills partner, the Jack of Diamonds. Before we got away we had a shooting contest. I beat them all & it sure filled me full of hot air. Then the change driver was killed & i took his place. Everyone blamed the Indians but they were white men who did the killing & murdering & robbed the boys of gold dust. Your father dared me to drive the stage that trip after the killing. I did & found it was myself in one hell of a fix Janey. The outlaws were back of me it was getting dark & I knew something had to be done, so I jumped off the driver's seat on to the nearest horse then on my saddle horse which was tied to the side & joined up in the dark with the outlaws. Your Father was bringing up the rear but I couldnt see it in the darkness but after they got the coach stopped and found no passengers but heaps of gold dust they got careless. Your Father & I got the whole bunch There were 8 of them & of course they had to be shot for they wouldnt give up. Your Father counted 3 with their right arm shot through. He said, "thats your work Jane. You never aim to kill." The other 5 he shot to kill. He never seemd to mind killing, but I do. I've never killed anyone yet, but I would like to knock some of Deadwoods women in the head. There is only I woman in that mess of crums & that is Missus Bander. Deadwood is full of crums but Missus Bander is different. I hope some day you can come to this Country then you will know how I had too exist. In 2 more years I will go to see you dear, then I know I will feel better about you. Perhaps then you will think of me sometimes not as your mother but as some lonely woman who once loved & lost a little girl like you. I shall take you on my lap & tell you all about that little girl. Of course you wont know its you. I have been trying to educate myself so I can spell & read & write ever since your

Daddy Jim gave me the school books & dictionary to bring home with me that time in Omaha. Giving you up nearly killed me Janey. Your folks named you Jane for me. That is why I call you Janey. I take one book at a time & look in the Dictionary for every word I dont know the meaning of. I only went as far as the third grade in school, & although I have those books to study it is no easy task.

I want to be able to act like a white person when I do visit you. Everybody thinks I can neither read or write even my name, so I just let them think so. It is better so, I find it. Your Grand Pa & Grand Ma were educated even if I was not & it wasnt there fault I ran off the first chance I got. You see your Grand Pa was a Preacher. He was like Preacher Smith, he thought he could fight the whole Indian Nation with a Bible. Im not afraid to face them as long i have 2 guns under my belt but Id sure as Hell hate to face them with a Bible under my arm instead. You will understand all this some day. Good night Janey.

September 1880, Deadwood

Janey, a letter from your Daddy Jim came today & another picture of you. Your birthday is this month, you are 7 years old. I like this picture of you, your eyes & forehead are like your Father, lower jaw, mouth & hair like me. Your expression in your blue eyes with their long black eyelashes are exactly like your fathers. It is nice that you dont have to atend a public school You are lucky to have a man like Captain O'Neil to give you so much of everything. I had nothing Janey & when I think of you being on board ship with your Daddy Jim with a teacher all your own & lovely clothing & he says you are taking lessons on the piano Be nice to him darling, & love him forever for all he has done for you. When he had you write your name on his letter to me it was so kind of him. You write such a nice hand, it made me ashamed of mine.

Your picture brought back all the years I have lived with your Father & recalled how jealous I was of him. I feel like writing about him to night so I will tell you somthings you should know. I met James Butler Hickok, "Wild Bill," in 1870 near Abeline, Kansas. I heard a bunch of outlaws planning to kill him. I couldnt get to where my horse was so I crawled on my hands & knees through the brush past the outlaws for over a mile & reached the old shack where he was staying that night. I told him & he hid me back of the door while he shot it out with them. They hit him, cutting open the top of his head & them they heard him fall & lit matches to see if he was dead. Bill killed them all. I'll never forget what he looked like with blood running down his face while he used 2 guns. He never aimed & I guess he was never known to have missed anyone he aimed at, I mean wanted to kill, & he only shot in self defense Then he was quite sure. I nursed him several days & then while on the trip to Abeline we met Rev. Sipes & Rev. Warren & we were married. There will be lots of folks doubt that but I will leave you plenty of proof that we were. You were not a woods colt Janey. Dont let any of these pus gullied [women] ever get buy with that lie.

I am ashamed of this writing but I cant do any better. I must tell you about this marriage certificate of ours. Your Father planned to have it transfered to a real one, printed. I aim to get it fixed up some day like he wanted it. Even if I do, always keep this one Janey, anyway. It may not look as nice but it was the only one Rev Warren & Rev Sipes could fix up so far from civilization. You will find a photograph of your Fathers parents in the album, also a gold pin in the shape of a horseshoe which belonged to your Father's Mother. He gave them to me. Take care of them darling. They are so old too & will be valuable as keepsakes when you are old. The gun I am keeping for you was one your father gave me. He bought this ring for my wedding ring. I shall put it amoung my treasures for you. It was bought at Abeline, Kansas while I was there with him. I was so jealous of every woman there. One I always call his common law Wife was Mamie Werly, a dance hall girl. I used to get mad & call her that to him. He would only laugh & say, "Foolish Jane, lets kiss and make up." He would never quarrell about Mamie Werly & paid no attention to her, I was jealous just the same & imagined lots. Dont let jealousy get you Janey. It kills love & all the nice things in life. It drove your father from me. When I lost him I lost everything I ever loved except you. I gave him a divorce so he could marry Agnes Lake. I was trying to make amends for the jealous times & my spells of meanness. If she had loved him she would have come out here with him but she didnt & I was glad to have him again even if he was married & she so far away. I always excused our sin by knowing he was mine long before he was hers. A man can love 2 women at 1 time. He loved her & still he loved me. He loved me because of you Janey. That first picture of you which your Daddy Jim sent your Father wanted. I gave it to him & it was in his pocket the day he was killed. His family thought I wasnt good enough for him. That & my jealousy was all our trouble. When he came back after marrying Agnes Lake I thought I would snub him, but we met again one day & both found we still loved each other better than ever. I forgot everything when I was near him. No one else.

FURTHER READINGS

Roberta Beed Sollid, *Calamity Jane*, Montana Historical Society Press, 1995; James D. McLaird, "Calamity Jane's Diary and Letters," *Montana The Magazine of Western History*, vol. 45, #4, 20–35; "The Story of Martha Cannary Burke, in Her Own Words," in Robert J. Casey, *The Black Hills and Their Incredible Characters* (Bobbs-Merrill, 1949).

Mary Hallock Foote (1847–1938)

Mary Hallock, born into a Quaker family, went to school at the Female Collegiate Seminary in Poughkeepsie and then to the Cooper Union Institute School of Design in New York City. She earned her living as a book illustrator before her marriage in 1876 to a Yale-educated civil engineer, Arthur Foote. Along with other young men after the Civil War, Foote imagined his future in the West, but youthful optimism was tested as the couple moved through a series of mining camps in Leadville, Colorado, in what she termed "darkest" Idaho, and in the Grass Valley in California. The settlements were raw and lonely outposts, hard on women and sometimes devastating to men. Mary Foote raised three children (her second daughter delivered with only her sister to help) and suffered several miscarriages. The 1880s brought disappointment as her husband's schemes for irrigation ditches failed again and again, and he sank first into depression and then into alcoholism. Mary became the family breadwinner, and turned back to her training as an illustrator. She worked on woodcuts, and she was, from the first, recognized as "one of the best designers in the wood."

Her stories of miners and "ditchdiggers" held little of the romantic exuberance found in the paintings of Frederic Remington. She focused most often upon the struggles of women and children, and of their lives filled with loneliness and isolation. Her landscapes, she once said, were horizons marked by "great black buzzards" that seemed to hang in the sky.

Mary Hallock Foote felt herself an exile in the west. Helen Hunt Jackson visited her briefly, but she relied most on her passionate friendship with Helena Gilder, wife of the editor of *Scribner's Magazine.* Over a period of thirty-five years, in 540 letters, she poured out her despair at becoming "an artist." Their correspondence was the basis for Carroll Smith-Rosenberg's essay, "The Female World of Love and Ritual," and a source for Carl Degler's history of the family, *At Odds* (1980). Yet, for all her doubt, the substantial canon of her work—fifteen titles of fiction and short stories—her work established a literature where women—not cowboys or gamblers—are the center of attention. The effort to make "a home" is a heroic enterprise in her stories, although that effort is sometimes both disheartening and difficult.

Hetty's story is a small gem, at once a frontier romance and an almost mystical rendering of lovers who escape into the dark western night. "Pretty Girls" is a wry comment on beauty that flowers briefly in the West. Foote's stories and illustrations appeared in *St. Nicholas* and *Scribner's* magazines. "The Rapture of Hetty" was published in a collection called *In Exile and Other Stories* (1894), and "Pretty Girls in the West" was part of a series published in *Century Magazine* in 1888 and 1889; both were later published as *The Idaho Stories and Illustrations.*

THE RAPTURE OF HETTY

The dance was set for Christmas night at Walling's, a horse-ranch where there were women, situated in a high, watered valley shut in by foothills, sixteen miles from the nearest town. The cabin with its roof of shakes, the sheds and corrals, can be seen from any divide between Packer's ferry and the Payette.

The "boys" had been generally invited with one exception to the usual company. The youngest of the sons of Basset, a pastoral and nomadic house, was socially under a cloud, on the charge of having been "too handy with the frying-pan brand."

The charge could not be substantiated, but the boy's name had been roughly handled in those wide, loosely defined circles of the range where the force of private judgment makes up for the weakness of the law, in dealing with crimes that are difficult of detection and uncertain of punishment. He that has obliterated his neighbor's brand or misapplied his own, is held as, in the age of tribal government and ownership, was held the remover of his neighbor's land-marks. A word goes forth against him potent as the levitical curse, and all the people say amen.

As society's first public and pointed rejection of him the slight had rankled with the son of Basset, and grievously it wore on him that Hetty Rhodes was going, with the man who had been his earliest and most persistent accuser: Hetty, prettiest of all the bunch-grass belles, who never reproached nor quarreled, but judged people with her smile and let them go. He had not complained, though he had her promise,—one of her promises,—nor asked a hearing in his own defense. The sons of Basset were many and poor; their stock had dwindled upon the range; her men-folk condemned him, and Hetty believed, or seemed to believe, as the others.

Had she forgotten the night when two men's horses stood at her father's fence,—the Basset boy's and that of him who was afterward his accuser; and the other's horse was unhitched when the evening was but half spent, and furiously ridden away, while the Basset boy's stood at the rails till close upon midnight? Had the coincidence escaped her that from this night, of one man's rage and another's bliss, the ugly charge had dated? Of these things a girl may not testify.

They met in town on the Saturday before the dance, Hetty buying her dancing-shoes at the back of the store, where the shoe-cases framed in a snug little alcove for the exhibition of a "fit." The boy, in his belled spurs and "shaps" of goat-hide, was lounging disconsolate and sulky against one of the front counters; she wore a striped ulster, an enchanted garment his arm had pressed, and a pink crocheted tam-o'-shanter cocked bewitchingly over her dark eyes.

Her hair was ruffled, her cheeks were red, with the wind she had faced for two hours on the spring-seat of her father's "dead axe" wagon. Critical feminine eyes might have found her a trifle blowzy; the sick-hearted Basset boy looked once,—he dared not look again.

Hetty coquetted with her partner in the shoe bargain, a curly-headed young Hebrew, who flattered her familiarly and talked as if he had known her from a child, but always with an eye to business. She stood, holding back her skirts and rocking her instep from right to left, while she considered the effect of the new style; patent-leather foxings and tan-cloth tops, and heels that came under the middle of her foot, and narrow toes with tips of stamped leather;—but what a price! More than a third of her chicken-money gone for that one fancy's satisfaction. But who can know the joy of a really distinguished choice in shoe-leather like one who in her childhood has trotted barefoot through the sage-brush and associated shoes only with cold weather or going to town? The Basset boy tried to fix his strained attention upon anything rather than upon that tone of high jocosity between Hetty and the shiny-haired clerk. He tried to summon his own self-respect and leave the place.

What was the tax, he inquired, on those neck-handkerchiefs; and he pointed with the loaded butt of his braided leather quirt to a row of dainty silk mufflers, signaling custom from a cord stretched above the gentlemen's-furnishing counter.

The clerk explained that the goods in question were first class, all silk, brocaded, and of an extra size. Plainly he expected that a casual mention of the price would cool the inexperienced customer's curiosity, especially as the colors displayed in the handkerchiefs were not those commonly affected by the cow-boy cult. The Basset boy threw down his last half-eagle and carelessly called for the one with a blue border. The delicate "baby blue" attracted him by its perishability, its suggestion of impossible refinements beyond the soilure and dust of his own grimy circumstances. Yet he pocketed his purchase as though it had been any common thing, not to show his pride in it before the patronizing salesman.

He waited foolishly for Hetty, not knowing if she would even speak to him. When she came at last, loitering down the shop, with her eyes on the gay Christmas counters and her arms filled with bundles, he silently fell in behind her and followed her to her father's wagon, where he helped her unload her purchases.

"Been buying out the store?" he opened the conversation.

"Buying more than father 'll want to pay for," she drawled, glancing at him sweetly. Those entoiling looks of Hetty's dark-lashed eyes had grown to a habit with her; even now the little Jewish salesman was smiling over his brief portion in them. Her own coolness made her careless, as children are in playing with fire.

"Here's some Christmas the old man won't have to pay for." A soft paper parcel was crushed into her hand.

"Who is going to pay for it, I'd like to know? If it's some of your doings, Jim Basset, I can't take it—so there!"

She thrust the package back upon him. He tore off the wrapper and let the wind carry his rejected token into the trampled mud and slush of the street.

Hetty screamed and pounced to the rescue."What a shame! It's a beauty of a handkerchief. It must have cost a lot of money. I shan't let you use it so."

She shook it, and wiped away the spots from its delicate sheen, and folded it into its folds again.

"*I* don't want the thing." He spurned it fiercely.

"Then give it to some one else." She endeavored coquettishly to force it into his hands, or into the pockets of his coat. He could not withstand her thrilling little liberties in the face of all the street.

"I'll wear it Monday night," said he. "May be you think I won't be there?" he added hoarsely, for he had noted her look of surprise, mingled with an infuriating touch of pity. "You kin bank on it I'll be there."

Hetty toyed with the thought that after all it might be better that she should not go to the dance. There might be trouble, for certainly Jim Basset had looked as if he meant it when he had said he would be there; and Hetty knew the temper of the company, the male portion of it, too well to doubt what their attitude would be toward an inhibited guest who disputed the popular verdict, and claimed social privileges which it had been agreed that he had forfeited. But it was never really in her mind to deny herself the excitement of going. She and her escort were among the first couples to cross the snowy pastures stretching between her father's claim and the lights of the lonely horse-ranch.

It was a cloudy night, the air soft, chill, and spring-like. Snow had fallen early and frozen upon the ground; the stockmen welcomed the "chinook wind" as the promise of a break in the hard weather. Shadows came out and played upon the pale slopes, as the riders rose and dropped past one long swell and another of dim country falling away like a ghostly land seeking a ghostly sea. And often Hetty looked back, fearing, yet half hoping, that the interdicted one might be on his way, among the dusky, straggling shapes behind.

The company was not large, nor, up to nine o'clock, particularly merry. The women were engaged in cooking supper, or were above in the roof-room brushing out their crimps by the light of an unshaded kerosene lamp, placed on the pine washstand which did duty as a dressing-table. The men's voices came jarringly through the loose boards of the floor from below.

About that hour arrived the unbidden guest, and like the others he had brought his "gun." He was stopped at the door and told that he could not come in among the girls to make trouble. He denied that he had come with any such intention. There were persons present,—he mentioned no names,—who were no more eligible, socially speaking, than himself, and he ranked himself low in saying so; where such as these could be admitted, he proposed to show that he could. He offered, in evidence of his good faith and peaceable intentions, to give up his gun; but on the condition that he be allowed one dance with the partner of his choosing, regardless of her previous engagements.

This unprecedented proposal was referred to the girls, who were charmed with its audacity. But none of them spoke up for the outcast till Hetty said she could not think what they were all afraid of; a dozen to one, and that one without his weapon! Then the other girls chimed in and added their timid suffrages.

There may have been some twinges of disappointment, there could hardly have been surprise, when the black sheep directed his choice without a look elsewhere to Hetty. She stood up, smiling but rather pale, and he rushed her to the head of the room, securing the most conspicuous place before his rival, who with his partner took the place of second couple opposite.

"Keep right on!" the fiddler chanted, in sonorous cadence to the music, as the last figure of the set ended with "Promenade all!" He swung into the air of the first figure again, smiling, with his cheek upon his instrument and his eyes upon the floor. Hetty fancied that his smile meant more than merely the artist's pleasure in the joy he evokes.

"Keep your places!" he shouted again, after the "Promenade all!" a second time had raised the dust and made the lamps flare, and lighted with smiles of sympathy the rugged faces of the elders ranged against the walls. The side couples dropped off exhausted, but the tops held the floor, and neither of the men was smiling.

The whimsical fiddler invented new figures, which he "called off" in time to his music, to vary the monotony of a quadrille with two couples missing.

The opposite girl was laughing hysterically; she could no longer dance nor stand. The rival gentleman looked about him for another partner. One girl jumped up, then, hesitating, sat down again. The music passed smoothly into a waltz, and Hetty and her bad boy kept the floor, regardless of shouts and protests warning the trespasser that his time was up and the game in other hands.

Three times they circled the room; they looked neither to right nor left; their eyes were upon each other. The men were all on their feet, the music playing madly. A group of half-scared girls was huddled, giggling and whispering, near the door of the dimly lighted shed-room. Into the midst of them Hetty's partner plunged, with his breathless, smiling dancer in his arms, passed into the dim outer place to the door where his horse stood saddled, and they were gone.

They crossed the little valley known as Seven Pines; they crashed through the thin ice of the creek; they rode double sixteen miles before daybreak, Hetty wrapped in her lover's "slicker," with the blue-bordered handkerchief, her only wedding-gift, tied over her blowing hair.

PRETTY GIRLS IN THE WEST

The wish so often expressed by mothers in the West that their daughters should have a "good time," suggests an inquiry as to what precisely is meant by this fond aspiration.

A mother's idea of a "good time" for her daughter usually signifies the sort of time she has failed to have herself. If she has been a hardworking woman, with many children to care for, she will desire that her daughter shall live easy and be blessed, in the way of offspring, with something less than a quiver-full. Where in the past labor has urged her, often beyond her strength, pleasure in the future shall invite her child.

So the mothers of the West, women of the heroic days of pioneering, unconsciously tell the story of their own struggles and deprivations in the ambitions which they indulge for their children.

Along the roads over which her parents journeyed in their white-topped wagon, their tent by night, their tabernacle, their fortress in time of danger, the settler's daughter shall ride in a tailor-made habit, or fare luxuriously in a drawing-room car. Where the mother's steadfast face grew brown with the glare of the alkali

Mary Hallock Foote, "Pretty Girls in the West," from *Century Magazine* (1888/9).

plain, the daughter shall glance out carelessly from behind the tapestry blind of her Pullman "section." Where the mother's hands washed and cooked and mended, and dressed wounds, and fanned the coals of the camp-fire, the daughter's shall trifle with books and music, shall be soft and "manicured" and daintily gloved.

It is one of the curious sights in the shops of a little town of frame houses—chiefly of one story, where the work of the house is not unfrequently done by the house-mother, not from poverty, but from the want in a new community of a servant class—to behold about Christmas time the display of sumptuous toilet articles implying hours spent upon the care of the feminine person, especially the feminine hands. This may be one of the indications of the sort of good time that is preparing for the daughters of the town. There are other and more hopeful suggestions, but none that seriously counteract the plainly projected revolt, on the part of the mothers, against a future of physical effort for their girls.

There are girls and girls in the West, of all degrees and styles of prettiness; but here, as elsewhere, and in all her glory, is seen the preeminently pretty girl—who by that patent exists, to herself, to her world, and in the imagination of her parents. The career of this young lady in her native environment is something amazing to persons of a sober imagination as to what should constitute a girl's "good time." The risks that she takes, no less than her extraordinary escapes from the usual consequences, are enough to make one's time-honored principles reel on the judgment seat of propriety.

It is true she does not always escape; but she escapes so often that it is quite impossible to draw any wholesome deductions from her. The only thing that can be done with her is to disapprove of her (with the consciousness that she will not mind in the least) and forgive her, because she knows not what she does. Why should she not take the good time for which, and for little else, she has been trained—the life of pleasure for which some one else pays!

In the novels she goes abroad and marries an English duke; in real life not quite so often; but she is an element of confusion, morally, in all one's prophecies with regard to her. She may have talent and make an actress or a singer, if she has any capacity for work; or she may marry the man she loves and become an exemplary wife. That which in her history appeals most deeply to one's imagination is the contrast between her fortunes and those of her mother.

If Creusa had survived the fall of Troy to accompany Aeneas on his wanderings, with a brood of fast-growing boys and girls, whose travel-worn garments she would have been mending while her hero entertained Dido with the tale of his misfortunes, it is not unlikely that that much-tried woman would have had her ideas as to those qualities in her sex that make for a "good time," and those which mostly go to supply a good time for others. And we may be sure that in planning the futures of the Misses Aeneas she would not have chosen for them the virtues that go unrewarded; rather shall they sit, white-handed and royally clad, and turn a smiling face upon some eloquent adventurer—who shall not be, in all respects, a copy of father Aeneas.

Whoever has lived in the West must have observed that here it is the unexpected that always happens; therefore it will be a mistake to take the pretty girl too seriously, or to regard her as a fatal sign of the tendency of the life she is so fitted to enjoy. She is merely a phase,—an entertaining if not an instructive one,—for which her parents' hard lives and changes of fortune are mainly responsible. Her children will reverse the tendency, or carry it to the point of fracture, where nature steps in, in her significant way, and rubs out the false sum.

But as often as not nature permits the whole illogical proceeding to go on, and nothing happens of all that we have prophesied. We see that the fountain *does* rise higher than its source, that grapes *do* grow upon thorns and figs upon thistles, on some theory of cause and effect unknown to social dynamics.

The pretty girl from the East is hardly enough of a "rusher" to please the young Western masculine taste; but there will not be wanting pilgrims to her shrine. Her Eastern hostess will be proud of the chance to demonstrate that she isn't at all the same sort of pretty girl as her sister of the West,—it is the shades of difference that are vital,—and she will receive an almost pathetic welcome at the hands of her young countrymen, stranded upon cattle-ranches, or in railroad or mining camps, or engaged in hardy attempts of one sort or another wherein there is room for feminine sympathy.

Whether she takes her pleasure actively, in the saddle or in the canoe, or sits out the red summer twilights on the ranch piazza, or tunes her guitar to the ear of a single listener who has ridden over miles of desert plain for the privilege, she will be conscious that she supplies a motive, a new meaning to the life around her.

All this is very dangerous. She is in a world of illusions capable of turning into ordeals for those who put them to the proof—ordeals for which there has been no preparation in the life of the pretty girl. Even the ordeal of taste is not to be despised—taste, which environs and consoles and unites and stimulates women in the East, and which disunites and tortures and sets them at defiance, one with another, in the West.

The life of the men may be large and dramatic, even in failure; but the life of women, here, as everywhere, is made up of very small matters—a badly cooked dinner, a horrible wall-paper, a wind that tears the nerves, a child with something the matter with it which the doctor "doesn't understand," an acquaintance that is just near enough *not* to be a friend: it is the little shocks for which one is never prepared, the little disappointments and insecurities and failures and postponements, the want of completeness and perfection in anything, that harrows a woman's soul and makes her forget, too often, that she has a soul.

So let our pretty Eastern girl remember, before she pledges herself irrevocably to follow the fortunes of some charming young man she has had a "good time" with on the frontier, that—all good times and masculine assurances to the contrary notwithstanding—the frontier is not yet ready for her kind of pretty girl. There is more than one generation between her and the mother of a new community—unless she be minded to offer herself up on the altar of social enlightenment, or for the particular benefit of her particular young man. This is a fate which will always have a baleful fascination for the young woman who is capable of arguing that, if the frontier be not ready for her, the young man is.

The pity of it is that these young gentlemen always will pick out the pretty girl, when a less expensive choice would be so much more serviceable and fit the conditions of their lives so much better. But they are all potential millionaires, these energetic dreamers. They do not pinch themselves in their prospective arrangements, including the prospective wife. Between them both, the girl who expects to have a good time, and the young man who is confident that he can give it to her, there will probably be a good deal to learn.

FURTHER READINGS

Melody Graulich, "Profile of Mary Hallock Foote," *Legacy* 3:2 (1986): 43–52; Shelley Armitage, "The Illustrator as Writer: Mary Hallock Foote and the Myth of the West," in *Under The Sun: Myth and Realism in Western American Literature*, ed. Barbara Howard Meldrum (Whitston Pub. Co., 198): 150–174; Mary Ellen Walsh, "Angle of Repose and the Writings of Mary Hallock Foote: A Source Study," *Critical Essays on Wallace Stegner*, ed. Anthony Arthur (G.K. Hall, 1982): 184–209; Richard W. Etulain, "Mary Hallock Foote, 1847–1938," *American Literary Realism* 5 (Spring 1972): 144–150; Rodman W. Paul, ed., *A Victorian Gentlewoman in the Far West: The Reminiscences of Mary Hallock Foote* (Huntington Library, 1972); Lee Ann Johnson, *Mary Hallock Foote* (Twayne, 1980); Barbara Cragg, ed., *Idaho Stories and Far West Illustrations of Mary Hallock Foote* (Idaho State University, 1988); Rodman W. Paul, *When Culture Came to Boise: Mary Hallock Foote in Idaho* (Idaho State Historical Society, 1977); James H. Maguire, *Mary Hallock Foote* (Boise State College Press, 1972).

Mary Hallock Foote, *Woman and Child.*

Used by permission of Idaho State University-Pocatello.

Helen Hunt Jackson (1830–1885)

Helen Jackson devoted herself to righting the wrongs of the United States government in what she saw as the illegal seizure of Indian lands. She was an Easterner, born in Amherst, Massachusetts, in 1830, and in her early years she was a friend of Emily Dickinson. She married in 1852, but within a decade, her husband and two young sons died, and Jackson was left to find a center for her energies and a way of supporting herself. Like other women of her time, she turned to writing and before long, her poems and sketches appeared in virtually every eastern magazine and newspaper of note. In 1875 she remarried a westerner, William Sharpless Jackson, a banker and railroad promoter of Colorado Springs. When her first husband died, she began to write short pieces for the *New York Evening Post,* for *The Nation,* and for *Hearth and Home,* often publishing under the pseudonym Saxe Holm. When she remarried, she moved west to Colorado and learned of the U.S. government's treatment of the Indian tribes.

When Helen Hunt Jackson wrote the novel *Ramona,* she was already well-known for her nonfiction work, *Century of Dishonor* (1881), which chronicled the plight of the Indians in the West. Jackson used writing as a political platform and her most effective form of "speech," much the same way men ran for political office. In *Ramona,* she took on the struggle of the California Mission Indians, who eked out a meager existence on land left to them after court claims filed by white settlers had stolen most of what they once had. Moved by their plight, Jackson was indefatigable in her research into their claims, working at the Bancroft Library and with land office records in Los Angeles. A single event reported in the newspapers focused her attention. On March 24, 1883, Juan Diego, a Cahuilla Indian, was murdered by Sam Temple, who turned himself in claiming self defense. A Justice of the Peace and a six-man coroner's jury ruled the shooting justifiable homicide. Jackson saw the event as comparable to a case where the murderer of a Winnebago Indian was freed because, said the press, "only" an Indian was killed.

The injustice of Juan Diego's murder fired Jackson's imagination. She wrote her western romance *Ramona* in the hope that it would result in political change. "My life blood went into it—All I had thought, felt, and suffered for five years on the Indian Question." Ramona, which Jackson meant to serve as a fictional counterpart to *Century of Dishonor,* became her best-known fictional work. Often dismissed as "sentimental" fiction, along the lines of Louisa May Alcott's *Little Women, Ramona* is nonetheless an important work of women's writing. In fact, Jackson aimed for the same sort of impact achieved by Stowe's abolitionist novel: "If I could write a story that would do for the Indian a thousandth part of what *Uncle Tom's Cabin* did for the Negro, I would be thankful for the rest of my life."

In the half-Indian and half-Scottish Ramona, Jackson created a sympathetic "mixed-blood" heroine who illustrates both the nobility of non-Anglo cultures and the intolerance of mainstream American society. Ramona, although raised by a Spanish land grant family headed by The Capitan, falls in love with Alessandro Assis, a Cahuilla Indian, and runs away with him. When Alessandro borrows an Anglo man's horse, he is summarily shot as a rustler. Alone, ill, and devastated by Alessandro's death, Ramona is rescued by The Capitan's son, Felipe, who has always loved her. They marry, and, unable to find acceptance of their interracial relationship in the United States, move together to Mexico.

The novel had more than 300 printings and was made into a motion picture at least three different times, but Jackson's hope it would have any effect on government policies did not come to pass. The story of Ramona, however, may have done a good deal to gain public sympathy for Native peoples.

RAMONA

"I thought that the news about our village must have reached you," he said, "and that you would know I had no home, and could not come, to seem to remind you of what you had said. Oh, Señorita, it was little enough I had before to give you! I don't know

---

Helen Hunt Jackson, from *Ramona* (1884).

how I dared to believe that you could come to be with me; but I loved you so much, I had thought of many things I could do; and—" lowering his voice and speaking almost sullenly—"it is the saints, I believe, who have punished me thus for having resolved to leave my people, and take all I had for myself and you. Now they have left me nothing;" and he groaned.

"Who?" cried Ramona. "Was there a battle? Was your father killed?" She was trembling with horror.

"No," answered Alessandro. "There was no battle. There would have been, if I had had my way; but my father implored me not to resist. He said it would only make it worse for us in the end. The sheriff, too, he begged me to let it all go on peaceably, and help him keep the people quiet. He felt terribly to have to do it. It was Mr. Rothsaker, from San Diego. We had often worked for him on his ranch. He knew all about us. Don't you recollect, Señorita, I told you about him,—how fair he always was, and kind too? He has the biggest wheat-ranch in Cajon; we've harvested miles and miles of wheat for him. He said he would have rather died, almost, than have had it to do; but if we resisted, he would have to order his men to shoot. He had twenty men with him. They thought there would be trouble; and well they might,—turning a whole village full of men and women and children out of their houses, and driving them off like foxes. If it had been any man but Mr. Rothsaker, I would have shot him dead, if I had hung for it; but I knew if he thought we must go, there was no help for us."

"But, Alessandro," interrupted Ramona, "I can't understand. Who was it made Mr. Rothsaker do it? Who has the land now?"

"I don't know who they are," Alessandro replied, his voice full of anger and scorn. "They're Americans—eight or ten of them. They all got together and brought a suit, they call it, up in San Francisco; and it was decided in the court that they owned all our land. That was all Mr. Rothsaker could tell about it. It was the law, he said, and nobody could go against the law."

"Oh," said Ramona, "that's the way the Americans took so much of the Señora's land away from her. It was in the court up in San Francisco; and they decided that miles and miles of her land, which the General had always had, was not hers at all. They said it belonged to the United States Government."

"They are a pack of thieves and liars, every one of them!" cried

Alessandro. "They are going to steal all the land in this country; we might all just as well throw ourselves into the sea, and let them have it. My father had been telling me this for years. He saw it coming; but I did not believe him. I did not think men could be so wicked; but he was right."

■ ■ ■

". . . the sheriff's men were in great hurry; they gave no time. They said the people must all be off in two days. Everybody was running hither and thither. Everything out of the houses in piles on the ground. The people took all the roofs off their houses too. They were made of the tule reeds; so they would do again. Oh, Señorita, don't ask me to tell you any more! It is like death. I can't!"

Ramona was crying bitterly. She did not know what to say. What was love, in face of such calamity? What had she to give to a man stricken like this?

"Don't weep, Señorita," said Alessandro, drearily. "Tears kill one, and do no good."

"How long did your father live?" asked Ramona, clasping her arms closer around his neck. They were sitting on the ground now, and Ramona, yearning over Alessandro, as if she were the strong one and he the one to be sheltered, had drawn his head to her bosom, caressing him as if he had been hers for years. Nothing could have so clearly shown his enfeebled and benumbed condition, as the manner in which he received these caresses, which once would have made him beside himself with joy. He leaned against her breast as a child might.

"He! He died only four days ago. I stayed to bury him, and then I came away. I have been three days on the way; the horse, poor beast, is almost weaker than I. The Americans took my horse," Alessandro said.

"Took your horse!" cried Ramona, aghast. "Is that the law, too?"

"So Mr. Rothsaker told me. He said the judge had said he must take enough of our cattle and horses to pay all it had cost for the suit up in San Francisco. They didn't reckon the cattle at what they were worth, I thought; but they said cattle were selling very low now. There were not enough in all the village to pay it, so we had to make it up in horses; and they took mine. I was not there the day they drove the cattle away, or I would have put a ball into Benito's head before any American should ever have had him to ride. But I was over in Pachanga with my father. He would not stir a step for anybody but me; so I led him all the way; and then after he got there he was so ill I never left him a minute. He did not know me any more, nor know anything that had happened. I built a little hut of tule, and he lay on the ground till he died. When I put him in his grave, I was glad."

"In Temecula?" asked Ramona.

"In Temecula!" exclaimed Alessandro, fiercely. "You don't seem to understand, Señorita. We have no right in Temecula, not even to our graveyard full of the dead. Mr. Rothsaker warned us all not to be hanging about there; for he said the men who were coming in were a rough set, and they would shoot any Indian at sight, if they saw him trespassing on their property."

"Their property!" ejaculated Ramona.

"Yes; it is theirs," said Alessandro, doggedly. "That is the law. They've got all the papers to show it.

■ ■ ■

But, my Señorita, it is very dark, I can hardly see your beloved eyes. I think you must not stay longer. Can I go as far as the brook with you, safely, without being seen? The saints bless you, beloved, for coming. I could not have lived, I think, without one more sight of your face;" and, springing to his feet, Alessandro stood waiting for Ramona to move. She remained still. She was in a sore strait. Her heart held but one impulse, one desire,—to go with Alessandro; nothing was apparently farther from his thoughts than this. Could she offer to go? Should she risk laying a burden on him greater than he could bear? If he were indeed a beggar, as he said, would his life be hindered or helped by her? She felt herself strong and able. Work had no terrors for her; privations she knew nothing of, but she felt no fear of them.

"Alessandro!" she said, in a tone which startled him.

"My Señorita!" he said tenderly.

"You have never once called me Ramona."

"I cannot, Señorita!" he replied.

"Why not?"

"I do not know. I sometimes think 'Ramona,'" he added faintly; "but not often. If I think of you by any other name than as my Señorita, it is usually by a name you never heard."

"What is it?" exclaimed Ramona, wonderingly.

"An Indian word, my dearest one, the name of the bird you are like,—the wood-dove. In the Luiseno tongue that is Majel; that was what I thought my people would have called you, if you had come to dwell among us. It is a beautiful name, Señorita, and is like you."

Alessandro was still standing. Ramona rose; coming close to him, she laid both her hands on his breast, and her head on her hands, and said: "Alessandro, I have something to tell you. I am an Indian. I belong to your people."

Alessandro's silence astonished her. "You are surprised," she said. "I thought you would be glad."

"The gladness of it came to me long ago, my Señorita," he said. "I knew it!"

"How?" cried Ramona. "And you never told me, Alessandro!"

"How could I?" he replied. "I dared not. Juan Canito, it was told me."

"Juan Canito!" said Ramona, musingly. "How could he have known?" Then in a few rapid words she told Alessandro all that the Señora had told her. "Is that what Juan Can said?" she asked.

"All except the father's name," stammered Alessandro.

"Who did he say was my father?" she asked.

Alessandro was silent.

"It matters not," said Ramona. "He was wrong. The Señora, of course, knew. He was a friend of hers, and of the Señora Ortegna, to whom he gave me. But I think, Alessandro, I have more of my mother than of my father."

"Yes, you have, my Señorita," replied Alessandro, tenderly. "After I knew it, I then saw what it was in your face had always seemed to me like the faces of my own people."

"Are you not glad, Alessandro?"

"Yes, my Señorita."

What more should Ramona say? Suddenly her heart gave way; and without premeditation, without resolve, almost without consciousness of what she was doing, she flung herself on Alessandro's breast, and cried: "Oh, Alessandro, take me with you! take me with you! I would rather die than have you leave me again!"

There was no real healing for Alessandro. His hurts had gone too deep. His passionate heart, ever secretly brooding on the wrongs he had borne, the hopeless outlook for his people in the future, and most of all on the probable destitution and suffering in store for Ramona, consumed itself as by hidden fires. Speech, complaint, active antagonism, might have saved him; but all these were foreign to his self-contained, reticent, repressed nature. Slowly, so slowly that Ramona could not tell on what hour or what day her terrible fears first changed to an even more terrible certainty, his brain gave way, and the thing, in dread of which he had cried out the morning they left San Pasquale, came upon him. Strangely enough, and mercifully, now that it had really come, he did not know it. He knew that he suddenly came to his consciousness sometimes, and discovered himself in strange and unexplained situations; had no recollection of what had happened for an interval of time, longer or shorter. But he thought it was only a sort of sickness; he did not know that during those intervals his acts were the acts of a madman; never violent, aggressive, or harmful to any one; never destructive. It was piteous to see how in these intervals his delusions were always shaped by the bitterest experiences of his life. Sometimes he fancied that the Americans were pursuing him, or that they were carrying off Ramona, and he was pursuing them. At such times he would run with maniac swiftness for hours, till he fell exhausted on the ground, and slowly regained true consciousness by exhaustion. At other times he believed he owned vast flocks and herds; would enter any enclosure he saw, where there were sheep or cattle, go about among them, speaking of them to passers-by as his own. Sometimes he would try to drive them away; but on being remonstrated with, would bewilderedly give up the attempt. Once he suddenly found himself in the road driving a small flock of goats, whose he knew not, nor whence he got them. Sitting down by the roadside, he buried his head in his hands. "What has happened to my memory?" he said. "I must be ill of a fever!" As he sat there, the goats, of their own accord, turned and trotted back into a corral near by, the owner of which stood, laughing, on his doorsill; and when Alessandro came up, said goodnaturedly, "All right, Alessandro! I saw you driving off my goats, but I thought you'd bring 'em back."

Everybody in the valley knew him, and knew his condition. It did not interfere with his capacity as a worker, for the greater part of the time. He was one of the best shearers in the region, the best horse-breaker; and his services were always in demand, spite of the risk there was of his having at any time one of these attacks of wandering. His absences were a great grief to Ramona, not only from the loneliness in which it left her, but from the anxiety she felt lest his mental disorder might at any time take a more violent and dangerous shape. This anxiety was all the more harrowing because she must keep it locked in her own breast, her wise and loving instinct telling her that nothing could be more fatal to him than the knowledge of his real condition. More than once he reached home, breathless, panting, the sweat rolling off his face, crying aloud, "The Americans have found us out, Majella! They were on the trail! I baffled them. I came up another way." At such times she would soothe him like a child; persuade him to lie down and rest; and when he waked and wondered why he was so tired, she would say, "You were all out of breath when you came in, dear. You must not climb so fast; it is foolish to tire one's self so."

In these days Ramona began to think earnestly of Felipe. She believed Alessandro might be cured. A wise doctor could surely do something for him. If Felipe knew what sore straits she was in, Felipe would help her.

■ ■ ■

The baby had thrived; as placid, laughing a little thing as if its mother had never known sorrow. "One would think she had suckled pain," thought Ramona, "so constantly have I grieved this year; but the Virgin has kept her well."

If prayers could compass it, that would surely have been so; for night and day the devout, trusting, and contrite Ramona had knelt before the Madonna and told her golden beads, till they were well-nigh worn smooth of all their delicate chasing.

At midsummer was to be a fête in the Saboba village, and the San Bernardino priest would come there. This would be the time to take the baby down to be christened; this also would be the time to send a letter to Felipe, enclosed in one to Aunt Ri, who would send it for her from San Bernardino. Ramona felt half guilty as she sat plotting what she should say and how she should send it,—she, who had never had in her loyal, transparent breast one thought secret from Alessandro since they were wedded. But it was all for his sake. When he was well, he would thank her.

■ ■ ■

All her preparations were completed, and it was yet not noon. She seated herself on the veranda to watch for Alessandro, who had been two days away, and was to have returned the previous evening, to make ready for the trip to Saboba. She was disquieted at his failure to return at the appointed time. As the hours crept on and he did not come, her anxiety increased. The sun had gone more than an hour past the midheavens before he came. He had ridden fast; she had heard the quick strokes of the horse's hoofs on the ground before she saw him. "Why comes he riding like that?" she thought, and ran to meet him. As he drew near, she saw to her surprise that he was riding a new horse. "Why, Alessandro!" she cried. "What horse is this?"

He looked at her bewilderedly, then at the horse. True; it was not his own horse! He struck his hand on his forehead, endeavoring to collect his thoughts. "Where is my horse, then?" he said.

"My God! Alessandro," cried Ramona. "Take the horse back instantly. They will say you stole it."

"But I left my pony there in the corral," he said. "They will know I did not mean to steal it. How could I ever have made the mistake? I recollect nothing, Majella. I must have had one of the sicknesses."

■ ■ ■

When she went into the house, Alessandro was asleep. Ramona glanced at the sun. It was already in the western sky. By no possibility could Alessandro go to Farrar's and back before dark. She was on the point of waking him, when a furious barking from Capitan and the other dogs roused him instantly from his sleep, and springing to his feet, he ran out to see what it meant. In a moment more Ramona followed,—only a moment, hardly a moment; but when she reached the threshold, it was to hear a gunshot, to see Alessandro fall to the ground, to see, in the same second, a ruffianly man leap from his horse, and standing over Alessandro's body, fire his pistol again, once, twice, into the forehead, cheek. Then with a volley of oaths, each word of which seemed to Ramona's reeling senses to fill the air with a sound like thunder, he untied the black horse from the post where Ramona had fastened him, and leaping into his saddle again, galloped away, leading the horse. As he rode away, he shook his fist at Ramona, who was kneeling on the ground, striving to lift Alessandro's head, and to stanch the blood flowing from the ghastly wounds. "That'll teach you damned Indians to leave off stealing our horses!" he cried, and with another volley of terrible oaths was out of sight.

With a calmness which was more dreadful than any wild outcry of grief, Ramona sat on the ground by Alessandro's body, and held his hands in hers. There was nothing to be done for him. The first shot had been fatal, close to his heart,—the murderer aimed well; the after-shots, with the pistol, were from mere wanton brutality. After a few seconds Ramona rose, went into the house, brought out the white altar-cloth, and laid it over the mutilated face. As she did this, she recalled words she had heard Father Salvierderra quote as having been said by Father Junipero, when one of the Franciscan Fathers had been massacred by the Indians, at San Diego, "Thank God!" he said, "the ground is now watered by the blood of a martyr!"

■ ■ ■

Taking the baby in her arms, she knelt by Alessandro, and kissing him, whispered, "Farewell, my beloved. I will not be long gone. I go to bring friends." As she set off, swiftly running, Capitan, who had been lying by Alessandro's side, uttering heart-rending howls, bounded to his feet to follow her. "No, Capitan," she said; and leading him back to the body, she took his head in her hands, looked into his eyes, and said, "Capitan, watch here." With a whimpering cry, he licked her hands, and stretched himself on the ground. He understood, and would obey; but his eyes followed her wistfully till she disappeared from sight.

■ ■ ■

Alessandro had warm friends among them, and the news that he had been murdered, and that his wife had run all the way down the mountain, with her baby in her arms, for help, went like wild-fire through the place. The people gathered in an excited group around the house where Ramona had taken refuge. She was lying, half unconscious, on a bed. As soon as she had gasped out her terrible story, she had fallen forward on the floor, fainting, and the baby had been snatched from her arms just in time to save it. She did not seem to miss the child; had not asked for it, or noticed it when it was brought to the bed. A merciful oblivion seemed to be fast stealing over her senses. But she had spoken words enough to set the village in a blaze of excitement. It ran higher and higher. Men were everywhere mounting their horses,—some to go up and bring Alessandro's body down; some organizing a party to go at once to Jim Farrar's house and shoot him: these were the younger men, friends of Alessandro. Earnestly the aged Capitan of the village implored them to refrain from such violence.

"Why should ten be dead instead of one, my sons?" he said. "Will you leave your wives and your children like his? The whites will kill us all if you lay hands on the man. Perhaps they themselves will punish him."

■ ■ ■

As Farrar rode slowly down the mountain, leading his recovered horse, he revolved in his thoughts what course to pursue. A few years before, he would have gone home, no more disquieted at having killed an Indian than if he had killed a fox or a wolf. But things were different now. This Agent, that the Government had taken it into its head to send out to look after the Indians, had made it hot, the other day, for some fellows in San Bernardino who had maltreated an Indian; he had even gone so far as to arrest several liquor-dealers for simply selling whiskey to Indians. If he were to take this case of Alessandro's in hand, it might be troublesome. Farrar concluded that his wisest course would be to make a show of good conscience and fair-dealing by delivering himself up at once to the nearest justice of the peace, as having killed a man in self-defence. Accordingly he rode straight to the house of a Judge Wells, a few miles below Saboba, and said that he wished to surrender himself as having committed "justifiable homicide" on an Indian, or Mexican, he did not know which, who had stolen his horse. He told a plausible story. He professed not to know the man, or the place; but did not explain how it was, that, knowing neither, he had gone so direct to the spot.

He said: "I followed the trail for some time, but when I reached a turn, I came into a sort of blind trail, where I lost the track. I think the horse had been led up on hard sod, to mislead any one on the track. I pushed on, crossed the creek, and soon found the tracks again in soft ground. This part of the mountain was perfectly unknown to me, and very wild. Finally I came to a ridge, from which I looked down on a little ranch. As I came near the house, the dogs began to bark, just as I discovered my horse tied to a tree. Hearing the dogs, an Indian, or Mexican, I could not tell which, came out of the house, flourishing a large knife. I called out to him, 'Whose horse is that?' He answered in Spanish, 'It is mine.' 'Where did you get it?' I asked. 'In San Jacinto,' was his reply. As he still came towards me, brandishing the knife, I drew my gun, and said, 'Stop, or I'll shoot!' He did not stop, and I fired; still he did not stop, so I fired again; and as he did not fall, I knocked him down with the butt of my gun. After he was down, I shot him twice with my pistol."

The duty of a justice in such a case as this was clear. Taking the prisoner into custody, he sent out messengers to summon a jury of six men to hold inquest on the body of said Indian, or Mexican; and early the next morning, led by Farrar, they set out for the mountain. When they reached the ranch, the body had been removed; the house was locked; no signs left of the tragedy of the day before, except a few blood-stains on the ground, where Alessandro had fallen. Farrar seemed greatly relieved at this unexpected phase of affairs. However, when he found that Judge Wells, instead of attempting to return to the valley that night, proposed to pass the night at a ranch only a few miles from the Cahuilla village, he became almost hysterical with fright. He declared that the Cahuillas would surely come and murder him in the night, and begged piteously that the men would all stay with him to guard him.

At midnight Judge Wells was roused by the arrival of the Capitan and head men of the Cahuilla village. They had heard of his arrival with his jury, and they had come to lead them to their village, where the body of the murdered man lay. They were greatly distressed on learning that they ought not to have removed the body from the spot where the death had taken place, and that now no inquest could be held.

Judge Wells himself, however, went back with them, saw the body, and heard the full account of the murder as given by Ramona on her first arrival. Nothing more could now be learned from her, as she was in high fever and delirium; knew no one, not even her baby when they laid it on her breast. She lay restlessly tossing from side to side, talking incessantly, clasping her rosary in her hands, and constantly mingling snatches of prayers with cries for Alessandro and Felipe; the only token of consciousness she gave was to clutch the rosary wildly, and sometimes hide it in her bosom, if they attempted to take it from her.

Judge Wells was a frontiersman, and by no means sentimentally inclined; but the tears stood in his eyes as he looked at the unconscious Ramona.

Farrar had pleaded that the preliminary hearing might take place immediately; but after this visit to the village, the judge refused his request, and appointed the trial a week from that day, to give time for Ramona to recover, and appear as a witness. He impressed upon the Indians as strongly as he could the importance of having her appear. It was evident that Farrar's account of the affair was false from first to last. Alessandro had no knife. He had not had time to go many steps from the door; the volley of oaths, and the two shots almost simultaneously, were what Ramona heard as she ran to the door. Alessandro could not have spoken many words.

The day for the hearing came. Farrar had been, during the interval, in a merely nominal custody; having been allowed to go about his business, on his own personal guarantee of appearing in time for the trial. It was with a strange mixture of regret and relief that Judge Wells saw the hour of the trial arrive, and not a witness on the ground except Farrar himself. That Farrar was a brutal ruffian, the whole country knew. This last outrage was only one of a long series; the judge would have been glad to have committed him for trial, and have seen him get his deserts. But San Jacinto Valley, wild, sparsely settled as it was, had yet as fixed standards and criterions of popularity as the most civilized of communities could show; and to betray sympathy with Indians was more than any man's political head was worth. The word "justice" had lost its meaning, if indeed it ever had any, so far as they were concerned.

FURTHER READINGS
Antoinette May, "Helen of California," in *The Annotated Ramona* (Wide World Publishing, 1989); Rosemary Whitaker, *Helen Hunt Jackson* (Boise State University Press, 1987); Antoinette May, *Helen Hunt Jackson: A Lonely Voice of Conscience* (Chronicle Books, 1987); John R. Byers, Jr., "The Indian Matter of Helen Hunt Jackson's *Ramona*: From Fact to Fiction," *American Indian Quarterly* 11 (Winter 1975/76): 331–346; Evelyn I. Banning, Helen Hunt Jackson (Vanguard, 1973); Ruth Odell, *Helen Hunt Jackson (H.H.)* (D. Appleton-Century Co., 1939).

Photograph of Ramona Lubo, said to be the model for *Ramona*, on the Cahuilla Reservation.

Courtesy of Seaver Center for Western History Research,
Los Angeles County Museum for Natural History.

Mourning Dove (Christal Quintasket) (1888–1936)

Mourning Dove was born in 1888 near Bonner's Ferry, Idaho, the daughter of an Okanogan father and a Scho-yel-pi or Colville mother. Raised with the English name Christal Quintasket and the Okanogan name Hum-ishu-ma (Mourning Dove), Mourning Dove was raised mostly by her paternal grandmother, who had married an Irish employee of the Hudson's Bay Company, who deserted her. White men's betrayals of Indian women later became an important theme in her works, including *Cogewea, the Half-Blood.*

In addition to her grandmother's teachings, Mourning Dove studied for three years in the Sacred Heart Convent in Ward, Washington, and briefly attended U.S. government Indian schools before enrolling in a business school where she learned typing and improved her English.

Mourning Dove married twice, although she never had children. With her second husband, she became a migrant farm laborer, following the harvests of apples and hops throughout the Pacific Northwest. Carrying along her typewriter, Mourning Dove worked steadily on her writing. In 1914, she met Lucullus V. McWhorter, founder of the *American Archaeologist,* who had a deep impact on the novel *Cogewea* as it was being written, inserting ethnographic explanations into it as well as critiques of Christian hypocrisy and government corruption. With McWhorter's assistance, Mourning Dove published *Cogewea* in 1927, and *Coyote Stories* in 1933. Mourning Dove died in 1936.

Cogewea, the first published novel by a North American Native American woman, is the story of three "half-blood" sisters, and the varying strategies adopted by mixed-blood women. One sister assimilates to white culture by marrying a white man and leaving Native American culture behind; another rejects her white background and embraces the most traditional stances in resistance to any sort of cultural change; the third, Cogewea, tries to live in both worlds, but finds herself always an outsider, asked repeatedly to choose her "real" identity.

COGEWEA THE HALF-BLOOD

It was sunset on the river Pend d'Oreille. The last rays of the day-God, glinting through the tangled vines screening the great porch of the homestead of the Horseshoe Brand Ranch, fell upon a face of rare type. The features were rather prominent and well defined. The rich olive complexion, the grave, pensive countenance, proclaimed a proud descent from the only true American—the Indian. Of mixed blood, was Cogewea; a "breed"!—the socially ostracized of two races. Her eyes of the deepest jet, sparkled, when under excitement, like the ruby's fire. Hair of the same hue was as lustrous as the raven's wing, falling when loose, in great billowy folds, enveloping her entire form. Her voice was low and musical, with a laugh to madden the gods.

Cogewea's mother had died when she was but a small child, and her father, Bertram McDonnald, had followed the gold rush to Alaska, leaving her and two sisters to be cared for by the old Indian grandmother. Through the aid of friends—an inherent principle in Indian life—the wolf was kept from the tepee door. During all the long years no word had come from the silent North, and it was supposed that this father had succumbed to death in the realms of storms and ghastly whiteness.

Ofttimes the *camas* and *salmon* were not plentiful in the smoky lodge, and the little orphans were no strangers to hunger. But despite this, the children were endowed with good health and vigorous constitutions, due to the devoted care of the primitive-minded grandmother. Life in the open, the sweat house and cold river baths, had stamped their every fiber with bounding vitality.

Cogewea, more than her two sisters, was own-headed and at times wilful. She could ride well and made long strolls into the bordering mountains. These runaway-trips were not unattended with danger and consequently were a source of considerable solicitude on the part of the old grandparent. Unlike other children, the repeated warnings that *Sne-nah* would catch her, had no effect. Contrary to all precedent, the little "breed" defied this dreaded devourer of children by extending her rambles farther and still farther into the luring wilder-

Morning Dove (Christal Quintasket), "Cogewea The Half-Blood," from *Cogewea* (1927).

ness. Like some creature born of the wild, neither fancied nor actual dangers deterred her from her set course.

At last, notwithstanding her antipathy to the culture of the pale face, the aged squaw was constrained to listen to the pleadings of the good Sisters, and at the age of twelve the little "woods-savage" and her two sisters were placed in the convent school. This measure was resorted to only after Cogewea returned one evening, her horse bearing an ugly cut on its hip, received from the claws of a cougar. The fierce animal had leaped from a tree and the child escaped only through the agility of her mount. With a mighty bound the horse had thwarted the hungry cat of its prey, with no other injury than the knife-like wound, neither deep nor serious.

The weaning process from the old life was slow, but in time Cogewea adapted herself to the new conditions and was an apt student. She seemed to imbibe knowledge, and not content with the scant learning there afforded, and looking to the future, she crossed the Continent and entered the Carlisle Indian School, from which she graduated with high honors at the age of twenty-one.

Such was Cogewea: "Chip-munk," of the Okanogans; the "breed" girl with the hypnotic eyes, who stood dreaming on the vine-clad porch of the "H-B" Ranch, the home of her oldest sister, Julia Carter. An ambitious girl, and, although having passed through the mill of social refinement, she was still—thanks to early training—whole hearted and a lover of nature. The wild appealed to her. Since her return from school her every day companions had been the cowboys of the range. With them or alone, she took many a thrilling dash on the back of a Wan-a-wish, across the low swelling plains or among the buttes and coulees of the broken uplands. Fond of books, the best authors claimed her attention when she was not riding or helping with the routine work of the house.

Cogewea was liked by all the rangers. She was close to their rough natures, for had she not been nurtured by the same elements? She commanded their respect as but few women of her blood could command it. While ready to die for her, they knew the demarcation between harmless friendship and gross familiarity. She understood the "beast" in man and how to subdue it with the same daring confidence which had characterized her younger days of mountain riding.

The sun dipped lower, as Cogewea, gazing out over the undulating hills to the west, dreamed on. What had the future in store for her? What would it bring? Would it, through her, illuminate the pathway of others? Could she fill any sphere of usefulness; or would she, like the race whose hue she had inherited, be brushed aside, crushed and defeated by the cold dictates of the "superior" earthlords? She had struggled hard to equip herself for a useful career, but seemingly there was but one trail for her—that of mediocrity and obscurity. Regarded with suspicion by the Indian; shunned by the Caucasian; where was there any place for the despised breed!

The girl's reveries were broken as the range riders burst into view over a distant swell. She saw them thrown into sharp silhouette against the sun, leaving its last crimson touch to plain and the beautiful Pend d'-Oreille, as its blue waters swept southward around the Horseshoe, from which the ranch derived its name. She thought of the canoe which ruffled its bosom no more. The huge Clay Banks on its eastern shore loomed grey and sombre in the shadowy gloaming, never again to reflect gleam of signal or camp-fire. The buffalo no longer drank of its cooling flood, nor thundered over the echoing plain.

Cogewea turned to the east, where the great Rockies, towering and majestic, were still bathed in the ruddy glow of the sunset. For a moment the topmost pinnacle stood clothed in scarlet flame, then the dusky wing of night, sweeping from eastern realms, fell darkening over all. Cogewea imagined that the time-grizzled peak beckoned a parting farewell, and a chill of loneliness struck to her heart. The world was receding!—and she buried her face in her hands to suppress the sob which welled to her lips. Then the sound of hoof-beats broke upon her ear as the riders came cantering to the barn corrals.

There is magic in the rhythmical chime of hoof-music— inspiration—exhilaration. Instantly the girl of moods forgot her brooding and with light-hearted impulsiveness, ran down the intervening slope to where the five cowboys were unsaddling their mounts.

No prudishness marked the movements of this strange, self-reliant girl. The product of an epoch, false modesty—the subterfuge of the weak—had no part in her makeup. Before reaching the gate she was greeted with the cheery: *"Hell-o Sis"* from James

LaGrinder, the ranch foreman. Cogewea returned the greeting in the same free way. Jim, as he was commonly called, was also a half-blood. He was a tall, spare built man of sinewy limb, wiry in action. His black eye was keen and restless. A scanty mustache adorned his sensitive lip, which he was wont to pull and twist when in deep thought or anger. When this danger signal was observed, the "boys" steered clear of their foreman. With strong, well-chiseled features, his bronze face was handsome for one of its type. As a rider, he had no equal on the range and was an artist with the rope. Quick-tempered and a dead shot, with his suspicious Indian nature, he was not regarded as a safe man to cross; although the handle of his six-shooter at his belt bore no notches. His schooling was limited to indifferent reading and writing. Twenty-seven years of age, with a life on the range, he was a typical Westerner—a rough nugget—but with an unconscious dignity peculiar to the Indian. All in all, Jim was hardly the social equal of the Carlisle maiden. He assumed the role of a "brother protectorate" over Cogewea, hence the "Sis" with which he addressed her. He betrayed his love for her in his own simple way, which at times appeared to the other boys as not exactly brotherly. Cogewea had not resented this attention. She was coquettishly blind and had encouraged poor Jim with her jokes which he took as reciprocal. Had she realized the true emotions in that strong impulsive bosom, she certainly would have been more careful. She was toying with fire.

Cogewea waited till Jim had his horse rubbed-down and stabled before they walked to the house side by side, under the knowing glances of the other riders. "Lucky dog," declared the white owner of the stock ranch, John Carter, who regarded Jim as a suitable match for his favorite sister-in-law. He hoped some day that his foreman would become a junior partner of the "H-B" brand.

John Carter was of Scotch descent, a well built man of middle age, good natured and amiable. Marrying his half-blood wife when she was but sixteen, he was more of a father to Cogewea than otherwise. Nor was she slow to take advantage of his fondness for her and was seldom refused any favor she might ask. Her escapades sometimes annoyed him, but she never failed to get back into his good graces with an additional link forged about his great, affectionate heart.

FURTHER READINGS

Mourning Dove, *Mourning Dove: A Salishan Autobiography*, ed. Jay Miller (University of Nebraska Press, 1990); Kathleen M. Donovan, "Owning Mourning Dove: The Dynamics of Authenticity," in *Feminist Readings of Native American Literature: Coming to Voice* (University of Arizona Press, 1998); Alanna Brown, "Looking Through The Glass Darkly: The Editorialized Mourning Dove," in *New Voices in Native American Literary Criticism*, ed. Arnold Krupat (Smithsonian Institution Press, 1993).

Katherine Anne Porter
(1890–1980)

The Porters left Kentucky in 1857 with "1 slave age 38 male, 1 slave age 21 female/ 1 slave age 4 male/ and 1 slave age 1 Male." They moved to Indian Creek, in Brown County, Texas where Katherine Anne was born in 1890 into a "god-forsaken, wilderness of lions, monkeys and snakes." Her given name was Callie Russell for a childhood friend of the mother. Texas was both heartache and home, a landscape filled with memories of family and of grief.

Porter began writing for newspapers in Denver and Chicago and published her first story, "Maria Conception" in 1922. *Flowering Judas* (1930) was followed by a series of collections of her short stories, *Hacienda* (1934), *Noon Wine* (1937) and *Pale Horse, Pale Rider* (1939). The life she led had something of the itinerant about it. She supported herself by fellowships, by retreats at the writers colony at Yaddo, at a series of universities as writer-in-residence, as an uncredited screenwriter in Hollywood. She had the curious ability to set herself in the midst of historical events; she was in Greenwich Village in the 1920s, in Mexico City during the Obregón revolution, in Berlin during Hitler's rise to power, in Paris just before the outbreak of World War II. Her biographer notes that when she was eighty-two, she was at Cape Canaveral for the launch of the rocket to the moon, covering the event for *Playboy* magazine.

Porter was a writer of subtlety, one for whom landscape was always full of suggestion and mystery. The title of the collection which contained "The Journey," *The Leaning Tower* (1944), may have come from Canto XXXIII of Dante's *Inferno*, and the story of Ugolino of Pisa, who starved to death in a tower. But "The Journey" is of two old women, one black and one white, talking about "god, about heaven, about planting a new hedge of rose bushes ." Time has erased color, and even the family about them have become a "tangled world, half white, half black, mingling steadily and the confusion growing ever deeper."

Her first novel, *Ship of Fools* (1962), was a tale of an ocean voyage of a group of Germans going back to Germany in 1931, after living as exiles in Mexico. Identities were ambiguous, and place had given way to changing and placeless ocean. She won both a Pulitzer Prize and a National Book Award, but many among her readers have always preferred the stories of Texas and the landscapes close to her roots have always held particular luminosity.

Although Porter is not always included in lists of "western" writers, her Texan roots shine through, as they do in the story of two old women.

THE JOURNEY

In their later years, the Grandmother and old Nannie used to sit together for some hours every day over their sewing. They shared a passion for cutting scraps of the family finery, hoarded for fifty years, into strips and triangles, and fitting them together again in a carefully disordered patchwork, outlining each bit of velvet or satin or taffeta with a running briar stitch in clear lemon-colored silk floss. They had contrived enough bed and couch covers, table spreads, dressing table scarfs, to have furnished forth several households. Each piece as it was finished was lined with yellow silk, folded, and laid away in a chest, never again to see the light of day. The Grandmother was the great-granddaughter of Kentucky's most famous pioneer: he had, while he was surveying Kentucky, hewed out rather competently a rolling pin for his wife. This rolling pin was the Grandmother's irreplaceable treasure. She covered it with an extraordinarily complicated bit of patchwork, added golden tassels to the handles, and hung it in a conspicuous place in her room. She was the daughter of a notably heroic captain in the War of 1812. She had his razors in a shagreen case and a particularly severe-looking daguerreotype taken in his old age, with his chin in a tall stock and his black satin waistcoat smoothed over a still-handsome military chest. So she fitted a patchwork case over the shagreen and made a sort of envelope of cut velvet and violet satin, held together with briar stitching, to contain the portrait. The rest of her handiwork she put away, to the relief of her grandchildren, who had arrived at the awkward age when Grandmother's quaint old-fashioned ways caused them acute discomfort.

Katherine Anne Porter, "The Journey," from *The Leaning Tower* (1944).

In the summer the women sat under the mingled trees of the side garden, which commanded a view of the east wing, the front and back porches, a good part of the front garden and a corner of the small fig grove. Their choice of this location was a part of their domestic strategy. Very little escaped them: a glance now and then would serve to keep them fairly well informed as to what was going on in the whole place. It is true they had not seen Miranda the day she pulled up the whole mint bed to give to a pleasant strange young woman who stopped and asked her for a sprig of fresh mint. They had never found out who stole the giant pomegranates growing too near the fence: they had not been in time to stop Paul from setting himself on fire while experimenting with a miniature blowtorch, but they had been on the scene to extinguish him with rugs, to pour oil on him, and lecture him. They never saw Maria climbing trees, a mania she had to indulge or pine away, for she chose tall ones on the opposite side of the house. But such casualties were so minor a part of the perpetual round of events that they did not feel defeated nor that their strategy was a failure. Summer, in many ways so desirable a season, had its drawbacks. The children were everywhere at once and the Negroes loved lying under the hackberry grove back of the barns playing seven-up, and eating watermelons. The summer house was in a small town a few miles from the farm, a compromise between the rigorously ordered house in the city and the sprawling old farmhouse which Grandmother had built with such pride and pains. It had, she often said, none of the advantages of either country or city, and all the discomforts of both. But the children loved it.

During the winters in the city, they sat in Grandmother's room, a large squarish place with a small coal grate. All the sounds of life in the household seemed to converge there, echo, retreat, and return. Grandmother and Aunt Nannie knew the whole complicated code of sounds, could interpret and comment on them by an exchange of glances, a lifted eyebrow, or a tiny pause in their talk.

They talked about the past, really—always about the past. Even the future seemed like something gone and done with when they spoke of it. It did not seem an extension of their past, but a repetition of it. They would agree that nothing remained of life as they had known it, the world was changing swiftly, but by the mysterious logic of hope they insisted that each change was probably the last;

or if not, a series of changes might bring them, blessedly, back full-circle to the old ways they had known. Who knows why they loved their past? It had been bitter for them both, they had questioned the burdensome rule they lived by every day of their lives, but without rebellion and without expecting an answer. This unbroken thread of inquiry in their minds contained no doubt as to the utter rightness and justice of the basic laws of human existence, founded as they were on God's plan; but they wondered perpetually, with only a hint now and then to each other of the uneasiness of their hearts, how so much suffering and confusion could have been built up and maintained on such a foundation. The Grandmother's rôle was authority, she knew that; it was her duty to portion out activities, to urge or restrain where necessary, to teach morals, manners, and religion, to punish and reward her own household according to a fixed code. Her own doubts and hesitations she concealed, also, she reminded herself, as a matter of duty. Old Nannie had no ideas at all as to her place in the world. It had been assigned to her before birth, and for her daily rule she had all her life obeyed the authority nearest to her.

So they talked about God, about heaven, about planting a new hedge of rose bushes, about the new ways of preserving fruit and vegetables, about eternity and their mutual hope that they might pass it happily together, and often a scrap of silk under their hands would start them on long trains of family reminiscences. They were always amused to notice again how the working of their memories differed in such important ways. Nannie could recall names to perfection; she could always say what the weather had been like on all important occasions, what certain ladies had worn, how handsome certain gentlemen had been, what there had been to eat and drink. Grandmother had masses of dates in her mind, and no memories attached to them: her memories of events seemed detached and floating beyond time. For example, the 26th of August, 1871, had been some sort of red-letter day for her. She had said to herself then that never would she forget that date; and indeed, she remembered it well, but she no longer had the faintest notion what had happened to stamp it on her memory. Nannie was no help in the matter; she had nothing to do with dates. She did not know the year of her birth, and would never have had a birthday to celebrate if Grandmother had not, when she was still Miss Sophia Jane, aged ten, opened a calendar at random, closed her eyes, and marked a date unseen with a pen. So it turned out that Nannie's birthday thereafter fell on June 11, and the year, Miss Sophia Jane decided, should be 1827, her own birth-year, making Nannie just three months younger than her mistress. Sophia Jane then made an entry of Nannie's birth-date in the family Bible, inserting it just below her own. "Nannie Gay," she wrote, in stiff careful letters, "(black)," and though there was some uproar when this was discovered, the ink was long since sunk deeply into the paper, and besides no one was really upset enough to have it scratched out. There it remained, one of their pleasantest points of reference.

They talked about religion, and the slack way the world was going nowadays, the decay of behavior, and about the younger children, whom these topics always brought at once to mind. On these subjects they were firm, critical, and unbewildered. They had received educations which furnished them an assured habit of mind about all the important appearances of life, and especially about the rearing of young. They relied with perfect acquiescence on the dogma that children were conceived in sin and brought forth in iniquity. Childhood was a long state of instruction and probation for adult life, which was in turn a long, severe, undeviating devotion to duty, the largest part of which consisted in bringing up children. The young were difficult, disobedient, and tireless in wrongdoing, apt to turn unkind and undutiful when they grew up, in spite of all one had done for them, or had tried to do: for small painful doubts rose in them now and again when they looked at their completed works. Nannie couldn't abide her new-fangled grandchildren. "Wuthless, shiftless lot, jes plain scum, Miss Sophia Jane; I cain't undahstand it aftah all the raisin' dey had."

The Grandmother defended them, and dispraised her own second generation—heartily, too, for she sincerely found grave faults in them—which Nannie defended in turn. "When they are little, they trample on your feet, and when they grow up they trample on your heart." This was about all there was to say about children in any generation, but the fascination of the theme was endless. They said it thoroughly over and over with thousands of small variations, with always an example among their own friends or family connections to prove it. They had enough material of their own. Grandmother had borne eleven children, Nannie thirteen. They boasted of it. Grandmother would say, "I am the mother of eleven children," in a faintly amazed tone, as if she hardly expected to be believed, or could even quite believe it herself. But she could still point to nine of them. Nannie had lost ten of hers. They were all buried in Kentucky. Nannie never doubted or expected anyone else to doubt she had children. Her boasting was of another order. "Thirteen of 'em," she would say, in an appalled voice, "yas, my Lawd and my Redeemah, thirteen!"

The friendship between the two old women had begun in early childhood, and was based on what seemed even to them almost mythical events. Miss Sophia Jane, a prissy, spoiled five-year-old, with tight black ringlets which were curled every day on a stick, with her stiffly pleated lawn pantalettes and tight bodice, had run to meet her returning father, who had been away buying horses and Negroes. Sitting on his arm, clasping him around the neck, she had watched the wagons filing past on the way to the barns and quarters. On the floor of the first wagon sat two blacks, male and female, holding between them a scrawny, half-naked black child, with a round nubbly head and fixed bright monkey eyes. The baby Negro had a potbelly and her arms were like sticks from wrist to shoulder. She clung with narrow, withered, black leather fingers to her parents, a hand on each.

"I want the little monkey," said Sophia Jane to her father, nuzzling his cheek and pointing. "I want that one to play with."

Behind each wagon came two horses in lead, but in the second wagon there was a small shaggy pony with a thatch of mane over his eyes, a long tail like a brush, a round, hard barrel of a body. He was standing in straw to the knees, braced firmly in a padded stall with a Negro holding his bridle. "Do you see that?" asked her father. "That's for you. High time you learned to ride."

Sophia Jane almost leaped from his arm for joy. She hardly recognized her pony or her monkey the next day, the one clipped and sleek, the other clean in new blue cotton. For a while she could not decide which she loved more, Nannie or Fiddler. But Fiddler did not wear well. She outgrew him in a year, saw him pass without regret to a small brother, though she refused to allow him to be called Fiddler any longer. That name she reserved for a long series of saddle horses. She had named the first in honor of Fiddler Gay, an old Negro who made the music for dances and parties. There was only one Nannie and she outwore Sophia Jane. During all their lives together it was not so much a question of affection between them as a simple matter of being unable to imagine getting on without each other.

Nannie remembered well being on a shallow platform out in front of a great building in a large busy place, the first town she had ever seen. Her father and mother were with her, and there was a thick crowd around them. There were several other small groups of Negroes huddled together with white men bustling them about now and then. She had never seen any of these faces before, and she' never saw but one of them again. She remembered it must have been summer, because she was not shivering with cold in her cotton shift. For one thing, her bottom was still burning from a spanking someone (it might have been her mother) had given her just before they got on the platform, to remind her to keep still. Her mother and father were field hands, and had never lived in white folks' houses. A tall gentleman with a long narrow face and very high curved nose, wearing a great-collared blue coat and immensely long light-colored trousers (Nannie could close her eyes and see him again, clearly, as he looked that day) stepped up near them suddenly, while a great hubbub rose. The red-faced man standing on a stump beside them shouted and droned, waving his arms and pointing at Nannie's father and mother. Now and then the tall gentleman raised a finger, without looking at the black people on the platform. Suddenly the shouting died down, the tall gentleman walked over and said to Nannie's father and mother, "Well, Eph! Well, Steeny! Mister Jimmerson comin' to get you in a minute." He poked Nannie in the stomach with a thickly gloved forefinger. "Regular crowbait," he said to the auctioneer. "I should have had lagniappe with this one."

"A pretty worthless article right now, sir, I agree with you," said the auctioneer, "but it'll grow out of it. As for the team, you won't find a better, I swear."

"I've had an eye on 'em for years," said the tall gentleman, and walked away, motioning as he went to a fat man sitting on a wagon tongue, spitting quantities of tobacco juice. The fat man rose and came over to Nannie and her parents.

Nannie had been sold for twenty dollars: a gift, you might say, hardly sold at all. She learned that a really choice slave sometimes cost more than a thousand dollars. She lived to hear slaves brag about how much they had cost. She had not known how little she fetched on the block until her own mother taunted her with it. This was after Nannie had gone to live for good at the big house, and her mother and father were still in the fields. They lived and worked and died there. A good worming had cured Nannie's pot-belly, she thrived on plentiful food and a species of kindness not so indulgent, maybe, as that given to the puppies; still it more than ful-filled her notions of good fortune.

The old women often talked about how strangely things come out in this life. The first owner of Nannie and her parents had gone, Sophia Jane's father said, hog-wild about Texas. It was a new Land of Promise, in 1832. He had sold out his farm and four slaves in Kentucky to raise the money to take a great twenty-mile stretch of land in southwest Texas. He had taken his wife and two young chil-dren and set out, and there had been no more news of him for many years. When Grandmother arrived in Texas forty years later, she found him a prosperous ranchman and district judge. Much later, her youngest son met his granddaughter, fell in love with her, and married her—all in three months.

The judge, by then eighty-five years old, was uproarious and festive at the wedding. He reeked of corn liquor, swore by God every other breath, and was rearing to talk about the good old times in Kentucky. The Grandmother showed Nannie to him. "Would you recognize her?" "For God Almighty's sake!" bawled the judge, "is that the strip of crowbait I sold to your father for twenty dollars? Twenty dollars seemed like a fortune to me in those days!"

While they were jolting home down the steep rocky road on the long journey from San Marcos to Austin, Nannie finally spoke out about her grievance. "Look lak a jedge might had better raisin'," she said, gloomily, "look lak he didn't keer how much he hurt a body's feelins."

The Grandmother, muffled down in the back seat in the corner of the old carryall, in her worn sealskin pelisse, showing coffee-brown at the edges, her eyes closed, her hands wrung together, had been occupied once more in reconciling herself to losing a son, and, as ever, to a girl and a family of which she could not alto-gether approve. It was not that there was anything seriously damag-ing to be said against any of them; only—well, she wondered at her sons' tastes. What had each of them in turn found in the wife he had chosen? The Grandmother had always had in mind the kind of wife each of her sons needed; she had tried to bring about better marriages for them than they had made for themselves. They had merely resented her interference in what they considered strictly their personal affairs. She did not realize that she had spoiled and pampered her youngest son until he was in all probability unfit to be any kind of a husband, much less a good one. And there was something about her new daughter-in-law, a tall, handsome, firm-looking young woman, with a direct way of speaking, walking, talk-ing, that seemed to promise that the spoiled Baby's days of clover were ended. The Grandmother was annoyed deeply at seeing how self-possessed the bride had been, how she had had her way about the wedding arrangements down to the last detail, how she glanced now and then at her new husband with calm, humorous, level eyes, as if she had already got him sized up. She had even sug-gested at the wedding dinner that her idea of a honeymoon would be to follow the chuck-wagon on the round-up, and help in the cattle-branding on her father's ranch. Of course she may have been joking. But she was altogether too Western, too modern, something like the "new" woman who was beginning to run wild, asking for the vote, leaving her home and going out in the world to earn her own living . . .

The Grandmother's narrow body shuddered to the bone at the thought of women so unsexing themselves; she emerged with a start from the dark reverie of foreboding thoughts which left a bit-ter taste in her throat. "Never mind, Nannie. The judge just wasn't thinking. He's very fond of his good cheer."

Nannie had slept in a bed and had been playmate and work-fellow with her mistress; they fought on almost equal terms, Sophia Jane defending Nannie fiercely against any discipline but her own. When they were both seventeen years old, Miss Sophia Jane was married off in a very gay wedding. The house was jammed to the roof and everybody present was at least fourth cousin to every-body else. There were forty carriages and more than two hundred horses to look after for two days. When the last wheel disappeared down the lane (a number of the guests lingered on for two weeks), the larders and bins were half empty and the place looked as if a troop of cavalry had been over it. A few days later Nannie was married off to a boy she had known ever since she came to the family, and they were given as a wedding present to Miss Sophia Jane.

Miss Sophia Jane and Nannie had then started their grim and terrible race of procreation, a child every sixteen months or so, with Nannie nursing both, and Sophia Jane, in dreadful discomfort, suppressing her milk with bandages and spirits of wine. When they each had produced their fourth child, Nannie almost died of puerperal fever. Sophia Jane nursed both children. She named the black baby Charlie, and her own child Stephen, and she fed them justly turn about, not favoring the white over the black, as Nannie felt obliged to do. Her husband was shocked, tried to forbid her; her mother came to see her and reasoned with her. They found her very difficult and quite stubborn. She had already begun to develop her implicit character, which was altogether just, humane, proud, and simple. She had many small vanities and weaknesses on the surface: a love of luxury and a tendency to resent criticism. This tendency was based on her feeling of superiority in judgment and sensibility to almost everyone around her. It made her very hard to manage. She had a quiet way of holding her ground which convinced her antagonist that she would really die, not just threaten to, rather than give way. She had learned now that she was badly cheated in giving her children to another woman to feed; she resolved never again to be cheated in just that way. She sat nursing her child and her foster child, with a sensual warm pleasure she had not dreamed of, translating her natural physical relief into something holy, God-sent, amends from heaven for what she had suffered in childbed. Yes, and for what she missed in the marriage bed, for there also something had failed. She said to Nannie quite calmly, "From now on, you will nurse your children and I will nurse mine," and it was so. Charlie remained her special favorite among the Negro children. "I understand now," she said to her older sister Keziah, "why the black mammies love their foster children. I love mine." So Charlie was brought up in the house as playmate for her son Stephen, and exempted from hard work all his life.

Sophia Jane had been wooed at arm's length by a mysteriously attractive young man whom she remembered well as rather a snubby little boy with curls like her own, but shorter, a frilled white blouse and kilts of the Macdonald tartan. He was her second cousin and resembled her so closely they had been mistaken for brother and sister. Their grandparents had been first cousins, and sometimes Sophia Jane saw in him, years after they were married, all the faults she had most abhorred in her elder brother: lack of aim, failure to act at crises, a philosophic detachment from practical affairs, a tendency to set projects on foot and then leave them to perish or to be finished by someone else; and a profound conviction that everyone around him should be happy to wait upon him hand and foot. She had fought these fatal tendencies in her brother, within the bounds of wifely prudence she fought them in her husband, she was long after to fight them again in two of her sons and in several of her grandchildren. She gained no victory in any case, the selfish, careless, unloving creatures lived and ended as they had begun. But the Grandmother developed a character truly portentous under the discipline of trying to change the characters of others. Her husband shared with her the family sharpness of eye. He disliked and feared her deadly willfulness, her certainty that her ways were not only right but beyond criticism, that her feelings were important, even in the lightest matter, and must not be tampered with or treated casually. He had disappeared at the critical moment when they were growing up, had gone to college and then for travel; she forgot him for a long time, and when she saw him again forgot him as he had been once for all. She was gay and sweet and decorous, full of vanity and incredibly exalted daydreams which threatened now and again to cast her over the edge of some mysterious forbidden frenzy. She dreamed recurrently that she had lost her virginity (her virtue, she called it), her sole claim to regard, consideration, even to existence, and after frightful moral suffering which masked altogether her physical experience she would wake in a cold sweat, disordered and terrified. She had heard that her cousin Stephen was a little "wild," but that was to be expected. He was leading, no doubt, a dashing life full of manly indulgences, the sweet dark life of the knowledge of evil which caused her hair to crinkle on her scalp when she thought of it. Ah, the delicious, the free, the wonderful, the mysterious and terrible life of men! She thought about it a great deal. "Little day-dreamer," her mother or father would say to her, surprising her in a brown study, eyes moist, lips smiling vaguely over her embroidery or her book, or with hands fallen on her lap, her face turned away to a blank wall. She memorized and saved for these moments scraps of high-minded poetry, which she instantly quoted at them when they offered her a penny for her thoughts; or she broke into a melancholy little song of some kind, a song she knew they liked. She would run to the piano and tinkle the tune out with one hand, saying, "I love this part best," leaving no doubt in their minds as to what her own had been occupied with. She lived her whole youth so, without once giving herself away; not until she was in middle age, her husband dead, her property dispersed, and she found herself with a houseful of children, making a new life for them in another place, with all the responsibilities of a man but with none of the privileges, did she finally emerge into something like an honest life: and yet, she was passionately honest. She had never been anything else.

Sitting under the trees with Nannie, both of them old and their long battle with life almost finished, she said, fingering a scrap of satin, "It was not fair that Sister Keziah should have had this ivory brocade for her wedding dress, and I had only dotted swiss . . ."

"Times was harder when you got married, Missy," said Nannie. "Dat was de yeah all de crops failed."

"And they failed ever afterward, it seems to me," said Grandmother.

"Seems to me like," said Nannie, "dotted swiss was all the style when you got married."

"I never cared for it," said Grandmother.

Nannie, born in slavery, was pleased to think she would not die in it. She was wounded not so much by her state of being as by the word describing it. Emancipation was a sweet word to her. It had not changed her way of living in a single particular, but she was proud of having been able to say to her mistress, "I aim to stay wid you as long as you'll have me." Still, Emancipation had seemed to set right a wrong that stuck in her heart like a thorn. She could not understand why God, Whom she loved, had seen fit to be so hard on a whole race because they had got a certain kind of skin. She talked it over with Miss Sophia Jane. Many, times. Miss Sophia Jane was always brisk and opinionated about it: "Nonsense! I tell you, God does not know whether a skin is black or white. He sees only souls. Don't be getting notions, Nannie—of course you're going to Heaven."

Nannie showed the rudiments of logic in a mind altogether untutored. She wondered, simply and without resentment, whether God, Who had been so cruel to black people on earth, might not continue His severity in the next world. Miss Sophia Jane took pleasure in reassuring her; as if she, who had been responsible for Nannie, body and soul in this life, might also be her sponsor before the judgment seat.

Miss Sophia Jane had taken upon herself all the responsibilities of her tangled world, half white, half black, mingling steadily and the confusion growing ever deeper. There were so many young men about the place, always, younger brothers-in-law, first cousins, second cousins, nephews. They came visiting and they stayed, and there was no accounting for them nor any way of controlling their quietly headstrong habits. She learned early to keep silent and give no sign of uneasiness, but whenever a child was born in the Negro quarters, pink, worm-like, she held her breath for three days, she told her eldest granddaughter, years later, to see whether the newly born would turn black after the proper interval . . . It was a strain that told on her, and ended by giving her a deeply grounded contempt for men. She could not help it, she despised men. She despised them and was ruled by them. Her husband threw away her dowry and her property in wild investments in strange territories: Louisiana, Texas; and without protest she watched him play away her substance like a gambler. She felt that she could have managed her affairs profitably. But her natural activities lay elsewhere, it was the business of a man to make all decisions and dispose of all financial matters. Yet when she got the reins in her hands, her sons could persuade her to this and that enterprise or investment; against her will and judgment she accepted their advice, and among them they managed to break up once more the stronghold she had built for the future of her family. They got from her their own start in life, came back for fresh help when they needed it, and were divided against each other. She saw it as her natural duty to provide for her household, after her husband had

fought stubbornly through the War, along with every other man of
military age in the connection; had been wounded, had lingered
helpless, and had died of his wound long after the great fervor and
excitement had faded in hopeless defeat, when to be a man
wounded and ruined in the War was merely to have proved oneself, perhaps, more heroic than wise. Left so, she drew her family
together and set out for Louisiana, where her husband, with her
money, had bought a sugar refinery. There was going to be a fortune in sugar, he said; not in raising the raw material, but in manu-
facturing it. He had schemes in his head for operating cotton gins,
flour mills, refineries. Had he lived . . . but he did not live, and
Sophia Jane had hardly repaired the house she bought and got the
orchard planted when she saw that, in her hands, the sugar refinery
was going to be a failure.

She sold out at a loss, and went on to Texas, where her husband had bought cheaply, some years before, a large tract of fertile
black land in an almost unsettled part of the country. She had with
her nine children, the youngest about two, the eldest about seventeen years old; Nannie and her three sons, Uncle Jimbilly, and two
other Negroes, all in good health, full of hope and greatly desiring
to live. Her husband's ghost persisted in her, she was bitterly outraged by his death almost as if he had willfully deserted her. She
mourned for him at first with dry eyes, angrily. Twenty years later,
seeing after a long absence the eldest son of her favorite daughter,
who had died early, she recognized the very features and look of
the husband of her youth, and she wept.

During the terrible second year in Texas, two of her younger
sons, Harry and Robert, suddenly ran away. They chose good
weather for it, in mid-May, and they were almost seven miles from
home when a neighboring farmer saw them, wondered and asked
questions, and ended by persuading them into his gig, and so
brought them back.

Miss Sophia Jane went through the dreary ritual of discipline
she thought appropriate to the occasion. She whipped them with
her riding whip. Then she made them kneel down with her while
she prayed for them, asking God to help them mend their ways and
not be undutiful to their mother; her duty performed, she broke
down and wept with her arms around them. They had endured
their punishment stoically, because it would have been disgraceful

to cry when a woman hit them, and besides, she did not hit very hard; they had knelt with her in a shamefaced gloom, because religious feeling was a female mystery which embarrassed them, but when they saw her tears they burst into loud bellows of repentance. They were only nine and eleven years old. She said in a voice of mourning, so despairing it frightened them: "Why did you run away from me? What do you think I brought you here for?" as if they were grown men who could realize how terrible the situation was. All the answer they could make, as they wept too, was that they had wanted to go back to Louisiana to eat sugar cane. They had been thinking about sugar cane all winter . . . Their mother was stunned. She had built a house large enough to shelter them all, of hand-sawed lumber dragged by ox-cart for forty miles, she had got the fields fenced in and the crops planted, she had, she believed, fed and clothed her children; and now she realized they were hungry. These two had worked like men; she felt their growing bones through their thin flesh, and remembered how mercilessly she had driven them, as she had driven herself, as she had driven the Negroes and the horses, because there was no choice in the matter. They must labor beyond their strength or perish. Sitting there with her arms around them, she felt her heart break in her breast. She had thought it was a silly phrase. It happened to her. It was not that she was incapable of feeling after-ward, for in a way she was more emotional, more quick, but griefs never again lasted with her so long as they had before. This day was the beginning of her spoiling her children and being afraid of them. She said to them after a long dazed silence, when they began to grow restless under her arms: "We'll grow fine ribbon cane here. The soil is perfect for it. We'll have all the sugar we want. But we must be patient."

By the time her children began to marry, she was able to give them each a good strip of land and a little money, she was able to help them buy more land in places they preferred by selling her own, tract by tract, and she saw them all begin well, though not all of them ended so. They went about their own affairs, scattering out and seeming to lose all that sense of family unity so precious to the Grandmother. They bore with her infrequent visits and her advice and her tremendous rightness, and they were impatient of her tenderness. When Harry's wife died—she had never approved of Harry's wife, who was delicate and hopelessly inadequate at housekeeping, and who could not even bear children successfully, since she died when her third was born—the Grandmother took the children and began life again, with almost the same zest, and with more indulgence. She had just got them brought up to the point where she felt she could begin to work the faults out of them—faults inherited, she admitted fairly, from both sides of the house—when she died. It happened quite suddenly one afternoon in early October, after a day spent in helping the Mexican gardener of her third daughter-in-law to put the garden to rights. She was on a visit in far western Texas and enjoying it. The daughter-in-law was exasperated but apparently so docile, the Grandmother, who looked upon her as a child, did not notice her little moods at all. The son had long ago learned not to oppose his mother. She wore him down with patient, just, and reasonable argument. She was careful never to venture to command him in anything. He consoled his wife by saying that everything Mother was doing could be changed back after she was gone. As this change included moving a fifty-foot adobe wall, the wife was not much consoled. The Grandmother came into the house quite flushed and exhilarated, saying how well she felt in the bracing mountain air—and dropped dead over the doorsill.

FURTHER READINGS

Katherine Anne Porter, *The Collected Essays and Occasional Writings of Katherine Anne Porter* (Delacorte Press, 1970); Isabel Bayley, ed., *Letters of Katherine Anne Porter* (Atlantic Monthly Press, 1990); Ruth M. Alverez and Thomas F. Walsh, eds., *Uncollected Early Prose of Katherine Anne Porter* (University of Texas Press, 1993); Darlene Harbour Unrue, ed., *Critical essays on Katherine Anne Porter* (G.K. Hall & Co., 1997); Thomas F. Walsh, *Katherine Anne Porter and Mexico: The Illusion of Eden* (University of Texas Press, 1992); Joan Givner, *Katherine Anne Porter: A Life* (Simon and Schuster, 1982; rev. ed., University of Georgia Press, 1991); James T.F. Tanner, *The Texas Legacy of Katherine Anne Porter* (University of North Texas Press, 1991); Clinton Machann and William Bedford

Clark, eds., *Katherine Anne Porter and Texas: An Uneasy Relationship* (Texas A&M University Press, 1990); *Katherine Anne Porter: Conversations* (University Press of Mississippi, 1987); Enrique Hank Lopez, *Conversations with Katherine Anne Porter: Refugee from Indian Creek* (Little, Brown, 1981); Robert Penn Warren, ed., *Katherine Anne Porter: A Collection of Critical Essays* (Prentice-Hall, 1979).

Linda Hogan (1947–   )

Linda Hogan is a Chickasaw poet, novelist, essayist who teaches at the University of Colorado at Boulder. Her books of poetry and stories include *Calling Myself Home* (1978), *Eclipse* (1983), *Seeing Through the Sun* (1985), *Savings* (1988), *Book of Medicines* (1993), and *Red Clay: Poems and Stories* (1994), and her novels include *Mean Spirit* (1990), *Solar Storms* (1995), and *Power* (1998). She has also written a collection of essays about nature, called *Dwellings: A Spiritual History of the Living World* (1995). In her writing, powerful images and great emotional depth are some-times held by gauzy "dreamcatcher" words and ideas. The wooden birds in "Making Do" represent the time when the people believed in the spirit and the power of the animals they so carefully carved. For the woman who carves the birds, the old ways provide a kind of healing and grace. In the smallest signs of belief, life starts again.

MAKING DO

Roberta James became one of the silent people in Seeker County when her daughter, Harriet, died at six years of age.

Harriet died of what they used to call consumption.

After the funeral, Grandmother Addie went to stay with Roberta in her grief, as she had done over the years with her children and grandchildren. Addie, in fact, had stayed with Roberta during the time of her pregnancy with Harriet, back when the fif-teen-year-old girl wore her boyfriend's black satin jacket that had a map of Korea on the back. And she'd visited further back than that, back to the days when Roberta wore white full skirts and white blouses and the sun came in the door, and she lay there in the hot sun like it was ironed flat against the floor, and she felt good with clean hair and skin and singing a little song to herself. There were

Linda Hogan, "Making Do," from "The Grace of Wooden Birds," in *The New Native American Novel: Works in Progress*, ed. Mary Dougherty Bartlett (1986).

oak trees outside. She was waiting. Roberta was waiting there for something that would take her away. But the farthest she got was just outside her skin, that black jacket against her with its map of Korea.

Addie never told Roberta a word of what she knew about divided countries and people who wear them on their backs, but later Roberta knew that her grandmother had seen way down the road what was coming, and warned her in little ways. When she brushed Roberta's dark hair, she told her, "You were born to a different life, Bobbie."

After the funeral, Roberta's mother offered comfort in her own way. "Life goes on," Neva said, but she herself had long belonged to that society of quiet Indian women in seeker, although no one would have guessed this of the woman who wore Peach Promise lipstick, smiled generously, and kissed the bathroom mirror, leaving a message for Roberta that said, "See you in the a.m. Love."

Grandma Addie tended Angela, Roberta's younger daughter. She fed the baby Angela spoonsful of meals, honey, and milk and held her day and night while Roberta went about the routines of her life. The chores healed her a little; perking coffee and cleaning her mother's lipstick off the mirror. She swept away traces of Harriet with the splintered broom, picking up threads from the girl's dress, black hair from her head, wiping away her footprints.

Occasionally Neva stopped in, clasped her daughter's thin cold hands between her warm ones, and offered advice. "That's why you ought to get married," she said. She wrapped Roberta's shoulders in a large gray sweater. "Then you'd have some man to help when things are down and out. Like Ted here. Well, any-way, Honey," she said at eye level to Roberta, "you sure drew a good card when Harriet was born. Didn't she, Ted?"

"Sure sugar, an ace."

But when Roberta wasn't looking, Neva shook her head slowly and looked down at the floor, and thought their lives were all hopeless.

Roberta didn't get married like her mother suggested. She did take some comfort on those long nights by loving Tom Wilkins. Each night she put pieces of cedar inside his Red Wing boots, to keep him close, and neatly placed them beneath her bed. She knew how to care for herself with this man, keeping him close in almost the same space Harriet had abandoned. She wept slightly at night after he held her and he said, "There now. There now," and patted her on the back.

He brought her favorite Windmill cookies with him from town and he sang late at night so that the ghost of Harriet could move on more easily, like he eventually moved on when Roberta stopped placing cedar in his boots.

"Why didn't that Wilkins boy come back?" Grandma asked.

"Choctaw, wasn't he?"

Roberta shrugged as if she hadn't left his boots empty of cedar. "He was prettier than me." She pushed her straggly hair back from her face to show Grandma what she meant.

A month later, Roberta was relieved when the company summoned Tom Wilkins to Louisiana to work on a new oil field and she didn't have to run into him at the store any longer.

Roberta's next child, a son she named Wilkins after the father, died at birth, strangled on his own cord. Roberta had already worn a dark shawl throughout this pregnancy. She looked at his small roughbox and said, "He died of life and I know that can happen."

She held her grandmother's hand.

Grandma Addie and Neva talked about Roberta. "A woman can only hold so much hurt," Grandma said.

"And don't think I don't know it," said Neva.

Roberta surfaced from her withdrawal a half year later, in the spring of 1974, when Angela looked at her like a little grandmother and said, "Mother, I know it is hard, but it's time for me to leave you" and immediately became feverish. Roberta bathed her with alcohol and made blessing-root tea, which she dropped into little Angela's rose-petal mouth with an eye dropper. She prayed fervently to God or Jesus, she had never really understood which was which, and to all the stones and trees and gods of the sky and inner earth that she knew well, and to the animal spirits, and she carried her little Angel to the hospital in the middle of praying, to that house made of brick and window and cinders where dying bodies were kept alive, carried the girl with soft child skin in a small quilt decorated with girls in poke bonnets, and thought how funny it was to wrap a dying child in such sweetness as those red-cheeked girls in the calico bonnets. She blamed herself for ignoring Angela in her own time of grief. Four days later Angela died, wearing a little corn necklace Roberta made, a wristlet of glass beads, and covered with that quilt.

"She even told Roberta she was about to die," Neva told Ted. "Just like an old woman, huh, Bert?"

Roberta went on with her silence through his third death, telling herself over and over what had happened, for the truth was so bad she could not believe it. The inner voice of the throat spoke and repeated the words of loss and Roberta listened hard. "My Angel. My Harriet. All my Life gone and broken while I am so young. I'm too young for all this loss."

She dreamed of her backbone and even that was broken in pieces. She dreamed of her house in four pieces. She was broken like the country of Korea or the land of the tribe.

They were all broken, Roberta's thin-skinned father broken by the war. He and Neva raised two boys whose parents had "gone off" as they say of those who come under the control of genie spirits from whiskey bottles, and those boys were certainly broken. And Neva herself had once been a keeper of the gates; she was broken.

In earlier days she read people by their faces and bodies. She was a keeper of gates, opening and closing ways for people to pass through life. "This one has been eating too much grain," she'd say, or "That one was born too rich for her own good and is spoiled. That one is broken in the will to live by this and that." She was a keeper of the family gates as well. She closed doors on those she disliked, if they were dishonest, say, or mean, or small. There was no room for smallness in her life, but she opened the doors wide for those who moved her slightly, in any way, with stirrings of love or pity. She had lusty respect for belligerence, political rebellion, and for vandalism against automobiles or business or bosses, and those vandals were among those permitted inside her walls.

And now she was broken, by her own losses and her loneliness.

Roberta cried against Addie's old warm shoulders and Grandma Addie stayed on, moving in all her things, cartons of canning jars, a blue-painted porcelain horse, her dark dresses and aprons, pictures of her grandchildren and great-grandchildren, scented candles of the virgin of Guadalupe, even though she was never a Catholic, and the antlers of the deer.

Roberta ignored her cousins from the churches of the brethren this and that when they came to comfort her in their

ways, telling her that all things were meant to be and that the Lord
gives and takes.

Uncle James was older and so he said nothing, and she sat
with him, those silent ones together.

Roberta's mother left messages on the bathroom mirror. There
is a time for everything in heaven."

With Grandma there to watch over Neva and the house,
Roberta decided one day to pack her dishes, blankets, and clothes
into the old Chevy she had bought from Ted, and she drove away
from the little square tombstones named Angela, Wilkins, and
Harriet, though it nearly broke her heart to leave them. She drove
away from all those trying to comfort her with what comforted
them. The sorrow in her was like a well too deep for young ground;
the sides caved in with anger, but Roberta planned still to return
for Grandma Addie. She stopped once, on the flat, neutral land of
Goodland, Kansas, and telephoned back

"You sure you don't want to come with me? It's kind of pretty
out this way, Grandma," she lied. She smelled truck exhaust from
the phone booth and she watched the long, red-faced boys walking past, those young men who had eaten so much cattle they
began to look like them.

"Just go and get settled. I'll be out to visit as soon as you get the
first load of laundry hung on the line."

Roberta felt her grandma smile. She hung up the phone and
headed back to the overloaded, dusty white car.

She headed for Denver, but wound up just west of there, in a
mountain town called The Tropics. Its name was like a politician's
vocabulary, a lie. In truth, The Tropics was arid. It was a mine town,
uranium most recently. Dust devils whirled sand off the mountains.
Even after the heaviest of rains, the water seeped back into the
ground, between stores, and the earth was parched again. Still,
Tropics conjured up visions of tall grasses in outlying savannas,
dark rivers, mists, and deep green forests of ferns and trees and
water-filled vines. Sometimes it seemed like they were there.

Roberta told herself it was God's acres, that it was fate she had
missed the Denver turn-offs from the freeway, that here she could forgive and forget her losses and get on with living. She rented a cabin,
got a part-time job working down at the Tropics Grocery where she
sold single items to customers who didn't want to travel to town. She

sold a bag of flour to one, a can of dog food to another, candy to schoolchildren in the afternoon. She sold boxed doughnuts and cigarettes to work crews in the mornings and 32 beer to the same crews after five. She dusted and stacked the buckling shelves, and she had time to whittle little birds, as her Uncle James had done. She whittled them and thought of them as toys for the spirits of her children and put them in the windows so the kids would be sure and see them. "This one's for Harriet," she'd tell no one in particular.

When she didn't work she spent her time in bed, completely still and staring straight at the ceiling. They used to say if a person is motionless, their souls will run away from the body, and Roberta counted on that. They say that once a soul decides to leave, it can't be recalled. Roberta lay in that room with its blue walls and blue-flowered blanket. She lay there with her hair pulled backed from her round forehead. She held the sunbonnet quilt in her hands and didn't move.

To her disappointment, she remained alive. Every night she prayed to die and join her kids, but every morning she was still living, breathing. Some mornings she pulled at her flesh just to be certain, she was so amazed and despairing to be still alive.

Her soul refused to leave. It had a mind of its own. So Roberta got up and began a restless walking. There were nights in The Tropics that she haunted the dirt roads like a large-shouldered thin-hipped ghost, like a tough girl with her shoulders held high to protect her broken heart Roberta Diane James with her dark hair that had seen worn thin from the hours she spent lying down trying to send her soul away. Roberta, with her eyes the color of dark river water after a storm when the gold stirs up in it. The left eye still held the trace of a wink in it, despite the thinness of skin stretched over her forehead, the smell of Ivory soap on her as she tried over and over to wash the grief from her flesh.

When I First heard how bad things were going for Roberta, I thought about going home, but I heard my other voices tell me it wasn't time. "There is a season for all things," Mom used to say, and I knew Mom would be telling Roberta just that, in her own words, and that Roberta would be fuming inside as I had done with Mom's fifty-cent sayings.

I knew this much: Roberta would need to hold on to her grief and her pain.

Us Chickasaws have lost so much we hold on to everything. Even our muscles hold on to their aches. We love our lovers long after they are gone, better than when they were present.

When we were girls, Roberta and I saved the tops of Coke bottlecaps and covered them with purple cloth like grapes. We made clusters of grapes sitting out there on the porch, or on tire swings in the heat, and we sewed the grapes together. We made do. We drank tea from pickle jars. We used potato water to starch our clothes. We even used our skinny dark legs as paper for tic-tac-toe. Now the girls turn bleach containers into hats, cutting them in fours and crocheting them together.

Our Aunt Bell is famous for holding on and making do. There's a nail in her kitchen for plastic six-pack rings, a box for old jars, a shelf or box for everything, including all the black and white shoes she's worn out as a grown woman. Don't think these boxes or nails mean she's neat, either. She's not. She has hundreds of dusty salt and pepper shakers people gave her, and stacks of old magazines and papers, years of yellowed history all contained in her crowded rooms. And I love her for it, for holding on that way. I have spent hours of my younger life looking at those shakers and reading those papers. Her own children tell her it is a miracle the viruses of science aren't growing to maturity in there.

We save ourselves from loss in whatever ways we can, collecting things, going out to Danceland, getting drunk, reading westerns or finding new loves, but the other side of all this salvation is that we deny the truth. When some man from town steals our land, we say, "Oh, he wouldn't do that. Jimmy Slade is a good old boy. I used to work for the Slades during the Depression." Never mind that the Slades were not the hungry ones back then.

Some of us southern Indians used to have ranches and cattle. They were all lost piece by piece, or sold to pay for taxes on some land that was also lost. Now and then someone comes around and tells us we should develop our land like we once did. Or they tell us just to go out in the world. We nod and smile at them.

Now and then some of us young people make a tidal wave in the ocean of our history, an anxiety attack in the heart monitor of our race. We get angry and scream out. We get in the news. We strip ourselves bare in the colleges that recruited us as their minority quota and we run out into the snowstorm naked and we get talked about for years as the crazy Indian that did this or that, the one that drove to the gas station and went straight to Canada, the girl who took out the garbage and never turned and went back. We made do.

I knew some people from up north. You could always tell they were from up north because my friend's daughter had a wall-eye with a hook tattooed on her forearm. Once we went to a pow-wow together and some of the women of the People wore jingle dresses, with what looked like bells. What are those?" I asked my friend.

They were snuff can lids. Those women of the forests and woodlands, so much making do just like us, like when we use silver salt cans in our dances instead of turtle-shell rattles. We make music of those saltshakers, though now and then some outsider decides we have no culture because we use store-bought shakers and they are not traditional at all.

I defy them: Salt is the substance of our blood, sweat, our secretions, our semen. It is the ocean of ourselves.

Once I saw a railroad engineer's hat in a museum. It was fully headed. I thought it was a new style like the beaded tennis shoes or the new beaded trucker's hats. But it was made in the late 1800s when the Lakota were forbidden to make traditional items. The mothers took to beading whatever was available, hats of the engineers of death. They covered colony cotton with their art.

We make art out of our loss.

That's why when I heard Roberta was in Colorado and was carving wooden birds, I figured it made sense. Besides, we come from a long line of whittlers and table carvers, people who work with wood, including the Mexican great-grandfather who made santos and a wooden mask that was banned by the priests. It's presence got him excommunicated.

Uncle James carves chains out of trees. We laugh and say it sounds like something they would do.

Roberta was carving wooden birds, crows, mourning doves, and even a scissortail or two. She sent some of the birds back home to have aunt bell put them on the graves of her little ones.

I think she was trying to carve the souls of her children into the birds. She was making do.

**Evelyn Cameron, *"Scholars"* at Knowlton,
35 Miles South of Terry, Montana, 1907.**

*The Haynes Foundation Collection, The Montana Historical Society,
Helena, Montana.*

First Person

In the women's West, as elsewhere, memory is never complete, but is instead the record only of what we choose to remember. Our memories may mask sadness or emphasize suffering, but in the process of sharing that memory, we are forced to reevaluate the meanings of our lives. This chapter presents a variety of women's ways of remembering their pasts in the West, drawn from memoirs, oral histories, narratives, and letters. Though what is chosen to be remembered varies greatly, common to each is the importance of the land on which one's life is made.

Here we present a selection from the often-neglected memoir of Mary Austin, in which long-hidden memories burn on the page with an anguish undiminished by the passage of time. Sometimes within women's first-person accounts are complex interplays between the rememberer and the recorder of the memory, as in the collaboration between anthropologist Ruth Underhill and Tohono O'Odham informant María Chona, and between Donna Gray and the ranch women whose stories she collects and preserves. As Teresa Jordan illustrates, memory can reclaim what is lost; in the memory of a granddaughter, a grandmother emerges not as the cantankerous creature experienced firsthand, but instead as understandable, justified, and heroic. In memories lie the roots of daughters' struggles, as in Elizabeth Hampsten's contemplation of her mother's letters, and of the differences that kept them apart. The process of remembering, too, can make a woman a warrior, ready to fight for her home, as Maxine Hong Kingston demonstrates. Sometimes what is remembered is a moment which passed so fleetingly that it becomes clear only in retrospect, as Mabel Dodge Luhan realizes. In memoir are discovered stories often left out of the history books, as reflected in the narratives of former slaves, now free, recalling their days before emancipation.

What is remembered inevitably shapes who we are, and in these first-person accounts of women, we see the origins of contemporary definitions of the West and of the lives of western women.

Mary Austin (1868–1934)

Most readers know Mary Austin through her novels and stories of the American West. Fewer know her later work, *The American Rhythm: Studies and Reëxpressions of Amerindian Songs* (1923, 1930), in which Austin argued the dance of Isadora Duncan, and the poetry of T. S. Eliot, E. E. Cummings, Ezra Pound, D. H. Lawrence, and Robinson Jeffers carried in them the rhythms of American speech and of Indian dance. Few readers know her autobiography *Earth Horizon* (1932), every bit as eccentric and surprising. She "thought there might be a great deal to be got out of being a woman; but she definitely meant neither to chirrup nor twitter."

Austin was sixty-four when she wrote *Earth Horizon,* and with the novelist's will to see her "heroine" at some distance, she devised two voices for herself—the I-Mary and Mary-by-herself. I-Mary is "the confident and outspoken Mary, with her witty, angry and imaginative voice." I-Mary is original and independent, but although *Earth Horizon* is a profoundly honest book, it holds its own counsel. In it one finds stories that never entered the novels, that are revisited in secret, but never forgotten. The following episodes occurred in the autumn of 1895, when she first went to live in the Owens Valley, and although each was "intimately connected with my life as an artist," neither was included in *The Land of Little Rain.*

TROUBLESOME MEMORIES

In the autumn of '95, Mary took Ruth and settled in Bishop, the most northerly of the Valley towns, of about one thousand inhabitants, with a large farming contingent. The ostensible reason for her going was to be easily accessible to medical attention, for herself as well as for the child. There was also the need of reorganizing her life in view of contingencies which she could never persuade her husband to make explicit items in their joint future. Incredible

Mary Austin, from *Earth Horizon: An Autobiography* (1932).

today that a life should be planned in which the wife's capabilities, her health and fitness for the part assigned to her to play, should be negligible properties, but the strange thing would have been that it could have been otherwise. Men made their own plans and endured the wife's unsuitability to them with magnanimity or impatience according to their natures. Mary's husband was uncomplaining and kind, but it simply did not enter into his calculation that his own adjustments should take into account her want of physical endowment for the life of pioneer housekeeping on a small income and the combined care of a permanently ailing child. It was a situation which Mary by this time fully realized she must meet herself, and for that she wanted a little space of detachment. At Bishop a plan for reviving a so-called Academy offered her a teaching possibility. She was to teach English, literature, and art.

The educational episode proved of no particular moment, owing in part to inexpert management and in part to its being undertaken under the least propitious circumstances. Those who live through them will recall Coxey's Army and the panic of the two preceding years, and in Inyo the gradual draining away of the mining interests which left the farmers with no market for their produce. This was how it came about that the most dramatic incident of Mary's first year at Bishop was the Free Silver Movement. The most intellectually intriguing incidents of her stay in Bishop clustered around the sheep interests and the Indian school. There were a number of wool-growers about Bishop—name for an old partner of Beale's—of whom Waterson, who figures in "The Flock" as the Manxman, was the largest. Two of the Waterson young people were pupils of Mary's and the acquaintance so formed led on to her completing at the Waterson Ranch the experiments begun several years earlier with hunting-dogs at Mountain View. It had been for a long time in Mary's mind that the story—that knot of related and inter-consequential incidents which make up the pattern called experience—must have come down to man by more intimate ancestral inheritance than the poem even. What she needed for uncovering the line of descent was a vocabulary expressive of experience—that is, things done leading to appreciable consequences, by which stories could be conveyed. She was finally to discover that vocabulary in the languages of signs—arm signs

chiefly and two or three vocables—invented by herders for communication with their dogs. This is much more than the vocabulary
of verbal commands such as are used in the hunting-fields; a
vocabulary of sentences expressive of the whole phase of an experience such as Sheep missing on the left, go and find them; Round
the flock and hold; Round and bed the flock. What Mary discovered that winter was that, by piecing these sentences and signs
together in the pattern of an incident which had happened often
enough to come easily to mind, and by narrating the incident in
this fashion on occasions on which was plain to the dogs that it
could not refer to a present circumstance, she could afford them
pleasure, such as they learned to invite in the same way a young
child invites the re-telling of a favorite tale. Of course there were
dogs who remained always uneasily in doubt as to the relevance
of such a narrative to the momentary reality, and dogs, who, convinced that it did not refer to anything actually going on at the
time among their charges, were always a little suspicious of your
intention, so to speak, of "pulling their leg." Curiously, although the
certainty so arrived at, that given the proper vocabulary there can
be transmissions of experience between man and dog is probably
the most important contribution to the story-teller's art that Mary
will ever make, I have found no story-teller in American in the least
interested. Indirectly it opens up the whole question of the communication of experience among animals, and alters the comparative values of instinct and training in animal behavior. It led on, for
Mary, to a renewed curiosity about Indian sign languages and their
experience-carrying possibilities, which made for many years a
stimulating minor intellectual interest.

There was a large campody at Bishop and the largest Indian
school in the valley. It was from the teacher, a more than ordinarily
competent and intelligent woman, that Mary began to learn the
sort of thing that made of her a fierce and untiring opponent of the
colossal stupidities, the mean and cruel injustices, of our Indian
Bureau. I have thought this over and intend not to say too much in
detail of that long and not yet entirely triumphant struggle. It is a
story in itself which will yet have to be written as those other stories of labor, of suffrage, of religious and intellectual freedom, all
the deeply felt and determined effort to realize in our communal
relations the constitutional guarantees of democracy. There are

other Indian episodes that are so intimately connected with my life as an artist, with what ultimately I came to understand, and stand for, in the structure and meaning of human society, that they cannot be omitted. But the whole business of affecting the governmental policy toward Indians, as the Government itself is now willing to admit it has been affected, might just as well have been any other of those half-unconscious starts of my generation toward the realization and rescue of the underdog, which has been its characteristic concern. At the same time that my contemporaries were joining labor organizations and aligning themselves with wage-strikes, I took to the defense of Indians because they were the most conspicuously defeated and offended against group at hand. I should have done as much even without what I afterward discovered among them of illumination and reformation of my own way of thought. I am consoled by the certainty, which nobody denies me, not even the Government which I fought, of having been of use to them. I got out of the actual activities involved precisely what my contemporaries in cities got, a knowledge of the persisting strain of bruteness, of emotional savagery, of greed and hypocrisy which taints the best of our Western civilization; precisely what my contemporaries learned by seeing strikers beaten up by policeman; citizens deprived by violence of their constitutional liberties; the lowly and underprivileged stripped of their economic opportunities. As for the other things that came to me by way of my Indian acquaintances, they are the gifts of a special grace which has been mind from the beginning, the persistence in me, perhaps, of an uncorrupted strain of ancestral primitivism, a single isolated gene of that far-off and slightly mythical Indian ancestor of whose reality I am more convinced by what happened to me among Indians than by any objective evidence.

What set me off on that trail was dreadful enough, a flagrant instance of a local pastime, known as mahala chasing. Many of the younger Indian women were employed in the town as household help, and it was no uncommon experience for them, on their way home unattended, to be waylaid by white men—in this instance two young girls, who had lingered behind to sweep the schoolhouse, and were afterward captured and detained for the greater part of the night by a gang of youths, of whom the only extenuating thing that can be said is that they were still very young, and instigated by an older man not a native of the community. The Indian girls closed their part of the episode by eating wild parsnip root—the convulsions induced by that bane being mercifully shorter than the sufferings already endured—and though the community did actually take measures to prevent the recurrence of such incidents, nothing was done to the offenders, who were sons, some of them, of the "best families." And not only at Bishop—I recall at Lone Pine a young wife kicked to death by a white man in a drunken fury at her resistance, and the Indian husband weeping in the broken measures of remediless despair. "My wife . . . all the same one dog." And the Ghost Dance . . . and Warner's Ranch . . . plenty of incident to set off less sensitive natures than Mary's against Christian pretense and democratic inadequacy.

These things had their part in the discovery Mary made that winter of '96–'97 that she was not only not a Methodist, but that she couldn't in the orthodox sense of the word, go on calling herself a Christian.

FURTHER READINGS

Melody Graulich, "Editor's Introduction," to Mary Austin, *Earth Horizon: An Autobiography* (University of New Mexico Press, 1991); Esther Lanigan, ed., *A Mary Austin Reader* (University of Arizona Press, 1996); Rueben J. Ellis, ed., *Beyond Borders: The Selected Essays of Mary Austin* (Southern Illinois University Press, 1996); Mary Austin, *Earth Horizon: An Autobiography* (Houghton Mifflin, 1932).

WPA Oklahoma Slave Narratives

Many parts of the West are also parts of the South; this is especially evident in Texas and Oklahoma, where the area's history resonates with the forces that shaped both regions in the nineteenth century. Southern-style slavery existed in parts of what we now think of as the trans-Mississippi West. Many parts of the West became sites of refuge and opportunity for free Blacks, who went West to work in mining, farming, ranching, and other western enterprise. One former slave woman, known as Aunt Clara Brown, came to the Rocky Mountains where she set up a successful laundry business in the goldfields; she was so successful and careful with her money that she was able to return to Kentucky with a bankroll which she used to bring out west a large number of slaves—including the daughter she had been sold away from. Other African Americans came to the West originally as slaves, and after the Civil War, worked to build communities and new lives for themselves in the region. These pioneers—from the Kansas "exodusters" of the 1860s to the San Francisco Bay Area war production workers of the 1940s—made a deep and lasting impact on the region. The stories of their coming to the West and of their subsequent histories are only now being recovered and told by historians.

Here we offer two narratives collected as part of the Depression-era WPA Slave Narratives project. In her narrative, Easter Wells tells of being a slave in Texas; she was interviewed by WPA field worker Mrs. Jessie R. Ervin at McAlester, Oklahoma, in September of 1937. Mary Grayson tells the story of childhood as a slave to the Creek Indians; she was interviewed by WPA employee Robert Vinson Lackey in Tulsa, Oklahoma, in the spring or summer of 1937. These narratives testify to the resilience and continuity of these women's lives in their new homes.

Easter Wells

A SLAVE IN TEXAS

I was born in Arkansas, in 1854, but we moved to Texas in 1855. I've heard 'em tell about de trip to Texas. De grown folks rode in wagons and carts but de chaps all walked dat was big enuff. De men walked and toted their guns and hunted all de way. Dey had plenty of fresh game to eat.

My mother's name was Nellie Bell. I had one sister, Liza. I never saw my father; in fact, I never heard my mammy say anything about him and I don't guess I ever asked her anything about him for I never thought anything about not having a father. I guess he belonged to another family and when we moved away he was left behind and he didn't try to find us after de War.

My mammy and my sister and me belonged to young Master Jason Bell. We was his onliest slaves and as he wasn't married and lived at home wid his parents; we was worked and bossed by his father, Cap'n William Bell and his wife, Miss Mary.

After we moved to Texas, old Master built a big double log house, weather-boarded on de inside and out. It was painted white. Dey was a long gallery clean across de front of de house and a big open hall between de two front rooms. Dey was three rooms on each side of de hall and a wide gallery across de back. De kitchen set back from de house and dey was a board walk leading to it. Vines was planted 'round de gallery and on each side of de walk in de summer time. De house was on a hill and set back from de big road about a quarter of a mile and dey was big oak and pine trees all 'round de yard. We had purty flowers, too.

We had good quarters. Dey was log cabins, but de logs was peeled and square-adzed and put together with white plaster and had shuttered windows and pine floors. Our furniture was home made but it was good and made our cabins comfortable.

Old Master give us our allowance of staple food and it had to run us, too. We could raise our own gardens and in dat way we had purty plenty to eat. Dey took good care of us sick or well and old Mistress was awful good to us.

Easter Wells (1937), from T. Lindsay Baker and Julie P. Baker, eds., *The WPA Oklahoma Slave Narratives* (1996).

My mammy was de cook. I remember old Master had some purty strict rules and one of 'em was iffen you burnt de bread you had to eat it. One day mammy burnt de bread. She was awful busy and forgot it and it burnt purty bad. She knowed dat old Master would be mad and she'd be punished so she got some grub and her bonnet and she lit out. She hid in de woods and cane brakes for two weeks and dey couldn't find her either. One of de women slipped food out to her. Finally she come home and old Master give her a whipping but he didn't hurt her none. He was glad to git her back. She told us dat she could'a clipped off to de North but she didn't want to leave us children. She was afraid young Master would be mad and sell us and we'd a-had a hard time so she come back. I don't know whether she ever burnt de bread any more or not.

Once one of de men got his 'lowance and he decided he'd have de meat all cooked at once so he come to our cabin and got Mammy to cook it for him. She cooked it and he took it home. One day he was at work and a dog got in and et de meat all up. He didn't have much food for de rest of de week. He had to make out wid parched corn.

We all kept parched corn all de time and went 'round eating it. It was good to fill you up iffen you was hungry and was nourishing, too.

When de niggers cooked in dere own cabins dey put de food in a sort of tray or trough and everybody et together. Dey didn't have no dishes. We allus ate at de Big House as mammy had to do de cooking for de family.

I never had to work hard as old Master wanted us to grow up strong. He'd have mammy boil Jerusalem Oak and make a tea for us to drink to cure us of worms and we'd run races and get exercise so we would be healthy.

Old Mistress and old Master had three children. Dey was two children dead between Master Jason and Miss Jane. Dey was a little girl 'bout my age, named Arline. We played together all de time. We used to set on de steps at night and old Mistress would tell us about de stars. She'd tell us and show us de Big Dipper, Little Dipper, Milky Way, Ellen's Yard, Job's Coffin, and de Seven Sisters. I can show 'em to you and tell you all about 'em yet.

I scared Arline and made her fall and break her leg twice. One time we was on de porch after dark one night and I told her dat I heard something and I made like I could see it and she couldn't so she got scared and run and hung her toe in a crack and fell off de high porch and broke her leg. Another time while de War was going on we was dressed up in long dresses playing grown-ups. We had a playhouse under some big castor-bean bushes. We climbed up on de fence and jest for fun I told her dat I seen some Yankees coming. She started to run and got tangled up in her long dress and fell and broke her leg again. It nigh broke my heart for I loved her and she loved me and she didn't tell on me either time. I used to visit her after she was married and we'd sure have a good visit talking 'bout de things we used to do. We was separated when we was about fifteen and didn't see each other any more till we was both married and had children. I went to visit her at Bryant, Brazos County, Texas and I ain't seen her since. I don't know whether she is still living or not.

I 'members hearing a man say dat once he was a nigger trader. He'd buy and trade or sell 'em like they was stock. He become a Christian and never sold any more.

Our young Master went to de War and got wounded and come home and died. Old Master den took full charge of us and when de War ended he kept us because he said we didn't have no folks and he said as our owner was dead we wasn't free. Mother died about a year after de War, and some white folks took my sister but I was afraid to go. Old Master told me iffen I left him he would cut my ears off and I'd starve and I don't know what all he did tell me he'd do. I must abeen a fool but I was afraid to try it.

I had so much work to do and I never did git to go anywhere. I reckon he was afraid to let me go off de place for fear someone would tell me what a fool I was, so I never did git to go anywhere but had to work all de time. I was de only one to work and old Mistress and de girls never had done no work and didn't know much about it. I had a harder time dan when we was slaves.

I got to wanting to see my sister so I made up my mind to run off. One of old Master's motherless nephews lived with him and I got him to go with me one night to the potato bank and I got me a lap full of potatoes to eat so I wouldn't starve like old Master said I would. Dis white boy went nearly to a house where some white folks lived. I went to de house and told 'em I wanted to go to where my sister was and dey let me stay fer a few days and sent me on to my sister.

I saw old Master lots of times after I run away but he wasn't mad at me. I heard him tell de white folks dat I lived wid dat he raised me and I sure wouldn't steal nor tell a lie. I used to steal brown sugar lumps when mammy would be cooking but he didn't know 'bout dat.

On holidays we used to allus have big dinners, 'specially on Christmas, and we allus had egg-nog.

We allus had hog-jowel and peas on New Years Day 'cause iffen you'd have dat on New Years Day you'd have good luck all de year.

Iffen you have money on New Years Day you will have money all de year.

My husband, Lewis Wells, lived to be one-hundred and seven years old. He died five years ago. He could see witches, spirits and ghosts but I never could. Dere are a few things dat I've noticed and dey never fail.

Dogs howling and scritch owls hollering is allus a warning. My mother was sick and we didn't think she was much sick. A dog howled and howled right outside de house. Old Master say, "Nellie gonna die." Sure nuff she died dat night.

Another time a gentle old mule we had got after de children and run 'em to de house and den he lay down and wallow and wallow. One of our children was dead 'fore a week.

One of our neighbors say his dog been gone 'bout a week. He was walking and met de dog and it lay down and stretch out on de ground and measure a grave wid his body. He made him git up and he went home jest as fast as he could. When he got dere one of his children was dead.

Iffen my left eye quiver I know I'm gwineter cry and iffen both my eyes quiver I know I gwinter laugh till I cry. I don't like for my eyes to quiver.

We has allus made our own medicine. Iffen we hadn't we never could astood de chills and fevers. We made a tea out'n bitter weeds and bathed in it to cure malaria. We also made bread pills and soaked 'em in dis tea and swallowed 'em. After bathing in dis tea we'd go to bed and kiver up and sweat de malaria out.

Horse mint and palm of crystal (Castor-bean) and bullnettle root boiled together will make a cure for swelling. Jest bathe de swollen part in dis hot tea.

Anvil dust and apple vinegar will cure dropsy. One tea cup of anvil dust to a quart of vinegar. Shake up well and bathe in it. It sure will cure de worse kind of a case.

God worked through Abraham Lincoln and he answered de prayers of dem dat was wearing de burden of slavery. We cullud folks all love and honor Abraham Lincoln's memory and don't you think we ought to?

I love to hear good singing. My favorite songs are: "Am I A Soldier Of The Cross," an "How Can I Live In Sin and Doubt My Savior's Love." I belongs to de Baptist church.

Mary Grayson
BORN INTO SLAVERY IN THE CREEK NATION

I am what we colored people call a "native." That means that I didn't come into the Indian country from somewhere in the Old South, after the War, like so many negroes did, but I was born here in the old Creek Nation, and my master was a Creek Indian. That was eighty three years ago, so I am told.

My mammy belonged to white people back in Alabama when she was born—down in the southern part I think, for she told me that after she was a sizeable girl her white people moved into the eastern part of Alabama where there was a lot of Creeks. Some of them Creeks was mixed up with the whites, and some of the big men in the Creeks who come to talk to her master was almost white, it looked like. "My white folks moved around a lot when I was a little girl," she told me.

When mammy was about 10 or 12 years old some of the Creeks begun to come out to the Territory in little bunches. They wasn't the ones who was taken out here by the soldiers and contractor men— they come on ahead by themselves and most of them had plenty of money, too. A Creek come to my mammy's master and bought her to bring out here, but she heard she was being sold and run off into the woods. There was an old clay pit, dug way back into a high bank, where the slaves had been getting clay to mix with hog hair

Mary Grayson (1937), from T. Lindsay Baker and Julie P. Baker, eds., *The WPA Oklahoma Slave Narratives* (1996).

scrapings to make chinking for the big log houses that they built for the master and the cabins they made for themselves. Well, my mammy run and hid way back in that old clay pit, and it was way after dark before the master and the other man found her.

The Creek man that bought her was a kind sort of a man, mammy said, and wouldn't let the master punish her. He took her away and was kind to her, but he decided she was too young to breed and he sold her to another Creek who had several slaves already, and he brought her out to the Territory.

The McIntosh men was the leaders in the bunch that come out at that time, and one of the bunch, named Jim Perryman, bought my mammy and married her to one of his "boys," but after he waited and she didn't have a baby he decided she was no good breeder and he sold her to Mose Perryman.

Mose Perryman was my master, and he was a cousin to Legus Perryman, who was a big man in the Tribe. He was a lot younger than Mose, and laughed at Mose for buying my mammy, but he got fooled, because my mammy got married to Mose's slave boy Jacob, the way the slaves was married them days, and went ahead and had ten children for Mr. Mose.

Mose Perryman owned my pappy and his older brother, Hector, and one of the McIntosh men, Oona, I think his name was, owned my pappy's brother William. I can remember when I first heard about there was going to be a war. The older children would talk about it, but they didn't say it was a war all over the country. They would talk about a war going to be "back in Alabama," and I guess they had heard the Creeks talking about it that way.

When I was born we lived in the Choska bottoms, and Mr. Mose Perryman had a lot of land broke in all up and down the Arkansas river along there. After the War, when I had got to be a young woman, there was quite a settlement grew up at Choska (pronounced Choe-skey) right across the river east of where Haskell now is, but when I was a child before the War all the whole bottoms was marshy kind of wilderness except where farms had been cleared out. The land was very rich, and the Creeks who got to settle there were lucky. They always had big crops. All west of us was high ground, toward Gibson station and Fort Gibson, and the land was sandy. Some of the McIntoshes lived over that way, and my Uncle William belonged to one of them.

We slaves didn't have a hard time at all before the War. I have had people who were slaves of white folks back in the old states tell me that they had to work awfully hard and their masters were cruel to them sometimes, but all the Negroes I knew who belonged to Creeks always had plenty of clothes and lots to eat and we all lived in good log cabins we built. We worked the farm and tended to the horses and cattle and hogs, and some of the older women worked around the owner's house, but each Negro family looked after a part of the fields and worked the crops like they belonged to us.

When I first heard talk about the War the slaves were allowed to go and see one another sometimes and often they were sent on errands several miles with a wagon or on a horse, but pretty soon we were all kept at home, and nobody was allowed to come around and talk to us. But we heard what was going on.

The McIntosh men got nearly everybody to side with them about the War, but we Negroes got word somehow that the Cherokees over back of Ft. Gibson was not going to be in the War, and that there were some Union people over there who would help slaves to get away, but we children didn't know anything about what we heard our parents whispering about, and they would stop if they heard us listening. Most of the Creeks who lived in our part of the country, between the Arkansas and the Verdigris, and some even south of the Arkansas, belonged to the Lower Creeks and sided with the South, but down below us along the Canadian River they were Upper Creeks and there was a good deal of talk about them going with the North. Some of the Negroes tried to get away and go down to them, but I don't know of any from our neighborhood that went to them.

Some Upper Creeks came up into the Choska bottoms talking around among the folks there about siding with the North. They were talking, they said, for old man Gouge, who was a big man among the Upper Creeks. His Indian name was Opoeth-le-ya-hola, and he got away into Kansas with a big bunch of Creeks and Seminoles during the War.

Before that time, I remember one night my uncle William brought another Negro man to our cabin and talked a long time with my pappy, but pretty soon some of the Perryman Negroes told them that Mr. Mose was coming down and they went off into the woods to talk. But Mr. Mose didn't come down. When pappy came back Mammy cried quite a while, and we children could hear them arguing late at night. Then my uncle Hector slipped over to our cabin several times and talked to pappy, and mammy began to fix up grub, but she didn't give us children but a little bit of it, and told us to stay around with her at the cabin and not go playing with the other children.

Then early one morning, about daylight, old Mr. Mose came down to the cabin in his buggy, waving a shot gun and hollering at the top of his voice. I never saw a man so mad in all my life, before nor since!

He yelled in at mammy to "git them children together and git up to my house before I beat you and all of them to death!" Mammy began to cry and plead that she didn't know anything, but he acted like he was going to shoot sure enough, so we all ran to mammy and started for Mr. Mose's house as fast as we could trot.

We had to pass all the other Negro cabins on the way, and we could see that they were all empty, and it looked like everything in them had been tore up. Straw and corn shucks all over the place, where somebody had tore up the mattresses, and all the pans and kettles gone off the outside walls where they used to hang them.

At one place we saw two Negro boys loading some iron kettles on a wagon, and a little further on was some boys catching chickens in a yard, but we could see all the Negroes had left in a big hurry.

I asked mammy where everybody had gone and she said. "Up to Mr. Mose's house, where we are going. He's calling us all in."

"Will pappy be up there too?" I asked her.

"No. Your pappy and your Uncle Hector and your Uncle William and a lot of other menfolks won't be here any more. They went away. That's why Mr. Mose is so mad, so if any of you younguns say anything about any strange men coming to our place I'll break your necks!" Mammy was sure scared!

We all thought sure she was going to get a big whipping, but Mr. Mose just looked at her a minute and then told her to get back to the cabin and bring all the clothes, and bed ticks and all kinds of cloth we had and come back ready to travel.

"We're going to take all you black devils to a place where there won't no more of you run away!" he yelled after us. So we got ready to leave as quick as we could. I kept crying about my pappy, but mammy would say, "Don't you worry about your pappy, he's free now. Better be worrying about us. No telling where we all will end up!" There was four or five Creek families and their Negroes all got together to leave, with all their stuff packed in buggies and wagons, and being toted by the Negroes or carried tied on horses, jack asses, mules and milk cattle. I reckon it was a funny looking sight, or it would be to a person now; the way we was all loaded down with all manner of baggage when we met at the old ford across the Arkansas that lead to the Creek Agency. The Agency stood on a high hill a few miles across the river from where we lived, but we couldn't see it from our place down in the Choska bottoms. But as soon as we got up on the upland east of the bottoms we could look across and see the hill.

When we got to a grove at the foot of the hill near the agency Mr. Mose and the other masters went up to the Agency for a while. I suppose they found out up there what everybody was supposed to do and where they was supposed to go, for when we started on it wasn't long until several more families and their slaves had joined the party and we made quite a big crowd.

The little Negro boys had to carry a little bundle apiece, but Mr. Mose didn't make the little girls carry anything and let us ride if we could find anything to ride on. My mammy had to help lead the cows part of the time, but a lot of the time she got to ride an old horse, and she would put me up behind her. It nearly scared me to death, because I had never been on a horse before, and she had to hold on to me all the time to keep me from falling off.

Of course I was too small to know what was going on then, but I could tell that all the masters and the Negroes seemed to be mighty worried and careful all the time. Of course I know now that the Creeks were all split up over the War, and nobody was able to tell who would be friendly to us or who would try to poison us or kill us, or at least rob us. There was a lot of bushwhacking all through that country by little groups of men who was just out to get all they could. They would appear like they was the enemy of anybody they run across, just to have an excuse to rob them or burn up their stuff. If you said you was with the South they would be with the North and if you claimed to be with the Yankees they would be with the South, so our party was kind of upset all the time we was passing through the country along the Canadian. That

was where old Gouge had been talking against the South. I've
heard my folks say that he was a wonderful speaker, too.

We all had to move along mighty slow, on account of the ones
on foot, and we wouldn't get very far in one day, then we Negroes
had to fix up a place to camp and get wood and cook supper for
everybody. Sometimes we would come to a place to camp that
somebody knew about and we would find it all tromped down by
horses and the spring all filled in and ruined. I reckon old Gouge's
people would tear up things when they left, or maybe some
Southern bushwhackers would do it. I don't know which.

When we got down to where the North Fork runs into the
Canadian we went around the place where the Creek town was.
There was lots of Creeks down there who was on the other side, so
we passed around that place and forded across west of there. The
ford was a bad one, and it took us a long time to get across.
Everybody got wet and a lot of the stuff on the wagons got wet.
Pretty soon we got down into the Chickasaw country, and everybody was friendly to us, but the Chickasaw people didn't treat their
slaves like the Creeks did. They was more strict, like the people in
Texas and other places. The Chickasaws seemed lighter color than
the Creeks but they talked more in Indian among themselves and
to their slaves. Our masters talked English nearly all the time
except when they were talking to Creeks who didn't talk good
English, and we Negroes never did learn very good Creek. I could
always understand it, and can yet, a little, but I never did try to talk
it much. Mammy and pappy used English to us all the time.

Mr. Mose found a place for us to stop close to Fort Washita, and
got us places to stay and work. I don't know which direction we
were from Fort Washita, but I know we were not very far. I don't
know how many years we were down in there, but I know it was
over two for we worked on crops at two different places, I remember. Then one day Mr. Mose came and told us that the War was over
and that we would have to root for ourselves after that. Then he just
rode away and I never saw him after that until after we had got
back up into the Choska country. Mammy heard that the Negroes
were going to get equal rights with the Creeks, and that she should
go to the Creek Agency to draw for us, so we set out to try to get
back.

We started out on foot, and would go a little ways each day, and mammy would try to get a little something to do to get us some food. Two or three times she got paid in money, so she had some money when we got back. After three or four days of walking we came across some more Negroes who had a horse, and mammy paid them to let us children ride and tie with their children for a day or two. They had their children on the horse, so two or three little ones would get on with a larger one to guide the horse and we would ride a while and get off and tie the horse and start walking on down the road. Then when the others caught up with the horse they would ride until they caught up with us. Pretty soon the old people got afraid to have us do that, so we just led the horse and some of the little ones rode it.

We had our hardest time when we would get to a river or big creek. If the water was swift the horse didn't do any good, for it would shy at the water and the little ones couldn't stay on, so we would have to just wait until someone came along in a wagon and maybe have to pay them with some of our money or some of our goods we were bringing back to haul us across. Sometimes we had to wait all day before anyone would come along in a wagon.

We were coming north all this time, up through the Seminole Nation, but when we got to Weleetka we met a Creek family of freedmen who were going to the Agency too, and mammy paid them to take us along in their wagon. When we got to the Agency mammy met a Negro who had seen pappy and knew where he was, so we sent word to him and he came and found us. He had been through most of the War in the Union army.

When he got away into the Cherokee country some of them called the "Pins" helped to smuggle him on up into Missouri and over into Kansas, but he soon found that he couldn't get along and stay safe unless he went with the Army. He went with them until the War was over, and was around Gibson quite a lot. When he was there he tried to find out where we had gone but said he never could find out. He was in the battle of Honey Springs, he said, but never was hurt or sick. When we got back together we cleared a selection of land a little east of the Choska bottoms, near where Clarksville now is, and farmed until I was a great big girl.

I went to school at a little school called Blackjack school. I think it was a kind of mission school and not one of the Creek nation schools, because my first teacher was Miss Betty Weaver and she was not a Creek but a Cherokee. Then we had two white teachers, Miss King and John Kernan, and another Cherokee was in charge. His name was Ross, and he was killed one day when his horse fell off a bridge across the Verdigris, on the way from Tullahassee to Gibson Station.

When I got to be a young woman I went to Okmulgee and worked for some people near there for several years, then I married Tate Grayson. We got our freedmen's allotments on Mingo Creek, east of Tulsa, and lived there until our children were grown and Tate died, then I came to live with my daughter in Tulsa.

FURTHER READINGS

T. Lindsay Baker and Julie P. Baker, eds., *The WPA Oklahoma Slave Narratives* (University of Oklahoma Press, 1996); Charles T. Davis and Henry Louis Gates, Jr., eds., *The Slave's Narrative* (Oxford University Press, 1985).

Russell Lee, *Family of Farm Workers Living at the Farm Security Administration Farm Worker's Mobile Unit, Friendly Corners, Arizona,* 1942.

Library of Congress, Prints and Photographs Division, Washington, DC, Negative #LC-USF34-72137-D.

Ruth Underhill (1884–1984)

Born into a Quaker family in upstate New York in 1884, Ruth Underhill first went West to undertake anthropological research in Arizona in the early 1930s. After receiving her PhD from Columbia University in 1939, she went on to a career with the Bureau of Indian Affairs, where she wrote the textbooks used to teach Indian children about their own histories, as well as several studies of the Tohono O'Odham (or Papago) tribe. She is best-known for her study *Papago Woman* (1936), which resulted from an extraordinary collaboration between Underhill and an elderly Tohono O'Odham informant, María Chona. María Chona was born at Mesquite Root, or *kiutatk*, just below Quijotoa Mountain in Southern Arizona, in approximately 1846; she was in her nineties when she told her autobiography in the 1930s. Several years of interviews between Underhill and Chona yielded Chona's autobiography, published in 1936 as *Papago Woman*, the first published Southwestern Native American woman's autobiography.

The text of *Papago Woman* records the meeting of two worlds: Underhill's world of a feminist social scientist and Chona's world of O'Odham ways undergoing rapid transition. While most outsiders thought of the O'Odham, whose reservation lies in the heart of Arizona's Sonoran Desert, as an especially "primitive" tribe. However, when Chona told her autobiography, the O'Odham had begun to live in wattle and daub, wood, or cement houses. Many lived away from the reservation, in Tucson, or in the areas surrounding the reservation. Many, especially those who worked outside the reservation, received wages for their labors and used U.S. currency. The Papago barter economy was at least partially replaced by a capitalist market system. The O'Odham replaced their breach clouts with cotton dresses and sandals for the women and khaki or denim pants, cotton shirts, and, if they could afford them, cowboy boots for the men. Guns, purchased or traded for, replaced bows and arrows, and trucks and cars began to make an appearance.

Still, it was important for Underhill to hide this evidence of cultural change underway in Chona's life. Like many early anthropologists, she wanted to "salvage" the authentic (non-European) aspects of Indians' cultures before contact with outside cultures erased them; as a result, Underhill tended to play down evidence that the Tohono O'Odham had learned to cope with the presence of Europeans and had even found some of their tools and ways worth adopting as their own.

In this selection from *Papago Woman,* Ruth Underhill expresses her surprise when she learns of the power that O'Odham women feel in their own culture. This was especially striking to Underhill because she wanted to learn how to get this sense of power for women in her own culture, and because she saw O'Odham women as, in fact, powerless in their own society. The discussion that takes place between Chona and the other O'Odham women and Ruth Underhill demonstrates just a few of the important exchanges among women of different cultures in the American Southwest.

WOMEN

My first weeks among the Papago were spent almost entirely with women. This was a fortunate accident. It provided an insight into one side of tribal life not usually explored by my male colleagues.

The women were usually in groups. No matter what house Chona and I were in, these relatives—for they all seemed some kind of kin—flowed in like water into a depression. They brought ground sheets, handwork, and female children of all ages.

Of course there was no spoken greeting. They could sit in the ramada, smiling, for at least half an hour. Then a toddling child might need attention, or a baby left alone for a moment might start to cry. Any woman might pick the baby up, even nurse it if she were able. Their closeness to one another seemed to me almost that of identical twins. Perhaps that closeness was normal among ancient people whose lives often depended on mutual help.

It was not only for housework that they stayed together. Their gathering of basketry materials or clay for pots was done in groups.

Ruth Underhill, "Women," from *Papago Woman* (1979).

So was their play. All the Papagos played, both old and young. They played gambling and guessing games; they raced and jumped; but always males of any age with males, females with females.

"The men were friendly," Chona had told me. "They cleared the race track, they cheered us and bet on us."

"But they did not race with you?"

"Of course not. We were too unlike. It would be like putting quails and hawks together."

"And you were the quails, I suppose. Didn't you think the hawks had more fun?"

I had strayed into the sort of talk heard from my own female friends. It did not register with Chona. I found myself going on with the old argument: "Well, you're at home all the time with babies and cooking. The men travel and—and—"

"But we're not always home. We make our trips for basketry and greens."

So they did. I had been talking about a modern situation which had not yet confronted the Papago. Perhaps the early differentiation between men's work and women's was more sensible.

I let the companionable silence calm us all, then began again: "But the ceremonies! They are mostly at night when you would have time to go. Won't the men let you?"

In fact, I had been somewhat nettled by finding that at many ceremonies the sex separation was as complete as at games. When I arrived with the troop of women, I found that we must all sit in a certain place, good view or not. And if I had been using a male interpreter, he could not come to help.

The women were smiling as I have smiled at pestering children. I tried to defend my position: "I can see that you don't want to go on the men's hunting expeditions, but why could you not take part in ceremonies?"

They laughed. "Oh, ceremonies are something the men made up, you know. They have the dreams, they make the stories, then they perform the ceremony."

"But don't you dream?"

No, it seemed the women did not dream very much; and finally I got the explanation: "You see, we *have* power. Men have to dream to get power from the spirits and they think of everything they can—songs and speeches and marching around, hoping that the spirits will notice them and give them some power. But we *have* power." When I looked a little surprised, the answer was: "Children. Can any warrior make a child, no matter how brave and wonderful he is?"

"Warriors *do* take a little part in starting the children."

They sniffed. "A very small part. It's nothing compared to the months that a woman goes through to make a child. Don't you see that without us, there would be no men? Why should we envy men? We *made* the men."

That delightful attitude I should have been glad to take home with me. Perhaps it was the basis for the dignified composure that I saw women exhibit when in public. For Papago women, at least the older ones, are beginning to take some public positions. Very recently, one was appointed a judge above male candidates. Another is active in social reform. And San Xavier has a women's club, the first in America made up entirely of native American women. Must they go through a long battle of fighting for their place, or will the peaceful Papago attitude prevail?

FURTHER READINGS
Joyce Griffen, "Ruth Murray Underhill," in Ute Gacs, Aisha Khan, Jerrie McIntyre, and Ruth Weinberg, eds., *Women Anthropologists: Selected Biographies* (Urbana: University of Illinois Press, 1988, 1989), pp. 355–360; Catherine Lavender, "Bringing Down the Clouds: María Chona, Ruth Underhill, and *Papago Woman*," M.A. Thesis, University of Colorado–Boulder, 1991; Catherine Lavender, "Storytellers: Feminist Ethnography and the American Southwest, 1900–1940," Ph.D. Thesis, University of Colorado–Boulder, 1997; Gretchen M. Bataille and Kathleen Mullen Sands, *American Indian Women, Telling Their Lives* (University of Nebraska Press, 1984).

Mabel Dodge Luhan (1879–1962)

Mabel Ganson was born and educated in Buffalo, New York. Her first marriage ended when her husband died, and then she remarried Edwin Dodge, a Boston architect. They lived in Florence where Mabel kept a salon frequented by such artists as Eleonora Duse, and Isadora Duncan. She divorced Dodge and returned to New York, where in Greenwich Village, she began to display her great skills as hostess to radical intellectuals and avant garde artists. She offered hospitality to John Reed, Lincoln Steffens, Amy Lowell, Walter Lippmann, Margaret Sanger, Max Eastman, Gertrude Stein, Alice B. Toklas, Willa Cather, and others, and was the major force behind the Armory Show of Post-Impressionist artists in 1913.

In 1916 she married artist Maurice Sterne, and they moved to Taos, New Mexico. She wrote of Taos "My life broke in two right then, and I entered into the second half, a new world more strange and terrible and sweet than any I had ever been able to imagine." She studied the customs of the Pueblo Indians and found in that culture answers she had searched for in the psychoanalytical theories of Freud and A. A. Brill. She divorced Sterne and in 1923 she married Tony Luhan, a Tiwa Indian. Their home was the center for artists D. H. Lawrence, Jean Toomer, Elsie Clews Parsons, Mary Austin, of men like John Collier, Carl Jung, Leopold Stokowski, and Thornton Wilder. The American Southwest, she said, was a place where the "land is a source of inspiration."

Mabel Dodge Luhan was a writer whose essays appeared in *Theatre Arts Monthly,* in "little magazines" like *Laughing Horse*, published in Santa Fé, and, later, in the four-volume autobiography *Intimate Memories* (1933–1937). Attention is always paid to her wide circle of artists and intellectuals, to her ideas of equality between the sexes—"For the mature woman…There is only herself, free and alone, bearing her own security within her own soul." Less notice is given to her gifts as a writer. The lovely *Winter in Taos* (1935) is offered here both for its intensely personal revelations, and for the poetry of its descriptions of landscape.

SEASONS

The fantastic house that has grown slowly, room by room, stretches and sprawls out beneath me. First there was a long, coffin-shaped, bare box of a place containing the four original rooms that I bought when I came eighteen years ago. Jose's father lived in them and offered to sell when Tony approached him about it.

Tony always loved this piece of rising ground above the town on the edge of the Indian land. When he was a little boy, he came down here with his father, who knew how to do carpenter work, and he held the nails when his father cut a hole in the thick *adobe* wall and fitted a new window into one of the rooms for Jose's father.

This same window is in Tony's room, now; it is the room where his guns and hunting knives are locked in the carved guncase Manuel made for his Christmas present two years ago, and where all his Indian things are. In this room he has many confabulations with Indians who come to talk over things, sitting before the corner fireplace. On the chimney place there are some things people have given him, a bronze horse, a bronze deer, and a golden buffalo!

The old beamed ceiling is painted sky-blue and the walls are whitewashed. There are white muslin curtains on the long window that looks eastward over the desert, but on Tony's father's tall, narrow window, there is none, so one can see out onto the portal through the small, uneven panes.

There is a bed beside this window, where sometimes one of the nephews or a visiting Indian friend sleeps. It has a red and white patchwork quilt on it, made of little pieces of old-fashioned calico.

On the wall over the bed, there is a crucifix carved out of ivory, that Clarence gave Tony, and upon it hangs a small rusty rosary he found in the ground here on the place. There are some Indian paintings hanging on the walls; also a fishing basket, a coiled-up hair rope, a pair of beaded moccasins and some other Indian things.

The long, narrow window his father set in the wall looks out upon the portal that stretches from the front door to John's jutting log cabin. It is a little crooked, and its wooden frame, ten or twelve inches wide, is somewhat warped, but he would not have it changed and neither would I.

Mabel Dodge Luhan, from *Winter in Taos* (1935).

■ ■ ■

And how I have loved it, this house built on different levels, a room or two at a time. The gatherings of all my past life are deposited here. Besides the regular furniture and pictures and books that came from Italy and France and New York, letters, in packets, that date all the way back to Buffalo, are stuffed into cabinets and drawers, and all kinds of curious odds and ends that have followed me down the years are tucked away in corners and shelves. Bits of china, silk, scraps of carving, parts of Buddhas, lacquer, incense, parchment and tooled leather throw out odd scents when one opens a cupboard door, or opens the heavy lid of some chest.

■ ■ ■

So the house is a kind of treasure trove, but it is treasure that needs a key, and I am the only one who has it. No one else could possibly understand the origin and use of all the mingled fragments hidden away in it, and I can never catch up with it all or get it really assembled. When one is my age, and has never had the heart to throw away a pretty box or an interesting letter, or get around to having all the breakages of journeys and the daily wear and tear on delicate antiques repaired, it may be imagined what accumulation gathers about one.

■ ■ ■

That is what the Big House is made up of. It is my home, it holds me, works me to death, bores me and will not let me go! The trees we planted have almost buried it, now; they tower in a great, green wall between us and the town. When I first came to live here in two or three rooms with Tony, we could look down the road and see all the way to the turn at the corner, and I said to him, then:

"I bet I'm going to spend all the rest of my life looking down that road!" I looked down along it for years, watching for him to come home, but now it is hidden. Nothing can be seen of it, not even the lights of an approaching car in the summertime, so thick are the leaves of the cottonwoods and elder trees along the "mother ditch" that curves along in front of the house below the flagstones that pave the courtyard.

The house grew slowly and it stretches on and on. At one end it piles up, for over the Big Room there is the bedroom where Tony sleeps, next to my room, and a big sleeping porch off of it; and from this room one climbs a steep little stairway up into a kind of look-out room, made of helioglass set in wooden columns on all four sides, where one has the views of all the valley, down to the village and beyond it to the horizon, up to the Pueblo and the Sacred Mountain, north to Frieda's ranch on the side of Lobo Mountain, and the Colorado mountains beyond it.

There is nothing on this bare, blue-painted floor but some *serapes,* and up here under the sky, winter and summer, one can lie in the sunshine and bathe in it until "untied are the knots in the heart," for there is nothing like the sun for smoothing out all difficulties.

■ ■ ■

Tony is naturally patriarchal and born to be a head of a family. It is a pity he has no sons of his own; but he never did have any, though Molly said she heard that all these nephews are really his sons! A most interesting thought to outsiders, I presume.

That morning, when Tony came upstairs, he sat down in the red rocking chair beside the bed. He looked serene and ample and strong as a dike. When Frieda and Lorenzo first came and we were driving them up to Santa Fe from the train, Frieda, I remember, looked wonderingly at his broad back in front of her and exclaimed:

"Don't you feel he is like a *rock* for you to lean on?"

And I said, "No," uncertainly. But we had only been together five years then. Now, twelve years later, he seems like a rock; more than that, a mountain, that will support all the weight I can put on him. Nothing can really hurt a woman who has a man like this, to give her moral and emotional support. We could lose our houses and our horses, our friends, our health and our strength, but as long as we are together, we are immune from essential loss.

■ ■ ■

I always knit in the wintertime, and I can't endure doing that in the summer! But as soon as the days grow shorter, I hunt for my bag of wools and all my amber needles, and I am perfectly content to sit in the window and knit and knit and knit and ponder and remember and get into a kind of even rhythm of thinking, feeling, breathing, knitting; that is, somehow, a very satisfactory activity, like a dance, or like the slow, sure motion of a constant star.

Out of this purring intensity there are produced many little sweaters. Not being proficient in sleeves or necks, they are merely slip-ons with a hole at the top and two holes for the arms. All over the Pueblo they can be seen every winter on the little boys. Turquoise blue, pink, emerald green, sapphire, red, they are dots of bright color running against the snow. At the beginning, they are of a fair proportion, coming to below the waist, but with each washing they grow longer and longer, so finally they come well below the knees and look like cylinders—but nobody seems to mind!

I was watching a little cloud floating over the Sacred Mountain, no bigger than a man's hand, as the saying goes, firmer, the iron frost in the ground would deepen, and in the early morning the rime would coat every branch and twig and stiffen the pale stubble in the fields.

Something like a shiver went over me at the thought of the winter thickening still more, covering us, clamping us down, until I remembered what I learned long ago, but always forget and have to learn anew each year: that if one gives up and lets it come right down over one, if one sinks into the season and is a part of it, there is peace in this submission. Only in resistence there is melancholy and a sort of panic.

It doesn't take long for the aspect of the world to change here, and in a short time great galleons of cloud sailed over the sky and soon covered the sun. Then everything looked sad indeed. We depend so much on the high key of light for illumining things.

When the sun shines, it colors every tree and hummock of earth near-by and in the distance the ether seems of ponderable blue and violet and mauve; the mountain changes from pansy purple to periwinkle blue, and great cloud-shadows shaped like eagles move over it, or it turns ink black splashed with white, behind the pale, radiant fields that glisten and flash. All day long there are changes of color and mood, startling and strange, and one never grows accustomed to the endless variety of the hours.

But when the sun is gone, the earth looks widowed and drear.

The winter fields seem shabby and dirty, splashed with manure and trodden into dinginess by the horses. The Mountain shrinks and crouches until it seems only half as high as usual, and it loses all its majesty. The landscape might be in New England instead of on a high and halcyon tableland in a region of magic.

■ ■ ■

When the grass is green and the iris are moving purple and quiet, like women gossiping with their heads together, it is hard to remember the deep, woolly snow and how hard it is to walk through it in the winter.

Tony and I used to go out hunting together sometimes when there was a new snowfall. Then the fresh tracks showed up where the animals had passed and the way they went. Tony would go on ahead through the woods, breaking a trail, and I would try to follow in his steps.

A still wood, with the new white covering, can be wonderful and as though the earth were remade that day; and the trees, standing bowed a little by the weight they have to bear until a wind comes that will shake it off, seem patient and trustful.

On the ground we saw many little writings, left delicately by the animals, lovely patterns in a rhythm of movement and ease, soft as the imprint of waves upon the sand, sensitive as the record of the heartbeat, written by the electrocardiograph.

One day in particular that I remember, Tony was tracking a deer. The hard, cleft marks of the hooves sprang upward in pairs, showing how he had run through the trees. Tony moved more rapidly and ever more silently, holding his gun in both hands, and I thought we would never come to the end of it, it was such hard going in the snow; but all of a sudden there was a flurry and a flapping ahead of us, high up in a pine tree. An eagle rose, head low, and heavily climbed into the sky between the thick branches; and the minute Tony saw it, he raised his gun with an involuntary movement and fired. He missed, and another sound followed the report of the gun. Ahead of us somewhere, we heard the quick crackle of broken twigs and the hasty departure of an animal running.

Tony gave an exclamation of impatience. "I so stupid!" he said in a low voice.

"Why? What was it?" I asked him, not understanding what had taken place.

"That eagle saw us coming first, and got up to warn the deer!" he said. "See? Here is where the deer was lying down, and the eagle, she was up on the tree."

"Do you mean to say that that eagle made you fire your gun so the deer would know we were close?"

"Yes, she made us tell, *some* way, we comin'. The eagle always take care of the deer. . . ." And he told me of other friendships between the wild animals and how they help each other. When he tells me things, it seems to me there is as much of coöperation as there is of cruelty in that world, and we usually think only of the cruel side of their habits, and how they prey upon each other and live in perpetual fear. We know very little.

■   ■   ■

October, and all the tourists have departed. Hardly an outside license to be seen on a car!

After the trees are fully turned and are like torches of fiery yellow, often with coral red tips, and others are big round balls of radiant, sun-colored loveliness, they have a long quiet pause before the end. Day after day of Indian summer passes, breathless, when the whole valley is immobile and every leaf is motionless, shining golden and still. What days! One moves in a dream through the country, scarcely able to believe one's eyes, for the wonder of it.

On a crisp morning in October when the hills are veiled soft with smoke from burning leaves, it is delicious to ride up to the cedars and get an armful of branches covered with blueberries. We pile them in a corner of the Big Room to dry and every day Albidia will burn a piece after she has swept and dusted the rooms. The sweet wholesome fragrance penetrates every part of the house, refreshing the air, and it has a curious effect of composing the life and the nerves of everyone, and establishing a feeling of order and clarity for the whole day.

The hills are misty and blue with the autumn haze—the Sacred Mountain is intensely somber with purple depths in its canyons, and the sun moves serenely uninterrupted across the cloudless, deep blue sky.

■ ■ ■

Sometimes the heart tightens up, though....

Now I went out to the kitchen to the telephone, but who should I call up? I had done that, once or twice, long ago, when Tony didn't come home; I had called a garage and sent a car out looking for him, and this made him so mad I never repeated it.

"I sitting there with my friends, and a Mexican come knock at the door and ask if they seen me, and say you been sending for me! Make me feel very foolish! I not a child that you send for me!"

"But I thought maybe you had an accident and needed help!"

"I not the kind that have accidents. You know me very well— how careful."

Yes, it was true, but why couldn't I feel it? And why do I go on year in and year out, feeling frightened if he stays away late at night? Most of the other women here turn off their lights and go to sleep, whether their men are home or not. Why can't I learn to do so?

I sat down before the fire and smoked a cigarette and began to feel sorry for myself, and this took the edge off the worry. It really isn't worth it, I thought, to live here in this solitude, shut in by the winter, when everyone has gone somewhere else and is having an interesting time! But, alas! I remembered that I was here because I chose to be, and that no other kind of time anyone was having meant a thing to me, compared with my life, the way I had built it here. This was best for me, this home in the valley, where my work stretches far out ahead of me.

Yes, this was my bed I had made, and I would lie on it, and for the most part it was better than the others', only the hard parts sometimes seemed harder than theirs, as I believe they are. But even in the summers, the worst things happen, I consoled myself.

■ ■ ■

I returned to my warm, serene room upstairs, and let anxiety rise in me until I was flooded with it. I ceased to oppose it, and let the trouble possess me.

Suddenly, outside my window, there was a loud, long-drawn-out howl, followed by a startling chorus of barks, rising like shrill laughter. It sounded like a hundred throats giving tongue in the still, cold night.

Coyotes down from the hill! Often we heard them in the distance, like fiends gathering as winter deepened and hunger drove them near, but rarely so close as this. The smell of fresh meat must have attracted them until they padded stealthily down through the unbroken snow to the wire-screened door of the meat-room.

Zero hour in truth, it seemed to me, now, as midnight showed on the little clock beside the bed, and I wondered if I would ever feel happy and at ease again. No matter that tomorrow the house would be full of voices, or that yesterday, only yesterday, we had such fun with Alexandra and Spud and the others, dancing here all the evening, and doing puzzles. There was only Now, and I was unable to endure it.

Then I was driven to the center of being, as always before in hard moments, all through my life: in, in, until the point was reached that is the most living kernel of us all, and I said: "Please make him come. *Now!*" over and over, and this loosened the constraint within and lighted me up with peace. I knew beyond doubt that everything was all right, so I would not have worried any more, even if Tony hadn't come until morning.

But I didn't have long to wait after that. Far below in the house I heard the front door bang shut, and then his slow, steady step through the house, till it was mounting the stairs.

I flew through the rooms to meet him.

"Oh, Tony!" I cried, "I was so afraid something had happened to you. Why are you so late?"

His face looked smooth and benevolent as he put his kind hand on my shoulder.

"What can happen?" he asked, gently.. "I wish you not worry like that! I had a nice time with my friends and we gambled a little: two, three dollars. I took my beans out to the Pueblo to Sofina, then she gave me coffee. Why you frightened like that?"

"Such a night—the storm—"

"Don't you know the moon is shining?" he said, smiling; and he pulled the curtain back from the window to show me.

Sure enough, it was shining, and the desert was spread out so clear and visible that I could see the shadow of a whole house, a dark reflection of itself upon the snow.

FURTHER READINGS

Mabel Dodge Luhan, *Intimate Memories: The Autobiography of Mabel Dodge Luhan*, ed. Lois P. Rudnick (University of New Mexico Press, 1999); Lois P. Rudnick, *Utopian Vistas: The Mabel Dodge Luhan House and the American Counterculture* (University of New Mexico Press, 1998); Lois P. Rudnick, *Mabel Dodge Luhan: New Woman, New World* (University of New Mexico Press, 1984); Winifred L. Frazer, *Mabel Dodge Luhan* (Twayne, 1984); Jane V. Nelson, *Mabel Dodge Luhan* (Boise State University Press, 1982); Mabel Dodge Luhan, *Taos and its Artists* (Duell, Sloan and Pearce, 1947); Patricia R. Everett, ed., *A History of Having a Great Many Times Not Continued to Be Friends: The Correspondence Between Mabel Dodge and Gertrude Stein, 1911–1934* (University of New Mexico Press, 1996).

Teresa Jordan, *Marie Scott's Hands*, from *Cowgirls: Women of the American West, An Oral History* (Doubleday, 1982).

Donna Gray

Donna Gray lives with her husband on a small ranch near Pray, Montana, in the heart of Paradise Valley, between the Absoroka and Gallatin ranges. A midwesterner by birth, Donna is a Montanan by choice. Her interviews with Montana ranch women—her neighbors—were tape recorded, and the stories shaped after listening to them for the cadences of speech, and for the bright images and details. These ranch women "kept house" over fifty years ago. "Without exception, every woman I approached felt that her life had not been of particular interest, that there was really 'nothing to tell.'"

Portions of these stories were performed in a readers' theater presentation, "Four Women From Pray," in Livingston, Montana, in 1989, 1990, and 1991.

ORAL HISTORIES OF RANCH WOMEN

Urma DeLong Taylor

Urma DeLong Taylor was born in North Dakota in 1911. Her parents and her mother's family, the Geers, were to become part of Montana's great homestead saga. When she speaks of those years, 1915–1919, it is sometimes with sadness, but also with nostalgia, pride, triumph. Given a great deal of responsibility for her age, she told me that by the age of 10½ she baked and cooked for her family. She asked some other little girls one day, "How many of you can dress a chicken from the feathers out, cut it up and have a meal on the table at night? They could none of them say it, of course."

In 1915, when she was 3½, Urma travelled with her parents, John and Elata DeLong, and her older sister, in a covered wagon, from their home in Mott, North Dakota, to Colorado. The covered wagon was built and outfitted by John, a carpenter by trade.

Donna Gray, "Oral Histories of Ranch Women" (1997).

It looked like all the pictures of covered wagons. It had bows up over the top with canvas. It was certainly waterproof, 'n' had that little puckerin' string that we'd peek out and watch the scenery as we'd gone past it. He (John) built the cupboards. It was all cupboards on the inside. They were along the side, had doors on 'em, so things wouldn't rattle out. Some was shelving, part drawers. Ever'thing had to have a door on it. On the outside he built shelves to carry the barrels of water and feed for the horses.

In the cupboards there were cans of all descriptions, for size, according to the food that was in 'em. You could put 50 pounds of flour in one of those cans. They nearly always bought flour in 50's, sugar in 25. She (Elata) had an old-fashioned Dutch oven. It had three little legs, a lid, and a handle to pick it up by. She made her biscuits in it, over the campfire, and you never ate such biscuits. There was a hot cake griddle, skillets, coffee pot 'n' such.

She had a lovely feather bed and homemade quilts. We all slept in that little space that was in the center between the cupboards. A wagon is not too awfully wide, either.

On that trip, we did what many a person couldn't say they'd done—they're so fussy about water nowadays—we took a cup and reached into a foot track. It had rained pretty hard in this one area, and cattle had crossed there and where they stepped down kinda deep, it was nothin' at all to dip in and get a drink. When you're out of water, wet is wet.

One time we crossed—I think Mother called it the Little Missouri River—it was in the spring, and it was pretty swollen. The horses had to swim some before they got to the edge. When they went to pull up out of there, onto the bank, us girls rolled right down and hit the tailgate of the wagon. Mother thought, out we went to drown! It was just the noise of a heavy chain from the outside hittin' the back end. It held, of course, but she just about had a heart attack.

When the DeLongs finally reached their destination, a great disappointment awaited them. They had travelled that great dis-

tance on the strength of an advertisement for a new town. This is
how Urma remembers it:

*They had advertised for carpenters to make a town. You had to
have $2,000 cash or the equivalent of it. He (Father) didn't have that
much; I think it was $500. He figured with that fine team and wagon
and his tools he made up more than $2,000. They didn't want a
bunch of poor people comin' in there. After we got to the town, they
had decided to change their minds; they didn't make the town, so
there's nothin' to do but turn around and go back.*

The DeLongs headed north to Sheridan, Wyoming, where John
DeLong worked briefly as a carpenter. From Sheridan, they went to
Broadus, Montana to join Elata's parents and siblings.

*My father put in for a homestead out of Broadus where my
grandparents' ranch was. My mother's brothers and sisters, all of
them, was living right in that same area. Father went to a land office
and made out the papers for the homestead, come home, and
Mother's brothers helped him get the logs out and make it. I have a
picture of the house they built.*

*We wintered in it, and the next spring along come a man, and
he said, "What are you folks doing here?" "Why," my father said, "This
is my homestead. We built the house and wintered here."*

*"Well, I'm sorry," he said, "but you're on my land." And my father
says, "All right, where did you put in for yours?" And I think they said it
was some 20 or 30 miles away at another land office. So, to prove the
thing, they go over to the land office, and they get the timing, because
it was put down right to the minute when you signed the paper, and
then they got the timing at that other one. Three hours difference,
and it was his land. We had to pick up and leave, go someplace. There
was no more land right around there. It was a fam'ly thing . . . we
had our house to live in, but we all worked together; we all shared*

our food. Food and some clothes was all you thought of anyhow.

After the homestead, we went down eastward from Sheridan (Wyoming). Got a 80 acre place there thirteen miles out of Arvada.

It would get so HOT in the summertime, and of course we'd go barefoot. It'd feel like it was burning your feet on the floor in the house. Right after breakfast, my mother and sister and I, we'd plan what we was goin' to have for lunch, and we'd hurry up and fix it, and take it down in the root cellar. We'd spend the whole day there! They crocheted, and I played with frogs. I diapered them and everything. They reminded me of a little child. When I lay them down to put their diapers on, they just lay there and let me do it. I had more fun with my little frogs!

I never rode in a car once in the time we lived there near Arvada. Oh, if us kids didn't look forward to the day when it was time to go to town. I don't recall ever going to town in the wintertime. It'd always be so cold, but in the summertime, my mother drove the team, and we went in the wagon to town . . . oh, boy . . . you'd get a few sticks of candy, little odds and ends like that. We sent to the catalog for things. Practically everything you got you got outta catalogs. I never will forget, there in the post office in town, some new shoes for me. Oh, those leather shoes! You know what new leather smells like . . . that was the best perfume I'd ever smelled. As we went along, ever few minutes, I'd take 'em out—oh—put 'em on, look 'em over, then put 'em back in the box. That was my fun, all the way home. 'Course, you never wore 'em around home. You only wore 'em when you went somewhere. Set 'em on the shelf; I'd pert near wear 'em out takin' 'em down to smell 'em.

The things that would please a child then, they wouldn't even think of today.

We went out to Washington after the hard winter, 1918 going into '19. It ruined the Geer family's big cattle business. They died like flies. There was nothin' for them to eat. We couldn't afford hay. That old swamp hay that they was bringin' in from North Dakota was all there was to be had, and we couldn't afford it. Cattle wasn't worth enough. They saved a few, but it was nothing but a handful. It was over 300 head that they had always run. It broke their hearts. They sold out to a neighbor—their land and their cattle, their equipment 'n' everything. They just pulled out. The boys spread out wherever they could find work.

The grandparents went out to—it was a ways from Seattle, but in that general area. They wrote back and says, "Say, there's fruit picking and things to make a living at out here. You better, any of you that wants something to do, come." My mother and her sister and us two girls, we went out there. My dad didn't come right then; he wanted to see whether we just ended up a visit, or what.

We got in right at raspberry time, and then it went to cherry picking. Us kids would do whatever the grownups was doing. It felt so funny to be makin' some money! When it come fall, we went down to Vancouver—that one across from Portland. They had this big Del Monte plant that canned every type of fruit, vegetable, anything in season, and they got on there.

I was 8½, and Mother showed me how I could boil spuds or fry 'em, usually it was boil. Then when they came home to lunch— nearly always it was hamburger; that was the quickest thing, that, or bacon, sump'n on that order, to fix real quick. By that time we had tent houses that we lived in.

In the Arvada segment, Urma tells a story about Pete, a little orphaned chicken. The little girl who was on her own day after day in the Vancouver tent village, must have had empathy for Pete . . . "a teeny guy . . . having to babysit himself."

Down there out of Arvada was a place where the road went right through a man's barn lot. You had to open the gate, go through it, then open another. This one day there was a poor little chicken, and he couldn't keep up with Mama for the reason that he'd gotten into some horse hair, and it had wound around and made hobbles of his little feet. Mother went to the house to tell 'em about it. There was not a soul nowhere, at the barns or anywhere, so we took the little orphan home with us instead. We got that old hair off . . . we named him Pete, and he was a spoiled child. He lived right in the house with us; he's one of us. We didn't put him in a cage . . . put him in a box . . . for the night. But in the daytime—I never will forget this one time—we was doing things outside and had just left him there in the house, and he jumped upon the table. To this good day I do what my mother did: on my table here's salt 'n' sugar 'n' everything. Sugar bowl settin' there, it was quite a big one. He jumped upon the table, and the highest thing he found was the sugar bowl. When we come in he was perched there on the edge. He wasn't even half grown, just a teeny guy yet, havin' to babysit himself! Oh, kid, such funny things. . . .

Madge Switzer Walker

Madge Switzer Walker was born in Montana in 1891. Her paternal grandparents, Andrew and Elizabeth Switzer, were early pioneers who settled in the Madison Valley in 1865, one year after the region was organized as the Montana Territory, twenty-four years before Montana entered the union as the 41st state in 1889.

The recollections in this account are from Madge's first eleven years, when the family lived in the small town of Jeffers, Montana.

My grandparents, Andrew and Elizabeth Switzer, came from Victor, Iowa, and that's in Powshiek County, in the southeastern corner of the state. They started with four oxen and three covered wagons. Grandpa Switzer had one wagon; Malpheus Switzer, Grandpa's brother, rode horseback along beside them. Law (another relative) had the second wagon. I can't remember about the third wagon . . .

They left Iowa the first of May, 1865, and they got to Virginia City September 30. They came to the Madison (Valley) the next day, October 1. That was . . . five months.

Grandma had a girl 10, and a girl 8. My dad was a year and a half, and she had a six weeks' old baby. She was afraid to go into a dark room. Think what she must have suffered; it must have been terrible. And she didn't want to come! *When they left Iowa, she went over to the railroad, a little ways from their farm, and rode for seven miles. I think she thought that would be the last time she'd ever see a railroad.*

When they got to the Platte River, she and Aunt Ellen cut their hair off. They had long hair, and it was just too much trouble, so they cut it off and laid it across a stump. They said, "Now they'll think we've been scalped!"

Grandma Switzer told me a story about an indian. Nez Perce

*were coming through the valley. They had their women and children
with them, but this young fellow came to her house. It was a one-room
cabin, with one window, one door, and she was washing on the board
in the tub. The indian—she was afraid of him—took out his knife. The
children were crying; she was afraid she was going to be scalped. He
sharpened the knife on a rock, then he pulled a hair out of his head
and cut it to see if it was sharp. Now she was really scared! I said,
"What did you do?"And she said,"I washed as hard as I could."*

The indian took a turnip out of his pocket and peeled it!

*She thought how foolish she was to have been afraid. The Nez
Perce were travelling with their women and children; they wouldn't
be on the war path and they wouldn't be up to any mischief. She
was just so frightened, and she had those little children. Well, my
goodness, what do we know about hard times?*

*Grandpa Switzer had a herd of purebred Brown Swiss cows, the
first in the valley. He milked about a dozen cows. I don't think
Grandma ever milked; he brought the milk in. She put it in pans, tin
pans about that big around (indicates a sizeable pan). He'd built her
a rack that let these pans fit in. She'd leave the milk till the next day,
and then she'd take the cream off the top. By that time it was stiff;
you could almost lift it up. She skimmed the cream and made butter;
she used the skim milk to make cottage cheese.*

*Grandma made butter in a barrel churn. That's the kind that goes
around and turns over. She turned it with a handle, over and over. She
put her butter in two-pound wooden molds, and sold it for 25¢ a pound.*

*To make cottage cheese, she put the milk on the back of the
stove in a fair-sized vessel, a kettle, and left it there overnight. By
morning it would have clabbered. Then she put it in a cheesecloth
bag and drained it. The curds were pretty hard and small.*

*Later on, they got a separator, and that was quite a something.
We would have that separated cream on fresh currants. The cream
was, oh, it was too rich!*

*The separator was an innovation. It was an iron rack, and there
was a bowl at the top of it with twenty-four discs that dipped into
the bowl. You'd crank until you got it to the point where it didn't
whine. You could tell by the sound of it if you were going fast
enough. It separated the cream from the milk. Centrifigal, you see.
The cream went to the outside, the skim milk went to the inside.
There were two spouts, one for the skim milk, one for the cream. It*

could be adjusted so the cream was very thick or very thin.

Grandma was a persevering woman. She raised chickens, sold cottage cheese, butter and eggs. She put her girls through school, a school for young ladies in Virginia City. She didn't bother about the boy. My dad probably went to school six months in his life, but he was a pretty smart man.

I remember once—I was just a little thing—going down to Grandma Switzer's house. When I got there, she had taken baby chickens away from a setting hen. She had them in a basket, and she let me look at them. Oh, they were cunning, just little puffs. I covered them up carefully, too carefully. When she uncovered them, they were all dead. Those chickens meant something to her; they were dollars and cents. As well as being sorry for the chickens. But she didn't scold me; she didn't say a word.

At Grandma Switzer's they didn't eat in the kitchen. They had a dining room (this was a large house built after the one-room log cabin) and sometimes they didn't have enough chairs to go around, so they sat on boxes and tree stumps. Her kitchen had a wood stove with a reservoir in the back and a big oven. She made loaves and loaves and LOAVES of bread. And cookies—she made lots of cookies in the fall when she had eggs and butter and cream. They were raised sugar cookies, about two inches across, and they puffed up in the middle. She put them in a barrel, and they lasted through the winter.

When I was about six, there was a general store in Jeffers. (Montana). I can remember a barrel of gingersnaps, and I remember a knife they used to cut tobacco. They had a wheel of cheese with a glass cover, and a knife inside that worked on a pivot. There were oyster crackers in one barrel, dill pickles in another. You just dipped in and got you some pickles. The barrel that had the gingersnaps was open to the public and to the flies! How did we live? And we thrived!

The other side of the store was dry goods: bolts of cloth, needles, pins, thread and lace.

I remember going to Virginia City one time in a horse and buggy with my mother and grandmother. Just the three of us went. Grandma was quite a hand to sing; they sang "Fling Out the Banner Far and Wide." I sat down in the bottom of the buggy, right at their feet. I think it was Nell we drove; she was a gray mare. We started early in the morning and we didn't get home till late at night. We bought a rocking chair for me, and where that rocking chair went, I don't know. . . .

Elizabeth Hampsten (1932–   )

Elizabeth Hampsten has written about western lives and western landscapes all of her life, although her own identity as a "westerner" had a long and circuitous path. She was born in Stuttgart, Germany, where her father was in the Foreign Service. The family lived in Marseilles and Montevideo before they returned to the United States in 1945. They went to live on the Double A ranch in northern Arizona, where she read voraciously, spent two years in public school before being sent off to boarding school. Most of her real learning came from the ranch, where she and her younger brother built a "human" skeleton out of the bones of a horse and a cow.

Mother and daughter were distanced from each other, strangers by temperament. Her mother wrote of Hampsten, then only three months old, "I think she has a sweet disposition but a nasty temper," and Hampsten later wrote of her family, "When I lived with my family, it seemed to me I fit in less well than the rest." Although it was not an era when "talented girls were being told how they might themselves become artists," Elizabeth went east to Wellesley, her mother's college, left, and finished at Northern Arizona University in Flagstaff. She earned a doctorate in English at the University of Washington, in Seattle, and teaches in the English Department of the University of North Dakota in Grand Forks.

When her mother died in 1970, Elizabeth was given a hatbox of her mother's letters, posted from Guadalajara, Stuttgart, Marseilles, Montevideo, and Williams, Arizona. The letters offered a chance to "read" family relationships and to discover that family often hides the distances between parents and children, between husband and wife. With some asperity and frustration, Hampsten writes of human separation, one from another, and from the land they live on, and of "that affinity to place and people that so mystifies me. . . ." Reading through *Mother's Letters,* it is often difficult to determine which voice is the more arresting—the mother's voice or the daughter's.

Between 1981 and 1989 Hampsten edited the magazine *Plainswoman*, publishing the prose and poetry and the photography of rural women, keeping their art alive. An editor with a fine ear for good writing, Hampsten included in the 1987 issue of *Plainswoman* a poem by a new poet named Linda M. Hasselstrom, then living in Hermosa, South Dakota.

***

THE DOUBLE A RANCH

While riding horseback on the ranch one afternoon of the summer I was sixteen, I very nearly was struck by lightning. Storms come suddenly in Northern Arizona, and I knew one was close, but put off turning toward home. When a bolt hit the wire fence just yards away, it was as if we stood, the mare and I, in the core of an explosion of light. A little closer to the fence, and the lightning might have killed us both; less forbearance on her part, and she could have killed me. But neither happened, and when the mare unshuddered herself, we went on, sloshing through the downpour.

Although I was close enough to feel electricity through the trembling of the mare and to be properly frightened, it was the fence was hit, not we. Everything was light, as though bursting away from us and brighter than any noon. (I was not aware of sound.) I have thought of that ride through the junipers and cliff roses at other times when I felt that sense of being, by accident, just to the side of an event that belonged to someone else but caught me also in its force. I watch and listen—to my parents and brothers and sister, to my husband and our children, to friends and relations and people I work and pass the time with—and I sense the force of these personalities. They, and the places where we knew each other, have and continue to form me. It is as though I move, from time to time, within fields like the electrical one—fields of love, or sorrow, or humor, or adventure—not necessarily meant to include me, but there I am.

For my family of parents and brothers and sisters, the eleven years on the Double A Ranch, just north of Ashfork, Arizona, were the major years of our being a family, and made "family" nearly synonymous with adventure. This adventure began in early June 1945, in an old Buick that my father, Shiras Morris, had managed to buy

Elizabeth Hampsten, from *Mother's Letters: Essays* (1993).

in spite of wartime scarcity; gasoline came thanks to coupons he had saved. I had just finished seventh grade, Shiras had resigned from the Foreign Service, and we were on our way to the ranch he and Mother had bought in Northern Arizona—partly to be nearer her parents who lived in Tucson, partly because "it would be good for the children," and partly I suspect because my father liked to do the unpredictable.

Uncle Bill was to be my father's partner and his first instructor in ranch management. Uncle Bill had grown up in Canada, had gone to the University of Arizona College of Agriculture, and had married my mother's younger sister. He had managed a number of ranger stations around the state when he and my father agreed to join in a ranching venture. Uncle Bill had stocked the Double A with Hereford bulls and half-wild cows from Mexico, an experiment in bargain breeding with limited success. (Shiras spent years rounding up the last of those Mexican cows.)

The Double A is one of the older ranches in that part of Arizona. Where we were to live was in the center of its two sections, divided by a fence that pastured cattle in the northern half in summer and in the lower southern canyons in the winter. Near the house was a sandstone dam (this was in the midst of sandstone quarry country) that was said to be one of the first dams for miles around, and reputed never to have gone dry. The house consisted of two rooms of hand-cut sandstone that we used as living room and bedroom, with window sills more than a foot deep. Attached was a frame kitchen, a shack really, moved from the other side of the dam. The house had six doors to the outside; Shiras replaced one with a window, and built on a large room with a fireplace as a bedroom for my mother and himself. The two boys had the sandstone bedroom and my sister and I the separate frame bunkhouse with a tin roof, truly alarming during thunder storms. Juniper trees grew everywhere—they were considered weeds destroying rangeland—and particularly enormous ones brooded over and cooled the house. The house faced south, to the road that led eighteen miles to Williams; in back to the north was the spillway from the dam and a ravine with cliffs and grapevines and Indian petroglyphs scratched on sandstone slabs. Across the dam rose Home Again Mountain, for when we saw its volcanic palisades, we knew we were home again.

■ ■ ■

Little by little things did get fixed. I helped paint the rooms, all of them white. The furniture from our parents' foreign service life may have looked odd in this rural setting, but to us it made things home. The curved sideboard with the sheet of glass on top; my father's victrola from his room at college; the wing chair; the desk with the secret drawer (postage stamps were kept there); the smooth, curved, rather art-deco bedstead; the spool beds—all these had been shipped during the war from the last post in Montevideo. Mother loved this furniture, and the houses, I think, where it had stood, and she dusted and polished and cared for it as best she could in the heat and grit of the ranch.

Outside along the front of the house we built a low wall of sandstone blocks from a shed that had been taken down—each of us assigned a daily quota of stones to carry. Mother planted zinnias along the wall, and for years we hauled buckets of water to them in the evening. A hop vine clung improbably to the kitchen overhang and thrived on dousings of dishwater. More sandstone slabs went to a terrace against the north side, the coolest place in the summer, with a Virginia creeper that spread bravely against the stone house. I'd sit on the steps to read by the last of the evening light. There was even a swing from a branch of the juniper tree against the kitchen. The bunkhouse we whitewashed—you could see through the knotholes and between some of the better-warped boards—and we decorated the four corners of the roof with deer antlers, pagoda-like. Against the side that faced the house, we hung an elegantly bleached horned cow skull.

Though the house was the main thing for us children and for my mother, of course there was more. There was the barn, for one—hay, tools, odd bits of machinery, saddles, and the sign on the door from the Department of Labor, *Aviso a los Empleados* (Notice to Employees), warning against industrial accidents, in two languages. Log corrals, the uneven sides much higher than we were, looped against the back side of the barn, where children could sit on the top rails watching a branding, a butchering, or a corral full of frantic wild horses that had been rounded up in the canyons. Behind the barn I milked the domesticated range milk cow, Antilles, her offspring in successive years named Lesser Antilles. I had learned to milk goats on my grandmother's farm in New Hampshire, where we had been sent in the summers to relieve my mother of us for a few weeks, and as I was the only member of the family who knew how to milk, I set myself up on one side of the cow with a bucket, and Lesser Antilles provided competition on the other. As often as Antilles did not knock me or the bucket over, we had a quart or so of milk a day. Mother sometimes even coaxed butter out of a small glass churn from Sears. But she put her foot down about chickens—they were noisy, and dirty, and stupid, and a tyranny, because once you started, you could never leave the premises. She would not have them.

Horses were indispensable to the work of the ranch, and I became not able to imagine a horse existing except to work. Our horses were fairly ordinary range animals. A brown-and-white spotted one my father liked to ride had been poisoned by locoweed and would tear off through the brush when a fit struck. A steadier horse, Mutt, was considered safe enough for children; he was old and came with the ranch. Mutt had been a first-rate cow horse, and by the time he was relegated to carrying me around, had a lot to teach. I was allowed to ride with the men, which meant starting early in the morning before it got hot, and riding until midafternoon, when it was very hot. We'd move cattle from one watering place to another, or gather calves for branding, or check fences, or, when my father replaced the original herd of Mexican cows with more conventional Herefords, stalk, and coax, and sometimes wildly chase long-legged, long-necked aging cows, no longer encumbered by calves, up and down rocky canyon sides. Mutt never flagged, even though I might have.

■ ■ ■

"The ranch" also meant the men who worked there. The Double A was of a size to need two men, and two or three more at roundups, these usually recruited in a quick tour of the bars in Williams and Ashfork. But to hire his full-time assistant, my father took great care. He found Richard Bargeman—we children called him always Mr. Bargeman—who had developed cowboying to an elegant profession. He was soft-spoken, and kindly, and infinitely patient with animals. A small house was built for him, and his wife

Leona and two little girls lived there. Before coming to the Double A, he had been an agent on the Navaho reservation, and Leona a nurse at the government hospital in Kayenta. He spoke Navaho, and taught us to count to ten. Mr. Bargeman was doubtless bemused by the vagaries of our family. Before his own house was built and his family joined him, he ate meals with us, he and my father at opposite ends of the table in the kitchen: mother and I sat on one side, Charly and Fifi on a bench against the wall, and Pancho on my father's lap, eating off his plate. Mr. Bargeman was full of stories about a roundup of wild cattle that had lasted for years on a ranch called the Hashknife. These tales, their names of places and people, took on the quality of mythology.

It was from Richard Bargeman that Shiras learned how to work a ranch, and learned also what he did not have to know how to do: he never roped. Roping was skilled and delicate work; it also was very competitive among those who did it well, and could be dangerous for those who did not, so he wisely left roping to Mr. Bargeman, who even enjoyed goat-roping competitions in town on Sunday afternoons. It was Mr. Bargeman who found a young quarter-horse mare for me, and brought her home without my parents' really deciding whether or not I should have more than a child's horse. She was named Coco. Mr. Bargeman broke her before I got home from school for the summer, but he never persuaded her to give up bucking, so my riding days often included tempestuous dumpings on the rocks. His professionalism about cowboying was wonderful to watch, and I wanted to see it all. We'd talk about what a "real" Western movie might be if anyone bothered to describe the truth; how close to move behind a cow and calf; how to know if your horse was getting tired; and mostly how to watch and listen and see "signs" of what animals had gone through the brush and how long ago. Day after day I rode with him, sometimes entire days with hardly any conversation.

■ ■ ■

I learned to sew those summers, but because yard goods were hard to come by in the last years of the war, Mother and I cut up outgrown dresses and pieced them into blouses. We also became inventive with flour and sugar sacks, and one year I fashioned

Shiras and Mr. Bargeman each a flour-sack suit, in a vaguely imi-
tated cutaway design, to be worn at one celebration or other of
family invention. One such event was graduation from Calvert
School. Charly and I were sent away to school during the years at
the ranch, but Fifi and Pancho learned at home with correspondence courses from the Calvert School of Baltimore, Maryland,
until they went to the Verde Valley School in Sedona, Arizona. Fifi
joined Verde Valley's first class, which helped construct the buildings and plan the school.

■ ■ ■

For me, in what were supposed to be the terrible teenage
years, the ranch was wonderful. To be sure, there were hot, desperate, long afternoons of boredom when I stretched out on the bed
and read all of Galsworthy, three trilogies in a single summer. My
grandfather had ridden horseback with John Galsworthy when
Galsworthy was on a lecture tour to the United States and found
himself in Tucson. Galsworthy's thank-you note is tucked in a book
of short stories. I read the miscellaneous collections of books my
father's mother sent from Brentano's at Christmas: a critical biography of Sidney Lanier; the letters from Jane Mecomb and her
brother Benjamin Franklin; histories of the cowboy; a book about
Traveler, reputedly the first quarter horse, who had drawn milk wagons somewhere in New York state. (In college these books made
my reputation as a near prodigy of the obscure.) I sewed, and did
algebra by correspondence, and in the bunkhouse learned to play
the recorder to myself, I being the single nonmusical member of
the family who was begged not to sing.

More often, I was out of doors, and whether working or hanging around afterwards, I found a great deal to watch and listen to.
Karo Jim lived in a covered truck and would ask my father every
few months to bring him a gallon can of Karo syrup (hence our
name for him). Jim Bennett was a small, bowlegged man, who one
thought of as very old until he began speaking of his mother,
whom he supported and visited often. Jim Bennett had swum the
Rio Grande when he was eight years old driving cattle with his
father to Denver, and he had worked cattle ever since. All the cowboys deferred to him. His tales inevitably were cautionary, ending

with Jim's tilting the back of his hat brim forward and saying, "I could have told 'em, and I did tell 'em"—implying too few took to heart what he told them, to their loss. He went to work on a large ranch owned by people my parents knew, where the Duke and Duchess of Windsor were entertained on their American visit. To show the royals a real cowboy, Jim was brought out and introduced: "Jim, this is the Duke and Duchess of Windsor." "Who-o-o?" Jim Bennett asked in a loud drawl.

■ ■ ■

Indeed I realized at the Double A that people living in a place could form their identities in it, they could make themselves part of that place. I longed to participate in such alchemy, to belong, in some secret way, to the mountains and canyons and small towns of Northern Arizona. Some of Mr. Bargeman's relatives worked on the Santa Fe railroad, and when I'd hear them list section houses along the line, it was as though these residents were joined into the names. Such intimacy was exotic to me, seductive, but it did not take me long to realize I was not likely to achieve it. Nothing in my past had allowed such connections. The "Foreign Service life" did not permit very long residence anywhere; and in addition, I knew that while the Consular Service in Stuttgart had provided me with papers alleging I had been born "on American soil," it was no soil to stand upon. Yet those are merely happenstances, and even I could tell that belonging to a place had to be a deeper phenomenon.

■ ■ ■

I find myself now after twenty-some years of living in the same house, in Grand Forks, and teaching in the same English department, at the University of North Dakota, longer than I have ever lived in any one place. Five children have grown and left home, and thirty years of marriage to my husband Richard have not matched this semblance of permanence. Right now, it suits me well to be a stranger, puzzling my way among a society that looks fixed and of long habit, with the stranger's privilege of exploring other people's haunts, and permission to be inept. North Dakota, lost at the top of the map, is a state that no one even wants to drive through if they can help it. Nevertheless, I prize living there. I have built friendships and enough familiarity with the state that I look forward to returning. Yet for now, it is a relief to be obviously from away; even living in someone else's house makes me feel at home.

■ ■ ■

Thus to be "from" somewhere I have supposed must be a gift, like the ability to carry a tune, that comes irrespective of class, educational experience, or whether one moves often, or travels. It is not particularly connected to knowing the history, the topography, or the origin of place names, but comes, it is my guess, with a kinetic sense of space. In North Dakota people identify not the town they live in or near, but name the county. In Uruguay people locate a school, a town, or their bus stop at the kilometer marker on the highway radiating from Montevideo, where at the capitol building begins kilometer 0. To such a method of thinking, other kinds of place-name information must seem arcane. In North Dakota, I have yet to find anyone among classrooms of students or audiences in other towns I might be talking to who knows the origin of the name of the town of Carpio. But even as people smile while I tell them (according to a WPA state guide, the first post office was in a railway car, so one went to the Car P.O.), they know that they are the ones "from" North Dakota, and I am not.

■ ■ ■

But certain regions attract me strongly, others I resist living in. The West draws me: the ranch in Northern Arizona, and Flagstaff where I went to college; Montana and Washington that gave me graduate school; and North Dakota where I feel I thrive now. To the East and Midwest I sense little connection. The New England landscape is beautiful, but my grandmother was too stern and dour for me to want to linger. The Hudson River Valley, where the boarding school was located, in the 1940s was tree-filled, but I desperately resisted being at that school. And the agricultural Midwest, the much-sung heartland of America, sunk me into faculty-wifery. I felt alien to those parts.

This attraction toward or alienation from places is certainly colored not only by topography and landscape, but by the people or events associated with a place. One's "sense of place," I would assume, is inevitably confounded or enriched or at least complicated by whatever social situations or elements of personal affection happen to go with it. For me, the Mississippi River makes none too removed a boundary from territories I do not really want to inhabit again if I can help it.

■ ■ ■

I expect one's sense of place is deeply psychic; I doubt we are moved by or drawn to mountains, deserts, rivers, woodlands, coast lines, or amber waves of grain alone and in a vacuum, but imperceptibly respond to them in combination with whatever human circumstances connect us to them. Hardly anything can be more lovely than the New England landscape—the view from the almost secret lookout beyond the lawn at Dingleton, New Hampshire could grace a Christmas card—yet the briefest visit east of the Hudson renews my conviction that that is where medieval monsters lie.

FURTHER READINGS
Elizabeth Hampsten, *Read This Only to Yourself: Writings of Midwestern Women 1880–1910* (1982); coeditor, *Far From Home: Families of the Westward Migration* (1989); *Settlers' Children: Growing up on the Great Plains* (1991).

Teresa Jordan

Teresa Jordan was the fourth generation raised on the family cattle ranch in the Iron Mountain country of southeastern Wyoming. Fifty miles from town, with no phone or television, storytelling was everything—"our social life, our entertainment, how we passed the time on long rides to distant pastures." When Jordan left the ranch, she traveled in a wide arc, far from the West of her childhood. She studied at Northwestern University and Colorado State University, and then went to Yale University where she was graduated Phi Beta Kappa.

She came back to the West and traveled over 60,000 miles to interview ranch women for her amazing book *Cowgirls: Women of the American West* (1982). She is also a professional photographer, whose exhibition if western women toured many cities. More recently, she is the author of *Riding the White Horse Home: A Western Family Album* (1993). She has edited *Graining the Mare: The Poetry of Ranch Women* (1994) and co-editor of *The Stories That Shape Us: Twenty Women Write about the West.* (1995). Jordan has recently added a new dimension to her skills—she is a "radio illustrator" along with her husband Hal Cannon, as they do "The Open Road," a regular feature for Public Radio International. In words and music they describe the "unexpected look of familiar places," from Yellowstone to Alaska, from the Grand Canyon to Hawaii. They make their home in eastern Nevada.

Jordan writes that her understanding of "the more interior stories of family, of grief, of loneliness, of emotional trial, survival, and even triumph" came after she had served her apprenticeship with stories of western women and how they lived their lives in "the outside world."

WRITING MY GRANDMOTHER'S LIFE

In the first photograph I have of my grandmother, she is reaching for something. Eight months old, she wears a christening gown

---

Teresa Jordan, "Writing My Grandmother's Life," from *Riding the White Horse Home* (1993).

of Irish lace and sits on a Persian rug. She is smiling and her large brown eyes show not the astonishment common in infant expressions but something more: something deep, intelligent, intensely present. Still, it is her hand, that grasping hand, that most intrigues me. What is she reaching for? The camera? The diamond of light reflected in the photographer's spectacles? Her arm stretches its full length, but three fingers curl to the palm as if to deny the reach. As if she knows, already, that a woman can ask for too much.

The woman I called Gran did not resemble this endearing infant. Effie Lannen Jordan was what was known politely as a "difficult woman." She lived in the same community all her life, but I have never heard an affectionate story about her. She managed to undermine even her generous impulses. When she gave my brother and me gifts, she would announce we were to come to her apartment to receive them. If we came too quickly, we were greedy. If we came too slowly, we showed disrespect. Nor could we thank her properly. If we wrote a note right away, we were fishing for more. And if we wrote too slowly—or God forbid, not at all—we were ungrateful.

Effie died at the age of eighty-three with only two accomplishments: she had raised a son and completed needlepoint seat covers for a dozen dining-room chairs. Her son, my father, cannot remember a single comfortable moment spent in her company, and the needlepoint, my grandmother always complained, had ruined her beautiful eyes.

For years, I seldom mentioned my grandmother—why talk about such bitterness? But a few years after her death, I was stalled on a project I had worked on for years. The frustration was familiar—I'd had trouble completing projects before. Unable to finish, unwilling to give up, I saw life passing me by. During the midst of this personal hell, I had a dream, and it was this dream that made me think about my grandmother's life.

In the dream, twin girls lived in an old Victorian house. The girls were six or seven years old and they wore white dresses. Their hair was tied back and they were pretty, yet sad. They never spoke. The interior of the house was murky and dark: the girls' dresses seemed to glow.

A set of railroad tracks passed through the house. A post about four feet high stood on either side of the tracks with an electric eye mounted on top of each post. A beam of light passed between the two eyes.

When the girls heard the train, their job was to run to the posts and hold their fingers in front of the electric eyes to break the beam. If they failed, the train would come to a crashing halt. Their job was to see that this never happened.

A train came rushing through. The girls were at their stations, and the passage was very pretty, very eerie: the line of the headlight piercing the murkiness and illuminating the girls in their white dresses; the shadows from the girls' fingers dancing in the mist; the way the train, so fast and streamlined, rushed through on its shimmering wheels, dust and steam roiling all around. The girls stood close to the train, frightened yet excited by the knowledge that people were being swept past to fascinating and unimaginable lives. With the train between them, the girls couldn't see one another. When it disappeared into the night, they receded back into their shadowy silence.

A second train approached, but this time the girls didn't get to the electric eyes in time and the beam stretched across the tracks unbroken. The engine smashed into it, grinding to a screeching halt, all the cars buckling up behind. Sparks flew everywhere and the air filled with the smell of scorched metal. The girls couldn't see one another but they both knew that they had done something terribly wrong.

The dream carried one final image. The doors to the cars were open. The girls could get on the train if they wanted to. Everything was quiet again. As long as the train stood still, its open doors beckoning, the girls couldn't see one another.

I woke with the knowledge that I had had an Important Dream. I didn't know who the girls were. Only the dresses were familiar, those turn-of-the-century white dresses with broad sashes and lace trim. In my attic, I had a half-dozen apple boxes filled with family photographs. Among the photographs were pictures of girls dressed in white.

I dug out the boxes and found a picture of my grandmother at the age of three, wearing a white dress. I found, too, a snapshot of myself at the same age, taken in my grandmother's apartment. I was wearing white flannel pajamas with ribbon trim. I set the two photographs side by side. We looked exactly alike. We could have been twins. This recognition did nothing to comfort me. The worst insult one member of my family could hurtle at another was "You are just like Gran."

Gran: even the word seemed acid and thin. Through the years, I had tried to eradicate anything about myself that might recall her. She was lethargic; I hardly ever sat down. She was critical; I was complimentary, sometimes to the point of obsequiousness. She never forgot a slight; I never held a grudge. My greatest fear had always been that Gran would somehow manifest herself in me, that I was condemned, as if genetically, to her bitterness and lethargy. I sometimes caught myself at the mirror, trying to reassure myself that I bore no trace of her cynical sneer, her perpetual pout.

In my memory, Gran was a witch: ugly and mean. But I looked at her picture at age three. She wasn't a witch then. She was beautiful, endearing, charismatic. Something had happened.

I pawed through the boxes and pulled out every photograph of my grandmother. I set them out on my dining-room table and arranged them in chronological order. In the earliest pictures, Effie's hands grabbed my attention. First was that christening photograph, taken at three months, where she reached for something. In the next picture, at one-and-a-half years, she stood between her parents, supported by her father's arm. She looked directly into the camera—again, those clear, perceptive eyes—and she held onto her own ear as if to say, "This is mine." In a third photograph, taken at age three, her hands rested passively, one in her lap and the other at her side, but she looked into the camera with complete openness and with something I could only describe as knowingness. I was struck by the personality present in those early photographs, and by the undercurrent of mirth. And I noticed, too, how joy and accessibility never surfaced again.

At five, she was photographed once again with her parents, and this time a sense of wariness had come into her eyes. They still shone, but they knew something—they had seen something—that they hadn't before. They revealed reticence, self-consciousness. I recognized, too, the beginning of a tightness around the mouth that she would wear the rest of her life.

At seven or eight, Effie was once again photographed alone, in another white dress. She had a child's body, but the face could have belonged to someone much older. She wore a measure of determination and perhaps of rebellion. This was the first photograph where the pose seemed obvious, an important turning point, I suppose, for a woman who would become known as a great *poseur.*

Two school photos—sad, resigned, wary. Then came a series of six photographs matted in a single frame, taken with her much younger sister, my Great-aunt Marj. Effie must have been about fifteen and Marjorie five. Both girls wore beautiful white dresses. Effie was alone in the first and last pictures, playing the piano. In the first, she looked at the camera, the tightness around her mouth bent into a smile. In the last, she leaned to her music in what seemed a parody of concentration. Almost all the photographs seemed staged. In three of the shots with Marj, the toddler seemed but a prop against which Effie could play good sister. But in one photograph, Effie's mask was completely absent and she seemed as guileless as she had in her earliest portraits, but ever so much sadder.

Then there were the photographs taken during college at the University of Kansas. Here Effie was all style and attitude. In one, with a cloche, she looked like an Inuit. In another, hand cocked on hip and outrageous, corded "cap," she looked like a flapper. And in a third, dark-brimmed hat pulled low over her sensuous eyes, she had the sultry elegance of a film star. Each portrait seemed distinct, as if a separate personality resided behind its ruse.

Effie never finished college. She always became "too ill" to take exams. She returned to Cheyenne and married my grandfather, Sunny. No wedding photographs have survived. Probably, she burnt them in one of her periodic fits of rage against the man she would neither live with nor divorce for forty years of a fifty-year marriage.

The visual chronicle picked up again in the midtwenties and showed a change so pronounced as to be shocking. Gone was all the stylishness, the air. A formal portrait revealed a rather plain woman with a look of defeat. The snapshots from the era were even more disturbing. Several showed her in 1928 with her newborn baby, Larry, my father. Effie looked fifty years old. She was twenty-seven. She smiled in the photos, but it was a pained sort of smile. I tried to figure out why she looked so awkward and finally it came to me. She nestled the baby against her right breast. Most women, even left-handed ones, hold their babies close to the heart. In another photo, she tried to adjust the baby's sweater and her clumsiness was painful. Even when she held her son in his christening gown when he was eight months old, she looked like she had never held a child before.

And then there was the Christmas photo with the family, one of the rare photographs that showed Effie and Sunny together. The tree glittered in the background, but Effie slumped in her chair in an attitude of utter defeat, Sunny looked at the camera with a wry tenseness, Effie's sister Marj was almost hidden—as she was in most family photographs—and seemed to be trying to appear pleasant, and Marj and Effie's parents, Nana and Papa Dick, sat stiffly in their chairs. Little Larry, six or seven years old, sat on the floor inspecting his new rifle, but even this activity brought no joy. He looked absorbed but miserable, as if wishing only for escape.

The visual record skipped the forties. The next photograph was taken at the same time as portraits of Nana and Marj. By this time, Marj's marriage had ended in divorce and all three women lived together in Cheyenne. My grandmother looked ineffably sad. The three women were together again in the next photo, taken in 1960. This was the Gran I knew, sharp and witchlike, with something truly nasty in her face. Finally, the last photos, taken at my father's second wedding in 1977: Effie was short and shrunken, but in one picture she was actually laughing. In nearly eighty years of photographs, this was the only one that caught her laughing. I knew that laugh, that bitter laugh: it was her witch's cackle.

There is danger in reading too much into snapshots, but I felt safe in drawing a few conclusions. Effie was born with a personality that tended more to the active than the passive; she had some desire to make a mark or at least be noticed; she did not fare well in marriage; and she was almost crazy with unhappiness.

"Lives do not serve as models," wrote Carolyn Heilbrun in her landmark study of women's biographies and autobiographies, *Writing a Woman's Life.* "Only stories do that. We can only retell and live by the stories we have read or heard. They may be read, or chanted, or experienced electronically, or come to us, like the murmurings of our mothers, telling us what conventions demand. Whatever their form or medium, these stories have formed us all. . . ."

Was there some clue to my grandmother in the stories that shaped her, the stories that shaped women of her time? As Heilbrun noted, until recently a woman had only one primary story to live by and it instructed her to put a man at the center of her life "and . . . allow to occur only what honors his prime position. Occasionally, women have put God or Christ [or social work or teaching] in the place of a man; the results are the same: one's own desires and quests are always secondary. For a short time, during courtship, the illusion is maintained that women, by withholding themselves, are central. . . . And courtship itself is, as often as not, an illusion: that is, the woman must entrap the man to ensure herself a center for her life. The rest is aging and regret."

Aging and regret: surely, that described Effie's life after marriage. My grandmother did not put her husband at the center of her life; she never put anyone at the center of her life except herself. She was criticized for this; she was also dreadfully unhappy and she made everyone around her unhappy as well. For the first time, I began to have sympathy for my grandmother. What if she didn't *want* to put someone else at the center of her life? What if she were virtually incapable of it? She had been, after all, a child with a distinct personality, an infant who held on to her own ear. What if she wanted something that was uniquely hers? It's possible to imagine a woman my age making this choice, and having a rich and admirable life. It was virtually *impossible* to imagine a woman—at least a conventional woman—in Effie's time doing so.

■ ■ ■

Unconventionality was not the only option open to my grandmother. Many women had succeeded while living apparently within convention. Still, they did not provide stories my grandmother or other women could live by, because the stories available about them did not reveal the truths of their lives. Eleanor Roosevelt's life stood as an extraordinary model of achievement, but the story of her life stressed that she took up her work only to help her husband—"doctors urged her to busy herself with a career in part to encourage [her husband] to involve himself again with the world around him [after he was stricken with polio in 1921]." As Heilbrun pointed out, "Well into the twentieth century, it continued to be impossible for women to admit into their autobiographical narratives the claim of achievement, the admission of ambition, the recognition that accomplishment was neither luck nor the result of the efforts or generosity of others. . . . Each woman set out to find her life's work, but the only script insisted that work discover and pursue her, like the conventional romantic lover."

I always had the feeling that Effie was angry at the world for not making her happy; I was angry at Effie for not making *herself* happy. I realize now that she didn't have the slightest idea what she wanted. Nothing she had seen or heard told her that her happiness was her own responsibility or that, if the conventional life did not satisfy her, she should search for one that did. No wonder she was crotchety.

Would she have been happier had she been raised with other possibilities? She was extremely intelligent—she had an incisive wit, played a wicked hand of bridge, and would regularly recall entire passages from *Wall Street Journal* articles she had read weeks before. She quite possibly had other talents as well. John Briggs, in *Fire in the Crucible*, a study of creative genius, notes the necessity of coincidence for talent to flourish: "A computer prodigy born into a culture where there are no computers or a musical prodigy born into a family where music is forbidden would be like sparks falling into the desert. . . . Most often, however, the prodigy's special spark is 'lost' because it finds no tinder. . . ." My grandmother was not a prodigy, but coincidence is necessary for more modest talents as well. Whatever embers she possessed fell in a desert where they did not extinguish so much as smolder until they marked her and everything she touched.

If she had been a man born to similar class and circumstance, she could have strode out into the world and taken hold of something that satisfied her; as a woman, she was instructed to remain passive. Everyone who talks about Gran says, "She really thought she was something, didn't she?" and they say it—each member of my family has said it, I have said it—with a tone of anger and bitterness. Who did she think she was to think she was so great? I have seldom heard this tone of voice applied to a man—a man who thought he was something could go out and *become* something. The only thing Effie could become was the wife of a man who was something. Her culture instructed her to stand mute in the shadows and make it possible for someone else's train to speed through.

It's easy to be angry at her for not "making the best of the situation," finding a way to be happy within marriage or club work or social causes. So very many women did. And yet many women didn't. As I began to talk about my grandmother, I was constantly told "I had a grandmother like that," or "You are writing about my great-aunt." One out of five women my age will never marry. Demographics play a role, but a good number of contemporary women *choose* not to marry because marriage is not the context within which they want to live their lives. The shoe doesn't fit, so they don't wear it. Few women my grandmother's age had that choice. They shoehorned themselves into the only lives they could imagine and somewhere along the line they started to grumble and complain.

But what did this all have to do with me? I was not my grandmother's twin. Possibilities were open to me that my grandmother could never imagine, because I had other stories to guide me. I could get on the train. I could drive the train. And yet I seemed reluctant to do so. I was caught in an odd paralysis. I was freed of the stories that shaped my grandmother, but her own story was still shaping me.

I remember staying with Gran when I was a child. My brother stayed across the hall in Nana and Marj's apartment and slept on their sofa bed, but I had to stay with Gran and sleep in her back bedroom, a small, dark room where the yellowed shades were always pulled. I spent a lot of time in that room. I slept there, but I was also sent there when I was naughty. Gran kept one of her cherished dining-room chairs in that bedroom, and she would set me down on it in the corner. The plastic seat cover that protected the needlepoint had gone brittle with age and bit into my legs even through my clothing. The room was dark and—the word comes to me now—murky. It smelled of cracked plastic and of the cigarette smoke that permeated everything in the apartment.

I could never please my grandmother and she often disciplined me, digging into my shoulder with her long red fingernails, shaking me the way a mother cat will shake a kitten. "You always have to have the last word," she'd tell me before she banished me to the bedroom. "You really think you're something. Don't show off. Don't get the big head. Straighten Up. Pipe Down. Be Still."

Be still. This command, more than any other, I remember. I remember her own extraordinary stillness as she sat day after day during her last decades in her light blue, crushed-velvet recliner, perfectly motionless except for the gesture it took to change channels with her remote control or light another cigarette and suck it down. She would exhale smoke from her mouth and then inhale it through her nostrils. "The French do it this way," she told me once.

As an adult, I had fought against her stillness tooth and nail. I was so seldom still that my cats had a preternatural preference for company—they had learned that there was a good chance I would sit down when strangers came and provide a rare lap and a welcoming hand. But I was not accomplishing what I most wanted to achieve, and the reason was more complex than the messages my grandmother passed down to me so directly.

The simple fact was, I feared ending up miserable and alone. I had stories of female success that gave me alternatives inconceivable for my grandmother. But the most powerful of stories, the family stories, did not give me examples of individual success intertwined with love. The stories that had shaped me informed me that I could have personal accomplishment or a happy marriage—I could not have both.

I grew up with three stories for women. The first was, of course, the story of Gran and Marj and Nana, the Three Witches of the West. The problem started with Nana, who was so powerful she chased the priest away and so controlling she wouldn't let her daughters go, and extended through her daughters and their failed marriages. In the story the family told about them, they were managerial women. They put themselves before their partners, they wanted to be in control of their own lives.

The second narrative was my mother's story, a traditional marriage. My mother was happy in her marriage and felt fulfilled as a full-fledged partner in the family enterprise. Still, it was my father's enterprise. Without him, the ranch meant little and she would not have kept it. Her creative accomplishment was the life they had built together. My parents talked openly about death and my mother often expressed the desire to die first. If my father were to precede her, she would have lost the center of her life.

The third story was that of my Great-aunt Marie's marriage to John Bell. I doubt John was an easy man to live with—surely, by today's standards, he was supremely self-centered—but Marie found with him the way to create the life she wanted. The success of their widespread business dealings was due to John, but the ranch was largely Marie's accomplishment. Marie herself, though, took no credit and asserted no visible authority. "I can't remember Marie ever giving me a direct order," a man who worked for her for thirty years once told me. "Even the first day we went out to move cattle, she said, 'How do you think we ought to do this?' I said, 'I don't know, Mrs. Bell. I've never been in this pasture before.' "

As long as I had only these three stories to guide me, I would remain stuck. I didn't have a story that told me I could be visible and not end up alone. But once I understood these stories and the power they held over me, I was free to search out other narratives or write my own. For the first time, I could perceive a relationship fundamentally different from any in my family so far. I could imagine a peer relationship in which I had my work, my partner had his, and we built a home and family together.

Lives don't serve as models, Heilbrun reminded us, only stories do. It was important what I understood of my grandmother's story. If I believed she was miserable and alone because she had a self, I had to believe that I would be miserable and alone because I had one, too. The story told me to destroy myself. But if I believed she was miserable and alone because she had no way to assert her self—in fact, she didn't have any evidence such assertion was possible—then I had to find a way not to diminish myself but to be as large as I was able.

I needed to understand the story of my grandmother's life in order to be free to fully live my own. I had to return to that dark Victorian house, cross the tracks for the first time, and embrace her. Then I could get on the train.

Maxine Hong Kingston (1940–)

Born in Stockton, California, Maxine Hong Kingston has become one of the most widely-read woman authors living today. Her writings reflect her sense of being poised between two worlds—China and the United States—and not feeling quite at home in either. The fate of her parents, who lost status in their move to the United States, illustrated for her some of the problems of being between worlds; her mother, a doctor and midwife in China, found herself working as a laundress and field hand in America, while her father, who had been a teacher in China, ran a laundry and managed a gambling house after he emigrated. Beyond this, Kingston's writings demonstrate her frustration about being a disappointment to her parents because she was born female.

Kingston studied literature at the University of California at Berkeley before moving with her family to Hawai'i, where she lived for nearly twenty years. In Hawai'i, she wrote a number of books, starting with *The Woman Warrior: Memoirs of a Girlhood Among Ghosts* (Knopf, 1976), which won the National Book Critics Circle Award for Nonfiction. She later published *China Men* (Knopf, 1980), which won the American Book Award, and *Tripmaster Monkey: His Fake Book* (Random House, 1989). She currently teaches creative writing at the University of California at Berkeley.

In *The Woman Warrior,* Kingston talks back in a powerful voice, raging at the sexism of Chinese culture and the racism of white-dominated American culture. Beaten down by constant devaluation, Kingston nonetheless rallies her troops to mount a spirited defense of her right to call this place her own.

In this selection from her "memoir of a girlhood among ghosts," Kingston talks about her struggle for self-esteem among relatives who express disappointment at her being a girl, and about coming to view her home as the place where she must take her stand and become the woman warrior who is inside her.

MY AMERICAN LIFE

My American life has been such a disappointment.

"I got straight A's, Mama."

"Let me tell you a true story about a girl who saved her village."

I could not figure out what was my village. And it was important that I do something big and fine, or else my parents would sell me when we made our way back to China. In China there were solutions for what to do with little girls who ate up food and threw tantrums. You can't eat straight A's.

When one of my parents or the emigrant villagers said, "'Feeding girls is feeding cowbirds,'" I would thrash on the floor and scream so hard I couldn't talk. I couldn't stop.

"What's the matter with her?"

"I don't know. Bad, I guess. You know how girls are. 'There's no profit in raising girls. Better to raise geese than girls.'"

"I would hit her if she were mine. But then there's no use wasting all that discipline on a girl. 'When you raise girls, you're raising children for strangers.'"

"Stop that crying!" my mother would yell. "I'm going to his you if you don't stop. Bad girl! Stop!" I'm going to remember never to hit or to scold my children for crying, I thought, because then they will only cry more.

"I'm not a bad girl," I would scream. "I'm not a bad girl. I'm not a bad girl." I might as well have said, "I'm not a girl."

"When you were little, all you had to say was 'I'm not a bad girl,' and you could make yourself cry," my mother says, talking-story about my childhood.

I minded that the emigrant villagers shook their heads at my sister and me. "One girl—and another girl," they said, and made our parents ashamed to take us out together. The good part about my brothers being born was that people stopped saying, "All girls," but I learned new grievances. "Did you roll an egg on *my* face like that when I was born?" "Did you have a full-month party for *me*?" "Did you turn on all the lights?" "Did you send *my* picture to Grandmother?" "Why not? Because I'm a girl? Is that why not?" "Why didn't you teach me English?" "You like having me beaten up at

Maxine Hong Kingston, from *The Woman Warrior: Memoirs of a Girlhood Among Ghosts* (1975).

school, don't you?"

"She is very mean, isn't she?" the emigrant villagers would say.

"Come, children. Hurry. Hurry. Who wants to go out with Great-Uncle?" On Saturday mornings my great-uncle, the ex-river pirate, did the shopping. "Get your coats, whoever's coming."

"I'm coming. I'm coming. Wait for me."

When he heard girls' voices, he turned on us and roared, "No girls!" and left my sisters and me hanging our coats back up, not looking at one another. The boys came back with candy and new toys. When they walked through Chinatown, the people must have said, "A boy—and another boy—and another boy!" At my great-uncle's funeral I secretly tested out feeling glad that he was dead—the six-foot bearish masculinity of him.

I went away to college—Berkeley in the sixties—and I studied, and I marched to change the world but I did not turn into a boy. I would have liked to bring myself back as a boy for my parents to welcome with chickens and pigs. That was for my brother, who returned alive from Vietnam.

If I went to Vietnam, I would not come back; females desert families. It was said, "There is an outward tendency in females," which meant that I was getting straight A's for the good of my future husband's family, not my own. I did not plan ever to have a husband. I would show my mother and father and the nosey emigrant villagers that girls have no outward tendency. I stopped getting straight A's.

And all the time I was having to turn myself American feminine, or no dates.

There is a Chinese word for the female I—which is "slave." Break the women with their own tongues!

I refused to cook. When I had to wash dishes, I would crack one or two. "Bad girl," my mother yelled, and sometimes that made me gloat rather than cry. Isn't a bad girl almost a boy?

"What do you want to be when you grew up, little girl?"

"A lumberjack in Oregon."

Even now, unless I'm happy, I burn the food when I cook. I do not feed people. I let the dirty dishes rot. I eat at other people's tables but won't invite them to mine, where the dishes are rotting.

If I could not-eat, perhaps I could make myself a warrior like the swordswoman who drives me. I will—I must—rise and plow the fields as soon as the baby comes out.

Once I get outside the house, what bird might call me; on what horse could I ride away? Marriage and childbirth strengthen the swordswoman, who is not a maid like Joan of Arc. Do the women's work; then do more work, which will become ours too. No husband of mine will say, "I could have been a drummer, but I had to think about the wife and kids. You know how it is." Nobody supports me at the expense of his own adventure. Then I get bitter: no one supports me; I am not loved enough to be supported. That I am not a burden has to compensate for the sad envy when I look at women loved enough to be supported. Even now China wraps double binds around my feet.

When urban renewal tore down my parents' laundry and paved over our slum for a parking lot, I only made up gun and knife fantasies and did nothing useful.

From the fairy tales, I've learned exactly who the enemy are. I easily recognize them—business-suited in their modern American executive guise, each boss two feet taller than I am and impossible to meet eye to eye.

I once worked at an art supply house that sold paints to artists. "Order more of that nigger yellow, willya?" the boss told me. "Bright, isn't it? Nigger yellow."

"I don't like that word," I had to say in my bad, small-person's voice that makes no impact. The boss never deigned to answer.

I also worked at a land developers' association. The building industry was planning a banquet for contractors, real estate dealers, and real estate editors. "Did you know the restaurant you chose for the banquet is being picketed by CORE and the NAACP?" I squeaked.

"Of course I know." The boss laughed. "That's why I chose it."

"I refuse to type these invitations," I whispered, voice unreliable.

He leaned back in his leather chair, his bossy stomach opulent. He picked up his calendar and slowly circled a date. "You will be paid up to here," he said. "We'll mail you the check."

If I took the sword, which my hate must surely have forged out of the air, and gutted him, I would put color and wrinkles into his shirt.

It's not just the stupid racists that I have to do something about, but the tyrants who for whatever reason can deny my family food and work. My job is my own only land. . . .

■ ■ ■

I live now where there are Chinese and Japanese, but no emigrants from my own village looking at me as if I had failed them.
Living among one's own emigrant villagers can give a good
Chinese far from China glory and a place. "That old busboy is really
a swordsman," we whisper when he goes by, "He's a swordsman
who's killed fifty. He has a tong ax in his closet." But I am useless,
one more girl who couldn't be sold. When I visit the family now, I
wrap my American successes around me like a private shawl. I am
worthy of eating the food. From afar I can believe my family loves
me fundamentally. They only say. "When fishing for treasures in the
flood, be careful not to pull in girls," because that is what one says
about daughters. But I watched such words come out of my own
mother's and father's mouths; I looked at their ink drawing of poor
people snagging their neighbors' flotage with long flood books
and pushing the girl babies on down the river. And I had to get out
of hating range. I read in an anthropology book that Chinese say,
"Girls are necessary too." I have never heard the Chinese I know
make this concession. Perhaps it was a saying in another village. I
refuse to shy my way anymore through our Chinatown, which tasks
me with the old sayings and the stories.

Further Readings

Sau-Ling Cynthia Wong, *Maxine Hong Kingston's The Woman
Warrior: A Casebook* (Oxford University Press, 1999); Diane
Simmons, *Maxine Hong Kingston* (Twayne, 1999); Paul Skenazy
and Tera Martin, eds., *Conversations With Maxine Hong Kingston*
(University Press of Mississippi, 1998); Laura E. Skandera-Trombley,
ed., *Critical Essays on Maxine Hong Kingston* (G K Hall, 1998);
Maxine Hong Kingston, *Hawaii One Summer* (University of Hawaii
Press, 1998); King-Kok Cheung, *Articulate Silences: Hisaye
Yamamoto, Maxine Hong Kingston, Joy Kogawa* (Cornell Univ-
ersity Press, 1993); Donna Perry, *Backtalk: Women Writers Speak
Out: Interviews* (Rutgers University Press, 1993); Maxine Hong
Kingston, "Cultural Mis-Reading by American Reviewers," in *Asian
and Western Writers in Dialogue: New Cultural Identities*, ed. Guy
Amirthanayagam (Macmillan, 1982).

Laura Gilpin, *Navajo Woman, Child, and Lambs*, 1932.

Used by permission of The Amon Carter Museum, Fort Worth, Texas.

7

Rewriting History

Four of the five selections in this chapter are largely forgotten by the reading public. Helen Hunt Jackson's "Indian Reform Letters," and the biographies of Crazy Horse, Sitting Bull, and Geronimo are the works of a handful of talented and determined women who understood the fatal flaw in the national predilection to deride the Indian as a "savage." Each understood the long injustice done to peoples driven off the land. Like George Catlin's elegant portraits of people he saw as the "aristocrats" of the Plains, the separate biographies are executed with historical accuracy and literary flair. But where Catlin was painting a "vanishing" people, Helen Hunt Jackson, Mari Sandoz, Dorothy Johnson, and Angie Debo understood their subjects as contemporaries, and as men of vision and intelligence, and they endeavored in their writing to find a public voice, to affect legislation, and shape public policy.

Old Jules and *Crazy Horse* are the twin masterworks of Mari Sandoz's career, and what is interesting about them is that they were "in the making" in her mind at the same time. Working in the Nebraska Historical Society in 1932, Sandoz took on the job of typing legible portions of a handwritten manuscript known as "The Life of Red Cloud." It had been recorded by Charles W. Allen in 1893 at the Pine Ridge Agency. She published *Old Jules* in 1935, but kept parts of that typescript and used them in writing *Crazy Horse,* finished in 1942. The resonance between the two books is astonishing.

Once she decided to write *Crazy Horse,* Sandoz went to work with energy and determination. With Eleanor Hinman, she set off

on an expedition that covered three-thousand miles through Sioux
country, locating Indian sites, living wherever they could find shelter, interviewing old buffalo-hunters and relatives like Short Bull
and He Dog. Hinman wrote the first drafts of the story, but gave the
writing over to Sandoz, who spent two winters in Washington reading the files of the Indian Bureau. She read everything she could
find in the historical societies in Nebraska, Colorado, and
Wyoming. And even then, she tore up the manuscript three times
because she wanted the narrative to sound as if it were written
from an Indian point of view.

Sandoz had five thousand index cards in boxes on her kitchen
table—where almost all women writers work. She knew she was
onto "a major work." She wrote to Helen Blish, "the story is tremendous." The aim of the book was to make a place for Crazy Horse in
the history of the nation, to carve for him, in words, the mountain
sculpture now taking form in the Black Hills, larger than the "white
faces" on Mount Rushmore. The sculpted Crazy Horse sits on his
horse, a great arm outstretched, pointing the way for his people.
Black Elk once prophesied that a great wind from the north and
the west would signal Crazy Horse's return, and the sounds of
eagle-bone whistles would scream, "Crazy Horse is coming! Crazy
Horse is coming! Sandoz, and Angie Debo, and Dorothy Johnson
heard those eagle-bone whistles fifty years ago, as each woman
wrote about the chief who led his people with wisdom and care,
before he was defeated by what Helen Hunt Jackson called "A
Century of Dishonor."

The final selection, "Sitting on Red Cloud's Grave" by Delphine
Red Shirt, suggests that the "heroes" of the past do not wait for
restoration by national legislation or recognition. Their feats are
celebrated by the daughters who retell the grandfather's stories. "I
realize that Red Cloud was right ... He knows all things and knows
that we are still true to Him. 'Ho he,' as Kah-kah used to say, and as
Mom-mah says now: 'That please me. It is good.' "

Helen Hunt Jackson (1830–1885)

Attending the seventieth birthday celebration of Oliver Wendell Holmes, Helen Hunt Jackson chanced to attend a lecture in Boston by Ponca Chief Standing Bear. He recounted the ways in which tribal lands had been taken from his people, and that when he attempted to bury the body of his young son in ancestral lands in Dakota Territory, he and thirty of his people were arrested on orders of Secretary of the Interior Carl Schurz. Jackson took up the Poncas' cause, and helped Standing Bear bring his case to trial. In *Standing Bear v. Crook*, the federal district court declared that an Indian had the right to sue for a writ of *habeas corpus*, and the Ponca were set free. Jackson and Thomas Henry Tibbles, one of the editors of the *Omaha Daily Herald*, organized a six-month lecture tour for Standing Bear in Chicago, Boston, New York, Philadelphia, and Baltimore, hoping that influential easterners would come forward to right the wrongs done to Indians.

Jackson began to educate herself about tribal history, poring over government documents in the Astor Library in New York City, learning the histories of the Delaware, the Cheyenne, Nez Perce, Sioux, Ponca, Winnebago, and Cherokee. The more she learned, the more she became an advocate of people without a voice. When he came to trial, she wrote a scathing condemnation of Colonel J. M. Chivington's 1864 massacre of Black Kettle's Cheyenne Village at Sand Creek. In 1878, when the Northern Cheyenne surrendered and were imprisoned at Fort Robinson in Nebraska, Jackson wrote to major newspapers condemning Secretary of Interior Schurz and his methods. The Jackson/Schurz letters, printed between 1879 and 1880, appeared in the New York *Tribune*, the *Boston Daily Advertiser*, the *New York Evening Post*, and the *New York Times*. She called Schurz a "blockhead," an "arch hypocrite," "stupid," "unprincipled," an "adroit liar," a "false souled," wicked, and insincere man. She demanded from Congress legislative reform in order to remove from national history "the stain of a century of dishonor." In 1881, Harper published her book *A Century of Dishonor*, in which she recorded, tribe by tribe, the national seizure of Indian lands.

Jackson waged war with the government at a time when few

women dared direct assaults on men in political power. What she hoped for—a rising swell of protest by the American people, a reappraisal of the government's Indian policy, and restitution of Indian lands—did not come to pass. Most Americans were well-satisfied by the country's "march of progress," and relentless in their goal of clearing the Indians from the western territories. Her letters were historical "relics" almost as they were written and read.

INDIAN REFORM LETTER

[January 31, 1880]
To the Editor of The Tribune.

SIR: In your capital editorial note this morning, you say: "The two most serious hindrances to a satisfactory solution of the Indian question are Indians and white men." Any problem is embarrassing when one of its factors is addicted to scalping men, torturing women, and braining children. The problem becomes still more embarrassing when "one" of the "factors" has no way of making known to the people what the other "factor" has done to him. In connection with the present attempt to rouse a sweeping sentiment of indignation and denunciation against the band of 4,000 well-nigh helpless Utes in Colorado, because twelve of their number have committed murder and rape, and some 300 or 400 of them undertook to prevent the marching of United States troops into their lands, I wish to tell to the American people a few of the atrocities which Colorado white men committed upon Indians only fifteen years ago.

In June, 1864, Governor Evans, of Colorado, sent out a circular to the Indians of the Plains, inviting all friendly Indians to come into the neighborhood of the forts and be protected by the United States troops. Hostilities and depredations had been committed by some bands of Indians, and the Government was about to make war upon them. This circular says:

Printed in the *Tribune*, Feb. 5, 1880, p. 5, as "The Starving Utes: More Questions for the people by 'H.H.': What White Men Have Done and Are Doing to Indians in Colorado."

In some instances they (the Indians) have attacked and killed soldiers, and murdered peaceable citizens. For this the Great Father is angry, and will certainly hunt them out and punish them; but he does not want to injure those who remain friendly to the whites. He desires to protect and take care of them. For this purpose I direct that all friendly Indians keep away from those who are at war, and go to places of safety. Friendly Arapahoes and Cheyennes belonging on the Arkansas River will go to Major Colby [Colley], United States Agent at Fort Lyon, who will give them provisions and show them a place of safety.

In consequence of this proclamation of the governor, a band of Cheyennes, several hundred in number, came in and settled down near Fort Lyon. After a time they were requested to move to Sand Creek, about forty miles from Fort Lyon, where they were still guaranteed "perfect safety" and the protection of the Government. Rations of food were issued to them from time to time. On the 27th of November, Colonel J. M. Chivington, a member of the Methodist Episcopal Church in Denver, and Colonel of the 1st Colorado Cavalry, led his regiment by a forced march to Fort Lyon, induced some of the United States troops to join him, and fell upon this camp of friendly Indians at daybreak. The chief, White Antelope, always known as friendly to the whites, came running toward the soldiers, holding up his hands and crying "Stop stop!" in English. When he saw that there was no mistake, that it was a deliberate attack, he folded his arms and waited till he was shot down. The United States flag was floating over the lodge of Black Kettle, the head chief of the tribe. Below it was tied also a small white flag as additional security, a precaution Black Kettle had been advised by United States officers to take if he met troops on the Plains. In Major Wynkoop's testimony given before the committee appointed by Congress to investigate this massacre, is the following passage:

Women and children were killed and scalped, children shot at their mother's breasts, and all the bodies mutilated in the most horrible manner. . . .The dead bodies of females profaned in such a manner that the recital is sickening, Colonel J. M. Chivington all the time inciting his troops to their diabolical outrages.

Another man testified as to what he saw on the 30th of November, three days after the battle, as follows:

> I saw a man dismount from his horse and cut the ear from the body of an Indian and the scalp from the head of another. I saw a number of children killed; they had bullet holes in them; one child had been cut with some sharp instrument across its side. I saw another that both ears had been cut off. . . . I saw several of the 3d Regiment cut off fingers to get the rings off them. I saw Major Sayre scalp a dead Indian. The scalp had a long tail of silver hanging to it.

Robert Bent testified:

> I saw one squaw lying on the bank, whose leg had been broken. A soldier came up to her with a drawn sabre. She raised her arm to protect herself; he struck, breaking her arm. She rolled over, and raised her other arm; he struck, breaking that, and then left her without killing her. I saw one squaw cut open, with an unborn child lying by her side.

Major Anthony testified:

> There was one little child probably three years old, just big enough to walk through the sand. The Indians had gone ahead, and this little child was behind following after them. The little fellow was perfectly naked, travelling in the sand. I saw one man get off his horse at a distance of about seventy-five yards and draw up his rifle and fire. He missed the child. Another man came up and said: "Let me try the son of a b——. I can hit him." He got down off his horse, kneeled down, and fired at the little child, but he missed him. A third man came up, and made a similar remark, and fired, and the little fellow dropped.

The Indians were not able to make much resistance, as only a part of them were armed, the United States officers having required them to give up their guns. Luckily they had kept a few.

When this Colorado regiment of demons returned to Denver they were greeted with an ovation. The *Denver News* said: "All acquitted themselves well. Colorado soldiers have again covered themselves with glory;" and at a theatrical performance given in the city, the scalps taken from three Indians were held up and exhibited to the audience, which applauded rapturously.

After listening, day after day, to such testimonies as these I have quoted, and others so much worse that I may not write and THE TRIBUNE could not print the words needful to tell them, the committee reported: "It is difficult to believe that beings in the form of men, and disgracing the uniform of the United States soldiers, and officers could commit or countenance the commission of such acts of cruelty and barbarity"; and, of Colonel Chivington: "He deliberately planned and executed a foul and dastardly massacre, which would have disgraced the veriest savage among those who were the victims of his cruelty."

This was just fifteen years ago, no more. Shall we apply the same rule of judgment to the white men of Colorado that the Government is now applying to the Utes? There are 130,000 inhabitants of Colorado; hundreds of them had a hand in this massacre, and thousands in cool blood applauded it when it was done. There are 4,000 Utes in Colorado. Twelve of them, desperate, guilty men, have committed murder and rape, and three or four hundred of them did, in the convenient phrase of our diplomacy, "go to war against the Government"; *i.e.,* they attempted, by force of arms, to restrain the entrance upon their own lands—lands bought, owned and paid for—of soldiers that the Government had sent there, to be ready to make war upon them, in case the agent thought it best to do so! This is the plain English of it. This is the plain, naked truth of it.

And now the Secretary of the Interior has stopped the issue of rations to 1,000 of these helpless creatures; rations, be it understood, which are not, and never were, a charity, but are the Utes' rightful dues, on account of lands by them sold; dues which the Government promised to pay "annually forever." Will the American people justify this? There is such a thing as the conscience of a nation—as a nation's sense of justice. Can it not be roused to speak now? Shall we sit still, warm and well fed, in our homes, while five hundred women and little children are being slowly starved in the bleak, barren wildernesses of Colorado? Starved, not because storm, or blight, or drouth has visited their country and cut off their crops; not because pestilence has laid its hand on them and slain the hunters who brought them meat, but because it lies within the promise of one man, by one word, to deprive them of one-half their necessary food for as long a term of years as he may please; and "the Secretary of the Interior cannot consistently feed a tribe that has gone to war against the Government."

We read in the statutes of the United States that certain things may be done by "executive order" of the President. Is it not [now] time for a President to interfere when hundreds of women and children are being starved in his Republic, by the order of one man? Colonel J. M. Chivington's method was less inhuman by far. To be shot dead is a mercy, and a grace for which we would all sue, if to be starved to death were our only other alternative.

    H.H.
New-York, Jan. 31st. 1880.

FURTHER READINGS

Helen Hunt Jackson, *A Century of Dishonor: A Sketch of the United States Government's Dealings with Some of the Indian Tribes* (Harper, 1885); Valerie Sherer Mathes, *Helen Hunt Jackson and Her Indian Reform Legacy* (University of Oklahoma Press, 1990); Rosemary Whitaker, *Helen Hunt Jackson* (Boise State University Press, 1987); Antoinette May, *Helen Hunt Jackson: A Lonely Voice of Conscience* (Chronicle Books, 1987); Evelyn I. Banning, *Helen Hunt Jackson* (Vanguard, 1973); Ruth Odell, *Helen Hunt Jackson (H.H.)* (D. Appleton-Century Co., 1939); Valerie Sherer Mathes, ed., *The Indian Reform Letters of Helen Hunt Jackson, 1879–1885* (University of Oklahoma Press, 1998).

Mari Sandoz (1896–1966)

When Mari Sandoz was a girl, buffalo hunters of the Oglala and Brule Sioux brought their guns to Old Jules for repair. They camped across the road, staying a while, telling stories of hunting grizzly along the Big-Horn River, and of wars with the Snake and the Crow. Through all the stories ran the name of Crazy Horse, "like a painted strip of rawhide in a braided rope." He was called the Strange Man, the leader who rallied his warriors, fought off his enemies, walked in silence among the tents of his villages. No account of him in American histories as a blood-thirsty warrior corresponded to the tales Sandoz heard as a child.

Crazy Horse was born in 1840 to the Oglala Lakota tribe near Bear Butte, South Dakota. In time, the young man became a war chief. He was an elegant fighter, who joined Red Cloud in Wyoming, and took part in the Fetterman Massacre (1866), but whatever battles he fought, the name Crazy Horse (His Horse is Crazy) would always be linked to the Little Big Horn and to the Indian's defeat of General George Armstrong Custer.

There are dozens of accounts—many contradictory—of the battle that took place in 1876, on the eve of the national centennial celebration of independence. Custer's military mistakes—how he divided his men, how he came upon an encampment of many thousand of Cheyenne, Hunkpapas, Miniconjous, Oglalas, Blackfeet and Arapahos, how he disobeyed orders and went forward with an attack—all of this is the stuff of military debate. When the battle ended, 197 U. S. soldiers lay dead on the field and the story could be pieced together only by the Sioux who survived.

The Oglala medicine man, Black Elk, then only thirteen years old, remembered hiding in the brush and seeing Crazy Horse come thundering onto the field on his white-faced pony, but there are no accounts of combat between Custer and Crazy Horse. Historian Stephen Ambrose, writing *Crazy Horse and Custer*, relied on Eleanor H. Hinman's 1930 interview with Short Bull, who said Crazy Horse was late getting into the field.and that much of the fighting by that time was over. But myth is as powerful as fact, and Crazy Horse and Custer remain twin stars of military history.

By 1877, the time had come to end the fighting. He agreed to surrender, but he left the agency without a pass when he took his sick wife, Black Shawl, back to her parents. He was arrested, handcuffed and when he resisted, he was pinned down by a jealous warrior, and bayoneted by a U.S. soldier. Sandoz's story ends with Crazy Horse's death, father and friends shedding "tears like rain washing over live rocks." The body disappeared, and no burial site has ever found. Crazy Horse rises today in the Black Hills of South Dakota, where a mountain-sized sculpture is being blasted out of the rock.

Sandoz's biography of Crazy Horse, appearing in 1942, during the Second World War, met with mixed reviews. The *New Yorker* saw it as too sympathetic to the Indian viewpoint. "Miss Sandoz writes with great drive and passion—more perhaps than the average reader will think the theme deserves." *The New York Times* ridiculed "the writing woman's book."

But there is reason to believe that Sandoz was less concerned with Crazy Horse as a military leader, and more concerned with the love story she told about Crazy Horse and the woman he took as his wife. He had been in love with Black Buffalo Woman—"Mostly it was just having her close, the smell of the sweet grass on her dress, feeling her shy, quick breathing inside the dark folds of the blanket he held about them with his bow arm." When she married another, Crazy Horse married Black Shawl, who rode behind him on her spotted pony, "her buckskin dress deep-yoked in beads, her saddle hangings long-fringed and beaded too, in the design of her family. It was true that she was not Black Buffalo Woman, but it was better to be second with such a man than first with another, and so she rode with her vermillioned face woman-strong and proud."

If you place that portrait next to Sandoz's description of Jules and his first wife—"he closed her mouth with the flat of his long muscular hand," and with his second wife, "his hand shot out, and the woman slumped against the bench"—Black Shawl, "with her vermillioned face woman-strong and proud," is Sandoz's incandescent portrait of what life on the edge of western settlement might have held.

Sandoz's work on the history of the West included *These Were the Sioux* (1951), *Cheyenne Autumn* (1953), *The Beaver Men* (1954), *The Cattlemen* (1958), *Son of the Gamblin' Man* (1960), *Love Song to the Plains* (1961).

MANY SOLDIERS FALLING INTO CAMP

Battle of the Rosebud, June 17, 1878

The night was thinning in the east when Crazy Horse stopped his Oglalas for a little resting. They were not far from the Rosebud now, and once a little wind brought a smell of water that stirred the tired horses and once the sweetness of the roses blooming so thick in that valley. But soon there was the soft owl hoot of another war party coming, so they rode in closer, for the soldiers must not escape them now.

Daylight came upon the warriors behind the ridge north and west of the bend of the Rosebud. Stopping there, they ate of their *wasna* and made ready for the fight. Crazy Horse loosened his long hair, tied on the calfskin cape, and threw dust over his spotted war horse while not far away the eighteen-year-old son of Red Cloud shook out a long-tailed war bonnet and put it on as though he were really a bonnet man of the *akicita,* the other young men standing away from him, even the older ones silent, for this son of the agency could be told nothing at all.

While the horses rested, the scouts were sent out to locate the soldiers, bring back word of them; but as they crossed the ridge they rode into the Crows coming up from the other side. There was shooting, a Lakota fell, two Crows were wounded, and all the warriors, forgetting about the resting horses, whipped them to the ridge and stopped there in dark rows against the sky.

Below him Crazy Horse saw the Crow scouts fleeing down the slope into the valley of the Rosebud, full of soldiers and Indians, so many they looked like a resting, cud-chewing herd of buffalo, the horses grazing, the men in dark little bunches. Beyond them was the willow-lined creek, with more soldiers on the other side, and then the bluffs and the far ridge, so far that a horseman would look like one of the scattering of little trees. And between him and that place, as in the palm of a browning hand, were the soldiers, and once more Crazy Horse wished for guns, plenty of good rifles and warriors who would strike together in waves like flying hail.

As the Crows fled howling back to the soldiers, they stirred into moving, running to catch their horses or lining up and then

---

Mari Sandoz, from *Crazy Horse: The Strange Man of the Oglalas* (1942).

going off every way in little bunches, many horse and walking soldiers hurrying up towards the hostiles, coming in rows, a flag waving, a bugle sounding clear in the warm air. Behind them the Indian scouts were riding hard up and down, raising a great dust, making ready to fight too, now that the soldiers had gone ahead, shooting into the hostiles.

Crazy Horse held his warriors together for a long time but there were so many soldiers and their rifle-fire was so close among them that finally they fell back to the rocks of the second ridge, hoping to draw the whites along. And they came, off their horses now, crawling from rock to rock, and when they were well scattered, Crazy Horse led a charge. It was a hot little fight, many men going down, some even from arrows. Then more soldiers, followed by the Snakes, came galloping up from the side. In the smoke and dust the Lakotas couldn't tell their friends from the scouts, so they withdrew awhile to rest their horses and to see how the fighting was going in other places.

The Crows had been getting bolder too, and when young Red Cloud lost his horse and ran away without stopping to take off the war bridle to show that he was unafraid, they rode upon him and whipped him hard, grabbing his father's rifle from him and jerking off the war bonnet, saying he was a boy, with no right to wear it. Crazy Horse and two others charged the Crows and got the young Bad Face back, not looking at him, shamed that they had seen one of their young men crying to his enemies for pity.

By now the sun was high and the fighting had spread off to the opposite ridge, the charges going back and forth over miles of rough ground, with many brave things done, many afoot and wounded ones being carried off the field by warriors whose horses were so tired they could barely be whipped out of a walk. The Hunkpapas were helping strong now. They came late, their horses were fresher and their guns still loaded. Crazy Horse was with them awhile, shooting from the ground as always. When his spotted horse was played out, he got his bay and went to the bluffs where the Cheyennes seemed to be making a very good fight. Once, when the smoke and dust lifted, Crazy Horse saw the sister of Chief Comes in Sight charge forward to where he was afoot and surrounded. With him on behind her she zigzagged back through the soldiers, bullets flying, the warriors making a great chanting for this brave thing done.

Ahh-h, the Cheyennes were indeed a strong people, Crazy Horse thought, but not the strongest heart and the longest arm, Lakota or Cheyenne, with only a bow was enough against these rifles. The warriors fought hard but always they were driven back. It was happening right now to his own Lakotas, his bravest men breaking into retreat before the bullets whistling hot around them, whipping hard to get away.

Then suddenly they found Crazy Horse before them, his horse turned into their faces, crying out to them: "Hold on, my friends! Be strong! Remember the helpless ones at home!" And with his Winchester held high as a lance he charged through them towards the coming soldiers. "This is a good day to die!" he called back over his shoulder, the calfskin flying out like bat wings behind him. "Hoka hey!"

"Hoka hey!" the strong voice of Good Weasel answered him as he turned to follow, and then Bad Heart Bull, Black Bear, and Kicking Bear. "Hoka hey!" the warriors roared out together, thundering close behind them, charging back into the soldiers among the rocks, lifting their arrows to fall among the horses. When the frightened animals began to break from the holders the soldiers jumped back on and now even the youngest Loafer could see that the whites were afraid and so pressed them harder, charging through them, shooting under the necks of the puffing horses, or from flat on their backs, until the Crows and Snakes fled from this wild charging, whipping, crying, towards the little bunch of soldier chiefs and traders' sons down around Three Stars.

Soon the whites were breaking as their scouts had, the Lakotas right among them, knocking the men from the saddles with their empty guns and the swinging war clubs, riding them down, never stopping except to pick up the dropped carbines, Crazy Horse ramming the stuck shells from them. So they drove the whole party like scattering antelope back into the valley, the warriors chasing after them. Here Crazy Horse saw many hurt ones, and many brave ones, too, particularly a little soldier chief sitting against a tree, his face all blood, still shooting with his revolver.

Now there was a loud bawling of bugles and the soldiers fell back together and made a thick new line that would be hard to break. Besides, the sun was moving away and so Crazy Horse decided it was time to try something else. Turning, he led his war-

riors around over the creek and down the other side, letting their
tired horses walk, making it seem they were giving up. As he
hoped, a bunch of soldiers and some Crow scouts saw them go
and followed down the other side, and once more Crazy Horse
became the old thing he was so often—a decoy, making little
stands behind the others, little charges towards the soldiers across
the creek, as if to hold them back. So they came faster.

As the Oglalas neared the bend of the Rosebud, signals were
sent back, calling the others to come down to the narrow place in
the valley, where it would be easier to fight with bows and tired
horses. More and more hostiles began to string out down the creek
behind the whites, who did not seem to notice these Lakota warriors coming.

But before the soldiers got to the place for fighting, the Crows
with them stopped, making the wild Crow howling, pointing
ahead, refusing to go to where the ridge came towards the creek,
with rocks and brush for the enemy to hide. And when a messenger from Three Stars came galloping after them, the soldiers swung
far out around the Indians following them and hurried back in
time to strike the rear of the warriors still fighting.

So the Indians scattered. The shells were gone, even those they
had got with the new guns, and the horses worn out. It had been a
hard fight.

The daybreak star was in the sky when the warriors got back
to the camp on the creek that flowed into the Little Big Horn. The
news had been sent ahead from where they stopped to make
travois for the wounded and so they were brought home in the
good way, two of the older chiefs from each circle leading them in.
The great encampment was fine to see, with cooking fires burning
every-where, the women moving dark about them, ready to feed
the hungry warriors. There were some bad things to tell—eight
men who would never charge the soldiers again, two from the
Oglalas, and more wounded. It was bad, too, about young Red
Cloud sneaking away to the agency like a shamed little boy, without the borrowed war bonnet or his father's fine gun. It must be
hard to have a son come home like that. But that was only the act

of one foolish young man, and the Indians killed were very few for so many in the fight, and the soldiers had been hurt too.

By the time the warriors had rested, scouts came riding with good news. Three Stars had fifty-seven men to haul away, dead and bad-wounded to need hauling, and it seemed that his ammunition was almost gone too. Anyway, he was turning his dust around and going back to Goose Creek, not so hungry to chase more Indians now. When the heralds rode through the camps with this word, even the mourning people stopped to make a little sound of joy.

After the news was talked over, Crazy Horse went out to sit on a ridge above the great camp, to think about the fight. There had indeed been something new among the warriors, as he had asked. The old Lakota way of fighting for coups and scalps and horses, of a man riding out alone and doing foolish things to show how strong he was, seemed gone. Yesterday most of them had charged in bunches, straight into the soldiers, breaking their lines, almost nobody stopping for coups or scalps until the fighting in that place was done. And they had driven Three Stars back. It was the biggest thing the Lakotas had ever done against soldiers who really came fighting, not just sneaking like coyotes through the canyons, trying to keep from being seen. Perhaps it was really bigger than the fight on the Piney, for the soldier chief there was no warrior like Three Stars.

And there was still the vision of Sitting Bull: Many Soldiers Falling into Camp.

The next day the whole camp moved down to the Little Big Horn, leaving the death lodges of the Lakotas behind, the women keening as they looked back from the first rise. That night the victory dances began, only the scalps of the Indian scouts hanging from the women's staffs, those of the short-haired soldiers thrown away as no better than so much horse skin. They danced the things taken too, the guns, including many of the short saddle ones, some thrown away by the soldiers when they jammed in the heat of the fighting. But one called Good Hand, who had helped the blacksmith at the agency, knew how to make them work very well, even those the soldiers had broken whipping their horses.

The drumming and dancing and singing lasted all night, the people going from one camp to the next to hear all the great things done on the Rosebud. But the best of all was down among the Cheyennes, where the story of Buffalo Calf Road, the woman who carried her brother from the battle, was told and retold. Their dancing lasted four days; the sacred buffalo hat was brought out, a new scalp tied to it, and the ceremonial of its renewal made before all the people.

Crazy Horse never helped with the dances, but there was work and planning to be done. Scouts were sent to follow Three Stars, to shoot into his night camps and keep the soldiers watching and afraid. Runners went to the young men of the agencies, north and south, carrying the good news of the fighting in their mouths and the pay-money taken from the soldiers in their pipe cases for powder from Boucher and others who traded in the night. One morning he took a little party of Oglala boys over to the Rosebud to pick up the scattered ammunition, for it was well known that the soldiers often take handfuls from their belts, lay it down handy, and then move on with the fighting. The boys filled several unborn buffalo calf skin sacks and got very many empty shells to reload, some lead too, from bullets flattened against the rocks, and many arrow points and the shoes from the dead American horses.

"Nothing must be forgotten when iron is so scarce," he said, and told the boys some stories of the stone arrow makers, a people so long gone they seemed forgotten, the Crows claiming they were a small people like eight-year-olds that lived in the cave rocks near the Yellowstone.

"Guns are better—" a Loafer son said impatiently.

"Guns are as the eyes and the hearts behind them," the Hunkpatila said, and then spoke no more.

In the great camp were many kettles to be filled and so hunters packed in fresh meat from the buffalo herds west of the river and some went clear beyond the Big Horn to where the antelope were like a great cloud shadow running over the grass. And every day more people came from the agencies, those from the north telling of soldiers marching up the Yellowstone like the black singing cricket, so many. Ahh-h? Then the women and children must be taken to a good place, with the river between them and these new guns. There seemed no danger now from Three Stars. He was headed into the mountains to hunt the big-horn, and his Crow scouts had gone home in anger right after the Rosebud fight, and the Snakes too. So his soldiers hunted, fished, and pulled arrows from the rumps of their horses, reminders that the hostiles were watching.

On the sixth day after the Rosebud fight the great encampment moved across the Little Big Horn, the old herald on the far bank calling out where the people were to go—the Cheyennes, leading, going farthest down the stream, the Hunkpapas at the back stopping near the mouth of Ash Creek, all the others between. It was an old-time moving camp, the councilors ahead, the women fine with their bright saddle trappings, the warriors singing, the young men playing tricks and showing off before the girls, the boys racing up and down, the great horse herds a thunder on the ground as they came. By evening the five great circles and several small ones were spread along three miles of river as orderly as after weeks of living.

That night there was dancing everywhere, not of ceremonies but for the young people. Groups moved from camp to camp, singing, joining around the drums in the light of the great fires, and then going on, the prettiest girls choosing their partners from among the young warriors who had done big things on the Rosebud. It was a night of fun lasting until the stars faded into dawn.

The next morning the camps slept late, many going straight to the river for bathing when they awoke, men and women and children splashing and laughing in little parties all up and down the swift, cool water of the Little Big Horn. As the climbing sun burned hotter, they scattered, some to move the grazing camp horses, many to the shade of the trees along the stream, most of the women going to the lodges to some easy, visiting work like rubbing the buckskin or waving the fly brush over the sleeping children, some of the younger ones taking the turnip-diggers to the hills north of the river. Many of the warriors loafed in the shade of the rolled-up lodges, talking lazily about the fighting the other day. Even the few boys around the camps were quiet, the whole great encampment like a dog lying in the sun.

It was true that the Cheyenne prophet, Box Elder, had sent out a crier a few days ago to warn the people to keep enough horses up, that he saw soldiers coming in a dream, and yesterday a No Bow went around saying the soldiers would be here the next day. Then there was Sitting Bull's vision of soldiers falling into camp. But the people were not uneasy. The scouts said Three Stars was going farther away and that the soldiers from the north were still far down the Rosebud. Even Crazy Horse had left his lodge, to visit in the Cheyenne camp.

But an Oglala crossing the ridge on his way to Red Cloud happened to see a dust hanging like smoke on the breaks up beyond Ash Creek, with many men moving under it. He whipped his horse back across the river and to his lodge, crying out: "Soldiers coming here! Soldiers coming here!"

It was like the shot of a wagon gun over the quiet valley of the Little Big Horn, setting the Indians into a swarming. Runners started to the other camps, warriors hurried out for the herds, or got their fighting things together, and the turnip-diggers were signaled in, for already the women were crying of danger close. There was dust to be seen from here, a great pile of it just up the river, on this side, with many fast-riding horse soldiers in it.

That was true, for already they were near the upper, the Hunkpapa circle, stretching themselves into a line of blue riders from the river to the hills, their Ree Indian scouts on the higher end. A row of smoke puffs came from the soldier guns, bullets tore through the lodges, the echoes roaring all over the great camp as they moved slowly ahead, shooting. And before the soldiers' coming the women grabbed up their little ones and fled down the river, the old men and the camp dogs following. The Big Bellies hurried out too, some going along to quiet the afraid ones, others staying to help make a wall between the people and the soldier guns until the warriors could come up with their arms and horses to stand off the whites. And as the herds came flying in from the hills, the young men caught up the first good horses they reached, jumped on, and with a whooping charged off into the fight.

With many Hunkpapas facing them and more Lakotas and Cheyennes coming hard, the soldiers got off to fight on foot, and when the warriors saw this done they felt very strong. First they struck the Rees, driving them from the fight, making them drop some Hunkpapa horses they had cut off, and leaving the whole end of the soldier line open. Only one, a half-Lakota that the northern people knew as Bloody Knife, stayed with the whites, and him they cut down like a sneaking Crow found in the woman's lodge.

By the time Crazy Horse and Big Road with some Oglala warriors reached the Hunkpapa camp there was already much damage done, the lodges torn by the bullets, many knocked down, some burning. And just beyond where the fighting was several hundred warriors stood against the soldiers, with Sitting Bull, Black Moon, and Gall leading them. Crazy Horse was on his yellow pinto, stripped to breechcloth, a splattering of hailstone marks on his body, the lightning streak down his face, and the red-backed hawk on his head. And when the warriors saw him coming they made a roaring and lined up for a charge. But he remembered their need to save ammunition, and all the jammed guns they got from the horse soldiers on the Rosebud.

"Be strong, my friends!" he called out. "Make them shoot three times fast, so their guns will stick and you can knock them down with your clubs!"

He said this over and over, as another would sing a song, holding the warriors back while he rode up and down before the soldiers, drawing their fire to him as the man in his vision had, bullets like hail around him, and not touching. And when the shooting slowed down, the men beginning to jerk at their guns, making loud words, the Indians charged and the scared soldiers broke and ran like crazy men for a patch of brush and trees near the river, the warriors getting many on the way. But now they had a little hiding-place and the Indians had to crawl up over flat ground, so the fighting slowed.

But it seemed the soldiers couldn't stay still. They kept coming out and looking back up the trail and finally they jumped on their horses and retreated through the warriors between them and the river. There was no crossing, but they spurred their horses to jump the high bank into the water, with the Indians after them as after buffalo caught in shifting quicksand, knocking them from their horses with war clubs as they tried to get out on the other side, their horses slipping and falling back, the Indians making the "Yi-hoo!" the game-killing cry, each time they struck. But many got away, and with the little soldier chief in the lead they headed towards a hill, some of the warriors after them, others going back to finish the scattered soldiers and to pick up the guns and shells and round up the horses.

While they were stripping the whites one of the Cheyennes from the south country stopped to look carefully at the markings on a soldier coat. It was the same as on the one he had got in the Washita fight, where Long Hair had killed his mother and his wife. So these must be the same soldiers, these who were laying on the ground here, and who died like buffalo in the river. With the blue coat held out in his hands he ran from one to another, showing it, crying for all the valley of the Little Big Horn to hear: "My heart is good! This day my heart is good!" the water running as with a raining down his dusty face.

But now a messenger came riding, his arm pointing off across the river. More soldiers! Many more soldiers going down along the ridge on the other side, just across the river from the lower camps, where the helpless ones were. There was a fork-tailed flag ahead, and behind it a long double row of soldiers and dust, so much dust that one could hardly see the bunch of gray horses that were among them.

Hoh! It was indeed as in Sitting Bull's vision—soldiers come falling into camp. Crazy Horse saw that the big fight would be made down there. Good, let it come. He felt very strong today because the warriors were as they had been on the Rosebud, not after coups and showing off, but striking hard, striking to kill. That was what had scared the many soldiers of Three Stars away, and broke those who came here. So Crazy Horse and Gall and Knife Chief called their warriors together with their bone whistles and spoke a few words for a charge on those soldiers going against the lower camps, already so close to the fleeing people.

"A few stay here to watch those on the hill, the rest go against the new ones," Gall told his Hunkpapas, and started off down the soldier side of the river.

"Remember the helpless ones down there! This is a good day to die!" Crazy Horse said to his Oglalas. But they needed no heating words now. "Hoka hey!" they cried, lifting the new soldier guns high as they swept off down the river behind the Hunkpapas while Crazy Horse hurried to gather up the warriors still scattered over the fighting ground and to bring up as many as he could from below. By the time they got to the half-struck lodges of the lower camps he saw four men ride out of the river and up towards the soldiers. They were half a mile away but they looked like Cheyennes, four Cheyennes, going out alone to hold hundreds of soldiers back from the river crossing until the Lakotas coming hard along the bottoms got there. They rode in a brave little row, their horses moving together as in a dance, their guns blooming into smoke together and making a stir among the soldiers as if some were hit. Then there was a long row of smoke puffs from their guns, but the Cheyennes kept riding, shooting together again, four guns against almost three hundred. It was a great thing and Crazy Horse whipped his tiring pinto faster to where Black Shawl, indeed a warrior's wife, had another horse waiting.

He stopped for a word of counciling with Sitting Bull and the other Big Bellies holding the people together, making plans for a stand or flight and a scattering if more soldiers came, too many more soldiers. He saw Worm and Little Hawk and limping Black Elk among the women and children, speaking calm and quieting to them, showing them all the guns and bows and war clubs ready among them if the soldiers came near.

"Hoka hey!" a small boy tied to his anxious mother's back cried when he saw Crazy Horse. The women heard and made the trilling to see that even a little one on the back knew this man.

"Hoka hey!" answered Crazy Horse as he threw a handful of fooling gopher dust over his fresh war horse and put some little grass spears through his braids because they were like the driving snow of the winter storm. Then he led his warriors off across the river. By now many Indians too late for the fight at the Hunkpapa camp were over the crossing and charging up the ridge towards the front of the soldiers as Gall and the others came sweeping along the slope, driving some of the back ones before them. Soon the two streams of warriors would have come together among the enemy as they did in the battle on the Piney. But the soldiers were stopping along the ridge in little bunches, many off their horses, the warriors already charging the horse-holders and getting a hard-shooting defense, the guns of the whites making a roar like a hailstorm before a wind, a great cloud of smoke and dust rising to hang along the ridge.

With his heart singing the war song of the drums back among

the helpless ones, his Winchester ready in his hand, the Oglala led his warriors through the river, around the end of the soldier ridge, and up a ravine behind it to cut off their retreat. And as he rode, more and more Indians fell in behind him, until the fresh war horse was the point of a great arrow, growing wider and longer, the dust of its moving standing in the air.

They reached the head of the ravine just as the Indians from the river side pushed the soldiers to the crest of the ridge, and with a great whooping the fresh warriors charged the back of the retreating blue line, using mostly arrows, spears, and clubs. They were hot for this fight today, and the soldier guns seemed little more than grease popping on the winter fire, their horses jumping a Lakota that fell among them like so much sagebrush or stone. The first charge by the Crazy Horse warriors broke the line, cut down horses and men on that hill before the soldiers could make a circle. At the next charge a few Indian horses were hit, another man or two—nothing at all in the fight of this summer day on the Little Big Horn. As the hundreds of warriors circled and charged and circled again, many brave deeds were probably being done everywhere, but nobody had time to see them in this great roar of fighting that deafened the ear, the dust and powder smoke that made a darkness as of evening.

There were some good men on that hill, some still trying to shoot carefully from the knee even as the Indians closed in, but the circle was getting smaller, the dead horses and men piling up around the soldiers as their guns stuck, the breath of their revolvers died in their hands. One bold warrior rode through them, followed by a whole charge, and so the whites went down under the hoofs and spears until it seemed nobody could be alive in that bloody pile. But there were a few, and jumping up together, they headed towards the brush of the river, so very far away, the whooping warriors running them down like new-born buffalo calves, striking them to the ground, looking for more, until suddenly there were no more.

While the warriors were still sitting around on their horses, almost not believing this easy thing, two young Lakotas came back from the breaks disappointed to miss the finish. They had been chasing a soldier who got away on horseback and were feeling cheated because he put the revolver against his head and fired.

Now all the others were rubbed out and they only got the killed-himself one between them, and so no plunder at all.

Yes, it was truly a strange thing that only a little while ago there had been several hundred soldiers and now suddenly there were no more to kill. Even the horses were gone, rounded up down along the river by boys from the camps. They had been so worn out that they were not afraid of Indians as American horses usually are, just stood to be caught.

When every brush patch had been whipped through for any hiding ones, Crazy Horse went back to the ridge of the dead. By now they were all stripped, lying naked and white as buffalo fat where the clothes had kept off the sun, looking so pitiful, so help-less. It made him feel bad for them, so many and dying so foolishly. Why did they have to come shooting the people?

Slowly he went among them to see if there were any more he knew besides the one who had died fighting so hard down at the river, the small white man called Reynolds, who used to be a boy living with his family in the upper Platte country. Crazy Horse had been told that the Cheyennes liked his little-girl sister and stole her. California Joe, the old mountain man with the red hair on his face, had helped get her back, it was said.

There was a trader's son among the dead too, Mitch Bouyer, the one they had seen in the fight with the Crows. Crazy Horse was sorry about killing him, but if the Cheyennes were right, these sol-diers were the ones who had struck their people in the winter camp on the Washita, who came to the Yellowstone three years ago, and later made the Thieves' Road into the Black Hills. He found nothing of their long-haired chief called Custer, the man with the yellow hair falling loose over his shoulder, yet they were bad people and the trader's son should not have been with them.

Stopping his horse at the end of the ridge, Crazy Horse looked down upon the scattered camp circles of his people, the women back among them, hurrying like dark ants to gather up their pos-sessions, a few of them crossing the river and stringing up towards the battleground to seek their own dead, to strike the soldiers who had made it so. Crazy Horse felt almost dead too, so tired. Finally he started towards the crossing and home, the warriors who had been held away by his standing coming up beside him from this side and that, all talking of the great things done this day, especially of the four Cheyennes who rode out alone against the hundreds of soldiers, holding them until the others got there, four against so many—a truly great thing.

Yes, Crazy Horse had seen it.

Then there was Moving Robe, the Cheyenne woman who carried the staff of her brother killed on the Rosebud into the fight today, and Yellow Nose, the Ute captive among them who had been brave, and the strong Lakotas, too many to count. But the greatest deed of all was cutting off the retreat of the soldiers.

That was not a thing done by one man but by many, following the plannings as they were made, Crazy Horse told them.

Hou! and the plannings of the surround were good ones, and came from one man—

But Crazy Horse had not stayed to listen. Remembering now the other bunches of soldiers he had seen along the ridge, he went back to look at them, particularly those where a very brave little soldier chief had held the warriors off a long time. Most of these whites, too, had been struck down close together. Truly it seemed that almost nothing was done for glory or personal power today, but all for the protection of the people. It was a great battle, and it should make any man feel good.

But there were Indians lost too, their people coming to haul them away with the travois now. Then there would be keening in the villages, and angry relatives riding for revenge against those other soldiers still waiting on the hill above the Hunkpapa circle. Crazy Horse was surprised to remember them now; they had been so forgotten.

At the river crossing he saw an American horse standing alone with many bloody wounds. He thought of shooting it but he had no bow along and a bullet might be worth very much after today. So he rode away to his camp. Black Shawl was back, if she had ever fled very far, and came running out to meet her man, to see that the blood mixed with the dust and sweat and paint was not his own; that he was not scratched.

She brought him hot water and a piece of soapweed root for washing, fed him, and had another fresh horse ready so he could go to the hill where the live soldiers were. On the way Crazy Horse saw some young warriors dressed in soldier clothes, with flags and bugles, riding around in twos like the soldiers. It seemed some whites left hidden in the brush from the morning had come out when they saw the blue coats and then ran back into the bushes when the warriors began shooting with the captured guns that were good after they knocked the stuck shells loose. They had shot at some of the soldiers from the hill who tried to come down for water, too. Maybe they had hurt them but they hadn't tried very hard. After the big fight they felt too good for much more killing.

When Crazy Horse got up on the hill, he saw it was true that more whites had come there, bringing pack mules, as the watching warriors said, and that they had really been digging themselves down into the stony hill as a turtle digs into sand. But it seemed they were, not satisfied with that place either, and while Crazy Horse signaled for more warriors, some of the soldiers came out and started off along the ridge towards the ground of the big fight, several miles away. They stopped on a high point where they could see very many Indians sitting on their horses down there, the smoke and dust like a wind cloud high above them. There were warriors coming across the river too, and the ones the soldiers had been fighting on the hill were trying to cut them off, so the little soldier chief led his men in a gallop back to their hole. The Indians attacked there, trying to scare them as they had done in the morning, to get at the horses. They made a few good hits but the whites seemed different now, much stronger, and they had a good place to defend. After going against them several times, afoot too, the tired Indians gave it up for that day. When the sun stood red on the hills west of the Little Big Horn, a night guard was set around the soldiers, and most of the warriors went back to the mourning camps across the river, where the death lodges had been put up for the twenty warriors killed, the medicine men working over the many wounded.

As soon as he could, Crazy Horse went to cover his head in his sleeping robe so he need not hear the keening; he tried to sleep so he need not think about the fight today and why it did not seem as good as the one on the Piney ten years ago. Many, many more were killed here, and he had lost no one like Lone Bear, and yet it seemed almost that he wished this hadn't happened. Could it be that his warrior days were over?

The next morning some of the headmen went up to look at the soldiers dug in on the hill. There was talk of making a great charge to finish the fight right away, but some were against it, saying good men would be lost, and their little ammunition used up.

"Wait," these advised. "The whites will soon come out for water."

Crazy Horse was there too, planning a few charges to try the hearts of the soldiers today, but the scouts signaled that another great army was coming up the river, many more than they had been fighting, with wagon guns. Short Bull and some of the others had stayed behind to shoot into their camps, to charge the horse herds, to make them move slower so the people would have time to get away, for they were already very close.

Once more the great encampment set out upon the trail, going up the river this time, and fast, with no beaded saddle hanging on the women's horses, no gay singing, no jokes and showing off. When the last travois pulled away past the Hunkpapa camp ground the grass of the valley began to burn, the pale smoke rolling up like midsummer thunder clouds behind them. So the long line of people hurried away towards the shelter of the White Mountains, leaving the places of the soldier fights behind—the ridge with the dead ones bloated fat in the hot sun, and the hole with the live ones, too, the last of the watching warriors from there falling in with those who guarded the rear of the people as the camp disappeared into the breaks along the river.

The battle of the Little Big Horn was done.

FURTHER READINGS

Mari Sandoz, *Crazy Horse: The Strange Man of the Oglalas* (University of Nebraska Press, 1942); Mari Sandoz, *The Battle of the Little Bighorn* (James F. Carr, 1966); Mari Sandoz, *Hostiles and Friendlies: Selected Short Writings* (University of Nebraska Press, 1959); Helen Staffer, *Mari Sandoz, Story Catcher of the Plains* (University of Nebraska Press, 1982); Wallace Stegner, "*Crazy Horse* by Mari Sandoz," *Atlantic Monthly* (January, 1943): 140.

Angie Debo (1890–1988)

Angie Debo, called "The First Lady of Oklahoma History," was born in 1890 in Beattie, Kansas, into a farming family. At the age of nine, she moved with her family in a covered wagon to a new farm near Marshall, Oklahoma Territory. As she had in Kansas, Debo attended one-room schools in Oklahoma, excelling as a student and becoming the teacher herself at seventeen. Over the next decades, she received an AB degree at the University of Oklahoma (1918), AM degree from the University of Chicago (1924), and a PhD degree from the University of Oklahoma (1933), all while working variously as a teacher in one-room schools, high schools, colleges and universities in Oklahoma and Texas. However, Debo's career was deeply marked by assumptions that a woman should not take academic positions away from men—even if that woman had a PhD when the male candidate did not—and she was unable to secure a full time position at a university. Instead, Debo taught sporadically at the university level after earning her doctorate, and focused her attentions on research and publishing.

What followed was a long and controversial career, during which Debo transformed the study of Native American and Western history. Her *Rise and Fall of the Choctaw Republic* (1934) traced the political formation of an influential confederation of tribal groups in the "Old Southwest." Her controversial *And Still the Waters Run: The Betrayal of the Five Civilized Tribes* (1940) was an eloquent and meticulously researched examination of the history of the Cherokee people in Oklahoma. She is remembered today for her several studies of Native American cultures, including *The Road to Disappearance: A History of the Creek Indians* (1941), *The Five Civilized Tribes of Oklahoma* (1961), *A History of the Indians of the United States* (1970), and *Geronimo: The Man, His Time, His Place* (1976). She is also known for several studies of Oklahoma's development: *Tulsa: From Creek Town to Oil Capital* (1943), *Prairie City: The Story of an American Community* (1944), and *Oklahoma: Foot-Loose and Fancy-Free* (1949).

Debo's frank discussion of land swindles and mistreatment of Native Americans by prominent Oklahomans raised terrific controversy surrounding her work. About her writing, Debo said, "I have only one goal: to discover truth and publish it. My research is objective, but when I find all the truth on one side, as has sometimes happened in my study of Indian history, I have the same obligation to become involved as any other citizen." In the years since her death in 1988, historians have re-examined Debo's works and have found them to be largely accurate and, in fact, fairhanded accounts of events as reflected in the documentary evidence.

In this selection from her biography of Geronimo, she presents the chief in the context of his culture, demonstrating his place among the Apache in direct contradiction to the more common representation of him as a "bloodthirsty savage." Emphasizing Geronimo's place within his family, she humanizes the mythological warrior of the Plains, even while she presents him as statesman and hero, standing with his people and their lands against the waves of settlers and soldiers who meant to swallow up both.

THE APACHES SETTLE DOWN AS PRISONERS

The War Department decided to remove the [Apache] prisoners from Fort Marion, but chose to bring only the families of the Fort Pickens prisoners to join them there while sending the main body on to Mount Vernon Barracks, a military post in Alabama on the west side of the Mobile River about thirty miles north of the city of Mobile. On April 19 [1887] Langdon was notified by telegram to prepare for his contingent. The train passed through Pensacola on April 27, and the families of the Fort Pickens prisoners were removed and taken by launch to the island. They numbered twenty women and eleven children. The families of two or three of the men chose to go on with the main body. It is safe to assume, however, that Geronimo's three wives and their children were among those who joined their men. Geronimo was thus reunited with his little son Fenton, captured with his mother Zi-yeh in the Sierra Madre almost two years before, and for the first time

---

Angie Debo, "The Apaches Settle Down as Prisoners," from *Geronimo: The Man, His Time, His Place* (1976).

he saw his infant daughter, Lenna. Probably he learned only then of the death of the little girl he had sent back with Maus in anticipation of the surrender he failed to carry out. Chappo's young wife went on to Mount Vernon. Her name appears in a list of the prisoners there in 1887 or early 1888. Probably her baby had died by this time. She herself must have died shortly after. Dohn-say, of course, went to Alabama with her husband, but Geronimo must have received news of her and of other family members and friends in the band. He always showed a surprising ability to keep in touch with relatives and associates from whom he was separated.

One can be sure that Naiche was reunited with his three wives and that Dilth-cley-ih, the daughter of Victorio, also joined her husband, Mangus. Huera came, too, but apparently Mangus did not welcome her. An especially well informed observer who visited the prisoners later referred to her as Mangus' divorced wife, with whom, however, the kindly Mangus did not quarrel although she was "confined within the same precincts." This perceptive visitor found Naiche gentlemanly, though dignified and reticent; he "responds to summons, smiles gravely, shakes hands cordially," ignoring the stares and comments of the curious with studied indifference. He found Mangus "more genial, smiles broadly" in friendly greeting, while "Geronimo steals up unannounced—sly and silent as a mountain lion. Feline is his eye." But he observed that even Geronimo, as well as Naiche, was a good husband and father, and that the affection of the mothers for their children was plainly apparent.

The general public, accustomed to think of Apaches as subhuman, had no conception of what it meant to the Fort Pickens prisoners to be reunited with their families. A letter written the following year by a tourist is revealing: "I had good luck today. . . . Saw Geronimo. . . . He is a terrible old villain, yet he seemed quiet enough today nursing a baby." The baby, of course, was Lenna. Now he could hold her in his arms.

Langdon settled the families in the dilapidated casemates formerly used as officers' quarters. Thus, each family had a separate apartment. (The men without families were grouped together as before in the company quarters at the opposite end of the structure.) The women performed the household labors while their men worked outside—clearing the ditch of a dense growth of wild indigo, digging and cleaning wells, and clearing a new parade ground and planting it with Bermuda grass. This division of labor accorded with Apache custom, which did not differ materially from that observed in white society; but Langdon, holding the stereotype of Indian women serving as "slaves" doing all the work, while "the men hunt, smoke, and loaf," was amazed that "there has never been a word of remonstrance on the subject."

There had, in fact, been "no occasion to reprimand, much less to punish a single one of these Indians since their arrival here." Their good conduct went beyond an enforced submission. Langdon commended them "for their cheerfulness of demeanor, for their prompt alacrity in obeying orders and for the zeal and interest shown in the duties assigned to them." But upon a return to more normal living with the presence of their wives and children they were emboldened to express hopes for their future. Two or three of them—no doubt Naiche, Geronimo, and perhaps Mangus—went to Wratten and asked him to tell Langdon that "they were very desirous of going into permanent homes on lands they could cultivate as their own."

Langdon was not ready to encourage even such timidly expressed demands. He sent back the stern message "that they had had that chance" once and had "lost it deservedly." Their lives had been "spared by a strong but merciful government and they should be thankful" to be forgotten for a while. Otherwise, "it might be remembered they had not as yet been punished for their crimes." After that warning, as Langdon reported it, "nothing more has been said about farms." So *he* thought! They got Wratten to write to General Stanley at San Antonio asking him how much longer they would have to stay in prison and when they would get the good land Miles had promised them. It would be twenty-six more weary years before their hopes would be realized. "I am an old man now," said Naiche at Fort Sill, and he still asked for "homes to ourselves where we can be to ourselves."

Langdon, of course, was unware of these promises, and it was undeniable that these warriors had raided and killed. He did, however, try to salvage the youngest of them. Very soon he became interested in Goso, whose age he estimated at seventeen, and recommended that he be sent to Carlisle. Afterwards he sought the same opportunity for Chappo. His recorded impressions give the only known characterization of this tragic warrior son of Geronimo. In his first list of prisoners Chappo stood out as "a very intelligent young Indian." More than a year later, in recommending him for Carlisle, the officer gave this description: "Chappo. Age 23. This Indian is unusually intelligent; has learned considerable English and is ambitious to improve his mind and study subjects that will [be] of use to him in the future." No doubt his father concurred. Throughout his later life Geronimo advocated equipping the youth of his band with the white man's techniques.

Sheridan gave his immediate approval to Langdon's first request regarding Goso. And eventually four of the young warriors were selected for educational training, but the red tape was not untangled until after the prisoners were removed from Fort Pickens. And now, with the arrival of their families, Langdon found three of their children who needed schooling. One was a son of Naiche, almost certainly the boy known as Paul. He was eventually sent to Hampton Normal and Agricultural Institute, the famous Virginia school for the training of Negroes, which at that time also accepted Indian students. The others were a brother and a sister (or possibly cousins) of Hunlona, orphans with no other relatives: a fifteen-year-old girl known as Katie and a small boy called Mike.

Langdon soon became disturbed about Katie. An observance celebrated by the band in early June was unquestionably her womanhood ceremony. The Indians had wanted to hold it earlier, but Langdon, cooperating with the local tourist business, set a later date and invited visitors. About three hundred spectators joined the excursion, arriving on two steamers from Pensacola the evening of June 10. They thought they were seeing a Corn Dance designed to keep evil spirits from damaging the crop—a custom foreign to Apache practice—but in spite of his gross misinterpretation the reporting journalist unwittingly gave a clear description of the puberty rites. The party arrived late and missed part of the ceremony. No mention was made of the ritual involving the girl—it is even possible that the Indians managed to carry it out in private—but the Dance of the Mountain Spirits was clearly depicted.

A huge fire was blazing in the center of the parade ground so that even the interior of the extensive old fortress was lighted. A large buffalo robe had been placed on the ground with the skin side up, and Geronimo, Naiche, and about eight other men with switches in their hands formed a circle around it. In front of one of the men was a rude drum. As the spectators waited, they were startled by a strange cry rising in unison from the women inside the fortress—a reverent imitation, if they had known it, of the cry of White Painted Woman when her son, Child of the Water, returned from slaying the monsters of Apache mythology. As the reporter described it, "It was a peculiar cry, commencing very low and rising until it became very shrill, then dying away with a low wailing sound."

This was the signal for the men in the circle to begin "a wild kind of chant" accompanied by rhythmic beating on the hide and drum. Then two masked dancers appeared wearing the ceremonial costumes and pronged headdresses of the Mountain Spirits and performed the rite of "worshiping the fire"—to the undiscerning spectators, "a mimic warfare with the evil spirits." They were accompanied, as always, by a clown, whose actions were designed to create merriment but who at the same time was supposed to be invested with curative Power.

After about two hours the visitors returned to the city, but the Indians continued through the night. To the spectators it had been an entertaining exhibition of savage customs. In actuality, it can be seen as a moving revelation of the Apache spirit. Circumscribed as they were, these prisoners, far from their mountains and facing an unknown future, living in a grim old fortress on a narrow strip of sand with the sea closing them in, were still true to their ancient faith.

As for Katie, she was now eligible for marriage. Although Langdon did not report his making an exhibit of the prisoners, he expressed his concern about her "in the interest of morality." He stated that Ahnandia, "who is living in the fort with his present wife wants to marry Katie—and her people [these would include Hunlona's relatives in Naiche's family] are said to be not averse to the 'marriage' so called." After a year of struggle with official regulations, he succeeded in sending her to Carlisle. She arrived on April 22, 1888, and died a year later—on May 27, 1889.

Eventually, the four young warriors were also sent to Carlisle. Ira Goso, Chappo Geronimo, Eli Hunlona, and Calvin Zhonne entered the school on July 8, 1888. With them was Hunlona's young brother, who was enrolled as Bruce Patterson. He remained there until 1898, when, having developed tuberculosis, he was transferred to the Indian service school at Albuquerque in the hope that the change of climate would benefit him. But he died there after slightly more than a month from a hemorrhage of the lungs, at about the age of seventeen. Three of the four young warriors were also to succumb to the tuberculosis that lay in wait for them at Carlisle. Hunlona was to die at the school, Goso was to end his life while working on a Pennsylvania farm during vacation, and Chappo Geronimo was to rejoin his band to die with his family. Five out of six was an unusually high death rate even for Apache youths at Carlisle.

But at Fort Pickens the prisoners, including the children, continued in good health. The post surgeon visited them at least twice a week and found few cases of illness. There was one exception. Geronimo's wife She-gha had been "very ill" when she came, and she never recovered her health. She died on September 28. Geronimo and a few other Indians were permitted to accompany the body across the strait to Fort Barrancas, where it was buried in the post cemetery. The cause of her death was ascribed in a current news account to Bright's disease, but the cemetery records show it to have been pneumonia. In June a woman who may have been She-gha had been reported as ill with "cold or rheumatism in the chest." It seems probable that she had become infected with tuberculosis at Fort Marion. Hers was the only death that occurred during the entire period at Fort Pickens.

Finally, the War Department decided to remove this party also to Mount Vernon Barracks. On May 13, 1888, they were taken across the bay to Pensacola and placed on the train. They reached their destination on the same day, leaving the train at the railway station in the small town of Mount Vernon, one-half mile from the military post. Thus, they got their first view of the locality that was to become drearily familiar to them in the ensuing years.

The post was built on a ridge in a location considered healthful. Its buildings, constructed in the 1830's, were of brick, and it was enclosed by a massive brick wall. The military reservation of 2,160 acres and the surrounding land were covered with small pine timber growing on sand ridges interspersed with low-lying swales and swamps. The soil was unsuited for agriculture, and the region was sparsely populated, with here and there a log cabin occupied by a poor white or black family supported by working at a sawmill or by gathering turpentine.

The newly arrived prisoners, with Geronimo leading, were taken up the hill to the post. There, in front of one of the gates of the barracks wall, they were grouped, sitting on their baggage awaiting orders and looking down on the village that had been built to house their compatriots. For some obscure reason these friends and relatives had not come out to meet them. This may have been a formal decision. Sam Kenoi remembered a council in which some members, blaming the holdout band for their own plight, objected to their return. But this tribal division, if it occurred, was soon to disappear.

At the time, Geronimo advanced a few steps and surveyed the encampment. Not a soul was in sight. Finally, a woman emerged from a distant dwelling and came toward him with slow steps and bowed head. It was his daughter Dohn-say. Still following Apache convention, he appeared to be oblivious to her approach. But when she came close, her feelings overcame her. She ran to him, threw her arms around his neck, and burst into wild weeping. Not a muscle of his face relaxed, but his emotion must have been as deep as hers.

Other reunions as keenly felt took place throughout the group. Except for the exiled youths at Carlisle, the band was one. But the years ahead would be bleak.

FURTHER READINGS

Shirley Leckie, *Angie Debo: Pioneering Historian* (University of Oklahoma Press, 2000); Suzanne Schrems and Cynthia Wolff, "Politics and Libel: Angie Debo and the Publication of *And Still the Waters Run*," *Western Historical Quarterly* 22 (May 1991): 184–203; Kenneth McIntosh, "Geronimo's Friend: Angie Debo and the New History," *Chronicles of Oklahoma* 66 (Summer 1988): 164–177; Glenna Matthews and Gloria Valencia-Weber, "Against Great Odds: The Life of Angie Debo," *OAH Newsletter* 13 (May 1985): 8–11.

Dorothy Johnson (1905–1984)

Dorothy Johnson was born in McGregor, Iowa, in 1905, and when she was four, the family moved west to Montana and eventually settled in the town of Whitefish, which was "still being hacked out of the woods." In an age when few young women received much education, Johnson graduated from Montana State University in 1928, and with a degree in English, she took a series of secretarial jobs in Okanogan, Washington, and in Menasha, Wisconsin. She moved to New York, where an emerging publishing industry provided work for talented young women. Like Willa Cather who had been managing editor of *McClure's*, Johnson became executive editor of a magazine called *Woman*.

In 1930, Johnson's first short stories appeared in the *Saturday Evening Post*. In 1949 *Cosmopolitan* published "The Man Who Shot Liberty Valance," and the following year *Colliers* published "A Man Called Horse." What came to be called "the western" was immediately popular. Warner Brothers filmed her novel *The Hanging Tree* in 1957 and Johnson became a screenwriter when "Liberty Valance" and "Horse" were made into western films.

Johnson's picture of Indian life was more historically accurate than that which usually filled the pages of pulp fiction. She wrote *Indian Country* (1953) and *Buffalo Woman* (1977) and in 1969 she wrote a full biography of the Sioux chief Sitting Bull, *Warrior for a Lost Nation*. Dorothy Johnson's book told readers who were willing to listen that Native Americans were neither "savages" nor "varmints," that these same men were care-worn leaders of their people, family men who held the lives of their wives and children in their hands. She was one of the few whites to be made an honorary member of the Blackfeet Tribe. In the last decade of her life, she taught journalism at the University of Montana in Missoula, living there until her death in 1984.

In the chapter excerpted here, Johnson describes the intervention of Mrs. Catherine Weldon on behalf of the Sioux, who were "defeated, cheated, and sometimes hungry." Like Helen Hunt Jackson, Mrs. Weldon had as little success with the army as Jackson.had with congressmen. But the excerpt adds a fillip—the sneering newspaper headlines suggesting that a white woman who defends a "red man" must be deranged, or sexually perverse. The detail recalls newspaper derision of the efforts of the Indian Defense Association in 1923, alleging that a member of that association, Mabel Dodge Luhan, was "Bohemia's Queen [who] Married an Indian Chief." Mrs. Weldon packed her bags and went home to Brooklyn, but Dorothy Johnson fought back in the ways she could, by writing Sitting Bull into the American canon of heroes.

SHE LOVES SITTING BULL

Buffalo Bill," Colonel William F. Cody, was an inspired showman who never missed a chance to make his traveling Wild West Show exciting. "Buffalo Bill's Wild West" packed 'em in with attractions that kept audiences bug-eyed throughout the colorful action and left them hoarse from yelling and sore-handed from clapping.

What could be more attractive to these city audiences than a good look at the nation's most talked-about, feared, and hated Indian chief, Sitting Bull?

So in the spring of 1885, Buffalo Bill's show manager, Major John M. Burke, traveled to the Sioux reservation to call on Sitting Bull. Burke had a proposition to present and a contract to be signed. Would Sitting Bull travel with the Wild West Show for four months?

Burke offered him fifty dollars a week; five other Hunkpapa men would get twenty-five dollars a month. Three women would receive fifteen dollars a month, and an interpreter would be paid sixty dollars. After considerable discussion, Sitting Bull agreed—if the contract included a clause that he insisted upon: he would have the sole right to sell his autograph and copies of his picture. In his dealings with white men, he had come to understand the use of money.

The Indians joined the show in Buffalo, New York, on June 12. Buffalo Bill's publicity shouted that Sitting Bull was the chief who had been responsible for the "massacre" of the Seventh Cavalry at

Dorothy Johnson, from *Warrior For a Lost Nation: A Biography of Sitting Bull* (1969).

the Little Bighorn. Gaudy posters claimed that he had personally scalped General Custer. (He hadn't; Custer was not scalped, and to this day nobody even knows who killed him.)

Sitting Bull was exhibited at the show, riding around the arena in a buggy, while ten thousand people in the audience jeered at him as Custer's murderer. He didn't understand English, but he knew the sound of hatred.

Probably the only thing that kept him from canceling his contract then and there was an exhibition of sharpshooting by a girl named Annie Oakley. She was a marvel. She shot and shattered glass balls as they were thrown into the air. Riding a buckskin pony, she snatched a pistol from the ground, fired three times, and broke three targets.

Sitting Bull cheered wildly along with everybody else. He adopted her as his daughter and gave her a Sioux name that translates as Little Straight Shooter, or Little Sure Shot. She was indeed little—five feet tall, weighing ninety-eight pounds. Annie Oakley's fame grew because of Sitting Bull's admiration for her skill. Buffalo Bill's publicity releases said that the Hunkpapa chief had joined the show because Little Sure Shot was in it. This wasn't true, but it made a good story.

This was a wild, exciting show, with Annie Oakley shooting, Indians and cowboys and buckskin-clad frontiersmen riding madly, and Buffalo Bill himself reenacting a famous fight he had had with an Indian named Yellow Hand. Newspapers gave the Wild West Show plenty of publicity. The *Boston Transcript* called Sitting Bull "Sedentary Taurus," and a reporter said he looked something like Daniel Webster.

The show went on to Montreal, where it had a wild welcome. Canadian audiences did not jeer at Sitting Bull. To them he seemed a wise man, for he had taken refuge in their country when the United States army had harassed him.

Reporters kept asking him about the Custer fight. He told one of them (at least the reporter said he did), "Nobody knows who killed Custer. Everybody fired at him. Custer was a brave warrior, but he made a mistake. The Indians honored him and did not scalp him. I fought for my people. My people said I was right. I will answer for the dead of my people. Let the palefaces do the same on their side."

The Canadians bought thousands of photographs showing Sitting Bull and Buffalo Bill standing together. The show moved to Detroit, then to Saginaw, then to Columbus. It closed in St. Louis on October 11, and Sitting Bull and his party returned to their agency at Standing Rock. With them went a gift to Sitting Bull from Buffalo Bill, a gray circus horse trained to do tricks.

Two years after that tour Buffalo Bill Cody took his show to England. Twice, by royal command, he put on a special performance for Queen Victoria and her family. But Sitting Bull was not there. He refused Buffalo Bill's invitation, saying, "It is bad for me to parade around awakening the hatred of white men. I am needed here. There is more talk of taking our land away from us."

Major McLaughlin's wife was half Sioux. She yearned to go to England. But if Sitting Bull did not go, nobody from the agency could go. So Sitting Bull's refusal irritated McLaughlin—like everything else the old chief did.

As the dismal years passed, just about every custom the defeated Sioux tried to retain was forbidden by somebody with authority over them.

They remembered sadly the great buffalo hunts—the hard riding and straight shooting, the excitement and triumph of the chase. There were no buffalo herds anymore. The last big hunt had been in 1883. Now there was only beef from the steers driven in by white contractors, and compared to the rich flavor of buffalo meat, beef was not very good. But on beef ration day, when cowboys drove the steers in, the Indians tried to recapture some of the delight of the old-time hunt by chasing the long-horned cattle on horseback and killing them as they had once killed buffalo.

The Indian Bureau prohibited even this. One of the commissions that came out to investigate the Sioux problem had described this chase as "a disgrace to our civilization" and said it would "perpetuate in a savage breast all the cruel and wicked propensities of his nature." After that, steers were slaughtered one at a time.

The Sioux, even defeated, cheated, and sometimes hungry, continued to be a great problem for everybody else. White settlers kept looking jealously at their big reservation: *Those lazy loafers are living off the government and they're not using the land—Why shouldn't we have it?*

In the West there were plenty of people who hated the Indians. In the East there were vociferous, organized, powerful groups who loved them from a safe distance and constantly gave advice to Congress, through paid lobbyists, on how to handle them. These "Indian friends" had been moved by Helen Hunt Jackson's book, *A Century of Dishonor,* but they didn't agree among themselves on what should be done for the Indians.

A former minister, Dr. T. A. Bland, founder of the National Indian Defense Association, went west to visit Red Cloud, Oglala chief, at the Pine Ridge Agency—and was stopped cold.

The agent there, V. T. McGillicuddy, was a good man for his job, but very strict. Nobody could set foot on his reservation without his consent, and he had signs posted all over, ordering visitors to get permission from him. Dr. Bland saw the signs, but he had permission from the Secretary of the Interior, who was McGillicuddy's superior, to visit Red Cloud. Intending to call on the agent very soon, Bland went into an eating place and ordered a meal. Before he had finished it, McGillicuddy came in and ordered him off the reservation.

Dr. Bland went indignantly back to Washington and published in his society's magazine, *The Council Fire,* a statement that McGillicuddy was one of the corrupt Indian agents. This caused a nationwide sensation and plenty of hard feelings, but it didn't do the Sioux any good.

White men continued to demand the land that was supposed to belong to the Sioux forever. Congress passed a law in 1887, the Dawes Act, that was supposed to satisfy both the whites and the Indians.

Under this law Sioux families could own land allotments individually instead of as part of the tribe. When all the Indians had chosen their land, the government would buy the rest—some nine million acres—from the tribe for fifty cents an acre and open it up to homesteading by white farmers.

But under the Treaty of 1868 the Dawes Act could not take effect until three fourths of the adult Indian men agreed to the idea. A tough army officer, Captain Richard Henry Pratt, headed a commission that visited the Sioux in 1888 to talk them into signing. They had no reason to love Captain Pratt. He was head of the Carlisle Indian School in faraway Pennsylvania, where many of the

frightened, homesick Indian children had been sent to be educated and civilized. He ran the school as if the children were bud-
ding criminals.

Pratt's commission argued for days with the Sioux. Four of the
tame chiefs appointed by Agent McLaughlin would have signed
the agreement, but Sitting Bull used his considerable eloquence
and lined them up firmly against it.

McLaughlin was furious. He was used to having those tame
chiefs do just what he told them to do.

Captain Pratt was furious too. He made threats. He even recommended that the Sioux beef ration be stopped so the Indians
would have to eat salt pork, which they hated. Thus they would be
starved into submission. One former Indian agent commented sarcastically that the government might as well issue arsenic instead
and "get the poisoning process finished with decent expedition."

Pratt's commission failed utterly, thanks to the stubbornness
and arguments of Sitting Bull.

Soon after this, Sitting Bull went with a delegation of Indians to
Washington, D.C., to see the Secretary of the Interior. He got the
offer for the land increased to $1.25 an acre—but he still did not
want to sell it.

The following year General Crook brought another land commission to the Sioux reservation—and Sitting Bull blocked the sale
again for a while. Then it was up to McLaughlin to make the
Indians agree somehow; if he failed, he would look like an incom-
petent to these important men sent out by the federal government.
McLaughlin persuaded the tame chiefs—by meeting with them
secretly.

When the time came for the public signing, Sitting Bill arrived
late—not to sign, but to try again to stop the docile, confused
chiefs. He had just heard that this ceremony was planned.
McLaughlin had kept him in the dark about it.

The Indians became panicky in the midst of confusion and
veiled threats from the commission. Enough Sioux men finally
signed the agreement to make it legal. The great Sioux reservation
was broken up.

The commissioners hadn't been gone for two weeks when the
beef ration at all the Sioux agencies was brutally reduced. This was
no fault of the commission; it was due to an economy move by

Congress. But the Sioux who had refused to sign blamed those who had agreed. *You can never trust a white man!* they said. *You should know that. You're fools!*

Someone asked Sitting Bull how the Indians felt about the land cession, and he replied bitterly, "Indians! There are no Indians left but me!"

Sitting Bull, of course, signed no agreements with the white men. While the Indians on his reservation were gathered for talks with General Crook, Sitting Bull used to ride around the camp circle in the evening, singing:

> *The tribe named me,*
> *So in courage I shall live.*

He wore a bunch of buffalo hair, painted red, fastened to one side of his head, in memory of the time when buffalo were plentiful.

Another song that he used to sing in those days, remembering when his people were happy, was this:

> *A warrior I have been.*
> *Now it is all over.*
> *I have a hard time.*

Arguments about the land cession didn't all take place in Dakota Territory. The "Indian friends" back east argued, too. All but one of these organizations favored the agreement, with the idealistic reasoning that if every Sioux family had to settle down and farm its own 160 acres, all the Sioux would become civilized in a hurry.

Dr. Bland's National Indian Defense Association disagreed with this theory. Wild people needed time, they believed. They should not be hurried into a shockingly unfamiliar way of living. The N.I.D.A. fought the land grab with all its power and considerable money. Dr. Bland had informative circulars printed up, in English type but in the Sioux language, and distributed to every Sioux family. Most of them knew somebody who could figure out what the printed matter said.

He wrote letters to Red Cloud and other Sioux chiefs, and in the spring of 1889 he sent out a crusading woman, Mrs. Catherine

Weldon, to help the Sioux chiefs hold out against the blandishments of the commission.

Mrs. Weldon was a wealthy widow, zealous and determined. She was an artist, and the reason she gave publicly for making the trip was that she wanted to paint a portrait of the famous Sitting Bull.

She reached Dakota Territory; then she ran into bureaucratic interference. A letter she wrote to Red Cloud never reached the old Oglala chief. It came into the hands of Agent McLaughlin instead. She wrote to Sitting Bull, and he answered with a letter that he entrusted to an Indian messenger—but Mrs. Weldon never received that answer.

It was easy for the agents to pry into the personal affairs of their charges, because the Sioux had to have their letters written and read by educated young Indians. Many of these people were convinced that it was to their advantage to cooperate with the agents.

Finally some letters got through the agency blockade, and Mrs. Weldon waited at Standing Rock Agency for Sitting Bull to meet her. He had been sick, and he was in mourning for the death of a daughter he loved, but he drove a team and wagon forty miles over rough country to talk with this white-woman stranger.

While Mrs. Weldon waited, Major McLaughlin came along, started a conversation with her, and began to make derisive remarks about Sitting Bull. Mrs. Weldon had not even mentioned the old chief—but Agent McLaughlin had been reading other people's mail.

He told Mrs. Weldon that Sitting Bull was a coward, selfish, nobody's friend, of no importance, and a heavy burden on the younger Sioux who were more progressive. "Progressive" was the word used to describe Indians who did just what the agent wanted them to do. It was never used in connection with Sitting Bull!

McLaughlin also brought Dr. Bland, head of the N.I.D.A., into the conversation, remarking that he had no influence or standing at the agency. Mrs. Weldon hadn't even mentioned him. She took an immediate dislike to McLaughlin.

When Sitting Bull arrived, Mrs. Weldon went with him, bag and baggage, to his camp on Grand River. She lived in his cabin with his two wives, helped with the housework, painted his portrait, and—fulfilling her major purpose—acted as his secretary, writing letters to help him in his effort to keep the Sioux lands for the Sioux.

The white men who detested Sitting Bull attacked Mrs. Weldon with lies and slander. A sneering news story in the *Bismarck Daily Tribune* for July 2, 1889, was headed:

SHE LOVES SITTING BULL
A NEW JERSEY WIDOW FALLS VICTIM
TO SITTING BULL'S CHARMS

Mrs. Weldon was justifiably furious. She was sure that Major McLaughlin was responsible for the lie. But she was determined to block the land grab. She suggested that Sitting Bull and his wives go with her to the other Sioux agencies to talk to the Indian leaders there. He agreed—but Major McLaughlin did not. Sitting Bull, like other Indians, could not leave his own area without a pass, and the agent would not issue one. He gave the excuse that the chief's signature might be needed on important documents. Furthermore, McLaughlin wouldn't even let Mrs. Weldon travel alone—she might not be safe, he said.

Mrs. Weldon lost her temper. She asked with bitter sarcasm, "Are you afraid of a woman and a woman's influence?" She threatened to report McLaughlin to Washington. Then she indignantly marched out of his office.

Sitting Bull came to the agency, although Mrs. Weldon had sent him a message warning him not to do so. The chief was angry. He tried to see the agent, but McLaughlin would not talk to him. Instead he sent another man who walked Sitting Bull over to the guardhouse and hinted that he might be sent to the penitentiary, because probably he intended to kidnap Mrs. Weldon. Sitting Bull indignantly replied that he looked on her as his own daughter.

Mrs. Weldon gave up and went home to Brooklyn, and the newspapers near the reservation published more sneering stories about her. The land cession went through.

But she was not yet defeated. The following April she wrote an apology to McLaughlin:

"You will doubtless be surprised to receive a letter from me after our not very amicable conversations. . . . And indeed it is with reluctance that I humble myself to address you, knowing that you cannot feel friendly disposed toward me. . . . Even enemies can act magnanimously towards each other, and I hope you will extend to me the courtesy of a gentleman to a lady. . . . It has been my intention to spend the rest of my life in Dakota among or near my Indian friends."

But she didn't accept too much humiliation. She remarked sarcastically, "It is such a brave noble deed for a strong powerful man (created to protect woman) to trample upon, to annihilate woman."

Mrs. Weldon planned to build a house and to give instruction in "useful domestic accomplishments" to Indian women and girls.

McLaughlin didn't try to block her visit to Sitting Bull this time. Again she moved in with his family. This time she brought along her only child, a boy named Christy, not quite fourteen. She studied the Sioux language and earned an honorable Sioux name, which she treasured: Woman Walking Ahead.

But she moved into a situation that was building up to tragedy, for this was the year 1890, when a strange religion known as the Ghost Dance was rampant among the desperate, bewildered Sioux.

FURTHER READINGS
Dorothy M. Johnson, *When You and I Were Young, Whitefish* (Montana Historical Society Press, 1997); Judy Alter, *Dorothy Johnson* (Boise State University Press, 1980).

Delphine Red Shirt

Delphine Red Shirt was born in Nebraska and grew up in Porcupine, South Dakota, on the Pine Ridge Reservation in the 1960s and 1970s. She is an enrolled member of the Oglala Sioux tribe, and represents the Oglala as a non-governmental representative at the United Nations. She attended the Red Cloud Indian School in Pine Ridge, and received a BA degree in liberal studies from Wesleyan University. In the years since graduating from college, Red Shirt has been a Marine reservist, an accountant, and a writer. After publishing poetry in high school, Red Shirt turned seriously to writing while at Wesleyan, and after working on her stories for many years, she completed *Bead on an Ant Hill* and published it in 1998. She is currently completing a narrative of her mother's life, taken down from her mother in Lakota and translated by Red Shirt into English; the working title for Red Shirt's second book is "Winyan Isnala," or "woman alone." A columnist for *Indian County Today*, Red Shirt now lives in Guilford, Connecticut.

SITTING ON RED CLOUD'S GRAVE

We would climb the hill, past the old church with the buffalo painted on the high ceilings, and walk up a dirt road to the cemetery. The road was the one they used for funerals. I had never been to a Catholic funeral until I went to that high school. One of the students died, and our whole class went to the funeral. He died on a weekend, and they buried him during the week. He was a junior. To me, it seemed he had a lot of promise. He was my cousin. My father and his father came from the same ancestor, Chief Lone Elk, a Brulé. My father's and his father's grandmothers were sisters. His father had been an artist who depicted life among the Lakota in the early part of the century. He tried to show what it was like for the reservation people. I remembered how my father and I went to

Delphine Red Shirt, "Sitting on Red Cloud's Grave," from *Bead on an Ant Hill: A Lakota Childhood* (1998).

visit his family. They lived in the same small town in which I lived in Nebraska. When he died, it was hard to believe that I had just seen him in our homeroom the Friday before. They said he had been shot by a bootlegger. It is illegal to sell alcohol on the reservation, but it was well known that there were certain houses in town where one could buy liquor. At his funeral, the priest burned incense, and we all stood unbelieving while they nailed his coffin inside another box, what we called a "rough" box made of unfinished pine. Over that they slowly shoveled dirt. They buried him on the other side of the highway where the newer cemetery was. It was the first and last time I went to that side.

I knew the old side, the side where Red Cloud is buried. The old side was where we went on slow afternoons, after school let out and all the day-students went home. Those of us who boarded at the school had free time between three o'clock and five o'clock. We would check in with the matron, the older woman who was in charge. Then we would buy a candy bar at the snack stand the nuns had in the recreation room, and if the weather permitted, we walked up to the graveyard. Our lives at the school were regimented to breakfast, school, lunch, school, free time, five o'clock mass, dinner, study hall, free time, bedtime, and lights out in the dorm at ten o'clock. The only block of free time we had was that time when we could walk up to the cemetery, sit down, and talk. It was the only private place, the only spot where we could be irreverent and no one would hear us. We found solace there as we grew older, and our lives changed from the shallow and frivolous years as freshmen to the somewhat more mature introspective years as juniors and seniors. The time I remember the best was my junior year.

It was my best year at that school. I went there, following in my brother's footsteps. He honored Mom-mah and Kah-kah by finishing second in his graduating class. As always, I had a more difficult time. It was not that the studies were hard; they were not, as I was able to prove to myself in my junior year when I won awards in my classes, signifying that the teachers gave me the highest honor. I had not expected it and was working at the library the night they had the awards banquet. My friends came running to tell me that I should have gone to the awards ceremony because my name had been called out for the different awards. I was surprised and pleased. The small gold pins were important to me. My junior year was the year I finally accepted who I was. All of my life, I had been less sure of myself than my brother was.

It was a time when I felt suspended between the safe and sure footing of childhood and the ever-shifting quagmire of adolescence. I felt uncomfortable feeling like that, unable to choose the side I knew best—childhood. When I had first gone to the high school, it felt like I was giving up the things I loved the most about childhood: the games I played, like "Red Rover, Red Rover," in the alfalfa field with my cousins; the comic books we kept in brown paper boxes under our beds and read over and over; the cold days when we played jacks and cards on the kitchen table in the lamplight, when the days grew shorter in the winter. My favorite cousins grew up in the log cabin near where Kah-kah had lived most of his life. They had no electricity. I remember dancing to Roy Orbison on a portable radio. It was those cousins I missed the most when I left home for the first time to board at the Catholic school. It was they who in their Lakota ways embraced me when I first came to the reservation. We played, pretended, dreamed, laughed, and joked in Lakota. They will always remind me of those carefree times I enjoyed as a child, before I had to go away to boarding school.

I had to leave home like the kids that they stole and put into boarding schools when Kah-kah was growing up, only I went voluntarily. It was one of two high schools on the reservation, and by the time I was ready for high school, I knew that I would go to that school named after Red Cloud. They said that he was buried there in the graveyard of the "Sapa ų pi" or "they that wore black," which is what Kah-kah called the Catholics. Kah-kah was a "Ska ų pi," or "they that wore white," which is what someone from the Episcopal church is called.

Red Cloud, who was buried in the Sapa ų pi cemetery, had first invited the Catholics to the reservation. He chose the land where our reservation was established; he and a Brulé chief named Spotted Tail selected the sites where our respective reservations now stand. Red Cloud invited the Sapa ų pi to educate the generations that would call this place home, this small area of land far from the H Sapa. He knew that these generations, including my own, would never know the kind of freedom that he and Crazy Horse and Sitting Bull had known. Red Cloud knew that our spirits would be subdued by this place, by the reservation. He wanted

freedom for us, the kind that only they knew. So, he invited the
Sapa u to give us freedom of a different kind, that of the mind, for
we Lakota believed that mind and spirit were one and the same.

He knew that in the time after the Sapa u were summoned and
had come to build their school and church, that we Lakota, being a
spiritual people, would naturally embrace them. He knew also that
in this new world forged by the government, our physical selves
would be limited to the boundaries set by the reservation, and we
would fare better if we were educated. He knew that our spirits
would never accept this limited life, the way he tried not to, even
when everything fell apart and our people were ordered to abandon forever their way of life. In the years I attended the school
named after him, I never knew how much foresight he had had, how
much he understood what life would be like for my generation.

I remember those autumn days after school, how the light
seemed dimmer and the air colder as we trekked up past the head-
stones to our favorite spot at the graveyard. I don't remember stopping to read the other gravestones. We didn't have time for that. We
usually walked directly to the gravestone at the far eastern end,
where the entire grave was covered by a cement block that stood
about three feet high. It was our favorite spot because we could all
sit on it side by side, looking off toward town, watching the cars
come and go.

It was a favorite pastime for the town kids to cruise the road
between the school and town. We watched the cars coming and
going until we saw the five o'clock bus returning from town, which
meant that if we wanted, it was time to go down to mass. The group
of us sometimes went to the five o'clock mass with the volunteers
who lived at the school. They were our teachers, some of them
young Jesuits and priests. We liked our teachers, and they seemed
to like us. So we sought them out. We joined their mass, and they
invited us into their circle where they held hands as they sang
along with a guitar. If we didn't go to the five o'clock mass, we
would get ready to go to dinner. It wasn't our favorite thing to do
because the food was lacking in quality. The cook at the school
believed that fresh baked bread was not good for you, so he kept
the bread in metal garbage cans until it was quite stale. Next to the
stale bread, he always served up some main dish that no one ate.
His assistant was a Puerto Rican man from New York City. Between

the two of them, they cooked very unappetizing meals. I stopped eating meat altogether and became a vegetarian.

I worked part-time at the library, and I would find time during the week to log in hours, for which I was paid. I liked my life there. If I wanted to borrow money, I would go to the Jesuit who everyone knew kept a set of books for that purpose. He would pencil in my name and the amount I borrowed, usually less than five dollars, and then when I came back to pay him, he would take a ruler and cross out my name. He kept his books meticulously, and I liked the way he puffed on his pipe when I came to borrow money for the weekend and the way he never declined my request. I liked the predictability of the place: the dorm, the library, the dining hall, the school bus ride home on the weekends, and the way I never felt I lacked for anything there, except a sense of the real world.

When I was a freshman at the school, the math teacher, a woman from New Jersey, announced that she wanted to invite four students from our school to try something new, to go home with her to teach the Lakota language and culture at the high school where she had taught the year before. She said the four students selected would go that summer, in early June, returning in time for the annual Sun Dance in August. I remember sitting in the gym when she made the announcement at the student assembly, the one we called the "little boys' gym," a term left over from the old days when the younger kids boarded at the school, too.

Mom-mah had boarded there as a young girl. She hated it. She said she admired the older girls who grew proficient at throwing large buns at the nuns when they turned their backs. They were given freshly baked buns for a snack, and many of the older girls kept theirs until they hardened. Then they used them as missiles, which they launched and fired at nuns they didn't like. She said by the time the nuns turned around in their heavy habits, the girl hurling the bun was standing silent and still. She said the hardest thing about her experience there was kneeling for so long at mass. She said sometimes she would use one of the hats they were given to wear at mass as a cushion for her aching knees. By the time I came to the high school, the nuns no longer wore habits, except for a stubborn few, and the younger students, those below the ninth grade, no longer boarded there. Everything had changed. The Lakota language was being taught by Lakota teachers, and the requirement to go to daily mass was no longer in place. We still attended mass on all the Catholic feast days, but the church was no longer an integral part of the school. It was no longer forced upon us the way it had been for Mom-mah.

The math teacher made the announcement and recruited students to fill out applications for the four slots. I filled out an application and handed it in, not really thinking about what it meant, other than the fact that it was a fully paid summer job. A summer job was important in our family. It was one of the only ways I was able to afford school clothes and a decent jacket to wear in the fall. At the next student assembly the math teacher announced the names of the four students selected, along with an alternate if one of the four declined. I was chosen among the four. When my name was announced, I felt uncomfortable being singled out in my group of friends. I did not want to bring attention to myself.

My friends were very familiar to me. We had been together since elementary school. All of our parents spoke Lakota, and our last names were not English or French like the half-bloods at the school, but Lakota. Our Lakota last names, combined with the fact that we came from isolated communities, meant that we were somehow different from the half-bloods. The difference was subtle, which made life even more complex for us. We were a group of full-blood Lakota girls whose self-image was determined by many other factors, not excluding this one. It was one more difficulty that my older brother had not had to deal with. He played football, liked politics, and could easily pass for an "iye ska," what Mom-mah called the "half-breeds." It means "translator," a name carried over from the time many of their ancestors translated Lakota for the government and English for our forefathers. I, on the other hand, looked like what I considered myself to be, a full-blood Lakota adolescent, floundering in a non-Lakota world. It was a time when I still thought in Lakota.

When school ended in my freshman year, and before I had a chance to breathe, I began my new job with the math teacher. I wasn't sure what going away from home for a summer job would mean, but I knew that I would be homesick. I had never been away for very long, at least not that far away. The night before I left, Mom-mah came to see me. My brother, six years my senior, drove her to the house at the school where we were staying, just before we were to begin our trip east. Mom-mah brought me a small cassette recorder. My brother, who was home from college, gave me a tape of Buffy St. Marie songs. I knew they had both scraped together all the money they had to buy me those things. I hugged Mom-mah and said good-bye, promising that I would write often. "Iyokśice śni ye. Iyokpiya omani ye," Mom-mah had said. "Do not be sad. Travel with a glad heart." I did not want my older brother to see the tears in my eyes. I was glad it was dusk when they came to say good-bye. I watched the taillights of their car grow dimmer as they pulled away on their way home. I knew that I could very easily have refused the summer job in New Jersey and stayed at home, but I went even though I was homesick before I left.

That summer, I felt like Red Cloud on a tour of Washington, DC I saw everything with intensely curious eyes. We drove east in a small Ford Mustang. Five of us, including the math teacher, squeezed into that small car loaded with our belongings. We made our way to New Jersey via Milwaukee, Chicago, Detroit, Charleston, Washington, DC and finally New York City. I do not remember being fond of any one city except for Washington, DC as I ran through the museums and monuments, feeling happy to be on the go. By that time, the four of us, two of us freshman girls, a freshman boy, and a sophomore girl, felt at home together. We all had known one another at the school by sight but not as well as one would think in such a small school.

When summer ended, we drove home. We had accrued experiences that no one on the reservation would believe that four kids from our high school could have had. We had even spent a week on Cape Cod and been to the shore along the Atlantic coast in a small yacht. My summer had been full of everything from my first banana split to my first taste of champagne and caviar at an art gallery near Cape Cod and even a small cup of wine shared with the cast of a play on Broadway in New York City. When I returned that autumn to the high school, I felt embarrassed when the math teacher showed slides of our experiences that summer. I had forgotten that I was coming home to high school at the end of the summer, and how I had acted as if I were a tourist on vacation. I was embarrassed by my own expectations after my summer there. I looked around me, at the kids in that small classroom, and realized how foolish I had been that summer, that my life was probably never going to be that way again.

I realize now that the year after I went east was a turning point for me. It was then that I became restless. I wanted something more, and I was never really sure what it was until I went away to college. I didn't realize that the morning I loaded my gear in that car and headed for the East Coast, that I would never really unpack my suitcase on the reservation again. I would, from that day forward, always look for the next opportunity to leave the reservation and see what lay beyond its borders.

I left the high school for a semester after that. I went to live with my older brother in a city near the Black Hills. I lived with him and attended the high school there. I did not like the school but kept going because I did not want to be labeled as a "dropout." I worked part-time at a local motel as a maid, cleaning rooms and changing beds. I knew I had to stay in school. If I didn't stay, I could expect only jobs like the maid's job I had that winter. I wanted to return to the reservation, back to my old school, but I had left because of fighting there. An older girl, an "iye ska," had taken a great dislike to me, and rather than fight, I left. I did not like the violence that erupted when the kids drank alcohol. I did not readily accept violence. I had inherited Mom-mah's gentle heart, and although I had been involved in fights, I felt greatly dishonored by any violent act. I could not comprehend what it meant. I remember when an older girl gave me my first bloody nose. She jumped me while I was viewing exhibits at a science fair. I felt dazed. How unreal it felt to feel the thud of skin against skin. I could not understand what it meant, perhaps because I did not grow up that way. It seemed foreign to me.

While I lived, worked, and went to school in the city, my older brother and others were restless as well. A new movement had come into our midst. It was a new political movement that was gaining momentum. My only contact with it was through my brother. I attended a few of the political rallies sponsored by the new movement, but I, like Mom-mah, was cautious and stayed back, not knowing what it would bring for the people in the end. When I look back now, I realize that what it meant for the people in my community was a loss of innocence. I remember the way it was before they came and the way it was after.

In my small community, before the movement came, we were insulated from the world. The boys, including my youngest brother, rode Shetland ponies up and down an old wagon trail that ran next to the highway. It was called the Big Foot Trail. It was named after the chief whose people died at Wounded Knee. The boys raced their ponies along that trail. They could be seen in groups of seven or eight, riding everywhere together. We girls walked up the road on warm summer evenings to the white bluffs across from the community center. I still remember the smell of fresh hay on those evenings. Our families all knew one another. We all lived in houses set a mile or so apart. There were distinct "tio śpaye" or "extended families," and elders who presided over them, both male and female. The local policeman was a very large man with a big belly hanging over his belt. He had a family in our community. Although no one had a telephone, he always seemed to know when someone digressed and had had too much alcohol to drink. We lived like that, isolated but serene in our innocence.

The changes brought by the movement were more apparent during and after the occupation of Wounded Knee in 1973, when followers of the movement barricaded themselves in a Catholic church there in a stand-off with the federal government. I can still see the federal marshals in their blue suits, toting guns and coffee as they milled about in our community. I was a high school student, and I watched it all in silence. When the occupation was finally over, someone came to Mom-mah and asked her if she would smuggle one of the leaders out in her car trunk. Mom-mah said "No," not because she was against them, but because it was wrong. I admired her for that, and like her, expected life to be like that, everything black and white, right or wrong, innocent or guilty.

Now that I look back on what happened to my community, I realize that because we were so close to Wounded Knee, we were all indicted. We were all guilty of aiding and abetting. Whom? I was not sure because from where Mom-mah and others in our community stood, both sides in the stand-off were at fault. Rightfully, we felt like the pawns that we were in that conflict. Once we perceived that, we lost our innocence.

The time after the occupation, chaos came and settled in our midst. Guns and drugs became available. Life grew more complex. Mom-mah came close to being wounded when she stepped into the line of fire in a drive-by shooting as she walked out of our post office. She was fortunate that the bullet only grazed her forehead. A few years earlier, I was not so lucky. I stepped right into the line of fire when someone who had access to a gun began randomly shooting. The bullet went through the right side of my chest. I survived, although at the time I thought, as only an adolescent would, that I had done something wrong even though I had been only guilty of being in the wrong place at the wrong time. These things happened after the occupation of Wounded Knee in 1973.

It was a time when these occurrences seemed common, "wo kope ya," Mom-mah would say, "frightfully so." A few days after graduation ceremonies were held at my high school, I was shot. I didn't attend the ceremonies, vowing that I would attend my college graduation—a seemingly impossible dream for someone coming from where I did.

It was a Sunday morning, the morning I woke up and thought I was going to die. Someone was randomly shooting a gun, and I awoke to find everyone in the house hiding on the floor. They were trying to dodge bullets flying through the house. I didn't believe or couldn't believe what was happening, and while I stood in a half-awake stupor, I felt something tear into my right chest. At first I thought it was happening to someone else; then I realized it was happening to me. When I began to bleed, I did not want to lie down. I thought if I did, I would never stand up again.

What I learned from that experience was that I was no longer safe there, in that place I had taken for granted as my childhood haven. At the time I was shot, I was an adolescent coming into young adulthood, and that fact put me into a category I considered more dangerous in that place. I knew I had to leave.

Long before this event occurred and I was still in high school, I had contradictory feelings about the movement, particularly during and after the occupation of Wounded Knee in 1973. On the one hand I identified with those who supported it, and on the other hand I did not like the violence. I did not know then that I would be directly affected by the violence that I so disdained.

When everything was over and the leaders of the movement were on trial or in jail, I felt guilty. After all, they had come to fight for us, for the full-bloods, the traditional people. When I wrote the following poem, I felt solace in the fact that they taught me something after all. I did what I knew best: I watched and waited, gleaning as much knowledge as I could from what I saw, the way Lakota children are supposed to learn. I wrote this poem for them:

Up on top of the prairie hill where sky meets earth,
High among the pine trees where the four winds blow,
A generation, lost in its search for identity, is asking,
"Who are we, we need to know. We have to know."

Descendants of people with an unwritten history,
So the answer was hard to find.
Only the old ones who preserved the history in their
  memories seemed to know.
Confused they turn to the ones who remember,
"Grandfather, show us the way, the road that will lead us all
  home."
Perhaps the answer lies hidden in the past.

Grandfather teaches them the ancient ways so they may not
  be forgotten.
He points out the road, but he refuses to lead.
He spoke these words to them:
"Do not walk backward for you will surely fall.
Learn from what is past, but look to tomorrow's dawn and
  follow the sun.
Walk frontward and learn of the white man's ways, of his
  writings, his books, and his language.
But most important, learn to walk side by side with him, as a
  friend.
Perhaps his books will tell you what you wish to know."

The generation listens to his words for he does not speak
  foolishly, as all old ones are wise.
But when he finished, some turned their backs and closed
  their eyes and refused to see or hear.
Others bravely walked ahead, straight and tall.
The four winds warned, "Do not separate. You are brothers
  and you are strong, together, as one."
It was too late. The words were not heard.
Those who walked ahead were over the next ridge.
They did not bother to look back, only ahead.
Those who walked blindly and mutely backward had fallen,
  obscure figures in the past.
Grandfather stood alone. He sang a mourning song, high on
  the hill.

I wrote the poem as a senior at the Catholic high school, and
the Catholic Church paid me twenty-five dollars for that poem and
used it in their mailings. Their mailings were what my older brother

called "begging letters" and were part of what he had disliked about the school. Back then I did not mind. Even if my understanding was limited, I felt that I understood. My brother had Kah-kah and Mom-mah to turn to in his arrogance. When he first discovered that the Catholic school was sending out the letters and had labeled them "begging letters," it was because he had felt outraged by them. He did not like the words "poor" and "Indian" in the same context. He felt that we were neither of those things. He knew who he was. I didn't. By the time I finished high school, Kah-kah had been dead seven years and Mom-mah and I were no longer living under the same roof. I was on my own, and I was not so sure what the future would bring.

I was grateful to the Catholic school for providing a safe place for me to learn and grow. I understood that without it I would not have known that I preferred John Steinbeck to any other writer. I would not have known that I could write poetry. I would not have known that Red Cloud was buried there, and that he, too, understood these things: how hard it was to be Lakota in a world where Lakota is not the language of choice. He understood that although we Lakota children were educated by the waśicu, we were first and foremost born of Lakota parents like Mom-mah and my father and that as a result we thought as they did, and still do.

Red Cloud tried to pass on what he had learned in his extraordinary life. At the end of his life, he realized that the true meaning of the Lakota people rested solely on their relationship to their Creator—"T'ųkaśila" or "Grandfather." He knew that our meaning did not lie anywhere else and that there was nothing else but this. Red Cloud saw this relationship with the Creator as one of perfect union and unbroken continuity.

He contemplated, in his last days, whether what the Sapa ų pi said, was true. How they said that we lived wickedly before they brought their God. Yet, as he watched them, he saw that the relationship they said they had with their God was often contradictory to what he saw. Their religion, to him, seemed partial, self-centered, fragmented, and full of fear. He saw his own relationship with T'ųkaśila as self-encompassing and self-extending. The relationship he saw among the new religions, including the Sapa ų pi's, was self-destructive and self-limiting to the Lakota. He said that when we Lakota relied only on our relationship with T'ųkaśila and lived according to the old beliefs, which dictated that we demonstrate in our daily lives compassion, truthfulness, fortitude, bravery, and true generosity, that we would live happily and die satisfied. He looked at what the wasicu brought to us, after they put us on the reservation, and he saw how inadequate it was for the Lakota, how insufficient. He tried to convince us that we Lakota had within us our own beliefs, our own relationship with our God, Tȟaku šką ška, our Creator. He wanted us to remain true to these things that had been sufficient for us since the beginning of time. The way Mom-mah, Kah-kah, and my brother, six years my senior, wanted me to be true to my Lakota self.

Red Cloud looked forward to seeing his ancestors in the spirit world. He knew that because the Sapa ų pi said we had lived evil lives before they came and brought salvation, our ancestors might not be in the wasicu's heaven. He felt solace in the fact that in the Lakota world view—the law of cause and effect—that as long as he remained true to Tȟųkašila, he would see his ancestors, there where Mom-mah said they lived "cąte wašteya,""with glad hearts."

I remember how the night comes there where there are no city lights, like a thick blanket falling over me. I remember how I sat on Red Cloud's grave until the shadows grew long. Like any adolescent, I felt invincible in my irreverence. Even Red Cloud's grave did not seem real to me. I was firmly rooted in the here and now. I did not know what my future would bring for me. I did not think about those things. I did not even think about whose grave it was that I was sitting upon. I wonder, now, as I sat there on his grave, if I was like a young sapling grafted onto an ancient tree, whether I absorbed some nourishment from him, my ancestor whose spirit remains firmly planted there. When I look back now, I realize that Red Cloud was right, that Tȟųkašila, the Lakota God whom Mom-mah and Kah-kah believed in, still lives in everything that is Lakota. He knows all things and knows that we are still true to Him. "Ho he," as Kah-kah used to say, and as Mom-mah says now: "That pleases me. It is good."

FURTHER READING
Mark Fogarty, "Finding Beads in an Unlikely Place," *Indian Country Today* (August 10–17, 1998).

"Mother" Mary Jones.

Courtesy of West Virginia and Regional History Collection, West Virginia University Libraries.

Walking the Line

8

Women and children who worked in the raw industries of the West, like canning, meat-packing, and mining, have tended to disappear from view. The tendency is to think of industrial labor as a nightmare of eastern cities, and that "West" meant open spaces and freedom.

When Helen Campbell wrote *Prisoners of Poverty: Women Wage-Workers, Their Trades and Their Lives* (1887), she described New York, where "nine thousand children under twelve years of age are ... adding their tiny contribution to the great stream of what we call the prosperity of the nineteenth century." Young girls worked in the textile mills of Lowell, Massachusetts, in the 1820s and 1830s, and by the turn of the century, in the needle trades and in the garment industries, but as far as women working in the West, "few historians have followed [Richard] Wade's example in describing the lives of urban western women, and no theoretical framework has been developed which would include women as an integral part of the urbanization in the West." That was written by Darlis Miller and Joan Jensen twenty years ago, in their influential essay "The Gentle Tamers Revisited." Even Upton Sinclair's powerful novel of the Chicago stockyards, *The Jungle* (1906), was about the work of men.

The chronicle of working women is held in a slim library of scholarship, but the images that bring that story to life are found in other places—in the songs and stories of "Aunt" Molly Jackson in

Appalachia in the 1920s. Midwife and union organizer, she carried a .38 and once threatened a storekeeper as she backed out of his store with a sack of flour for hungry children. Stories of working women find their way into the *Autobiography* of "Mother" Jones, union organizer "extraordinaire" in Cripple Creek and Ludlow, Colorado, where striking workers were massacred. Tillie Olsen's account of longshoremen and their families in San Francisco is part reportage and part literature, as are Barbara Kingsolver's interviews with Latina women who "held the line" against Phelps Dodge. That literary heritage—the literature of resistance in all its curious forms—takes shape in the songs of cannery workers in California, who were determined to make a different life for their children. It can be heard in Edith Summers Kelley's poem "The Head-Cutters."

The selections in this chapter are testimonies of women moved by desperate events. If the extraordinary moment had not moved them, they would not have raised their voices. Resistance was thrust upon them. Women "walked the line" because their children were hungry and their men were out of work.

These testimonies—some of them tape- recorded interviews, some poetry, some song, some reportage—have been shaped by literary artists, but the voices are authentic, full of passion and eloquence. They comprise a kind of proletarian literature that is sometimes just beneath the surface of western history. They tell about the experience of work and the importance of work to women who are wives and mothers. These voices tell about the separation of people into rich and poor, into farmer and industrial worker, into "foreigner" and "American." As historians look for sources, as literary critics look for texts, these working class women bring their experiences forward and ask to be accounted for in our histories of the West.

Mary "Mother" Jones
(1830–1930)

The American labor movement has had its share of fiery women, although their voices are often forgotten and their work uncelebrated. Annie Clemence was president of the ladies' auxiliary of the Western Federation of Miners in Michigan, when 15,000 copper miners earning $1 a day went on strike in 1913.against the Calumet and Hecla Mining Company. Ella Reeve Bloor, "Mother Bloor," then a Socialist organizer, recalled that at a strikers' Christmas party that was broken up, panic broke out, children were trampled, and mine operators had Annie Clemence locked up in the courthouse.

Like other women drawn to the labor movement, Mary Harris Jones, known as "Mother" Jones, saw the desperation of workers who could not feed their children. Mary Harris was born in County Cork, Ireland, before her family settled in Toronto. As a young woman she worked as a dressmaker and a convent schoolteacher until 1861 when she married a member of the Iron Molders' Union in Memphis. After only a few short years, her husband and four young children died in a yellow fever epidemic. She moved to Chicago, where disaster pursued her, and in 1871, the great fire left her homeless and destitute.

She began to attend meetings of the newly formed Knights of Labor, and to see the labor movement as a woman's cause, and to travel wherever strikes were brewing—She was in Pittsburgh during the railroad strike in 1877, in Chicago, where the leaders of the Haymarket strike were hung in 1887. She worked with strikers in Birmingham in 1894, and among the anthracite miners of Pennsylvania in 1900–1902. In 1902 she led "an army" of women in Pennsylvania.when they routed strikebreakers with their mops and brooms. She led a march of textile workers—women and children—from Kensington, Pennsylvania to President Theodore Roosevelt's Long Island home in 1903.

She was in the Colorado coalfields in 1903–6, in the copper mine strike in Idaho in 1906, and in Ludlow, Colorado, in 1913–14. To twelve hundred striking workers, living in tents through the win-

ter, Mother Jones said "We will lick the hell out of the operators."
She was in New York City in 1915–16, organizing garment workers
and streetcar conductors, and in 1923, at ninety-three, she was still
trying to organize coal miners in West Virginia.

In Cripple Creek, Colorado, in 1903, workers had demanded an
eight-hour day, ventilation for the mines and a standard measure
for a ton of coal. As winter came on, workers living in tents worried
as they saw their children sick and hungry, and women grew as
fierce as the men. The governor declared martial law; Agnes
Smedley, who grew up in nearby Trinidad, Colorado, recalled in
Daughter of Earth that daughters of foreign-born miners were
raped: "Ignorant, lousy foreigners, the officials in the town called
them."

Strikers dynamited the railroad station and the governor put
them in bull pens. Seventy-three men were taken to the Kansas border and left to freeze or starve on the prairie. By midsummer, the
strike at Cripple Creek was broken.

The *Autobiography* has been called "a completely undocu-
mented record of an old woman's uncertain memories," but
Jones's account of the strikes at Cripple Creek and at Ludlow
(1913–14) when strikers and their families were fired upon is
borne out by historical texts. The *Autobiography* brings into sharp
focus the kinds of western violence that had nothing to do with
Indians or with outlaws.

THE CRIPPLE CREEK STRIKE

The state of Colorado belonged not to a republic but to the
Colorado Fuel and Iron Company, the Victor Company and their
dependencies. The governor was their agent. The militia under Bell
did their bidding. Whenever the masters of the state told the governor to bark, he yelped for them like a mad hound. Whenever they
told the military to bite, they bit.

The people of Colorado had voted overwhelmingly for an
eight-hour day. The legislature passed an eight-hour law but the
courts had declared it unconstitutional. Then when the measure

---

Mary Harris Jones, from *The Autobiography of Mother Jones* (1925).

was submitted directly to the people, they voted for it with 40,000 votes majority. But the next legislature, which was controlled by the mining interests, failed to pass the bill.

The miners saw that they could not get their demands through peaceful legislation. That they must fight. That they must strike. All the metal miners struck first. The strike extended into New Mexico and Utah. It became an ugly war. The metal miners were anxious to have the coal miners join them in their struggle.

The executive board of the United Mine Workers was in session in Indianapolis and to this board the governor of Colorado had sent a delegation to convince them that there ought not to be a strike in the coal fields. Among the delegates, was a labor commissioner.

I was going on my way to West Virginia from Mount Olive, Illinois, where the miners were commemorating their dead. I stopped off at headquarters in Indianapolis. The executive board asked me to go to Colorado, look into conditions there, see what the sentiments of the miners were, and make a report to the office.

I went immediately to Colorado, first to the office of The Western Federation of Miners where I heard the story of the industrial conflict. I then got myself an old calico dress, a sunbonnet, some pins and needles, elastic and tape and such sundries, and went down to the southern coal fields of the Colorado Fuel and Iron Company.

As a peddler, I went through the various coal camps, eating in the homes of the miners, staying all night with their families. I found the conditions under which they lived deplorable. They were in practical slavery to the company, who owned their houses, owned all the land, so that if a miner did own a house he must vacate whenever it pleased the land owners. They were paid in scrip instead of money so that they could not go away if dissatisfied. They must buy at company stores and at company prices. The coal they mined was weighed by an agent of the company and the miners could not have a check weighman to see that full credit was given them. The schools, the churches, the roads belonged to the Company. I felt, after listening to their stories, after witnessing their long patience that the time was ripe for revolt against such brutal conditions.

I went to Trinidad and to the office of the Western Federation of

Miners. I talked with the secretary, Gillmore, a loyal, hard-working man, and with the President, Howell, a good, honest soul. We sat up and talked the matter over far into the night. I showed them the conditions I had found down in the mining camps were heart-rending, and I felt it was our business to remedy those conditions and bring some future, some sunlight at least into the lives of the children. They deputized me to go at once to headquarters in Indianapolis.

I took the train the next morning. When I arrived at the office in Indianapolis, I found the president, John Mitchell, the vice-president, T. L. Lewis, the secretary, W. B. Wilson of Arnot, Pennsylvania, and a board member, called "old man Ream," from Iowa. These officers told me to return at once to Colorado and they would call a strike of the coal miners.

The strike was called November 9th, 1903. The demand was for an eight hour day, a check weighman representing the miners, payment in money instead of scrip. The whole state of Colorado was in revolt. No coal was dug. November is a cold month in Colorado and the citizens began to feel the pressure of the strike.

Late one evening in the latter part of November I came into the hotel. I had been working all day and into the night among the miners and their families, helping to distribute food and clothes, encouraging, holding meetings. As I was about to retire, the hotel clerk called me down to answer a long distance telephone call from Louisville. The voice said, "Oh for God's sake, Mother, come to us, come to us!"

I asked what the trouble was and the reply was more a cry than an answer, "Oh don't wait to ask. Don't miss the train."

I got Mr. Howell, the president, on the telephone and asked him what was the trouble in Louisville.

"They are having a convention there," he said.

"A convention, is it, and what for?"

"To call off the strike in the northern coal fields because the operators have yielded to the demands." He did not look at me as he spoke. I could see he was heart sick.

"But they cannot go back until the operators settle with the southern miners," I said. "They will not desert their brothers until the strike is won! Are you going to let them do it?"

"Oh Mother," he almost cried, "I can't help it. It is the National Headquarters who have ordered them back!"

"That's treachery," I said, "quick, get ready and come with me."

We telephoned down to the station to have the conductor hold the train for Louisville a few minutes. This he did. We got into Louisville the next morning. I had not slept. The board member, Ream, and Grant Hamilton, representing the Federation of Labor, came to the hotel where I was stopping and asked where Mr. Howell, the president was.

"He has just stepped out," I said. "He will be back."

"Well, meantime, I want to notify you," Ream said, "that you must not block the settlement of the northern miners because the National President, John Mitchell, wants it, and he pays you."

"Are you through?" said I.

He nodded.

"Then I am going to tell you that if God Almighty wants this strike called off for his benefit and not for the miners, I am going to raise my voice against it. And as to President John paying me . . . he never paid me a penny in his life. It is the hard earned nickels and dimes of the miners that pay me, and it is their interests that I am going to serve."

I went to the convention and heard the matter of the northern miners returning to the mines discussed. I watched two shrewd diplomats deal with unsophisticated men; Struby, the president of the northern coal fields, and Blood, one of the keenest, trickiest lawyers in the West. And behind them, John Mitchell, toasted and wined and dined, flattered and cajoled by the Denver Citizens' Alliance, and the Civic Federation was pulling the strings.

In the afternoon the miners called on me to address the convention.

"Brothers," I said, "You English speaking miners of the northern fields promised your southern brothers, seventy per cent of whom do not speak English, that you would support them to the end. Now you are asked to betray them, to make a separate settlement. You have a common enemy and it is your duty to fight to a finish. The enemy seeks to conquer by dividing your ranks, by making distinctions between North and South, between American and foreign. You are all miners, fighting a common cause, a common master. The iron heel feels the same to all flesh. Hunger and suffering and the cause of your children bind more closely than a common tongue. I am accused of helping the Western Federation of Miners, as if that were a crime, by one of the National board members. I plead guilty. I know no East or West, North nor South when it comes to my class fighting the battle for justice. If it is my fortune to live to see the industrial chain broken from every workingman's child in America, and if then there is one black child in Africa in bondage, there shall I go."

The delegates rose en masse to cheer. The vote was taken. The majority decided to stand by the southern miners, refusing to obey the national President.

The Denver Post reported my speech and a copy was sent to Mr. Mitchell in Indianapolis. He took the paper in to his secretary and said, pointing to the report, "See what Mother Jones has done to me!"

Three times Mitchell tried to make the northern miners return to the mines but each time he was unsuccessful. "Mitchell has got to get Mother Jones out of the field," an organizer said. "He can never lick the Federation as long as she is in there."

I was informed that Mitchell went to the governor and asked him to put me out of the state.

Finally the ultimatum was given to the northern miners. All support for the strike was withdrawn. The northern miners accepted the operators' terms and returned to work. Their act created practical peonage in the south and the strike was eventually lost, although the struggle in the south went on for a year.

Much of the fighting took place around Cripple Creek. The miners were evicted from their company-owned houses. They went out on the bleak mountain sides, lived in tents through a terrible winter with the temperature below zero, with eighteen inches of snow on the ground. They tied their feet in gunny sacks and lived lean and lank and hungry as timber wolves. They received sixty-three cents a week strike benefit while John Mitchell went traveling through Europe, staying at fashionable hotels, studying the labor movement. When he returned the miners had been lashed back into the mines by hunger but John Mitchell was given a banquet in the Park Avenue Hotel and presented with a watch with diamonds.

From the day I opposed John Mitchell's authority, the guns were turned on me. Slander and persecution followed me like black shadows. But the fight went on.

One night when I came in from the field where I had been holding meetings, I was just dropping to sleep when a knock—a loud knock—came on my door. I always slept in my clothes for I never knew what might happen. I went to the door, opened it, and faced a military chap.

"The Colonel wants you up at headquarters."

I went with him immediately. Three or four others were brought in: War John and Joe Pajammy, organizers. We were all taken down to the Santa Fe station. While standing there, waiting for the train that was to deport us, some of the miners ran down to bid me good-bye. "Mother, good-bye," they said, stretching out their hands to take mine.

The colonel struck their hands and yelled at them. "Get away from there. You can't shake hands with that woman!"

The militia took us to La Junta. They handed me a letter from the governor, notifying me that under no circumstances could I return to the State of Colorado. I sat all night in the station. In the morning the Denver train came along. I had no food, no money. I asked the conductor to take me to Denver. He said he would.

"Well," I said, "I don't want you to lose your job."

I showed him the letter from the governor. He read it.

"Mother," he said, "do you want to go to Denver?"

"I do," said I.

"Then to Hell with the job;" said he, "it's to Denver you go."

In Denver I got a room and rested a while. I sat down and wrote a letter to the governor, the obedient little boy of the coal companies.

"Mr. Governor, you notified your dogs of war to put me out of the state. They complied with your instructions. I hold in my hand a letter that was handed to me by one of them, which says 'under no circumstances return to this state.' I wish to notify you, governor, that you don't own the state. When it was admitted to the sisterhood of states, my fathers gave me a share of stock in it; and that is all they gave to you. The civil courts are open. If I break a law of state or nation it is the duty of the civil courts to deal with me. That is why my forefathers established those courts to keep dictators and tyrants such as you from interfering with civilians. I am right here in the capital, after being out nine or ten hours, four or five blocks from your office. I want to ask you, governor, what in Hell are you going to do about it?"

I called a messenger and sent it up to the governor's office. He read it and a reporter who was present in the office at the time told me his face grew red.

"What shall I do?" he said to the reporter. He was used to acting under orders.

"Leave her alone," counselled the reporter. "There is no more patriotic citizen in America."

From Denver I went down the Western Slope, holding meetings, cheering and encouraging those toiling and disinherited miners who were fighting against such monstrous odds.

I went to Helper, Utah, and got a room with a very nice Italian family. I was to hold a meeting Sunday afternoon. From every quarter the men came, trudging miles over the mountains. The shop men were notified not to come but they came anyhow. Just as the meeting was about to open, the mayor of the little town came to me and said that I could not hold a meeting; that I was on company ground. I asked him how far his jurisdiction extended. He said as far as the Company's jurisdiction. He was a Company mayor.

So I turned to the audience and asked them to follow me. The audience to a man followed me to a little tent colony at Half Way that the miners had established when they had been evicted from their homes.

When the meeting closed I returned to Helper. The next day, although there was no smallpox in town, a frame shack was built to isolate smallpox sufferers in. I was notified that I had been exposed to smallpox and must be incarcerated in the shack. But somehow that night the shack burned down.

I went to stay in Half Way because the Italian family were afraid to keep me longer. Another Italian family gave me a bare room in their shack. There was only a big stone to fasten the door. No sooner was I located than the militia notified me that I was in quarantine because I had been exposed to smallpox. But I used to go out and talk to the miners and they used to come to me.

One Saturday night I got tipped off by the postoffice master that the militia were going to raid the little tent colony in the early morning. I called the miners to me and asked them if they had guns. Sure, they had guns. They were western men, men of the mountains. I told them to go bury them between the boulders; deputies were coming to take them away from them. I did not tell them that there was to be a raid for I did not want any bloodshed. Better to submit to arrest.

Between 4:30 and 5 o'clock in the morning I heard the tramp of feet on the road. I looked out of my smallpox window and saw about forty-five deputies. They descended upon the sleeping tent colony, dragged the miners out of their beds. They did not allow them to put on their clothing. The miners begged to be allowed to put on their clothes, for at that early hour the mountain range is the coldest. Shaking with cold, followed by the shrieks and wails of their wives and children, beaten along the road by guns, they were driven like cattle to Helper. In the evening they were packed in a box car and run down to Price, the county seat and put in jail.

Not one law had these miners broken. The pitiful screams of the women and children would have penetrated Heaven. Their tears melted the heart of the Mother of Sorrows. Their crime was that they had struck against the power of gold.

The women huddled beneath the window of the house where I was incarcerated for smallpox.

"Oh Mother, what shall we do?" they wailed. "What's to become of our little children?"

"See my little Johnny," said one woman, holding up a tiny, red baby—new born.

"That's a nice baby," I said.

"He sick. Pretty soon he die. Company take house. Company take my man. Pretty soon company take my baby."

Two days after this raid was made, the stone that held my door was suddenly pushed in. A fellow jumped into the room, stuck a gun under my jaw and told me to tell him where he could get $3,000 of the miners' money or he would blow out my brains.

"Don't waste your powder," I said. "You write the miners up in Indianapolis. Write Mitchell. He's got money now."

"I don't want any of your damn talk," he replied, then asked:

"Hasn't the president got money?"

"You got him in jail."

"Haven't you got any money?"

"Sure!" I put my hand in my pocket, took out fifty cents and turned the pocket inside out.

"Is that all you got?"

"Sure, and I'm not going to give it to you, for I want it to get a

jag on to boil the Helen Gould smallpox out of my system so I will
not inoculate the whole nation when I get out of here."

"How are you going to get out of here if you haven't money
when they turn you loose?"

"The railway men will take me anywhere."

There were two other deputies outside. They kept hollering for
him to come out. "She ain't got any money," they kept insisting.
Finally he was convinced that I had nothing.

This man, I afterward found out, had been a bank robber, but
had been sworn in as deputy to crush the miners' union. He was
later killed while robbing the post office in Prince. Yet he was the sort
of man who was hired by the moneyed interests to crush the hopes
and aspirations of the fathers and mothers and even the children
of the workers.

I was held twenty-six days and nights in that bare room, isolated for smallpox. Finally with no redress I was turned loose and
went to Salt Lake. During all those days and nights I did not
undress because of imminent danger.

All civil law had broken down in the Cripple Creek strike. The
militia under Colonel Verdeckberg said, "We are under orders only
from God and Governor Peabody." Judge Advocate McClelland
when accused of violating the constitution said, "To hell with the
constitution!" There was a complete breakdown of all civil law.
Habeas corpus proceedings were suspended. Free speech and
assembly were forbidden. People spoke in whispers as in the days
of the inquisition. Soldiers committed outrages. Strikers were
arrested for vagrancy and worked in chain gangs on the street
under brutal soldiers. Men, women and tiny children were packed
in the Bullpen at Cripple Creek. Miners were shot dead as they
slept. They were ridden from the country, their families knowing
not where they had gone, or whether they lived.

When the strike started in Cripple Creek, the civil law was
operating, but the governor, a banker, and in complete sympathy
with the Rockefeller interests, sent the militia. They threw the officers out of office. Sheriff Robinson had a rope thrown at his feet
and told that if he did not resign, the rope would be about his
neck.

Three men were brought into Judge Seeds' court—miners.
There was no charge lodged against them. He ordered them

released but the soldiers who with drawn bayonets had attended the hearing, immediately rearrested them and took them back to jail.

Four hundred men were taken from their homes. Seventy-six of these were placed on a train, escorted to Kansas, dumped out on a prairie and told never to come back, except to meet death.

In the heat of June, in Victor, 1600 men were arrested and put in the Armory Hall. Bullpens were established and anyone be he miner, or a woman or a child that incurred the displeasure of the great coal interests, or the militia, were thrown into these horrible stockades.

Shop keepers were forbidden to sell to miners. Priests and ministers were intimidated, fearing to give them consolation. The miners opened their own stores to feed the women and children. The soldiers and hoodlums broke into the stores, looted them, broke open the safes, destroyed the scales, ripped open the sacks of flour and sugar, dumped them on the floor and poured kerosene oil over everything. The beef and meat was poisoned by the militia. Goods were stolen. The miners were without redress, for the militia was immune.

And why were these things done? Because a group of men had demanded an eight hour day, a check weighman and the abolition of the scrip system that kept them in serfdom to the mighty coal barons. That was all. Just that miners had refused to labor under these conditions. Just because miners wanted a better chance for their children, more of the sunlight, more freedom. And for this they suffered one whole year and for this they died.

Perhaps no one in the labor movement has seen more brutality perpetrated upon the workers than I have seen. I have seen them killed in industry, worn out and made old before their time, jailed and shot if they protested. Story after story I could tell of persecution and of bravery unequalled on any battle field.

There was Mrs. M. F. Langdon of Cripple Creek. "The Victor Record," a newspaper giving the miners' side of the strike, had been arbitrarily suppressed by the militia, as were all journals that did not espouse the cause of the coal operators. Her husband had been arrested because he was the editor of The Record.

The military were surprised when the morning after the suppression of the paper and the jailing of the editor and his helpers, the paper came out as usual. Throughout the night Mrs. Langdon, working with a tiny candle, had set the type and run the sheets out on a hand press.

On November 19, 1903, two organizers, Demolli and Price, were going to Scofield when a short distance from town, a mob composed of members of the "citizens' alliance" boarded the train armed with high-powered rifles, and ordered the train crew to take the organizers back.

In December, Lucianno Desentos and Joseph Vilano were killed outright by deputy sheriffs at Secundo. Soon after their killing, the home of William G. Isaac, an organizer, was blown up. He was in Glenwood Springs when it occurred. Part of the house was wrecked by the explosion, the part in which his two little children usually slept. The night of the explosion, however, they slept in the back room with their mother. The family was saved from being burned to death in the fire that followed the explosion by crawling through a broken window. Isaac was arrested and charged with attempting the murder of his wife and children.

And so I could go on and on. Men beaten and left for dead in the road. The home of Sherman Parker searched without warrants, his wife in her nightclothes made to hold the light for the soldiers. And no arms found.

On Sunday in February of 1914, Joe Panonia and myself went to a camp out in Berwyn to hold a meeting, and William Farley and James Mooney, national organizers, went to Bohnn. Both settlements lay in the same direction, Berwyn being a little further on. As we drove through Bohnn after our meeting, three women ran out from a shack, waving their long, bony arms at us and shrieking and whirling around like witches. They jumped right in front of our automobile in the narrow road.

"Come in! Come in! Something bad!" They put their hands to their heads and rocked sidewise. They were foreigners and knew little English.

"Joe," I said, "we'd better drive on. They may have been drinking. It may be some sort of hoax to get us into the house."

"No! No!" shrieked the women. "No drink! Something bad!" They climbed on the running board and began pulling us.

"Come on, Mother," said Joe. "Let's go in. I think there has been trouble."

We followed the three lanky women into the shack. On a wretched bed covered with dirty rag-ends of blankets and old quilts lay Mooney, bleeding profusely and unconscious. Farley sat beside him, badly beaten.

Joe raced into Trinidad and got a doctor but although Mooney survived he was never quite right in the head afterward. Farley, however, recovered from his terrible beating.

He said that as they were returning from Bohhn, seven gun-men jumped out from the bushes along the road, had beaten them up, kicked them and stamped their feet upon them. All seven were armed and resistance was useless.

Organizers were thrown into jail and held without trial for months. They were deported. In April fourteen miners were arrested at Broadhead and deported to New Mexico. They were landed in the desert, thirty miles from food or water. Hundreds of others were deported, taken away without being allowed to com-municate with wives and children. The women suffered agonies not knowing when their men went from home whether they would ever return. If the deported men returned they were immediately arrested by the militia and put in jail. All organizers and leaders were in danger of death, in the open streets or from ambush. John Lawson was shot at but by a miracle the bullet missed him.

The strike in the southern fields dragged on and on. But from the moment the southern miners had been deserted by their northern brothers, I felt their strike was doomed. Bravely did those miners fight before giving in to the old peonage. The military had no regard for human life. They were sanctified cannibals. Is it any wonder that we have murders and holdups when the youth of the land is trained by the great industrialists to a belief in force; when they see that the possession of money puts one above law.

Men like President Howell and Secretary Simpson will live in history. I was in close touch with them throughout this terrible strike. Their descendants should feel proud that the blood of such great men flows in their veins.

No more loyal, courageous men could be found than those southern miners, scornfully referred to by "citizens' alliances" as "foreigners." Italians and Mexicans endured to the end. They were defeated on the industrial field but theirs was the victory of the spirit.

FURTHER READINGS
Elizabeth Jameson, *All That Glitters: Class, Conflict, and Community in Cripple Creek* (University of Illinois Press, 1998); Edward M. Steel, ed., *The Correspondence of Mother Jones* (University of Pittsburgh Press, 1985); Priscilla Long, *Where the Sun Never Shines: A History of America's Bloody Coal Industry* (Paragon House, 1989); Howard M. Gitelman, *Legacy of the Ludlow Massacre: A Chapter in American Industrial Relations* (University of Pennsylvania Press, 1988); Philip S. Foner, ed., *Mother Jones Speaks: Collected Writings and Speeches* (Monad Press, 1983); Zeese Papanikolas, *Buried Unsung: Louis Tikas and the Ludlow Massacre* (University of Utah Press, 1982); Dale Fetherling, *Mother Jones, The Miners' Angel* (Southern Illinois University Press, 1974); Harold Aurand, *From the Molly Maguires to the United Mine Workers*, Temple University Press, 1971; Emma Florence Langdon, *The Cripple Creek Strike: A History of Industrial Wars in Colorado* (Ayer Company Publishers, 1969).

Tillie Olsen (1913–)

Tillie Lerner Olsen, born in 1913 in Nebraska, grew up there and in Wyoming, shaped as much by Russian history as by middle America. Samuel and Ida Lerner left Russia in 1905, and in the United States, Samuel Lerner worked as a painter and paper-hanger, and as a farmer. He became state secretary of the Nebraska Socialist Party only a few years before Eugene V. Debs polled close to a million votes as the Socialist candidate for president in 1912 and Victor Berger was the Socialist congressman from Milwaukee. Yet the Socialist movement became suspect when, within a few short years, Debs and Berger were sentenced to prison for advocating the nation stay out of World War I. Tillie Lerner joined the Young Communist League, and was jailed in Kansas City for trying to organize packing house workers.

She had little formal schooling, but she began to know herself as a writer, beginning the novel that would be published years later as *Yonnondio: From the Thirties* (1974). Her poem, "I Want You Women Up North to Know" appeared in *Partisan* in March of 1934. It was written in response to an indictment brought by a Texas woman, Felipe Ibarro, against factory owners who employed Chicana workers, and "sweated them to death." The poem carried the names, ages, salaries of the women cited in Ibarro's indictment. Olsen's poem echoes Mother Jones's 1925 warning to middle-class women that their fancy dresses were sewn by eight-year-olds in Alabama working twelve-hour days on machines scaled down to children's size. Olsen's poetic skill is evident in her images—in "the blood embroidering the darkness," in the "bony children" and the "skeleton brother."

In 1934, as the Depression wore on, workers were demanding the right to collective bargaining and to form a union, but those rights were not won without a fight. In Minneapolis, the teamsters began a general strike that shut down the city, and in San Francisco, long-shoremen, tired of standing in the morning chill "like slaves in a slave market begging for a bidder," chose Harry Bridges to lead them and closed ports up and down the California coast. The police fought the strikers with guns and tear gas. "I write this on a battlefield," wrote Tillie Olsen. She saw men wounded in the streets, and frightened

scabs riding through picket lines in open trucks. Arrested for picket-
ing, Tillie Olsen wrote, "I am feverish and tired. Forgive me that the
words are feverish and blurred." Her account of the San Francisco
strike appeared in the September/October issue of *Partisan Review*.

Olsen married and raised four children and remained an
activist all her life. She was president of the Women's Auxiliary of
the CIO, and Director of CIO War Relief from 1944 to 1945. Over the
years, the focus of her writing began to shift to the struggle of
women trying to maintain their independent lives and their families. In the 1950s and 60s, her stories won national attention. "Tell Me
A Riddle" won first prize in the O. Henry Award in 1961. She published *Silences* (1978), *The Word Made Flesh* (1984), and she edited
Mother to Daughter, Daughter to Mother: A Daybook and Reader
(1984). Her short fiction has been published in over 200 anthologies, her books are translated into eleven different languages, and
she is the recipient of eight honorary doctorates. However much
the women in her stories struggle against the "silences," they inhabit
a place where home and politics are interwoven.

I WANT YOU WOMEN UP NORTH TO KNOW

I want you women up north to know
how those dainty children's dresses you buy
    at macy's, wannamakers, gimbels, marshall fields,
are dyed in blood, are stitched in wasting flesh,
down in San Antonio, "where sunshine spends the winter."

I want you women up north to see
the obsequious smile, the salesladies trill
    "exquisite work, madame, exquisite pleats"
vanish into a bloated face, ordering more dresses,
    gouging the wages down,
dissolve into maria, ambrosa, catalina,
    stitching these dresses from dawn to night,
    In blood, in wasting flesh.

Tillie Olsen, "I Want You Women Up North To Know," from *Partisan,* March 1934.

Catalina Rodriguez, 24,
    body shrivelled to a child's at twelve,
catalina rodriguez, last stages of consumption,
    works for three dollars a week from dawn to midnight.
A fog of pain thickens over her skull, the parching heat
    breaks over her body,
and the bright red blood embroiders the floor of her room.
    White rain stitching the night, the bourgeois poet would say.
    white gulls of hands, darting, veering,
    white lightning, threading the clouds,
this is the exquisite dance of her hands over the cloth,
and her cough, gay, quick, staccato,
    like skeleton's bones clattering,
is appropriate accompaniment for the esthetic dance
    of her fingers,
and the tremolo, tremolo when the hands tremble with pain.
Three dollars a week,
two fifty-five,
seventy cents a week,
no wonder two thousand eight hundred ladies of joy are spending
the winter with the sun after he goes down—for five cents (who
said this was a rich man's world?) you can
    get all the lovin you want
"clap and syph aint much worse than sore fingers, blind eyes, and
    t.b."

Maria Vasquez, spinster,
    for fifteen cents a dozen stitches garments for children she
    has never had,
Catalina Torres, mother of four,
    to keep the starved body starving, embroiders from dawn
    to night.
Mother of four, what does she think of,
    as the needle pocked fingers shift over the silk—
    of the stubble-coarse rags that stretch on her own brood,
    and jut with the bony ridge that marks hunger's landscape
    of fat little prairie-roll bodies that will bulge in the
    silk she needles?
(Be not envious, Catalina Torres, look!

on your own children's clothing, embroidery,
more intricate than any a thousand hands could fashion,
there where the cloth is ravelled, or darned,
designs, multitudinous, complex and handmade by Poverty
     herself.)
Ambrosa Espinoza trusts in god,
"Todos es de dios, everything is from god,"
through the dwindling night, the waxing day, she bolsters
     herself up with it—
but the pennies to keep god incarnate, from ambrosa,
and the pennies to keep the priest in wine, from ambrosa,
ambrosa clothes god and priest with hand-made children's dresses.

Her brother lies on an iron cot, all day and watches,
on a mattress of rags he lies.
For twenty-five years he worked for the railroad, then they
     laid him off.
     (racked days, searching for work; rebuffs; suspicious eyes of
     policemen.
     goodbye ambrosa, mebbe in dallas I find work; desperate
     swing for a freight,
     surprised hands, clutching air, and the wheel goes over a
     leg,
     the railroad cuts it off, as it cut off twenty-five years of his
     life.)
She says that he prays and dreams of another world, as he lies
     there, a heaven (which he does not know was brought to
     earth in 1917 in Russia, by workers like him).

Women up north, I want you to know
when you finger the exquisite hand-made dresses
what it means, this working from dawn to midnight, on what
strange feet the feverish dawn must come
     to maria, catalina, ambrosa,
how the malignant fingers twitching over the pallid faces jerk
them to work,
and the sun and the fever mount with the day—
     long plodding hours, the eyes burn like coals, heat jellies
     the flying fingers,

down comes the night like blindness.
  long hours more with the dim eye of the lamp, the breaking
  back,
  weariness crawls in the flesh like worms, gigantic like earth's
  in winter.
And for Catalina Rodriguez comes the night sweat and the blood
  embroidering the darkness.
  for Catalina Torres the pinched faces of four huddled
  children,
  the naked bodies of four bony children,
  the chant of their chorale of hunger.
And for twenty eight hundred ladies of joy the grotesque act gone
  over—the wink—the grimace—the "feeling like it baby?"
And for Maria Vasquez, spinster, emptiness, emptiness,
  flaming with dresses for children she can never fondle.
And for Ambrosa Espinoza—the skeleton body of her brother on
his mattress of rags, boring twin holes in the dark with his eyes to
the image of christ, remembering a leg, and twenty five years cut
off from his life by the railroad.

Women up north, I want you to know,
I tell you this can't last forever.

I swear it won't.

THE STRIKE

Do not ask me to write of the strike and the terror. I am on a battle-field, and the increasing stench and smoke sting the eyes so it is impossible to turn them back into the past. You leave me only this night to drop the bloody garment of Todays, to cleave through the gigantic events that have crashed one upon the other, to the first beginning. If I could go away for a while, if there were time and quiet, perhaps I could do it. All that has happened might resolve

Tillie Olsen, "The Strike," from *Partisan Review*, Volume 1 (September–October, 1934).

into order and sequence, fall into neat patterns of words. I could stumble back into the past and slowly, painfully rear the structure in all its towering magnificence, so that the beauty and heroism, the terror and significance of those days, would enter your heart and sear it forever with the vision.

But I hunch over the typewriter and behind the smoke, the days whirl, confused as dreams. Incidents leap out like a thunder and are gone. There flares the remembrance of that night in early May, in Stockton, when I walked down the road with the paper in my hands and the streaming headlines, LONGSHOREMEN OUT. RIOT EXPECTED; LONGSHORE STRIKE DECLARED. And standing there in the yellow stubble I remembered Jerry telling me quietly, ". . . for 12 years now. But we're through sweating blood, loading cargo five times the weight we should carry, we're through standing morning after morning like slaves in a slave market begging for a bidder. We'll be out, you'll see; it may be a few weeks, a few months, but WE'LL BE OUT, and then hell can't stop us."

H-E-L-L C-A-N-T S-T-O-P U-S. Days, pregnant days, spelling out the words. The port dead but for the rat stirring of a few scabs at night, the port paralyzed, gummed on one side by the thickening scum of prostrate ships, islanded on the other by the river of pickets streaming ceaselessly up and down, a river that sometimes raged into a flood, surging over the wavering shoreline of police, battering into the piers and sucking under the scabs in its angry tides. HELL CAN'T STOP US. That was the meaning of the lines of women and children marching up Market with their banners—"This is our fight, and we're with the men to the finish." That was the meaning of the seamen and the oilers and the wipers and the mastermates and the pilots and the scalers torrenting into the river, widening into the sea.

The kids coming in from the waterfront. The flame in their eyes, the feeling of invincibility singing in their blood. The stories they had to tell of scabs educated, of bloody skirmishes. My heart was ballooning with happiness anyhow, to be back, working in the movement again, but the things happening down at the waterfront, the heroic everydays, stored such richness in me I can never lose it. The feeling of sympathy widening over the city, of quickening—class lines sharpening. I armored myself with that on National Youth Day hearing the smash and thud of clubs around me, seeing boys fall to their knees in streams of blood, pioneer kids trampled under by horses. . . .

There was a night that was the climax of those first days—when the workers of San Francisco packed into the Auditorium to fling a warning to the shipowners. There are things one holds like glow in the breast, like a fire; they make the unseen warmth that keeps one through the cold of defeat, the hunger of despair. That night was one—symbol and portent of what will be. We League kids came to the meeting in a group, and walking up the stairs we felt ourselves a flame, a force. At the door bulls were standing, with menacing faces, but behind them fear was blanching—the people massing in, they had never dreamed it possible—people coming in and filling the aisles, packing the back. Spurts of song flaming up from downstairs, answered by us, echoed across the gallery, solidarity weaving us all into one being. 20,000 jammed in and the dim blue ring of cops back in the hall was wavering, was stretching itself thin and unseeable. It was OUR auditorium, we had taken it over. And for blocks around they hear OUR voice. The thunder of our applause, the mighty roar of it for Bridges, for Caves, for Schumacher. "Thats no lie" "Tell them Harry" "To the Finish" "We're with you" "Attaboy" "We're solid." The speeches, "They can never load their ships with tear gas and guns," "For years we were nothing but nameless beasts of burden to them, but now. . . .""Even if it means . . . GENERAL STRIKE," the voices rising, lifted on a sea of affection, vibrating in 20,000 hearts.

There was the moment—the first bruise in the hearts of our masters—when Mayor Rossi entered, padding himself from the fists of boos smashing around him with 60 heavyfoots, and bulls, and honoraries. The boos had filled into breasts feeling and seeing the tattoo of his clubs on the embarcadero, and Rossi hearing tried to lose himself into his topcoat, failing, tried to puff himself invincible with the majesty of his office. "Remember, I am your chief executive, the respect . . . the honor . . . due that office . . . don't listen to me then but listen to your mayor . . . listen," and the boos rolled over him again and again so that the reptile voice smothered, stopped. He never forgot the moment he called for law and order, charging the meeting with not caring to settle by peaceful means, wanting only violence, and voices ripped from every corner. "Who started the violence?" "Who calls the bulls to the waterfront?" "Who ordered the clubbing?"—and in a torrent of anger shouted, "Shut up, we have to put up with your clubs but not with your words, get out of here, GET OUT OF HERE." That memory clamped into his heart, into the hearts of those who command him, that bruise became the cancer of fear that flowered into the monstrous Bloody Thursday, that opened into the pus of Terror—but the cancer grows, grows; there is no cure. . . .

It was after that night he formed his "Citizens Committee," after that night the still smiling lips of the Industrial Association bared into a growl of open hatred, exposing the naked teeth of guns and tear gas. The tempo of those days maddened to a crescendo. The city became a camp, a battlefield, the screams of ambulances sent the day reeling, class lines fell sharply—everywhere, on streetcars, on corners, in stores, people talked, cursing, stirred with something strange in their breasts, incomprehensible, shaken with fury at the police, the papers, the shipowners . . . going down to the waterfront, not curious spectators, but to stand there, watching, silent, trying to read the lesson the moving bodies underneath were writing, trying to grope to the meaning of it all, police "protecting lives" smashing clubs and gas bombs into masses of men like themselves, papers screaming lies. Those were the days when with every attack on the picket lines the phone rang at the I.L.A.—"NOW—will you arbitrate?"—when the mutter GENERAL STRIKE swelled to a thunder, when everywhere the cry arose—"WE'VE GOT TO END IT NOW." Coming down to headquarters from the waterfront, the faces of comrades had the strained look of men in battle, that strangely intense look of living, of feeling too much in too brief a space of time. . . .

Yes, those were the days crescendoing—and the typewriter breaks, stops for an instant—to Bloody Thursday. Weeks afterward my fists clench at the remembrance and the hate congests so I feel I will burst. Bloody Thursday—our day we write on the pages of history with letters of blood and hate. Our day we fling like a banner to march with the other bloody days when guns spat death at us that a few dollars might be saved to fat bellies, when lead battered into us, and only our naked hands, the fists of our bodies moving together could resist. Drown their strength in blood, they commanded, but instead they armored us in inflexible steel—hate that will never forget. . . .

"It was as close to war . . . as actual war could be," the papers blared triumphantly, but Bridges told them, "not war . . . MASSACRE, armed forces massacring unarmed." Words I read through tears of anger so that they writhed and came alive like snakes, you rear in me again, "and once again the policemen, finding their gas bombs and gas shells ineffective poured lead from their revolvers into the jammed streets. Men (MEN) fell right and left." ". . . And everywhere was the sight of men, beaten to their knees to lie in a pool of blood." "Swiftly, from intersection to intersection the battle moved, stubbornly the rioters refused to fall back so that the police were forced. . . ." "and the police shot forty rounds of tear gas bombs into the mob before it would move. . . ."

Law . . . and order . . . will . . . prevail. Do you hear? It's war, WAR—and up and down the street "A man clutched at his leg and fell to the sidewalk" "The loud shot like that of the tear gas bombs zoomed again, but no blue smoke this time, and when the men cleared, two bodies lay on the sidewalk, their blood trickling about them"—overhead an airplane lowered, dipped, and nausea gas swooned down in a cloud of torture, and where they ran from street to street, resisting stubbornly, massing again, falling back only to carry the wounded, the thought tore frenziedly through the mind, war, war, it's WAR—and the lists in the papers, the dead, the wounded by bullets, the wounded by other means—W-A-R.

LAW—you hear, Howard Sperry, exserviceman, striking steve-dore, shot in the back and abdomen, said to be in dying condition, DEAD, LAW AND ORDER—you hear and remember this Ben Martella, shot in arm, face and chest, Joseph Beovich, stevedore, laceration of skull from clubbing and broken shoulder, Edwin Hodges, Jerry Hart, Leslie Steinhart, Steve Hamrock, Albert Simmons, marine engineer, striking seamen, scaler, innocent bystander, shot in leg, shot in shoul-der, chest lacerated by tear gas shell, gassed in eyes, compound skull fracture by clubbing, you hear—LAW AND ORDER MUST PRE-VAIL—it's all right Nick, clutching your leg and seeing through the fog of pain it is a police car has picked you up, snarling, let me out, I don't want any bastard bulls around, and flinging yourself out into the street, still lying there in the hospital today—

LAW AND ORDER—people, watching with horror, trying to comprehend the lesson the moving bodies were writing. The man stopping me on the corner, seeing my angry tears as I read the paper, "Listen," he said, and he talked because he had to talk, because in an hour all the beliefs of his life had been riddled and torn away—"Listen, I was down there, on the waterfront, do you know what they're doing—they were shooting SHOOTING—" and that word came out anguished and separate, "shooting right into men, human beings, they were shooting into them as if they were animals, as if they were targets, just lifting their guns and shooting. I saw this, can you believe it, CAN YOU BELIEVE IT? . . . as if they were targets as if . . . CAN YOU BELIEVE IT?" and he went to the next man and started it all over again. . . .

I was not down . . . by the battlefield. My eyes are anguished from the pictures I pieced together from words of comrades, of strikers, from the pictures filling the newspapers. I sat up in headquarters, racked by the howls of ambulances hurtling by, feeling it incredible the fingers like separate little animals hopping nimbly from key to key, the ordered steady click of the typewriter, feeling any moment the walls would crash and all the madness surge in. Ambulances, ripping out of nowhere, fading; police sirens, outside the sky a ghastly gray, corpse gray, an enormous dead eyelid shutting down on the world. And someone comes in, words lurch out of his mouth, the skeleton is told, and goes again. . . . And I sit there, making a metallic little pattern of sound in the air, because that is all I can do, because that is what I am supposed to do.

They called the guard out . . . "admitting their inability to control the situation," and Barrows boasted, "my men will not use clubs or gas, they will talk with bayonets" . . . Middlestaedt . . . "Shoot to kill. Any man firing into the air will be courtmartialed." With two baby tanks, and machine guns, and howitzers, they went down to the waterfront to take it over, to "protect the interests of the people."

I walked down Market that night. The savage wind lashed at my hair. All life seemed blown out of the street; the few people hurrying by looked hunted, tense, expectant of anything. Cars moved past as if fleeing. And a light, indescribably green and ominous was cast over everything, in great shifting shadows. And down the street the trucks rumbled. Drab colored, with boys sitting on them like corpses sitting and not moving, holding guns stiffly, staring with wide frightened eyes, carried down to the Ferry building, down to the Embarcadero to sell out their brothers and fathers for $2.00 a day. Somebody said behind me, and I do not even know if the voice was my own, or unspoken, or imagined, "Go on down there, you sonovabitches, it doesn't matter. It doesn't stop us. We won't forget what happened today. . . . Go on, nothing can stop us . . . now."

Somehow I am down on Stuart and Mission, somehow I am staring at flowers scattered in a border over a space of sidewalk, at stains that look like rust, at an unsteady chalking—"Police Murder.

Two Shot in the Back," and looking up I see faces, seen before, but utterly changed, transformed by some inner emotion to faces of steel. "Nick Bordoise . . . and Sperry, on the way to punch his strike card, shot in the back by those bastard bulls. . . ."

OUR BROTHERS

Howard S. Sperry, a longshoreman, a war vet, a real MAN. On strike since May 9th, 1934 for the right to earn a decent living under decent conditions....

Nickolas Bordoise, a member of Cooks & Waiters Union for ten years. Also a member of the International Labor Defense. Not a striker, but a worker looking to the welfare of his fellow workers on strike....

Some of what the leaflet said. But what can be said of Howard Sperry, exserviceman, struggling through the horrors of war for his country, remembering the dead men and the nearly dead men lashing about blindly on the battlefield, who came home to die in a new war, a war he had not known existed. What can be said of Nick Bordoise. Communist Party member, who without thanks or request came daily to the Embarcadero to sell his fellow workers hot soup to warm their bellies. There was a voice that gave the story of his life, there in the yellowness of the parched grass, with the gravestones icy and strange in the sun; quietly, as if it had risen up from the submerged hearts of the world, as if it had been forever and would be forever, the voice surged over our bowed heads. And the story was the story of any worker's life, of the thousand small deprivations and frustrations suffered, of the courage forged out of the cold and darkness of poverty, of the determination welded out of the helpless anger scalding the heart, the plodding hours of labor and weariness, of the life, given simply, as it had lived, that the things which he had suffered should not be, must not be. . . .

There were only a few hundred of us who heard that voice, but the thousands who watched the trucks in the funeral procession piled high with 50¢ and $1.00 wreaths guessed, and understood. I saw the people, I saw the look on their faces. And it is the look that will be there the days of the revolution. I saw the fists clenched till knuckles were white, and people standing, staring, saying nothing, letting it clamp into their hearts, hurt them so the scar would be there forever—a swelling that would never let them lull.

"Life," the capitalist papers marvelled again, "Life stopped and stared." Yes, you stared, our cheap executive, Rossi—hiding behind the curtains, the cancer of fear in your breast gnawing, gnawing; you stared, members of the Industrial Association, incredulous, where did the people come from, where was San Francisco hiding them, in what factories, what docks, what are they doing there, marching, or standing and watching, not saying anything, just watching. . . . What did it mean, and you dicks, fleeing, hiding behind store windows. . . .

There was a pregnant woman standing on a corner, outlined against the sky, and she might have been a marble, rigid, eternal, expressing some vast and nameless sorrow. But her face was a flame, and I heard her say after a while dispassionately, as if it had been said so many times no accent was needed, "We'll not forget that. We'll pay it back . . . someday." And on every square of sidewalk a man was saying, "We'll have it. We'll have a General Strike. And there won't be processions to bury their dead." "Murder—to save themselves paying a few pennies more wages, remember that Johnny . . . We'll get even. It won't be long. General Strike."

Listen, it is late, I am feverish and tired. Forgive me that the words are feverish and blurred. You see, If I had time, If I could go away. But I write this on a battlefield.

The rest, the General Strike, the terror, arrests and jail, the songs in the night, must be written some other time, must be written later. . . . But there is so much happening now. . . .

FURTHER READINGS

Constance Coiner, *Better Red: The Writing and Resistance of Tillie Olsen and Meridel Le Sueur* (University of Illinois Press, 1998); Nancy Huse and Kay H. Nelson, eds., *The Critical Response to Tillie Olsen* (Greenwood Publishing Group, 1994); Mara Faulkner, *Protest and Possibility in the Writing of Tillie Olsen* (University Press of Virginia, 1993); Mickey Pearlman and Abby H.P. Werlock, *Tillie Olsen* (Twayne, 1991); Elaine Neil Orr, *Tillie Olsen and a Feminist Spiritual Vision* (University Press of Mississippi, 1987); Deborah Rosenfeld, "From the Thirties: Tillie Olsen and the Radical Tradition," *Feminist Studies*, Vol. 7, No. 3 (Fall 1981): 371–406; Selma Burkom and Margaret Williams, "De-Riddling Tillie Olsen's Writings," *San Jose Studies* 2 (1976): 65–83.

Barbara Kingsolver (1955–)

Barbara Kingsolver was born in Kentucky in 1955, and has worked as a teacher, scientific writer, and journalist. Her first novel, *The Bean Trees* (1988) won critical acclaim, but when she moved to Arizona, she was still unsure of her future as a novelist. In Tucson, her "day job" was as a scientific writer, and then, in 1983, as a freelance journalist, she was sent to cover a "constellation of small, strike-gripped mining towns strung out across southern Arizona," where workers were locked in a struggle with Phelps Dodge. She spent the summer taping interviews with about seventy-five people, mostly Latina women. "I listened for more than a year to the stories of striking miners and their stunningly courageous wives, sisters, daughters. Sometimes I had to visit them in jail." For eighteen months, the strike was carried on by the women, as husbands and fathers traveled as far as Texas and California to keep their families fed. Kingsolver's account of the Latinas who held the line against a multinational corporate giant is an intimate and thoroughly exceptional portrait of the labor movement in America.

Her novels, *The Poisonwood Bible* (1998), *Animal Dreams* (1990) and *Pigs in Heaven* (1993), stories, *Homeland* (1989), and essays, *High Tide in Tucson* (1995), tell of women—Native American, Latina, Anglo—trying to find their way in the world. She has also published a bilingual collection of protest poetry, *Another America: Otra America* (1992). Her work has won a Los Angeles Times Book Award for fiction and an Edward Abbey Ecofiction Award in recognition of her concerns for the land.

WOMEN IN THE GREAT ARIZONA MINE STRIKE OF 1983

All the people and events in this book are real. In a few cases I've changed names to protect safety or family harmony; in those

---

Barbara Kingsolver, from *Holding the Line: Women in the Great Arizona Mine Strike of 1983* (1989).

instances I've used a first name only. I also changed the name of the woman identified as Flossie Navarro, at her request; after a long and remarkable life as a trendsetter in the Morenci mine and in her town, she still demurred from direct publicity. All others who speak here are identified by name. I've sometimes edited their narratives for brevity, but have dedicated my efforts to retaining the letter and spirit of their testimonies—mixed metaphors and all.

When it came to reconstructing the strike in the form of a book, I found there were two different kinds of truth I was after: human and historical. Many of the stories here are personal, describing an internal landscape. Sometimes the most important events were not "And then they threw me in jail," but rather, "For the first time I realized if newspapers are lying about us, they could be lying about places like the Middle East and Nicaragua." Sometimes I found it best to shut my mouth and record what I heard, trusting the integrity of my sources as the most credible witnesses to their own metamorphoses.

Even so, I knew these personal truths would mean more if I placed them into an accounting of the historical facts of the strike—just the facts, pure and simple. Given the unbelievable parameters of this story, I wanted to grant readers the confidence that they were reading actual history, not speculation. Pure enough a task but not so simple, as it turned out. Sorting fact from fiction was a test of wit, nerve, and a writer's endurance; tales ran rampant on both sides of the picket line, and while all of them would have made good copy, many of them simply had to be untrue. A typical example: during one of the showdowns between strikers and the police, a strike supporter named Alice who was in her ninth month of pregnancy became trapped inside the small store she owned. Riot police threw tear gas through her storefront window, entered the store, arrested her, and dragged her onto the bus that was being used as a paddy wagon. This much I witnessed before I was forced to leave the scene. Finding out what happened next took me through a maze of testimonies sworn on many a stack of Bibles. Some people told me she was beaten on the bus and went into labor on the spot. Some said she gave birth to a brain-damaged boy a few hours later, and that her doctor (a renowned strike supporter) vowed to sue Phelps Dodge. Some said the police let her out of the bus as soon as they realized she was pregnant, while others insisted that she was held in custody. When I asked Alice herself, she put her head in her hands and said, "I don't want to talk about it." (I couldn't blame her.) The story I eventually put together from accounts by the doctor who attended the birth, several of Alice's friends, witnesses on the bus, arrest records, and a local police officer, was this one: Alice was gassed in her store, abruptly questioned, handcuffed, put into the bus, let out a little while later, and detained overnight in the home of a police officer. Two days later she gave birth to a boy who developed meningitis but recovered fully. So all of the tales contained a bit of the real story, but only a bit.

Collecting rumors and trying to assemble truth, I sometimes felt like the foolish heroine of the Rumpelstiltskin story whose brash confidence got her into the job of trying to spin straw into gold. I became obsessed with verification because, as the strike wore on, the truth was shocking enough without embroidery. In this book I have attempted to make a clear distinction between interviewees' hyperbole and the events I was able to verify. Even when I was there myself to watch—sometimes through a haze of gas—I gathered as many independent accounts as possible, including the "official" version in state newspapers, which occasionally was the wildest fiction of all. I applied my training as a scientist, looking for replication of sequence and detail among the stories. I learned a great deal about this thing we casually call The Truth. I humbly offer the reader a story that really happened.

Since completing this book I have plied my trade mainly as a writer of fiction. Many people have asked me, since I appear to possess the skills of prevarication, why I didn't cast the story of *Holding the Line* as a novel rather than a work of nonfiction. "A lot more people would read it," they tell me, and they are probably right. And yet, as it stands, this story contains all the elements of a novel: lively characters, conflict, plot, resolution, even metaphor and imagery. When I submitted an early draft to a publisher (with no preface explaining my methods), the editors returned it saying "We like this a lot but sorry, we don't publish novels!" Very well then, it is novelesque, and if people would sooner read the very same story under the heading "Once upon a time" than the one that begins, "Listen: this really happened," then why not give them the novel?

That it really happened is exactly the point—and that's why

not. I believe the most important thing about this story is that it is true. In a place a few hours' drive from where I live, the government, the police, and a mining company formed a conspicuous partnership to break the lives of people standing together for what they thought was right. That ironclad, steel-toed partnership arrested hundreds of citizens on charges so ludicrous that the state, after having perfectly executed its plan of intimidating the leadership and turning public sympathy against the strikers, quietly dropped every case. When I begin to tell people what happened during the strike of '83, it often happens that they stop me and say, "This was *eighteen* eighty-three, right?" No. It was barely more than a decade ago, right here in the United States of America. Ronald Reagan was president, Michael Jackson's *Thriller* was on the radio. People who got crushed for organizing unions were thought to live in faraway lands like Poland and South Africa. This was the land of the free and the home of the brave. U.S. citizens had so much confidence in law enforcement, they merrily went along with the rallying cry of "More Police!" as an answer to most social ills. They would barely blink when the U.S. attorney general declared that innocent people don't get arrested in America.

A novel at its best sheds insight on life, but the reader may choose to take or leave its lessons. I would like in this case to narrow that choice, and so this is not a novel. It is a cautionary tale. Its lesson is: watch your back, America. Take civil liberty for granted at your own risk. Trust in leaders who arrive into power by means of wealth, and see what they protect when push comes to shove. What happened in Arizona could happen again and it will, somewhere, to someone. It will happen again and again, if we do not open our eyes and believe what we see.

This story's other lesson is hope. If a group of people who described themselves as "nobody really, just housewives" could endure so much without breaking, if they could bear the meanness of their nation without becoming mean-spirited themselves, if they could come away with a passion for justice instead of revenge, then ordinary people are better than they are generally thought to be. That all this, too, really happened is extremely important. I did not invent these women; they invented themselves. What happened to them could happen to you, or me, and perhaps sometime it will. For better and for worse, this is a story of what could become of us.

■ ■ ■

The Women

The story could begin on the day Flossie Navarro sashayed into the mine on the wind of World War II. Or it could begin much earlier than that. In every season since the earth's face was opened for dredging, women have worked in mines and they have fought for the safety and survival of miners. And always, it wasn't exactly supposed to be that way. The hostility Flossie stirred as a miner still persists in Arizona's copper pits, and is a tradition probably as old as mining itself, rooted in the mineral-rich soils of the Andes where the Incas opened mines before European ships ever touched the Americas' shores. The keepers of these ancient Andean mines in the Bolivian *altiplano* have always described their world as two separate domains: one above ground, and one underneath. A benevolent, matronly earth goddess oversees growing crops and family life. But the stony underground world carved out by miners seeking copper, tin, and silver—that is the devil's domain.

This devil's name is Supay, and he has ruled miners' lives from underneath their floors since before the Spanish conquest. When the mine shafts rumble and threaten to collapse, Bolivian miners assume it is Supay begrudging the ore they tap, little by little, from his glittering black veins. In the heart of Bolivia's mountainous mining region, the mining town of Oruro was the ancient ceremonial center for the Incas. High priests claimed to travel from Peru through tunnels, passing secretly under the core of the Andes, and in full ceremonial dress they leaped out of the ground in Oruro. Now the tunnel's mouth is blocked with boulders, but festivals still celebrate the powers of Supay. During the week of Carnival, Devil Dancers in red-tipped shoes and horned masks jam the streets in a wild procession leading to the Church of the Mine Shaft. The festivities end with a ceremonial offering to Supay held deep in the mine—where women can't go. The devil's domain is masculine, on Carnival days and on every working day of the year. Women in Bolivia may earn subsistence wages by picking through the slag heaps for overlooked bits of ore, but the central economic pursuit of the region—mining—is closed to them. Tradition holds that a female presence in this special corner of hell would anger Supay terribly and cause a cave-in. If a woman went into the mines, the miners say, disaster would follow.

In the open-pit mine in Morenci, Arizona, a steadily grazing herd of mechanized shovels raises a yellow haze of fine dust. This is the most productive copper mine in North America. In the best of years it has yielded nearly 300,000 tons of metal; clearly this is the domain of both devil and dollar. The copper smelter's two smokestacks rise like a pair of giant horns out of the mountain's granite pate. Below the horned promontory lies the pit. The earth's entrails are laid open there in a pattern of descending steps that expose the strange, delicate colors of a mountain's insides: lavender, pink, blue-gray. If the miners labor here in the belly of a beast, gutting it more deeply every day, then that beast is as tough as Prometheus, the thief in Greek mythology whose punishment was to be disemboweled every day for eternity. Morenci's miners—grandfathers, fathers, and sons—have worked this same scarred landscape for more than half a century.

Around the mine and in the river valley below it lie the ordinary mining towns of Morenci and Clifton. Each of the two small towns has its high school, its main drag, its dust-coated bouquet of blinking neon signs, its sundry handful of bars and drive-in restaurants. No devil dances for Carnival in these streets, but even so, the germinal social order of Supay's domain seems to hold sway over all that has come after. A mine is a masculine enclave, not just in the Andes—the exact same social prescriptions surface wherever the earth is scratched. Flossie Navarro heard constantly that female workers would jinx the mine. When women began working the Appalachian coal mines in the late 1970s, they confronted a centuries-old folk belief that a woman underground was bad luck and could cause a cave-in merely by her presence.

Who could blame miners for an excessive interest in bad luck? With or without a woman's presence, to mine ore is to flirt with disaster. Between 1961 and 1973, for example—years when most of us held an anxious eye on a perilous occupation overseas—more than half a million disabling injuries happened in U.S. mines. That's nearly twice as many as befell all U.S. soldiers in Vietnam. The mean death rate for miners during those years was approximately 1,080 per million, and for active-duty personnel, about 1,270 per million. (These figures are from the National Safety Council and Department of Defense Information, respectively). If war is hell, so is mining: underground shafts collapse, smelter furnaces explode, lung disease is endemic. In few other professions are the odds so stacked against living long enough to retire.

■　■　■

When eastern investors in the Phelps Dodge Corporation began to develop a profitable copper industry in the Southwest just after the turn of the century, the anti-alien laws they constructed were as utilitarian and malleable as the metal itself. For example: at the Copper Queen mine in Bisbee, Arizona, underground shafts reached precious deposits of silver and gold, and mining was regarded as a skilled, well-paying craft. Mexicans were explicitly forbidden to work underground. But in other Arizona mines where geology called for different methods and attitudes, the rules changed. In the Clifton-Morenci district the open-pit mine required an immense, unskilled labor force. In contrast to the all-European Bisbee mine, Morenci mine records from 1917 describe a work camp that was 80 percent Mexicans, 15 percent Spaniards and Italians, and only 5 percent "whites"—meaning European Anglo-Saxons. Workers for the Morenci operation were imported from Mexico en masse. These laborers were regarded as beasts of burden and paid only slightly better than the average mule, even though their descendants say that many who crossed the border from Sonora were skilled miners and smelters. The *mineros* from the south brought more than strong backs. Outside the mining museum at Jerome, Arizona, sits an old "Chilean wheel"—an efficient ore-crushing technology that was used extensively in Latin America before being introduced into Arizona, probably by Mexican miners. Their stories have been lost, in the main, but their knowledge enriched the industry.

■　■　■

Separated by a world of mountain and desert, the women of these disparate towns carried a single flag into battle when the time came. Nearly every one of them spoke of a grandfather who'd walked out of the Morenci mine in 1915 or left Bisbee by cattle car in 1917, or a father who struggled for a decent life while bearing discrimination like a scar. The threat to their standard of living was not just personally dangerous; they saw it as an insult to their ancestors. These tiny, isolated towns have steeped for half a century in their own labor traditions and extracted a sense of pride that provides their only medicine against hard times. Even for those women who weren't miners themselves, the union they'd grown up with was a tool as familiar to them as a can opener or a stove. They knew exactly where they would be without it: living in Tortilla Flats or Indian Town, barred from the social club, the library, and the swimming pool. Living with husbands who broke their backs and spirits for half a white man's wage. Regardless of age or color, they'd be women living with prospects no higher than car-hop and laundromat, women working against the odds, women damned as bad luck in a devil's domain. They marched for the union because they knew in their bones a union banner was the only curtain between themselves and humiliation. Being cursed by scabs or the National Guard is a lesser evil by far than the curse of a father's ghost.

■ ■ ■

The Strike

"Something's going to happen. They're taking in mattresses and taking in food, so we'd better have some people up there." Carmina Garcia went. Her husband, Willie, was away for the morning, so she called her friends Jessie and Velia, the mayor's wife. "We went around the side to check the Columbine gate and saw that the trucks were coming in and out through the back, bringing in food, cots, and whatnot. Then they told us there were more people going through the main gate, so we went to the main road and there we saw the people were coming in *buses*. They were scared to come to work. Don't you see, they shouldn't have been working—there was a strike! So P.D. hired those buses to bring in the scabs from Safford, and even a few from Clifton. They would stop and pick them up and drive them around back.

"We had to put a stop to it. People from Duncan, Safford, *everywhere*, were coming in to help us close it down. They said in the papers there were one or two thousand, but it was more than that, I know. As time went on you started seeing a little bit more and a little bit more.

"And P.D. was bringing in stuff left and right. The helicopter was coming in with food, because a lot of them were going to stay in the mine, once they got in. P.D. was telling them, 'They're going to kill you.' I know this because there was a guy working in there that my husband and I know real well—later on he quit. He told us that his foreman told him, 'Here, go kill those sons of bitches! Look at that mob, they're going to kill you anyway!' And threw a gun in his truck! David didn't want it—he threw it out of his truck and left it there. But they were trying to get everybody scared.

"We weren't going to kill them, honey. All we were asking was for them to *get out* of there. That's all we ever asked."

Berta Chavez and her sisters were there, of course. Berta was up above the mine. "We could look down into the mine where the scabs were. They had their hats over their faces; I guess they were afraid, because we had control. And they'd come in disguises. One guy came in with a paper sack over his head, with holes cut for the eyes. They were ashamed because they knew they shouldn't be in there scabbing for P.D.

"Outside, there were people from the mine gate all the way to the general office. It was full of people. A couple of thousand, I'd say. We had our trucks there—we backed them up—and we had our beer and our ice chests—it was just like a picnic. We were just waiting. We gave them till 12:00 to get the scabs out. We said after 12:00, nobody comes in or out."

■ ■ ■

News of the Morenci shutdown crossed the state in record time. Janie Ramon, the first woman in the Ajo mine, was now reporting secretary for her union, the International Chemical Workers Union Local 703. She took it upon herself to try and stir up some resistance to Phelps Dodge in Ajo.

I met Janie several weeks later in the Ajo Union Hall—a mobile home equipped with a few chairs and a rickety aluminum table, an ancient coffee machine, and a TV. "On August 8, when things started happening in Morenci," Janie said, rapping her knuckles precariously against the table, "the strikers up there claimed we didn't have any courage, that we were meek little mice. I was with a girlfriend and my boyfriend that day, and the three of us went around to the Ajo bars to tell people what we were doing on the line. There were a lot of scabs in some of the bars, but I thought if I talked to them and told them what harm they were doing the union, it might make them change their minds. But they weren't having anything to do with me. We ended up getting into a fight. We left.

"The next day, August 9, was when the women blocked traffic at the mine gate." The men, she said, were away from the gates trying to stop individual cars. "Everyone had bats, but no one used them. We didn't hurt anybody. We were there again the next day. I was on a side gate. All of a sudden six cars pulled up and a driver got out of every car with a machine gun—an M-16. That was ridiculous. Not one of us had any weapon."

Gloria Blase was there too and clearly remembers the M-16s. "It was the state troopers, the DPS. They jumped out with their machine guns pointing straight at us. They kept telling us, 'Move, you're next, go ahead. Just try us.' There were three women where I was standing, and they [DPS] were aiming right at our heads. A striker grabbed a camera and started taking pictures, so they pulled the machine guns back to their shoulders.

"I hadn't done anything; I was just at the picket line. Earlier, some guy threw a beer can at a DPS car. It was after that that all the DPS showed up. Then, later on, some windows were broken out of a scab van going by, so the cops came again, in four cars. They all jumped out with their batons, but they didn't know what to do. One of them said, 'Somebody without a shirt did it.' But all four guys had taken off their shirts, so they couldn't arrest anybody. It was just a show of force."

Later that morning Janie Ramon left for the union hall. On the way she was stopped and arrested for assault, as a result of the fight in the bar two nights before. "I just couldn't believe it. My boyfriend made a remark, and they said he was obstructing justice, so they arrested him too. That afternoon we were to be arraigned. They brought me in the hallway, and I stood there for an hour, and then they said the *paperwork* wasn't done and I couldn't be arraigned until the next day, so I had to spend the night in there. I was released the next day at 9:00 A.M. They told me if I touched the people who filed charges against me I would be thrown in jail for sixty days. No appeal."

■ ■ ■

The Judge

The judge, Ajo Justice of the Peace Helen Gilmartin, was widely regarded as a Phelps Dodge employee, and Ajo strikers complained about conflict of interest. They found it a bit galling that she drove around town in a car with vanity plates reading "PD AJO." When I called Gilmartin's office to ask about this, I was told only that prior to her appointment to the bench six months before the strike, she had indeed worked in the security division of Phelps Dodge. (Eventually, in September 1983, she agreed to excuse herself from hearing cases involving strikers.) According to Janie and others arrested at that time, the judge offered jailed strikers the choice of crossing the picket line or staying behind bars.

Judge Gilmartin and Janie Ramon are relatives, a fact that increased Janie's bitterness. "I told her, 'Don't tell me I'm going to sit in jail or go to work, because I'll sit in here and I'll rot before I cross a picket line!' I have two kids, six and nine, and they understood. I told them we were fighting for our rights—I've always told them we shouldn't be led around by the nose. If I crossed that picket line, it would be like letting the company slap me in the face every day. I wouldn't have any respect for myself. I told my kids it would be like bowing down to someone, and you don't have to bow down to anyone. You're a person, and everyone has rights. I've always taught them that.

"On August 19 I received a suspension letter from P.D. for strike misconduct on August 10. That's the day I was in jail. A few days later I was terminated for 'blocking mine gate traffic.' I'd been standing at gates that were already locked and chained. Nobody went by there, or through, or even attempted."

Gloria Blase was also terminated for alleged strike-related misconduct. "I was supposedly carrying a wrench. I wasn't—it was a crowbar that I picked up and put in my truck. I wanted to correct them, so I went to see the films at the general office."

Because the company couldn't legally fire strikers without cause, Phelps Dodge kept a file of films documenting activities for which they were being terminated. When Gloria viewed the films, she realized she wasn't in the cast; on the day for which her warrant had been issued, she wasn't even on the line. She had witnesses and decided to fight the termination.

Seventy-four other strikers in Ajo were fired and ordered to vacate their company-owned homes during the next weeks. Eleven Ajo strikers, including Janie, were arrested on charges of rioting, obstructing traffic, or "interfering with the judicial process."

C. Pat Scanlon, vice-president of finance for the Phelps Dodge Corporation, felt that on balance the firings were good for the company. "We discharged throughout Arizona 188 of the strikers for strike-related misconduct," he commented later. "Our perception of that group is that in general it included a lot of the less desirable employees that were working, either because they were general troublemakers, or unreliable, or drunks, or whatever. So it had the effect of purging the work force of a lot of people who were not really on the company's side . . . so in that respect, we upgraded the work force."

Soila Bom, in the very first arrest of the strike, was jailed for using her telephone to tell a former friend that she now considered him a scab. Those arrested were booked into the Ajo annex of the Pima County Jail, but most were later moved to a jail in Tucson. For the three-hour drive they sat handcuffed in the back of a van without water or air-conditioning. The arrests were a shock, and the extremely high bonds set—up to $20,000—bankrupted union coffers overnight. Union attorney Duane Ice reported that the unions planned to fight back and would seek jury trials. Years later, Soila and every one of the others would be vindicated by appalled juries. But at the time, and in the months to come, being legally in the right did them no more good than if they had been pedestrians run down in a crosswalk.

■ ■ ■

The Governor

Since Arizona's population is primarily urban, the majority of the governor's constituents couldn't easily relate to the inhabitants of remote blue-collar mining towns and were probably inclined to distrust the bred-in-bone union loyalty that led the strikers to seemingly desperate measures. But the people of Clifton and Morenci saw Gov. Bruce Babbitt's "first obligation," a frightening military occupation of their town, as excessive; the punishment didn't fit the crime. They felt that the anti-assembly injunctions had been unfairly invoked in the first place. What they saw more than anything was a clear alliance between their governor, the troops, and Phelps Dodge. When the mine gates reopened on August 19, National Guardsmen were lined up on Phelps Dodge property, guns pointing out. Patrolling activity was stepped up for the shift changes when, after the ten-day "cooling-off" period, Phelps Dodge again began bringing busloads of nonstrikers in and out of the mine. When Phelps Dodge reopened the employment office, armed National Guardsmen were standing on the roof. The sensation of being stared at through a riflescope is unsettling, to say the least. When strikers and their families walked the picket lines, uniformed sharpshooters followed their movements with automatic weapons. Strike sympathy still ran high in the town, and the memory of the shutdown—the astonishing power of their numbers—was fresh in the strikers' minds. But they reluctantly came to understand, as many have learned before them, that a majority opinion means nothing against guns.

Trudy Morgan, the wife of a striking miner, summed up the town's emotions. "I felt defeated, just lost. I think we all felt that way. I have to say our town was raped."

Flossie Navarro's memories of the occupation are vivid. Having survived clamorous days as a union miner during World War II and after, she never expected to see the same battles fought again, like a rerun of an old war film, in her retirement. She didn't care for the show.

"I was here when the National Guard came in, yes, ma'am. I saw them helicopters come in. We had eighteen up here in the air—*eighteen helicopters*. We went out there in the yard, and I counted them as they went over. They circled and circled; it was just like a battle. You'd just like to have got a gun and shot 'em all down! That's really what I'd like to of done. All night you'd hear them—brrr, brrr, brrr, like they was taking the top of the house off. At night, and of a day, for the three o'clock shift change. And of a morning, when the early-morning shift was coming up, them helicopters would wake you up, here they'd come. It was as bad as during the war when those planes would come down drilling. That's just what it put me in mind of. Just like war.

"When those National Guard were here I kept the grandkids right with me every minute cause there was no telling what was going to happen to them. One time we went up Old Chase Creek to the fruit stand up there. While we was there at the truck stop, there was a cop car come down, one of those DPS, and there was six of them in that sucker. They stopped right over here and got out, and they took off their shirts and put on those bullet-proof vests. Then they got in the car and come on down the highway. Right there, *ignorantly*, in front of us. I didn't say anything to them, but I sure would have liked to. But I was just one woman there; they probably would have beat the hell out of me. Now, why couldn't they have done that in a motel room, up in Morenci? At least I have the guts to drive through town without no bullet-proof vest!

"They was all over the place, all up the road and on top of the stores, pointing their guns down at people like it was a battle. They had all their jeeps, whatever you call them, and those old stupid-looking outfits. At the lines they'd have four or five of them ganged up on one striker. That's not fair, is it? Why didn't they take them man to man? Why didn't they give them both a gun, stand them up there, and let them go at it—if it was a war they wanted?"

■ ■ ■

Jean Lopez spent her entire childhood in sight of the smoke-stacks of the Morenci smelter. "The governor sent the National Guard in so that P.D. could open the plant without any incident. It was as simple as that. People knew it wasn't just an ordinary strike, and they were scared. The newspaper said they were being trained up here at the National Guard armory in Safford, practicing their . . . whatever it is they have to practice. It just wasn't *necessary*. These people all grew up here. You *know* the people here, and they're not bad people. I was so angry when I saw all these guys here, and we pay for that with our own tax money! I called Governor Babbitt, and I told him I do not appreciate that he sent these people up here, against us, and *my* taxes are paying for *them* to threaten me and my people? I say that's wrong!

"I was angry that our own country would turn our own people against us. A lot of these strikers are Vietnam vets; they fought for this country—for what? I had an uncle who got killed in Vietnam. It just doesn't make sense to me. This is an American against an American. That didn't seem like it should be happening here. These are horror stories you hear from somewhere else—South America,

Poland, or someplace—but not here in the United States. We like to think we're better off—you know, patriotism and all that. I'm not saying I'm not glad I'm an American, but at this moment I don't feel that I'm 100 percent. I'm sorry, but that's the way it is."

Fina Roman, head of the Women's Auxiliary, expressed similar doubts about truth, justice, and the American Way. "I think this has been a learning process for us. We have always been proud of our country and believed in the democratic system. Try to imagine the disappointment of having had such faith in that system that's turning against us now. We taught our children that if you do right and don't break the laws, the system in place is your defense: you can't lose if you work within that system—you can defend what you think is right, and not be punished for it. But we *have* been punished, and that's been damaging to the values we tried to instill.

"This town has been here over a hundred years, and for all that time we have been law-abiding citizens who raised our children, supported our town, and produced many valuable, worthwhile human beings. All of a sudden, as soon as we stand to defend what we believe is right, they call us law-breaking animals."

Fina confided these thoughts one evening as we sat in the Machinists' Hall in Clifton, after she'd spent a long afternoon standing on the picket line and trying to organize some emergency relief for a striker family with five kids in danger of having their home foreclosed. The huge, dimly lit hall, which ordinarily buzzed with people and projects as the nerve center of the strike, was nearly empty now as people went home to supper. Fina looked worried and tired.

"The greatest disappointment for me was that I campaigned for Governor Babbitt door to door. I thought he was the best thing that could happen to Arizona. Now I feel betrayed. He was a guest at our graduation, in May of last year, and applauded unions. Three months later he sent in troops to destroy them. We remember these things.

"It was such an excessive show of force. It's frightening. We're facing people armed with destructive weapons, and we don't know—would they take our life? Our children are impressionable. They go out and taunt them, sometimes acting immature, thinking they're defending their parents, and one day they might overstep." She paused for a minute as four small girls in blue jeans, their long black hair flying, tore into the union hall and chased each other up the stairs, screaming and giggling. Fina asked me, as if I knew, "Would these men shoot our kids away? People think about it every day. Would they shoot them for throwing a rock? We don't know."

■ ■ ■

The occupation of Clifton and Morenci left indelible marks. The character of the strike, and the tactics of its supporting organizations, were forced to change. The Women's Auxiliary in particular hardened its core.

According to Jean Lopez, the auxiliary used to be "a group where the ladies would get together and air their complaints." She says it made them feel better to see that other families were in the same boat. "You'd come feeling depressed and leave feeling great. And it was kind of a support group for the men—the women would get together and make tortillas to take to the picketers up at the mine. And parties for the children at Christmas, that kind of thing. This is basically what it was. But it changed. The women were forced to take a stand. We were always behind the lines, and the men were up in front. But in this strike, the women had to move to the front."

Fina Roman explained how this had come about. "Everybody was on the line at first, including the women. But the women are the ones who have never stayed away from it. Partly this is because there was an injunction against the men, but also because it was very important to us to keep that picket line active. The men, after the injunction, were in danger of being arrested for just being there. The women took over."

■ ■ ■

The Women

And so, in the face of a considerable army, the women of Clifton and Morenci began rolling their groggy children out of bed at 4:00 A.M. and making their way in the predawn light to the top of the hill. Most of them now groan remembering the difficulty of organizing their households around this strange new schedule— Phelps Dodge's "state-of-emergency" twelve-hour shift change—but they also agree that the all-women pickets were "kind of fun." It had never been their habit to go anywhere but the grocery store without their husbands—socializing spots like the bar were traditionally off limits to women alone or in groups—so the female camaraderie on the line was a heady discovery.

The Women's Auxiliary received notice that it was technically barred from the lines along with the strikers, because of its legal affiliation with the unions. Undaunted, the women organized under a new title, "Citizens for Justice," and refused to stay home. Carrying hand-painted signs that declared such things as "WHO IS GOVERNOR, PHELPS DODGE OR BRUCE SCABBITT?" housewives, waitresses, mothers, and daughters came out to the roadside to make the most public stand of their lives.

"We had to try and keep the number *down* to ninety-nine," says Shirley Randall. "All women. We knew we couldn't just quit. We asked the men not to go, so they couldn't say we were doing anything wrong. The men were more rowdy—the rock throwers."

This last point is debatable; Cleo Robledo said the opposite. "You better believe the women turned out. And oh, they were brave! The scabs, the DPS, all of them hate facing the women worse than they hate facing the men. Even if there were just five, seven women up there in that little island, they'd call out the DPS. Oh, yes. 'Get them up here, we can't stand these women!' They were afraid of the women because I think we're much more . . . verbal."

Their "verbs" were sharply curtailed, though, by the presence of armed guards. "When we were on the line," Diane McCormick said, "you really had to maintain. You couldn't be rowdy—you knew they were watching. I remember one time we were on the line and I looked up and said, 'They have snipers on the hill!' Everyone turned and, sure enough, they were all up there, right above the mine. There's a little shack up there. Always before we had just seen the Guard and the DPS when they were right there near us. When I saw the snipers up there, with their guns ready, I felt like, man, we don't have a chance; don't do anything. I felt they would shoot us, I honestly did—that they wouldn't hesitate."

■ ■ ■

"For just innumerable years," Fina Roman says, "Clifton was a safe community; people knew everyone else; everyone looked after everyone else's children. There was just a family atmosphere throughout the community. Now that no longer is true. Unfortunately it isn't always those who have crossed the picket line, but the law enforcement agencies, who are causing the problems. They are forever questioning people who they meet walking down the street. We're used to walking everywhere—it's a small community, and people enjoy walking. Now we're questioned when we are found walking. This is strange to us. I think an investigation has to be undertaken to find the reasons for our rights being violated. There is a right-to-work law in Arizona, but that doesn't mean that we must forfeit all other rights."

The sentiment among strikers was the same everywhere. "We *are* going to see the end of this," Carmina Garcia declared. "Come hell or high water. The river can take us, but we're not giving in to P.D."

FURTHER READINGS

Mary Jean Demarr, *Barbara Kingsolver: A Critical Companion* (Greenwood Publishing Group, 1999); Donna Perry, *Backtalk: Women Writers Speak Out: Interviews* (Rutgers University Press, 1993); Judy Aulette and Trudy Mills, "Something Old, Something New: Auxiliary Work in the 1983–1986 Copper Strike," *Feminist Studies* (Summer, 1988): 251–268; Barbara Kingsolver, and Jill Barrett Fein, "Women on the Line," *Progressive* (March 1984): 5.

Cannery Women's Songs from the *UCAPAWA News*

Throughout the first decades of the twentieth century, struggles for fair and safe working conditions in western industries were intense and prolonged. Miners and oil workers, migrant farm laborers, shipyard workers, cannery laborers and needleworkers, and others organized, demanded betterment of their conditions, and went out on strike; over and over again, state militias, privately-funded factory militias, and even federal troops responded and ended the strikes. Many of the workers who went out on strike and marched on the picket lines were women. In some industries, women workers made up the majority of the labor force, as in the case of canneries in the Southwest. One cannery, the California Sanitary Canning Company, had a workforce of four hundred and thirty, mostly women and mostly Mexican American. In August of 1931, almost all of these workers walked out, demanding higher wages and better wages, as well as the recognition of their union, The United Cannery, Agricultural, Packing and Allied Workers of America, Local 75, and the establishment of a closed shop. In the middle of a record-breaking heat wave, the women set up a twenty-four-hour picket line, marking, according to historian Vicki L. Ruiz, "the beginning of labor activism by Mexicana cannery and packing workers in Los Angeles."

As they walked the line, the women sang songs set to popular folk melodies which put forward their demands and buoyed their spirits as local authorities moved in to put down the strike. After the strike was over, and they continued to push for improvements, the Escuela de Obreras (worker's school) encouraged continued vigilance against the return of the poor conditions which prevailed before the 1939 strike. These songs reflect Mexicana workers' views of themselves as fighters for justice and their families' futures.

Cannery Women's Songs from the *UCAPAWA News* (1939–1941).

"CIFRA Y DATOS," ESCUELA DE OBRERAS, BETABELEROS, ABRIL DE 1940

Alerta betabeleros
Escuchen con atención
Y tengan en la memoria
Lo que es organización

Estudiantes adelante
Adelante sin tropiezo
El estudio de este grupo
Es la base del progreso

Con muy grande sacrificio
Y empeño del CIO
La compañera Moreno
Esta Escuela organizó

Fijémonos en lo pasado
Comprendamos la razón
Divididos no hay progreso
Solamente con la Unión

Adelante, compañeros
Y luchemos como un león
No se valgan de pretextos
Ingresemos a la Unión

Las locales nos esperan
Con una gran ansiedad;
Llevamos cifras y datos
De lo que es la realidad

Con un estrecho saludo
De Unión y fraternidad
La compañera Moreno
Salud y felicidad

Ya con esta me despido
Mi corrido terminó
Aclamando en alto voz
Adelante el CIO!

"UNION SHOP AND $22," SUNG TO THE TUNE OF *YANKEE DOODLE* (1941)

The walnut girls aren't satisfied
They're asking for more money,
They're getting sixteen bucks a week
And think it isn't funny.

(Chorus)
  Union shop and twenty-two!
  Twenty-two is jake!
  Union shop and twenty-two!
  To get the girls some steak!

The prices are all going up
And soon they'll be outrageous,
Everything is being raised,
Except our meager wages.
  (Union shop, etc.)

They tell us that we want too much
That we are merely playing
But aching backs and straining eyes,
Are worth more than they're paying.

"CLUBBED BUT WE STILL STRIKE," (1939), SUNG TO THE TUNE OF *I'VE BEEN WORKING ON THE RAILROAD*

Fight for Union recognition
Fight for better pay
Fight to better our condition
In the democratic way
Eighty cents won't even feed us,
A dollar and a quarter would be fine,
Show the farmers that they need us,
JOIN THE PICKET LINE.

FURTHER READINGS
Vicki L. Ruiz, *Cannery Women, Cannery Lives: Mexican Women, Unionization, and the California Food Processing Industry 1930–1950* (University of New Mexico Press, 1987); Vicki L. Ruiz, "A Promise Fulfilled: Mexican Cannery Workers in Southern California," *Pacific Historian* 30 (Summer 1986); Vicki L. Ruiz, *From Out of the Shadows: Mexican American Women in the Twentieth-Century America* (Oxford University Press, 1999).

Edith Summers Kelley
(1884-1956)

Few writers are so little-known to the reading public as Edith Summers Kelley. Her novel *Weeds* was first published in 1923. It was reissued in 1972 by the Southern Illinois University Press in a series called "Lost American Fiction." Matthew J. Bruccoli wrote its Afterword, including three paragraphs from the November 4, 1923, *San Diego Union* with the information that Kelley and her husband C. Fred Kelley were living as chicken farmers, having given up their dreams of being artists, he a sculptor, and she a writer.

Edith Summers was born and educated in Toronto. She went to New York where for two years she worked as a secretary to Upton Sinclair, who remembered her as "an unpretentious little woman, red-haired and bespectacled.... She had been a wage-slave at the Standard dictionary, and her eyesight was ruined...." For a brief time in 1906 and 1907, she was engaged to Sinclair Lewis, but she married his roommate, Allan Updegraff, in 1908. After that marriage ended in divorce, she married C. Fred Kelley, and the couple began an itinerant life, moving from New Jersey to California, often living out of their car. For a time, they raised tobacco as tenant farmers in Kentucky, years which are drawn with deadly accuracy in *Weeds*.

When both the novel and the farming failed, the Kelleys went to California, ending up north of San Diego on a chicken ranch, and when that failed too, Edith Kelley was doing daywork as a housemaid. Her husband took a job in a slaughterhouse, where he had to pull the wool from the decaying hides of sheep. Her poem "The Head-Cutters" is a description of the cannery workers' grisly labors. Their "feet freeze fast to the slimed and rotted floor."

In Upton Sinclair's 1906 novel *The Jungle*, Naturalism was hailed as a new strain of American fiction, but in the writing of women, there was as yet no welcoming voice. Kelley's second novel, *The Devil's Hand*, was published posthumously in 1974. When the Feminist Press reprinted Kelley's masterpiece *Weeds* in

1996, it finally restored to the novel the chapter long excised, "Billy's Birth." Perhaps Kelley's time has come among a new generation of readers.

THE HEAD-CUTTERS

When the harsh cannery whistle shatters
  the air at midnight,
Or in the frozen black hours of
  the near dawn,
To tell that a sardine boat had come
  to dock,
The rich people on the hill turn
  over on their pillows,
Mutter and yawn,
And say what they will do to end this
  pest:
They'll sleep at night, or know just why
  they can't.
They'll have that whistle stopped or
  make them move their plant.

But the dark folk on the flats are
  glad and rise up quickly
From the warm bed into the biting cold:
Father and mother and Manuel and Jose,
And Joachim and Dolores and little Angelina,
And run, buttoning their clothes to the
  cannery,
Teeth chattering all the way,
Leaving only the babies at home with
  the grandma,
Sleeping till day.

Edith Summers Kelley, "The Head-Cutters," 1941, Manuscript in the Kelley file, Carton 4, Carey McWilliams Collection, Special Collections, University of California, Los Angeles, quoted in Vicki L. Ruiz, *Cannery Women, Cannery Lives: Mexican Women, Unionization, and the California Food Processing Industry, 1930–1950* (1987).

It is cold in the cannery and a wet,
*   salt wind blows through,*
And the feet freeze fast to the
*   slimed and rotted floor,*
And the fingers grow stiff on the knife,
*   numb, jointless, and sore,*
Cutting the heads and guts from the little sardines as they pour
Out of the chutes that is always
*   belching sardines, always more, always more.*

It is no time now for idle chatter and talk
The wagging tongues of the women are
*   still and the children as dumb.*
Only the knives that chop, the feet that
*   walk,*
The whirring song of the belt and the
*   boilers' hum;*
And through the floor cracks, sullen, undertone
Of the black waves' incessant go-and-come.
It is cold and they shiver and cough,
*   and the hands become slow;*
And here a boy's finger the keen
*   knife slits to the bone,*
And there a girl totters,
Gone faint from the icy chill of the
*   blood-freezing water.*
And yon at the end of the row,
An old man slumps to his knees
*   like a felled ox waiting for slaughter.*

But here and there some dark-eyed
*   Angelo,*
Proud in his youth, seeks out his Rosa's
*   glance.*
And by the age-old miracle of love,
These two are all alone and far away.
Even here such miracles are free to come.

And still the little slippery sardines
slide down the chute, a silver river
    of fish
That seems to have no end.
Ghastly the gray hag, dawn, stalks
    in from the water,
Dims the electric lamps and shows all
    haggard the faces.
Sodden the clothes, and reeking with
    filth and with offal.
The long, black, rotted floor and
    the tables splattered with fishgut.

But the chute is empty at last,
The silver stream has ceased flowing.

Out of the black and stinking hole,
Their eyes puffy with wakefulness,
The head-cutters come forth into
    the dawn.
No gray hag now, but all in coral and
    pearl,
A lovely mermaid rising from the bay,
Flinging the veils of morning to the
    breeze.
No dawn so blue as dawn upon the
    sea.
The sky an abalone shell,
The sea a pearl,
Mackerel cloudlets, and the foam-white
    swirl
Of gull flight over the smooth rippling
    shore.
Brightness and calm. No shadow anywhere;
And a warm sun, so kind to the chilled
    blood and body sore.
There will be money now for the men
    to guzzle and gamble,
Silk stockings for the girls and
    high-heeled shoes,

Candy and gum to make the children gay.
And for the mothers,
The bread to buy and the meat,
And the rent to pay.

FURTHER READINGS

Edith Summers Kelley, *Weeds* (Feminist Press, 1996); Edith Summers Kelley, *The Devil's Hand* (Feminist Press, 1974); "The Head-Cutters," Carey McWilliams Collection, Special Collections, University of California, Los Angeles; Vicki L. Ruiz, *Cannery Women, Cannery Lives: Mexican Women, Unionization, and the California Food Processing Industry 1930–1950* (University of New Mexico Press, 1987); Vicki L. Ruiz, "A Promise Fulfilled: Mexican Cannery Workers in Southern California," *Pacific Historian* 30 (Summer 1986); Vicki L. Ruiz, *From Out of the Shadows: Mexican American Women in the Twentieth-Century America* (Oxford University Press, 1999).

Seniors' Hike, May 17, 1922, Whitefish Hish School.

from K. Ross Toole Archives, Mansfield Library, University of Montana–Missoula.

Talking Back

In her introduction to *Off the Reservation*, Paula Gunn Allen writes of herself, "I was raised in a family that assumed resistance to be the bedrock of its reality." In this chapter, women express themselves in different forms of resistance because that is the crucible of their identity.

For Mary Crow Dog and Angela Davis resistance is born in a political movement; it means defense of tribe and of race. For Jeanne Wakatsuki Houston resistance lies in the refusal to let memory die. For Nancy Mairs, resistance is the refusal to allow physical pain to limit the act of social protest. For Terry Tempest Williams, protest means bearing witness. Each of these selections is autobiographical, but self revelation is not the purposed end of the telling. The passionate voice of protest sometimes overwhelms the individual. What is important is to be heard, to be seen, to be effective. What is important is to break the silence. That impulse to speak out goes back to Tillie Olsen's little book *Silences*, which awoke a generation of women. It is still heard. It is in Teresa Jordan's portrait of the women in her family whose failed marriages were the result of their refusal to be silent. "They put themselves before their partners. They wanted to be in control of their own lives." Jordan and Elizabeth Hampsten write of themselves as girls "who could never please" their mothers. As Jordan writes, "As an adult, I fought against her stillness tooth and nail." And Terry Tempest Williams fought against her Mormon upbringing that a young girl does not "make waves" or "rock the boat."

Paula Gunn Allen speaks of herself as a "maverick," as an outsider whose "quest most closely approximates the American journey." It is a new persona for American women, eastern and western. These voices are sometimes strident, and sometimes impassioned for the plight of others. The poet is multiple. She hears the voices of "whatever color, class, gender, or sexual orientation." Resistance is to life on the "reservation," to life defined by compliance.

Sor Juana Inés de la Cruz
(ca. 1648–1694)

Sor Juana Inés de la Cruz was born Juana Asbaje in San Miguel de Nepantla, in the Spanish Viceroyalty of Mexico, sometime between 1648 and 1651, the daughter of a Spanish-born father and a "criollo," or Mexican-born, mother. At the time of her birth, the Mexican New Spain stretched across the western part of North America, extending far north into California. Her father's social standing afforded her access to education through private tutors; she learned to read at the age of four, and at the age of ten she began writing poetry, both in Latin and in Spanish. Spanish colonial convents provided the chief destinations for women of Sor Juana's intellectual achievement and inclination, and she took her novitiate vows in 1667 at the Carmelite convent of San José. While she left no accounting of her precise reasons for entering the convent, she wrote often of the loss of freedom that women experienced on marrying; it is likely that she embraced convent life because it afforded her at least minimal physical and intellectual freedom. She took her final vows at the Convent of San Jerónimo in 1669 and officially took the name Sor (Sister) Juana Inés de la Cruz.

Life in the convent included not only private study and reflection but also the convivial company of like-minded women, with whom Sor Juana enjoyed roundtable discussions (*tertulias*) and even lively philosophical debates with her superiors, including male archbishops with whom she debated women's equality. She also engaged classic philosophers's criticisms of women, especially taking Aristotle to task for his misogyny. She argued that had he known how to cook, the mysteries of chemistry would not have eluded him. Her poems were statements of her belief in women's equality, and they have reverberated in Latin American, Mexican, and Chicana women's writings in the more than three hundred years since her death in 1694.

We make available here one of her most famous writings, a letter written to the "Most Illustrious Poetess, Sor Filotea de la Cruz" in 1691. In this eloquent defense of a woman's right to think and to write about her knowledge, Sor Juana challenges the condemnation of a senior nun who has criticized Sor Juana for her "prideful" intelligence. In the section that has been excerpted, Sor Juana argues that as God has made her intelligence what it is, then it cannot be a sin for her to demonstrate his exceptional handiwork. No consideration of Western women's writing can be complete without a recognition of the West's Spanish colonial past or without an acknowledgment of the literary legacies that Spanish colonial women have provided to Western women writing today.

RESPONSE TO THE MOST ILLUSTRIOUS POETESS, SOR FILOTEA DE LA CRUZ

I have never written of my own choice, but at the urging of others, to whom with reason I might say, *You have compelled me.* But one truth I shall not deny (first, because it is well-known to all, and second, because although it has not worked in my favor, God has granted me the mercy of loving truth above all else), which is that from the moment I was first illuminated by the light of reason, my inclination toward letters has been so vehement, so overpowering, that not even the admonitions of others—and I have suffered many—nor my own meditations—and they have not been few— have been sufficient to cause me to forswear this natural impulse that God placed in me: the Lord God knows why, and for what purpose. . . .

■   ■   ■

Continuing the narration of my inclinations, of which I wish to give you a thorough account, I will tell you that I was not yet three years old when my mother determined to send one of my elder sisters to learn to read at a school for girls we call the *Amigas.* Affection, and mischief, caused me to follow her, and when I observed how she was being taught her lessions I was so inflamed with the desire to know how to read, that deceiving—for so I knew

---

Sor Juana Inés de la Cruz, "Response to the Most Illustrious Poetess, Sor Filotea de la Cruz," (1691), trans. Margaret Sayers Peden (1982).

it to be—the mistress, I told her that my mother had meant for me
to have lessons too. She did not believe it, as it was little to be
believed, but, to humor me, she acceded. I continued to go there,
and she continued to teach me, but now, as experience had dis-
abused her, with all seriousness; and I learned so quickly that
before my mother knew of it I could already read, for my teacher
had kept it from her in order to reveal the surprise and reap the
reward at one and the same time. And I, you may be sure, kept the
secret, fearing that I would be whipped for having acted without
permission. The woman who taught me, may God bless and keep
her, is still alive and can bear witness to all I say.

I also remember that in those days, my tastes being those common to that age, I abstained from eating cheese because I had
heard that it made one slow of wits, for in me the desire for learning was stronger than the desire for eating—as powerful as that is
in children. When later, being six or seven, and having learned how
to read and write, along with all the other skills of needle-work and
household arts that girls learn, it came to my attention that in
Mexico City there were Schools, and a University, in which one
studied the sciences. The moment I heard this, I began to plague
my mother with insistent and importunate pleas: she should dress
me in boy's clothing and send me to Mexico City to live with relatives, to study and be tutored at the University. She would not permit it, and she was wise, but I assuaged my disappointment by
reading the many and varied books belonging to my grandfather,
and there were not enough punishments, nor reprimands, to prevent me from reading: so that when I came to the city many mar-
veled, not so much at my natural wit, as at my memory, and at the
amount of learning I had mastered at an age when many have
scarcely learned to speak well.

I began to study Latin grammar—in all, I believe, I had no
more than twenty lessons—and so intense was my concern that
though among women (especially a woman in the flower of her
youth) the natural adornment of one's hair is held in such high
esteem, I cut off mine to the breadth of some four to six fingers,
measuring the place it had reached, and imposing upon myself
the condition that if by the time it had again grown to that length I
had not learned such and such a thing I had set for myself to learn
while my hair was growing, I would again cut it off as punishment

for being so slow-witted. And it did happen that my hair grew out and still I had not learned what I had set for myself—because my hair grew quickly and I learned slowly—and in fact I did cut it in punishment for such stupidity: for there seemed to me no cause for a head to be adorned with hair and naked of learning—which was the more desired embellishment. And so I entered the religious order, knowing that life there entailed certain conditions (I refer to superficial, and not fundamental, regards) most repugnant to my nature; but given the total antipathy I felt for marriage, I deemed convent life the least unsuitable and the most honorable I could elect if I were to insure my salvation. Working against that end, first (as, finally, the most important) was the matter of all the trivial aspects of my nature that nourished my pride, such as wishing to live alone, and wishing to have no obligatory occupation that would inhibit the freedom of my studies, nor the sounds of a community that would intrude upon the peaceful silence of my books. These desires caused me to falter some while in my decision, until certain learned persons enlightened me, explaining that they were temptation, and, with divine favor, I overcame them, and took upon myself the state which now so unworthily I hold. I believed that I was fleeing from myself, but—wretch that I am!—I brought with me my worst enemy, my inclination, which I do not know whether to consider a gift or a punishment from Heaven, for once dimmed and encumbered by the many activities common to Religion, that inclination exploded in me like gunpowder, proving how *privation is the source of appetite*. . . .

■   ■   ■

This manner of reflection has always been my habit, and is quite beyond my will to control; on the contrary, I am wont to become vexed that my intellect makes me weary; and I believed that it was so with everyone, as well as making verses, until experience taught me otherwise; and it is so strong in me this nature, or custom, that I look at nothing without giving it further examination. . . .

■   ■   ■

And what shall I tell you, lady, of the natural secrets I have discovered while cooking? I see that an egg holds together and fries in butter or in oil, but, on the contrary, in syrup shrivels into shreds; observe that to keep sugar in a liquid state one need only add a drop or two of water in which a quince or other bitter fruit has been soaked; observe that the yolk and the white of one egg are so dissimilar that each with sugar produces a result not obtainable with both together. I do not wish to weary you with such inconsequential matters, and make mention of them only to give you full notice of my nature, for I believe they will be occasion for laughter. But, lady, as women, what wisdom may be ours if not the philosophies of the kitchen? Lupercio Leonardo spoke well when he said: how well one may philosophize when preparing dinner. And I often say, when observing these trivial details: had Aristotle prepared victuals, he would have written more. And pursuing the manner of my cogitations, I tell you that this process is so continuous in me that I have no need for books. And on one occasion, when because of a grave upset of the stomach the physicians forbade me to study, I passed thus some days, but then I proposed that it would be less harmful if they allowed me books, because so vigorous and vehement were my cogitations that my spirit was consumed more greatly in a quarter of an hour than in four days' studying books. And thus they were persuaded to allow me to read. And moreover, lady, not even have my dreams been excluded from this ceaseless agitation of my imagination; indeed, in dreams it is wont to work more freely and less encumbered, collating with greater clarity and calm the gleanings of the day, arguing and making verses, of which I could offer you an extended catalogue, as well as of some arguments and inventions that I have better achieved sleeping than awake. I relinquish this subject in order not to tire you, for the above is sufficient to allow your discretion and acuity to penetrate perfectly and perceive my nature, as well as the beginnings, the methods, and the present state of my studies.

FURTHER READINGS
Stephanie Merrim, *Early Modern Women's Writing and Sor Juana Inés de la Cruz* (Vanderbilt University Press, 1999); Octavio Paz, *Sor Juana Or, the Traps of Faith*, translated by Margaret Sayers Peden

(Belknap Press, 1990); Sor Juana Inés de la Cruz, *Woman of Genius: The Intellectual Autobiography of Sor Juana de la Cruz* (Lime Rock Press, 1982); Norma Salazar, *Foolish Men: Sor Juana Inés de la Cruz As Spiritual Protagonist, Educational Prism, and Symbol for Hispanic Women* (Educational Studies Press, 1993); Pamela Kirk, *Sor Juana Inés de la Cruz: Religion, Art, and Feminism* (Continuum Publishing Group, 1998).

Jeanne Wakatsuki Houston
(1934–   )

Jeanne Wakatsuki was born in 1934 in California, the "nisei," or American-born, daughter of "issei" immigrants from Japan. Her family was interned at Manzanar during World War II, an experience she recalled in her memoir *Farewell to Manzanar* (1973), cowritten with her husband, James Houston. After the war, Wakatsuki completed a BA degree at the University of San Jose, and went to work for several years as a group worker and juvenile probation officer in San Mateo, California. She later left this position and focused on writing, travelling to France to study at the Sorbonne and the University of Paris. She then published her Manzanar memoir, as well as wrote the screenplay for the film adaptation of the book. In 1985, she published *Beyond Manzanar*, in which she examined the ways her experiences as a person trapped somewhere between Japanese and American cultures had shaped her identity as a woman. She lives today in Santa Cruz, California, with her family.

In *Farewell to Manzanar*, Jeanne Wakatsuki Houston recalls the experiences of her family during the internment. Forced from their home in Long Beach, where her father and brothers were fishermen, the Wakatsuki family spent the duration of the war with ten thousand other Japanese-Americans in the Manzanar internment camp, a dusty and barren site in the desert of Southern California. Seven years old in 1942, Jeanne Wakatsuki sometimes saw life in the camp as an adventure, but the impact of it on her parents—and especially on her father—was not lost on her. In this selection from her memoir, she writes about the ways in which internment transformed her father, and how it caused the ground to shift beneath the Wakatsuki family.

SHIKATA GA NAI

In December of 1941 Papa's disappearance didn't bother me nearly so much as the world I soon found myself in.

Jeanne Wakatsuki Houston and James D. Houston, "Shikata Ga Nai," from *Farewell to Manzanar* (1973).

He had been a jack-of-all-trades. When I was born he was farming near Inglewood. Later, when he started fishing, we moved to Ocean Park, near Santa Monica, and until they picked him up, that's where we lived, in a big frame house with a brick fireplace, a block back from the beach. We were the only Japanese family in the neighborhood. Papa liked it that way. He didn't want to be labeled or grouped by anyone. But with him gone and no way of knowing what to expect, my mother moved all of us down to Terminal Island. [My brother] Woody already lived there, and one of my older sisters had married a Terminal Island boy. Mama's first concern now was to keep the family together; and once the war began, she felt safer there than isolated racially in Ocean Park. But for me, at age seven, the island was a country as foreign as India or Arabia would have been. It was the first time I had lived among other Japanese, or gone to school with them, and I was terrified all the time.

This was partly Papa's fault. One of his threats to keep us younger kids in line was "I'm going to sell you to the Chinaman." When I had entered kindergarten two years earlier, I was the only Oriental in the class. They sat me next to a Caucasian girl who happened to have very slanted eyes. I looked at her and began to scream, certain Papa had sold me out at last. My fear of her ran so deep I could not speak of it, even to Mama, couldn't explain why I was screaming. For two weeks I had nightmares about this girl, until the teachers finally moved me to the other side of the room. And it was still with me, this fear of Oriental faces, when we moved to Terminal Island.

In those days it was a company town, a ghetto owned and controlled by the canneries. The men went after fish, and whenever the boats came back—day or night—the women would be called to process the catch while it was fresh. One in the afternoon or four in the morning, it made no difference. My mother had to go to work right after we moved there. I can still hear the whistle—two toots for French's, three for Van Camp's—and she and Chizu would be out of bed in the middle of the night, heading for the cannery.

The house we lived in was nothing more than a shack, a barracks with single plank walls and rough wooden floors, like the cheapest kind of migrant workers' housing. The people around us were hardworking, boisterous, a little proud of their nickname, *yo-go-re,* which meant literally *uncouth one,* or roughneck, or dead-end kid. They not only spoke Japanese exclusively, they spoke a dialect peculiar to Kyushu, where their families had come from in Japan, a rough, fisherman's language, full of oaths and insults. Instead of saying *ba-ka-ta-re,* a common insult meaning *stupid,* Terminal Islanders would say *ba-ka-ya-ro,* a coarser and exclusively masculine use of the word, which implies gross stupidity. They would swagger and pick on outsiders and persecute anyone who didn't speak as they did. That was what made my own time there so hateful. I had never spoken anything but English, and the other kids in the second grade despised me for it. They were tough and mean, like ghetto kids anywhere. Each day after school I dreaded their ambush. My brother Kiyo, three years older, would wait for me at the door, where we would decide whether to run straight home together, or split up, or try a new and unexpected route.

None of these kids ever actually attacked. It was the threat that frightened us, their fearful looks, and the noises they would make, like miniature Samurai, in a language we couldn't understand.

At the time it seemed we had been living under this reign of fear for years. In fact, we lived there about two months. Late in February the navy decided to clear Terminal Island completely. Even though most of us were American-born, it was dangerous having that many Orientals so close to the Long Beach Naval Station, on the opposite end of the island. We had known something like this was coming. But, like Papa's arrest, not much could be done ahead of time. There were four of us kids still young enough to be living with Mama, plus Granny, her mother, sixty-five then, speaking no English, and nearly blind. Mama didn't know where else she could get work, and we had nowhere else to move *to.* On February 25 the choice was made for us. We were given forty-eight hours to clear out.

The secondhand dealers had been prowling around for weeks, like wolves, offering humiliating prices for goods and furniture they knew many of us would have to sell sooner or later. Mama had left all but her most valuable possessions in Ocean Park, simply because she had nowhere to put them. She had brought along her pottery, her silver, heirlooms like the kimonos Granny had brought from Japan, tea sets, lacquered tables, and one fine old set of china, blue and white porcelain, almost translucent.

On the day we were leaving, Woody's car was so crammed with boxes and luggage and kids we had just run out of room. Mama had to sell this china.

One of the dealers offered her fifteen dollars for it. She said it was a full setting for twelve and worth at least two hundred. He said fifteen was his top price. Mama started to quiver. Her eyes blazed up at him. She had been packing all night and trying to calm down Granny, who didn't understand why we were moving again and what all the rush was about. Mama's nerves were shot, and now navy jeeps were patrolling the streets. She didn't say another word. She just glared at this man, all the rage and frustration channeled at him through her eyes.

He watched her for a moment and said he was sure he couldn't pay more than seventeen fifty for that china. She reached into the red velvet case, took out a dinner plate and hurled it at the floor right in front of his feet.

The man leaped back shouting, "Hey! Hey, don't do that! Those are valuable dishes!"

Mama took out another dinner plate and hurled it at the floor, then another and another, never moving, never opening her mouth, just quivering and glaring at the retreating dealer, with tears streaming down her cheeks. He finally turned and scuttled out the door, heading for the next house. When he was gone she stood there smashing cups and bowls and platters until the whole set lay in scattered blue and white fragments across the wooden floor.

■ ■ ■

The American Friends Service helped us find a small house in Boyle Heights, another minority ghetto, in downtown Los Angeles, now inhabited briefly by a few hundred Terminal Island refugees. Executive Order 9066 had been signed by President Roosevelt, giving the War Department authority to define military areas in the western states and to exclude from them anyone who might threaten the war effort. There was a lot of talk about internment, or moving inland, or something like that in store for all Japanese Americans. I remember my brothers sitting around the table talking very intently about what we were going to do, how we would keep the family together. They had seen how quickly Papa was removed, and they knew now that he would not be back for quite a while. Just before leaving Terminal Island Mama had received her first letter, from Bismarck, North Dakota. He had been imprisoned at Fort Lincoln, in an all-male camp for enemy aliens.

Papa had been the patriarch. He had always decided everything in the family. With him gone, my brothers, like councilors in the absence of a chief, worried about what should be done. The ironic thing is, there wasn't much left to decide. These were mainly days of quiet, desperate waiting for what seemed at the time to be inevitable. There is a phrase the Japanese use in such situations, when something difficult must be endured. You would hear the older heads, the Issei, telling others very quietly, "*Shikata ga nai*" (It cannot be helped). "*Shikata ga nai*" (It must be done).

Mama and Woody went to work packing celery for a Japanese produce dealer. Kiyo and my sister May and I enrolled in the local school, and what sticks in my memory from those few weeks is the teacher—not her looks, her remoteness. In Ocean Park my teacher had been a kind, grandmotherly woman who used to sail with us in Papa's boat from time to time and who wept the day we had to leave. In Boyle Heights the teacher felt cold and distant. I was confused by all the moving and was having trouble with the classwork, but she would never help me out. She would have nothing to do with me.

This was the first time I had felt outright hostility from a Caucasian. Looking back, it is easy enough to explain. Public attitudes toward the Japanese in California were shifting rapidly. In the first few months of the Pacific war, America was on the run. Tolerance had turned to distrust and irrational fear. The hundred-year-old tradition of anti-Orientalism on the west coast soon resurfaced, more vicious than ever. Its result became clear about a month later, when we were told to make our third and final move.

The name Manzanar meant nothing to us when we left Boyle Heights. We didn't know where it was or what it was. We went because the government ordered us to. And, in the case of my older brothers and sisters, we went with a certain amount of relief. They had all heard stories of Japanese homes being attacked, of beatings in the streets of California towns. They were as frightened of the Caucasians as Caucasians were of us. Moving, under what appeared to be government protection, to an area less directly threatened by the war seemed not such a bad idea at all. For some it actually sounded like a fine adventure.

Our pickup point was a Buddhist church in Los Angeles. It was very early, and misty, when we got there with our luggage. Mama had bought heavy coats for all of us. She grew up in eastern Washington and knew that anywhere inland in early April would be cold. I was proud of my new coat, and I remember sitting on a duffel bag trying to be friendly with the Greyhound driver. I smiled at him. He didn't smile back. He was befriending no one. Someone tied a numbered tag to my collar and to the duffel bag (each family was given a number, and that became our official designation until the camps were closed), someone else passed out box lunches for the trip, and we climbed aboard.

I had never been outside Los Angeles County, never traveled more than ten miles from the coast, had never even ridden on a bus. I was full of excitement, the way any kid would be, and wanted to look out the window. But for the first few hours the shades were drawn. Around me other people played cards, read magazines, dozed, waiting. I settled back, waiting too, and finally fell asleep. The bus felt very secure to me. Almost half its passengers were immediate relatives. Mama and my older brothers had succeeded in keeping most of us together, on the same bus, headed for the same camp. I didn't realize until much later what a job that was. The strategy had been, first, to have everyone living in the same district when the evacuation began, and then to get all of us included under the same family number, even though names had been changed by marriage. Many families weren't as lucky as ours and suffered months of anguish while trying to arrange transfers from one camp to another.

We rode all day. By the time we reached our destination, the shades were up. It was late afternoon. The first thing I saw was a yellow swirl across a blurred, reddish setting sun. The bus was being pelted by what sounded like splattering rain. It wasn't rain. This was my first look at something I would soon know very well, a billowing flurry of dust and sand churned up by the wind through Owens Valley.

We drove past a barbed-wire fence, through a gate, and into an open space where trunks and sacks and packages had been dumped from the baggage trucks that drove out ahead of us. I could see a few tents set up, the first rows of black barracks, and beyond them, blurred by sand, rows of barracks that seemed to spread for miles across this plain. People were sitting on cartons or milling around, with their backs to the wind, waiting to see which friends or relatives might be on this bus. As we approached, they turned or stood up, and some moved toward us expectantly. But inside the bus no one stirred. No one waved or spoke. They just stared out the windows, ominously silent. I didn't understand this. Hadn't we finally arrived, our whole family intact? I opened a window, leaned out, and yelled happily. "Hey! This whole bus is full of Wakatsukis!"

Outside, the greeters smiled. Inside there was an explosion of laughter, hysterical, tension-breaking laughter that left my brothers choking and whacking each other across the shoulders.

We had pulled up just in time for dinner. The mess halls weren't completed yet. An outdoor chow line snaked around a half-finished building that broke a good part of the wind. They issued us army mess kits, the round metal kind that fold over, and plopped in scoops of canned Vienna sausage, canned string beans, steamed rice that had been cooked too long, and on top of the rice a serving of canned apricots. The Caucasian servers were thinking that the fruit poured over rice would make a good dessert. Among the Japanese, of course, rice is never eaten with sweet foods, only with salty or savory foods. Few of us could eat such a mixture. But at this point no one dared protest. It would have been impolite. I was horrified when I saw the apricot syrup seeping through my little mound of rice. I opened my mouth to complain. My mother jabbed me in the back to keep quiet. We moved on through the line and joined the others squatting in the lee of half-raised walls, dabbing courteously at what was, for almost everyone there, an inedible concoction.

After dinner we were taken to Block 16, a cluster of fifteen barracks that had just been finished a day or so earlier—although finished was hardly the word for it. The shacks were built of one thickness of pine planking covered with tarpaper. They sat on concrete footings, with about two feet of open space between the floorboards and the ground. Gaps showed between the planks, and as the weeks passed and the green wood dried out, the gaps widened. Knotholes gaped in the uncovered floor.

Each barracks was divided into six units, sixteen by twenty feet, about the size of a living room, with one bare bulb hanging from the ceiling and an oil stove for heat. We were assigned two of these for the twelve people in our family group; and our official family "number" was enlarged by three digits—16 plus the number of this barracks. We were issued steel army cots, two brown army blankets each, and some mattress covers, which my brothers stuffed with straw.

The first task was to divide up what space we had for sleeping. Bill and Woody contributed a blanket each and partitioned off the first room: one side for Bill and Tomi, one side for Woody and Chizu and their baby girl. Woody also got the stove, for heating formulas.

The people who had it hardest during the first few months were young couples like these, many of whom had married just before the evacuation began, in order not to be separated and sent to different camps. Our two rooms were crowded, but at least it was all in the family. My oldest sister and her husband were shoved into one of those sixteen-by-twenty-foot compartments with six people they had never seen before—two other couples, one recently married like themselves, the other with two teenage boys. Partitioning off a room like that wasn't easy. It was bitter cold when we arrived, and the wind did not abate. All they had to use for room dividers were those army blankets, two of which were barely enough to keep one person warm. They argued over whose blanket should be sacrificed and later argued about noise at night—the parents wanted their boys asleep by 9:00 p.m.—and they continued arguing over matters like that for six months, until my sister and her husband left to harvest sugar beets in Idaho. It was grueling work up there, and wages were pitiful, but when the call came through camp for workers to alleviate the wartime labor shortage, it sounded better than their life at Manzanar. They knew they'd have, if nothing else, a room, perhaps a cabin of their own.

That first night in Block 16, the rest of us squeezed into the second room—Granny, Lillian, age fourteen, Ray, thirteen, May, eleven, Kiyo, ten, Mama, and me. I didn't mind this at all at the time. Being youngest meant I got to sleep with Mama. And before we went to bed I had a great time jumping up and down on the mattress. The boys had stuffed so much straw into hers, we had to flatten it some so we wouldn't slide off. I slept with her every night after that until Papa came back.

FURTHER READINGS

Page Smith, *Democracy on Trial: The Japanese American Evacuation and Relocation in World War II* (Simon & Schuster, 1995); Maria Hong, ed., *Growing Up Asian American: An Anthology* (W. Morrow, 1993); Mei Takaya Nakano, *Japanese American Women: Three Generations, 1890–1990* (Mina Press, 1990); John Tateishi, ed., *And Justice For All: An Oral History of the Japanese American Detention Camps* (Random House, 1984); Jeanne Wakatsuki Houston, *Beyond Manzanar: Views of Asian American Womanhood* (Copra Press, 1985); Elaine Kim, *Asian American Literature: An Introduction to the Writings and Their Social Context* (Temple University Press, 1984); Jessie A. Garrett and Ronald C. Larson, eds., *Camp and Community: Manzanar and the Owens Valley* (California State University, Japanese American Oral History Project, 1977).

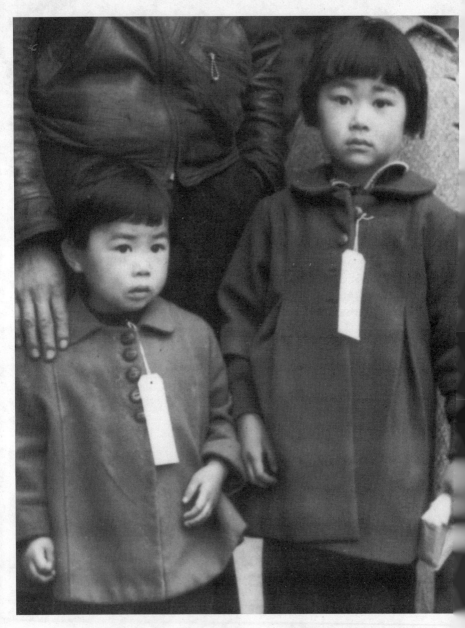

Dorothea Lange, *Hayward, California, Members of the Mochida Family Awaiting Evacuation Bus*, 1942 (detail).

National Archives, Still Picture Branch, College Park, Maryland. Control #NWDNS-210-G-C153.

Season's Greetings

Joan Myers, *Christmas Card from Japanese Relocation Camp,* 1985.

From Joan Myers and Gary Okihiro, Whispered Silences: Japanese Americans and World War II. University of Washington Press, *1996. Copyright © 1996 Joan Myers, used by permission of artist.*

Joan Myers, *Entry Station, Manzanar, California*, 1985.

Mary Crow Dog (1953–)

Mary Brave Bird was called *iyeska*, half blood. She was born on the Rosebud Reservation in South Dakota in 1953, and grew up in a one-room cabin without running water or electricity. Her grandfather fed the family by hunting rabbits, deer, squirrels, and porcupines. At the missionary school, sisters "taught" Indian children with a leather strap, and by the time she was ten, she could hold down a pint of whiskey. Raped at fifteen, despairing of the future, she was a rebel looking for a life that offered some meaning and purpose.

The American Indian Movement that came into existence in 1968 "hit the reservations like a tornado...." In 1971 Mary met Leonard Crow Dog, a Lakota peyote priest and medicine man who would later become her husband. Through him, she found a place in the American Indian Movement, and joined the sit-in in Washington, D.C., at the Bureau of Indian Affairs. In 1972, she was among the two thousand Indians who occupied Wounded Knee for seventy-one days. The occupation was an effort to take back control of the reservation from tribal leaders who had "sold out" to Uncle Sam, and to remind Indians and whites alike of the slaughter of Big Foot's tribe in 1893 when the Ghost Dance fever swept the reservations. During the siege, under fire, Mary gave birth to a son. "They put me in jail at Pine Ridge and took my baby away.... In 1975 the feds put the muzzles of their M-16's against my head, threatening to blow me away. It's hard being an Indian woman."

Lakota Woman is Mary Crow Dog's autobiography, but it is also the history of the siege at Wounded Knee, and the story of Crow Dog's friend Annie Mae Aquash, who was found dead in the snow at the bottom of a ravine on the Pine Ridge Reservation, her hands cut off by the FBI and sent to Washington for fingerprint identification.

Lakota Woman was told to and written with Richard Erdoes, author of *Lame Deer*, *The Sun Dance People*, and *The Pueblo Indians*.

TWO CUT-OFF HANDS

They won't let Indians like me live. That's alright. I don't want to grow up to be an old woman.

—*Annie Mae Aquash*

Nobody could ever say anything bad about my friend Annie Mae, because she never did anything bad in her life. She never walked into my home, she always burst in, full of energy. She was a small woman, hardly more than five feet tall, but she dominated those around her by the force of her personality. She was pretty, too, with her wide, smiling mouth, her Indian eyes and cheekbones, her flowing black hair.

She was always the first up in the morning, making sure that everybody got fed. She saw to it that all the men had clean clothes. She often took dirty clothes to the river and washed them herself. She combed and braided all the men's hair. Whenever she saw young girls just sitting around and gossiping, doing nothing all day but lying on a couch putting on makeup, she would tell them to get off their asses and start doing something worthwhile. She was happy to clean house, have everybody sweeping up and mopping. She was a good cook. She taught me and a lot of other women some good Indian recipes. Once she danced into my kitchen, danced around the table with a whole basket full of frogs she had caught in the river and killed. She cooked us up some frog's legs French-Canadian style. She would do fine bead-work for you. All you had to do was ask her. She learned how to make Sioux moccasins from Leonard's mother. She was gifted and had a flair for designing clothes, for creating very imaginative Indian fashions. She even modeled them for white customers. She was a natural-born leader. She had held responsible positions as director of Indian youth and antialcohol programs. She played a very active role within the Indian movement, both at national AIM headquarters in Minneapolis and on the West Coast. For me she was a rock to lean on, a rock with a lot of heart. She did not deserve to die.

Mary Crow Dog with Richard Erdoes, from *Lakota Woman* (1990).

Annie Mae was a Micmac Indian, born and raised on a tiny reservation in Nova Scotia, not far from Halifax. Though she lived in Canada, two thousand miles from Rosebud, her life was almost a copy of mine, or of that of thousands of other young Indian girls and women. Instead of on a reservation, she lived on a reserve. Instead of a Bureau of Indian Affairs regulating and interfering with her existence, it was a department. The white boss lording it over the Micmacs was an agent, not a superintendent. The men who harassed her were mounties, not state troopers. Otherwise everything was the same north of the border. She lived in the same kind of tar paper shack that I did. She too had to do without electricity, indoor plumbing, central heating, running water, and paved roads. She too was often hungry, down to one meal a day, eating anything she could find. Her mother had the same name as I— Mary Ellen. All she could tell me about her father was that he was a good fiddler who one day vamoosed. Her mother then married a good, hard-working, sober-minded man, but he got sick and died. Her mother then came apart, did hardly anything but gamble and smoke, and took off to marry again, abandoning her half-grown children, leaving them to fend for themselves.

Annie Mae had two sisters and one brother. One of the sisters, Mary, was especially close to her. She told me that Mary was very much like herself. The kids helped each other, Annie Mae having to take the part of her absent mother. Annie Mae could live off the sea, clamming and fishing. She worked as a berry picker and spud picker at one dollar per hour. Spud picking was back-breaking work. When she was seventeen she decided there was nothing to hold her on the Micmac reserve. She was eager and determined to make something of herself, to find out things. For many Micmacs, Boston was the mecca, the big city with a capital B, and to Boston she went.

She had met a young Micmac, Jake Maloney, and married him. They had two daughters. For a while she lived like a white middle-class housewife in a middle-class home. She was a sharp dresser, even wore dyed beehive hairdos, but she wanted to remain an Indian. She wanted her daughters to grow up as Indians. Jake's and her beliefs conflicted. They started to quarrel. He beat her. She left and divorced him. She had to fight him for the custody of her daughters. In the end she won. Her own children, at one time, told her that they preferred living with their father because he could give them the many things they wanted, things Annie Mae would not be able to give them if they lived Indian style on Boston's skid row. They preferred their white stepmother to their real one. Annie Mae grew into a Native American militant. She got into the same kind of fights that Barb and I had fought. She gave herself to the cause and that meant giving her children to her sister Mary to care for. That was hard and heart-wrenching. It was the sacrifice Annie Mae made to the movement—her motherhood. One thing she got out of her marriage: her husband was a martial arts freak and a professional karate teacher. Annie Mae became his sparring partner and learned some good chops and kicks. She knew when and on whom to use them.

Annie Mae met her first AIM people on November 26, 1970, when Russell Means and two hundred militants buried Plymouth Rock under a ton of sand, as a "symbolic burial of the white man's conquest." Among the tribes represented were New England Wampanoags, Narraganset, and Passamaquoddy, as well as a group of Micmacs, Annie Mae among them, calling themselves the "first victims of the wrath of the WASP." Later Annie Mae was among those who with war whoops boarded *Mayflower II*, the replica of the vessel that had brought the pilgrims to the New World. She watched Russell climb up the rigging, waving a pirate's blunder-buss, shouting: "Don't let us pick this up! We don't want to take up the gun again. But if you force us to, watch out!" This first meeting with AIM had on Annie Mae the same effect my first encounter had on me. It decided her fate. It decided when and how she would die.

In the beginning of 1972, or thereabouts, Annie Mae found her-self a lover, Nogeeshik Aquash. Nogeeshik was a Canadian Indian who, Annie Mae told me, came from an island in the Great Lakes area. He looked and acted like an Indian, but at the same time was unlike any other Indian I knew. He was good-looking in a sinister way. His face was very pale with a sort of Fu-Manchu mustache and a tiny, scraggly goatee. He was very slim, elegantly emaciated. He had the movements of a cat, or maybe a spider. Paleness contrast-ing with his black hair, he sometimes reminded me of a handsome ghost. He is a good artist and lithographer. He dressed Indian, but again in a strange, unique way. He always wore a special sort of little, flat black hat with a feather stuck in it. Together they worked in the movement. On the side they started Indian fashion shows and became involved in exhibiting and sponsoring Indian crafts and jewelry. Annie Mae took part in the takeover of the BIA building and later she and Nogeeshik went to Wounded Knee. Right after Annie Mae helped me give birth, she and Nogeeshik were married in the Indian way. As Leonard was then with Russell Means in Washington trying to arrange a cease-fire, our friend the medicine man Wallace Black Elk performed the ceremony. They were joined together with the pipe and the star blanket. They were cedared up and smoked the sacred tobacco while four men and four women made a flesh offering for them. "A marriage like this," Black Elk told them, "lasts forever."

It did not work out that way. Their relationship turned sour. For a while they lived in Ottawa and that town was not good for them. Nogeeshik did a lot of barhopping and sometimes took Annie Mae along. He was moody to begin with, but when drunk he became abusive. Annie Mae told me, "He was torturing my mind. He did not treat me right." White women were attracted to him and he flaunted them in Annie Mae's face. Once or twice, she said, he beat her, or at least tried to. She could take care of herself if it came to physical confrontations. They split up a few times but always got together again until finally she got to a point where she could not take it anymore. She told me, "We had a quarrel and he broke the pipe, the sacred pipe we were married with at the Knee. For no reason at all. Then I knew that it was all over and I left him for good."

After that she stayed on and off with us at Crow Dog's Paradise. She got very high up in the councils of AIM, to the extent of helping set movement policies. She had no luck with men. She was a very strong-hearted woman and that made some men uncomfortable. In the months before her death she got really close to Leonard Peltier. She admired him, and could not do enough for him. I still think that he would have been the ideal man for her, but things turned out tragically for both of them.

Annie Mae came to us to take part in the 1974 and 1975 Sun Dance. She came alone. She put up a tipi in back of our house and there she lived. She liked being with us Sioux. She tried learning to speak our language. She started making Sioux arts and crafts. Tough in a fight, she was gentle and comforting to any of the people who were sick or in despair. Everybody liked her, and many depended on her. She pared her existence down to the very basics, to the simplest way of tipi living.

At that time many other people besides her were camping on our place, and someone stole a necklace and earrings she had, worth about five or six hundred dollars. She said, "I have no need of such things anymore. Whoever took them is welcome to the stuff. I am only sorry that skins are ripping off skins." She came over to the house and dumped all her clothes and possessions on the table, telling me, "Keep these. This is for you. I'd rather not have anything at all, just whatever I have on my back. That's good enough for my execution." Ever since Wounded Knee she had had premonitions of approaching death. "I've fought too hard," she said. "They won't let Indians like me live. That's all right. I don't want to grow up to be an old woman." She talked that way often, almost cheerfully, without a trace of sentimentality. All she was left with then were her jeans, ribbon shirt, and Levi's jacket. That was all.

She wanted to take Leonard and me to the Micmac country, to Nova Scotia, to Shubenakadie, to Pictou's Landing, to all the tiny Micmac reserves which, as she jokingly said, are not much larger than a football field—the king-size ones. She told me that her Micmac people were losing their culture and their language. She said that every year her people go to an island and have ceremonies there, but that these rituals are becoming Christianized. She wanted to take Leonard to her tribe to teach them, to let them see that the old Indian ways still exist.

Leonard taught her the way of Grandfather Peyote. She liked to come to the meetings and was learning the songs. During a half-moon ceremony she had a vision. She was sitting beside me when it came to her. She said that she saw the moon turn into a prison, a jail with round walls, and inside it she saw the tiny figures of Indians leaving this prison, walking toward a big fire, walking right into the flames. And inside the fire was a man beckoning to her. And so she also walked into the flames. She told me: "I have experienced pain and the ecstasy and the glory of the fire which will consume me soon. A fire that will make me free."

Annie Mae still traveled a lot. Wherever Indians fought for their rights, Annie Mae was there. She helped the Menominee warriors take over a monastery. She told me that she was packing a gun. She said, "If any of my brothers are in a position where they're being shot at, or being killed, I go there to fight with them. I'd rather die than stand by and see them destroyed." No matter how often Annie Mae left us, she always showed up again at our place.

I read somewhere in an anthropology book that we Sioux "thrive on a culture of excitement." During the years from 1973 to 1975 we had more than enough excitement for even the most macho warrior, more than we could handle. Wilson, the tribal chairman at Pine Ridge, had established a regime of terror. Being shot at or having one's house fire-bombed were daily occurrences Pine Ridge people had to live with. Pine Ridge and our own reservation have a common border, and the violence spilled over onto Rosebud. Many people who either opposed Wilson, belonged to AIM or OSCRO, or had been at Wounded Knee were brutally murdered. Some estimate that as many as two hundred and fifty people, women and children among them, were killed during this time—out of a population of eight thousand! Between forty and fifty of these murders have been listed in official government files. The vast majority of these killings were never investigated. Among the victims was one of our best friends, Pedro Bissonette, leader of OSCRO, the Oglala Sioux Civil Rights Organization. He was shot to death by tribal police on a lonely road, "resisting arrest" as they claimed. One of his relatives, Jeanette Bissonette, was shot and killed driving home from the burial of another victim. Byron De Sersa was shot to death on account of an article critical of the Wilson regime his father had written in a local Indian newspaper. Wallace Black Elk's brother was killed in a mysterious explosion when entering his home and turning on the light. Our oldest and most respected medicine man, Frank Fools Crow, was firebombed and had his horses killed and his sweat lodge with all his sacred things destroyed. Leonard's family suffered too. His niece, Jancita Eagle Deer, was killed in an unexplained "accident" after having been savagely beaten. She had last been seen in the car of her lover, who later turned out to be an informer and who had brutally mistreated her many times before. Jancita was then suing a high South Dakota official for rape. Her mother, Delphine, Leonard's older sister, wanted to take up the suit, but was beaten to death by a BIA policeman who claimed "drunkenness" as his excuse. Her battered corpse, her arms and legs fractured, was found in the snow, the tears frozen on her cheeks. A nephew went up into the hills and never came back. His body was found with a bullet in it. And so it went, on and on.

It came to a point where nobody felt safe anymore, not even in their own homes. Once, when a car backfired near our house, all of our children immediately took cover under beds and behind walls. They thought the goons had arrived. The situation was aggravated by the fact that the movement became an object of attention for the FBI's Cointelpro and Cablesplicer projects. AIM was infiltrated by a number of informers and agents provocateurs. I hardly think that AIM deserved that much attention. This infiltration, together with the never-ending violence, brought on a general state of paranoia. The agents stirred up mistrust among us until nobody trusted anybody anymore. Husbands suspected their wives, sisters their brothers. Old friends who had fought many civil rights battles together began to be afraid of each other. Those inside prisons suspected those who remained free. Men sentenced to longer terms suspected those who were released sooner. Even some of the leaders began doubting each other—and by then Annie Mae was a leader.

It did not surprise me when the rumors started that she was an FBI undercover agent. People were saying: "Look at that woman, she is always traveling. Wherever something happens, she's there. So she must be an informer." Annie Mae came to me and cried. She said, "The goons are after me. They might kill me as they have killed so many others. I don't know what to do. If I get killed I don't want my children to think that I died working for the enemy. Promise me, if the goons blow me away, to tell my girls that I died true to my beliefs, fighting for my people."

For a while Annie Mae stayed at the point of greatest danger. She was helping Sioux women intimidated by the goons in Oglala, on the Pine Ridge Reservation, where Dennis Banks had set up a camp of opponents to Wilson's rule. That was like going into the lions' den. On June 26, 1975, the FBI invaded the little settlement in force under the pretext of investigating, of all things, the theft of an old pair of boots. Whether the FBI people were just dumb or whether they wanted to provoke an incident, I cannot say. What is sure is that their wading into that explosive situation was the spark that blew up the whole powder keg. A firefight started. It ended with one Indian and two agents dead. It may have been pure coincidence that this happened on the ninety-ninth anniversary of the Custer battle. Among those accused of having shot the feds was Leonard Peltier, Annie Mae's close friend. The witnesses against him later withdrew their testimony, saying that they had been nowhere near and that they had testified against him only under threats and compulsions. Peltier is now doing two lifetimes in the white man's prisons.

In the aftermath of this incident, the situation at Pine Ridge got totally out of hand. The whole reservation was in a state of panic. Annie Mae did not even dare use her own name anymore. She took refuge with us, again staying in the tipi behind our house. She was at Crow Dog's place when the big bust occurred. On September 5, 1975, the whole SWAT team, about a hundred and eighty agents in bulletproof vests with M-16s, rubber boats, helicopters, heavy vehicles, and artificial smog fell upon our and Old Man Henry's homes, as well as upon Annie Mae's little tent and the cabin of Crow Dog's sister and brother-in-law, less than a mile away. It was an Omaha Beach type of assault, like the movies one saw on TV of actions in Vietnam. We found out, much later, that the FBI thought that Peltier was hiding out at our place, which was completely untrue.

When the feds saw Annie Mae, they said, "We've been looking for you." They handcuffed her, throwing her around like a rag doll. When they were dragging her into the squad car she smiled at me and gave me the Indian Power sign with her fists even though she was handcuffed. They questioned her and questioned her although she had not been any where near the scene of the shootout. The FBI was convinced that she knew where Peltier was hiding. They knew how close she was to him. Then, suddenly, they let her go for lack of evidence. She came to see me. She related to me what had happened to her. The agents had told her that she would not live long if she did not tell them everything she knew and some things she could not have known—where some people had gone to ground, for instance. If she did not talk and if she did not do everything they wanted. she wasn't going to live. They would make sure she'd be dead—or put her away for the rest of her life, which would be worse.

She said to me: "They offered me my freedom and money if I'd testify the way they wanted. I have those two choices now. I chose my kind of freedom, not their kind, even if I have to die. They let me go because they are sure I'll lead them to Peltier. They're watching me. I don't hear them or see them, but I know they're out there somewhere. I can feel it."

I told her to stay with us if she wanted to, she was welcome to move in with me anytime. I told her to take care of herself. She said: "Maybe this is the last time we can talk together. Remember, your husband is an important man to his people. Love him and protect him from all bad things. Don't let this white man's culture destroy him. Don't let him drink. Don't let him go with people who might do him harm. Watch him. He is a good man. He is needed."

I saw her one more time in Pierre, South Dakota, when Leonard went on trial. She had come to support him and to comfort me, to give us courage. We were all staying at the Holiday Inn. She came to my room. She did not say anything much, she was just sitting on the bed looking at me. She said, "I just wanted to see you. You won't see me again." We talked about a few unimportant things, said our goodbyes, shook hands, hugged each other, and she cried and cried. That was the last time I saw her. It was as if she had heard Hinhan, the owl, hoot for her, death calling her. She knew and she accepted it.

In the last days of November, 1975, she just disappeared. Everybody said, "Annie Mae has gone underground." At the same time I had to take leave of my husband, who was sent to prison on Wounded Knee-related charges. Leonard was held in Lewisburg, Pennsylvania, a maximum-security prison. I went with my little son Pedro to New York to stay with white friends so that I could be close to him, within visiting distance. It was there, in New York, in early March 1976, that I got a phone call from a friend in Rapid City, telling me that Annie Mae Aquash had been found dead in the snow at the foot of a steep bluff near Wanblee on the Pine Ridge Reservation. The FBI was there at once, swarming over her. They shipped her to Scotts Bluff for an autopsy. They cut her hands off to send to Washington for identification—a needless cruelty as they could have made fingerprints on the spot without mutilating her. It seems that those who killed her had also raped her. She was buried in a pauper's grave. After the FBI had identified her, an official report was issued that she had died of exposure. The implication was that here was just another drunken Indian passing out and freezing to death. But no alcohol or drugs had been found in the autopsy.

Annie Mae's friends and relatives were not satisfied. They obtained a court order to exhume the body and had their own pathologist perform a second autopsy. He at once found a bullet hole in her skull, found the bullet, too, a .32-caliber slug. He also found the cut-off hands thrown with the body into the coffin. William Janklow, the attorney general of the State of South Dakota, had said that the only way to deal with renegade AIM Indians was to put a bullet through their heads, and someone had taken the hint. Leonard could occasionally call me collect from the prison. When I told him that Annie Mae had died, and how, he wept over the phone. We cried together. He would have liked to be the one to bury her, but that could not be.

Annie Mae Aquash is dead. Leonard Peltier is doing two life-times. Maybe the prison hacks let him wear the moccasins she made for him. Nogeeshik was in a bad car accident and is now a wheelchair case. Leonard and I still have a lot of things she once treasured, which she gave to us. Someday I am going to find out who killed this good, gently tough, gifted friend of mine who did not deserve to die. Someday I will tell her daughters that she died for them, died like a warrior. Someday I will see Annie Mae. In a strange way I feel that she died so that I, and many others, could survive. That she died because she had made a secret vow, like a Sun Dancer who, obedient to his vow, pierces his flesh and under-goes the pain for all the people so that the people may live.

FURTHER READINGS
Mary Crow Dog and Richard Erdoes, *Lakota Woman* (Grove Weidenfeld, 1990); Mary Brave Bird (Mary Crow Dog) with Richard Erdoes, *Ohitika Woman* (Grove Press, 1993); Leonard Crow Dog and Richard Erdoes, *Crow Dog: Four Generations of Sioux Medicine Men* (HarperCollins, 1995); Paul Chaat Smith & Robert Allen Warrior, *Like a Hurricane: The Indian Movement from Alcatraz to Wounded Knee* (New Press, 1996).

Terry Tempest Williams
(1955–   )

Western naturalist, storyteller, writer, and feminist, Terry Tempest Williams was born in Corona, California, in 1955. Raised in a Mormon family in Salt Lake City, Utah, she received a BA in English and an MA in Environmental Education from the University of Utah. She has worked as Curator of Environmental Education and Naturalist-in-Residence at the Utah Museum of Natural History.

Williams writes eloquently in defense of the wild places around her. She has called herself "a naturalist first and a writer second," and her writing reflects her deep sense of the importance of seeing humans as in and not above nature. Many of her earliest writings were aimed at children; *The Secret Language of Snow* (1984), written with Ted Major, was a study of Inuit and Kobuk ways of seeing their environment, and *Between Cattails* (1985) tells the story of her grandmother's fostering of Williams's childhood interests in bird-watching and marshland ecology. However, Williams is best known for her collections of interrelated essays, published as *Pieces of White Shell: A Journey to Navajoland* (1984), *Coyote's Canyon* (1989), *Earthly Messengers* (1989), *Refuge: An Unnatural History of Family and Place* (1991), *An Unspoken Hunger: Stories from the Field* (1994), and *Desert Quartet: An Erotic Landscape* (1995).

In addition to her concern for ecology, Williams's writings are deeply informed by her Mormon upbringing and her feminism. From Mormonism, she draws a sense of the sacredness of everyday life, of the mystical qualities associated with connecting to one's place on this earth and to the history which lies behind it. But Williams, who is not an Orthodox Mormon herself, has also been critical of the subservient role which Mormon women have been forced to play in their communities. Her sense of women's centrality and their intrinsic connectedness to the earth resonates in her writing. Describing *Refuge*, she argued that she wrote the book "to remember my mother and grandmothers and what it was that we shared, and as a way of recalling how women conduct their lives in the midst of family, in the midst of illness, in the midst of death—in the midst of day-to-day living. I wrote *Refuge* to celebrate the correspondence between the landscape of my childhood and the landscape of my family, to explore the idea of how one finds refuge in change. And it is *Refuge* that gave me my voice as a woman."

In this selection from the book *Refuge*, "The Clan of One-Breasted Women," Williams examines life as a Mormon woman and as a Westerner concerned about the environmental degradation of her home. She tells the story of the women of her family, bearers of the desert West's atomic legacy. Williams bears witness to what is buried beneath the shifting sands of Western bombing ranges. Through all of Williams's writing runs a strong connection between self and landscape, between one's fate as a Western woman and the fate of Western places.

THE CLAN OF ONE-BREASTED WOMEN

I belong to a Clan of One-Breasted Women. My mother, my grandmothers, and six aunts have all had mastectomies. Seven are dead. The two who survive have just completed rounds of chemotherapy and radiation.

I've had my own problems: two biopsies for breast cancer and a small tumor between my ribs diagnosed as a "borderline malignancy."

This is my family history.

Most statistics tell us breast cancer is genetic, hereditary, with rising percentages attached to fatty diets, childlessness, or becoming pregnant after thirty. What they don't say is living in Utah may be the greatest hazard of all.

We are a Mormon family with roots in Utah since 1847. The "word of wisdom" in my family aligned us with good foods—no coffee, no tea, tobacco, or alcohol. For the most part, our women were finished having their babies by the time they were thirty. And only one faced breast cancer prior to 1960. Traditionally, as a group of people, Mormons have a low rate of cancer.

Is our family a cultural anomaly? The truth is, we didn't think about it. Those who did, usually the men, simply said, "bad genes."

Terry Tempest Williams, "The Clan of One-Breasted Women," from *Refuge* (1991).

The women's attitude was stoic. Cancer was part of life. On February 16, 1971, the eve of my mother's surgery, I accidently picked up the telephone and overheard her ask my grandmother what she could expect.

"Diane, it is one of the most spiritual experiences you will ever encounter."

I quietly put down the receiver.

Two days later, my father took my brothers and me to the hospital to visit her. She met us in the lobby in a wheelchair. No bandages were visible. I'll never forget her radiance, the way she held herself in a purple velvet robe, and how she gathered us around her.

"Children, I am fine. I want you to know I felt the arms of God around me."

We believed her. My father cried. Our mother, his wife, was thirty-eight years old.

A little over a year after Mother's death, Dad and I were having dinner together. He had just returned from St. George, where the Tempest Company was completing the gas lines that would service southern Utah. He spoke of his love for the country, the sandstoned landscape, bare-boned and beautiful. He had just finished hiking the Kolob trail in Zion National Park. We got caught up in reminiscing, recalling with fondness our walk up Angel's Landing on his fiftieth birthday and the years our family had vacationed there.

Over dessert, I shared a recurring dream of mine. I told my father that for years, as long as I could remember, I saw this flash of light in the night in the desert—that this image had so permeated my being that I could not venture south without seeing it again, on the horizon, illuminating buttes and mesas.

"You did see it," he said.

"Saw what?"

"The bomb. The cloud. We were driving home from Riverside, California. You were sitting on Diane's lap. She was pregnant. In fact, I remember the day, September 7, 1957. We had just gotten out of the Service. We were driving north, past Las Vegas. It was an hour or so before dawn, when this explosion went off. We not only heard it, but felt it. I thought the oil tanker in front of us had blown up. We pulled over and suddenly, rising from the desert floor, we saw it, clearly, this golden-stemmed cloud, the mushroom. The sky seemed to vibrate with an eerie pink glow. Within a few minutes, a light ash was raining on the car."

I stared at my father.

"I thought you knew that," he said. "It was a common occurrence in the fifties."

It was at this moment that I realized the deceit I had been living under. Children growing up in the American Southwest, drinking contaminated milk from contaminated cows, even from the contaminated breasts of their mothers, my mother—members, years later, of the Clan of One-Breasted Women.

It is a well-known story in the Desert West, "The Day We Bombed Utah," or more accurately, the years we bombed Utah: above ground atomic testing in Nevada took place from January 27, 1951 through July 11, 1962. Not only were the winds blowing north covering "low-use segments of the population" with fallout and leaving sheep dead in their tracks, but the climate was right. The United States of the 1950s was red, white, and blue. The Korean War was raging. McCarthyism was rampant. Ike was it, and the cold war was hot. If you were against nuclear testing, you were for a communist regime.

Much has been written about this "American nuclear tragedy." Public health was secondary to national security. The Atomic Energy Commissioner, Thomas Murray, said, "Gentlemen, we must not let anything interfere with this series of tests, nothing."

Again and again, the American public was told by its government, in spite of burns, blisters, and nausea, "It has been found that the tests may be conducted with adequate assurance of safety under conditions prevailing at the bombing reservations." Assuaging public fears was simply a matter of public relations. "Your best action," an Atomic Energy Commission booklet read, "is not to be worried about fallout." A news release typical of the times stated, "We find no basis for concluding that harm to any individual has resulted from radioactive fallout."

On August 30, 1979, during Jimmy Carter's presidency, a suit was filed, *Irene Allen v. The United States of America*. Mrs. Allen's case was the first on an alphabetical list of twenty-four test cases, representative of nearly twelve hundred plaintiffs seeking compensation from the United States government for cancers caused by nuclear testing in Nevada.

Irene Allen lived in Hurricane, Utah. She was the mother of five children and had been widowed twice. Her first husband, with their two oldest boys, had watched the tests from the roof of the local high school. He died of leukemia in 1956. Her second husband died of pancreatic cancer in 1978.

In a town meeting conducted by Utah Senator Orrin Hatch, shortly before the suit was filed, Mrs. Allen said, "I am not blaming the government, I want you to know that, Senator Hatch. But I thought if my testimony could help in any way so this wouldn't happen again to any of the generations coming up after us . . . I am happy to be here this day to bear testimony of this."

God-fearing people. This is just one story in an anthology of thousands.

On May 10, 1984, Judge Bruce S. Jenkins handed down his opinion. Ten of the plaintiffs were awarded damages. It was the first time a federal court had determined that nuclear tests had been the cause of cancers. For the remaining fourteen test cases, the proof of causation was not sufficient. In spite of the split decision, it was considered a landmark ruling. It was not to remain so for long.

In April, 1987, the Tenth Circuit Court of Appeals overturned Judge Jenkins's ruling on the ground that the United States was protected from suit by the legal doctrine of sovereign immunity, a centuries-old idea from England in the days of absolute monarchs.

In January, 1988, the Supreme Court refused to review the Appeals Court decision. To our court system it does not matter whether the United States government was irresponsible, whether it lied to its citizens, or even that citizens died from the fallout of nuclear testing. What matters is that our government is immune: "The King can do no wrong."

In Mormon culture, authority is respected, obedience is revered, and independent thinking is not. I was taught as a young girl not to "make waves" or "rock the boat."

"Just let it go," Mother would say. "You know how you feel, that's what counts."

For many years, I have done just that—listened, observed, and quietly formed my own opinions, in a culture that rarely asks questions because it has all the answers. But one by one, I have watched the women in my family die common, heroic deaths. We sat in waiting rooms hoping for good news, but always receiving the bad. I cared for them, bathed their scarred bodies, and kept their secrets. I watched beautiful women become bald as Cytoxan, cisplatin, and Adriamycin were injected into their veins. I held their foreheads as they vomited green-black bile, and I shot them with morphine when the pain became inhuman. In the end, I witnessed their last peaceful breaths, becoming a midwife to the rebirth of their souls.

The price of obedience has become too high.

The fear and inability to question authority that ultimately killed rural communities in Utah during atmospheric testing of atomic weapons is the same fear I saw in my mother's body. Sheep. Dead sheep. The evidence is buried.

I cannot prove that my mother, Diane Dixon Tempest, or my grandmothers, Lettie Romney Dixon and Kathryn Blackett Tempest, along with my aunts developed cancer from nuclear fall-out in Utah. But I can't prove they didn't.

My father's memory was correct. The September blast we drove through in 1957 was part of Operation Plumbbob, one of the most intensive series of bomb tests to be initiated. The flash of light in the night in the desert, which I had always thought was a dream, developed into a family nightmare. It took fourteen years, from 1957 to 1971, for cancer to manifest in my mother—the same time, Howard L. Andrews, an authority in radioactive fallout at the National Institute of Health, says radiation cancer requires to become evident. The more I learn about what it means to be a "downwinder," the more questions I drown in.

What I do know, however, is that as a Mormon woman of the fifth generation of Latter-day Saints, I must question everything, even if it means losing my faith, even if it means becoming a member of a border tribe among my own people. Tolerating blind obedience in the name of patriotism or religion ultimately takes our lives.

When the Atomic Energy Commission described the country north of the Nevada Test Site as "virtually uninhabited desert terrain," my family and the birds at Great Salt Lake were some of the "virtual uninhabitants."

One night, I dreamed women from all over the world circled a blazing fire in the desert. They spoke of change, how they hold the

moon in their bellies and wax and wane with its phases. They
mocked the presumption of even-tempered beings and made
promises that they would never fear the witch inside themselves.
The women danced wildly as sparks broke away from the flames
and entered the night sky as stars.

And they sang a song given to them by Shoshone grandmothers:

Ah ne nah, nah	*Consider the rabbits*
nin nah nah—	*How gently they walk on the earth—*
ah ne nah, nah	*Consider the rabbits*
nin nah nah—	*How gently they walk on the earth—*
Nyaga mutzi	*We remember them*
oh ne nay—	*We can walk gently also—*
Nyaga mutzi	*We remember them*
oh ne nay—	*We can walk gently also—*

The women danced and drummed and sang for weeks, preparing
themselves for what was to come. They would reclaim the desert for
the sake of their children, for the sake of the land.

A few miles downwind from the fire circle, bombs were being
tested. Rabbits felt the tremors. Their soft leather pads on paws and
feet recognized the shaking sands, while the roots of mesquite and
sage were smoldering. Rocks were hot from the inside out and dust
devils hummed unnaturally. And each time there was another
nuclear test, ravens watched the desert heave. Stretch marks
appeared. The land was losing its muscle.

The women couldn't bear it any longer. They were mothers.
They had suffered labor pains but always under the promise of
birth. The red hot pains beneath the desert promised death only, as
each bomb became a stillborn. A contract had been made and
broken between human beings and the land. A new contract was
being drawn by the women, who understood the fate of the earth
as their own.

Under the cover of darkness, ten women slipped under a
barbed-wire fence and entered the contaminated country. They
were trespassing. They walked toward the town of Mercury, in
moonlight, taking their cues from coyote, kit fox, antelope squirrel,
and quail. They moved quietly and deliberately through the maze

of Joshua trees. When a hint of daylight appeared they rested, drinking tea and sharing their rations of food. The women closed their eyes. The time had come to protest with the heart, that to deny one's genealogy with the earth was to commit treason against one's soul.

At dawn, the women draped themselves in mylar, wrapping long streamers of silver plastic around their arms to blow in the breeze. They wore clear masks, that became the faces of humanity. And when they arrived at the edge of Mercury, they carried all the butterflies of a summer day in their wombs. They paused to allow their courage to settle.

The town that forbids pregnant women and children to enter because of radiation risks was asleep. The women moved through the streets as winged messengers, twirling around each other in slow motion, peeking inside homes and watching the easy sleep of men and women. They were astonished by such stillness and periodically would utter a shrill note or low cry just to verify life.

The residents finally awoke to these strange apparitions. Some simply stared. Others called authorities, and in time, the women were apprehended by wary soldiers dressed in desert fatigues. They were taken to a white, square building on the other edge of Mercury. When asked who they were and why they were there, the women replied, "We are mothers and we have come to reclaim the desert for our children."

The soldiers arrested them. As the ten women were blindfolded and handcuffed, they began singing:

> *You can't forbid us everything*
> *You can't forbid us to think—*
> *You can't forbid our tears to flow*
> *And you can't stop the songs that we sing.*

The women continued to sing louder and louder, until they heard the voices of their sisters moving across the mesa:

> *Ah ne nah, nah*
> *nin nah nah—*
> *Ah ne nah, nah*
> *nin nah nah—*

Nyaga mutzi
oh ne nay—
Nyaga mutzi
oh ne nay—

"Call for reinforcements," one soldier said.

"We have," interrupted one woman, "we have—and you have no idea of our numbers."

I crossed the line at the Nevada Test Site and was arrested with nine other Utahns for trespassing on military lands. They are still conducting nuclear tests in the desert. Ours was an act of civil disobedience. But as I walked toward the town of Mercury, it was more than a gesture of peace. It was a gesture on behalf of the Clan of One-Breasted Women.

As one officer cinched the handcuffs around my wrists, another frisked my body. She did not find my scars.

We were booked under an afternoon sun and bused to Tonopah, Nevada. It was a two-hour ride. This was familiar country. The Joshua trees standing their ground had been named by my ancestors, who believed they looked like prophets pointing west to the Promised Land. These were the same trees that bloomed each spring, flowers appearing like white flames in the Mojave. And I recalled a full moon in May, when Mother and I had walked among them, flushing out mourning doves and owls.

The bus stopped short of town. We were released.

The officials thought it was a cruel joke to leave us stranded in the desert with no way to get home. What they didn't realize was that we were home, soul-centered and strong, women who recognized the sweet smell of sage as fuel for our spirits.

FURTHER READINGS
Jocelyn Bartkevicius and Mary Hussman, "A Conversation with Terry Tempest Williams, " *Iowa Review* 27 (Spring 1997): 1–23; Karla Armbruster, "Rewriting a Genealogy with the Earth: Women and Nature in the Works of Terry Tempest Williams," *Southwestern*

American Literature 22 (1995): 209–220; Laura L. Bush, "Terry Tempest Williams's *Refuge*: Sentimentality and Separation," *Dialogue: A Journal of Mormon Thought* 28 (Fall 1995): 147–160; Edward Lueders, "Landscape, People, and Place: Robert Finch and Terry Tempest Williams," in Edward Lueders, ed., *Writing Natural History: Dialogues with Authors* (University of Utah Press, 1989): 37–65.

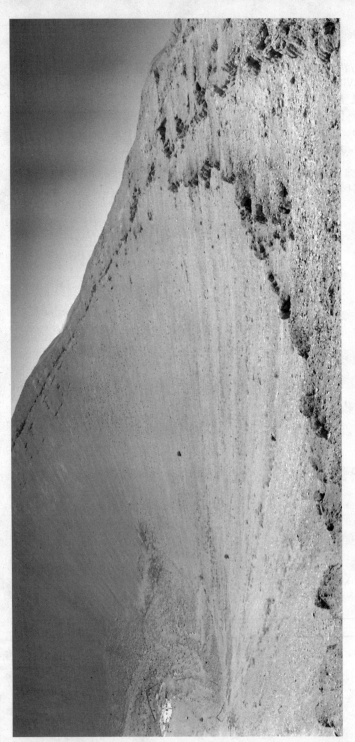

Carole Gallagher, *Sedan Crater at the North End of Yucca Flat*, 1990.

Copyright © 1990, Carole Gallagher. From Carole Gallagher, American Ground Zero: The Secret Nuclear War (Massachusetts Institute of Technology Press, 1993); used by permission of the artist.

Carole Gallagher, *"Atomic" Street Sign, Amargosa Valley, Nevada, Ten Miles South of the Nevada Test Site*, 1988.

Nancy Mairs (1943–   )

Nancy Mairs was born in California in 1943, raised in New England, and then returned west to Tucson in 1972. Two years later, she was diagnosed with multiple sclerosis, a chronic, incurable, degenerative disease of the central nervous system. In spite of physical hardship, she earned an MFA and PhD at the University of Arizona, and, more recently, an honorary doctorate from Wheaton College in 1994. When her daughter joined the Peace Corps, Mairs and her husband traveled to Zaire.

Her output has been prodigious—*Plaintext* (1986), *Remembering the Bone House* (1989), *Carnal Acts* (1990), *Ordinary Time: Cycles in Marriage, Faith and Renewal* (1993) and *Voice Lessons: On Becoming a (Woman) Writer* (1994)—making her one of the nation's leading feminist voices. At the conclusion of "Waist-High in the West," one of her best-known essays, she wrote, "The tale of westward migration has always been premised on possibility [but] I moved into a West of impossibility. . . . [It's] an honest-to-God Western adventure I'm having here. Trust me."

In the story reprinted here, Mairs and her husband joined with Catholic Workers and others in Mercury, Nevada, on November 8, 1987, to celebrate Catholic radical Dorothy Day's birthday, and get themselves arrested for protesting at the nuclear testing site.

FAITH AND LOVING IN LAS VEGAS

If we are to be pilgrims for peace and justice, we must expect the desert.

—*Dom Helder Cámara*

Lorenzo is holding my left hand, and Jim is holding my right. Behind me, George holds hands with Jack and Mimi, the three together nudging the wheelchair forward. In the chill, bright desert

Nancy Mairs, "Faith and Loving in Las Vegas" from *Carnal Acts* (1990).

air our voices float up and mingle with those of the couple of hundred people still behind us:

"Be not afraid. I go before you always. Come, follow Me, and I will give you rest."

A plywood platform has been laid across the wide bars of the cattle guard. The wheelchair bumps up onto the plywood and rolls forward. We have crossed the line.

We are the fourth group to cross. A dozen or more groups will follow us. We are Catholic Workers who have gathered in Las Vegas from all over the country to celebrate the ninetieth anniversary of founder Dorothy Day's birth. We spent yesterday at a Catholic high school in the city, holding workshops and listening to speakers, among them Dom Helder Cámara, the Brazilian archbishop whose labors for the political rights of the poor have transformed the Church throughout the world. He is a figure for whom the simile *birdlike* might have been coined, a tiny aged sparrow of a man in his tan cassock and wooden pectoral cross, his eyes small and bright above dark pouches, his slender fingers gnarled and curved. His accent is thick and his voice is creaky, making his message hard to decipher. But we all understood instantly and cheered when, his right hand inscribing a wide arc above his head, he told us, "We cannot have a First World and a Second World and a Third World and a Fourth World. . . . We must create only One World!"

This morning, Dom Helder among us, we set out from the school in a long caravan across sixty miles of desert, past range after range of humped and spiny mountains, to the Nevada Nuclear Test Site. Beneath this vast sweep of earth, tinted in colors the language has never quite captured (something like rose, like smoke, gray-green, buff), beyond the barbed-wire fence, the United States routinely sets off nuclear explosions, testing what is known already: that We can kill off Them a hundred-fold anytime They step out of line. To protest the deadly provocative desire these explosions signify, some of us have chosen to trespass onto the site, others to blockade access to it with their bodies, still others to line the route and provide support. Although we trespassers are entering federal land, which as taxpayers we have helped to pay for, we are denied any rights in it. We, like the blockaders, know that we will be arrested for our act.

Those of us from Casa María, the Catholic Worker house in Tucson, have clustered together. Despite nearly two decades of social activism, George and I have never committed civil disobedience before, and we are glad to be surrounded by loving and oft-arrested friends. We have been joined for the crossing by Fred and Mimi, a couple in their sixties. Mimi's a writer, and now that he's retired from social work Fred, his polio-damaged legs patched up with steel and Teflon, cooks for the soup kitchen at St. Joseph's on Manhattan's Lower East Side. Once, he's just been telling us, the soup kitchen came into a load of Brie, a dozen or more wheels, and then the hungry and homeless at St. Joseph's got vegetable crêpes with Brie for lunch. The workers found one of the women who lives there seated on her pallet on the floor in her nightgown with a whole wheel of Brie in her lap, gazing far into some other world as she consumed it bite by bite with a teaspoon.

Facing the group of us, the sheriff of Nye County, a slim man with graying temples, says, "First I am going to ask you not to do this." We say nothing. "Then I am going to tell you that if you do it, I will have to arrest you for trespassing." He meets our eyes. "Do you all understand that?"

"Yes," we answer. "Yes, we understand." I don't, I discover, feel as though I'm responding to a question. I feel more the way I do during a baptism, when we break the Nicene Creed into questions and answers: "Do you believe in one God, the Father, the Almighty, Maker of heaven and earth, of all that is seen and unseen?" the priest asks at that time, and the people respond, "I do." Here, acknowledging that I understand that this weathered man with the tired eyes is going to arrest me sounds oddly like a profession of faith.

Deputies begin to handcuff the members of our group. I had envisioned clanking metal circles, the sort that marshals might use to subdue great train robbers, but these are plastic straps like elongated versions of the fasteners we use to close our trash bags before lugging them out to the alley. I hold my wrists up to be strapped, but the deputy passes me over.

"I'd like to be handcuffed too," I say. My voice sounds ridiculously sedate, as though I'd just asked for two lumps of sugar in my tea. Little did my grandmother suspect, when she drilled me in the tones of a Yankee lady, that I'd find them handy when I got arrested.

"Uh-uh." The deputy shakes his head. "The sheriff doesn't want you handcuffed." Just then the sheriff looks down at me. "We can't take you in there," he says. "We can't handle a wheelchair on the bus."

"It's all right," I tell him. "Don't worry. I can walk a little. I'll get out of the wheelchair and climb on the bus."

Plainly he's not happy, but he assents.

"My wheelchair," I say. "You will take care of it for me? You won't let anything happen to it, will you?" I haven't for an instant felt afraid of mistreatment by these somber uniformed men, but suddenly I'm scared they might punish me through my wheelchair.

"Don't worry. We'll take good care of it."

It's hard, George discovers, to push a wheelchair across gravel with your hands in cuffs. With Lorenzo, Jim, and Jack helping out, we make a drunken progress toward the bus. Mimi has her cuffed hands full helping Fred, who can't use his Canadian crutch with his hands bound. I don't know how he managed to get handcuffs and I didn't. I suppose it was because he was erect and I was folded up. There is a subtle taxonomy of crippledness.

At the bus I'm glad I don't have handcuffs, though. The steps are very steep, and even holding onto railings on either side, with people in front and back of me for support, I can barely haul myself up. I will be sore for days. Fred has a hard time too, we can see, but he makes it. George and I are given the front seat. He clutches my hand. In a broad-brimmed straw hat and bug-eye sunglasses and a UCLA sweatshirt he looks funny and boyish. "Well," I say, squeezing his hand in return, "this is it. We're across."

Why, I find myself wondering in the first elated rush at being safely on the other side, have we postponed for so long crossing the line between peaceful protest and nonviolent direct action? For me, the progression first from apathy to protest and now from protest to civil disobedience seems hooked somehow to the lives of my children. I crossed that first line in the autumn of 1969, about six months after the birth of my second child, Matthew, when I spotted a full-page advertisement in the *Boston Sunday Globe* protesting the war in Vietnam. Something jolted me then, as it never had before, like a sudden electrical connection: perhaps it was the presence of a small squalling draftable boy whom I was supposed to raise to kill for his country. Whatever the reason, the following day I called the telephone number printed at the bottom of that page.

Thereafter, the small boy and his slightly larger sister riding on our backs and shoulders, George and I began a life of moderate activism. In the intervening years, as the boy and his sister grew astonishingly, we've attended meetings, painted posters, picketed army and air force bases, stood in candlelit vigils. In 1970 we worked to elect an antiwar candidate, the Jesuit priest Robert Drinan, to Congress. We've written letters to editors and legislators. We've boycotted grapes and Campbell products in support of the United Farm Workers. A decade ago, having found a community of people living out their values in ways that inspired us, we converted to Roman Catholicism and later joined Catholics for Peace and Justice. We help to provide food for the hungry, shelter for the homeless, clothing, household equipment, and medical supplies for the poor in Tucson and Central America. To support their economic self-sufficiency, we buy Nicaraguan coffee and crafts made by cooperatives throughout the world. These are worthy enough gestures, and I don't think I'm debasing them by pointing out that they're easy enough as well: they're *safe*. We may encounter—have encountered—familial disapproval and the skepticism of friends. But only rarely have we been physically accosted, and no one has ever threatened to haul us off to jail.

I think that this sense of safety was important to me while I had dependent children. To risk going to jail seemed irresponsible to me while I had to provide for their daily needs. But now Anne has gone off to the Peace Corps. Matthew, at eighteen, has moved out of the house. In fact, he is struggling just now to decide whether or not to register for the draft. And six months after his eighteenth birthday, here I am in Mercury, Nevada, stepping up my activism, stepping across the next line in my path. Or, in this case, rolling across the next cattle guard.

When the bus is full, we drive a quarter of a mile or so up a straight road, stopping beside a long white trailer. At one end, an area fenced off by posts and wire holds a galvanized metal trash barrel, a couple of white Rent-a-Cans, and the first busloads of the arrested. George and I wait for the others to get off. Just as we are about to follow, a security officer tells me, "You stay right here. We'll ticket you on the bus."

I look at George. I look out the window at the crowd in the pen.

"I don't want to be separated from the others," I say. "I don't want to be left alone. I want to get off the bus."

"There's no place for you to sit." He's right. My wheelchair is back at the crossing.

"I'll sit on the steps," I say. "Or we can turn the trash barrel over and I'll sit on that. I'll sit on one of the toilets. Please. I don't want to be left." The security officer glances at George, who nods, and shrugs. As I head for the steps, the bus driver starts speaking to me softly.

"Do you know what they really do here?" he asks. "They test drugs to help people like you." Actually, no one I know of is working on multiple sclerosis at the atomic level, but I believe that medical research goes on here. "Eighty percent of the testing has nothing to do with weapons."

"It's the twenty percent I'm here about." I find myself speaking softly too. "That's the part that scares me." Some people express anger at his laying such a "trip" on me, but though I'm shocked, I don't feel angry. I feel touched. He's tried to reach out for me as best he can.

I get separated from the others whether I want to or not. A stolid woman in brown trousers and a striped blouse leads me to the steps exiting the trailer, at the opposite end from the holding pen. Those in the pen cheer me as I walk away, and I shrink inwardly in embarrassment. People with whole bodies sometimes mistake cripples for heroes. They forget that I'm doing just what they're doing, only more clumsily. Such self-deprecation denies, however, my real use to them as an emblem of the value of this action. What they are doing is hard. My presence assures them that it is not too hard, that all of us can do whatever we must, here, now, and wherever else we are called. This seems a good enough use to be put to.

Seating me on the gray wooden steps, the woman writes me a ticket for trespassing on federal land "after being advised not to." The fine is $250 plus a $65 processing fee. My court date is December 21, 1987. Some people are giving false identification—many, for this birthday celebration, are being "Dorothy Day"—but I have decided, this time at least, against noncooperation. Naming myself accurately feels like taking responsibility for my act.

When she has finished filling in the blanks and given me my pink copy, she tells me to get back on the bus. I hesitate, looking over at the others. I can't see George.

"Go on," she says. "You can't stay out here. It's not safe."

I am inclined to balk. But, as the sheriff's reluctance to arrest me and my brief interchange with the bus driver have demonstrated, my reality is skewed from the others'. I want to be treated exactly like them. In truth, though, I'm not exactly like them. I'm getting more and more different from them almost by the day. I can't divorce myself, morally or otherwise, from my failing body. I am she. And I have, as a consequence, some responsibilities they can't even grasp. Hell, I can scarcely grasp them myself. All I know is that my crossing the line bears another kind of weight from theirs. It is not a straightforward individual act of civil disobedience. Like it or not, I cross not foremost as a private citizen but as a representative of those people who, despite their disparities, get lumped as the result of their physical disabilities into a single class. Poor people! They haven't asked me to represent them. Most of them would probably shudder at the very idea. But, in a sense, here we all are on a Sunday morning out in the middle of the Nevada desert. Whatever I do will reflect on them.

I feel constrained to be a "good cripple," cheerful and patient, so that whoever might roll along in my wake someday will find the way eased: a stance wholly at odds with the disobedience I am here to practice. I don't know how to resolve this conflict, which has cut me off, quite literally, from the other demonstrators, leaving me as sober and bleak as the landscape I admire from the bus window. The farthest mountain range, bluish and blurred, marks the southern lip of Death Valley, the bus driver explains to me. He is friendly now, maybe conciliatory, though not apologetic.

Slowly the bus is filling. A beautiful young security officer called Bambi jumps up the steps. One of the demonstrators, practicing noncooperation, has given her a hard time, and she's flushed from chasing after him each time he has wandered off toward the desert.

"Which one of you is Dorothy, the one who gave me the cross?" she calls out. The white-haired woman across the aisle from me raises her hand. "I just want to thank you and give you a hug," says Bambi, grinning. "But don't tell anyone I did that or I'll get taken off the line. They know I love this duty so that's how they punish me if

I act up. Once they caught me singing and dancing with the people on the bus, and they took me off for *six months*." We laugh and applaud her.

I wish George were with me. I don't feel alarmed by our separation, as I often do, because I know that everyone here will watch over me until we're back together. In that sense, though I don't know anyone in this group, I'm not among strangers. But I want everything happening here to happen to us together. That's the mark of marriage for me: George's presence roots me more deeply in my own experience. As if my wish had power, he climbs on the bus and hugs me quickly before heading for the last seat, in the back. The doors close, and we turn back to the entrance, stopping there to pick up my wheelchair. If we can put it on the bus now, I don't see why we couldn't have had it with us all along. Oh, well. We are driven back across the line, past the cheering group of demonstrators who have chosen not to be arrested and the silent groups of counterdemonstrators and site workers who are on strike, to the area where we left our cars. George settles me in the wheelchair and, tilting me back, rolls me away from the road. Looking up, I see a white van with the door open, Dom Helder perched on the front seat. I wave to him, and he waves back.

We have made a round trip, across the line and back again, and yet I know that in a way we can never come back. A line, once crossed, can never be *un*crossed. We have, in trespassing, entered new moral terrain, and we will inevitably be transformed in it, though it's too early to tell precisely how. I can glimpse a couple of points already, though. I can tell, for one thing, that I am not the same woman who took up her posters and candles to protest the Vietnam War in 1969. In those days I believed in the efficacy of action. I believed that if I, and others like me, protested emphatically enough, we could sway all right-minded people to our point of view. We could create change. And in a limited way—the only way I started out knowing—I guess I was right. In large measure because of the pressure of popular opinion, the role of the United States in the war in Southeast Asia ground to its ugly and dishonorable close. Perhaps I even believed then that, having learned the error of such ways, the United States would turn utterly from war as a means of structuring human relationships. I was awfully young, remember, not even thirty, and even more ignorant than I am today.

Now I'm not at all sure that I can do anything to prevent the evil—of which nuclear weapons testing, like CIA covert activities, the trading of arms for hostages, the building of B-1 bombers, the gobbling of federal funds for "defense" rather than the enhancement of human life, is only an emblem—which gnaws at the world's heart. I just don't know. I've come up here to the wilderness to plant my feet on the other side of an invisible line and earn a black mark on my hitherto unbesmirched record without the promise of anything in return. Anything at all.

This terrain seems, at least from where I stand now, foggy and rugged indeed. We are a time-ridden, an ends-addicted society, and no action is valued unless it produces results. By this standard, I have just committed a nonaction. I have just wasted my time. I must be a fool. And yet, smiling foolishly up into Dom Helder's little wrinkled fool's face, I feel certain that something's happening here. I can't change the world. I got lucky once and helped to stop a war, but the world didn't change. The fact that I still confuse Nixon and Reagan is more than a slip of the tongue or the sign of a loose cog somewhere. The men in power, and the women beginning to join them, are, beyond the personal level, indistinguishable: Republican/Democrat, American/Russian, Protestant/Catholic/Muslim/Jew, black/white/yellow/red/brown, all tend to run together. They all thrive on the adrenaline rush triggered by believing one is menaced by An Enemy. They project Enemies right and left to maintain the high. I've got no thrill to offer them to keep their juices pumping like that.

Why, then, do anything at all? If I really believe that no act of mine can break the addiction of those in power, why not lapse into quiescence, accept the world as it is, make the best of a bad thing? Because I have begun to recognize the possibility of relating differently to that world: in the role of witness. I am being transformed by this new understanding from a hot young crusader into a bony finger, pointing: *Here,* the body I have permitted to be arrested testifies, *we are doing wrong. Here we have been unjust. Let's choose another life.* If those in power choose, over my testimony, to blow the world to smithereens instead, I'll be lost with all the rest. I don't believe that right choice confers immunity. I no longer believe in reward. I simply believe that choices must be made regardless of their chances of success. And so I've come here.

The other point I've begun to descry is that although I was arrested for stepping *in*to a giant ring of barbed wire, my true direction is *out*ward. This is not a new movement, of course, but a leap along the trajectory of one I began years ago. I've been shoved and spat on and given the finger—and, in my own more polite circle of family and friends, sighed over—plenty often enough to know that my beliefs do not hold social sway. But my act of civil disobedience has further shrunk the circle of people who understand and share my commitments. I could swagger and say that all others don't matter; but the fact is that they do. Though I don't care much anymore for the world's approval, I yearn for its understanding. Now I've increased the distance between myself and most of the people I come into contact with. They may write me off as a zealot, or a crank. A position on society's margins strengthens one's capacity for the kind of witness I've chosen, I know. All the same, I'm feeling lonely and a little scared. I shiver. George helps me pull on a heavy black sweater and hands me an apple and some almonds.

Late at night, back in Tucson, the weekend's images and insights tumble over and over inside my skull, each turn polishing them to new clarity. In time, I will add them to my hoard. They will travel with me across the next line, and the next. Ahead I've got a lot of moral territory to explore, I know. From where I stand, at the foot of my bed tugging my arms out of my sweater, that territory stretches boundlessly, as shadowy and severe as I imagine the test site to lie at this moment, under tonight's full moon. This sense of vastness both daunts and exhilarates me. In my early activist days, I'm sure I thought that by the time I was forty-four, I'd have all life's ambiguities sorted out and resolved. Now I know that such work goes on forever. To finish it not only isn't possible but—more important—isn't even the point.

"That was a fine experience," I mumble to George through the folds of the nightgown I'm struggling into. "Thank you for pushing me to it, and through it. I guess I can't even get arrested by myself anymore."

"Oh, I don't know." He and the black cat have already snugged down under the covers, and his voice is muffled by blankets and sleep. "Knowing you the way I do, I think you'd manage to find some way to get arrested on your own."

500	The Western Women's Reader

Doubtless he's right. But why, after all, would I want to? Getting arrested, like any of life's necessary tasks, is eased and enriched by company. And one cannot make the world's peace, by its very nature, in solitude. Peace must be woven intentionally, meticulously, clasped hand by clasped hand, across all the desert spaces between us.

Holdings hands, with the black cat tucked between us, George and I sleep.

FURTHER READINGS

Nancy Mairs, *Waist-High in the World: A Life Among the Nondisabled* (Beacon Press, 1996); Nancy Mairs, "Waist-High in the West," in *The Stories That Shape Us: Contemporary Women Write About the West*, ed. Teresa Jordan and James R. Hepworth (W. W. Norton & Co, 1995): 233–240.

Angela Davis (1944–   )

Angela Davis was born in Birmingham, Alabama, in 1944. She attended Brandeis University in Boston, and spent her junior year in France. She studied with Herbert Marcuse in Germany, and returned to the United States where she joined the Philosophy Department at UCLA. Her political conscience was shaped by the Civil Rights movement of the 1960s; she joined SNCC and then the all-black Che-Lumumba Club and the Communist Party U.S.A. When George Jackson, John Clutchette, and Fleeta Drumgo, imprisoned at Soledad Prison in California, were accused of murdering a white guard, Davis joined the movement to "Free the Soledad Brothers." Jackson's seventeen-year old brother, Jonathan, staged a one-man raid on the San Rafael courthouse in Marin County in an attempt to trade hostages for the prisoners. Jonathan, two prisoners and a judge were killed.

Davis, who was not at the scene, was accused of supplying weapons for the raid, and the FBI added her name to its Most Wanted List on charges that included murder, kidnapping, and conspiracy. She went underground, but in 1970 she was arrested in New York City, extradited to California, and jailed for sixteen months until her trial. In 1972, she was found not guilty.

In the fall of 1969, already a member of the Black Panther Party and of the Communist Party, she was hired to teach in the Philosophy Department of UCLA, but before she could teach her first class, the Regents of the University fired her. After her acquittal in 1972, she won reinstatement, but the experience of prison in Marin County was the start of a lifelong commitment to prison reform. "Virtually every black person [has] some personal relationship to the prison system." Davis is presently a member of the National Alliance Against Racist and Political Repression, and a member of the National Black Women's Health Project. She is on the Advisory Board of the Prison Activist Resource Center, and is at present working on a comparative study of women's imprisonment in the US, the Netherlands, and Cuba. Davis has lectured in all of the fifty United States, as well as in Africa, Europe, the Caribbean, and the former Soviet Union. Her writing includes the *Autobiography*,

Blues Legacies and Black Feminism, and *The Angela Y. Davis Reader*. She is a tenured professor in the History of Consciousness Department at the University of California, Santa Cruz. In 1994, she was appointed to the University of California Presidential Chair in African American and Feminist Studies.

AN AUTOBIOGRAPHY

In July 1968, I turned over my fifty-cents—the initial membership dues—to the chairman of the Che-Lumumba Club, and became a full-fledged member of the Communist Party, U.S.A. Shortly thereafter I had to retreat to La Jolla in order to do the last intensive preparations for my Ph.D. qualifier examinations. For weeks and weeks I only studied. Days, I studied in my office at the university. Evenings, I worked—often well into the night—in the isolated house in Del Mar which friends lent me for the last part of the summer. My thoughts became so thoroughly wedded to philosophical things that I even found myself dreaming sometimes about the ideas of Spinoza, Kant, Hegel. I had wanted to pass the exams at this time and not wait until after my second year of classes, as was the normal procedure. This meant that I had to study on my own works that I would have ordinarily read in connection with courses. I had to work, work and work—until the point of absolute saturation.

As exam week approached, the simmering desperation among graduate students preparing to take the test exploded into open panic. In the middle of a discussion, for example, someone might break into tears for no apparent reason. The fear of not passing was omnipresent. And there was something that was feared even more than flunking the exams: passing them with a terminal master's degree and thus being shut out of the Ph.D. program entirely. If one simply flunked the exams, one could always take them again in the spring. But a terminal master's was the end.

It was a great relief to learn that I had done quite well on the examinations. Having passed them, I began to work on the prospectus for my dissertation, and became a teaching assistant in

---

Angela Davis, from *Angela Davis: An Autobiography* (1989).

the Philosophy Department, a further requirement for the Ph.D. About half of each week I spent researching and teaching in La Jolla and the other half I devoted to my political work in Los Angeles.

I was glad to be in a position to resume attending the weekly Che-Lumumba meetings. It was an extremely important period for us. In June, Charlene Mitchell, our founding chairperson, had been selected by the national convention to be our Party's candidate for President, thus becoming the first Black woman ever to run for that office. We were immensely proud that the first Black woman presidential candidate was also a Communist. Because it had been twenty-eight years since the Communist Party had participated in the presidential elections, her candidacy marked the beginning of a new era for the Party. The vestiges of McCarthyism were being repudiated, and more and more people were realizing that they had to be defeated once and for all.

If I still retained any of the elitism which almost inevitably insinuates itself into the minds of college students, I lost it all in the course of the Panther political education sessions. When we read Lenin's *State and Revolution*, there were sisters and brothers in the class whose public school education had not even allowed them to learn how to read. Some of them told me how they had stayed with the book for many painful hours, often using the dictionary to discover the meaning of scores of words on one page, until finally they could grasp the significance of what Lenin was saying. When they explained, for the benefit of the other members of the class, what they had gotten out of their reading, it was clear that they knew it all—they had understood Lenin on a far more elemental level than any professor of social science.

At the beginning of the second quarter, the sisters and brothers in the leadership of the Black Student Council all agreed that something was needed to set our membership in motion once more. We needed an issue around which to struggle. But what was the right issue? What was the most magnetic and most dramatic issue? Each of us thought seriously and intensely; our individual proposals were argued out in meetings that seemed never to end.

Finally, we reached unanimous agreement. Since the San Diego Campus of the university was to consist, ultimately, of a series of separate colleges, we decided that it would be just and appropriate to demand that the next college—the third college—be expressly devoted to the needs of students from oppressed social groups. Specifically, it should serve the needs of Black students, Chicano students and white students of working-class origin. While tightening our already close relationship with the Chicano students in the Mexican-American Youth Association, we drew up plans for our college. In order to project the radical character of our demands, we decided to call it Lumumba-Zapata College—after the assassinated Congolese revolutionary leader, Patrice Lumumba, and the Mexican revolutionary, Emiliano Zapata. We wanted our goals to be transparent: Lumumba-Zapata College, in our theoretical formulation, was to be a place where our peoples could acquire the knowledge and skills we needed in order to more effectively wage our liberation struggles.

After a brief period of strategy planning sessions, we decided that the time was right to confront the university administration. One afternoon the members of our two organizations streamed into the chancellor's office, insisting that he listen to our demands. I had been designated by the sisters and brothers to read the statement collectively drawn up by the BSC and MAYA. Along with our demands for Lumumba-Zapata College, we issued a very serious warning: in the event that the chancellor refused to negotiate, we would not guarantee that the university would continue to function undisturbed.

We had put up a fierce struggle. Large numbers of UCSD students had experienced the radicalization that was occurring on campuses throughout the country. The university hierarchy decided, apparently, that it was best to make the concessions we were demanding, rather than risk a prolonged disruption of campus activities. To tell the truth, we had not really expected them to agree so readily to our notion of the third college. And when they did, those of us leading the movement knew that despite our victory—of which all of us were proud—Lumumba-Zapata College would never become the revolutionary institution we had originally projected. Concessions were going to be inevitable, however the creation of the college would bring large numbers of Black, Brown and working-class white students into the university. And it would be a real breakthrough to have a college in which students would exercise more control over the education they received.

At the end of the school year, as I prepared to leave for a conference in Oakland, and go from there to Cuba, students selected by our organizations were settling down to a summer of drawing up concrete curriculum, faculty and administrative proposals for the college. The fight was not over. On the contrary, it had just begun. The most important responsibility resting with us was to ensure that whoever became involved in the college—students and faculty alike, carried on the legacy of struggle out of which the idea of Lumumba-Zapata was born.

The stage was set for the battle. The first step was to answer the chancellor's letter asking me whether I was a member of the Communist Party. Only my lawyer—John McTernan—and a few close friends and comrades were aware of the way I was going to reply to the question. Most people assumed that I would invoke the Fifth Amendment to the Constitution, declining to answer on the grounds that I might incriminate myself. During the McCarthy era, this had been the strategy of most Communists, for at that time, if it could be established that a person was a Communist, he or she could be sentenced, under the Smith Act, to many years in prison. Gus Hall and Henry Winston, the General Secretary and the Chairman of our Party, had spent almost ten years of their lives behind walls.

Since there was going to be a fight in any event, I preferred to pick the combat area, and to determine myself the terms of the struggle. The Regents had moved in with an attack on me. Now I would assume the offensive and would move in with an attack on them.

I answered the chancellor's letter with an unequivocal affirmation of my membership in the Communist Party. I strongly protested the posing of the question in the first place, but made it clear to them that I was prepared to fight openly, as a communist.

My reply caught the Regents unawares, and some of them considered my announcement of my membership in the Communist Party a personal affront. I am sure that they had taken for granted that I would call upon the Fifth Amendment. Their strategy, in turn, would have been to publicly ransack my immediate past in order to prove that I was in fact a Communist.

They countered my move with an impetuous, angry response: they announced their intention to fire me.

As time went by, it became clear that the assault on my job was only a tiny part of a systematic plan to disarm and destroy the Black Liberation struggle and the entire radical movement. The fight for my job had to be interwoven with a larger fight for the survival of the movement.

Repression was on the rise throughout the country. The worst victims of judicial frame-ups and police violence were members of the Black Panther Party. Bobby Seale and Ericka Huggins had been indicted in New Haven. Fred Hampton and Mark Clark were murdered by Chicago policemen as they slept in their beds. And in Los Angeles, the Black Panther Party headquarters was raided by the Los Angeles Police Department and their special tactical squad, with the National Guard and the Army on alert.

The fight for my job raged on and was sending me up and down the California coast, exposing and challenging Ronald Reagan, and seeking support for our side. I was active in the Che-Lumumba Club, working in the area of political education. And, of course, I had to prepare for the two sets of lectures I was giving at UCLA. I was already killing myself trying to fulfill all these responsibilities. How could I possibly find time to be active on a day-to-day basis in the Soledad Brothers Defense Committee?

Even though these were my thoughts as the subcommittees were being constituted, my arm shot up when they asked for volunteers for the subcommittee on campus involvement. Something more elemental than timetables and prior commitments had seized me and made me agree to coordinate the committee's efforts in the local colleges and universities.

The decision had been made. How to find time was a secondary question. I thought about my initial reluctance to take on a substantial role. How presumptuous it had been to weight the outcome of the fight for my job against the outcome of the fight for the lives of these men. At UCLA I was fighting for my right as a Black woman, as a Communist, as a revolutionary, to hold on to my job. In Soledad Prison, George Jackson, John Clutchette, Fleeta Drumgo were fighting for their rights as Black men, as revolutionaries, to hold on to their *lives*. Same struggle. Same enemies.

FURTHER READING

Bettina Aptheker, *The Morning Breaks: The Trial of Angela Davis* (Cornell University Press, 1999); Joy James, ed., *The Angela Y. Davis Reader* (Blackwell, 1998).

Paula Gunn Allen (1939–   )

Paula Gunn Allen is sometimes called a Laguna-Pueblo/Sioux, but she says of herself that she was born "a mixed-blood Laguna girl on the border of the mixed-blood Laguna Reservation and the Cubrero Land Grant, to a mix-blood Laguna mother, grandmother, great-grandmother, and perhaps great-great-grandfather to Oak clan, to the Sunrise/summer people, and to a Maronite-American father born and raised around the mountain to the east of the Cubrero, north of Laguna's mother village." She says her relatives and close friends are Spanish Americans, Mexican Americans and Anglos, German Jews and German Christians, Lebanese Maronites and Spaniards, Italian-Americans, Greek Americans, Basque immigrants, and Japanese Americans. "We [Native Americans] are global by blood . . . American through and through."

Like Gertrude Stein, Allen possesses an authentic American voice. "Wyrds" and "orthographies" capture her imagination, and her great gift has been to bring the Native American presence into the cannon of American literature. "E'me haah kosha si'ano Kawaike/ shrai' ena schat-chen-ni-ni Sti'its'tsi-naku/ F'me haah kosah si'ano Kawaike." (For I am born Kawaike/ Let this little writing go to Thought Woman/ For I am born Kawaike).

She has written both poetry and prose, and her books include *The Blind Lion* (1974), *Star Child* (1981), *A Cannon Between My Knees* (1981), *Shadow Country* (1982), *The Woman Who Owned the Shadows* (1983), *The Sacred Hoop* (1986), *Wyrds* (1987), *Skins and Bones: Poems, 1979–87* (1988), *Grandmothers of the Light* (1991), and *Life Is A Fatal Disease: Collected Poems, 1962–1995* (1997).

In the collection she edited, *Spider Woman's Granddaughters: Traditional Tales and Contemporary Writing by Native American Women* (1989), Allen described a change overtaking Native American women writers. They are no longer writing the recognizable "drum and feathers" stories. Native American women are beginning to "strike out and reoccupy territory stereotypically off-limits...."The new narrator is indigenous American and contemporary American at the same time. The Native American woman is "judging, assessing, [the] icons of American history." Those words were written a decade before the publication of *Off the Reservation*, where all that is "off limits" is the subject of the book. The *Declaration of Independence*, Thoreau's *Walden*, Emerson's *American Scholar*—all these belong to the writer who is Laguna Pueblo/Sioux. and contemporary American, to the "global" native American woman.

THE SAVAGES

> *As we rowed from our ships and set foot on the shore*
> *In the still coves,*
> *We met our images.*
>
> *Our brazen images emerged from the mirrors of the world*
> *Like yelling shadows,*
> *So we searched our souls,*
>
> *And in that hell and pit of everyman*
> *Placed the location of their ruddy shapes.*
> *We must be cruel to ourselves.*

The first thing that they did after landing was to steal all the corn they could carry from a nearby Wampanoag village. The natives of that place had seen them coming and, having been previously treated to the visits of white men, had fled into the forest. The next day the Puritans came back; yesterday's haul had been too little, they felt, so they took what was left in the storage bins.

> They had now no friends to welcome them nor inns to entertain or refresh their weather-beaten bodies; no houses or much less towns to repair to, to seek for succor . . . All things stand upon them with a weather-beaten face, and the whole country, full of woods and thickets, represented a wild and savage hue.
>
> —*WILLIAM BRADFORD*

Paula Gunn Allen, "Savages in the Mirror: Phantoms and Fantasies in America," from *Off the Reservation: Reflections on Boundary-Busting, Border-Crossing, Loose Canons* (1998).

There was a Wampanoag village that had been emptied by previous contact with the Europeans; the inhabitants had died of some disease the year before. These poor, "weather-beaten bodies" repaired thereto and made themselves at home. The village that succored them was one filled with houses covered by elm-bark of generous size, walled around by a "stockade" fence, which thus nicely separated from home that which they most feared: woods and thickets that, to their minds, represented a wild and savage face.

It is strange that accounts of early American experience overlook the presence of other human communities—a negligible presence, we are led to believe, all but gone right after the first Thanksgiving dinner. Despite American folklore that is all too often offered to children and adults alike as "fact," there were thousands upon thousands of people living in settled, agricultural communities along the Atlantic seaboard. And it was these societies—or, one may fairly say, this civilization—from which the colonials drew the strength, courage, and concepts upon which to base both their revolutions against England and, much later, Spain and to devise a form of nationhood that recognized the equal rights of all adult citizens, male and female, "high born" or "common," to have a voice in their own governance. And though it took them well over a century, from 1776 to 1947, eventually they recognized their founding ideals in law. "The shot heard round the world," as the American Revolution of 1776 was termed by pundits and philosophers of the eighteenth and nineteenth centuries, was fired from an Algonquin and Haudenoshonee gun.

Whoever the first Americans were, they weren't the Puritans, whose idea of social organization was to lock all citizens within the palisades, whip and chain people to stockades or to wagons or horses from which they were dragged out of town, or to banish them, alone, to the wilderness for in any way disagreeing with the "town fathers," who were the sole recognized authorities. Thus, it is strangest of all that "our images" were suitable mirrors of being, while we were and still are not allowed to be there at all.

I have sat through more hours of American History and American Literature than I care to contemplate, and seldom is the word "Indian" (even that misshapen idol) mentioned. "With all due respect, ma'am," ever the courtly professorial expert of white

supremacy, "Indians never had any effect on America at all."
(America's a self-made Marlborough man, ma'am).

Did you know that the Cherokee tipped the balance of
Spanish power that gave the south Atlantic coast to the English?

That the Haudenoshonee ("Iroquois") dominated the power
struggle among France, England, and Spain for over two hundred
years?

That the Chickasaw platoons who ran missions for Andrew
Jackson during the War of 1812 were the reason for the victory of
the United States over England?

I didn't.

I spent twenty-two years in school, and I didn't know that.

Nor in all those years was I ever given this moving speech to
memorize. Delivered by Ta-ha-yu-ta (Logan), the lone survivor of
his community and family during the French and Indian War, this
bit of eloquence was featured in the McGuffy Reader, used for several generations in American public schools as exemplary oratory.

> I appeal to any white man to say, if he ever entered Logan's cabin
> hungry, and he gave him not meat; if ever he came cold and
> naked, and he clothed him not. During the course of the last long
> and bloody war, Logan remained idle in his cabin, an advocate of
> peace. Such was my love for the whites, that my countrymen
> pointed as they passed, and I said, "Logan is the friend of white
> man." I had even thought to have lived with you but for the injuries
> of one man. Colonel Cresap, the last spring, in cold blood and
> unprovoked, murdered all the relations of Logan, not even sparing
> my women and children. There runs not a drop of my blood in the
> veins of any living creature. This called on me my revenge. I have
> sought it; I have killed many; I have fully glutted my vengeance. For
> my country, I rejoiced at the beams of peace. But do not harbor a
> thought that this is the joy of fear. Logan never felt fear. He will not
> turn on his heel to save his life. Who is there to mourn for
> Logan?—Not one!

> —*TAH-HA-YU-TA [LOGAN], IROQUOIS*

The French and Indian War was fought in the mid-1700s, before
the founding of the Republic. The Puritans, historically deemed the

nation's forefathers, had come ashore not two centuries before. But they were not the first Europeans to colonize what is now the United States. New Mexico was colonized long before Plymouth. Why was Puritan Colony designated the earliest American settlement? Why do chronological history or literature books start with the Puritans? In terms of the present boundaries of the United States, the Southwest was entered first and subdued (more or less). Then Florida. Then New England and New France. Then California, Navajoland/Apache. Then the Plains. But American history marches ever westward, from the northern Atlantic coast of the United States to California. Let us be ever mindful that that history speaks English. But that it does so is accidental. English was made the national language by one vote over German because a cart carrying two delegates to the Continental Congress meeting on the issue broke down. Those two delegates, who were prepared to cast their votes for the German language, missed the meeting. These instances of historians' oversights can be explained, of course: Europeans didn't invade, conquer, and "settle" America; Yale and Harvard—with barely perceptible assists from Andover, William and Mary, Dartmouth, and Princeton—did. There is more than a grain of truth in this explanation, but there is another, more intriguing, one: America has amnesia.

The American myth, for some reason, depends on an "empty" continent for its glory, and for its meaningfulness to Americans. The Adam who names the beasts and the birds, who tends God's garden, wasn't to be beat out of his place, dethroned as "Firstborn of God" by Spaniards, Dutchmen, Frenchmen, or, heaven forbid, savages.

> President Jackson asked,
> What good man would prefer a forested country ranged with savages
> To our extensive republic studded with cities
> With all the improvements art can devise or industry execute?

The question that has haunted me for several years now is: What did they see when they saw their images emerge "from the mirrors of the world"? People don't develop amnesia for the love of forgetfulness—or do they? Certainly, there is a passion for memory loss in American thought. Thoreau speaks with indignation of the grip of history on the free growth of the (civilized) soul. "One generation abandons the enterprises of another like stranded vessels." And his construction is not unique to himself nor to Americans. He was aware of the Aztec ceremonial renewal of all possessions every fifty-two years (but probably not of its meaning as renewal). He confused history with bondage, perhaps because the history of Europeans was the history of the bondage of others as well as themselves.

> Then through the underbrush we cut our hopes
> Forest after forest to within
> The inner hush where Mississippi flows
> And were in ambush as the very source,
> Scalped to the cortex. Yet bought them off
> It was an act of love to seek their salvation.

The mind is a curious instrument—that of a culture no less so than that of a person—and its existential messages are more profoundly illuminating than its protestations. This amazing trick of memory-loss is such a case. It might tell us why America is ambivalent at best, schizoid or schizophrenic at worst. For how can one immediately experience the present without regard to the shaping presence of the past? Yet Americans have been, at least in the expressions of their artists and scholars, profoundly present-oriented and idea- or fantasy-centered. Their past has fascinated them, in a made-up form, but the real past is denied as though it is too painful—too opposed to the fantasy, the dream, to be spoken.

> Pastor Smiley inquired,
> What good man would allow his sins or his neighbors'
> To put on human dress and run in the wilds
> To leap out on innocent occasions?

Is that what they saw—their ideal of sin personified?

It is fairly clear that the European transplants did not see "Indians." It is possible that they did, as Josephine Miles (whose poem I've been quoting) suggests, see themselves. Certainly, this connection is borne out by the curious scholarly amnesia regarding the tribes who, contrary to popular American opinion, covered this continent as "the waves of a wind-ruffled sea cover its shell-paved floor," to quote Sealth (Seattle). Until recently, American figures have estimated the entire contact population of the tribes to be around 450,000. The numbers now estimated are around ten million, and this figure is rising. Some maverick researchers have put it as high as fifty or sixty million (present in what is now the United States).

I suppose if I saw myself as murdering, one way or another, several million people and hundreds of cultures, I'd long to forget my past, too.

> President Jackson asked,
> What good man would prefer a forested country ranged with savages
> To our extensive republic studded with cities
> With all the improvements art can devise or industry execute?

"The only good Indian is dead," they said; now that the Indian is presumed dead, he gets better and better all the time. The "Indian" can be interjected into the American dream, transformed, un-humanized, a sentimentalized sentinel of America's ideal of virtue. Nobody loves a drunk Indian because a drunk Indian is real, alive, and not at all ideal. The "Indian" was one with nature, they say; and who can be more "one with nature" than a corpse?

> Miss Benedict proposed,
> The partial era of enlightenment in which we live.
> Brings Dionysus to the mesa and the cottonwood grove,
> And floats Apollo to the barrows of the civic group
> To ratify entreaties and to harp on hope.

Americans may be the world champion forgetters. Yet their story has a strange logic of its own, and that logic is solidly based on the unconscious motives that propelled the actions and the rhetoric in the first place. And America has cultural amnesia, at least with regard to the Tribes. He, "American Adam," is born innocent, purer than Christ, having neither mother nor (legitimate) father. Yet all that is born on earth has parents: why is it so important that America pretend to be different in this respect, to reject her commonality with all things? The mother, the land, is forgotten and denied, but the father, Europe, is not forgotten so much as attacked, as in a Freudian Oedipal drama, conquered over and over, a recurrent bad dream.

> The question, whether one generation of men has a right to bind another, seems never to have started on this our side of the water. Yet it is a question of such consequence as not only to merit decision, but place, also, among the fundamental principles of government.

> —*THOMAS JEFFERSON, 1789*

The mother: Indian, earth, and Nature (seen as one thing, according to Brandon in *The Last Americans*) were submerged into "the infinite pool of the unconscious," hopefully never to be recovered. Perhaps this is Oedipal also, Frank Waters tells us in *Pumpkin Seed Point*, that the Indian represents the lost unconscious that Americans must reclaim and redeem.

It was an act of love to seek their salvation.

The eternal Mother is forever forbidden to man, the story goes. The gulf between mother and son is enormous and widening. And this is the schizophrenic split: Americans are forever forbidden to love the source of their being and so, their being in itself. Since Mother can't be loved, her falsified image, a grotesque fantasy, must be forever conquered and possessed. However violent the fantasization process, violence is a necessary component of the repression: Indians won't be fantasized and erased; they endure in spite of everything. History persists as well, but the fantasy is out of control, threatened with exposure (and annihilation) by ever-present reality: another recurrent nightmare.

The Americans separated themselves from their paternal heritage, or so they believed. They removed their maternal heritage from sight and embarked on the expediencies of treaty, fraud, murder, mass enslavement, duplicity, starvation, infection—deliberate as well as accidental—whipping, torture, and removal. They needed land, it is said. They were greedy, it is said.

But to my mind, neither need nor greed can explain the genocide. Neither can explain the raging destruction of the earth. Neither can explain the single-minded, horrifying assault on the tribes as tribal entities, long after Indian presence was reduced to nostalgic memory, long after Indians could possibly be a military or economic threat, so long after that even today the assault continues. What obscure drive causes this single-minded pursuit of destruction?

America, the lonely hero, sprung full-blown out of the mind of God. The moral condition. The righteous imperative. Without father or mother, alone, divided, singular, driven to destroy all that speaks of cooperation, sharing, communality. The Puritans' own communes couldn't last a single generation. I am told that "thirty years is a long time for a Utopia to last." (In America, I silently add. Other utopias have lasted millennia. But they weren't based on the idea that a single individual was more than God.) It seems that Americans, loving loneliness best of all freedoms, die from it. Perhaps the central truth of early colonial experience in New England was the enormity of their sense of isolation. Far from all that was familiar, the colonials learned, perforce, to view alienation as rugged individualism, making it their defining virtue. Isolation and self-referencing became "self-reliance," providing the basic theme for American civilization for the ensuing two centuries.

The loneliness of exploration was, and is, a compelling idea for Americans. The lone hero still wanders, determined and self-assured, however lost, across the pages of America. Ronald Reagan in the forties and Robert Redford in the seventies flicker in their autistic heroism across the projected screens of American life. The Great American Cowboy is cheered for his self-reliance; the most hated American is the one who accepts society's help through a welfare allotment. And it isn't a matter of virtue in the Protestant sense that creates this peculiarity: It is not that taking care of oneself is a virtue. It is that the hero is, above all things, lonely and happy in his estrangement from all bonds that bind and cling, depend and shape. Andrew Jackson was idolized for his singular determination to let no considerations of social need or wish, of moral or legal *noblesse oblige*, interfere with his isolated, splendid determination.

In America, law substitutes for custom. In America, society substitutes for love of family, comrade, village, or tribe. *Walden* is the self-proclaimed triumph of the isolated, superior individual. Alone with nature, not in it. Not of it. One can be with it as a scholar is with a book, but as an observer, not a creative participant.

Indians are called primitive and savage not because they commit atrocities; everyone commits atrocities one way or another. Indians are designated primitive because they place the good of the group and the good of the earth before that of the self. Mexicans are denigrated not because they speak with an accent, not because they take siestas, not because they routed American heroes at the Alamo, not because they have what Americans want—a large share of North America—but because they think *sangre* is more important than reason, that *la familia* is more important than fame. The community is the greatest threat to the American Individual Ethic; and it is the community that must be punished and destroyed. Not because Americans take much conscious notice of community, but because community is what a human being must have to be human in any sense, and community is what Americans deny themselves—in the name of progress, in the name of growth. In the name of Freedom. In the name of the Hero.

A person can't cherish glorious loneliness from within a community. So, most women, as keepers of community, are also despised: Remember "Momism?" We are a constant reminder of the lonely male's need to belong to others so that he can belong to himself. And it was the natural and necessary belonging of the Native American that so infuriated the Americans, so that those men who are America's greatest heroes rose to commit mass murder of the tribes. The difference between Native Americans and Americans, William Brandon says (*The Last of the Americans*), is that belonging is most important to the Indians, while belongings are most important to the Whites. But what are belongings but a badge of isolation, a mountain of clutter that walls one off from those around? Thoreau revealed the most about himself (and his admirers) by saying that he felt that the name Walden was originally "walled in." He was most taken by the idea that Walden (or White) Pond had no apparent source for its water, and no outlet. Entire unto itself. A very moist desert dependent on nothing. Caused by nothing. Surrounded by smooth, regular stones. A wall to keep its pristine clarity, its perfect isolation. Secure.

It is not so strange that everyman-America hates and fears Communism. The very word strikes at the root of the American way and at the heart of the American sickness: a communist is one who must depend on others. A communist is one who must cooperate. A communist is one who must share.

And it is no wonder that the American Scholar is believed to live in an "ivory tower"; that utopians invariably take themselves off to splendid isolation from the contamination of others; that Americans are obsessed with the terror of "infectious disease"; that we are obsessed with "privacy"; that our proudest document is entitled, "The Declaration of Independence."

I have always wondered why Americans never cooperate on anything. Why even a corporation, a company of many persons, is defined as a "legal individual." I begin to see why. Strange that Dionysus is relegated to the "mesa and to the cottonwood grove" and Apollo to "the barrows of the civic group"—neither of which are considered American by rugged-individual Americans. And today, Dionysus is dying of thirst on the mesas and in the dying cottonwood grove, while Apollo is on his way to outer space. They cut off Dionysus's water supply and sent Apollo to the moon. Both are thus beyond the reach of encounter or confrontation. All that is left for America to deal with, to find itself with, are myths and mirrors and shadowy reflections that twist in on themselves and on time and space so that truth, the truth about America's past and America's identity, can never be found, never be affirmed or renewed. And in this way everything becomes relative, nothing related instead of the other way around, the only way we can remain sane.

> Reading today this manual of wisdom,
> In the still coves
> We meet our images
>
> And, in ambush at the very source,
> Would buy them off. It is an act of love
> To seek their salvation.

It is not that Americans are lonely that matters here, but that Americans cherish loneliness disguised as solitude as though it were a wife. They take her to their breasts and cleave to her with the determined clutch of catatonia. They will not let her go. They protect her with all the ferocious murderousness of a jealousy-crazed lover and will kill anything that threatens to tear their loneliness away.

It occurs to me that governments are instituted among men to keep them apart. And so is capitalism. And its fodder, money. And so are "nuclear" families—highly mobile, of course. And so is progress, the touchstone of corporationism, of the nation, and of every American's life. It occurs to me that the "melting pot" never worked because it was not intended to work and that schools and other institutions are designed to teach and reinforce the principle that group experiences are painful, anti-human, demoralizing, like the infants in Orwell's *1984* were taught through pain to fear music and flowers. Loneliness, the beloved of the American Hero, is a coiling clinging snake. It is strangling the life out of the people, the families around us, killed by the murderous creation of our own minds. Yet it is seductive, hypnotic in its murderous intent, because however fiercely loved, solitude is not really possible, in this world after all.

> . . . And when the last Red Man shall have perished and the mem-
> ory of my tribe shall have become a myth among the White men,
> these shores will swarm with the invisible dead of my tribe, and
> when your children's children think themselves alone in the field,
> the store, the shop, upon the highway, or in the silence of the path-
> less woods, they will not be alone. In all the earth there is no place
> dedicated to solitude. At night when the streets of your cities and
> villages are silent and you think them deserted, they will throng
> with the returning hosts that once filled them and still love this
> beautiful land. The White Man will never be alone.
>
> *—SEALTH*

Why is it essential that the American be self-reliant, commu-nityless—without a place to belong, a past to remember, a begin-ning in the roots of time, a heritage that would give them a mean-ingful place in the living circle that is life on this earth? Americans have an overwhelming, consuming need to be different. Do we cling to loneliness because nothing can be so peculiar as this monstrous love affair with isolation?

> Professor Roy Harvey Pearce quoted,
> These savages are outlandish Tartars and Cain's children,
> Though someone reported once, "They do not withold assent
> From the truth set forth in a credible manner."
> Is it possible?

In 1974, Americans can no longer afford the masochistic love of loneliness. The problems that confront us cannot be solved by a lone hero riding into town, a "law unto himself." No *one* can save us, but we must learn how to save ourselves—all of ourselves. We cannot do it unless we have models of community; America needs to become a tribe.

In our history we have pursued a consistent policy of exterminating Indians; that guilt rests as heavy as would matricide. Along with Indians, America has relentlessly destroyed the Earth and Earth's creatures—Indians, Nature, Earth, all of these are America's mother who must be denied. The lone/lonely hero must be more than god; he must be entire unto himself, "walled-in." But the destruction wrought by individual initiative necessarily haunts us now, because everywhere we look, we see death: past, present, and future. And death is what America has fled for five hundred years.

There is something that can be done; there is a way around the destruction, but it requires giving up America's real love: loneliness. This time, America can't do it herself. She needs models for community; for a rational place for femininity in the community; for ways to integrate diverse lifestyles and ethnic values into the national community; for regaining deteriorating neighborhoods; for ways to handle "deviance" so that the deviant can be allowed to continue as a participant in the community's life, and so that most "deviance" just won't occur. America needs child-rearing models and models for communities that integrate and support families in their economic, interpersonal, and child-rearing tasks. America needs a guide to the overhauling of institutions so that they can foster persons and communities instead of dividing and destroying them. America needs to find ways to preserve identity that do not result in destruction of the community: an individual who has no home, no place, is not a human being, but a prey of every vagrant whim and demagoguery. Humans cannot exist in isolation; they go insane. America needs to learn ways to preserve the individual's sense of identity, and the nation's, in a pluralistic, culturally diverse society. America needs to resolve the "leadership" problems (crisis, say some); to learn how to live in balance and harmony with the living environment; to learn creative, participatory ways of meeting the challenges of survival and technology instead of destructive, apathetic reactions toward them.

America needs a way to understand how society and community can function harmoniously and how a person can fit meaningfully into the massive body of this century's life. Above all, America needs a tradition that is relevant to this continent and the life upon it; America needs a sense of history, a sense of America's place in eternal time, a way to use history as renewal, not as denial. To do this, America must absolve herself of the historic guilt toward her predecessors and heal the split in her soul.

> *One party to the purchase*
> *Receipts the purchase price and hands us back*
> *His token of negotiation which redeems:*
> We Cannibals must help these Christians.

America has a ready way to find those models so desperately needed, assuming America intends to solve them. To do this, though, American scholars and officials have to stop looking at the American Indians as "primitives" or "curios." They will have to give up the concept of Indians as mirrors of idealizations and projections of imagined sinfulness and see us instead as peoples who know how to resolve the problems all of America faces. The tribes today and throughout history provide brilliant and solid models that America could learn from and build on. Instead of treating the tribes as "problems," America should relate to us as a potentially creative force in American life.

Most Native Americans see themselves as necessarily a part of America. Red and White have been through five hundred years of experience together; whether that experience was good or bad, it has been bonding. As for the partners in an American marriage, that bond has been born of pain, fantasy, love, and shared grief as much as of horror and death, punishment and guilt. Native America has lived through every attempt at conquest and annihilation and knows that the human spirit is, in the last analysis, unconquerable. That knowledge alone, given in blood, written all over this continent in agony, can free Americans from their fear of annihilation, if Americans are willing to share the agony and redemption with Native Americans.

For thousands and thousands of years, the tribes faced the problems of community and survival, growth and freedom, and

solved them; the only problem they could not solve was
America's passion for isolation, that ambivalence, that destruc-
tiveness, that "craziness," those policies, and that contempt.
Above all, the contempt, for, make no mistake—however benevolent America's patronage has been, it was always patronage; it is
still patronage. Indians don't need that patronage, they need
respect. They need to work together with greater America to
resolve that last dilemma, which, cannot be resolved without
cooperation.

It is easy to say *how* America can solve the cruel problems that
face us, but it is impossible to say that she *will*. For ever since white
men came here, they were torn. On the one hand, they loved freedom, and the Native Americans helped them in that love, supported them, taught them what freedom means. But on the other
hand, the immigrants hated freedom, feared it, feared to make the
adjustments and sacrifices and immolations of self that freedom
requires. They thought that the isolated self was the badge of
strength and glory; they didn't see that a free being is free as a
member of a universe of member-beings, and they feared that perception as they feared the Devil and death. So in their terror and
conflict, they tried to enslave all that was free-thinking, perhaps to
compromise between that love and that fear, that attraction toward
freedom and that repulsion from what it entails. But they could
never enslave the Indians; they had to resort to destruction in the
attempt, as they had to destroy their own emblem, Eagle, as they
destroyed Buffalo, Wolf, Whale; as they are presently determined to
destroy Coyote and Mountain Lion. And failing in that destruction
of Native peoples because they finally couldn't bring themselves
to do it, nothing was left but to deny the Tribes' existence, meaning,
and way of life.

But suppose they finally succeed; suppose all the free creatures are finally exterminated—dead or changed beyond all recognition; suppose all this Turtle Island is reduced to a wasteland of
dead waters and dead plants and dead mountains. Will America
have finally succeeded in realizing her dearest dream? For then
America will be alone, with only death and terror for comfort and
companionship.

We have finally reached that place: the seeds of destruction
and the seeds of life have reached their season of harvest. Whether

the one or the other is given to the people to eat depends in part on which seed grows hardiest in the soil that is America. It's reaping time; now we see how well we have sown.

FURTHER READINGS
Kathleen M. Donovan, "Storytelling Women: Paula Gunn Allen and Toni Morrison," in *Feminist Readings of Native American Literature: Coming to Voice* (University of Arizona Press, 1998); Paula Gunn Allen, "'Border' Studies: The Intersection of Gender and Color," in David Palumbo-Liu, ed., *The Ethnic Canon: Histories, Institutions, and Interventions* (University of Minnesota Press, 1995); Paula Gunn Allen, "Who is Your Mother?: Red Roots of White Feminism," in Ronald Takaki, ed., *From Different Shores: Perspectives on Race and Ethnicity in America* (2nd ed., Oxford University Press, 1994); Paula Gunn Allen, "Going home, December 1992," in *A Circle of Nations: Voices and Visions of American Indians*, ed. John Gattuso (Beyond Words, 1993); Donna Perry, *Backtalk: Women Writers Speak Out: Interviews* (Rutgers University Press, 1993); Maria Moss, *We've Been Here Before: Women in Creation Myths and Contemporary Literature of the Native American Southwest* (Lit, 1993); Elizabeth I. Hanson, *Paula Gunn Allen* (Boise State University Press, 1990); Laura Coltelli, ed., *Winged Words: American Indian Writers Speak* (University of Nebraska Press, 1990).

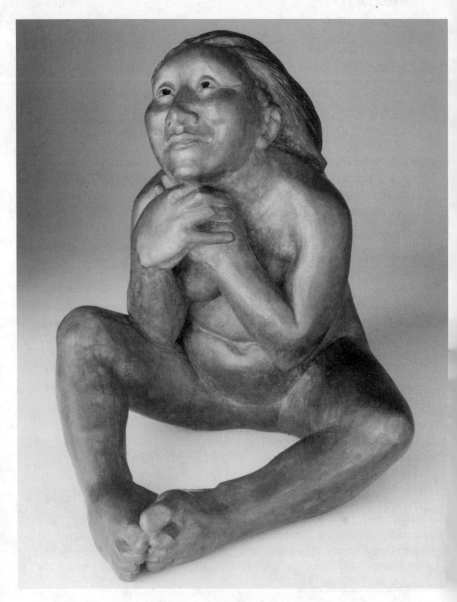

**Roxanne Swentzell, "In Love,"
photographed by Wendy McEahern.**

*Used by permission of Peter Wright, Wright Publishing Co.,
Albuquerque, New Mexico.*

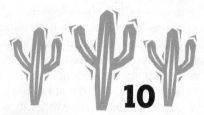

10

Looking Within Myself I Am Many Parts: Western Women's Writing Today

In thinking about Western women's writing today, we have been reminded of the painting of the late Santa Clara Pueblo artist Helen Hardin, who titled a portrait of a woman "Looking Within Myself I Am Many Parts." Looking within ourselves, Western women writers are many parts—Westerners, women, and a myriad of other identities as well. It is a joyous thing to admit that this scant selection of Western women's writing today only scratches the surface of what is now available. Nonetheless, here we present some of our favorite recent and contemporary writings by women, writings which provide at least a glimpse of the richness and breadth of western women's literary output today.

Through these stories and poems run a passion for the place and a sense of home. From Joan Didion's examination of California's "west of the West" status to Gretel Ehrlich's finely-drawn evocation of Wyoming's openness, from Janet Campbell Hale's exorcism of Custer's ghost to Sandra Cisneros's repossession of the Alamo, here are represented the vivid voices of Western women writing today.

Joan Didion (1934–   )

Born in Sacramento, California, in 1934, Joan Didion is a fifth-generation Californian for whom California (and the West which contains it) has become both a focal point and a vanishing point. The daughter of an Army Air Corps officer, Didion moved with her family all over the West, settling momentarily in Colorado before returning to Sacramento. In 1956, Didion graduated from the University of California at Berkeley, and took a job writing copy for *Vogue Magazine* in New York City, where she was soon promoted to editor. Didion later wrote that her seven year sojourn in New York had not changed her, as what happened there "seemed to impinge not at all upon the Sacramento mind." In 1963 she returned to California, settling in Los Angeles, and publishing the novel *Run River,* the story of the disintegration of a California family.

Didion's oft-mentioned compulsion to precision—she has said, of her work, "I'm not much interested in spontaneity, what concerns me is total control"—connects with many readers' stereotypical view of California as a site of neurosis, psychoanalysis, and obsessiveness. At least one critic has named California "the id of America." In California, which she portrays as chaos swirling about her calm and controlled self, Didion finds the perfect demonstration of her fears about the world spinning out of control. Perhaps this conviction that things fall apart is not surprising coming from the great, great, great-granddaughter of a member of the Donner Party, perhaps the greatest disaster of the overland trail.

Didion is known for her many collections of her magazine columns and essays, which include *Slouching Towards Bethlehem* (1968), *The White Album* (1979), *After Henry* (1992), and the longer essays published as volumes, *Salvador* (1983) and *Miami* (1987). Didion's short novels include *Play It as It Lays* (1970), *A Book of Common Prayer* (1977), *Democracy* (1984), and *The Last Thing He Wanted* (1996).

In this selection, taken from her 1979 volume *The White Album,* Didion examines an issue of deep significance in California, as in much of the West: water. In her evocation of the complicated engineering behind western communities' conquest of nature, she illustrates the precariousness of western settlement, even in the computer age.

HOLY WATER

Some of us who live in arid parts of the world think about water with a reverence others might find excessive. The water I will draw tomorrow from my tap in Malibu is today crossing the Mojave Desert from the Colorado River, and I like to think about exactly where that water is. The water I will drink tonight in a restaurant in Hollywood is by now well down the Los Angeles Aqueduct from the Owens River, and I also think about exactly where that water is: I particularly like to imagine it as it cascades down the 45-degree stone steps that aerate Owens water after its airless passage through the mountain pipes and siphons. As it happens my own reverence for water has always taken the form of this constant meditation upon where the water is, of an obsessive interest not in the politics of water but in the waterworks themselves, in the movement of water through aqueducts and siphons and pumps and forebays and afterbays and weirs and drains, in plumbing on the grand scale. I know the data on water projects I will never see. I know the difficulty Kaiser had closing the last two sluiceway gates on the Guri Dam in Venezuela. I keep watch on evaporation behind the Aswan in Egypt. I can put myself to sleep imagining the water dropping a thousand feet into the turbines at Churchill Falls in Labrador. If the Churchill Falls Project fails to materialize, I fall back on water-works closer at hand—the tailrace at Hoover on the Colorado, the surge tank in the Tehachapi Mountains that receives California Aqueduct water pumped higher than water has ever been pumped before—and finally I replay a morning when I was seventeen years old and caught, in a military-surplus life raft, in the construction of the Nimbus Afterbay Dam on the American River near Sacramento. I remember that at the moment it happened I was trying to open a tin of anchovies with capers. I recall the raft

---

Joan Didion, "Holy Water," from *The White Album* (1979).

spinning into the narrow chute through which the river had been temporarily diverted. I recall being deliriously happy.

I suppose it was partly the memory of that delirium that led me to visit, one summer morning in Sacramento, the Operations Control Center for the California State Water Project. Actually so much water is moved around California by so many different agencies that maybe only the movers themselves know on any given day whose water is where, but to get a general picture it is necessary only to remember that Los Angeles moves some of it, San Francisco moves some of it, the Bureau of Reclamation's Central Valley Project moves some of it and the California State Water Project moves most of the rest of it, moves a vast amount of it, moves more water farther than has ever been moved anywhere. They collect this water up in the granite keeps of the Sierra Nevada and they store roughly a trillion gallons of it behind the Oroville Dam and every morning, down at the Project's headquarters in Sacramento, they decide how much of their water they want to move the next day. They make this morning decision according to supply and demand, which is simple in theory but rather more complicated in practice. In theory each of the Project's five field divisions—the Oroville, the Delta, the San Luis, the San Joaquin and the Southern divisions—place a call to headquarters before nine A.M. and tells the dispatchers how much water is needed by its local water contractors, who have in turn based their morning estimates on orders from growers and other big users. A schedule is made. The gates open and close according to schedule. The water flows south and the deliveries are made.

In practice this requires prodigious coordination, precision, and the best efforts of several human minds and that of a Univac 418. In practice it might be necessary to hold large flows of water for power production, or to flush out encroaching salinity in the Sacramento-San Joaquin Delta, the most ecologically sensitive point on the system. In practice a sudden rain might obviate the need for a delivery when that delivery is already on its way. In practice what is being delivered here is an enormous volume of water, not quarts of milk or spools of thread, and it takes two days to move such a delivery down through Oroville into the Delta, which is the great pooling place for California water and has been for some years alive with electronic sensors and telemetering equipment and men blocking channels and diverting flows and shoveling fish away from the pumps. It takes perhaps another six days to move this same water down the California Aqueduct from the Delta to the Tehachapi and put it over the hill to Southern California. "Putting some over the hill" is what they say around the Project Operations Control Center when they want to indicate that they are pumping Aqueduct water from the floor of the San Joaquin Valley up and over the Tehachapi Mountains. "Pulling it down" is what they say when they want to indicate that they are lowering a water level somewhere in the system. They can put some over the hill by remote control from this room in Sacramento with its Univac and its big board and its flashing lights. They can pull down a pool in the San Joaquin by remote control from this room in Sacramento with its locked doors and its ringing alarms and its constant print-outs of data from sensors out there in the water itself. From this room in Sacramento the whole system takes on the aspect of a per-fect three-billion-dollar hydraulic toy, and in certain ways it is. "LET'S START DRAINING QUAIL AT 12:00" was the 10:51 A.M. entry on the electronically recorded communications log the day I visited the Operations Control Center. "Quail" is a reservoir in Los Angeles County with a gross capacity of 1,636,-018,000 gallons. "OK" was the response recorded in the log. I knew at that moment that I had missed the only vocation for which I had any instinctive affinity: I wanted to drain Quail myself.

Not many people I know carry their end of the conversation when I want to talk about water deliveries, even when I stress that these deliveries affect their lives, indirectly, every day. "Indirectly" is not quite enough for most people I know. This morning, however, several people I know were affected not "indirectly" but "directly" by the way the water moves. They had been in New Mexico shoot-ing a picture, one sequence of which required a river deep enough to sink a truck, the kind with a cab and a trailer and fifty or sixty wheels. It so happened that no river near the New Mexico location was running that deep this year. The production was therefore moved today to Needles, California, where the Colorado River nor-mally runs, depending upon releases from Davis Dam, eighteen to twenty-five feet deep. Now. Follow this closely: yesterday we had a freak tropical storm in Southern California, two inches of rain in a normally dry month, and because this rain flooded the fields and provided more irrigation than any grower could possibly want for several days, no water was ordered from Davis Dam.

No orders, no releases.

Supply and demand.

As a result the Colorado was running only seven feet deep past Needles today, Sam Peckinpah's desire for eighteen feet of water in which to sink a truck not being the kind of demand anyone at Davis Dam is geared to meet. The production closed down for the weekend. Shooting will resume Tuesday, providing some grower orders water and the agencies controlling the Colorado release it. Meanwhile many gaffers, best boys, cameramen, assistant directors, script supervisors, stunt drivers and maybe even Sam Peckinpah are waiting out the weekend in Needles, where it is often 110 degrees at five P.M. and hard to get dinner after eight. This is a California parable, but a true one.

I have always wanted a swimming pool, and never had one. When it became generally known a year or so ago that California was suffering severe drought, many people in water-rich parts of the country seemed obscurely gratified, and made frequent reference to Californians having to brick up their swimming pools. In fact a swimming pool requires, once it has been filled and the filter has begun its process of cleaning and recirculating the water, virtually no water, but the symbolic content of swimming pools has always been interesting: a pool is misapprehended as a trapping of affluence, real or pretended, and of a kind of hedonistic attention to the body. Actually a pool is, for many of us in the West, a symbol not of affluence but of order, of control over the uncontrollable. A pool is water, made available and useful, and is, as such, infinitely soothing to the western eye.

It is easy to forget that the only natural force over which we have any control out here is water, and that only recently. In my memory California summers were characterized by the coughing in the pipes that meant the well was dry, and California winters by all-night watches on rivers about to crest, by sandbagging, by dynamite on the levees and flooding on the first floor. Even now the place is not all that hospitable to extensive settlement. As I write a fire has been burning out of control for two weeks in the ranges behind the Big Sur coast. Flash floods last night wiped out all major roads into Imperial County. I noticed this morning a hairline crack in a living-room tile from last week's earthquake, a 4.4 I never felt. In the part of California where I now live aridity is the single most prominent feature of the climate, and I am not pleased to see, this year, cactus spreading wild to the sea. There will be days this winter when the humidity will drop to ten, seven, four. Tumbleweed will blow against my house and the sound of the rattlesnake will be duplicated a hundred times a day by dried bougainvillea drifting in my driveway. The apparent ease of California life is an illusion, and those who believe the illusion real live here in only the most temporary way. I know as well as the next person that there is considerable transcendent value in a river running wild and undammed, a river running free over granite, but I have also lived beneath such a river when it was running in flood, and gone without showers when it was running dry.

"The West begins," Bernard DeVoto wrote, "where the average annual rainfall drops below twenty inches." This is maybe the best definition of the West I have ever read, and it goes a long way toward explaining my own passion for seeing the water under control, but many people I know persist in looking for psychoanalytical implications in this passion. As a matter of fact I have explored, in an amateur way, the more obvious of these implications, and come up with nothing interesting. A certain external reality remains, and resists interpretation. The West begins where the average annual rainfall drops below twenty inches. Water is important to people who do not have it, and the same is true of control. Some fifteen years ago I tore a poem by Karl Shapiro from a magazine and pinned it on my kitchen wall. This fragment of paper is now on the wall of a sixth kitchen, and crumbles a little whenever I touch it, but I keep it there for the last stanza, which has for me the power of a prayer:

It is raining in California, a straight rain
Cleaning the heavy oranges on the bough,

Filling the gardens till the gardens flow,
Shining the olives, tiling the gleaming tile,
Waxing the dark camellia leaves more green,
Flooding the daylong valleys like the Nile.

I thought of those lines almost constantly on the morning in Sacramento when I went to visit the California State Water Project Operations Control Center. If I had wanted to drain Quail at 10:51 that morning, I wanted, by early afternoon, to do a great deal more. I wanted to open and close the Clifton Court Forebay intake gate. I wanted to produce some power down at the San Luis Dam. I wanted to pick a pool at random on the Aqueduct and pull it down and then refill it, watching for the hydraulic jump. I wanted to put some water over the hill and I wanted to shut down all flow from the Aqueduct into the Bureau of Reclamation's Cross Valley Canal, just to see how long it would take somebody over at Reclamation to call up and complain. I stayed as long as I could and watched the system work on the big board with the lighted checkpoints. The Delta salinity report was coming in on one of the teletypes behind me. The Delta tidal report was coming in on another. The earthquake board, which has been desensitized to sound its alarm (a beeping tone for Southern California, a high-pitched tone for the north) only for those earthquakes which register at least 3.0 on the Richter Scale, was silent. I had no further business in this room and yet I wanted to stay the day. I wanted to be the one, that day, who was shining the olives, filling the gardens, and flooding the daylong valleys like the Nile. I want it still.

FURTHER READINGS
Janis P. Stout, *Strategies of Reticence: Silence and Meaning in the Works of Jane Austen, Willa Cather, Katherine Anne Porter, and Joan Didion* (University Press of Virginia, 1990); Sharon Felton, *The Critical Response to Joan Didion* (Greenwood Publishing Group, 1993); Michelle Carbone Loris, *Innocence, Loss and Recovery in the Art of Joan Didion* (Peter Lang Publishing, 1989); Ellen Friedman, ed., *Joan Didion: Essays & Conversations* (Ontario Review Press, 1984); Katherine Usher Henderson, *Joan Didion* (Ungar, 1981); Mark Royden Winchell, *Joan Didion* (Twayne, 1980).

Gretel Ehrlich (1946–   )

Born in 1946 in Santa Barbara, California, Gretel Ehrlich was educated at Bennington College, the University of California, Los Angeles, Film School, and the New School for Social Research. After living in big cities like Los Angeles and New York City, Ehrlich relocated to Wyoming in 1976, after having gone to the state to make a film and finding herself transformed by her encounter with its landscapes. Amid the undulating hills of the Wyoming plains, Ehrlich found that, "Space has a spiritual equivalent and can heal what is divided and burdensome in us." Taking a job as a sheepherder, she learned to live in Wyoming's arid space, and found herself healed by the experience. As she writes of this time, "Friends asked when I was going to stop 'hiding out' in Wyoming. What appeared to them as a landscape of lunar desolation and intellectual backwardness was luxurious to me. For the first time I was able to take up residence on earth with no alibis, no self-promoting schemes." The result of this "residence on earth" was Ehrlich's first non-fiction work, *The Solace of Open Spaces* (1985).

In addition to *The Solace of Open Spaces*, Ehrlich has published several collections of poetry, including *Geode/Rock Body* (1970), *To Touch the Water* (1981), and *Arctic Heart: A Poem Cycle* (1992). She is also known for her collections of essays, which include *Wyoming Stories* (1986), *Drinking Dry Clouds: Stories from Wyoming* (1991), and *Islands, The Universe, Home* (1991). Her novel, *Heart Mountain* (1988), is set during World War II, when Japanese Americans were interned at the Heart Mountain Relocation Camp in Wyoming. In the early 1990s, she was struck by lightning near her Wyoming ranch; after a long rehabilitation from her injuries, she wrote *A Match to the Heart* (1995) about the experience. Ehrlich currently lives in California.

As Thomas Lyon has written of Ehrlich, "It is sometimes necessary now to go east to get to the West." Even though Ehrlich grew up in California, she did not feel she was really in "the West" until she landed in Wyoming, with its disorienting openness and aridity. In this selection from *The Solace of Open Spaces*, Ehrlich recounts her coming to what she thinks of as the West, and how she came to fall in love with it.

THE SOLACE OF OPEN SPACES

It's May and I've just awakened from a nap, curled against sage-brush the way my dog taught me to sleep—sheltered from wind. A front is pulling the huge sky over me, and from the dark a hailstone has hit me on the head. I'm trailing a band of two thousand sheep across a stretch of Wyoming badlands, a fifty-mile trip that takes five days because sheep shade up in hot sun and won't budge until it's cool. Bunched together now, and excited into a run by the storm, they drift across dry land, tumbling into draws like water and surge out again onto the rugged, choppy plateaus that are the building blocks of this state.

The name Wyoming comes from an Indian word meaning "at the great plains," but the plains are really valleys, great arid valleys, sixteen hundred square miles, with the horizon bending up on all sides into mountain ranges. This gives the vastness a sheltering look.

Winter lasts six months here. Prevailing winds spill snow-drifts to the east, and new storms from the northwest replenish them. This white bulk is sometimes dizzying, even nauseating, to look at. At twenty, thirty, and forty degrees below zero, not only does your car not work, but neither do your mind and body. The landscape hardens into a dungeon of space. During the winter, while I was riding to find a new calf, my jeans froze to the saddle, and in the silence that such cold creates I felt like the first person on earth, or the last.

Today the sun is out—only a few clouds billowing. In the east, where the sheep have started off without me, the benchland tilts up in a series of eroded red-earthed mesas, planed flat on top by a million years of water; behind them, a bold line of muscular scarps rears up ten thousand feet to become the Big Horn Mountains. A tidal pattern is engraved into the ground, as if left by the sea that

---

Gretel Ehrlich, "The Solace of Open Spaces," from *The Solace of Open Spaces* (1985).

once covered this state. Canyons curve down like galaxies to meet the oncoming rush of flat land.

To live and work in this kind of open country, with its hundred-mile views, is to lose the distinction between background and foreground. When I asked an older ranch hand to describe Wyoming's openness, he said, "It's all a bunch of nothing—wind and rattlesnakes—and so much of it you can't tell where you're going or where you've been and it don't make much difference." John, a sheepman I know, is tall and handsome and has an explosive temperament. He has a perfect intuition about people and sheep. They call him "Highpockets," because he's so long-legged; his graceful stride matches the distances he has to cover. He says, "Open space hasn't affected me at all. It's all the people moving in on it." The huge ranch he was born on takes up much of one county and spreads into another state; to put 100,000 miles on his pickup in three years and never leave home is not unusual. A friend of mine has an aunt who ranched on Powder River and didn't go off her place for eleven years. When her husband died, she quickly moved to town, bought a car, and drove around the States to see what she'd been missing.

Most people tell me they've simply driven through Wyoming, as if there were nothing to stop for. Or else they've skied in Jackson Hole, a place Wyomingites acknowledge uncomfortably because its green beauty and chic affluence are mismatched with the rest of the state. Most of Wyoming has a "lean-to" look. Instead of big, roomy barns and Victorian houses, there are dugouts, low sheds, log cabins, sheep camps, and fence lines that look like driftwood blown haphazardly into place. People here still feel pride because they live in such a harsh place, part of the glamorous cowboy past, and they are determined not to be the victims of a mining-dominated future.

Most characteristic of the state's landscape is what a developer euphemistically describes as "indigenous growth right up to your front door"—a reference to waterless stands of salt sage, snakes, jack rabbits, deerflies, red dust, a brief respite of wildflowers, dry washes, and no trees. In the Great Plains the vistas look like music, like Kyries of grass, but Wyoming seems to be the doing of a mad architect—tumbled and twisted, ribboned with faded, deathbed colors, thrust up and pulled down as if the place had been startled out of a deep sleep and thrown into a pure light.

I came here four years ago. I had not planned to stay, but I couldn't make myself leave. John, the sheepman, put me to work immediately. It was spring, and shearing time. For fourteen days of fourteen hours each, we moved thousands of sheep through sorting corrals to be sheared, branded, and deloused. I suspect that my original motive for coming here was to "lose myself" in new and unpopulated territory. Instead of producing the numbness I thought I wanted, life on the sheep ranch woke me up. The vitality of the people I was working with flushed out what had become a hallucinatory rawness inside me. I threw away my clothes and bought new ones; I cut my hair. The arid country was a clean slate. Its absolute indifference steadied me.

Sagebrush covers 58,000 square miles of Wyoming. The biggest city has a population of fifty thousand, and there are only five settlements that could be called cities in the whole state. The rest are towns, scattered across the expanse with as much as sixty miles between them, their populations two thousand, fifty, or ten. They are fugitive-looking, perched on a barren, windblown bench, or tagged onto a river or a railroad, or laid out straight in a farming valley with implement stores and a block-long Mormon church. In the eastern part of the state, which slides down into the Great Plains, the new mining settlements are boomtowns, trailer cities, metal knots on flat land.

Despite the desolate look, there's a coziness to living in this state. There are so few people (only 470,000) that ranchers who buy and sell cattle know one another statewide; the kids who choose to go to college usually go to the state's one university, in Laramie; hired hands work their way around Wyoming in a lifetime of hirings and firings. And despite the physical separation, people stay in touch, often driving two or three hours to another ranch for dinner.

Seventy-five years ago, when travel was by buckboard or horseback, cowboys who were temporarily out of work rode the grub line—drifting from ranch to ranch, mending fences or milking cows, and receiving in exchange a bed and meals. Gossip and messages traveled this slow circuit with them, creating an intimacy between ranchers who were three and four weeks' ride apart. One old-time couple I know, whose turn-of-the-century homestead was used by an outlaw gang as a relay station for stolen horses, recall that if you were traveling, desperado or not, any lighted ranch house was a welcome sign. Even now, for someone who lives in a remote spot, arriving at a ranch or coming to town for supplies is cause for celebration. To emerge from isolation can be disorienting. Everything looks bright, new, vivid. After I had been herding sheep for only three days, the sound of the camp tender's pickup flustered me. Longing for human company, I felt a foolish grin take over my face; yet I had to resist an urgent temptation to run and hide.

Things happen suddenly in Wyoming, the change of seasons and weather; for people, the violent swings in and out of isolation. But good-naturedness is concomitant with severity. Friendliness is a tradition. Strangers passing on the road wave hello. A common sight is two pickups stopped side by side far out on a range, on a dirt track winding through the sage. The drivers will share a cigarette, uncap their thermos bottles, and pass a battered cup, steaming with coffee, between windows. These meetings summon up the details of several generations, because, in Wyoming, private histories are largely public knowledge.

Because ranch work is a physical and, these days, economic strain, being "at home on the range" is a matter of vigor, self-reliance, and common sense. A person's life is not a series of dramatic events for which he or she is applauded or exiled but a slow accumulation of days, seasons, years, fleshed out by the generational weight of one's family and anchored by a land-bound sense of place.

In most parts of Wyoming, the human population is visibly outnumbered by the animal. Not far from my town of fifty, I rode into a narrow valley and startled a herd of two hundred elk. Eagles look like small people as they cat car-killed deer by the road. Antelope, moving in small, graceful bands, travel at sixty miles an hour, their mouths open as if drinking in the space.

The solitude in which westerners live makes them quiet. They telegraph thoughts and feelings by the way they tilt their heads and listen; pulling their Stetsons into a steep dive over their eyes, or pigeon-toeing one boot over the other, they lean against a fence with a fat wedge of Copenhagen beneath their lower lips and take in the whole scene. These detached looks of quiet amusement are sometimes cynical, but they can also come from a dry-eyed humility as lucid as the air is clear.

Conversation goes on in what sounds like a private code; a few phrases imply a complex of meanings. Asking directions, you get a curious list of details. While trailing sheep I was told to "ride up to that kinda upturned rock, follow the pink wash, turn left at the dump, and then you'll see the water hole." One friend told his wife on roundup to "turn at the salt lick and the dead cow," which turned out to be a scattering of bones and no salt lick at all.

Sentence structure is shortened to the skin and bones of a thought. Descriptive words are dropped, even verbs; a cowboy looking over a corral full of horses will say to a wrangler, "Which one needs rode?" People hold back their thoughts in what seems to be a dumbfounded silence, then erupt with an excoriating perceptive remark. Language, so compressed, becomes metaphorical. A rancher ended a relationship with one remark: "You're a bad check," meaning bouncing in and out was intolerable, and even coming back would be no good.

What's behind this laconic style is shyness. There is no vocabulary for the subject of feelings. It's not a hangdog shyness, or anything coy—always there's a robust spirit in evidence behind the restraint, as if the earth-dredging wind that pulls across Wyoming had carried its people's voices away but everything else in them had shouldered confidently into the breeze.

I've spent hours riding to sheep camp at dawn in a pickup when nothing was said; eaten meals in the cookhouse when the only words spoken were a mumbled "Thank you, ma'am" at the end of dinner. The silence is profound. Instead of talking, we seem to share one eye. Keenly observed, the world is transformed. The landscape is engorged with detail, every movement on it chillingly sharp. The air between people is charged. Days unfold, bathed in their own music. Nights become hallucinatory; dreams, prescient.

Spring weather is capricious and mean. It snows, then blisters with heat. There have been tornadoes. They lay their elephant trunks out in the sage until they find houses, then slurp everything up and leave. I've noticed that melting snowbanks hiss and rot, viperous, then drip into calm pools where ducklings hatch and live-stock, being trailed to summer range, drink. With the ice cover gone, rivers churn a milkshake brown, taking culverts and small bridges with them. Water in such an arid place (the average annual rainfall where I live is less than eight inches) is like blood. It festoons drab land with green veins; a line of cottonwoods following a stream; a strip of alfalfa; and, on ditch banks, wild asparagus growing.

I've moved to a small cattle ranch owned by friends. It's at the foot of the Big Horn Mountains. A few weeks ago, I helped them deliver a calf who was stuck halfway out of his mother's body. By the time he was freed, we could see a heartbeat, but he was strain-ing against a swollen tongue for air. Mary and I held him upside down by his back feet, while Stan, on his hands and knees in the blood, gave the calf mouth-to-mouth resuscitation. I have a vague memory of being pneumonia-choked as a child, my mother giving me her air, which may account for my romance with this windswept state.

If anything is endemic to Wyoming, it is wind. This big room of space is swept out daily, leaving a bone yard of fossils, agates, and carcasses in every stage of decay. Though it was water that initially shaped the state, wind is the meticulous gardener, raising dust and pruning the sage.

I try to imagine a world in which I could ride my horse across uncharted land. There is no wilderness left; wildness, yes, but true wilderness has been gone on this continent since the time of Lewis and Clark's overland journey.

Two hundred years ago, the Crow, Shoshone, Arapaho, Cheyenne, and Sioux roamed the intermountain West, orchestrat-ing their movements according to hunger, season, and warfare. Once they acquired horses, they traversed the spines of all the big Wyoming ranges—the Absarokas, the Wind Rivers, the Tetons, the Big Horns—and wintered on the unprotected plains that fan out from them. Space was life. The world was their home.

What was life-giving to Native Americans was often nightmar-ish to sodbusters who had arrived encumbered with families and ethnic pasts to be transplanted in nearly uninhabitable land. The great distances, the shortage of water and trees, and the loneliness created unexpected hardships for them. In her book *O Pioneers!*, Willa Cather gives a settler's version of the bleak landscape:

> The little town behind them had vanished as if it had never been, had fallen behind the swell of the prairie, and the stern frozen country received them into its bosom. The homesteads were few and far apart; here and there a windmill gaunt against the sky, a sod house crouching in a hollow.

The emptiness of the West was for others a geography of possibility. Men and women who amassed great chunks of land and struggled to preserve unfenced empires were, despite their self-serving motives, unwitting geographers. They understood the lay of the land. But by the 1850s the Oregon and Mormon trails sported bumper-to-bumper traffic. Wealthy landowners, many of them aristocratic absentee landlords, known as remittance men because they were paid to come West and get out of their families' hair, overstocked the range with more than a million head of cattle. By 1885 the feed and water were desperately short, and the winter of 1886 laid out the gaunt bodies of dead animals so closely together that when the thaw came, one rancher from Kaycee claimed to have walked on cowhide all the way to Crazy Woman Creek, twenty miles away.

Territorial Wyoming was a boy's world. The land was generous with everything but water. At first there was room enough, food enough, for everyone. And, as with all beginnings, an expansive mood set in. The young cowboys, drifters, shopkeepers, schoolteachers, were heroic, lawless, generous, rowdy, and tenacious. The individualism and optimism generated during those times have endured.

John Tisdale rode north with the trail herds from Texas. He was a college-educated man with enough money to buy a small outfit near the Powder River. While driving home from the town of Buffalo with a buckboard full of Christmas toys for his family and a winter's supply of food, he was shot in the back by an agent of the cattle barons who resented the encroachment of small-time stockmen like him. The wealthy cattlemen tried to control all the public grazing land by restricting membership in the Wyoming Stock Growers Association, as if it were a country club. They ostracized from roundups and brandings cowboys and ranchers who were not members, then denounced them as rustlers. Tisdale's death, the second such cold-blooded murder, kicked off the Johnson County cattle war, which was no simple good-guy-bad-guy shoot-out but a complicated class struggle between landed gentry and less afflu-ent settlers—a shocking reminder that the West was not an egali-tarian sanctuary after all.

Fencing ultimately enforced boundaries, but barbed wire abrogated space. It was stretched across the beautiful valleys, into the mountains, over desert badlands, through buffalo grass. The "anything is possible" fever—the lure of any new place—was con-stricted. The integrity of the land as a geographical body, and the freedom to ride anywhere on it, were lost.

I punched cows with a young man named Martin, who is the great-grandson of John Tisdale. His inheritance is not the open land that Tisdale knew and prematurely lost but a rage against restraint.

Wyoming tips down as you head northeast; the highest ground—the Laramie Plains—is on the Colorado border. Up where I live, the Big Horn River leaks into difficult, arid terrain. In the basin where it's dammed, sandhill cranes gather and, with delicate leg-work, slice through the stilled water. I was driving by with a rancher one morning when he commented that cranes are "old-fashioned." When I asked why, he said, "Because they mate for life." Then he looked at me with a twinkle in his eyes, as if to say he really did believe in such things but also understood why we break our own rules.

In all this open space, values crystalize quickly. People are strong on scruples but tenderhearted about quirky behavior. A friend and I found one ranch hand, who's "not quite right in the head," sitting in front of the badly decayed carcass of a cow, shak-ing his finger and saying, "Now, I don't want you to do this ever again!" When I asked what was wrong with him, I was told, "He's goofier than hell, just like the rest of us." Perhaps because the West is historically new, conventional morality is still felt to be less important than rock-bottom truths. Though there's always a lot of teasing and sparring, people are blunt with one another, sometimes even cruel, believing honesty is stronger medicine than sympathy, which may console but often conceals.

The formality that goes hand in hand with the rowdiness is known as the Western Code. It's a list of practical do's and don'ts, faithfully observed. A friend, Cliff, who runs a trapline in the winter, cut off half his foot while chopping a hole in the ice. Alone, he dragged himself to his pickup and headed for town, stopping to open the ranch gate as he left, and getting out to close it again, thus losing, in his observance of rules, precious time and blood. Later, he commented, "How would it look, them having to come to the hospital to tell me their cows had gotten out?"

Accustomed to emergencies, my friends doctor each other from the vet's bag with relish. When one old-timer suffered a heart attack in hunting camp, his partner quickly stirred up a brew of red horse liniment and hot water and made the half-conscious victim drink it, then tied him onto a horse and led him twenty miles to town. He regained consciousness and lived.

The roominess of the state has affected political attitudes as well. Ranchers keep up with world politics and the convulsions of the economy but are basically isolationists. Being used to running their own small empires of land and livestock, they're suspicious of big government. It's a "don't fence me in" holdover from a century ago. They still want the elbow room their grandfathers had, so they're strongly conservative, but with a populist twist.

Summer is the season when we get our "cowboy tans"—on the lower parts of our faces and on three fourths of our arms. Excessive heat, in the nineties and higher, sends us outside with the mosquitoes. In winter we're tucked inside our houses, and the white wasteland outside appears to be expanding, but in summer all the greenery abridges space. Summer is a go-ahead season. Every living thing is off the block and in the race: battalions of bugs in flight and biting; bats swinging around my log cabin as if the bases were loaded and someone had hit a home run. Some of summer's high-speed growth is ominous: larkspur, death camas, and green greasewood can kill sheep—an ironic idea, dying in this desert from eating what is too verdant. With sixteen hours of daylight, farmers and ranchers irrigate feverishly. There are first, second, and third cuttings of hay, some crews averaging only four hours of sleep a night for weeks. And, like the cowboys who in summer ride the night rodeo circuit, night-hawks make daredevil dives at dusk with an eerie whirring sound like a plane going down on the shimmering horizon.

In the town where I live, they've had to board up the dance-hall windows because there have been so many fights. There's so little to do except work that people wind up in a state of idle agitation that becomes fatalistic, as if there were nothing to be done about all this untapped energy. So the dark side to the grandeur of these spaces is the small-mindedness that seals people in. Men become hermits; women go mad. Cabin fever explodes into suicides, or into grudges and lifelong family feuds. Two sisters in my area inherited a ranch but found they couldn't get along. They fenced the place in half. When one's cows got out and mixed with the other's, the women went at each other with shovels. They ended up in the same hospital room but never spoke a word to each other for the rest of their lives.

After the brief lushness of summer, the sun moves south. The range grass is brown. Livestock is trailed back down from the mountains. Water holes begin to frost over at night. Last fall Martin asked me to accompany him on a pack trip. With five horses, we followed a river into the mountains behind the tiny Wyoming town of Meeteetse. Groves of aspen, red and orange, gave off a light that made us look toasted. Our hunting camp was so high that clouds skidded across our foreheads, then slowed to sail out across the warm valleys. Except for a bull moose who wandered into our camp and mistook our black gelding for a rival, we shot at nothing.

One of our evening entertainments was to watch the night sky. My dog, a dingo bred to herd sheep, also came on the trip. He is so used to the silence and empty skies that when an airplane flies over he always looks up and eyes the distant intruder quizzically. The sky, lately, seems to be much more crowded than it used to be. Satellites make their silent passes in the dark with great regularity. We counted eighteen in one hour's viewing. How odd to think that while they circumnavigated the planet, Martin and I had moved only six miles into our local wilderness and had seen no other human for the two weeks we stayed there.

At night, by moonlight, the land is whittled to slivers—a ridge, a river, a strip of grassland stretching to the mountains, then the huge sky. One morning a full moon was setting in the west just as the sun was rising. I felt precariously balanced between the two as I loped across a meadow. For a moment, I could believe that the stars, which were still visible, work like cooper's bands, holding together everything above Wyoming.

Space has a spiritual equivalent and can heal what is divided and burdensome in us. My grandchildren will probably use space shuttles for a honeymoon trip or to recover from heart attacks, but closer to home we might also learn how to carry space inside ourselves in the effortless way we carry our skins. Space represents sanity, not a life purified, dull, or "spaced out" but one that might accommodate intelligently any idea or situation.

From the clayey soil of northern Wyoming is mined bentonite, which is used as a filler in candy, gum, and lipstick. We Americans are great on fillers, as if what we have, what we are, is not enough. We have a cultural tendency toward denial, but, being affluent, we strangle ourselves with what we can buy. We have only to look at the houses we build to see how we build *against* space, the way we drink against pain and loneliness. We fill up space as if it were a pie shell, with things whose opacity further obstructs our ability to see what is already there.

FURTHER READINGS
Roger M. Valade III, "Gretel Ehrlich," in *Contemporary Authors* 140, ed. Donna Olendorf (Gale, 1993); Geoff Sadler, ed., *Twentieth-Century Western Writers* (St. James Press, 1991), pp. 205–206.

Roxanne Swentzell (1962–)

Roxanne Swentzell, born in Taos, lives in the Santa Clara Pueblo south of Santa Fé. She has been working in clay since she was a child. The "people" she shapes are at once a celebration of the old ways and a birthing into new ways. She says of herself, "I am a sculptor of human emotions."

Virginia Woolf wrote of a woman's need for a "room of one's own," but Swentzell's art emerges from the communal experience and is a family affair. "People would come together to collect materials, dig clay, sift, polish and fire pottery. This was done through and around other activities such as taking care of children, cooking, or visiting. There [are] no studios where 'art' is the sole activity. It was done in the flow of daily life, and every act [is] done in order to restate the place of humans within the cosmos." The artistic sense belongs to all people, not merely to people who call themselves "artists." "There was, and is, no word meaning 'art' or 'artist' in the Pueblo language."

Swentzell briefly attended the Institute of American Indian Arts in Santa Fé and the Museum Art School in Portland before she decided to go home. But living in the Santa Clara Pueblo doesn't eliminate the complexity of modern life. Most of the people in the pueblo "go off to work from eight to five just like everybody else and they want their new car and their TV and their VCR. What they really want is to be middle class white Americans. . . . Nobody has a center any more. . . . It is time for everybody to get back home. . . . The whole world needs to get back home."

Swentzell herself grew up in a home that was richly complex. Her mother, who is from the Santa Clara Pueblo, holds a doctorate in American Studies from the University of New Mexico, and her father, who is Anglo, teaches at St. John's College in Santa Fé. Growing up, Swentzell listened to Gregorian chants and studied Rubens and Michelangelo, and she also took part in the feast days, watched the clowns and joined with uncles, aunts and cousins in the dances of the pueblo. She learned to sculpt when she was four from an uncle who was blind.

Swentzell works in the traditional manner, which means her

figures are coiled like pots. Often her works include multiple figures. "I have to find very strong clays to be able to hold up arms and other things." The clay itself is a living element that shrinks and moves. "It's taken many, many years to be able to get close to what I want. . . ."

Swentzell's work can be seen in the Heard Museum in Phoenix, Arizona, and in the Smithsonian's Museum of the American Indian in New York City. In 1994 she won the Creative Excellence in Sculpture Award at the Santa Fé Indian Market. The Emergence of the Clowns has toured the United States, Canada, and New Zealand. Some of her newer pieces are being cast in bronze, and she has accepted a commission to do a large piece of public art in Santa Fé. Most recently, Swentzell writes, "I've been playing around more with humor to get a message across." Swentzell's figures—her clay people—are recognized today throughout the world.

CLAY PEOPLE

You clay people
who dance through
my soul
dance right on through
me.
My eyes
look upon you
out there
I know you
in here. Like
children
out in the world
I send you
and
hope
you find love
Out there.

Roxanne Swentzell, "Clay People" (1999).

Roxanne Swentzell, Clay Sculptor, Santa Clara Pueblo,
New Mexico, 1996, Photographed by Toba Tucker.

*From Pueblo Artists: Portraits by Toba Pato Tucker, Museum of New Mexico Press,
1998. Copyright © 1996 Toba Tucker, used by permission of the artist.*

IN A CIRCLE

In a circle we spin
All roads lead home
For are we not the mud
from whence we come?
And are we not the air,
and water and sunlight,
we take in?
Are we not the clouds
that also rise up from
the ground,
to rain down
upon ourselves?

FURTHER READINGS
Toba Pato Tucker, *Pueblo Artists: Portraits* (Museum of New Mexico Press, 1998); Lois Crozier-Hogle, *Surviving in Two Worlds* (University of Texas Press, 1997); Larry Abbott, "Interview with Roxanne Swentzell," *Indian Artist* (Fall 1997): 21–25.

Gloria Anzaldúa (1942–)

Born in the ranching community of Jesus Maria of the Valley of South Texas, Gloria Anzaldúa was a member of the seventh generation of her family born in Texas. When she was eleven years old, her family left the ranch for Hargill, Texas, which she later described as having "one signal light and 13 bars and 13 churches and maybe two mini-marts." For one year following her father's death when she was 16, Anzaldúa and her remaining family became migrant farm laborers, traveling throughout Texas and Arkansas, following the harvests. Fearful that her sons would miss their chance for an education if they continued as migrant workers, Anzaldúa's mother returned to Jesus Maria of the Valley of South Texas and settled there. After graduating from high school, Anzaldúa went on to earn a BA from Pan American University in 1969, an MA in English and Education from the University of Texas at Austin in 1972. In the years since, in addition to continuing in the PhD Program in the History of Consciousness at the University of California at Santa Cruz, she has written *Borderlands/La Frontera: The New Mestiza* (1987), and edited two anthologies of writings by women of color: *This Bridge Called My Back: Writings by Radical Women of Color* (1981), with Cherríe Moraga; and *Making Face, Making Soul/Haciendo Caras: Creative and Critical Perspectives by Women of Color* (1990).

Anzaldúa became a writer despite discouraging expectations she faced as a Chicana. As she writes, "good Chicanitas don't go to school, they drop out in the 6th, 7th, and 8th grade . . . [and] cook, clean, and sew." Anzaldúa refused to behave in this way, defending her thirst for knowledge against criticism that reading instead of scrubbing floors was a mark of laziness. Anzaldúa's openness about being a lesbian clashed with her mother's homophobia and made more difficult Anzaldúa's acceptance in her Chicana community.

In the book from which this selection is drawn, *Borderlands/La Frontera: The New Mestiza*, Anzaldúa addresses the formation of a new consciousness, which she terms "*mestiza*," out of the "radical, ideological, cultural and biological cross-pollenization" which takes place in the "Borderlands."

BORDERLANDS

In the 1800s, Anglos migrated illegally into Texas, which was then part of Mexico, in greater and greater numbers and gradually drove the tejanos (native Texans of Mexican descent) from their lands, committing all manner of atrocities against them. Their illegal invasion forced Mexico to fight a war to keep its Texas territory. The Battle of the Alamo, in which the Mexican forces vanquished the whites, became, for the whites, the symbol for the cowardly and villainous character of the Mexicans. It became (and still is) a symbol that legitimized the white imperialist takeover. With the capture of Santa Anna later in 1836, Texas became a republic. Tejanos lost their land and, overnight, became the foreigners.

> Ya la mitad del terreno
> les vendió el traidor Santa Anna,
> con lo que se ha hecho muy rica
> la nación americana.
>
> ¿Qué acaso no se conforman
> con el oro de las minas?
> Ustedes muy elegantes
> y aquí nosotros en ruinas.

   —from The Mexican Corrido, "Del peligro de la Intervención"

In 1846, the U.S. incited Mexico to war. U.S. troops invaded and occupied Mexico, forcing her to give up almost half of her nation, what is now Texas, New Mexico, Arizona, Colorado and California.

With the victory of the U.S. forces over the Mexican in the U.S.-Mexican War, *los norteamericanos* pushed the Texas border down 100 miles, from *el río Nueces* to *el río Grande*. South Texas ceased to be part of the Mexican state of Tamaulipas. Separated from Mexico, the Native Mexican-Texan no longer looked toward Mexico as home; the Southwest became our homeland once more. The border fence that divides the Mexican people was born on February 2, 1848 with the signing of the Treaty of Guadalupe-Hidalgo. It left 100,000 Mexican citizens on this side, annexed by conquest along

Gloria Anzaldúa, from *Borderlands/La Frontera: The New Mestiza* (1987).

with the land. The land established by the treaty as belonging to Mexicans was soon swindled a way from its owners. The treaty was never honored and restitution, to this day, has never been made.

> *The justice and benevolence of God*
> *will forbid that . . . Texas should again*
> *become a howling wilderness*
> *trod only by savages, or . . . benighted*
> *by the ignorance and superstition,*
> *the anarchy and rapine of Mexican misrule.*
> *The Anglo-American race are destined*
> *to be forever the proprietors of*
> *this land of promise and fulfillment.*
> *Their laws will govern it,*
> *their learning will enlighten it,*
> *their enterprise will improve it.*
> *Their flocks range its boundless pastures,*
> *for them its fertile lands will yield . . .*
> *luxuriant harvests . . .*
> *The wilderness of Texas has been redeemed*
> *by Anglo-American blood & enterprise.*
> —William H. Wharton

The Gringo, locked into the fiction of white superiority, seized complete political power, stripping Indians and Mexicans of their land while their feet were still rooted in it. *Con el destierro y el exilo fuimos desuñados, destroncados, destripados*—we were jerked out by the roots, truncated, disemboweled, dispossessed, and separated from our identity and our history. Many, under the threat of Anglo terrorism, abandoned homes and ranches and went to Mexico. Some stayed and protested. But as the courts, law enforcement officials, and government officials not only ignored their pleas but penalized them for their efforts, *tejanos* had no other recourse but armed retaliation.

After Mexican-American resisters robbed a train in Browns-ville, Texas on October 18, 1915, Anglo vigilante groups began lynching Chicanos. Texas Rangers would take them into the brush and shoot them. One hundred Chicanos were killed in a matter of months, whole families lynched. Seven thousand fled to Mexico, leaving their small ranches and farms. The Anglos, afraid that the *mexicanos* would seek independence from the U.S., brought in 20,000 army troops to put an end to the social protest movement in South Texas. Race hatred had finally fomented into an all out war.

> My grandmother lost all her cattle,
> they stole her land.

"Drought hit South Texas," my mother tells me. "*La tierra se puso bien seca y los animales comenzaron a morrirse de se'*. *Mi papá se murío de un* heart attack *dejando a mamá* pregnant *y con ocho huercos*, with eight kids and one on the way. *Yo fuí la mayor, tenía diez años*. The next year the drought continued *y el ganado* got hoof and mouth. *Se calleron* in droves *en las pastas y el* brushland, *pansas blancas* ballooning to the skies. *El siguiente año* still no rain. *Mi pobre madre viuda perdió* two-thirds of her *ganado*. A smart *gabacho* lawyer took the land a way *mamá* hadn't paid taxes. *No hablaba inglés*, she didn't know how to ask for time to raise the money." My father's mother, Mama Locha, also lost her *terreno*. For a while we got $12.50 a year for the "mineral rights" of six acres of cemetery, all that was left of the ancestral lands. Mama Locha had asked that we bury her there beside her husband. *El cemeterio estaba cercado*. But there was a fence around the cemetery, chained and padlocked by the ranch owners of the surrounding land. We couldn't even get in to visit the graves, much less bury her there. Today, it is still padlocked. The sign reads: "Keep out. Trespassers will be shot."

In the 1930s, after Anglo agribusiness corporations cheated the small Chicano landowners of their land, the corporations hired gangs of *mexicanos* to pull out the brush, chaparral and cactus and to irrigate the desert. The land they toiled over had once belonged to many of them, or had been used communally by them. Later the Anglos brought in huge machines and root plows and had the Mexicans scrape the land clean of natural vegetation. In my childhood I saw the end of dryland farming. I witnessed the land cleared; saw the huge pipes connected to underwater sources sticking up in the air. As children, we'd go fishing in some of those canals when they were full and hunt for snakes in them when they were dry. In the 1950s I saw the land, cut up into thousands of neat rectangles and squares, constantly being irrigated. In the 340-day growth season, the seeds of any kind of fruit or veg-

etable had only to be stuck in the ground in order to grow. More
big land corporations came in and bought up the remaining land.

To make a living my father became a sharecropper. Rio Farms
Incorporated loaned him seed money and living expenses. At harvest time, my father repaid the loan and forked over 40% of the earnings. Sometimes we earned less than we owed, but always the corporations fared well. Some had major holdings in vegetable trucking,
livestock auctions and cotton gins. Altogether we lived on three successive Rio farms; the second was adjacent to the King Ranch and
included a dairy farm; the third was a chicken farm. I remember the
white feathers of three thousand Leghorn chickens blanketing the
land for acres around. My sister, mother and I cleaned, weighed and
packaged eggs. (For years afterwards I couldn't stomach the sight of
an egg.) I remember my mother attending some of the meetings
sponsored by well-meaning whites from Rio Farms. They talked
about good nutrition, health, and held huge barbeques. The only
thing salvaged for my family from those years are modern techniques of food canning and a food-stained book they printed made
up of recipes from Rio Farms' Mexican women. How proud my
mother was to have her recipe for *enchiladas coloradas* in a book.

El cruzar del mojado/Illegal Crossing

> *"Ahora si ya tengo una tumba para llorar,"* dice Conchita,
> upon being reunited with her unknown mother just before
> the mother dies
> —from Ismael Rodriguez' film, *Nosotros los pobres*

La crisis. Los gringos had not stopped at the border. By the end
of the nineteenth century, powerful landowners in Mexico, in partnership with U.S. colonizing companies, had dispossessed millions
of Indians of their lands. Currently, Mexico and her eighty million
citizens are almost completely dependent on the U.S. market. The
Mexican government and wealthy growers are in partnership with
such American conglomerates as American Motors, IT&T and Du
Pont which own factories called *maquiladoras*. One-fourth of all
Mexicans work at *maquiladoras;* most are young women. Next to
oil, *maquiladoras* are Mexico's second greatest source of U.S. dollars. Working eight to twelve hours a day to wire in backup lights of

U.S. autos or solder miniscule wires in TV sets is not the Mexican way. While the women are in the *maquiladoras*, the children are left on their own. Many roam the street, become part of *cholo* gangs. The infusion of the values of the white culture, coupled with the exploitation by that culture, is changing the Mexican way of life.

The devaluation of the *peso* and Mexico's dependency on the U.S. have brought on what the Mexicans call *la crisis. No hay trabajo.* Half of the Mexican people are unemployed. In the U.S. a man or woman can make eight times what they can in Mexico. By March, 1987, 1,088 *pesos* were worth one U.S. dollar. I remember when I was growing up in Texas how we'd cross the border at Reynosa or Progreso to buy sugar or medicines when the dollar was worth eight *pesos* and fifty *centavos*.

La travesía. For many *mexicanos del otro lado,* the choice is to stay in Mexico and starve or move north and live. *Dicen que cada mexicano siempre sueña de la conquista en los brazos de cuatro gringas rubias, la conquista del país poderoso del norte, los Estados Unidos. En cada Chicano y mexicano vive el mito del tesoro territorial perdido.* North Americans call this return to the homeland the silent invasion.

> *"A la cueva volverán"*
> ——El Puma *en la cancion "Amalia"*

South of the border, called North America's rubbish dump by Chicanos, *mexicanos* congregate in the plazas to talk about the best way to cross. Smugglers, *coyotes, pasadores, enganchadores* approach these people or are sought out by them. *"¿Qué dice muchachos a echársela de mojado?"*

> "Now among the alien gods with
> weapons of magic am I."
> ——Navajo protection song, sung when going into battle.

We have a tradition of migration, a tradition of long walks. Today we are witnessing *la migración de los pueblos mexicanos,* the return odyssey to the historical/mythological Aztlán. This time, the traffic is from south to north.

El retorno to the promised land first began with the Indians from the interior of Mexico and the *mestizos* that came with the *conquistadores* in the 1500s. Immigration continued in the next three centuries, and, in this century, it continued with the *braceros* who helped to build our railroads and who picked our fruit. Today thousands of Mexicans are crossing the border legally and illegally; ten million people without documents have returned to the Southwest.

Faceless, nameless, invisible, taunted with "Hey cucaracho" (cockroach). Trembling with fear, yet filled with courage, a courage born of desperation. Barefoot and uneducated, Mexicans with hands like boot soles gather at night by the river where two worlds merge creating what Reagan calls a frontline, a war zone. The convergence has created a shock culture, a border culture, a third country, a closed country.

Without benefit of bridges, the "*mojados*" (wetbacks) float on inflatable rafts across *el rio Grande,* or wad or swim across naked, clutching their clothes over their heads. Holding onto the grass, they pull themselves along the banks with a prayer to *Virgen de Guadalupe* on their lips: *Ay virgencita morena, mi madrecita, dame tu bendición*.

The Border Patrol hides behind the local McDonalds on the outskirts of Brownsville, Texas or some other border town. They set traps around the river beds beneath the bridge. Hunters in army-green uniforms stalk and track these economic refugees by the powerful nightvision of electronic sensing devices planted it in the ground or mounted on Border Patrol vans. Cornered by flashlights, frisked while their arms stretch over their heads, *los mojados* are handcuffed, locked in jeeps, and then kicked back across the border.

One out of every three is caught. Some return to enact their rite of passage as many as three times a day. Some of those who make it across undetected fall prey to Mexican robbers such as those in Smugglers' Canyon on the American side of the border near Tijuana. As refugees in a homeland that does not want them, many find a welcome hand holding out only suffering, pain, and ignoble death.

Those who make it past the checking points of the Border Patrol find themselves in the midst of 150 years of racism in Chicano *barrios* in the Southwest and in big northern cities. Living in a no-man's-borderland, caught between being treated as criminals and being able to eat, between resistance and deportation, the illegal refugees are some of the poorest and the most exploited of any people in the U.S. It is illegal for Mexicans to work without green cards. But big farming combines, farm bosses and smugglers who bring them in make money off the "wetbacks'" labor—they don't have to pay federal minimum wages, or ensure adequate housing or sanitary conditions.

The Mexican woman is especially at risk. Often the *cóyote* (smuggler) doesn't feed her for days or let her go to the bathroom. Often he rapes her or sells her into prostitution. She cannot call on county or state health or economic resources because she doesn't know English and she fears deportation. American employers are quick to take advantage of her helplessness. She can't go home. She's sold her house, her furniture, borrowed from friends in order to pay the *cóyote* who charges her four or five thousand dollars to smuggle her to Chicago. She may work as a live-in maid for white, Chicano or Latino house-holds for as little as $15 a week. Or work in the garment industry, do hotel work. Isolated and worried about her family back home, afraid of getting caught and deported, living with as many as fifteen people in one room, the *mexicana* suffers serious health problems. *Se enferma de los nervios, de alta presión.*

La mojada, la mujer indocumentada, is doubly threatened in this country. Not only does she have to contend with sexual violence, but like all women, she is prey to a sense of physical helplessness. As a refugee, she leaves the familiar and safe homeground to venture into unknown and possibly dangerous terrain.

This is her home
this thin edge of
barbwire.

La Conciencia de la Mestiza—
Towards a New Consciousness

> *Por la mujer de mi raza*
> *hablará el espíritu.*

Jose Vascocelos, Mexican philosopher, envisaged *una raza mestiza, una mezcla de razas afines, una raza de color—la primera raza síntesis del globo.* He called it a cosmic race, *la raza cósmica,* a fifth race embracing the four major races of the world. Opposite to the theory of the pure Aryan, and to the policy of racial purity that white America practices, his theory is one of inclusivity. At the confluence of two or more genetic streams, with chromosomes constantly "crossing over," this mixture of races, rather than resulting in an inferior being, provides hybrid progeny, a mutable, more malleable species with a rich gene pool. From this racial, ideological, cultural and biological cross-pollinization, an "alien" consciousness is presently in the making—a new *mestiza* consciousness, *una conciencia de mujer.* It is a consciousness of the Borderlands.

Una lucha de fronteras / A Struggle of Borders

> Because I, a *mestiza,*
> continually walk out of one culture
> and into another,
> because I am in all cultures at the same time,
> *alma entre dos mundos, tres, cuatro,*
> *me zumba la cabeza con lo contradictorio.*
> *Estoy norteada por todas las voces que me hablan*
> *simultáneamente.*

The ambivalence from the clash of voices results in mental and emotional states of perplexity. Internal strife results in insecurity and indecisiveness. The mestiza's dual or multiple personality is plagued by psychic restlessness.

In a constant state of mental nepantilism, an Aztec word meaning torn between ways, *la mestiza* is a product of the transfer of the cultural and spiritual values of one group to another. Being tricultural, monolingual, bilingual, or multilingual, speaking a patois, and in a state of perpetual transition, the *mestiza* faces the dilemma of the mixed breed: which collectivity does the daughter of a dark-skinned mother listen to?

El choque de un alma atrapado entre el mundo del espíritu y el mundo de la técnica a veces la deja entullada. Cradled in one culture, sandwiched between two cultures, straddling all three cultures and their value systems, *la mestiza* undergoes a struggle of flesh, a struggle of borders, an inner war. Like all people, we perceive the version of reality that our culture communicates. Like others having or living in more than one culture, we get multiple, often opposing messages. The coming together of two self-consistent but habitually incompatible frames of reference causes *un choque,* a cultural collision.

Within us and within *la cultura chicana,* commonly held beliefs
of the white culture attack commonly held beliefs of the Mexican
culture, and both attack commonly held beliefs of the indigenous
culture. Subconsciously, we see an attack on ourselves and our
beliefs as a threat and we attempt to block with a counterstance.

But it is not enough to stand on the opposite river bank, shouting
questions, challenging patriarchal, white conventions. A counterstance locks one into a duel of oppressor and oppressed; locked in
mortal combat, like the cop and the criminal, both are reduced to a
common denominator of violence. The counterstance refutes the
dominant culture's views and beliefs, and, for this, it is proudly defiant.
All reaction is limited by, and dependent on, what it is reacting against.
Because the counterstance stems from a problem with authority—
outer as well as inner—it's a step towards liberation from cultural
domination. But it is not a way of life. At some point, on our way to a
new consciousness, we will have to leave the opposite bank, the split
between the two mortal combatants somehow healed so that we are
on both shores at once and, at once, see through serpent and eagle
eyes. Or perhaps we will decide to disengage from the dominant culture, write it off altogether as a lost cause, and cross the border into a
wholly new and separate territory. Or we might go another route. The
possibilities are numerous once we decide to act and not react.

A Tolerance For Ambiguity

These numerous possibilities leave *la mestiza* floundering in
uncharted seas. In perceiving conflicting information and points of
view, she is subjected to a swamping of her psychological borders.
She has discovered that she can't hold concepts or ideas in rigid
boundaries. The borders and walls that are supposed to keep the
undesirable ideas out are entrenched habits and patterns of
behavior; these habits and patterns are the enemy within. Rigidity
means death. Only by remaining flexible is she able to stretch the
psyche horizontally and vertically. *La mestiza* constantly has to
shift out of habitual formations; from convergent thinking, analyti-
cal reasoning that tends to use rationality to move toward a single
goal (a Western mode), to divergent thinking, characterized by
movement away from set patterns and goals and toward a more
whole perspective, one that includes rather than excludes.

The new *mestiza* copes by developing a tolerance for contradictions, a tolerance for ambiguity. She learns to be an Indian in Mexican culture, to be Mexican from an Anglo point of view. She learns to juggle cultures. She has a plural personality, she operates in a pluralistic mode—nothing is thrust out, the good the bad and the ugly, nothing rejected, nothing abandoned. Not only does she sustain contradictions, she turns the ambivalence into something else.

She can be jarred out of ambivalence by an intense, and often painful, emotional event which inverts or resolves the ambivalence. I'm not sure exactly how. The work takes place underground—subconsciously. It is work that the soul performs. That focal point or fulcrum, that juncture where the mestiza stands, is where phenomena tend to collide. It is where the possibility of uniting all that is separate occurs. This assembly is not one where severed or separated pieces merely come together. Nor is it a balancing of opposing powers. In attempting to work out a synthesis, the self has added a third element which is greater than the sum of its severed parts. That third element is a new consciousness—a mestiza consciousness—and though it is a source of intense pain, its energy comes from continual creative motion that keeps breaking down the unitary aspect of each new paradigm.

En unas pocas centurias, the future will belong to the mestiza. Because the future depends on the breaking down of paradigms, it depends on the straddling of two or more cultures. By creating a new mythos—that is, a change in the way we perceive reality, the way we see ourselves, and the ways we behave—*la mestiza* creates a new consciousness.

The work of *mestiza* consciousness is to break down the subject-object duality that keeps her a prisoner and to show in the flesh and through the images in her work how duality is transcended. The answer to the problem between the white race and the colored, between males and females, lies in healing the split that originates in the very foundation of our lives, our culture, our languages, our thoughts. A massive uprooting of dualistic thinking in the individual and collective consciousness is the beginning of a long struggle, but one that could, in our best hopes, bring us to the end of rape, of violence, of war.

La encrucijada / The Crossroads

> A chicken is being sacrificed
> at a crossroads, a simple mound of earth
> a mud shrine for *Eshu*,
> *Yoruba* god of indeterminacy,
> who blesses her choice of path.
> She begins her journey.

Su cuerpo es una bocacalle. La mestiza has gone from being the sacrificial goat to becoming the officiating priestess at the crossroads.

As a *mestiza* I have no country, my homeland cast me out; yet all countries are mine because I am every woman's sister or potential lover. (As a lesbian I have no race, my own people disclaim me; but I am all races because there is the queer of me in all races.) I am cultureless because, as a feminist, I challenge the collective cultural/religious male-derived beliefs of Indo-Hispanics and Anglos; yet I am cultured because I am participating in the creation of yet another culture, a new story to explain the world and our participation in it, a new value system with images and symbols that connect us to each other and to the planet. *Soy un amasamiento,* I am an act of kneading, of uniting and joining that not only has produced both a creature of darkness and a creature of light, but also a creature that questions the definitions of light and dark and gives them new meanings.

We are the people who leap in the dark, we are the people on the knees of the gods. In our very flesh, (r)evolution works out the clash of cultures. It makes us crazy constantly, but if the center holds, we've made some kind of evolutionary step forward. *Nuestra alma el trabajo,* the opus, the great alchemical work; spiritual *mestizaje,* a "morphogenesis," an inevitable unfolding. We have become the quickening serpent movement.

Indigenous like corn, like corn, the *mestiza* is a product of crossbreeding, designed for preservation under a variety of conditions. Like an ear of corn—a female seed-bearing organ—the *mestiza* is tenacious, tightly wrapped in the husks of her culture. Like kernels she clings to the cob; with thick stalks and strong brace roots, she holds tight to the earth—she will survive the crossroads.

Lavando y remojando el maíz en agua de cal, despojando el pellejo. Moliendo, mixteando, amasando, haciendo tortillas de masa. She steeps the corn in lime, it swells, softens. With stone roller on *metate*, she grinds the corn, then grinds again. She kneads and moulds the dough, pats the round balls into *tortillas.*

We are the porous rock in the stone *metate*
squatting on the ground.
We are the rolling pin, *el maíz y agua,*
la masa harina. Somos el amasijo.
Somos lo molido en el metate.
We are *the comal* sizzling hot,
the hot *tortilla,* the hungry mouth.
We are the coarse rock.
We are the grinding motion,
the mixed potion, *somos el molcajete.*
We are the pestle, the *comino, ajo, pimienta,*
We are the *chile colorado,*
the green shoot that cracks the rock.
We will abide.

El camino de la mestiza / The Mestiza Way

Caught between the sudden contraction, the breath sucked in and the endless space, the brown woman stands still, looks at the sky. She decides to go down, digging her way along the roots of trees. Sifting through the bones, she shakes them to see if there is any marrow in them. Then, touching the dirt to her forehead, to her tongue, she takes a few bones, leaves the rest in their burial place.

She goes through her backpack, keeps her journal and address book, throws away the muni-bart metromaps. The coins are heavy and they go next, then the greenbacks flutter through the air. She keeps her knife, can opener and eyebrow pencil. She puts bones, pieces of bark, *hierbas*, eagle feather, snakeskin, tape recorder, the rattle and drum in her pack and she sets out to become the complete *tolteca.*

Her first step is to take inventory. *Despojando, desgranando, qui-tando paja.* Just what did she inherit from her ancestors? This weight on her back—which is the baggage from the Indian mother, which the baggage from the Spanish father, which the baggage from the Anglo?

Pero es difícil differentiating between *lo heredado, lo adquirido, lo impuesto.* She puts history through a sieve, winnows out the lies, looks at the forces that we as a race, as women, have been a part of. *Luego bota lo que no vale, los desmientos, los desencuentos, el embrutecimiento. Aguarda el juicio, hondo y enraízado, de la gente antigua.* This step is a conscious rupture with all oppressive tradi-tions of all cultures and religions. She communicates that rupture, documents the struggle. She reinterprets history and, using new symbols, she shapes new myths. She adopts new perspectives toward the darkskinned, women and queers. She strengthens her tolerance (and intolerance) for ambiguity. She is willing to share, to make herself vulnerable to foreign ways of seeing and thinking. She surrenders all notions of safety, of the familiar. Deconstruct, construct. She becomes a *nahual,* able to transform herself into a tree, a coyote, into another person. She learns to transform the small "I" into the total Self. *Se hace moldeadora de su alma. Según la concepción que tiene de sí misma, así será.*

FURTHER READINGS

Alma M. Garcia, "The Development of Chicana Feminist Discourse," in Ronald Takaki, ed., *From Different Shores: Perspectives on Race and Ethnicity in America* (2nd ed., Oxford University Press, 1994); Donna Perry, *Backtalk: Women Writers Speak Out: Interviews* (Rutgers University Press, 1993); Héctor A. Torres, "Experience, Writing, Theory: The Dialects of Mestizaje in Gloria Anzaldúa's *Borderlands/La Frontera: The New Mestiza,*" in *Cultural and Cross-Cultural Studies and the Teaching of Literature,* eds. J. Trimmer and T. Warlock (1991); Gloria Anzaldúa, *Making Face, Making Soul/Haciendo Caras: Creative and Critical Perspectives by Women of Color* (Aunt Lute Foundation, 1990); Gloria Anzaldúa, *Borderlands/La Frontera: The New Mestiza* (Spinsters/Aunt Lute Books, 1987); Gloria Anzaldúa and Cherríe Moraga, eds., *This Bridge Called My Back: Writings by Radical Women of Color* (Persephone Books, 1981).

Janet Campbell Hale (1947–)

A member of the Coeur d'Alene tribe of Northern Idaho, Janet Campbell Hale grew upon the Coeur d'Alene Indian Reservation in Idaho, although after she was ten, her family moved often. She has said that she attended twenty-one schools in three western states before she finally dropped out of high school. A mother while still in her teens, Hale fled her abusive husband and hid out in the Haight-Ashbury District in San Francisco. A few years later, she attended the City College of San Francisco, and then transferred to the University of California–Berkeley, where she graduated with a BA in 1974. She later received an MA in creative writing from the University of California at Davis and studied law at the University of California at Berkeley. Hale published her first novel, *The Owl's Song*, in 1974, the same year she received her BA degree. Her 1985 novel, *The Jailing of Cecelia Capture*, was nominated for a Pulitzer Prize. In 1993, she published a collection of autobiographical essays, *Bloodlines*.

While living for a period in New York City, Hale stated, "if I don't ever see the West again, my heart and soul will always belong to its dramatic terrain. It is my own inner landscape." In the mid-1990s, Hale returned to Idaho, and now lives on the Coeur d'Alene Indian Reservation. Describing her life there since her return, she has said, "It has largely been a nightmare." Most recently, she has published *Women on the Run,* a collection of short stories.

In this selection of poems, she demonstrates the deep connections she feels with the western land and with the people who work it, across barriers of space and ethnicity. She examines the inheritance her history has given her, and confirms the continuities which connect today's western communities to their pasts.

SALAD LA RAZA

The crisp
Pale green
Lettuce
Caught the sunlight,
Glistened,
As I
Broke the leaves
For my salad,
Lettuce
I'd bought that morning at Safeway,
Remembering how
My family,
For a time,
And off and on,
Lived in dumpy cabin camps,
Moved around,
Picking berries
       beans,
       apples,
       cherries,
Stripping hops.
I remembered
The dirt,
And sweating
Under a blazing sun
For next to nothing,
And
The babbling,
Laughing
Mexican workers,
Who called themselves "Spanish"
(There were no Chicanos
    in those days)

Janet Campbell Hale, "Salad La Raza," "Desmet, Idaho, March 1969," and "Custer Lives in Humbolt County" (1975), from *Voices of the Rainbow,* ed. Kenneth Rosen (1975).

And looked down
On Indians so much,
"Los Indios" was enough
of a dirty name
In itself.
Eating my crisp and delicious
Safeway salad,
I tried not to think
Of Caesar Chavez.

DESMET, IDAHO, MARCH 1969

At my father's wake,
The old people
  Knew me,
  Though I
  Knew them not,
And spoke to me
In our tribe's
Ancient tongue,
Ignoring
The fact
That I
Don't speak
The language,
And so
I listened
As if I understood
What it was all about,
And,
Oh,
How it
Stirred me
To hear again
That strange,
  Softly
  Flowing
Native tongue,

So
Familiar to
My childhood ear.

CUSTER LIVES IN HUMBOLT COUNTY

What was it called,
When all that old-time white man trouble
was going on?
All that killing and taking away of home,
of country?
Justifiable genocide or some
such thing, no doubt.
Involuntary manslaughter,
they called it,
When that cop in Humbolt County
Shot the young Pomo last spring,
Shot him and left him
Lying by the roadside,
Hidden in the tall green grass,
Lying bleeding in the spring sunlight,
In the tall green grass,
Involuntary manslaughter,
they called it,
when the Pomo died at last.

All the old, wild-West white man trouble
is over now,
Should be forgotten, they say.
Wild grass grows again at Little Big Horn,
at Steptoe, at Wounded Knee,
Tall grass, swaying in the gentle wind,
covering the old battle scars,
The old healed wounds.
The sun shines warm in a big, clear sky,
All is quiet now,
The past is best forgotten.

FURTHER READINGS
Janet Campbell Hale, *Women on the Run* (University of Idaho Press, 1999); Janet Campbell Hale, *Bloodlines: Odyssey of a Native Daughter* (Random House, 1993); Frederick Hale, *Janet Campbell Hale* (Boise State University Press, 1996).

Sylvia Watanabe

Sylvia Watanabe has published one collection of her short stories, 1992's *Talking to the Dead,* but in its pages are the stories of
unforgettable Hawai'ian characters. Of Japanese and Hawai'ian
ancestry, Watanabe was raised in Hawai'i. She has said that in writing she "wanted to record a way of life which I loved and which
seemed in danger of dying away." The recipient of a Japanese
American Citizens League National Literary Award and a National
Endowment for the Arts Fellowship, Watanabe now lives in
Michigan.

TALKING TO THE DEAD

We spoke of her in whispers as Aunty Talking to the Dead, the
half-Hawaiian kahuna lady. But whenever there was a death in the
village, she was the first to be sent for; the priest came second. For
it was she who understood the wholeness of things—the significance of directions and colors. Prayers to appease the hungry
ghosts. Elixirs for grief. Most times, she'd be out on her front porch,
already waiting—her boy, Clinton, standing behind with her basket
of spells—when the messenger arrived. People said she could
smell a death from clear on the other side of the island, even as the
dying person breathed his last. And if she fixed her eyes on you
and named a day, you were already as good as six feet under.

I went to work as her apprentice when I was eighteen. That was
in '48, the year Clinton graduated from mortician school on the GI
bill. It was the talk for weeks—how he'd returned to open the
Paradise Mortuary in the heart of the village and had brought the
scientific spirit of free enterprise to the doorstep of the hereafter. I
remember the advertisements for the Grand Opening, promising to
modernize the funeral trade with Lifelike Artistic Techniques and
Stringent Standards of Sanitation. The old woman, who had waited
out the war for her son's return, stoically took his defection in

Sylvia Watanabe, "Talking to the Dead," from *Talking to the Dead* (1992).

stride and began looking for someone else to help out with her business.

At the time, I didn't have many prospects—more schooling didn't interest me, and my mother's attempts at marrying me off inevitably failed when I stood to shake hands with a prospective bridegroom and ended up towering a foot above him. "It would be bad enough if she just looked like a horse," I heard one of them complain, "but she's as big as one, too."

My mother dressed me in navy blue, on the theory that dark colors make things look less conspicuous. "Yuri, sit down," she'd hiss, tugging at my skirt as the decisive moment approached. I'd nod, sip my tea, smile through the introductions and small talk, till the time came for sealing the bargain with handshakes. Then, nothing on earth could keep me from getting to my feet. The go-between finally suggested that I consider taking up a trade. "After all, marriage isn't for everyone," she said. My mother said that that was a fact which remained to be proven, but meanwhile it wouldn't hurt if I took in sewing or learned to cut hair. I made up my mind to apprentice myself to Aunty Talking to the Dead.

The old woman's house was on the hill behind the village, just off the road to Chicken Fight Camp. She lived in an old plantation worker's bungalow with peeling green and white paint and a large, well-tended garden—mostly of flowering bushes and strong-smelling herbs.

"Aren't you a big one," a voice behind me said.

I started, then turned. It was the first time I had ever seen her up close.

"Hello, uh, Mrs. Dead," I stammered.

She was little, way under five feet, and wrinkled. Everything about her seemed the same color—her skin, her lips, her dress. Everything was just a slightly different shade of the same brown-gray, except her hair, which was absolutely white, and her tiny eyes, which glinted like metal. For a minute those eyes looked me up and down.

"Here," she said finally, thrusting an empty rice sack into my hands. "For collecting salt." Then she started down the road to the beach.

In the next few months we walked every inch of the hills and beaches around the village, and then some. I struggled behind, laden with strips of bark and leafy twigs, while Aunty marched three steps ahead, chanting. "This is *a'ali'i* to bring sleep—it must be dried in the shade on a hot day. This is *noni* for the heart, and *awa* for every kind of grief. This is *uhaloa* with the deep roots. If you are like that, death cannot easily take you."

"This is where you gather salt to preserve a corpse," I hear her still. "This is where you cut to insert the salt." Her words marked the places on my body, one by one.

That whole first year, not a day passed when I didn't think of quitting. I tried to figure out a way of moving back home without making it seem like I was admitting anything.

"You know what people are saying, don't you?" my mother said, lifting the lid of the bamboo steamer and setting a tray of freshly steamed meat buns on the already crowded table before me. It was one of my few visits since my apprenticeship, though I'd never been more than a couple of miles away, and she had stayed up the whole night before, cooking. She'd prepared a canned ham with yellow sweet potatoes, wing beans with pork, sweet and sour mustard cabbage, fresh raw yellowfin, pickled eggplant, and rice with red beans. I had not seen so much food since the night she tried to persuade Uncle Mongoose not to volunteer for the army. He went anyway, and on the last day of training, just before he was to be shipped to Italy, he shot himself in the head while cleaning his gun. "I always knew that boy would come to no good," was all Mama said when she heard the news.

"What do you mean you can't eat another bite?" she fussed now. "Look at you, nothing but a bag of bones."

The truth was, there didn't seem to be much of a future in my apprenticeship. In eleven and a half months I had memorized most of the minor rituals of mourning and learned to identify a couple of dozen herbs and all their medicinal uses, but I had not seen, much less gotten to practice on, a single honest-to-goodness corpse. "People live longer these days," Aunty claimed.

But I knew it was because everyone, even from villages across the bay, had begun taking their business to the Paradise Mortuary. The single event that had established Clinton's monopoly was the untimely death of old Mrs. Parmeter, the plantation owner's mother-in-law, who'd choked on a fishbone in the salmon mousse during a fund-raising luncheon for Famine Relief. Clinton had been chosen to be in charge of the funeral. After that, he'd taken to wearing three-piece suits, as a symbol of his new respectability, and was nominated as a Republican candidate for the village council.

"So, what are people saying?" I asked, finally pushing my plate away.

This was the cue that Mama had been waiting for. "They're saying that That Woman has gotten herself a pet donkey, though that's not the word they're using, of course." She paused dramatically; the implication was clear.

I began remembering things about living in my mother's house. The navy-blue dresses. The humiliating weekly tea ceremony lessons at the Buddhist temple.

"Give up this foolishness," she wheedled. "Mrs. Koyama tells me the Barber Shop Lady is looking for help."

"I think I'll stay right where I am," I said.

My mother fell silent. Then she jabbed a meat bun with her serving fork and lifted it onto my plate. "Here, have another helping," she said.

A few weeks later Aunty and I were called outside the village to perform a laying-out. It was early afternoon when Sheriff Kanoi came by to tell us that the body of Mustard Hayashi, the eldest of the Hayashi boys, had just been pulled from an irrigation ditch by a team of field workers. He had apparently fallen in the night before, stone drunk, on his way home from the La Hula Rhumba Bar and Grill.

I began hurrying around, assembling Aunty's tools and potions, and checking that everything was in working order, but the old woman didn't turn a hair; she just sat calmly rocking back and forth and puffing on her skinny, long-stemmed pipe.

"Yuri, you stop that rattling around back there," she snapped, then turned to the sheriff. "My son Clinton could probably handle this. Why don't you ask him?"

Sheriff Kanoi hesitated before replying, "This looks like a tough case that's going to need some real expertise."

Aunty stopped rocking. "That's true, it was a bad death," she mused.

"Very bad," the sheriff agreed.

"The spirit is going to require some talking to," she continued. "You know, so it doesn't linger."

"And the family asked especially for you," he added.

No doubt because they didn't have any other choice, I thought. That morning, I'd run into Chinky Malloy, the assistant mortician at the Paradise, so I happened to know that Clinton was at a morticians' conference in Los Angeles and wouldn't be back for several days. But I didn't say a word.

When we arrived at the Hayashis', Mustard's body was lying on the green Formica table in the kitchen. It was the only room in the house with a door that faced north. Aunty claimed that a proper laying-out required a room with a north-facing door, so the spirit could find its way home to the land of the dead without getting lost.

Mustard's mother was leaning over his corpse, wailing, and her husband stood behind her, looking white-faced, and absently patting her on the back. The tiny kitchen was jammed with sobbing, nose-blowing mourners, and the air was thick with the smells of grief—perspiration, ladies' cologne, the previous night's cooking, and the faintest whiff of putrefying flesh. Aunty gripped me by the wrist and pushed her way to the front. The air pressed close, like someone's hot, wet breath on my face. My head reeled, and the room broke apart into dots of color. From far away I heard somebody say, "It's Aunty Talking to the Dead."

"Make room, make room," another voice called.

I looked down at Mustard, lying on the table in front of me, his eyes half open in that swollen, purple face. The smell was much stronger close up, and there were flies everywhere.

"We'll have to get rid of some of this bloat," Aunty said, thrusting a metal object into my hand.

People were leaving the room.

She went around to the other side of the table. "I'll start here," she said. "You work over there. Do just like I told you."

I nodded. This was the long-awaited moment. My moment. But it was already the beginning of the end. My knees buckled, and everything went dark.

Aunty performed the laying-out alone and never mentioned the episode again. But it was the talk of the village for weeks—how Yuri Shimabukuro, assistant to Aunty Talking to the Dead, passed out under the Hayashis' kitchen table and had to be tended by the grief-stricken mother of the dead boy.

My mother took to catching the bus to the plantation store three villages away whenever she needed to stock up on necessaries. "You're my daughter—how could I *not* be on your side?" was the way she put it, but the air buzzed with her unspoken recriminations. And whenever I went into the village, I was aware of the sly laughter behind my back, and Chinky Malloy smirking at me from behind the shutters of the Paradise Mortuary.

"She's giving the business a bad name," Clinton said, carefully removing his jacket and draping it across the back of the rickety wooden chair. He dusted the seat, looked at his hand with distaste before wiping it off on his handkerchief, then drew up the legs of his trousers, and sat.

Aunty retrieved her pipe from the smoking tray next to her rocker and filled the tiny brass bowl from a pouch of Bull Durham. "I'm glad you found time to drop by," she said. "You still going out with that skinny white girl?"

"You mean Marsha?" Clinton sounded defensive. "Sure, I see her sometimes. But I didn't come here to talk about that." He glanced over at where I was sitting on the sofa. "You think we could have some privacy?"

Aunty lit her pipe and puffed. "Yuri's my right-hand girl. Couldn't do without her."

"The Hayashis probably have their own opinion about that."

Aunty dismissed his insinuation with a wave of her hand. "There's no pleasing some people," she said. "Yuri's just young; she'll learn." She reached over and patted me on the knee, then looked him straight in the face. "Like we all did."

Clinton turned red. "Damn it, Mama," he sputtered, "this is no time to bring up the past. What counts is now, and right now your right-hand girl is turning you into a laughingstock!" His voice became soft, persuasive. "Look, you've worked hard all your life, and you deserve to retire. Now that my business is taking off, I can help you out. You know I'm only thinking about you."

"About the election to village council, you mean." I couldn't help it; the words just burst out of my mouth.

Aunty said, "You considering going into politics, son?"

"Mama, wake up!" Clinton hollered, like he'd wanted to all along. "You can talk to the dead till you're blue in the face, but *ain't no one listening*. The old ghosts have had it. You either get on the wheel of progress or you get run over."

For a long time after he left, Aunty sat in her rocking chair next to the window, rocking and smoking, without saying a word, just rocking and smoking, as the afternoon shadows spread beneath the trees and turned to night.

Then she began to sing—quietly, at first, but very sure. She sang the naming chants and the healing chants. She sang the stones, and trees, and stars back into their rightful places. Louder and louder she sang, making whole what had been broken.

Everything changed for me after Clinton's visit. I stopped going into the village and began spending all my time with Aunty Talking to the Dead. I followed her everywhere, carried her loads without complaint, memorized remedies, and mixed potions till my head spun and I went near blind. I wanted to know what *she* knew; I wanted to make what had happened at the Hayashis' go away. Not just in other people's minds. Not just because I'd become a laughing-stock, like Clinton said. But because I knew that I had to redeem myself for that one thing, or my moment—the single instant of glory for which I had lived my entire life—would be snatched beyond my reach forever.

Meanwhile, there were other layings-out. The kitemaker who hanged himself. The crippled boy from Chicken Fight Camp. The Vagrant. The Blindman. The Blindman's dog.

"Do like I told you," Aunty would say before each one. Then, "Give it time," when it was done.

But it was like living the same nightmare over and over—just one look at a body and I was done for. For twenty-five years, people in the village joked about my "indisposition." Last fall, my mother's funeral was held at the Paradise Mortuary. While the service was going on, I stood outside on the cement walk for a long time, but I never made it through the door. Little by little, I'd begun to give up hope that my moment would ever arrive.

Then, a week ago, Aunty caught a chill, gathering *awa* in the rain. The chill developed into a fever, and for the first time since I'd known her, she took to her bed. I nursed her with the remedies she'd taught me—sweat baths; eucalyptus steam; tea made from *ko'oko'olau*—but the fever worsened. Her breathing became labored, and she grew weaker. My few hours of sleep were filled with bad dreams. Finally, aware of my betrayal, I walked to a house up the road and telephoned for an ambulance.

"I'm sorry, Aunty," I kept saying, as the flashing red light swept across the porch. The attendants had her on a stretcher and were carrying her out the front door.

She reached up and grasped my arm, her grip still strong. "You'll do okay, Yuri," the old woman whispered hoarsely. "Clinton used to get so scared, he messed his pants." She chuckled, then began to cough. One of the attendants put an oxygen mask over her face. "Hush," he said. "There'll be plenty of time for talking later."

On the day of Aunty's wake, the entrance to the Paradise Mortuary was blocked. Workmen had dug up the front walk and carted the old concrete tiles away. They'd left a mound of gravel on the grass, stacked some bags of concrete next to it, and covered the bags with black tarps. There was an empty wheelbarrow parked to one side of the gravel mound. The entire front lawn had been roped off and a sign had been put up that said, "Please follow the arrows around to the back. We are making improvements in Paradise. The Management."

My stomach was beginning to play tricks, and I was feeling shaky. The old panic was mingled with an uneasiness which had not left me ever since I'd decided to call the ambulance. I kept thinking that it had been useless to call it since she'd gone and died anyway. Or maybe I had waited too long. I almost turned back, but I thought of what Aunty had told me about Clinton and pressed ahead. Numbly, I followed the two women in front of me.

"So, old Aunty Talking to the Dead has finally passed on," one of them, whom I recognized as Emi McAllister, said. She was with Pearlie Woo. Both were old classmates of mine.

I was having difficulty seeing—it was getting dark, and my head was spinning so.

"How old do you suppose she was?" Pearlie asked.

"Gosh, even when we were kids it seemed like she was at least a hundred," Emi said.

Pearlie laughed. "'The Undead,' my brother used to call her."

"When we misbehaved," Emi said, "our mother always threatened to abandon us on the hill where Aunty lived. Mama would be beating us with a wooden spoon and hollering, 'This is gonna seem like nothing then.'"

Aunty had been laid out in a room near the center of the mortuary. The heavy, wine-colored drapes had been drawn across the windows and all the wall lamps turned very low, so it was darker indoors than it had been outside. Pearlie and Emi moved off into the front row. I headed for the back.

There were about thirty of us at the viewing, mostly from the old days—those who had grown up on stories about Aunty, or who remembered her from before the Paradise Mortuary. People got up and began filing past the casket. For a moment I felt dizzy again, but I glanced over at Clinton, looking prosperous and self-assured, accepting condolences, and I got into line.

The room was air conditioned and smelled of floor disinfectant and roses. Soft music came from speakers mounted on the walls. I drew nearer and nearer to the casket. Now there were four people ahead. Now three. I looked down at my feet, and I thought I would faint.

Then Pearlie Woo shrieked, "Her eyes!" People behind me began to murmur. "What—whose eyes?" Emi demanded. Pearlie pointed to the body in the casket. Emi cried, "My God, they're open!"

My heart turned to ice.

"What?" voices behind me were asking. "What about her eyes?"

"She said they're open," someone said.

"Aunty Talking to the Dead's eyes are open," someone else said. Now Clinton was hurrying over.

"That's because she's not dead," still another voice added.

Clinton looked into the coffin, and his face went white. He turned quickly around and waved to his assistants across the room.

"I've heard about cases like this," someone was saying. "It's because she's looking for someone."

"I've heard that too! The old woman is trying to tell us something."

I was the only one there who knew. Aunty was talking to *me*. I clasped my hands together, hard, but they wouldn't stop shaking.

People began leaving the line. Others pressed in, trying to get a better look at the body, but a couple of Clinton's assistants had stationed themselves in front of the coffin, preventing anyone from getting too close. They had shut the lid, and Chinky Malloy was directing people out of the room.

"I'd like to take this opportunity to thank you all for coming here this evening," Clinton was saying. "I hope you will join us at the reception down the hall."

While everyone was eating, I stole back into the parlor and quietly—ever so quietly—went up to the casket, lifted the lid, and looked in.

At first I thought they had switched bodies on me and exchanged Aunty for some powdered and painted old grandmother, all pink and white, in a pink dress, and clutching a white rose to her chest. But there they were. Open. Aunty's eyes staring up at me.

Then I knew. This was *it:* my moment had arrived. Aunty Talking to the Dead had come awake to bear me witness.

I walked through the deserted front rooms of the mortuary and out the front door. It was night. I got the wheelbarrow, loaded it with one of the tarps covering the bags of cement, and wheeled it back to the room where Aunty was. It squeaked terribly, and I stopped often to make sure no one had heard. From the back of the building came the clink of glassware and the buzz of voices. I had to work quickly—people would be leaving soon.

But this was the hardest part. Small as she was, it was very hard to lift her out of the coffin. She was horribly heavy, and unyielding as a bag of cement. I finally got her out and wrapped her in the tarp. I loaded her in the tray of the wheelbarrow—most of her, anyway; there was nothing I could do about her feet sticking out the front end. Then I wheeled her out of the mortuary, across the village square, and up the road, home.

Now, in the dark, the old woman is singing.

I have washed her with my own hands and worked the salt into the hollows of her body. I have dressed her in white and laid her in flowers.

Aunty, here are the beads you like to wear. Your favorite cakes. A quilt to keep away the chill. Here is *noni* for the heart and *awa* for every kind of grief.

Down the road a dog howls, and the sound of hammering echoes through the still air. "Looks like a burying tomorrow," the sleepers murmur, turning in their warm beds.

I bind the sandals to her feet and put the torch to the pyre.

The sky turns to light. The smoke climbs. Her ashes scatter, filling the wind.

And she sings, she sings, she sings.

FURTHER READINGS

Sylvia Watanabe, *Talking to the Dead, And Other Stories* (Doubleday, 1992); Sylvia Watanabe and Carol Bruchac, eds., *Into the Fire: Asian American Prose* (Greenfield Review Press, 1996); Sylvia Watanabe and Carol Bruchac, eds., *Home to Stay: Asian American Women's Fiction* (Greenfield Review Press, 1994).

Molly Ivins (1944–)

Born in 1944 in Texas, Molly Ivins has carved out a niche for herself as a political reporter, columnist and humorist, with the Houston *Chronicle,* the Minneapolis *Star-Tribune,* the Austin *Texas Oserver,* the N*ew York Times,* and the *Dallas Times Herald.* She has also contributed essays to numerous leading journals and magazines, including *Nation, New York Times Book Review, Mother Jones, Ms.,* and *Progressive.* Ivins received a BA from Smith College, an MA from Columbia University, and attended the Institute of Political Science, in Paris, France.

Throughout her career, Ivins has focused on Texas politics, which she once called the "finest form of free entertainment ever invented." Her essays have been collected in several books: *Molly Ivins Can't Say That, Can She?* (Vintage, 1992); *Nothin' But Good Times Ahead* (Vintage, 1994); and *You Got to Dance With Them What Brung You: Politics in the Clinton Years* (Random House, 1988). She is currently completing *Shrub: The Short but Happy Political Life of George W. Bush* (Random House, 2000)

IMPERSONATING THE LORD

We're having trouble again with that fellow who runs around impersonating the Lord. This cad, claiming to be God, told the Rodriguez family of Floydada, Texas, last month that if they didn't get naked, get in their car, and drive to Louisiana, he, God, would destroy Floydada (which is, incidentally, pronounced "Floy-*day*-da," *not* like the art movement).

Now, you know perfectly well that wasn't really God. Someone was just funnin' the Rodriguezes. God might destroy Floydada sometime, on aesthetic grounds, but He'd never tell anyone to go to Louisiana.

The upshot of this deplorable case of Lord impersonation was

Molly Ivins, "Lone Star Republic" and "Impersonating the Lord," from *You Got to Dance with Them What Brung You* (1998).

that the entire Rodriguez family, buck naked, drove to Vinton, Louisiana, Marcia Ball's hometown, where they were startled by a cop, drove into a tree, and then twenty nekkid folks piled out of a GTO (five kids in the trunk), which just astonished the hell out of the Vinton cops. The driver was incarcerated, the other Rodriguezes were remanded to the care of the Baptist church in nearby Sulphur, Louisiana, and the Vinton cops still haven't recovered.

I figure this Lord impersonator is the same guy who pulled that prank on Oral Roberts a few years back. Remember when Roberts said that God had told him to tell us, "Pay up or the preacher gets it"? Same joker. You notice he's concentrating on the Texas-Oklahoma area. I won't deny that we have an unusually high percentage of geeks in this neck of the prairie because, let's face it, we do. But I don't think it's fair for this prankster to be pickin' on our geeks.

I think the Texas Lege should pass a bill making impersonatin' the Lord a felony and then we should have a kind of neighborhood watch, with everyone callin' in suspected cases of Lord impersonation to the Texas Rangers.

I don't see why God should take the blame when preachers or citizens claim they've heard from him and then say somethin' idiotic. They can say it on their own, like my old preacher, who once observed, "My friends, to be a good Christian, you must, uuhhh, be a good Christian."   (1993)

LONE STAR REPUBLIC

Called upon once more in my capacity as the World's Leading Authority on blue-bellied, wall-eyed, lithium-deprived Texas lunatics, I step modestly but confidently into the breach.

Yes, friends, I can explain why almost a dozen mush-brained lint-heads holed up in the Davis Mountains demanding that Texas become a free country once again. I cannot explain why the national media chose to describe these oxygen-deprived citizens as "Texas separatists"—as though being a Texas separatist were something within the realm of loosely circumscribed sanity—but then, not even Slats Grobnik could explain everything.

The self-proclaimed "Republic of Texas" is a set of folks descended from the Texas property-rights movement. The property-rights movement, known further west as the Wise Use movement, surfaced here in the summer of 1994, born in a state of high indignation and profound misunderstanding.

The folks in property rights were upset over the prospect that the gummint might take their property without giving them any recompense. These folks were not reassured by the very words in the Constitution that say the gummint cannot take your property without giving you fair value for it. During one memorable exchange on this point, Marshall Kuykendall, president of the group Take Back Texas, replied to some legalistic quibbler who asked for a specific case of gummint taking property: "When Lincoln freed the slaves, he did not pay for them."

You have to admit, ol' Marshall has you there.

Now, while that story is quite true, in fairness, it makes the property-rights folks look a lot dumber than they actually are. It is widely understood and accepted, even in Texas, that you cannot do whateverthehell you damn please with your own property if it will have a seriously adverse effect on your neighbors. You cannot be building some plant with a lot of toxic emissions if it will cause the neighbors to die, for example. Reasonable people can agree on that.

But in central Texas, the slightly more communistic area of the state, environmentalists have successfully filed a bunch of lawsuits, leaving the courts pondering how much property has to be set aside to maintain a habitat for two endangered species: the black-capped vireo, a pretty songbird, and the Barton Creek salamander, a critter only a herpetologist could love.

Envision this from the property owner's point of view: Here you are settin' on several acres of increasingly valuable land on the edge of these boomin' cities—either Austin or San Antone. You got these high-tech companies—IBM, Texas Instruments, whoever—just beggin' you to let 'em build a nice, new plant on your place. And some fool is goin' to screw this up over a salamander? And while this salamander deal is bein' decided, is anybody goin' to pay you for the money you're losin'?

So there you have the nub of your property-rights movement, which also involves more generalized antienvironmentalist sentiment, plus a lot of fed-cussing.

So how'd we get from fair questions to *las cucarachas* in the Davis Mountains? Easy. The property-rights movement always did shade gradually from folks who sound just like every grump you've ever heard grousin' about the goddamn gummint to total fruitcakes. The fruitcake end of the spectrum naturally shaded into the militia movement. As Jim Hamblin of San Marcos, a member of the Texas Constitutional Militia, once inquired reasonably, "Why are they so afraid of a few hundred thousand people with assault rifles?"

But out there on the far end of the militia movement—mostly a bunch of guys who like to play soldier—you find your folks into *The Turner Diaries,* race war, and bombing federal buildings. Slippery slopes.

The Republic of Texas in turn has two branches: the nearly normal lunatics who claim to be the official Republic of Texas and the Richard Lance, McLaren branch. McLaren has been filing phony liens since 1985 and is splendidly obsessive: He has written thousands and thousands of pages of legal documents, briefs, appeals, warrants, liens, proclamations—a sort of vast parody of the law.

Two things worth noting about the ROT folks. One is, you listen to these guys long enough and they will start to remind you of the kids who used to get so heavily involved in the game Dungeons and Dragons that they lost track of reality. At some point, imagination becomes delusion. And this group delusion is spread through the Internet.

One cannot blame computers for this, since history is full of examples of not just the *folie à deux* but the *folie à large numbers*. But computers do facilitate the phenomenon.

The second important point about ROT and its followers is that they should not be dismissed with the old put-down "Get a life." That's the problem. They can't. Most of them don't have the education or the skills to get and keep a decent job. They're going to spend the rest of their lives in trailer parks. Basically, these guys are Bubba. A little stranger than Bubba usually is, but still Bubba. Maybe a high school education. Twenty, make that almost thirty, years of falling wages. No way to get ahead. And all day they listen to the establishment media tell them the economy is booming. Everyone else is getting rich. Mansions are selling like hotcakes. Big cigars and thick steaks are fashionable again. The angst of the soccer mom is the highest concern of our politicians.

There is so much anger out here. It is taking so many bizarre forms. And most of the media can't even see it: economic apartheid keeps the bottom half of this society well hidden from the top half. Texas Attorney General Dan Morales says ROT is "terrorism, pure and simple."

We all feel real bad about the one fella who was killed in the deal: we thought we'd gotten out of it without bloodshed, but two of 'em took to the hills. The official explanation is that Mike Matson, forty-eight, was shot by a Texas Department of Criminal Justice dog handler after he had fired on a state helicopter. But it should be noted that Matson had shot three dogs at that point.

"Dingbattery, pure and simple" I could buy. Terrorism? Because a lot of Americans cannot forgive what happened at Waco and Ruby Ridge? Why should they? Ever heard anyone apologize for those murders? A lot of Americans have no hope, get no help, and see their own government as an oppressive force. For them, it is, isn't it? Working-class people are getting screwed by their own government. Its latest start is to cut the capital-gains tax and the estate tax that kicks in after a person leaves more than $600,000. More tax breaks for the rich mean a larger share of the tax burden for everybody else.

What we have here is just a little case of misdirected anger. O.K., the U.N. and black helicopters are not the problem. But don't underestimate the anger itself.												(1997)

FURTHER READINGS
Nation, June 7, 1986: 786-787; *New York Times Book Review,* October 20, 1991: 13; *Women's Review of Books,* December 1991: 8–9.

Colleen McElroy (1935–)

Washington poet and short story author Colleen McElroy was born in St. Louis, Missouri, in 1935. As the daughter of an Army father, she moved often as a child, learning a habit of wandering that she maintains even today. Arriving in a new place and wanting to make friends, McElroy learned that telling stories opened doors for her, and she has told them ever since. She first moved across the Mississippi to attend Kansas State University, where she received BS and MS degrees. She moved to Seattle, Washington, to take her PhD at the University of Washington, where she is now Professor of English. Originally trained as a speech therapist, McElroy is probably best known as a poet, although her short stories are also popular with readers. McElroy started writing poetry in her mid-thirties, publishing numerous books of poems, including *Music from Home* (1976), *Bone Flames* (1987), and *What Madness Brought Me Here: New and Selected Poems, 1968–1988* (1990). Her short fiction collections include *Jesus and Fat Tuesday* (1987), *Driving Under the Cardboard Pines* (1990), and *A Long Way from St. Louie* (1997). She has received a National Endowment of the Arts Fellowship, a Rockefeller Foundation Fellowship, and a Fulbright Fellowship, as well as the Before Columbus American book award.

McElroy writes with passion about her experiences as an African American woman in the West, and in her travels far afield from her Pacific Northwest home. In this story from *A Long Way from St. Louie* (1997), she tells a funny, suspenseful, and ultimately heartwrenching story of American race relations on the borders.

HOW NOT TO CROSS THE BORDER

1964, the Mexican border. Nogales. It's hot, of course, and I've got all the windows open. The car still smells new, an overpowering

Colleen McElroy, "How Not to Cross the Border," from *A Long Way From St. Louie* (1997).

smell despite dust billowing behind approaching traffic, and the inevitable odor of human sweat and fruit gone bad from all the cargo trucks. I'm sweating, but I'm wearing my coolest smile.

"¿Habla español?," the agent smiles back.

"¿Qué pasa?," I mutter.

"¿Dónde vive?," he says slowly, as if he suspects I'm slow witted. In a bad movie, he'd twist his mustache, and although I feel as if I'm in a bad movie, he merely looks at me impatiently. I wonder how early he had to report to work that morning. He looks tired. He looks exasperated.

"¿Dónde vive?" he repeats, articulating carefully.

"¿Adónde?" I answer, just as carefully.

He opens the door. "Get out of the car, señora."

That I can do. I lean against the car, a Caddie, powder blue. I'm wearing a dress and heels, sling pumps. Obviously I have no plans to run.

He walks around to the front of the car, checks out the Kansas license plates. He shakes his head. Great. Now he thinks I'm a K.C. gangster, a black woman in a pimp blue Caddie. He looks me over and I'm wearing just the outfit to confirm his suspicions: fuschia dress, tight around the hips, and three inch heels to match. Nails long and lacquered red. My hair in the latest Kansas City curls. "What business do you have in Mexico?" he asks.

"I have no business in Mexico," I say. Little does he know, that's exactly what my mother had said when I left the kids with her. "You've got no business in Mexico. You oughta be here with these babies."

"What brings you to Mexico?"

"This car," I say.

Now he thinks I'm a smart ass. I want to correct myself, to say that I am delivering the car for someone else. I want to say that he's as scary as all the Southerners I saw working in gas stations when I was driving through Texas, places that kept the NO COLOREDS signs on the walls with the old license plates and posters for Dr. Pepper and Nehi grape soda. I want to say I don't know what possessed me to drive to Mexico in the first place except a free trip away from Kansas City and Swift's Packing House, a getaway from a job where my patients were more likely to fly to the moon than recover language functions. I want to say that I drove down with Shirley. She's in the next lane over, black Caddie. We're both divorced, and it's a vacation. "A chance to get out of Kansas City," I'd told my mother. "It will do us good." I want to say this to the agent, but before I can figure out how to put any of it into words that will help me slide across the border, he says, "Papers, please."

I stop myself from answering, "I don't got to show you no steenking pay-pers," but the agent is not Alphonso Bedoya and I'm not Leo G. Carroll and this is not a movie, despite the locked trunk that has kept the Caddie riding low all the way from Kansas. I show him what papers I have.

He looks at my driver's license and at the car registration. "This car does not belong to you?"

"No, my car is at home. I'm delivering . . ."

"Open the trunk, señora."

I gulp. "I don't have a key to the trunk," I say. Did he actually unbuckle his holster? I want to throw up my hands, scream: *Don't shoot!* and surrender immediately. "She has the key," I say quickly. I point to the car one lane over, where Shirley stands, sunlight beaming down on all of her six-foot blondeness.

He eyeballs her Cadillac. Same model, different color. "Señora, I would like you to open this car. The car you are driving."

I stare across at Shirley. She smiles and waves. The agent she is talking to looks in my direction. He is not smiling. "Ask her for the keys," I say. "I don't know nothing."

"This also is the car of the blonde señora?" he asks.

This is getting really bad, I think. "No, her brother's. When we finally deliver it."

"And where is the brother of the señora?"

Really bad. "I don't know," I say.

He's resting his hand on his gun. "Señora, please pull the car into the waiting area. Go into the office. Leave the keys in the car."

I step back into the Caddie, gentle it into a parking slip in the neutral zone between the U.S. and Mexico. As I get out of the car and head up the stairs into the customs office, Shirley waves at me again. But I am gallows-bound and have no friends. Two hours later, I am convinced that I will become the Woman Without a Country. Twice they've come in, asked me my name and Kansas City address, my place of employment, and marital status. But then suddenly, it is over.

"You may leave, señora. Your friend she is waiting."

At first, I think he must be talking to someone else, except I am the only one in the room. I have been the only one in the room for two hours. I almost trip at the door. Without chicken wire covering a window, the sunlight is bright, almost surgical. Shirley is wearing sunglasses. I put on my sunglasses. We drive to Nogales and I sulk all the way to the hotel. She chatters as if we're heading home from a shopping trip at the mall. Her brother now has the car, she tells me. "Next time, he can drive his own damn car," I tell her. "Was the trunk still locked?" I ask. She doesn't answer. I never see the blue Caddie again.

Blaine, Washington, five years later. I've crossed this border a hundred times or more. "How long do you plan on staying in Canada?" the agent drawls. I wonder what joker has sent this southern transplant to the Canadian border. All he needs are reflector glasses to complete the picture. On the other hand, all we need are love beads and incense to make us full-fledged hippies. I figure that means we're already in trouble.

"How far is New Wes?" Don asks.

"About half an hour," I remind him.

"About an hour," Don tells the agent.

The agent leans over and looks into the car. He doesn't say anything, just pokes his head in the window and takes a look-see. Don's wearing a fringed suede vest and jeans. He has just left a theater rehearsal and there are traces of stage makeup near his ears, but it's too late to tell him to wipe off the stuff. I'm wearing bell bottoms and a halter top, my midriff bare. I pat my Afro into shape in case there are dents in it. Don reaches over and turns off the radio. He pats my arm. I give his hand a squeeze—my black hand over his white. The agent raises his eyebrows. He sees we're both wearing wedding rings. "You two married?" he asks.

"To each other?" Don laughs. I laugh, too.

I think of my husband, off flying planes somewhere near the Arctic Circle. And Don's wife at home, bossing their two kids, who are smart enough to be inventing weapons that will blow us all to Kingdom Come. Fortunately, Don is trying to keep them interested

in theater, a safe, penniless career. I'm hoping some of his enthusiasm will rub off on my kids, although my daughter is the only one
who has taken the bait so far. That is, if you don't count me: I hang
around Don because he is in theater and I'm willing to beg my
way onto the stage. We're simpatico, but married—no.

"Are you married?" the agent repeats.

Don says "No" and I say "Yes." Don says "Yes" and I say "No." The
agent says, "Step out of the car."

Obediently, we open the doors.

"Let me see your driver's license," the agent says.

"For this I had to get out of the car," Don says.

I kick him. It's not the time to be a comedian. With all the
Vietnam war objectors heading across the border, it's not the time
to be anything but a U.S. resident on a couple of hours of R & R,
unless you have reason to be running. And if we were running, we'd
have our act together better than this.

"You have a driver's license, too?" the agent snarls, except it
sounds as if he's asking for my criminal record.

I'm almost tempted to flash my television press pass, but all we
want to do is buy a couple of bottles of Canadian Fifth and some
Indian smoked fish in New Westminister to take to the cast party
tomorrow night. So I'm not ready to make a federal case out of it.
Yet. I hand over my license.

"You don't have the same last name," he says.

We both say: "No." Don winks at me.

"But you're wearing wedding rings."

We both say: "Yes."

"Open the trunk," he says.

Don begins waving his hands, talking fast. His speech is clo-
quent. I don't know if he's doing Hamlet or Puck, but it's something
Shakespearean. The agent stares as if Don has just lost his mind. I
can't tell if he's listening or wondering how long it will take to subdue this Looney Tunes and handcuff him. I'm wondering why Don
doesn't just open the trunk. Instead, he's describing the theater, the
art of making drama, of making an audience believe they're somewhere else instead of in a room, in the dark, with a lot of strangers.

It's not a bad explanation, fit for a beginning drama class at the college where we both teach, but Don's doing this for the benefit of an overweight customs agent whose uniform shirt barely buttons up.

"What are you trying to tell me?" the agent says.

"Yeah. Just open the trunk," I say.

Don glowers at me. "Look, you don't want me to open the trunk," he whispers in a voice that's like Iago plotting Othello's downfall.

The agent whispers right back. "Open the trunk." There's doom in every word. I decide the agent is definitely doing Hamlet.

Don shrugs and takes the key from the ignition. "Don't say I didn't warn you," he announces, and clicks open the trunk.

At first, all I can see are naked bodies, fleshy pink arms and legs jumbled in every direction. Three arms going one way, four in another. A leg missing a foot. A foot coming out of the pile at an impossible angle. The agent groans. What must he be thinking: the gruesome remains of mass murder? A storehouse of body parts? A gull screams and passes overhead. The wind whispers in the evergreens, then flees toward Birch Bay. I have nowhere to go. Then I notice a head, the eyes staring and blank. Mannequins!

"You're crossing the border with stage props?" I ask. My eyes are stuck open as wide as the mannequin's.

Don grins, playing Puck again.

"If you have an explanation for this, I don't want to hear it," the agent says.

He makes us unload the trunk, but after a few hollow left arms and a foot or two, he's had enough. "Next time," he says, "take that crap out of your car before you get here."

"There's a man who doesn't appreciate theater," Don says, as we drive toward New Westminister.

"And you're the master of understatement," I say.

FURTHER READINGS

Colleen McElroy, "When the Shoe Never Fits: Myth in the Modern Mode," in *Poet's Perspectives: Reading, Writing, and Teaching Poetry,* eds. Charles R. Duke and Sally A. Jacobsen (Boynton/Cook, 1992); Colleen J. McElroy, *Travelling Music* (Story Line Press, 1998); Colleen J. McElroy, *Driving Under the Cardboard Pines, And Other Stories* (Creative Arts Book Company, 1990); Colleen J. McElroy, *What Madness Brought Me Here: New and Selected Poems, 1968–1988* (Wesleyan Univ Press, 1990); Colleen J. McElroy, *Bone Flames, Poems* (Wesleyan University Press, 1987); Colleen J. McElroy, *Jesus and Fat Tuesday, And Other Short Stories* (Creative Arts Book Company, 1987); Colleen J. McElroy, *Queen of the Ebony Isles* (Wesleyan University Press, 1984); Colleen J. McElroy, *Winters Without Snow* (Reed Cannon & Johnson Publishers, 1980); Colleen J. McElroy, *Music from Home, Selected Poems* (Southern Illinois University Press, 1976).

Sandra Cisneros (1954–)

Born in Chicago in 1954, Sandra Cisneros was raised in Humboldt Park, Illinois, the only daughter among seven children of a Chicana mother and a Mexican father. After earning a BA at Loyola University, she graduated from the Writing Program at the University of Iowa. In the years since, she was been Writer-in-Residence at several universities, including The University of Michigan at Ann Arbor, The University of California-Irvine, and The University of New Mexico in Albuquerque.

Sandra Cisneros has published a large number of poetry collections, including *Bad Boys* (Mango, 1980), *The Rodrigo Poems* (Third Woman Press, 1987), *Loose Woman: Poems* (Knopf, 1994), and *My Wicked Wicked Ways* (Turtle Bay Books, 1992). Still, she is best-known for her novels, written as collections of interconnected short stories and essays. The first of these, *The House on Mango Street* (1984), drew on her experiences in Chicago, and won the Before Columbus American Book Award. Her next novel, *Woman Hollering Creek* (1991), centered around San Antonio, Texas, and drew on narratives of people living in the area.

Writing in English generously peppered with Spanish phrases more evocative than their translations, Cisneros captures linguistically her mastery of both of her worlds. Spanish is, for Cisneros, a boon for the Chicana writer, who has "twice as many words to pick from [and thus] two ways of looking at the world." In this selection from *Woman Hollering Creek,* Cisneros plays with the idea of remembering the Alamo, the site of the siege commemorated in John Wayne's film version, looking at it from the other side of the story.

REMEMBER THE ALAMO

Gustavo Galindo, Ernie Sepúlveda, Jessie Robles, Jr., Ronnie DeHoyos, Christine Zamora . . .

Sandra Cisneros, "Remember the Alamo," from *Woman Hollering Creek* (1991).

When I was a kid and my ma added the rice to the hot oil, you know how it sizzles and spits, it sounds kind of like applause, right? Well, I'd always bow and say *Gracias, mi querido público,* thank you, and blow kisses to an imaginary crowd. I still do, kind of as a joke. When I make Spanish rice or something and add it to the oil. It roars, and I bow, just a little so no one would guess, but I bow, and I'm still blowing kisses, only inside.

Mary Alice Luján, Santiago Sanabria, Timoteo Herrera . . .

But I'm not Rudy when I perform. I mean, I'm not Rudy Cantú from Falfurrias anymore. I'm Tristán. Every Thursday night at the Travisty. Behind the Alamo, you can't miss it. One-man show, girl. Flamenco, salsa, tango, fandango, merengue, cumbia, cha-cha-chá. Don't forget. The Travisty. Remember the Alamo.

Lionel Ontiveros, Darlene Limón, Alex Vigil . . .

There are other performers, the mambo queens—don't get me wrong, it's not that they're not good at what they do. But they're not class acts. Daniela Romo impersonators. Lucha Villa look-alikes. Carmen Mirandas. Fruit department, if you ask me. But Tristán is very—how do I put it?—elegant. I mean, when he walks down the street, he turns heads like this. Passionate and stormy. And arrogant. Yes, arrogant a little. Sweetheart, in this business you have to be.

Blás G. Cortinas, Armando Salazar, Freddie Mendoza . . .

Tristán holds himself like a matador. His clothes magnificent. Absolutely perfect, like a second skin. The crowd throbbing—Tris-TAN, Tris-TAN, Tris-TAN!!! Tristán smiles, the room shivers. He raises his arms, the wings of a hawk. Spotlight clean as the moon of

Andalucía. Audience breathless as water. And then . . . *Boom!* The heels like shotguns. A dance till death. I will love you *hasta la muerte, mi vida.* Do you hear? Until death.

Brenda Núñez, Jacinto Tovar, Henry Bautista, Nancy Rose Luna . . .

Because every Thursday night Tristán dances with La Calaca Flaca. Tristán takes the fag hag by the throat and throttles her senseless. Tristán's not afraid of La Flaquita, Thin Death.

Arturo Domínguez, Porfiria Escalante, Gregory Gallegos Durán, Ralph G. Soliz . . .

Tristán leads Death across the floor. ¿ *Verdad que me quieres, mi cariñito, verdad que si? Hasta la muerte.* I'll show you how to ache.

Paul Villareal Saucedo, Monica Riojas, Baltazar M. López . . .

Say it. Say you want me. You want me. *Te quiero.* Look at me. I said *look* at me. *Don't* take your eyes from mine, Death. Yesssss. My treasure. My precious. *Mi pedacito de alma desnuda.* You want me so bad it hurts. A tug-of-war, a tease and stroke. Smoke in the mouth. *Hasta la muerte.* Ha!

Dorotea Villalobos, Jorge H. Hull, Aurora Anguiano Román, Amado Tijerina, Bobby Mendiola . . .

Tristán's family? They love him no matter what. His ma proud of his fame—That's my *m'ijo.* His sisters jealous because he's the pretty one. But they adore him, and he gives them tips on their makeup.

At first his father said What's this? But then when the newspaper articles started pouring in, well, what could he do but send photocopies to the relatives in Mexico, right? And Tristán sends them all free backstage passes. They drive all the way from the Valley for the opening of the show. Even the snooty relatives from Monterrey. It's unbelievable. Last time he invited his family they took the whole damn third floor of La Mansián del Rio. I'm not kidding.

He's the greatest live act in San Anto. Doesn't put up with bull. No way. Either loves you or hates you. Ferocious, I'm telling you. *Muy* hot-hot-hot or cold as a witch's tough *chichi*. Isn't tight with nobody but family and friends. Doesn't need to be. Go on, say it. I want you to. I'll school you. I'll show you how it's done.

See this ring? A gift from an art admirer and dance aficionado. Sent $500 worth of red roses the night of his opening. You should've seen the dressing room. Roses, roses, roses. Honey! Then he sent the ring, little diamonds set in the shape of Texas. Just because he was fond of art. That's how it is. Say it. *Te quiero.* Say you want me. You want me.

The bitch and Tristán are like this. La Flaca crazy about him. Lots of people love Tristán like that. Because Tristán dares to be different. To stand out in a crowd. To have style and grace. And *elegancia.* Tristán has that kind of appeal.

He's not scared of the low-rider types who come up at the Esquire Bar, that beer-stinking, piss-soaked hole, jukebox screaming Brenda Lee's "I'm Sorry." *¿Eres maricón?* You a fag? Gives them a look like the edge of a razor across lip.

Dresses all in white in the summer, all in black in the winter. No in-between except for the show. That's how he is. Tristán. But he's never going to be anything but honest. Carry his heart in his hand. You know it.

And when he loves, gives himself body and soul. None of this fooling around. A love so complete you have to be ready for it. Courageous. Put on your seat belt, sweets. A ride to the finish. So bad it aches.

A dance until death. Every Thursday night when he glides with La Flaca. Wraps his arms around her. La Muertita with her shit-eating, bless-her-heart grin. Doesn't faze him. La Death with her dress up the crack of her ass. The girl's pathetic.

What a pair! The two like Ginger and Fred tangoing across the floor. Two angels, heavenly bodies floating cheek to cheek. Or *nalga* to *nalga*. Ay, girl, I'm telling you. *Wáchale, muchacha.* With those maracas and the cha-cha-chá of those bones-bones-bones, she's a natural. *¿Verdad que me quieres, mi cariñito? ¿Verdad que si?*

Tristán? Never feels better than on Thursday nights when he's working her. When he's living those moments, the audience breathing, sighing out there, roaring when the curtains go up and the lights and music begin. That's when Tristán's life starts. Without ulcers or gas stations or hospital bills or bloody sheets or pubic hairs in the sink. Lovers in your arms pulling farther and farther away from you. Dried husks, hulls, coffee cups. Letters home sent back unopened.

Tristán's got nothing to do with the ugly, the ordinary. With screen doors with broken screens or peeling paint or raw hallways. The dirty backyards, the muddy spittle in the toilet you don't want to remember. Sweating, pressing himself against you, pink pink peepee blind and seamless as an eye, pink as a baby rat, your hand small and rubbing it, yes, like this, like so, and your skull being crushed by that sour smell and the taste like tears inside your sore mouth.

No. Tristán doesn't have memories like that. Only *amor del corazón,* that you can't buy, right? That is never used to hurt anybody. Never ashamed. Love like a body that wants to give and give of itself, that wants to create a universe where nothing is dirty, no one is hurting, no one sick, that's what Tristán thinks of when he dances.

Mario Pacheco, Ricky Estrada, Lillian Alvarado . . .

Say it. Say you want me. *Te quiero.* Like I want you. Say you love me. Like I love you. I love you. *Te quiero, mi querido público. Te adoro.* With all my heart. With my heart and with my body.

Ray Agustín Huerta, Elsa González, Frank Castro, Abelardo Romo, Rochell M. Garza, Nacianceno Cavazos, Nelda Therese Flores,

Roland Guillermo Pedraza, Renato Villa, Filemón Guzmán, Suzie A. Ybañez, David Mondragón . . .

This body.

FURTHER READINGS:
Sandra Cisneros, "From a Writer's Notebook," *The Americas Review* XV, No. 1 (Spring 1987): 69-79; Alvina E. Quintana, *Home Girls: Chicana Literary Voices* (Temple University Press, 1996); Alma M. Garcia, "The Development of Chicana Feminist Discourse," in Ronald Takaki, ed., *From Different Shores: Perspectives on Race and Ethnicity in America* (2nd ed., Oxford University Press, 1994); Erlinda Gonzáles-Berry and Tey Diana Rebolledo, "Growing Up Chicano: Tomás Rivera and Sandra Cisneros," *Revista Chicano-Riqueña* XIII, Nos. 3-4 (Fall-Winter, 1985): 109-119.

Biographical Information About Western Women Photographers in this Anthology

Evelyn Cameron

Evelyn Jephson Flower was born just south of London in 1868, into a well-to-do family. Living a gentrified country life until 1889, she married Ewen Cameron, with whom she journeyed to Terry, Montana, to start a horse ranch. Finding life there invigorating, Cameron wrote, "I like to break colts, brand calves, cut down trees, ride & work in a garden. . . ." To make riding astride easier for her, she often wore her husband's trousers, and in 1895 she introduced the split skirt into Montana; she was threatened with arrest for this "unconventional" behavior. In order to help supplement their meager ranching income, Cameron began taking in boarders, one of whom taught her the basics of photography. She persevered with this hobby, and by 1904 had, by her calculations, earned $94.40 from selling her photographs. The small town's post office became the hub of Cameron's growing photography business, with the postmistress taking orders and selling prints. Cameron was well aware that her images were precious records of a unique place, and she was very careful to take notes of the circumstances in which each photograph was taken. Also, her meticulous diaries would later yield further information about the people and places she captured on film. After her husband's death in 1915, Cameron continued to manage their ranch alone until her own death in 1928. Most of Cameron's work—along with Cameron herself—remained virtually unknown beyond Terry for more than fifty years, until Janet Williams, one of Cameron's friends, shared her amassed collection of the Camerons's personal effects, which included letters, manuscripts, 35 diaries, 1,800 negatives, and 2,500 original prints, with editor Donna M. Lucey. In 1990, Lucey published her book, *Photographing Montana, 1894–1928: The Life and Work of Evelyn Cameron*, a selection of Cameron's photographs accompanied by the story of Cameron's fascinating life.

Carole Gallagher

Carole Gallagher is a documentary photographer whose work has been exhibited in the United States and abroad. Living in New York City and the Pacific Northwest, she refers to herself as "bicoastal." Her groundbreaking book, *American Ground Zero: The Secret Nuclear War* (1993), is an eloquent examination of the aftermath of nuclear testing in the American West. In it, she became "a blank slate upon which the stories and images could be written." More than photographic essay, and more than history, her study tells the story of the Atomic West and its legacy.

Laura Gilpin

Laura Gilpin was born in Colorado Springs, Colorado, in 1891. In 1916, she paid her way to New York City with her earnings from raising chickens in order to study photography at the Clarence White School, then the leading American school of photography. After graduating in 1917, she returned to Colorado Springs, where she met Elizabeth Forster, a nurse, who also worked in Navajo country. With Forster, she took several trips South to photograph at Canyon de Chelly, Mesa Verde, and Chinle and Red Rock, Arizona. Gilpin made her living as a portrait and architectural photographer, but she is remembered today especially for her Southwestern landscapes and for her photography of the Navajo. She was working on a photographic survey of Canyon de Chelly and the Navajo people who live there when she died in 1979. Her photographs are collected in two major surveys: Laura Gilpin, *The Enduring Navaho* (1968), and Martha A. Sandweiss's *Laura Gilpin: An Enduring Grace* (1986).

Teresa Jordan

Teresa Jordan is a writer, poet, essayist, musician, and photographer. Although in recent years most readers know her as a writer, her photographs of Western women and their work on the land are filled with a special beauty, as if the women and the land belong to each other. The photographs in this collection come from her book *Cowgirls: Women of the American West* (1982). She and husband Hal Cannon currently produce Western travelogues for Public Radio International, and she calls herself a "radio illustrator."

Dorothea Lange

Born in Hoboken, New Jersey, in 1895, Dorothea Lange traveled with a friend to San Francisco in 1917 and settled there for the rest of her life. Working as a clerk in a camera shop, she met the noted California photographer Imogen Cunningham, who introduced her to the bohemian world of local photography. With Cunningham's encouragement, she soon became a professional photographer and started her own studio. When the Great Depression hit in the 1930s, she found work as a roving photographer for the Farm Security Administration (FSA), as part of a New Deal program intended to document the lives of America's agricultural workers. Like Russell Lee, whose FSA portrait of migrant farm workers in Arizona also appears in this collection, Lange traveled extensively throughout the West and South photographing Dust Bowl immigrants and farm workers. Her deep empathy for the suffering of workers during the Depression was perhaps the result of her own struggle to overcome the partial paralysis that resulted from a childhood bout with polio. During the 1940s, she took a similar position with the Office of War Information, documenting war production in California; her images of war workers are an indelible record of the demographic transformation of the Bay Area in the 1940s. She then went to work for the War Relocation Administration, and in this capacity, she recorded the internment of Japanese American families in California. Serious chronic illness forced her to give up photography after World War II for many years, but before she died in 1965 she had been able to produce several important documentary studies, including photo essays taken in Ireland and Vietnam, and a study of the Berryessa Valley in California, before it was flooded by a federal dam. Her work has been collected in many books, but the majority of her Western photographs appear in the following collections: *Dorothea Lange: American Photographs* (1994); *Photographing the Second Gold Rush : Dorothea Lange and the East Bay at War 1941–1945* (1995); and *Dorothea Lange: Photographs of a Lifetime* (1996).

Joan Myers

Joan Myers was born in Iowa and earned a master's degree in musicology from Stanford University in 1967. During the next years, however, she turned to photography, and has since been both writer and artist. Her books include *Whispered Silences* (1996), with Gary Okihiro, a contemporary revisiting of Japanese World War II reloca-tion camps. Some of her books record journeys—*Along the Santa Fé Trail* (1986), *The Mexican Road* (1989), and *Santiago: Saint of Two Worlds* (1991), which followed the medieval pilgrimage route across northern Spain to Santiago de Compostela. Myers's latest work, *Salt Dreams: Land and Water in Low-Down California*, (University of New Mexico Press, 1999) culminates a ten-year pho-tographic study of the Salton Sea with text by William DeBuys. Some of her exhibitions were the series called "Women of a Certain Age," and a new series of photographs on Western power, for the National Millennium Survey at the College of Santa Fé.

Toba Pato Tucker

Toba Pato Tucker's book *Pueblo Artists: Portraits* was published in 1998 by the Museum of New Mexico Press. It features 135 black and white photographs of Pueblo artists of all ages. Tucker, who considers herself a documentary portrait photographer, has been working in the Southwest for the past twenty years. In *Pueblo Artists*, she wanted to "record the remarkable and prevalent inci-dence where several generations in one family work together cre-atively, passing their traditions from one to the next, from the old to the young, creating a link from the past to the present."

Barbara Van Cleve

Barbara Van Cleve grew up on her family's Lazy K Bar Ranch, founded in 1880, on the East slopes of the Crazy Mountains near Melville, Montana. She earned an MA in English Literature at Northwestern University, and taught English and served as Dean of Women at DePaul University. She is the author and photographer of *Hard Twist: Contemporary Women Ranchers* (1995), and the co-author and photographer, with poet Paul Zarzyski, of *All This Way for the Short Ride* (1997). Her work is published in *Roughstock Sonnets* (1989), *Way Out West* (1991), and *Cowboys* (1993). Her ranch and her photography are the focus of a television documentary, *Barbara Van Cleve: Capturing Grace* (1993), and she was special still photog-rapher for Robert Redford's film, *The Horse Whisperer* in 1997. Van Cleve spends summers on the Montana ranch, and winters in Santa Fé, printing and preparing her work for exhibition.

Credits and Permissions

Photographic Credits

Teresa Jordan, "Cutting Out Heavy Heifers," from *Cowgirls: Women of the American West, An Oral History* (Doubleday, 1982). Copyright © 1982 Teresa Jordan, used by permission of the artist.

Amelda Ann Mansfield, 80, at the wheel of the car in which she retraced her overland journey by covered wagon. Used by permission of The San Antonio Light Collection, The Institute of Texan Cultures, University of Texas-San Antonio.

Evelyn Cameron, *Children's Day at Church, 1913*. The Haynes Foundation Collection, The Montana Historical Society, Helena, Montana.

Evelyn Cameron, *"Scholars" at Knowlton, 35 Miles South of Terry, Montana, 1907*. The Haynes Foundation Collection, The Montana Historical Society, Helena, Montana.

Evelyn Cameron, *Self-Portrait Standing on Jim, 1912*. The Haynes Foundation Collection, The Montana Historical Society, Helena, Montana.

Barbara Van Cleve, *Chinks, Oxbow and Jinglebobs*, 1984. Copyright © 1984 Barbara Van Cleve.

Calamity Jane with Rifle, Montana Historical Society, Helena, Montana.

Joan Myers, *Crossed Arms, 1992*. From the exhibition, *Women of a Certain Age*. Copyright © 1999 Joan Myers, used by permission of artist.

Mary Hallock Foote, *Woman and Child*, used by permission of Idaho State University-Pocatello.

Photograph of Ramona Lubo on the Cahuilla Reservation, Courtesy of Seaver Center for Western History Research, Los Angeles County Musuem for Natural History.

Russell Lee, *Family of Farm Workers Living at the Farm Security Administration Farm Workers' Mobile Unit, Friendly Corners, Arizona, 1942*. Library of Congress, Prints and Photographs Division, Washington, DC, Negative #LC-USF34–72137-D.

Teresa Jordan, *Marie Scott's Hands*, from *Cowgirls: Women of the American West, An Oral History* (Doubleday, 1982). Copyright © 1982 Teresa Jordan, used by permission of the artist.

Copyright © 1989 by Angela Davis. Used by permission of International Publishers Co., New York, New York.

Paula Gunn Allen, "Savages in the Mirror: Phantoms and Fantasies in America," from *Off the Reservation: Reflections on Boundary-Busting, Border-Crossing, Loose Canons* by Paula Gunn Allen. Copyright © 1998 by Paula Gunn Allen. Reprinted by permission of Beacon Press, Boston.

Joan Didion, "Holy Water," from *The White Album*. Copyright © 1979 by Joan Didion. Published by Simon & Schuster. Reprinted by permission of Janklow & Nesbit Associates Literary Services, New York. All rights reserved.

Gretel Ehrlich, "The Solace of Open Spaces," from *The Solace of Open Spaces* by Gretel Ehrlich. Copyright © 1985 by Gretel Ehrlich. Used by permission of Viking Penguin, a division of Penguin Putnam Inc.

Roxanne Swentzell, "Clay People." Copyright © 1999 Roxanne Swentzell. Used by permission of the author.

Gloria Anzaldúa, selection from *Borderlands/La Frontera: The New Mestiza*. Copyright © 1987 by Gloria Anzaldúa. Used by permission of Aunt Lute Books, San Francisco, California.

Janet Campbell Hale, "Salad La Raza," "Desmet, Idaho, March 1969," and "Custer Lives in Humbolt County" (1975), from *Voices of the Rainbow*, ed. Kenneth Rosen (Arcade Publishing, 1975). Copyright © 1975, 1993 by Kenneth Rosen. Published by Arcade Publishing, Inc., New York, New York by arrangement with Seaver Books, New York, New York.

Sylvia Watanabe, "Talking to the Dead," from *Talking to the Dead* by Sylvia Watanabe. Copyright ©1992 by Sylvia Watanabe. Used by permission of Doubleday, a division of Random House, Inc.

Molly Ivins, "Lone Star Republic" and "Impersonating the Lord," from *You Got to Dance with Them Which Brung You* by Molly Ivins, Copyright © 1998 by Molly Ivins. Reprinted by permission of Random House, Inc.

Colleen McElroy, "How Not to Cross the Border" from *A Long Way from St. Louie* by Colleen McElroy. Copyright © 1997 by Colleen McElroy. Used by permission of Coffee House Press.

Sandra Cisneros, "Remember the Alamo," from *Woman Hollering Creek*. Copyright © 1991 by Sandra Cisneros. Published by Vintage Books, a division of Random House, Inc., New York, and originally in hardcover by Random House, Inc. Reprinted by permission of Susan Bergholz Literary Services, New York. All rights reserved.

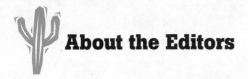 **About the Editors**

Lillian Schlissel received her PhD in American Civilization from Yale University in 1957. She has taught at Brooklyn College, where she was the director of the American Studies Program from 1974 to 1998. She is presently Professor *Emerita* of English and American Studies at Brooklyn College, CUNY. She has been visiting professor of American Studies at the University of New Mexico and the University of Santa Clara, California. She is the author of *Women's Diaries of the Westward Journey* (1982), coeditor of *Far from Home, Families of the Westward Journey* (1989), author of (for younger readers) *Black Frontiers* (1994), and editor of (for younger readers) *The Diary of Amelia Stewart Knight* (1992). She has also edited *Three Plays by Mae West* (1997), *Washington Irving's Journals* (vol. 2, 1981), *Conscience in America* (1970), and *The World of Randolph Bourne* (1965).

Catherine Lavender was born in Ukiah, California, and grew up near Denver, Colorado. She is the descendant of a long line of western women who settled in both the U. S. and Canada, including overlanders, miner's widows, railroad station "masters," midwives, suffragists, ranchers, and businesswomen. She received her doctorate in Western and Women's History in 1997 from the University of Colorado at Boulder, with a dissertation about feminist anthropologists in the early twentieth-century American Southwest. She is currently the Director of American Studies and an Assistant Professor of History at the College of Staten Island of the City University of New York.